WESTFIELD

Novels by
Roderick Thorp

WESTFIELD

RODERICK THORP

CROWN PUBLISHERS, INC.
New York

Printed in the United States of America

Published simultaneously in Canada by General Publishing Company Limited

Designed by Ruth Kolbert Smerechniak

Library of Congress Cataloging in Publication Data

Thorp, Roderick.
   Westfield.

   I. Title.
PZ4.T55We [PS3570.H67]   813'.5'4   77-23372
ISBN 0-517-52972-6

FOR
My Mother and Father

Contents

Part One

THE
INTRUDER

When I was a child, I spake as a child,
I understood as a child, I thought as a child:
but when I became a man, I put away childish things.

MICHAEL MONK

Rendezvous

I

EVERY GENERATION LEARNS IT MUST INVENT ITS OWN DEFINITIONS of love.

Our story begins on the first business day of the New Year, 1877, January 5, a Tuesday, in New York City. The weather is overcast and seasonably damp and cold, conditions familiar enough to New Yorkers today. The state of the traffic on Broadway to the west of City Hall is familiar, too: at a near-standstill, vehicles lurching a few feet and stopping, drivers glaring and muttering stolidly. We have seen the engravings: horsecars, carriages, wagons loaded with sacks, barrels, and wooden crates, and carts and barrows pushed and pulled by men as often as horses.

It is only a hundred years ago, but with the exceptions of the steamship and the railroad, applications of the invention of the steam engine one hundred years before, there has not been an advance in human transportation since the invention of the sail and the taming of the horse in prehistoric times. In 1877 New York is a city serviced by hundreds of sailing ships and quartering thousands upon thousands of horses. The smell of horses and cold, damp, badly tanned leather is everywhere. If you look up Broadway through the rising brownish dust, you can see in the distance, regal and ghostlike, a man on horseback, guiding his mount through the congestion. The start of our modern era shimmers with such visions—visions that delighted Western eyes for more than a thousand years.

Now they are about to be swept away. In fifty years they will all be gone, and in fifty more they will have receded into legend. In any event, a man pausing on the steps of the entrance of the Astor House opposite the post office at the foot of City Hall Park after a hearty lunch might be distracted by the beauty of the figure on horseback, whatever he knows of history. Let us say that there is such a man, and his name is Thomas Westfield.

Westfield is an emotional man, as free as any of us—the acts that most loudly proclaim his freedom also, inevitably most bitterly protest the ways he has been brought to heel. Well, Westfield is immersed in life. He has reached one of those moments of living in which all he has built is about to dissolve in a ruin of ironies, and so he perceives that this is a time for boldness. Ours has been a cruel age, and this is a world we cannot touch; we have to release Westfield to his fate.

In those days New York was already a great metropolis, a port, and a commercial center of more than a million people packed into three-, four-, and five-story wooden, brick, and brownstone structures on the lower half of the island of Manhattan. Consolidation was still twenty-one years away, and even though the bridge to Brooklyn was under construction, Brooklyn itself was a separate political entity—a rival—so that New Yorkers of the period took a feisty pride in their own bustling civic enterprise. From Fourteenth Street down, or half the then-existing city, the island was ringed with docks, and from almost every corner one could see, though in some places far off, the forest of masts and spars of the clippers, steamers, and coastal vessels. The city roared. As Westfield stood facing the post office, surveying the stalled traffic before him, he could hear the echo of a freight train puffing up Hudson Street. Suddenly the traffic moved, and the air was filled with the clatter of iron horseshoes on the cobblestones. At the same time, Westfield sucked a bit of food from between his teeth.

The doorman of the Astor House, who was drunk, took the several unrelated activities as a cue and ventured a step forward. He raised his voice to a near-shout that was almost drowned in the noise of the traffic.

"Hansom, Alderman?"

"Yes! Tell him Cherry Street!"

"Yes, sir, Mr. W.!"

As he turned away, the doorman relaxed and showed a small leering smile. Westfield saw it—for a moment he thought of turning back into the hotel and making a complaint. But then he gave it up and fished in his pocket for a quarter, which was his customary, extravagant tip for the situation. He kept his head turned to avoid the doorman's eyes, climbing into the hansom without another word. When he saw a newspaper lying on the leather seat, he decided he would read it from first page to last to keep from dwelling too much on the state of his nerves.

So what if the doorman took the obscure destination to be the location of some love nest? Being misunderstood was nothing new to Westfield. Basically he concurred with the doorman's underlying presumption, that he really was a timid man. More than timid—gentle, serious, and misunderstood. And today was so much a day he did not want to do anything he would regret, the noblest day of his life, and he was so nearly out of control, absolutely terrified, that he bathed himself in a special self-pity, reminding himself how serious and gentle he was—a gambler might go so far as to say that he was trying not to jinx his luck.

Nevertheless, nobility and sensitivity notwithstanding, the doorman was not far wrong about Westfield. Westfield, who was thirty-eight and married, had a mistress, the latest in a long line of them, and her name was Kate.

Westfield was tall, a fraction over six feet, one hundred and ninety pounds, with an athletic demeanor. He was not an athlete, but he tried to keep his weight down. The presentation he made was not so impressive as it was forbidding, for he had a tense expression. His blue eyes were deeply set and glaring, and his beard, which he shaved every day, was heavy. He kept his thinning brown hair fastened to his scalp with a pomade he had used for years but no longer actually needed. He fussed with himself as little as he could, and in a time when men tended everything from moustaches to muttonchops, this let him feel a secret glee.

He was like that, full of quiet unmalicious jokes. He loved to laugh, and as people were allowed to know him, they learned this fact, even if many of them did not always appreciate what he thought was funny. He had the childish sense of humor of a lonely man, but when he was stirred, his blue eyes sparkled. Currently he laughed most with Kate; she was years his junior and saw into him as most others did not.

His day had started badly. He had awakened at eight-thirty, shaving and dressing while his wife, Louise, and the maid, Hannah, packed the children off to school. The house was quiet when he came downstairs, and he ate alone. Louise had been speaking to him only in the presence of others since before Christmas; the anger the doorman had released had been created by her. Westfield knew it. He was at the front door, ready to leave, when she suddenly appeared at the top of the stairs.

"What time do you expect to be home?"

"About four, I suppose."

He never wanted to look at her when they were like this. She knew it, and her next words were a challenge to engage her eyes. "This is your day of days, isn't it, Thomas? Your day of glory—?"

The words faded: even she understood that he would not forgive her for sending him out in a fury today. But it was also a petty game, and he took his time looking up to her. She was of medium height, with straight yellow-blonde hair, and freckled skin. At thirty-five she was still insistently girlish when she was not being severe with him. She was considered a great beauty, but he had despised her so deeply for so long that he could not ever look at her for the pleasure of it or even in the sad consolation of husbandly proprietorship. She had a husky, breathy voice that was part of her charm with others, but it was his recollection that she had cultivated it for the additional attention it brought her. He had watched her carefully over the sixteen years of their marriage; left to herself, she had an endless capacity for deception. And self-deception. At the foot of the stairs he stayed silent, waiting.

Her hand reached for the balustrade, then pulled back. "You're determined to go through with this, aren't you?"

"I've explained it all. I've given you my reasons."

"But I don't understand any of them! They don't make sense to me!"

His voice rose until he was nearly screaming. "That's probably because you've been asked for the first time in your life to think of someone besides yourself, and you don't know how!"

When he turned away he smiled, but he was wishing again that she were dead, and in that way he knew that this was still another time that he had lost. At such moments he dared not look too closely at what he was doing.

I I

His business was printing. A century ago New York was the center of the expanding printing industry and the competition was ruthless; but Westfield had come to the city from Hartford at the age of nineteen with letters of introduction from his father and a bank draft amounting to most of what he had inherited from his mother, who was from Fall River and had been dead many years. Her people had operated steamers between New York and Boston. His father had wanted him to go to college, but young Westfield had revealed an iron streak. The letters of introduction were addressed to politicians and other men of importance, hope against hope—his father expected him home again within the year, whipped.

But the boy had luck, or took the opportunities he saw, and after some years, when he was married and established in business, he joined the

Democratic Party. He had no particular convictions or beliefs. He went to meetings, gave money, and offered his time, until gradually he was brought to the attention of the people who controlled the party's affairs. He knew Tweed, Oakley Hall, and the rest of the gang of thieves. Ready to run errands and do favors, he was rewarded with invitations and minor contracts and eventually appointments to positions in which, it was assumed, he would give and take kickbacks and bribes. He knew it was reckless, but he kept quiet, in part because he harbored secret ambitions. He envied Hall, and thought that if he could somehow press things harder, he could be mayor himself someday. When Tweed, Hall, and the others were ruined, the lesson of the biggest political scandal in the city's history was not lost on Westfield. He was frightened senseless for months, unable to eat or sleep. But he saw that what had pulled him through was his mediocrity. He had survived. In the flush of being released from his terror, he felt as though he had achieved a victory.

When the party needed fresh but still reliable faces for the board of aldermen, Westfield was an obvious choice. His opponent in his first election was a short, pear-shaped man with wet, fishy eyes, and Westfield beat him easily by standing up straight and enunciating clearly. In office he made sure to serve his constituents promptly and well, and in the next election he ran on his record. It was a continuation of the same mediocrity that had carried him through in the past and he knew it. It was the measure of him: he was a man who was frightened senseless whenever he was touched by something new. He could not help seeing that even if he became mayor someday he would be the same. So, acknowledging these insights as the wisdom that comes with maturity, he resigned himself to being comfortable and devoted his energies to his private life.

What tickled him most these days about his political activities was that Louise hated them—which meant that he was free to do as he pleased without her interference. There were benefits and privileges that she did not know about and which he exploited with relish. He was almost above the law, almost a celebrity, almost rich, and had enough of all of these perquisites to make it easy for him to keep his real self apart from her, her family, and her friends. He could talk about duty and the public good, the future and the need for vision, but it was all gibberish, given what he knew about New York. His career was something for her to boast about or deprecate, depending on whether she was speaking with family or friends. Her family felt secure and happy, seeing what a fine man she had married, and her friends were able to observe that he was a stuffed shirt and not a threat to their own little empires. In the light of what he knew of what the latter were in for with her, Westfield found their view of him quite amusing.

When he was finished in his office behind Park Row, Thomas Westfield walked around to City Hall, where the talk was still of the Hayes-Tilden election. There were only a few people there, reporters mostly, and no new information. Westfield had reconciled himself to Hayes, and he found the continuing debate tedious and hypocritical. His colleagues wanted to argue from principle, but Tilden was their man, and their voices rang out not so much with great sentiment as with the frustration of gluttons unable to believe that they were about to be turned away from the feast. When a young reporter from the *Tribune* who did not know him well tried to elicit a comment in the hope of building a story, Westfield nearly bolted. He had come to chat, but he kept going, out the side door with his coat still unbuttoned.

As he crossed Broadway and headed south, Westfield hoped that one of the older men would take the young reporter aside and put him wise. He was a printer, not a politician, he had told the press originally, and he didn't want to put on airs. It was not long before they understood that he really meant it, that he did not want to take chances. But it was in his nature to believe he was somehow in their debt. He would whisper something here or there, sometimes sending a reporter after a story that no one else knew. But he was generous in the saloons, where generosity was unnecessary, and he would have a word with a magistrate if the situation warranted or help a boy land a job. At the least, he thought, he was making friends.

He ate slowly—cream of barley soup, leg of mutton, succotash, beet salad, hot ginger cake, Neufchâtel cheese—and washed it down with three cups of strong black coffee. In Westfield's opinion the dining room of the Astor House was second only to Delmonico's in the entire city. He considered a liqueur but decided against it. He was a fair drinker, but alcohol affected him more before dinner than after, and he wanted to keep his head clear. With his last cup of coffee he had a small cigar. The Christmas decorations were still up in the dining room and out front in the lobby, and the cool fragrances of the evergreen boughs mixed pleasantly with the warm odors from the kitchens. Westfield sat quietly for a long time. He wanted to remember the meal. He wanted to fix the entire day in his memory to serve him the rest of his life.

When he stepped outside the leer of the old doorman triggered the anger inside him; it reminded him again that he was living in a dream, and that his wife's fears were more justified than she knew.

The newspaper in the hansom was the *Times;* its front page was no salvation after all, filled on one side with accounts from the various state legislatures on the Hayes-Tilden maneuverings, on the other with more of the train wreck in Ashtabula, Ohio. The death toll there was up to nearly two hundred. Among the dead were women and children, whole families, a pair of honeymooners married just a few hours. One woman pinned in the wreckage had been on her way to meet her husband; the reporter watched the flames consume her and recorded her screams of agony. He had her dying words, but Westfield turned the page as he realized he was about to read them.

Filling an inside page were summaries of what the city's leading ministers had said in their holiday sermons. All ministers were scoundrels, Westfield thought, too shrewd to work and too eager to poke their noses into other people's business. Over the weekend one of them, trying to make a name for himself, no doubt, had compared the country in its current crisis to ancient Israel on the eve of its destruction. If you really wanted to measure the rot in a city's social fabric, Westfield believed, all you needed to examine was the stupidity of its clergy.

When the cab turned off Park Row, Westfield sat back and gazed out the window. These were the most vicious, crowded slums in the world. The reports had it that New York was worse than any city in Europe, worse than anything yet known in the Orient. There was at least one murder a night in one building alone, the old brewery at Five Points. The police were afraid to enter even by day. Hoodlums controlled the whole area, brazen gangs that courted publicity with flamboyant styles. The Plug Uglies wore derby hats; the Dead Rabbits marched into battle with a hare impaled on a stick. There were gun battles that rattled the alleys and streets for hours. Bill Tweed had climbed out of this environment, bearing with him the neighborhood's distinctive morality. It took a special kind of human being to escape the place. Westfield was thinking of Kate more than anyone else now. She had come from this area, from Lombard Street down by the river.

Between the slowly passing buildings, Alderman Westfield could see the stone tower of the bridge to Brooklyn rising bright and gray, suffused with the pink of the afternoon sun. The workmen would be spinning the cables for years. The bridge was the stroke of genius that would ensure the city's prosperity for generations to come—everyone knew it. The chance to make money in land speculation in Brooklyn had long since passed. Business was going to be wonderful; there was no telling where the end would be. Tenements were going up by the hundreds, new ones every day. The future was going to be beautiful, everyone said: they could not see that they were creating the look of it themselves.

It always came down to money. The world was bound up in money. The poor and the damned were other people's mistakes. Westfield resurrected the image of the woman burning to death in the wreck in Ohio. It made him jump and squirm. As if he were there by the overturned railroad car, the smoke swirling around him, he could see and hear the woman screaming for her life, tearing at her clothes and even her flesh in the effort to escape death.

He took a breath and struggled to hold on to himself. For a split second he had wriggled like a puppet on twisted strings. He sat back. The cab rolled past a stable, and the smell was strong on the cold, moist air. His heart was pounding.

He had no right to expect otherwise and he knew it. He was going against his wife's wishes. His mistress was thrilled with what he was doing, but that had stopped being a factor a long time ago. He had been so many weeks in the fighting and planning that he wanted to believe that he hardly understood why he was doing it anymore. All he was certain of was that he was completely committed to it—if he didn't finish it to his satisfaction, he would never be the same.

He was going into Cherry Street, to the shelter Tweed himself had built, to take custody of a child he had never seen. A boy. Until shortly before Christmas, the child had lived with his parents in this neighborhood—on Lombard Street, in fact. A delicate boy, Westfield had been told. He was no longer sure that he was bringing the child into a better life. Westfield was not sure he could admit to himself what he really knew about this: that if he did not do it, he could consider himself destroyed.

Youth

I

THOMAS WESTFIELD WAS CERTAIN THAT THE ONLY MISTAKE HE HAD made in his life had been to marry Louise Lowe.

At nineteen, letters of introduction in hand, he had reported to the boardinghouse of his father's choice, off Madison Square, away from the roughhouse of the docks and just as far from the theatrical crowd at Union Square nine blocks to the south. If Thomas was determined to have his try at New York, it would be under his father's supervision. A suspicious and self-righteous New Englander who in his late age would curl over like a crook, the elder Westfield counseled all three of his sons through his "Saturday letters," demanding and receiving replies before the following Thursday. By 1877 the roles would nearly reverse, the thirty-eight-year-old son showing a forbearance that was almost paternal. The old man had not become senile; his opinions on the world and the proper conduct of an individual were merely variants on the opinions he had held all his life and which had become obsolete, even foolish in the light of changing times. In 1877 the adult Thomas Westfield could see that this was somehow part of the natural process.

Such wisdom comes at the age of thirty-eight. Nineteen is another matter.

In late 1857 Thomas Westfield was so frightened of his father and so obsessed with himself that he hardly knew that the country was moving toward a calamity that would tear it apart. He was as thin as his father, slack-jawed, and had a poor complexion. He carried on no conversation in which a skilled listener could not detect some fear or uncertainty. It was in his mind to go about his business with a scrupulous, deferential attitude; somehow he thought his honesty would be noticed by his betters.

His inheritance was out at interest. He was employed in a good position by a Pearl Street importer of woolens from England and Scotland. He had made his rounds with the letters of introduction, but for those first three months, there were no invitations for him to call again. He tried not to lose hope or patience. He attended lectures and plays, and he made sure he was seen with a book.

In the evenings he went from the parlor up to his room as late as he dared and as tired as he could make himself to ward off the temptations and perils of self-abuse. He was terribly afraid that he was too highly sexed and would drive himself insane. There was a maid in the boardinghouse, a chubby Irish girl named Mildred with bright red cheeks and a black fuzz on her upper lip, and since her duties often brought her so close to him that he could smell the soap on her skin or feel the warmth of her body, soon enough the simple rustle of her skirts sent the blood pumping into his loins and thoughts of her writhing fat thighs to the forefront of his mind. He was not an innocent. On the nights he was especially aware of her, if he could get to sleep without touching himself, he would be awake in an hour, his erection rock-hard in his nightshirt. Once after such an episode he had to get out of bed and light the lamp, only to discover at once that he had to wipe spots of the sticky goo from the carpet. He didn't get it all. On the following Saturday he found Millie on her hands and knees picking at the dried stuff with her thumbnail. "You shouldn't be eatin' food in your room, sir. It's against house rules, but don't worry, I won't snitch." He stood breathless with fear, the offending member drawn so far up into his belly that, a moment later, when she was gone, he could hardly grasp it with his fingertips through the fabric of his wool trousers. For hours afterward, he was afraid that the experience had injured him.

He took to the streets. He knew how to find a woman. His brothers had seen to that a year before, on his eighteenth birthday.

They were older, close to each other in age. They were as much under their father's jurisdiction as he was, but they had more experience in dealing with him. On this particular evening the elder Westfield thought the three of them had taken the train down to New Haven to see a production of *A Midsummer Night's Dream,* which they had all studied carefully in high school.

They were in a sporting house in East Hartford, an old, low-ceilinged structure so settled in the mud that it was almost tilted over. The front room was bare, smoky, and boisterous. Thomas perched anxiously on the edge of a chair while his brothers explained the situation to the madam, a bloated mulatto woman with breasts like pig bladders. As she waddled closer to Thomas, her eyes turned hard and curious. Her breath smelled of whiskey. "What do you have to say for yourself on yo' birthday, boy?"

He gulped, then suddenly remembered to stand in the presence of a lady. "They told you that?" he croaked.

She glanced at his brothers, then back to him, her eyelids drooping. "This is how ah get all mah best customers. Ah think ah know how to accommodate a young gennemum." She hooked a blubbery arm in his and thrust him toward the stairs. "Yo' brothers want the best for you. Is that all right with you, boy?"

"Yes'm." He thought he was going to faint. He felt his knees giving way. He grabbed for the bannister.

She preceded him up the stairs to a door that opened upon a bedroom wallpapered in pink. The bedstead was polished brass. "This' mah special room," she said. "If y'all have to relieve yo'sef, open the window. Get comfortable. Ah'll send up the girl."

He still felt dizzy. The room smelled heavily of scent and powder. Thomas removed his jacket and draped it carefully over the back of a chair. In another moment the door opened again, so silently it almost seemed like his imagination.

The woman was taller than he had hoped, dark-haired, wearing a gown and a heavy belted robe. She had circles under her eyes and drawn, sallow cheeks. She had been pretty once. It passed through his mind that she was consumptive. She started to undo her robe.

"What's your name, boy?"

He told her.

"You call me Becky. Happy Birthday."

He moved to turn down the lamp.

"No, leave it alone. I like the lamp on. Not everybody does, but I do." She seemed to be laughing. She drew him closer, laughing still, but tender. The robe opened. "Now press yourself against me," she said with a sly assurance.

Two weeks later, with his father believing he had gone up to Chicopee to visit a cousin his brothers' age, he went back to East Hartford. He wanted Becky, no one else, and resented having to pay ten dollars for the night, as if his desire for her were payment and sacrifice enough. He had to wait downstairs for her in the choking, noisy saloon. He had three cups of rum, and he was drunk when she came down. Her mouth twisted as soon as she saw him.

" 'lo, Becky."

"Your name is Thomas, isn't it? I guess you've come to tell me you've got the habit."

"*Show* you, more likely."

"You're to be a man all of a sudden? Well, come on, let's see how much you've had to drink."

"Do we get the same room back?"

"You don't want that room." She put her hand on his shoulder. "Your ten dollars don't pay for it, anyway."

The room she led him to was hardly a room at all; it was the size of a pantry, windowless, furnished with a bed, washstand, and chair. He could no longer conceal his pain. "You don't seem glad to see me."

"I'm just hoping that you haven't drunk so much that you're going to give me trouble."

He let his eyes go over the room again. Two weeks before she had ministered to him so surely and lovingly that he had whimpered like a sick dog. She had made him watch her, and at the moment of his own greatest pleasure and distress, she had smiled the most beautiful smile he had ever seen. He had wanted to believe that he had been permitted in that moment to understand everything. He thought he would die if he never saw that smile again. His voice quavered and he began to sob. "I'd rather go upstairs. I have the money."

She let out a shout and clapped her hands. "They didn't tell you, did they?"

"Who?"

"Your brothers! That room has peepholes! They watched us the whole time. You think they had your interests at heart? They paid for their own pleasure."

For a moment he couldn't move, the blow was so great, then he lunged at her. "What about you? You had your pleasure, too. I saw it!"

"I enjoyed you."

"Like that? Just like that?"

"Don't you know what I am yet, you damned fool?"

"Don't say it!" He took her arms to kiss her, but she twisted her face away. She got free of him. He wanted to see that smile. Did he have to beg for it, when she had given it so freely last time? His tears were strangled in his throat.

She saw. She touched his face, suddenly tender. "This isn't a good place for the likes of you. We'll see if you haven't had too much to drink."

It turned out that he had. "See me next time," she said brusquely, and flounced out. He did not get up from the bed until he was sure that no one would see that he had cried.

He did not go back. And he never told his brothers what he knew. He wanted to get even, but at the same time it seemed better to keep silent and do nothing. Perhaps they saw the change in him, that he no longer trusted them, but they failed to see the important thing: that they could not trust him. He was their brother, but he was also their enemy. As a consequence, everything they shared from then on, including the passage of time, gave him a special pleasure, precious, secret as a miser's glittering hoard.

In New York he kept to himself in the same way but for another reason: he did not know the ways of the city. If he was seen with a street girl in one of the smarter or more public sections, he might be ruined, he thought. His struggle to control himself led to a desperation that ordained failure; his encounters, when they came, on side streets with pitiful creatures, left him guilt-ridden and frightened of disease. He agonized over his defeat at the hands of the city, searching the faces of older men he suspected were alone, too, in the effort to learn what would become of him after more than just a few months of this miserable existence.

One evening after work he joined some other young men from the importer's at the Gem Saloon, and toward the end of the night, when they were all drunk, one suggested they adjourn to a sporting house. This was after Westfield had been in the city almost a year. There were six of them in the party and in their procession up Broadway to Canal Street he maintained the act of the man of experience, telling the others that he had been to such places in Hartford. It took him until the next day to realize what their questions revealed of their opinion of him.

The place was astonishing, bigger and more lavish than the one in East Hartford, a real home, with music and food, furniture and carpets. There was perfume, the rustle of skirts, whispers and laughter. The girls were young and pretty and acted full of love. When he went upstairs with a lovely little blonde girl, very drunk indeed, he asked her if the walls were drilled through. No, she said; if he wanted to put on a show, they would have to go down the hall. He laughed and said no easily, as if he were a man of genuine experience. She laughed, too, with a confidence in him that was thrilling.

The next morning was a different story. He had failed again because of the alcohol; he was hung over and in the grip of a suicidal remorse. His thoughts ran amok—to fear of discovery by the decent people of the city, by his father's friends, to realizing what his co-workers thought of him, to wondering what God thought of him. His mother's death before his eighth birthday had been a sign, the accusing finger of the Almighty Himself—young Westfield had thought it so many times in the past that he was actually tired of it. The truth, and he knew it, was that he had hardly noticed the event of his mother's death: he had been a child just discovering the world of school and playmates. People had had to tell him that he had suffered a grave loss. It was as if he had not been able to pay attention to his life. And now that he was older he saw that perhaps that was the clearest sign that he was doomed from the start, doomed for all time.

But then the following week something extraordinary happened: two of the people to whom his father's letters had introduced him invited him to their homes. What else did it mean but that he had succeeded with his original design? Now he saw he had escaped at last the superstitions of his childhood. His sense of the distance he had come from Hartford was so great he felt euphoric. Like a conqueror, he returned to the sporting house to celebrate, and when he had the best time ever, better even than the first time with Becky in East Hartford—that smile again, and beautiful, coming from a beautiful girl—he realized that his fate was sealed. He was in the city to stay, and he knew one of the reasons why.

What had happened to his father's friends was simple. They had not been waiting until he had established himself. Each had assumed he had other acquaintances and friends in New York. He hadn't even known he had pleased them. What he did not see, and needed the passage of time to understand, was that at almost twenty he was still a child, not very high at all on their list of priorities. They had expected nothing of him. There had been nothing of him to expect.

He continued to go about his business, public, private, and secret, sinking his roots deeper into the city, happier now, and it showed in his bearing and conversation. People told him he was mature for his age. He said that it was due to the experience of living in New York. He meant it in the most general sense, without humor, and believed that he was telling the truth completely.

II

He was twenty-two when he met Louise Lowe. The war he had hardly noticed coming was almost a year old, and because he had taken his father's advice and moved his inheritance into positions in commodities that were soon in short supply, he was established as a successful young man. He had been put up for membership in several business and social clubs. He was not fooled by his welcome into the company of the men who managed New York, for he was just as well known to them as a fellow patron of the city's sporting houses—not a bit the source of embarrassment he had originally imagined, but better, an opportunity to establish that he possessed a gentleman's discretion.

By the fall of 1861, then, he knew more people in positions of power in the city than he could count, and he was spoken of glowingly in drawing rooms far more frequently than ever was reported to him.

The young Westfield had been casually acquainted with Jedidiah Lowe for more than a year as a purchaser of his employer's woolens when the old man sent a message around inviting him to lunch. Lowe owned a department store on Canal Street, and Westfield had the impression that he was a moral, quick-judging man. And probably selfish, too, for he weighed over three hundred pounds. His yellowish muttonchops hung down over his collar. Beyond what he sensed, all Westfield really knew about Lowe was that he hated Lincoln to the point of treason. They met at Delmonico's.

"Well, boy, are you liquid?"

They had disposed of the main course, Lowe having lunched on calf's brains. Westfield had had the roast Long Island duckling. He said, "I have something put aside."

"Either you're liquid or you're not. I have my eye on a printing shop. The owner is going blind, dying, and he has nothing but daughters, so he's in a bad fix. Twenty thousand takes control, the rest to be paid out of profits for the next ten years. That should marry off the daughters and take care of the widow. I want to put up ten and have you in with me—"

"Why? I know nothing of printing."

"Business is business. I want you to learn *this* business and run it. I intend to be frank with you. The man whose shop this is is my wife's brother-in-law—her sister's husband. I have a premonition about myself, that I won't live through this insane war. I have a daughter and a son, but the boy is only nine years old. If I should die, two families will go to ruin."

"You have the store, sir."

"The clerks will pick it clean as soon as I'm gone. Under normal conditions, it would take years to turn it into a corpse, and the capital I've set aside might last a few years more, but ruin would come, and ruin it would be, in the fullness of time."

"Mr. Lowe, I'm afraid that I'd have to know a lot more about this—"

"I know, I don't take you for a fool. Come to my house this evening at eight. That's for dinner, so you'll need to dress. I have my brother-in-law's books already there and we can go over them afterward."

This was to be one of Westfield's evenings at Lillian's and he did not like having his plans changed for him. He stifled a sigh. "I'll be there at eight."

Later that afternoon, he went down into the street and found a boy to run a message over to Lillian's explaining that he would not be there that night. A message was not strictly necessary, but Westfield had made a habit each night of saying when he would return so that the girl he fancied at the time would be waiting for him. Currently she was a petite, tiny-breasted brunette named Lucy. She had grown up in an orphanage and believed that he was the finest gentleman she had ever met. The compliment meant little to him. He had already spent enough years listening to girls in whorehouses to know that he was a gentle and considerate lover. He liked Lucy, and he had learned that it was easier to send a note around than to have his feeling for her spoiled by having to listen to a half-baked, whining complaint. If she had a note—even if she couldn't read it—she would believe he treasured her, and act accordingly the next time she saw him.

The Lowe house on Thirteenth Street off Fifth Avenue was an older, wooden structure of two stories, with the servants' quarters in a dormer upstairs. The first-floor rooms were bright and spacious and elegantly and meticulously furnished. Jedidiah Lowe greeted Westfield in the parlor and offered him sherry. "The ladies will be along shortly. As you see, Mrs. Lowe is conscientious about the running of the household."

Westfield gave a small tight smile and Lowe waved him toward a chair. "What do you think of my proposal now?"

"I have some questions."

"Good. I'd be less sure of you if you didn't."

"Sir, I feel I must tell you, if you don't already know it, I won't make a decision about our business quickly. I want to gather the facts and take the time to think about them. A few days, a few clear, crisp mornings, and I may be able to grasp some questions that might be beyond me in the ambiance of good company in a happy home."

Lowe saw through his babble. " 'Procrastination is the thief of time,' said the poet."

" 'Know thyself,' said the philosopher. This is more than a business proposition. You have asked me to rearrange my life to fulfill the designs of your own."

"You don't mince words, Mr. Westfield—" There was a noise at the door, and Lowe looked up. Westfield rose and turned. The two women had hesitated, having heard the subject of the conversation. Lowe pulled his enormous weight out of his chair. "Come in, my dear, and Louise. Mr. Westfield, may I present my wife, Mrs. Lowe, and my daughter, Miss Lowe."

"How do you do?" Westfield tried to keep his eyes on Mrs. Lowe. He was afraid to look at the daughter. She realized it.

"What don't you mince words about, Mr. Westfield?"

Now he looked directly into her eyes. "I'm not certain that I can recall, after the introduction of such beauty, Miss Lowe." He wanted to say more but was afraid, even though she seemed pleased.

Mr. Lowe said, "Mr. Westfield is a young man who knows how to pull his fat out of the fire, Louise."

Mrs. Lowe looked faintly pained. "A coarse remark before dinner, don't you think, Jedidiah? It will be served in a minute, so may we join you?"

"You have," he said abruptly. Westfield concealed a smile. Like many tyrants in business, Lowe was not sovereign at home. It was useful to know. Following her mother, Louise stole another glance at Westfield, who nodded his head, a salute. He wanted it seen by her father. A little brazenness could work a sharper bargain. But better, if Louise could sense that he had the power to skin her father in a business deal, she might think twice about him.

She was beautiful—in that, the two women were alike. Mother and daughter, both young, about twenty years apart, blonde, freckled, moderately tall, delicately boned. Missing a night at Lillian's was having an effect on Westfield, for he thought that if he couldn't have the daughter, he would settle for the mother. The notion of fat, old Lowe on top of her, a firm, lovely woman perhaps twenty-five years his junior, was loathsome to contemplate, but Westfield couldn't help it. He knew nothing about marriage, but he was willing to believe that the sharpness between the Lowes had its origins in that aspect of their lives.

They were called to dinner. Westfield was seated opposite Louise—and it was as if Louise could read his thoughts, for she looked across the table with a smile that was almost a laugh. He could not let her defeat him so easily, but he dared not try to gain an advantage. He thought of it, of letting her see in his eyes how easily he could imagine her giving herself to him, but finally he was afraid to show her that side of himself.

Naturally the conversation at the table revolved around him. The women wanted to know where he was from and whom he knew and what his work was, and when it came time to know where he was living in New York, Louise reacted with glee.

"Oh, Mr. Westfield, I'm sure we've already met, after a fashion! I went to school on Madison Square. I finished my studies just last year. Do you happen to recall a group of schoolgirls out walking every fair afternoon? Until last year, I was one of them."

"Yes, I do seem to recall—"

"Well, did you know we had a game? If you saw us, we most certainly saw you. We used to try to describe the people we passed with a single word—"

"Louise! This is disgraceful!"

"No, it wasn't, Mother." Westfield could see that she had altered her mother's meaning. "A schoolgirl's game. Sometimes a person was a sparrow or a bear, and once we saw a man who was terribly short, with a funny round hat right on top of his head, and one of the girls said, 'Barge,' and just as quickly another girl said, 'Canoe,' and, do you know, he really was a canoe."

"I fail to see the point of all this, Louise, I really do."

Westfield kept his tone as casual and self-assured as he could. "How would you have described me, Miss Lowe?"

"I'm trying to think. Naturally, if we really did see you, I wouldn't remember what we said. I suppose the word could change from day to day with the person's clothing and humor and so forth. I know! I was trying to think of you as one of the great birds, an eagle, which you most certainly are not, or a hawk, but there are too many kinds of hawks and your idea of a hawk might not express the independence that I intend; no, you're a sailing ship, one of those big, noble ones that cross the ocean."

"I thank you. My family on my mother's side were sailors—sea captains, in fact. I think highly of ships."

"I wanted to express your self-reliance. You seem to be master of your destiny."

"Your father's business with me would seem to lay that open to question."

She sat back. "I'm so glad."

Through dinner and after, in the library with her father, Westfield pondered this. While Lowe talked of wages and overhead at the printing shop, and Westfield more in defense of his reputation than anything else scratched down all the figures he could, he became more and more intrigued with the nuances of Louise's remark. Only a fool would not recognize it as an invitation. Westfield wanted to think that she had already decided about him, even if she did not yet know it. Women were women: he had seen that clouded smile, that passing fragment of hope, before. For his part, he was delerious with her. When he left for the night, quite late, he told Jedidiah Lowe that he would give him his reply in a week. The old man grudgingly agreed, but he need not have been concerned. Westfield, papers thrust in every pocket, did not even see him, he was so caught up with Louise. He stumbled down the steps to the street. A carriage passed, the horses' hooves gently clopping. Love? Misery! The worst thing that had ever happened to him!

Westfield needed the week to consult with his father, for in truth he had never made a business decision in his life. As well and as favorably as he could, Westfield set out old Lowe's proposal, with several counter-proposals of his own. There was nothing to do but sit back and wait; but that simple thing was all but impossible. That weekend, while the letters were in transit, Westfield violated his rules of conduct and was seen in several spots across the city absolutely stinking drunk; two out of three nights he finished up at Lillian's, where he passed out cold and had to be put to bed until shortly before dawn.

He was singularly unsuited for love or, at least, courtship as it was practiced more than one hundred years ago: when he left the Lowes' the week before, his head full of thoughts of Louise, he had headed for his boardinghouse only for as long as that course remained the same as the one to Lillian's. At Fifth Avenue he turned downtown instead of up, and when he arrived at the whorehouse, Lillian herself said he looked like he had seen a ghost. She showed him upstairs quickly, even though his Lucy was busy with another gentleman. The girl Lillian sent in was a horse-faced, oversized German as stupid as they come. Westfield slept for a while, but he was far from at peace with himself. When he awakened, he felt as if he had lost all hope, like a man who had just been thrown into prison.

He met Lowe on Thursday, this time at the St. Nicholas, at Lowe's suggestion. Lowe was in good humor, and Westfield took it to mean that he expected a reply in the affirmative. Lowe looked pink and freshly groomed, and smelled of bay rum: he had treated himself to an hour at Phalon's on the other side of the hotel lobby. The food at the St. Nicholas was inferior, and both men ordered conservatively; but Lowe wanted to pretend that everything was as good as the week before, and Westfield, for his own reasons, went along with him. It soon became clear that there would be no mention of business until the meal was done.

Westfield's father had said no. His long-range plans for his son called for years more of careful, diversified investment. The war would provide opportunities for years to come. To put so much of his capital in one small shop was foolishness, but to commit his time as well was positively catastrophic. He would be spending his working hours learning a trade instead of standing above them all to see which could serve his purposes best. For no reason at all that the elder Westfield could see, Thomas was changing and narrowing the entire design of his life. What more could it amount to than that?

"I look upon the basic business proposition with favor," Westfield told Lowe when the waiter had taken their dishes away. "However, I have reservations about the long term, and there will have to be some modification of certain particulars."

"I expected no less from you," said Jedidiah Lowe benignly. "Tell me what you must have."

"For the first six months, the right to sell to you, at my option, my interest in the firm for the price I will have paid, plus mutually agreed-upon interest, in cash. At the end of that period, if I do not exercise that option, I want the option to buy from you an additional five percent of your interest."

"Must you have control?"

"Absolutely. I'm sorry, but there's more. If we pass the probationary period and I choose to exercise my option to buy five percent of your holdings, I want the further option to buy your remaining percentage at a future time at a price we agree upon now."

"Out of the question. All of it goes completely counter to the objectives I stated last week. You've taken leave of your senses."

Westfield smiled. "I admit it."

"I don't understand. If you've been having sport with me, Westfield, I'll see that the whole city hears about it!"

Now that the time to say what was really on his mind had come, Westfield lost his voice. He poured some water. "Excuse me," he whispered. He gazed at the high tin ceiling faintly blurred by cigar smoke. "I—I cannot do this at all unless I have your permission to court your daughter."

"You won't have your wife's family owning part of your business, is that it?"

"I won't have people saying that I made my way with my wife's money."

"Your honor is that important to you?"

"Would you prefer less in a business partner?"

"By your terms, you won't be my partner if you're unsuccessful with my daughter. Well, I suppose I shouldn't blame a man for trying for the best deal he can get under difficult circumstances. Put your terms in a letter—"

"I'm afraid you haven't heard it all," said Westfield. "You said that you wanted me to run the business. I want the appropriate title, salary, and percentage of the profits."

Lowe laughed until his eyes were wet. "I should have expected as much. I'm afraid I'm laughing, young man, because your business firmness simply melted when the talk turned to my daughter, but it doesn't seem to stop you one bit."

Westfield's ears burned. "I'm sorry. I don't have much experience—"

"At your age, I expect not. As I say, put your terms in a letter and I'll consider them. In the meantime, come around on Sunday afternoon. We're at home from four until six. I'll try to give you *my* answer as quickly as possible. You'll be suffering enough at the hands of others, that's clear."

Do not try to understand Westfield's lie about his inexperience too quickly. He saw it as a mild glossing over of facts, for he was talking not of Lillian's or the place before that, but rather of the two young ladies he had tried for, ineptly and feebly, in the past year. Westfield really did know nothing about respectable women. He had met them as he had met Louise, at dinner parties, and he had gone around to call in the days that followed, as he was ready to do with Louise. Listening to their prattle, seeing that they were constitutionally incapable of directness, he had grown nervous and bored. It is always a bad idea to look objectively at any human being in that condition. *Why am I here?* Since he had already found an answer to that question, and since the young ladies were numb to that part of life, and since they were not much in beauty or brains, either, the secret, rebellious part of him announced that it just wasn't worth the effort, and he dropped them. He was inept about that, too, winding up looking like the rejected suitor, but he had no real feelings about that, just the general relief he had been looking for. When he saw the disenchantment growing in the young ladies, he felt the surge of hope that precedes any victim's rescue.

So that was the lie he thought he was telling concerning two minor incidents. What of the lie beneath? He had become so used to paying young women for sexual attentions that he had come to regard it as his personal business, like his other private habits. He did not feel obliged to discuss it with anyone. Westfield regularly saw his friends at Lillian's. He was not ashamed. And because he was not ashamed, his feelings poured from him a bit more freely. He was not a licentious person. No, worse: he was looking for love and, worse still, from time to time he found it.

III

For a long time after the introduction of gunpowder to Europe, warfare continued in very much the manner in which it had been conducted in the medieval period. One of the first innovations that gunpowder made possible had to do with the siege of a walled and gated city. For this the French devised a metal cone packed with gunpowder. Because they did not have the means to deliver it from a distance, it was necessary for a man to run up to the gate, fasten the device, and light the fuse. Necessarily, the fuse was quite short, to prevent the besieged from emerging and snuffing it out. All too often, the fuse was shorter than its designers intended, and the man lighting it was blown up with the bomb. The bomb was called a petard, and we still have the expression that goes with it, "hoist by his own petard."

Some two or three years after the war, married five or six years and the

sole support of a wife, two children, and sending monthly checks to a
mother-in-law and a young brother-in-law in Philadelphia, where they
had joined the long-since widowed sister, Westfield heard the expression
in a business conversation over lunch. He had not heard it in more years
than he could remember, and it haunted him for days afterward. He
knew what it meant, but he did not know its origin. At last he sent a clerk
around to one of the newspaper offices on Park Row to find out for him.

He wore the expression around his neck like a horse collar for almost a
year. In those days he was so black and bitter about his marriage that it
was all he could do to bring himself to talk to Louise. In the years since
the wedding, his feelings had varied only by degree. They had married
too quickly, too young; that much was clear to him from the beginning.
The next year, when the conscription was instituted, both his father and
his father-in-law told him to find a substitute and pay him off; he found
one, a printer's devil in the shop, and before the year was out, Westfield
regretted it. (The printer's devil, a boy of seventeen, reported for duty
and jumped off a train in Pennsylvania: no one ever heard of him again.)
As the war went on, Westfield's brain filled with fantasies prodded by
Harper's Weekly and *Frank Leslie's Illustrated Newspaper.* Sometimes, in
the noise and smoke, he saw himself lying in the shell-ravaged mud, a
terrible wound in his stomach, gushing blood. It was infantile, and in his
more lucid moments he was wracked with self-loathing, but eventually
he saw that what he wanted was to be adored again. He wanted to stride
the city like the confident and self-possessed gentleman he thought he
had become. Going home was like visiting a tomb—the place was *darker*
than any other place in his life. Literally he had trouble holding his head
up. At times he wanted to strangle his wife; when her back was turned, he
glowered at her. And he had fits of temper, but he smashed not her
things, only his own.

That was the nadir, those early months. Gradually he became resigned.
It took cunning to assess every new opportunity for what it offered the
life he intended to live apart from her. It was necessary, he told her, to
join more clubs and to take a more active interest in politics. Finally he
claimed to have become a card player. He had lost his self-respect. He
didn't care, and then he forgot about it.

Not that it mattered much anyway. He came to see that the entire
structure of his life seemed to be founded on illusions he fostered in
others. If his own father kept a sinewy grip on the least important
portions of his life in the belief that he controlled it all, then Jedidiah
Lowe, while he was alive, had a view of him that was even more
fantastical—lunatic, finally.

Lowe had been right about one thing: he did not live out the war. In
the winter of 1864, rotting with cancer that had consumed more than half

of him, leaving a thin, translucent ghost of a creature in his stead, Lowe praised himself for having chosen Louise's husband well. He had had a design, he said. It was before Christmas, one of the last times the old man could come downstairs from the bedroom. All the family was present, and it was thought that he was raving with pain and the fear of death. His eyes glowed like those of an infant in the arms of a whiskey-drinking uncle. It was the first that Westfield had heard of any design. Later, when he was helping Jedidiah up the stairs again—the one member of the family able or willing to do so (he had already become the ox of the family; no job was too dirty or heavy for him)—he saw no reason why he couldn't ask about it, since the old man would be dead in a matter of days. Westfield was packing him into his bed.

"Oh, I had it in the back of my mind," Lowe said. "Nothing more than that."

"How did you come to choose me?"

"Originally I liked the way you handled bolts of cloth. I could see that you believed you were headed for better things. I make up my mind about people pretty quickly, you know. What I learned of your background was only confirmation. I believe in first impressions."

He closed his eyes to sleep, and there was never another opportunity to ask for more detail. At the funeral, where Louise was composed enough to show her displeasure with Westfield for having worn the wrong shoes, Westfield almost burst out laughing. First impressions? Better things? Even at the old man's funeral he was wondering when he would be able to slip away for another taste of his own, his real life.

The children were hers. The boy, Thomas, Jr., looked like his maternal grandfather, and, worse, he was a whiner; he clung to her. Perhaps it was Westfield's fault, he had let the boy see his temper. For a while Westfield believed he would come around, and he did, for an intermittent year or two, but when Thomas, Jr., was ten, he lost interest in his father again. He liked ships, but by then Westfield was lost in his own existence.

Westfield had hope for Julie. She was brown-haired, not like her mother, but pretty in her own way. Westfield thought that Louise was disappointed with her looks, and he took it upon himself to teach her that she was beautiful and would be a successful young woman. When he saw that Louise resented the attention he paid to Julie, he made it a game, embellishing it when Louise was around and creating jokes and secrets when she wasn't. Still, Louise was with Julie more than he was, and there were times when he suspected that she undermined much of what he did when she was alone with Julie, and for nothing but spite.

His outside interests were what saved him. Except for a few months before and after the wedding, he had always had them. There was a period at the start of the new decade when he was convinced that she was carrying on with other men; so he fell in love, installed the girl in a house far downtown, and saw her as much as he dared. Because of his suspicions about Louise, he became sex-obsessed and abused the girl in nasty ways. To save herself, the girl took up with another man. When Westfield realized what he had done, he kept track of her, taking her to lunch once or twice, but it was too late to start again. He knew; he simply wanted to show her that he was not as barbaric as he really had been with her.

He met Kate in the late summer of 1876, only a day or two after his thirty-eighth birthday. In the next weeks he fell wildly in love with her, and she with him. It was astonishing, beautiful, frightening, maddening. She would not leave the house in which he had found her; she would not be in his debt. On the other hand, if he was late for their appointment, she would burst into tears. Her youth gave her a naïveté and resilience that made her tears all the more heartbreaking. But they never lasted long: she was happy with him; she wanted to forget anything that made her unhappy when she was in his presence.

She was from the worst of the slums, the Sixth Ward, Lombard Street, where no sane man would go after dark, and she kept up with the people, her old friends. God knew how or why. Lombard, George, Cherry streets, Cheapside: he had gone through there often enough over the years on one errand or another. When he offered his help, she cried but asked to be given time to consider it. The next time he saw her, she said it was a bad idea. It was one thing to take his money and gifts for herself; she was a whore and they both knew it. They could handle such things. The people in the Sixth Ward hated people like him. Some who needed his charity most were the least equipped to understand it. She would refuse to hide the fact that it was a gentleman's money, and not because she wanted for him the small satisfaction of having them know that they had a benefactor. A whore's money always had another meaning for them, loot from minor victories in the war against the rich. Either way, she was able to hear their cackling as they spent it. She was in tears as she tried to explain it. "Don't you see? It will make them worse. It isn't the way."

When he came by in early December with his Christmas present—he couldn't stand waiting for the holiday to see the joy he hoped she would feel—she greeted him as if he had come to take her to view a corpse. The present, a gold bracelet, was in his pocket, and he left it there. Oppressed by her mood, he felt he had to make a joke.

"If you're going to be this way, I'll have to go back downstairs."

"Did you read the papers?" She was only beginning to learn to read.

"The parents of a boy I know were murdered last night, shot to death, and he saw it, I know he did. A man came to their door and shot them—"

He wanted her to calm herself. "Do I know these people?"

"I've never mentioned them to you. He was a ship's joiner. They came from the north of England."

"Do you want me to pursue it for you?"

She was sitting on the bed. "Could you? Could you really?"

"Of course I can."

"And my friend? Could you find out what they've done with him?"

"How old is he?" He felt the evil twinge of suspicion. He could not help himself; it was the way he had always been. She was staring.

"I don't know, still a boy, just a little thing. I haven't seen him in years."

He had been the victim of his own ugly thoughts too often to laugh. "What's his name?"

"Monk. Michael Monk."

He wanted to say it made him think of an orangutan, but he didn't. He went around to the other side of the bed and removed his jacket. She did not turn to him, so he put the bracelet on the table next to the lamp, where, if she didn't see it first, he could point it out to her. All he had to do was lie on the bed and in a moment she would curl up in the crook of his arm. She did not see the bracelet, but in a few minutes she murmured "Thank you." It took him a moment to realize she was still thinking of her friend. Now she unbuttoned his pants. Like many other women, she enjoyed her own contraction when a man ejaculated in her mouth. He closed his eyes and surrendered himself to the transport of his ecstasy. He loved her more than anyone on earth.

The next day, down at City Hall, he asked about the Monk family. No one had heard anything about a double killing. He had work to do in the shop and could not get back to do it until midafternoon. On the way to police headquarters he was stopped twice by acquaintances who wanted to hear what he knew of the Hayes-Tilden election. "Honestly, Alderman, strictly off the record, do you think we'll go to war again over this?"

The furor over the results of the Hayes-Tilden election was only the storm outside. There was an element to the Monk killings that distracted him completely: Kate. When he was shown to the captain who had received the reports of the incident, and the captain told him what he knew, Westfield was so lost in thoughts of Kate that he had to ask the man to repeat it, word for word, a full ten-minutes' recital.

The captain must have thought he was mad. "Tell you what, sir. See Alderman Sullivan. That's his ward. He—ah, you'd better see him about it, sir."

Westfield rose in a daze. He remembered a lot of what the captain had said, probably most of it. Absently and grimly he thanked the captain and headed for the door. When he reached it, he looked back: from behind his desk the captain still watched him, eyes wide, mouth agape. Certainly; he thought Westfield was out of his mind.

But as he walked back to City Hall, Westfield thought his way through the scene again. In all the daydreaming, he had kept his eyes locked on the captain's. Hadn't he seemed like an inquisitor? With his mind's eye, he studied the captain's face more carefully. Why the nervousness? In any event, a new meaning emerged: the captain had gotten at least some of his information from Sullivan, burly, wet-lipped swine of thirty or so, and the captain did not want to have trouble with him as a result of Westfield.

Well, Westfield had his own methods of dealing with men like Sullivan.

Two nights later, when he was supposed to be playing cards with friends, he told Kate what he had learned. He sat on the edge of a hard chair, his jacket still on, and described his comings and goings from City Hall and Police Headquarters to the Sixth Ward. He was indulging in detail not because he wanted Kate to be happy with how much he had tried to do, although that had been a consideration early in the errands themselves, but because the subject had swallowed him whole. She knew Sullivan and was as afraid of him as everyone else seemed to be, and when she showed alarm as he told her that he had gone directly to Sullivan, he laughed at her for not understanding the courtesies that all politicians must abide by to make their own lives tolerable.

"The fact that I love you, Kate, doesn't mean that I'm as powerless as you."

Her eyes were shining with pride in him.

"As I'm sure you know, Sullivan does his business out of a saloon. I haven't been in a place like that in fifteen years, and I don't think the patrons have seen a man in decent clothes in the place since it opened. Sullivan was holding his court at a table in the rear, drinking ale and eating pig's knuckles. He kept wiping his lips, but the grease kept reappearing, like magic. He was very polite and offered what hospitality he could. Normally I don't have much to do with him, and I suspect he has aspirations to rise socially. He never will, but that's beside the point. I told him that I was on an errand for a constituent I judged to be very influential in my corner of the world and I wanted to be able to go back with clear answers." He paused to accept her blushing smile. "I permitted him to understand that I would be in his debt. A man like Sullivan counts favors owed to him the way Jay Gould sizes up the value of what he can steal next. When I mentioned the family name, Monk, I could see something behind Sullivan's eyes. At that moment one of his toughs

came to the table with some request or other, and shouted at him. But
then he smiled, 'Can't you see I'm talking to a gentleman?' Jim Sullivan
may have his aspirations, but he doesn't seem to see that a gentleman
treats his servants with even more care—"

"The way you treat me," she said mischievously.

"I just described you as an influential constituent, young lady—"

"You love me," she said.

"I do. You know I do."

"Tell the rest."

"Sullivan got very confidential then. He wanted me to understand that
the way he did his business was different from the way I did mine, and if
he couldn't explain exactly how he knew things, it was not only because
he was required to keep his finger on the pulse of his ward just as I must
do, but also because the nature of his ward required him to accept the
confidences of people who, he said, lived a different life from his and
mine."

"He actually used those words?"

"Yes. Kate, I know what he is. The shooting was, he said, a matter of
mistaken identity. Apparently the killer, a professional who was paid
seventy-five or a hundred dollars, went to the wrong house, or door.
Sullivan said that he didn't know more about it, other than that his
neighborhood informants have told him that the killer himself has been
attended to for his mistake."

"Who hired him?"

"Sullivan didn't have that information. I'm sorry, Kate, but that is what
I was able to learn. Your friends were murdered by accident. You know
better than I how that can happen in the Sixth Ward."

She was weeping, tears spilling onto her cheeks. "And Michael?"

"He's in the new home in Cherry Street. Sullivan said he would check
on him, but I told him not to trouble himself."

"Find out, Thomas—please find out!"

In the days that followed, what he learned of Michael Monk became
confused in Westfield's mind with other, closer, issues.

From their beginnings the previous September he had wanted Kate to
be his mistress, and even though she had told him why she would not do
it, he had not stopped wanting it. He was determined to win her
completely, or as completely as he could. He had gone that far: his
emotions were out of control. But he was not frightened. He savored his
thoughts of her—he wallowed in them.

As for the boy, it appeared that he was not coming around. Two weeks
after the killings, he was still not eating. Westfield was told that the boy

spent his days sitting in a corner, his eyes closed as often as they were open.

It would have been simple to keep the information from Kate, but Westfield, for all his marital infidelities, had become more and more honest with the women he loved. He simply could not lie to Kate. And he could not keep silent, either. In her turn Kate had become his one connection with the real world. So even if she didn't ask, he told her whatever Sullivan had told him. One of the matrons in the home raised her voice to Michael in an attempt to make him work, and when he went for her, screaming and clawing like an animal, the woman was forced to beat him.

Westfield could see the pain on Kate's face, yet he couldn't stop himself. He began to wonder if in fact he intended it, this propulsion toward a new situation. The boy held Kate to him, and finally Westfield couldn't resist the challenge of it. It was a way to bind her to him completely.

"I've decided to take the boy in," he said to her the following week.

"What? You couldn't. Your wife—"

"I'll do it," he said firmly. He did not want to see her reaction, but not because he was too tempted to tell her what it really meant to him or because he had grown comfortable with the notion that winning her would take time, but because he had begun to contemplate Louise. It would be a contest of wills—he owed this to himself. It was a way of beginning life all over again.

He was peering into his future in that way when Kate flung her plump arms around his neck and began to kiss him all over his face.

I V

The planning and execution of the entire scheme was so intricate, laborious, and time-consuming that it was only Kate's continued joy that kept her more than just in the shadows of his life. Still, he was so weary with appointments with Sullivan, the magistrate, his lawyer, the police, and snoops of all descriptions that he went for as many as five days without seeing her. She understood.

It was like unraveling a snarled skein of yarn, juggling a dozen precious objects, and threading through a maze, all at the same time. No part of it was unimportant; it required all his tact and skill. Sullivan played his part under the impression that Louise was the instigator of the project, whereas the magistrate believed that the Westfields together were acting on some long-suppressed impulse to aid the city's homeless youth. When a reporter got hold of the story, Westfield had to go back to Sullivan to have it killed. The gossip that Sullivan was sure to start made Westfield nervous, but in the state he was in, growing more and more pleased with himself, nothing unhappy could fasten itself in his mind for long.

As for Louise, it took him all of ten days to concoct the story he wanted her to believe: that the Monk killings were the talk of City Hall, the Police Department, and the Democratic Party; that the child (Westfield hadn't seen him yet) had reduced the hardhearted matrons of the Cherry Street shelter to tears; that when he had heard the story himself, Westfield had broken down and cried.

He had briefed himself so well on his lie that his eyes moistened when he told it to her.

She was silent. He knew her tricks, so he didn't look at her: she was watching him to see what he really had on his mind. Staring at the floor, he told her that he wanted to give the boy a home.

She said no. He had expected as much. She always said no to anything new, anything he wanted to do. He stood up and looked down at her.

"I've already said that we would do it. There's no backing away from it now."

"How dare you?" she cried. "To bring a slum child into your own home to live with your own flesh and blood—?"

Although her argument made so much sense it made him feel afraid, he smiled. "Be quiet. I've told all these people I'm dealing with that you're the finest woman on earth. You wouldn't have them believe otherwise, would you?"

From that point on, through the holidays, she spoke to him only in front of others and only when she was spoken to. Unpleasant as it was, he saw that it was the best he could have achieved.

The estrangement from Kate created an odd effect: he had to overcome the feeling that her continuing interest was not an intrusion. At last he went around to see her with the intention of describing what had taken place inside him, but he wound up saying more than he thought he meant. The truth was that he could not sort out his feelings.

"At this point I would proceed with it anyway, even if you began to object. I have never wanted anything as much in my life. I could flatter you by saying that somewhere in my mind is the idea that he is our child, that we embarked on this together, but nothing of the sort is true—"

"You don't have to say it. I know."

"You don't seem unhappy."

"I'm not. Would you be unhappy if I did something like this?"

He smiled ruefully. "Probably." That much was clear to him.

"I don't feel excluded," she said. She kissed his cheek. "I love you more."

She had yet to hear that the boy was worse. Westfield had been told he had lost more weight, perhaps as much as fifteen pounds. He was being left alone because of Westfield's interest in him, but no positive steps were being taken with respect to his health. No steps were possible. It was assumed that he had fallen into melancholia, and it was hoped that Westfield's intervention would rescue him. The boy still did not know about Westfield.

He had not seen the boy as a concession to his own emotions. As confused as he was, he saw that it would be awful if everything simply melted away. He would remember it forever; how much more deeply would he be hurt if he remembered the boy's eyes? Brown eyes, they said, dark brown eyes. He was a handsome child, they told Westfield, physically sound, apparently intelligent. Westfield did not need to know more. With discipline, an eleven-year-old boy could be molded into any sort of man.

There was no more information on his parents' murders. The police held little hope. A hired assassin had made a mistake and had paid for it with his own life. Three lives lost—one day when Westfield went around, the police had even had trouble finding the file. It was a dead issue.

Westfield's business in Cherry Street went smoothly and about as quickly as he could have expected. The hansom he had taken from the Astor House waited at the curb below. The shelter itself was directed by one of Tweed's old cronies and staffed by the sort of women who have no memory whatever of their own youth. With groveling ceremony, Alderman Westfield was ushered into the director's office, where he was immediately praised for his Christian charity and profound human understanding. Then he was offered a drink from a bottle kept hidden in a drawer. Westfield declined.

The director was a rheumy-eyed old tosspot with stained moustaches and a double chin that ballooned an inch over his collar. He had a habit of rubbing his nose with his knuckle, as if his nose permanently itched. Westfield noted that his cuff had an expanse of dully glistening dried snot.

"Umph, I'm certain that your papers of guardianship are all in order, Alderman. Would you like to meet the boy while I go through them?"

"I'll wait, thank you."

The director cast a glance to the matron at the door. "Bring the boy upstairs and have him wait outside." He bared his teeth at Westfield. "We got him ready this morning, not wanting to keep a man such as yourself waiting."

"That's quite all right."

While he sat there, Westfield looked beyond the director to the small, narrow window behind him. The smudged, dirty glass gave a view of the back yards of the Sixth Ward. The welter of broken-down, ramshackle structures looked even less promising than from the street: some of them seemed ready to topple over. Chimneys issued uncertain threads of smoke that the mild breeze carried off. Washlines zigzagged in a dozen crazy directions, sagging with tattered shirts and shapeless pants frozen stiff in the January air. From one clapboard structure a downspout had broken loose and projected outward like a broken bone. It was only a matter of time before a boy came along and tugged it loose, perhaps bringing a load of debris down on top of him. A boy like Michael? Westfield frowned. For the first time he realized that Michael Monk had already lived a harder life than he himself had ever known, and that the murder of his parents might have been the culmination of years of unremitting poverty and violence.

The director sniffed. "The papers appear to be in order, Alderman."

"Let's get on with it, then."

The director caught the sharpness in Westfield's tone. He shuffled to the door and led Michael in.

Michael Monk was taller than Westfield had imagined, by three or four inches, and not merely a handsome child, but beautiful, with smooth, even features and large, soft eyes. He was so thin, pale, and sick-looking that his eyes and lips looked like painful swellings on his face. The blood vessels beneath his skin were plainly visible—soft, blue coursings at his temples, and down his neck. His black curly hair had grown thick and wild. He was wearing a plain black jacket with the lapels folded over to protect him against the cold outside.

"Michael, this is Mr. Westfield, who has been appointed your guardian. You're a lucky boy. You'll be living in his house from now on."

The boy glanced at the director, then back at Westfield. He didn't understand; for a horrible moment, Westfield felt sure that he didn't understand the words themselves, that they were only a noise that had drawn his attention away from the new figure sitting in the center of the room, and that his melancholia had reduced him to the level of a dumb animal.

"Are these all the clothes he has?" Westfield asked.

"That's right, sir."

"He wasn't a street arab. Surely there were more."

"He was brought here in the middle of the night. When someone thought to go back to where he lived, the place had been picked clean."

"What do you mean 'picked clean'? By whom?"

"By neighbors. You don't know how it is down here, sir."

Westfield got up and unbuttoned his own jacket. It was big enough to serve as a coat for the child. "Step up, boy. We're going out in the cold and I don't want you to get sick."

The director prodded him forward. At a distance of three feet Michael stopped and stood submissively, hands at his sides, eyes wary. Westfield draped the coat around him and began to button it. The boy's shoulders were so thin that Westfield thought he would cry.

"Does he have any belongings at all?"

"Yes. He brought it with him and it's in his pocket now. He won't part with it. A woman's comb."

Westfield sat down again. He reached for Michael's hand. "Is it your Mama's?"

The boy stared at him.

"I want you to keep it. My Mama died when I was younger than you, and I have nothing to remember her by."

There was a movement of his head, almost imperceptible, that Westfield, in a burst of elation, took as a nod of understanding. He motioned Michael forward.

"Do you remember Kate Regan?"

He did; there was a flash of recognition.

"Kate is the one who told me about you. She told me that if I could, I was to convey to you her regards. She wants you to know that you have nothing to worry about with me. She knows that I'm going to take good care of you."

Michael searched Westfield's eyes for a long moment. It was as if he were absorbing Westfield's words singly, as if in each of them he could see facets of his future.

Now there was a smile. His teeth were yellow and stained and his spittle clung to them, but it was a smile. Westfield wanted to hug him, he was so relieved.

Too many questions remain. For example, what of Louise? At the very moment Westfield is feeling his first authentic impulse toward his sad and strange newfound son, Louise is on the fourth floor of their home on East Thirty-eighth Street, arranging a bouquet of dried flowers in a vase on Michael's new (used, actually, but not marred) night table. The fourth floor is given over to servants' quarters, to be sure, but the room is her husband's choice, not hers—not so much a failure of his nerve as an inability to see more deeply than he can into the situation he has created. Like other women of her generation, whether he knows it or not, she has submitted to his direct orders as she always has, and as well as she knows how. Her lingering resentment is another matter. The flowers are just one of her decorative touches. Hannah, the maid, who understands these things better than Louise, has offered the information that the boy will be undernourished and probably sickly. Louise has told her to prepare the appropriate food.

So Hannah is far below, preparing the broth she always gives to the ill, brewed of chicken and pork and potatoes and onions. When he arrives, Michael will ask for more, and Louise will overrule Hannah's impulse to add on "substantial" things and instruct her to slice some cured ham, an unbelievable delicacy for Michael. Louise's heart will be cut deeply by the pathetic sight of the boy, and she will be awake tonight long after Westfield himself is asleep and dreaming of Kate's plump, rosy body. Louise will gaze fondly at Westfield—his mouth will be open, his thinning hair sticking out in bizarre directions; in the blessed dimwittedness of a man's dream of lust he will be wondering how such large breasts can be so firm—and Louise will think that she is married to one of the kindest, most noble men in the history of the world.

She has no idea that she was dismissed so many years ago from the part of his life that is most important to him—indeed, she does not know that there is anything else to him than what she sees. She was raised to be a lady and has been sheltered all her life by men seeking to preserve her fragile and mercurial charm. She cannot imagine an alternative. She knows nothing of the desperate poverty from which Michael has just been rescued: she has seen those people when she has been shopping, read about them in tracts and pamphlets, and they are more than she can bear. She refuses to read newspaper accounts of the crimes their degradation has forced upon them, and would deny houseroom to the many books published about them or the vice in the city it seems their lot to serve.

Her husband has never seen her with her hair let down, although he has touched it occasionally in the perfect darkness of their bedroom. He has never seen her nude. She does not know any names for the parts of her body that interest him so, and her thatch of pubic hair horrifies her.

With that sort of conditioning, Louise Lowe Westfield is thankful that her husband has apparently lost so much of his interest in sex. Contrary to anything he may have thought during their marriage, she has never experienced even one pleasurable feeling as a consequence of physical contact. "Don't expect too much," her mother said before the wedding, almost hysterical herself at having to speak of it.

Afterward, when Louise dutifully reported what she could of the honeymoon, her mother tried to learn how her daughter had fared. Louise—her loyalties now, and honestly, divided—could only look away. Mrs. Lowe, whose husband did not consort with whores and therefore inconvenienced her regularly, all three hundred pounds of him to exactly the effect on his wife that Westfield had intuited, felt compelled to express her views on sex for the first time in her life.

"It's part of God's design. He couldn't give men the drive to succeed in industry and business without making it part of the rest of them. They have to be the way they are, and we really should pity them. I'm sure that some of them, on reflection, feel mortally ashamed of their desire."

Notice that Mrs. Lowe did not actually discuss sex, but rather her view of men themselves. It should be noted, too, that she fudged on her very last word. Her thought was "lust," but she could not bring herself to let it pass her lips. It is still a potent and dangerous word. Thus the meaning, and Louise's understanding, was not what Mrs. Lowe might have wished.

The result is that, during the early, agonizing years of Louise's marriage, when Thomas hates her murderously, she sees him struggling manfully with his "desire"—that he loves her too much to subject her to carnal abuse. Out of love for him and profound respect for his ordeal, she endures his vile temper and resolutely does nothing that will threaten his virtue.

Fortified by the popular wisdom that life is never easy, Louise keeps their home happy and well ordered. She falls back on her training and stuffs their lives with culture and art. She becomes, against his befuddled protests, a minor patroness, buying, encouraging, and celebrating deservedly obscure sculptors and petulant, fainthearted watercolorists. And in the end, with the fawning attentions of a fast-talking Italian, she resumes playing the piano. In the last third of the nineteenth century the piano enjoyed a rush of popularity in the United States every bit as big as the television boom of the middle of the twentieth. Louise concentrates on Chopin, but she is hapless, and the house is filled with stumbling, halted noises that only hint at the never-never land of popularized romanticism that she believes to be the home of all art.

For all these new relationships, too, she falls back on her old training and is flirtatious, witty, and gay. When the Italian brings her tiny gifts, a china music box, a fan of French lace, her husband tells her not to encourage him, but she laughs and tells him that he does not understand the ways of the Old World. She never sees that the Italian makes himself scarce whenever her husband comes home, or that, even more sinister, her husband has lost his appetite for the food her hands have touched.

Through all this courses her resentment, but since she remembers it first as the only emotion she experienced on her wedding night, she has identified it not as resentment or, deeper, anger, or deeper still, rage, but as the core, even the bond, between a man and a woman. Central to the agony of the Industrial Age is the fact that we do not know what we are feeling. Since her parents seemed to have been married happily, Louise clings to her mother's advice, even unconsciously, and when the resentment rushes up in her, she sees it in sexual terms—it is her sexual metaphor, the way she understands sex—and she struggles against Thomas until she sees he cannot be denied or, just as often, he capitulates in a fit of despair that she interprets as the mortal shame her mother described.

So Louise will forgive misunderstanding, but she will not forgive rudeness; and when Thomas opens his newspaper in the room while she is having tea with a burly sculptor and his tiny wife, she feels—and properly, from her point of view—that her first obligation is to her guests, and she makes a remark designed to cut him dead. He rises, says in a strangled voice, "I should have expected nothing else from you," and leaves the house. She bids her guests a quick good-bye, but not quick enough: Thomas is gone for the rest of the week. She assumes that he is at one of his clubs, but when he returns to still another roomful of artists, he is red-eyed, unshaven, and dirty. Her vague contrition vanishes totally, and when she tries to hustle him out of view of the scurrying guests, she attacks him for disgracing her. Given what he has been thinking about the Italian, he is speechless, and it is not until they are in their bedroom that he makes any sound at all. The sound he makes then drives her out into the hall and down the stairs to tell Hannah not to worry. Thomas is screaming—a raw, rasping, snarling shriek, at the top of his lungs and for as long as one deep breath can last.

Later, when she feels it is safe, she ventures upstairs again. Thomas is asleep in the bed, smelling of his own sickness. For the next two days he stays in bed, and she suggests a doctor. No, he croaks, he is better now. But for a year she wonders, still afraid—and then observes that everything has slid imperceptibly back to normal.

It has occurred to no one who knows her that Louise is not very bright. Thomas has thought it, of course, but only in his fits of anger, and she remains as mysterious to him as she was at first. There is a mystery of sorts, a rather complicated one: her assets, meager as they are, are among the most valued of her era—even features, charm, manners, a certain girlish carriage. Since her childhood she has been praised for her witty and delightful conversation, and she is pleased that she has a reputation for the sudden devastating remark. It does not take much intelligence to make clever conversation, merely an ability to pay attention to the rhythm of words, and since nearly all words have two or three meanings, the knowledge to change their direction. Louise would say it was instinctive, and laugh it off. Charm and manners, which are learned, are only devices designed to conceal character and, not incidentally, intelligence or the lack of it. So Louise remains as mysterious—and as celebrated—as ever.

At the heart of that mystery and celebrity for Thomas is the question of whether she is faithful to him. He chooses to believe, finally, that she has been, but belief is no substitute for sure and certain knowledge. Louise is, simply, a coquette. No man but her husband has ever touched her, and she would be outraged if any dared try. The Victorian era, which tried so hard to deny the influence of sex on our lives, cranked out middle-class coquettes by the millions, just as our own society, influenced as it is by the Victorian, has produced millions more variations on the same theme.

A Girl

I

KATE WAS SIXTEEN.

At nine, when both of her parents were alive and drinking themselves into a stupor night after night, she was a skinny kid with streaks of dirt on her legs, and when she wasn't scavenging bits of coal from the barges along South Street in the winter or stomping barefoot through the muck around the pilings in the summer, she was playing street games with the other children, girls and boys together, on Lombard Street. They chased rats and killed them with sticks, set cats adrift on planks on the river, built fires and cooked food they had stolen, trooped through the streets tracing routes commanded, as often as not, by police they encountered along the way. They followed fire engines and cheered the different companies as we cheer athletes today. Her brother had gone to sea. Her sister was in a cathouse uptown somewhere, to be dead in another year, stabbed seventeen times by a Negro pimp. Kate herself had already discovered sex, at age seven, and had forgotten about it, as much, or as little, as any part of her exploration of the world around her. In her later life the clearest memory she had of her early experience was of standing on the corner of Lombard Street, talking with a boy her own age, with her finger up her nose as she tried to snag an elusive hard snot, when a fat biddy walked by and whispered, "Filthy!" The busybodyness of it so infuriated Kate that she ran after the woman and kicked her in the back of the ankle. Later, when she was sixteen, the incident made her blush; and when she was forty-five, in 1906, drunk from celebrating having missed the San Francisco earthquake, she told the story herself and led the raucous laughter.

At twelve and still not blooming, her father dead in a dock accident and her mother drunk every waking moment on stale beer, Kate was one of scores of children working in a celluloid collar factory. Three nights out of five she slept in the street, which is to say in a doorway or on a barge, where it was safer than at home. Her mother, a toothless harridan at forty-one, had surrendered all interest in her family, and anything was liable to happen in those two rooms. Kate knew everything there was to learn of life in the Sixth Ward; she had seen it herself, and she was well past worrying about her mother, her last solid connection with the world: no, her first concern, at twelve, was in staying alive.

At twelve she was untouchable, a remote, hard, little creature. When other children huddled together at night for warmth, she crawled off into a corner and piled up around her what she could to shield her from the wind, straw on a barge, oily rags in a warehouse. If she could have explained her behavior, she would have said that she was becoming afraid—more and more every day. In a city a small child has little reason to fear anything, except in rare instances; children from the ages of seven to twelve are both an ignored and carefully supervised part of the street scene, noisy pests needing a word now and then or perhaps a kick in the pants. At twelve she understood that that was changing for her. There were the gangs, and if she knew many of the members, she knew too that they were thieves, kidnappers, and murderers. That they knew her would not save her if they were drunk. She could remember her father's drunken gruntings at night; her mother had outlived them but had not survived them. The girls in the collar factory disappeared regularly with young men, men, even *old* men, and when they reappeared, sometimes they had money, a few greasy coins gleaming between their fingers. There were whores on the street, young ones with shrill cries and laughter, old ones with drawn skin and wild, searching eyes. Kate did not believe in God and had no religion in the sense that she was afraid certain acts would cause her to be hurled into eternal abandonment, but when she looked upon the life before her, she was filled with dread. It was inevitable. She would be one of them, a whore.

In another year she was no longer a child and had forgotten her fears. From a distance she loved a leader of one of the gangs, a thirty-year-old black-haired, blue-eyed Irishman named O'Rourke. He looked as if he had been carved from a rock, with a beard so dense that his smoothly shaven chin seemed a dark, shiny blue. He was solid muscle, like a draft horse, but his eyes—whose expression shifted between amusement and suspicion—and his hands—hard, square hands always nearly curled into fists—reminded her of a great, restless, primeval killer. She knew that that was what he was. He had beaten men to death.

On a Friday evening in March he stopped her in the street. It had been warm, but now the air was blustery and turning colder. He had her by the arm. His derby was tipped forward over his forehead and his chin jutted out so that his eyes, glittering down at her, seemed buried deep inside him. It was as if he were challenging her to look at him brazenly. She burned with self-consciousness.

"We should be talking to each other, little one," he said softly. There was gin on his breath. "I've seen you—I know what your business is. Tell me, what's your name?"

"Let go of me. I don't want to have anything to do with you."

"Your name is Kate Regan," he said with a smirk. "Your father was killed on the docks and you have no one to look after you." His grip on her arm tightened. "Don't you think you need looking after?"

"No! Let go of me!"

But she was standing still, not trying to pull away. He thrust her forward, his grip tighter. There were people on the street, women and older men, but it was as if they did not see what was happening. It was not that late at night. The lamps were lit and the sky glowed a brilliant purple. O'Rouke pushed her again and she stumbled. He held her upright and propelled her forward again. "My place is just around the corner. We'll have a drink and get to know each other."

It was useless to call for help. If no one would look at them, perhaps it was because they knew there were no police on patrol. She started to cry, for the first time in years. He saw it. "That's fine. I knew you weren't so tough."

She could not tell how drunk he was: some men could drink themselves crazy inside while giving only the faintest external signs. She tried to wrench free one last time, but his fingers squeezed her flesh so hard that she felt the pain all the way down to the back of her hand.

His flat was on the second floor, two tiny rooms, a table and some chairs in one and a bed in the other. Through the doorway she could see his clothes strewn on the floor. He lit a lamp, keeping himself between her and the door to the stairs. He was not so drunk that he could not see the movement of her eyes as she estimated her chances. He took a bottle and some glasses from the shelf, not letting his eyes leave her. "Do you like gin?"

"No." Her arm ached.

He gave her a glass. "You want to drink it fast; it won't burn so much. Don't think about throwing it at me. I didn't bring you up here to hurt you, but I'll knock your teeth down your throat if you don't behave."

She could see that he almost wanted her to give him the opportunity to do it. She drank the gin, which burned horribly. He laughed at her, had a drink himself, and moved to refill his glass. It was a chance to run for the door. As if she were an afterthought, he reached out with his left hand, caught her by the back of the neck, and held her. He pushed her downward until she was nearly on her knees. "Do you understand me yet?" he snarled. "Do you?"

"Y-yes."

"I don't think you do." He released her, and as she straightened up, he hit her with the back of his fist across the side of her head. She fell against the table, almost unconscious. There would be no more resistance, and the realization opened up inside her with all the frightening power of the birth of a new aspect of her personality.

Three and a half years later, when she was sixteen, she had already been in love a half dozen times in ways that ran the spectrum from her capitulation to O'Rourke on the one hand to her adoration of Westfield on the other. At sixteen, if she had been living a different sort of life, we would have said that she was a strapping girl in the bloom of her youth. She weighed nearly one hundred and forty pounds, and her skin glowed with the pink flush of good health. Her eyes were golden brown and her lips childishly small. In the days when she was not asleep she wore her straight, medium-brown hair in a bun; in the evenings, when she was working, she let it fall in disarray on her plump shoulders. She was beautiful with the beauty of youth; a little later in her life, when she would weigh thirty pounds less than in her teens, she would be handsome, beautiful with the beauty of maturity. At sixteen she was still childishly clumsy, needed guidance in her manners and choice of clothes, and was only beginning to assert what she thought was her real self. Recently another whore had taught her to read, and she was an avid, though unselective reader of newspapers. Through them and the conversations her reading provoked, she thought she was educating herself. She had no difficulty with being a whore, except when the customers were sadistic or foul-smelling or when she felt depressed, which she did more or less as frequently as anyone else. At sixteen, newly literate and still substantially untutored, she had a very large sum of money in the bank—so large, in fact, that Westfield, if he had known about it at all, would have been astonished and even covetous.

II

O'Rourke kept her his prisoner for more than two weeks, not leaving her alone until he was sure that she would not try to escape. That took four days. As hungry as she was, she would not have left: she had made up her mind to that by the morning after he had beaten and raped her, then had beaten her again for not being a virgin. It took her hours more to remember that she had had a sexual connection at the age of seven, but by that time O'Rourke was unconscious again and his inability to listen to the truth as she had finally remembered it gave her the opportunity to think through the meaning of the power of the hold her "secret" had over him. In the darkness of his fetid room she smiled as she realized that she would never tell him anything about herself. If O'Rourke could have seen that smile and the savoring of delicious ironies it reflected, he would have recoiled in horror and dashed for the door.

After the first, short, terrifying beating, the expectation of rape was almost a relief. She had thought she would be murdered. He tore at her clothes and she urinated down her thigh and into the tops of her cotton stockings; O'Rourke, admiring her half-developed body for the first time, burst into laughter. In another moment the vision intrigued him, and his attitude changed in a way she could see and in which she could take an odd and surprising pleasure. While she watched him struggle with his own clothes, she felt an unmistakable physical quickening. She would have broken him if she could have found the way, but the expression on his face almost gave the promise of a better revenge. He looked timid suddenly, vulnerable. If he were allowed to go his way, pursuing whatever it was inside him that made him appear as if he were staring into the details of his death rather than at her, she would somehow win over him. It was impossible to imagine, but she would win. She turned and walked naked into the bedroom.

She realized later that he thought that she was surrendering to him. That happened—again, when he was unconscious—but for the moment she had managed to stop his rough stuff. He entered the bedroom, parted her legs, and settled himself between them. He was, as she realized later, too, not as big as other men his size and age, but he was fully erect. He fumbled with her a while; she saw that she would have to lift her legs; he slid into her easily, completely, and had his pleasure at once, crooning, "Jesus! Oh, Jesus, you bitch! You fuckin' whore!" She felt nothing, expecting no more, but she was so delighted she wanted to laugh. It was not him; it was the world of sex and her own precious place in it. It was clear to her that the process had continued to strip him long after he was naked. Finally he was helpless in the need to cry out his love for her—he *did* love her, she would have sworn it. Out of control, defenseless, he had given voice to his heart's deepest need, whether he would ever admit it or not.

The slowed tempo of his breathing made her see that the moment had passed; her body awakened to his body on hers and the slippery fluid oozing out from inside her. The secret place he had just nearly filled now felt peculiarly more empty than it had when she had stared at him through the doorways of saloons. She moved her legs with the movement of his hips; he raised himself to look at her face, and she smiled in the blossoming of physical excitement that was beginning to take her. It was a mistake. Later, and especially with Westfield, she would learn that it did not have to be so. "You're some kind of a fuckin' whore, aren't you?" O'Rourke bellowed. She misinterpreted his emotion for more excitement, excitement they would share, and she lifted herself to him more, in the rhythm he had just taught her, and while he shouted his rage and more excitement than his spent member could stand, she had an orgasm, her first, and felt a new, unsuspected part of her soul open up, stretch its full length, and curl up like a kitten going to sleep.

Within the hour he had her arm twisted behind her back and her hair pulled down so that she felt as if it were going to be torn from her scalp. He wanted to know who had been with her before him, how many of them there had been, what they had done. She could not remember what had happened to her at the age of seven, and, terrified again, she begged him to stop. This pleased him and he made her get down on her knees and beg for her life; this, in turn, excited him. When he entered her a second time, the combination of her wetness and the effect of the alcohol he had consumed dulled his frenzy, and for what seemed to her like many minutes he labored to get done. She did not perceive it as laboring; for her, his movements had the precision of the escapement of a watch. She surrendered to it, and the anticipation of another confession of his love. This time he was not so talkative, as if he were somehow trying to defend himself against her, but it was nothing for her to move herself in a way that disarmed him. She almost giggled, but his ejaculation was more copious than before; she had forgotten that she would have that, and her response startled her. In seconds O'Rourke was out cold, and once again she was pondering the vulnerability she could evoke from him whenever she chose, it seemed, while simultaneously experiencing for the first time the spiritual refreshment of drifting into unconsciousness with a penis inside her.

What she could not have known, no more than a girl of her age in our time would know, but which any adult woman in our time senses within seconds, was that O'Rourke's sexuality was infantile, arrested, and as logical an expression and extension of the frustration and violence inside him as his hoodlumism, street-corner posing, or even the way his eyes glittered down on her, as they had on thirteen-year-olds before her and would again on even eleven-year-olds destined to follow. She could not understand the meaning of her age in relation to his—no, in that early evaluation of her circumstance, in which she reckoned the sixty–five hours she worked every week at the collar factory, there was the promise, already partially fulfilled, of a journey of exploration and discovery. That she could discount the brutality he had already inflicted on her was just as much a consequence of her experience with life as her age. The most recent part of that experience was the tantalizing glimpse of malehood, deformed as it was, that O'Rourke had given her. And because she was thirteen, she was even able to entertain a fantasy, however unclear, more an emotional heightening than anything she could see, of being important in his life.

After two weeks, she was not terribly surprised when he turned her over to the members of his gang. In the effort to maintain himself with her, in his own increasing childlike desperation, he had slapped and punched her, twisted her arms, pulled her down to her knees. The degradations were boring once she realized that he was not going to kill her. Finally she did not even enjoy the sex, and then it was he who was destroyed. She knew it. As she was to tell Westfield a few years later, when O'Rourke gave her one last beating for good measure, she had sensed it coming; and after that, when the gang sold her to a whorehouse on the far West Side for one hundred dollars, that did not surprise her either.

If the Kate Regan of three years later was no timid sparrow but a financially shrewd young woman whose eyes could not conceal her continuing belief in the promise of life, then the Thomas Westfield she met was nothing like the scared-stiff nineteen-year-old who had left Hartford four years before her birth. For him another lifetime had passed. He understood himself in superficial, socially advantageous ways, and had acquired talents for those assets that are specifically denied to the young, such as patience, the illusion of self-confidence, and a sense of strategy in dealing with others.

For her part, she had developed a taste for men who had lost their boyishness, men of thirty or more, whose skins did not glow, whose eyes hinted distraction or problems or even real mental activity. She admired success. Her previous lovers had carried it more or less easily, and as a consequence she expected good conversation in a love affair as much as interesting sex. What satisfied ordinary customers had nothing to do with her. She never responded to any of them when she was in love; and when she was not in love and did respond, she thought about the man until she saw him again or until the next one came along. Other girls said that it was the same for them, so she saw no need to trouble herself about it. Because she was young, she was only a fair judge of character, but because she was a whore, her judgment was getting better. She had made mistakes in love and she had been hurt in love, so that when she met Westfield she was slightly wary and needed strong emotions to overcome her fears.

He had been told that he would like her, just as she had been told that he was a real gentleman; but he did not come around for almost a week after she had established herself at Caroline's, whose place Westfield was frequenting at the time. Caroline had told him that a fresh young thing had appeared at her door, saying that she had heard that Caroline's was the best of its kind in the whole city and that she wanted work. Westfield vaguely understood the business. A girl could be sold by one place to another like a slave, but she received a percentage of her earnings in all but the lowest brothels. That was the ugly side of it. If a girl took her opportunities, she could make money, call herself an actress, rise in society as the mistress of one man or another, and even marry well. Caroline's story did not enchant him. He did not care for hard or ambitious young girls; they made him uneasy.

When he finally did come in, he was not alone. He and two other men settled into a bantering conversation at the bar. He saw her, in a corner of the parlor, talking animatedly with a handsome young man with a moustache. She was wearing a medium-blue velvet dress that showed a substantial portion of her bosom. Her skin was very fair, very fine. Her cheeks had just a touch of rouge, and she looked her age. On the basis of what he knew, he had decided to be careful with her. As she looked in his direction, he turned away. He had had so many years practice with the maneuver that he showed no stress or self-awareness and she did not think he had noticed her at all.

In a few minutes Caroline came down from upstairs, disengaged her from the young man, motioned to Westfield, introduced them, and excused herself to attend to the young man before his confusion boiled into anger. Westfield kept his eyes on the young man as Caroline led him into the other room, and as he turned to Kate, he allowed himself a wry smile.

"I'm afraid that you weren't done any favor. My friends and I just stepped in for a drink."

"I've heard so much about you, Mr. Westfield—I suspect if I were rude to you, I wouldn't be here tomorrow."

"You speak very well."

"I associate only with the best people."

"What have you heard about me?"

"Nothing but the best, obviously, I'm here, aren't I?"

"How long has it been since you said 'ain't'?"

"I think I said it yesterday. Not today."

Beneath all the practiced behavior, he found her charming. When he bade her good evening, they had an understanding that he would see her in a week. She asked if he wanted her to tell Caroline, but he said he would attend to it.

He did not keep the appointment. He made other arrangements, and the next morning sent around a messenger with an envelope containing, in addition to an appropriate amount of cash, a note explaining that he had had business requiring his attention and asking for another appointment the following week. But the next week, he sent around another note asking her to meet him in one of the private dining rooms at Delmonico's.

He was waiting for her. "I'm sorry about last week. You enjoy Delmonico's, don't you?"

"I've never been here before."

"I thought as much. I would have been disappointed if you had said otherwise."

"Lied, you mean?"

"That would have been unforgivable."

She overate. She had had good meals before, but nothing so rich or elaborate. She learned later that he urged it on her for a reason, just as he kept the conversation on her rather than him. When they had finished dessert, fresh strawberries from New Jersey, he told her that she did not have to worry about going to bed with him that night. She had not begun to feel the real effect of all the food and was afraid that she had offended him.

"No, it's been a delightful evening. I'll see you next week."

"Is it my manners? Is there something I don't know?"

"Your manners are perfect. I like you very much. There's nothing wrong, nothing. I only hope that I haven't bored you with my way of doing things."

"No! Oh, no! I don't know if I'll be able to wait until next week."

He sat back, propped his elbow on the arm of his chair, rested his chin on his fist, smiled, and gazed deeply into her eyes. She could hardly stand it. If he looked at her that way when he took her to bed, she thought she would die. For a long while he stayed silent, and then, gently, he asked, "Ah, should *you* say a thing like that to *me?*"

If he had not placed the careful emphasis on the "you" and "me," she believed she might not have understood him. She buried her face in her hands. "Now you hate me."

"Just the opposite. I'll be waiting, too. Tomorrow or the next evening, if you think of me, at that same moment I shall be sitting at home reading a book."

"I hate books! I don't understand them. Now I'll hate them more—"

He was laughing, this time out loud. She could not help smiling. He said, "Don't you see how genuinely funny it is?"

"Yes. It doesn't bother you?"

"I'm too old for that. It will be all the funnier for you tomorrow or the next evening, you can be sure."

She could see it. "Still, a *week!*"

He was laughing again.

It was not a week. Three nights later, approximately as he had planned it, at nearly ten o'clock, as she came down the stairs at Caroline's, she saw him sitting in the parlor, an untouched glass of creme de menthe on the table before him. The room was very crowded. He did not see her until she was standing in front of him, and then he rose.

"I'm sorry," he said quietly. "Are you surprised?"

"To see you? Yes—yes. You said a week."

He made a space for her on the couch, took her hand in his, and patted it. Their knees touched. "Would you like something to drink?" She shook her head no. "I lost patience with my own game," he said. "I didn't want to wait any longer."

"Thank you," she whispered. A full understanding came slowly. "I'm very happy." She wanted to kiss him, but the need to be mindful of his position stopped her—and made her think of something else. "Game? What game were you playing, Thomas?"

"That's the first time you've said my name." He looked around. "I'm much too old for this. I could have taken you upstairs the first night I saw you. You're a beautiful young girl, Kate. At my age—"

"That's the third time you've mentioned how old you are, Thomas. I wish you wouldn't. It makes me think that you see your life as nearly over, and it isn't."

"I don't think that, in fact. I come from long-lived stock. My father still writes every week, telling me what to do with my life. That's how *young* I am! What I mean is, at my age there's so much I've learned about life, or about myself, that I know exactly what I want. And if I can't have it, I don't want anything at all."

"And what is it you wanted, Thomas?"

He raised his eyes. She had never seen such a shy smile on the face of a grown man. "I wanted you attention."

"You have it." She was not sure he had heard her, she was so choked. It was as if he had reached inside her and put his hand on her heart. She stared at him, knowing she would not be able to save herself from loving him. Suddenly he was in command of himself again, and he surveyed the room.

"Shall we go upstairs, or shall we drink this together?"

"The best room is in use—"

He offered her the glass. "None of that matters," he said quietly.

For a long time he seemed to have nothing to say, and he stared off, and if he were remembering voyages to distant alien places, countries of beautiful languages and strange soul-satisfying customs, for whenever he looked to her his eyes would shine like a child's. It was the first time in years that she had been frightened by a man, but at the same time she found him beautiful. She had seen beauty in men before, young men, boys whose fathers had brought them to her for initiation, but she had been able to see through to their innocence, fear, and desire. When he began to touch her, taking her hand, pressing his knee against hers, she could see that he was still reaching for her, not indulging his curiosity or revealing a repertoire of sexual proficiencies. She wondered what he would be like when they were actually making love, and after; and then suddenly she remembered the thought she had had with O'Rourke and so many others since: that the experience continually revealed them, until it got them down to what they really were. Hoodlums, sailors, policemen, bureaucrats, judges, and even a few priests were all like children after they had shed layer after layer of pretense and disguise. This man was stripped away in advance. No one had ever been more vulnerable to her or less afraid of what she could do. He was giving himself to her as completely as she had always hoped she could give herself to a man, and she loved it because it raised her above herself.

As for Westfield, the man who had stood in his room a few years before and screamed for as long as one breath could last, and who had concluded afterward that this part of his life was all that was really his, he could not help laughing at himself. The joy and surrender in her eyes was more than he had bargained for. If in his conclusion about his life was the whisper that all he really wanted from what life could give was the opportunity to love someone, then he was a desperate and ridiculous figure indeed. He had done nothing with her by accident, but now he did not know if he could have acted any other way. He was old enough to be her father, but in spite of everything he had done since he had arrived in New York, he was still so innocent of the depth of love that until this moment he never suspected how much he was afraid of it.

He took her upstairs precisely because he was so afraid—and because everything inside him cried out for him to do it, regardless of the consequences. He knew he was not going to be what he had been, yet he was so ashamed of his past that he did not know he could stay worthy of such a blessing. He did not care where it took him. He did not care if he ever thought an old, clear thought again in his life.

Neither had ever felt such intense physical excitement. He could not remember climbing the stairs, she could not remember undressing. They reached each other in the center of the bed, both still kneeling, and fell back upon the pillows with their bodies joining naturally, not impatiently, but seemingly instantaneously, and they exploded together. He could feel the sensation race up his spine to the base of his neck; his legs twitched like a corpse's, and he thought he was going to die. For her the contractions were so violent that she feared for him; she felt that she was going to lift them both right off the bed, and she wanted it to last forever. All of it happened in a roar of sound that they did not understand until it was over, when they heard the laughter rising from downstairs, not faintly, followed by whistles and cheers. He knew at once what they had done; she had to raise her head and peer over his shoulder. The sound they had heard had been themselves. Kate saw Caroline's jeweled fingers wrap around the edge of the half-open door, but Westfield, who was rigid now with more than sex, only heard her voice, a soft and distinctly jealous purr: "Alderman, I think you were raised in a barn."

She closed the door as the two on the bed laughed so hard they shook themselves apart, which made them yelp again. The shock and lovely warmth of the hustled recoupling caused them to look into each other's eyes for perhaps the first time since their bodies began to touch. Each was happy and could see happiness in the other: she was wondering when he would visit her again; he was remembering his first time in Hartford a whole lifetime before, when the audience had had a far different effect on him. He wanted to tell her about it and there was no reason why he shouldn't. Under the thought was the notion that he had come full circle, that he had begun his sexual pilgrimage in these circumstances and that this was the finish. It was too important in his life for him not to be superstitious. He kissed her, aching with more love than even love could cure. He would tell her about Hartford, and if weakened, if he felt more afraid than he could stand, maybe he would tell her about the fear, too. He didn't want to, but he could see that if he loved her more than he did at this moment, he would not be able to help himself.

III

By the time Michael Monk moved into the fourth-floor room on East Thirty-eighth Street, his new guardian and his old friend from Lombard Street had been so long and richly in love that each had difficulty remembering what life had been like without the other. Leaving the door open on their first wacky night together had hurt neither of them. She had been regarded with a grudging respect by the other girls, good at her work, no man-stealer, not a prima donna. Her cries had filled her co-workers with laughter, but then with awe, for better than anybody they could recognize authenticity. In the next days, she did not act like a whore who had scored a coup but a girl in love. And she was loved. Two days later he looked stricken when he did not see her immediately, but then as her eyes lifted to his across the room, the other girls wanted to applaud, the exictement between them was so intense. There is a kind of love, illicit or not, that everybody celebrates. Caroline had resigned herself to losing her best girl, and when she found out that Kate had refused Westfield's offer of an apartment and all that went with it, she kept her relief to herself. The girls thought Kate was crazy. She just shrugged and flounced away, not even saying that she had her reasons— at sixteen, she already knew that that would only invite more questions.

She was afraid. As much as she knew, she thought she still didn't know enough. He was a big, powerful man, more powerful than he knew, more skilled, more accomplished. When they were alone, he would try to belittle his position, but she could see for herself. People deferred to him, solicited his opinion, moved in his direction when he entered a room. He told her it was nonsense, but he was absolutely wrong. In private he was gentle and considerate and loving in ways his public admirers would not have been able to imagine; but what they saw of him was all they had a right to see. She thought he was a great man, and finally that made her afraid.

She could not take what she thought was a new step in life. Her plans still took the form of childish dreams—five more years, saving as much as twenty-five thousand dollars, all she would need for the rest of her life. She dreamed of going to San Francisco and being a lady. If she stayed with this until she was twenty-six, for ten more years, she could have close to fifty thousand.

But if she went with him according to her new dreams and moved into an apartment near Union Square (dreams are always specific), she would have less money than she had now, would not be able to save, would be dependent on him, would have to drain him dry just to stay even with her original plan. She knew exactly what he had: he had told her, to the penny. He had told her, too, about his belief that he had come full circle, that he would never love again. It created another dream, that she could make him leave his wife (she could not help hating his wife—after all, who had made him unhappy?) and they could go off together and start a new life. She had heard the stories of too many men for that, but the dreams persisted, continued into her sleep. At odd moments with her customers the dreams would unravel suddenly like stitching on a cheap dress, and she would have an orgasm that would leave her so disgusted with herself that she wanted to vomit. If he saw her again soon enough, she would say she was down in the dumps, and he would try to cheer her out of her mood. He had given up trying to talk her into letting him set her up in her own apartment, but she knew it was only because he believed he would eventually win. She believed it, too, because she believed she loved him more than he loved her. He handled himself so much better than she did. She was afraid she was out of control, and because she did not know what it was like to lose at this, she was afraid of herself most of all.

She still did not know why she had allowed Westfield to take in Michael Monk, except that now she could look back and see that Michael's appearance in their lives had brought with it a pleasant, almost domestic calm. She could have stopped Westfield at any time, and she was not sure that she was right not to have done so. Caroline had warned her that if she ever wanted to stop seeing him, he might throw it back at her, or worse. Westfield could turn on her. Kate did not think that he would do that, but as she knew, and as Caroline reminded her, people changed. That was the worst of it, but the best was simpler: she and Westfield were in love, and they had done something about it. She couldn't imagine how she would ever be sorry.

There was not much that she knew about Michael Monk. She remembered him well enough—there was just not that much to him. His parents had come over at the end of the war, from Liverpool to Halifax, and then down from Canada. His father was a hard, silent man who acted as if he had once lived better than he did on Lombard Street, but his mother, a woman as tired as any other down there, had been nicer. Michael had taken after his father in looks and probably disposition as well, for he was silent, too, gentle and shy. He did not seem suited to the rough-and-tumble of the neighborhood. Kate thought she remembered something about Michael having trouble with one of the boys' gangs, but that had been years ago. At times when she wanted to congratulate herself for the role she had played in saving him from the workhouses, she caught herself thinking that perhaps the episode had worked out for the best. That sort of notion lasted only a moment because there was nothing wrong with her mind—she could remember that two people, Michael's parents, had died. She knew what Westfield had told her about the professional assassin being dead, too, but she didn't believe that. She knew too much about life in the Sixth Ward. She was not even sure that the killings had been an accident, but that was just a guess—she didn't know anything. She never heard anything important about Lombard Street, just the gossip girls passed along. A year ago she had burst into tears when she had learned that O'Rourke had been stabbed to death in a beer garden on the Bowery, and her reaction had so surprised her that she vowed aloud to forget where she had come from. It wasn't possible; she couldn't stop people from talking to her. To most things she was immune anyway, and she knew it, and the reminder of O'Rourke eventually finally aroused an anger in her that she didn't understand, for something about him made her feel small. What upset her about Michael Monk was what she had read in the papers, that his parents had been murdered in front of him. Her own parents had been animals, but other parents on the street had been better, and in her mind their homes had been places where people laughed and hugged one another. Michael Monk had lived in one of those friendly places. He had seen it blown apart with the lives of his parents; it was what he remembered of them—what he knew of life itself.

All through the rest of the winter and into the spring Westfield told her how Michael was progressing. It was a knotty problem because the boy needed more attention than his own children, and Westfield did not want them to think that Michael had intruded in their lives that way permanently. Kate kept her opinion to herself, but she didn't see how it could be otherwise. From Westfield's accounts she knew his children well, she thought, and she didn't like them. Thomas, Jr., was fifteen, Julie fourteen, very close to her own age, but she saw them as infants, overgrown, spoiled, and ignorant of life. Louise had taken it upon herself to prepare them for Michael. Westfield reported all this to Kate amiably; he saw nothing that could go awry. He did not discuss his life with Louise, and for all Kate knew, he went home and did with Louise exactly what he had done an hour before with her. But Kate did not think so. If he was happy at home, why did he want her? It seemed to her that Louise had seen an opportunity to set the children against him again. Time would tell. In any event, Westfield told her that Michael was coming along. Westfield did not have to be reminded of the blow Michael had sustained, and he remarked on the boy's large sad eyes. Michael had not said a word of his parents, and without his knowledge, Westfield had investigated what arrangements had been made for them. Potter's field. Kate kept her own counsel. For a while she thought of paying out of her own pocket to have them buried properly, but finally the idea slipped away. It was not her place. Later, when Michael became an adult, he might want to do something himself and might resent her having intruded—yes, even after she had engineered his rescue. For all she knew, he already hated her for that. Her powerlessness made her feel like the whore she was, closed out for good; for her own sake she had to turn away from all thoughts of the Michael of the future.

I V

As for Westfield, he was in his glory. Louise had taken to Michael, bought him clothing, hired a tutor, sent Westfield in search of his school records. Westfield passed the request along to Sullivan, who reported that there were no records to be found. Michael himself said that he had gone as far as the fourth grade, which was appropriate to an eleven-year-old. The tutor indicated that Michael had great natural aptitude and had added to his formal education on his own. Louise asked Westfield to see if he could arrange for Michael to start school in September at the grade the tutor thought appropriate. It did not seem to be a very large request. Westfield had thought of none of this, and he could not help feeling a kind of continuous relief as he saw these problems raised and then settled so easily. The excitement had been good for the entire household, with Hannah and Louise the happiest and busiest of all. Young Thomas was unhappy, but Westfield reckoned that the competition would be good for him eventually. Julie was at an impressionable age, intensely curious about the circumstances from which Michael had come. Westfield wanted to discourage her interest but could not see how; Louise had expressed no concern, and so Westfield was inclined to let the matter go. The truth was that now that he had gone ahead with it, the whole business left him feeling an unaccountable woe, not as if he had not done something right but as if he had done something unutterably wrong. He guessed that it was because he had misunderstood the magnitude of the thing. He had forgotten that so many human beings would be involved and that Michael's presence would have an effect on each of them.

And as for Michael, Westfield did not know yet how he felt about him. The boy was so quiet, for one thing: it was natural, Westfield supposed, but it was nerve-racking. He seemed all right, with manners good enough to surprise everybody. Louise was especially pleased to hear him say "Yes, sir" and "Please" and "Thank you." For the most part he stayed in the kitchen, where the tutoring was done and where, obviously enough, most of the day's activities took place. Westfield was no longer sure what he had ever expected of the child, but now he was content to let him find his own way. They would warm up to each other later, he imagined, and when Westfield took everything into account, he reckoned he was generally happy with the way things were going.

If he considered himself happy, he considered himself happiest with Kate. He was seeing her as often as he could—counting afternoons, as frequently as four times a week. He dreamed of her more than ever, and at odd moments at the printing shop he would discover that he had turned from his desk to stare through the window down into the street. As the weather warmed and the women came out in their bright dresses, he would see a sudden movement of color or some fine brown hair spilling unnoticed on the back of a smooth young neck, and he would tumble into thoughts of Kate so vivid he would have to catch his breath. When he was listening to one of his printers or drifting through a meeting at City Hall, in the darkness of his mind she would look over her shoulder at him and smile.

Nothing could help him. He had given up telling her when he would be around the next time. "I'll see you Tuesday, if not before" was the way it went now. Two or three times he had to wait for her to finish with a customer, and since she had not known he had been waiting, she would be sullen with him—she could not make love with him without wondering what he was thinking of her. The truth was that he was thinking nothing; he could not imagine her with anyone else if he tried. He deferred to her mood because it was the way of making love to her that was available to him, and as soon as she saw that he was making love to her, real love, she forgot everything. She knew that no one had ever loved her as much as he loved her, and as much as anyone she knew what love, real love, was worth. When they made love, it was the joy on his face that she responded to, not his body, but she did not know what she could tell him. It was the same for him—what made him happy was her response to his loving. As much as they could, they watched each other's eyes. She was the one who had to break it off, drawing him to her, holding onto him while her orgasm possessed her completely—*"Oh, Jesus Christ, Thomas!"*

She could curl up against him like the children who slept together on the barges, and occasionally she would think of them, melancholy, and wonder what had happened to them. She would press herself closer to him, run her hand through the black, wild hair on his belly, and wrap her legs around his thigh so she could rub her wet cunt against his skin. Sometimes she fell asleep, and sometimes he could hear her pursed lips sucking wetly, faintly, clucking, like a baby's, like a baby in the sweet, smooth, dreamless sleep of babies. It was the happiest Westfield had ever been in his life.

But sometimes, when he was asleep, she lay awake thinking about Michael. There was a lie at work, one to which Kate had inadvertently contributed, the one that had made Michael's redemption possible. She fully expected the lie to be found out, and was prepared to say that she was confused or misinformed. In the meantime she hoped Westfield would not think too carefully about what he knew—for instance, that Michael knows Kate, and knows she is a whore. Why should he, when according to all the other information, she left Lombard Street when he was seven or eight years old? Why should she remember him, if he had been a little kid, or know as much as she does about him? A city street turns over a generation of children in less than three years. No, they know each other because they are closer in age than Westfield realizes, and because, for a brief time, since he was quick and she was so slow and unruly as to be unteachable, they were in the same class in school.

When Westfield met him, whatever he thought, whatever he had been told, Michael Monk was really fourteen years old.

Book Two

MICHAEL WESTFIELD

On Thirty-eighth Street

I

IT WAS LOUISE WHO WORE DOWN MICHAEL'S TERROR, ALTHOUGH SHE didn't know it. He despised her at first, hating the sound of her voice. She was always talking, too close to him, her hands always fluttering. She seemed to be hovering over him constantly, asking if he was all right, if he had what he needed, if there was anything he wanted. She was like a golden, benevolent, but dimwitted bird, and at night upstairs in his room the misery inside him would part long enough to allow him to see her gracefully waving her arms and slowly rising through the window. He would imagine her flying over the roof and disappearing, but then with the first twinges of mirth the misery would return with a rush and clamp down on him like a lid.

He was afraid to talk. His mother had been right, they thought he was eleven, but he could see how easily anything he might say could give him away. He liked Hannah, and that made her a danger. She was so much like the women of Lombard Street that he found himself thinking of her as one of them. From there it was a simple thing to think of telling her the truth, but he saw the consequences so quickly that he ran out of the kitchen as if he were about to be sick. She chased him into the back garden.

"Michael! What happened?"

He covered his mouth with his hand and bobbed his head as if he had to vomit. Out of the corner of his eye he saw Louise appear at the door.

"Missus! Something's wrong with Michael!" She called Westfield's son Master Thomas. Even though Michael ate upstairs with the family, and Hannah ate in the kitchen, he was still not sure what the Westfields wanted of him. When he was most frightened of them, he thought that he would wake up someday to learn that he was their servant.

Together the women sat him down on one of the metal chairs and peered into his face. "He was just sittin' at the table studyin' his books when he jumped up and come out here!"

"Something you ate, Michael?"

He shrugged, then nodded. He had taken to watching younger children on the street for clues about how to behave, and sometimes what he did felt wrong—too young. Louise felt his brow, told Hannah that he did not feel warm, and asked if she thought he needed a doctor.

"No, castor oil should do it."

It did not bother him: he was trying to fix in his mind the cause for this difficulty. Even thinking of telling anybody anything would make trouble for him that would last the rest of his life.

That evening his bellyache was real and he was put to bed early. Louise came up and looked in on him. He was old enough to know better than to try to feign sleep.

"How are you feeling?"

"Better, thank you."

She put her lamp on the dresser and sat on the bed. Even in the darkness she looked as if she were made of gold. Again she put her hand to his forehead. "You're not warm. Do you like it here, Michael?"

"Yes, ma'am." He could smell her soap and perfume.

"I'm glad you're with us. Do you know what we do in August? Did anybody tell you?"

"Julie. She said you go to Saratoga."

"*We,* Michael. You'll be coming with us this year. Does that please you?"

"Yes." He wished she would go away now. Julie had told him about Saratoga, with elm trees so big they dwarfed the hotels, which were the biggest in the world. It sounded so beautiful and cool, the sun shining through such high branches, that he did want to see it. The pleasure made him think of his parents again.

"Michael, are you going to cry?"

He shook his head no. More than anything, he did not want to cry. When he was alone, he could control himself, but now he was not sure.

As if she could suddenly read his thoughts, she leaned over and kissed his cheek. He smiled, and smiling made him cry, and he had to smile again.

"You're a good boy," she said, and got up to leave.

The next night, when there was nothing wrong with his stomach, and late, after Thomas and Julie were in bed one floor below, Louise returned. This time he was asleep, and her weight on the edge of the bed awakened him. Before he could gather his thoughts, she said, "It's only me."

He lay still, watching her but not afraid. Later in his life, when he was thirty-one, he would tell Emily that this night was at the center of one of his happiest memories.

"I'm sorry I dusturbed you. I wanted to see how you were."

"I'm all right."

"You were, until I came in. Mr. Murphy says that you're very good in your studies. Do you like Mr. Murphy?"

"Yes."

"Good, well—I'm keeping you awake. If what I have to say is important, I'll remember it tomorrow." And she kissed him on the cheek again, but nearer his lips, and allowed him to breathe more deeply the odors of her soap and perfume. She did not smell like his mother, but she smelled warm and friendly and decent—and not as if she could fly out the window.

In the next days she did not come up to his room but set aside moments before Thomas and Julie came home from school. She had nothing to say but seemed to want only to take stock of him. At the end of the first session she kissed him, a peck, almost on his temple. He could hardly smell anything, but he was still pleased. The next time her lips actually rested momentarily on his skin. When he was thirty-one, he saw that she had to get accustomed to him and that, because he had been so dirty and uncared-for when she had first seen him, the idea of kissing him had probably revolted her. Emily saw his smile but dismissed it as something else.

He could get along with Murphy, even if he did have to be especially careful with him. Murphy was a redheaded, middle-sized, solidly built young man with small eyeglasses and hard calloused hands. He was a student at the City College and supported himself, when he was not tutoring, by working with his father, who was a bricklayer. Murphy held a book in his hands as carefully as he would have cupped a rose, and insisted that Michael do the same. Michael's mother had taught him how to handle a book, but he could not let on to Murphy. It was the same as his recitations, when he stumbled over words he knew perfectly well.

"I'm sorry, sir, but I don't know this word."

"Attribute," Murphy said, putting the accent on the second syllable. He pronounced it that way himself, deliberately stammering. He had to keep his eyes down when he did it, in fear that Murphy would catch on. He could not appear to be too quick or slow, but at the same time he had to make progress or else when he returned to school he would be forced to repeat subjects he had already mastered. He guessed that Kate Regan had had his school records removed—it had been clever of her to think of it. He had thought of it, too, but because he had seen no way to do it, he had expected to be found out. He still expected it, but he did not know how it would happen or from which direction it would come.

One day when they were alone in the kitchen Murphy removed his glasses and sat back and stared at Michael. It was an early afternoon in March, raining, gray, and the light coming in the windows carried with it the wetness of the rain.

"I'm beginning to wonder about you, son."

"In what way, sir?"

"For instance, what do you plan to do with your life?"

"Mr. Westfield will decide now."

"I suppose he will. You see, you happen to have a fine mind; there's no way of telling how fine. I'm beginning to wonder if I shouldn't talk to his lordship about you—"

"His lordship?"

"Mr. W. himself. If you tell him I said that, I'll deny it. Your own stock isn't so high and I think you know what a little suspicion about you at this point will do—"

Suspicion? Michael wanted to ask him what he meant, as clear as it seemed, but he couldn't. He watched Murphy's eyes, hoping that the Irishman could not see well enough to know that he was being studied.

"I want to tell Mr. W. that he should know that you might be bright enough for more than just the normal education you would have gotten—before. He should be put on notice."

"Do you think I should work harder?"

Murphy smiled. "You're not an ordinary boy. I don't see how you could work harder."

"I could try."

"I'd have to tell them. It would require more of my time."

"Tell Mrs. Westfield," Michael said. "Tell her that I said I wanted to get ahead a grade so I would be out of school and working that much sooner."

Murphy gazed at the sideboard on which lay the onions and potatoes that had been brought up from the cellar earlier in the day. "That isn't what I had in mind. You don't know what a precious thing a real education is."

"You can tell her I said it. It will give her an idea how serious I am. You'd have to say what you think, too," he added.

Now Murphy turned his eyes to him again. "You've already made up your mind? You want to go to college?"

"Yes."

He reached for his glasses. "Someday you will have to tell me about yourself, Michael."

It was several days before he began to believe that he did not have to worry about the meaning of Murphy's "suspicions" or whatever he might have asked himself about Michael's craftiness in pointing him toward Mrs. Westfield, but by then it didn't matter. Michael had already hardened himself to going back to the children's shelter on Cherry Street.

There was a hardness that ran all through him, the hardness of wild, animal terror. In the weeks and months since the night of his parents' murders, it had submerged and drawn back, but it had also convoluted with each new change in his circumstance, and finally, worst of all, it had grown. He watched everybody, and he watched himself. The best he could do was remind himself over and over that he was eleven years old. He could not remember what being eleven felt like; he could not remember what had happened in his own life in that year. He could remember events, but he could not be sure if they had happened three years before, or two, or four. And if the events themselves were too vivid, he could not remember his own reactions. It was hopeless.

He was alone, completely, unutterably, alone. His father had spoken of a brother living in Liverpool, but Michael did not even know his name. He could be alive or dead: in any case, the connection was lost. There was no one on his mother's side. She had not been willing to leave Birkenhead until her own mother had died. Michael could not think of what his parents had gone through without dissolving inside. They had waited years to marry, more years to emigrate, only to be destroyed before their dream had begun.

Everything his parents had worked for would be gone forever if he allowed his own life to disappear beneath the filth and horror of this city. The only relief he could find from his agony was in his resolve not to fail them. He still did not know what that meant or where success would carry him; he did not see success in terms of his own pleasure but in terms of moral justification. His mother had told him years ago that they had come across the Atlantic to escape the fierce, dark poverty of Liverpool, but that they had underestimated everything. They were not stopped in New York, she said then; they were starting again to save, to plan, to find a better place. That they had not reached it did not mean that they had been wrong. He could remember too clearly her happiness as she talked about what they wanted to do. There was no way that could have been wrong, in Michael's mind. Remembering it only deepened his resolve until the resolve itself was a place to which he could flee to be relieved of his grief.

His mother had been a governess in England, attending merchants' daughters, teaching them their manners and how to read and write. His father had been a ship joiner, a taciturn man, sensitive: she had known him all her life. He was ten years her senior. She had always loved him, she told Michael; there had not been a time when she had not loved him.

Almost as if she had known what was coming, she had taught him everything she could about himself, his father, her, and both their families as far back as the Bibles recorded. She had said that it was important for him to understand where he had come from, for the world was changing and nobody knew where he was going. She had been a wonderful teacher. He did not know everything; he was only a boy, but his head was filled with the richest and most beautiful stories that he could not tell anybody now. If he was able to follow her last instruction and save himself, he would never be able to tell them for the rest of his life.

Upstairs in his bed, he tried not to think of anything, but he could not help himself. If he thought too much of this new life he had with the Westfields, he would suddenly be stabbed with the memory of how he had come here. More than anything he did not want to think of it, but finally it seemed as if he thought of it always. It waited for him in the nights; it rose up before him in the days, the special meaning inside every loud sudden sound.

He remembered it perfectly, every detail.

He was in his own bed, still awake, when there was a knock at the door. His father got up from the table to answer it. Michael could see the door from where he was. The man was of medium height but heavy, wearing a brown bowler and brown greatcoat. He had a round face, a black handlebar moustache, and small eyes with dark circles under them.

"You know what I come for," he said.

His father was in his winter undershirt. He was holding a copy of *The Sun*. "No, I never saw you before."

"You know who sent me and what I come for," the man said.

Michael's mother blocked the view as she entered the darkened bedroom. As she turned back, the first shot was fired and she screamed—after the ringing report of the pistol, the scream sounded as if it were coming from under a pillow. Michael understood none of it, not even the bits of wet stuff that hit him in the face. She turned around again, and now he could see the man at the door, a monstrous nickel-plated, pearl-handled revolver in his hand. The room was blue with smoke. She had taken a step toward Michael.

"Here's one for you, Missus," the man said, and fired again.

There was another deafening explosion, and this time a blinding flash. The other room became thick with smoke. Michael saw his mother's body arch as the bullet struck her, her arms go upward. The glass in the window behind him fell to the floor. When he looked back from the window, his mother was pitching forward on her face, and the man was turning away.

He sat up, got to his knees, and leaned over the edge of the bed. There was a puddle of blood spreading around her neck. As she pushed herself over she let out a cry that made his bladder open.

"Aw—God, God. Michael, don't go out there. Is he gone? Is the door open?"

The door was open. "Do you want me to close the door?" He could see the blood pumping out of her chest.

"Wait!" There was a commotion in the street, a shout, and the sound of footsteps going away. "That would be him," she said. The blood was on her neck and her face.

"Mommy—!"

"Listen to me. Go to the door. Lock it. Whatever you do, don't look at your father. Come right back to me."

In a panic he ran to the door, pushed it shut, and threw the bolt. He turned the wrong way, toward his father, and saw that his father's head was split open down almost to between the eyes. The blood from him was mixed with gray matter, and it was on the walls and ceiling, lumps of it, glistening wet. It was what had hit him a moment before.

"*Michael!*"

He ran to her. "Oh, Mommy!"

"Listen to me. Your father's dead and I'm going to die. I don't know who that man was. Listen to me, Michael. They'll put you in a workhouse unless you lie about your age. Tell them you're under twelve—eleven, do you understand me? How old are you?"

"Eleven."

"The only proof of your age is the paper the captain of the ship gave me. It's in the metal box under our bed. I want you to get it and destroy it. Get it."

"I won't leave you, Mommy!"

"Do as I tell you. Get that paper and tear it up and throw it out the window. You'll never have any chance unless you do as I say."

She could not lift her head; she was bleeding to death, and now, as if she knew that she was as good as dead, she moaned. In horror he backed away, then ran to the other room. He did not look at his father. The box was under the bed with wooden crates and a bundle tied with string. He could hear people coming up the stairs as he found the document. He was crying; he tore at the paper, then pushed the large fragments into his mouth. His mother moaned again, louder; somebody pounded at the door. He ran back to the room and got on the bed. The blood was pumping in shining rivulets over her neck. Men were pushing at the door. He chewed on the paper, but nothing happened. As the door gave way he had his fingers down his throat, pushing the paper as far as he could reach. The people spilling into the flat gasped and cried out, and one of them, a man with a cap, stepped quickly toward the darker room.

"Jesus, Mary, and Joseph! She's still alive! There's a boy in here!"

The others fell silent. The people who crowded into the room listened to her as someone behind them passed a lamp forward. She was breathing long, deep gasps that rattled with blood. Michael was standing on the bed, leaning over her, his hands to his mouth. Her eyes were closed. No one moved, for they could see that she was about to die. The blood had stopped. Her chest went up and down more quickly, but they could hear nothing. Then she stopped moving.

He was eleven again.

I I

He was tall even for his true age, with fair, smooth skin and thick dark hair. He took after his father, as Kate had remembered, his large dark eyes his most conspicuous feature. He was at the beginning of puberty, his legs covered with long, dark down. He knew that he would have to avoid being seen for years to come. Since the first day the women in the house had given him complete privacy, and neither Westfield himself nor young Thomas had shown any curiosity about his life on the fourth floor. Westfield had asked once if he was comfortable in the room, and young Thomas made a point of ignoring him. Michael thought he did not have to worry about either of them stepping into the room at the wrong moment.

His clothes were new, but he guessed that that would change when it occurred to someone that he could just as well wear Thomas's hand-me-downs. That did not bother him, except that he disliked young Thomas and feared him. There was something cowardly and bullying in that soft fleshy face. Michael suspected that Thomas was only waiting for the opportunity to teach Michael who was going to be boss.

He had no defense. An eleven-year-old could not protect himself against a boy who was fifteen. No matter how he thought it through. Michael could see that he had no choice but to take whatever Thomas felt like giving him. There could be no settling in private, for if Thomas went to his mother and said that an eleven-year-old had whipped him, questions would be asked. A boy from the streets could have learned enough, but finally it was a matter of strength. It was one more thing he had to remember, that he was not supposed to be as strong as he was.

There was nothing he could do about Julie. He had calculated that she was three months his junior, but she completely believed that she was three years his senior. She had claimed him as her own, a pet, a toy child, and when she came home from school, she looked for him until she found him.

"How are you feeling today?"

"Very well, thank you."

"What did Mr. Murphy teach you?"

"We talked about Bismarck."

"Tell me everything you learned."

He would have to do it.

She was a tall girl with a straight back and narrow waist and a sudden, engaging smile. She was spoiled rotten and could not hide it; when she raised her voice to her mother, which she did frequently, there was no place in the house where Michael could not hear her piercing shriek.

Later, when her father came home, she was the first one to the door. She would fling her arms around him as if Westfield had been gone a month, and he would look at the others coming from upstairs or the back of the house with a kind of amused and stupid bafflement which, Michael suspected, was supposed to absolve him of responsibility for what his daughter was doing. Michael never looked at Louise during any of these scenes for fear Westfield would catch him. He knew about Kate, and it would not take much for Westfield to connect one thing and another and want to run Michael out of the house.

Another reason to be cautious with Julie. She would charge into his room without knocking, read his copybooks, look through the drawers of his dresser without permission, and ask him endless questions about Lombard Street.

Usually she was plopped on his bed while she did this, while he curled over his desk trying to read. An advantage to a room on the top floor was that the good light for reading lasted until it was time for dinner.

"Were you in any of those gangs, Michael?"

"Nope."

"Say no. You're not supposed to say nope. Why not?"

"They didn't ask me," he said.

She liked to bounce on the mattress during these inquisitions. He had given up trying to figure a way to keep her out of the room. Downstairs was the best library he had ever seen anywhere, and he could not risk taking a book because she might find it. Certainly she would prattle on and on about how well he could read.

"Did you get into fights?"

"Yes."

"Did you win?"

He had to think before he answered. If he told her the truth and she told her father, he might see him as a bad influence on her. Not Louise. Once Hannah, scolding him, had used the phrase "hoodlum ways," and Louise had become upset. If Michael had been a hoodlum, he heard Louise saying to Hannah later, she chose not to be reminded of it.

"Gee," he said to Julie, "I have a hard time remembering lots of things these days."

He thought it was a marvelous answer, but the next week she was back again: "Did you remember any more about those fights?"

Westfield called her his beauty. Michael thought she had a good smile. She had nice eyes and perfect posture. But her bosom had not begun to develop, and when it did, it would not be very big. And she was too thin. Even Louise was almost too thin for Michael's tastes.

Julie had precipitated the first real trouble between Michael and young Thomas.

It was late April, warm and moist, and the three of them were in the back garden. The sun was just disappearing behind the roofs of the buildings that faced East Thirty-seventh Street, and the light had faded to the reddish gold of a spring twilight. They were playing Blind Man, Michael was It, and he tripped over the brickwork bordering one of the plantings. Julie ran to his aid.

"Did you hurt yourself?"

He showed her his skinned hand. Thomas had been sitting on one of the iron chairs with his legs drawn up so that there could have been no chance of Michael's bumping him.

"What do you always have to go fussin' over him for? The game wasn't over—aw, I quit!"

He had to go by them to get into the house. They did not step aside quickly enough, and after Thomas knocked them back, he turned suddenly on Michael and pushed him down. Michael's hand skidded across the pavement; the added pain made him rage inside.

"I'm going to tell Mommy on you, Thomas!"

"See if I care! Go ahead, see if I care! You're always spoilin' things, fussin' over him!"

Michael was too busy picking grit out of his palm to pay much attention to either of them. Beads of blood appeared on his skin, and he sucked on them.

"You shouldn't do that. You should wash it. Don't you know any-thing?"

"Yup." He was smiling.

"What's so funny?"

It was better to stay quiet. She had asked him if he knew anything. The way Thomas had moved and used his hands, even Thomas knew that he couldn't fight. He wasn't afraid of an eleven-year-old, but he was terribly afraid of getting hurt. What Michael knew was that he didn't have to worry about him anymore.

The Westfield family gathered together every evening at dinner. Michael could not get used to it. He was expected to put on clean clothes, a jacket, collar and tie, and all three children were expected to sit quietly in the parlor with Mr. and Mrs. Westfield while Westfield and sometimes his wife as well had a glass of sherry. Westfield would ask the children about school, but would pay little attention to their answers. Michael took his cue from Thomas and let his eyes wander to the farthest corners of the room. The tin ceiling had a pattern composed of flowers, buds, and leaves, and Michael passed the time counting one and then another. If Westfield wanted to know how Michael was progressing, he asked his wife, who answered as if Michael were out of the room. It made Michael dislike Westfield even more.

Michael was the only one in the house who really knew the man. It was sickening to see Julie gush over him when there was Kate Regan— where? Michael wished he knew. And Louise treated Westfield almost as if he were a visiting prince. How would she react if she knew about Kate? Michael could not imagine. Nor could he imagine what went on in Westfield's mind. The organization of his entire life seemed to depend on the silence of a boy he did not even appear to care about. After that first day or so, hardly a word passed between them.

One evening Murphy returned for dinner, and the two men discussed Michael and his prospects as if he were a racehorse. If he raised his head, there was Julie staring at him, as if taking credit for her part in the miracle she thought they were performing with him. He could not help feeling sorry for Thomas: no one seemed to notice he was alive. Michael thought that he would not be surprised if he entered a room one day and found the fat kid crying.

Later, after Murphy had gone home, Westfield called Michael into the library. It was on the second floor, with the master suite. The children's bedrooms were one flight above, the servants' quarters above them. Westfield had Michael sit in one of the chairs facing his desk.

"Mr. Murphy tells me that you want to go to college."

"Yes, sir."

"You know that college is expensive."

"Yes, sir."

"Ah, I'm afraid that I'm going to have to ask you some questions about your life before—the life you had before. Will that upset you?"

He shrugged.

"Did your parents wish you to go to college?"

"Yes, sir."

"Who were they? All the police were able to learn was that your father was a ship joiner."

Michael honestly didn't understand the question.

"Where did they come from? Do you know anything about that?"

"They were from England. Near Liverpool." He knew that Birkenhead was across the Mersey from Liverpool; his mother had described it to him so many times that he could see it gleaming filthily in the morning air. What could he tell about his mother? "I think she was a governess, sir, or a children's maid."

"A nanny?"

"What's that?" He knew perfectly well what it was. Now he was afraid that the Westfields would conclude from his apparent ignorance and her situation here in America that in fact that was what she had been.

"We've all been curious about where you get your love of learning. I suppose it was from her."

Michael saw that he had to let it pass. It did not seem natural that he would understand that his father had had it in him too but had not had the formal education to allow him to show it in the usual ways. Michael did not know how Westfield would respond if he explained that his father had known everything there was to know about the sea, science, poetry, an endless number of stories.

"Do you like it here? Truly?"

"Yes, sir."

"Do you miss them much?"

"Yes."

"Do you say your prayers?"

"Yes, sir." He did not count it a lie; he could not say his prayers at night now without being reminded of them. If a God could let them die, what kind of an afterlife could there be?

"Mrs. Westfield has become attached to you. We still don't know how you lived before you came to us, although the signs are encouraging. Do you see what a responsibility you have?"

He suspected what it was, but he wanted to hear Westfield say it.

"You're going to have to do everything in your power to see that that attachment is protected and stays unspoiled." He sat back suddenly and stared at Michael coldly, as if challenging Michael to ask about Kate Regan. What would happen if he asked? What would Westfield do?

"I like Mrs. Westfield very much, sir."

Westfield's mouth worked. "Then you do understand what I just said? You'll do nothing to hurt her?"

"I never will."

"Good. If you mind your p's and q's, I'll see what I can do about fulfilling your parents' wishes for you."

Michael was silent.

"What do you say, boy?"

"Excuse me. Thank you."

"You can go now."

Climbing the stairs, Michael thought that he would never be able to understand Westfield. Why had he brought Michael here in the first place? If he was so clever, why couldn't he have said no to Kate? Michael had not seen Kate in more than three years, perhaps four, and the girl he remembered was not capable of having such a hold over a man.

Later that night he saw another side: there was no punishment Westfield could inflict on him that would irradicate the damage Michael could do in return. If Mrs. Westfield somehow learned that the boy her husband had brought home and to whom she had grown attached was in fact an old acquaintance of her husband's mistress, and further, that the mistress was only months older than the Westfield children, Westfield would be ruined. He would not be able to confine the scandal to this house. He would be brought down for good.

It took days more for it to come clear. It was dinnertime, and Hannah had called the family in to the dining room, after the interminable waiting in the front parlor while Westfield sipped his sherry. At the table Michael sat next to Thomas, with Julie opposite them. Hannah brought the platter of spring chicken from the serving table. She served Louise first, then Westfield. He was taking a leg and thigh when he spoke.

"Is something wrong, Michael?"

The children's heads wheeled. His casual tone had not concealed the fact that this was the first time he had spoken to Michael in front of them without condescension. It took Michael a moment to realize that he sounded exactly as if he thought that his position made him Michael's father, too.

"No, sir, there's nothing wrong."

Westfield's eyebrow went up. Michael felt a stab of terror: in his reaction he had forgotten to soften his voice as if he were eleven.

"Well, you were staring at me."

"I'm very hungry." The voice was perfect again.

Westfield smirked. "It's the mark of a gentleman not to show those things so noticeably."

"Sorry, sir."

"Oh Thomas, all boys love spring chicken," Louise said. "*All* boys," she added gently.

"Nobody denies that, dear," he said, still looking at Michael. "Thank you, Hannah. I was talking about gentlemanliness. I'm sure you agree that Michael needs to be a gentleman."

"Of course but—"

"It's a trivial thing Louise. Let it go." After a moment, he said, "You're right, we all love spring chicken."

Michael looked around the table, and then up to Hannah, who was serving Thomas. No one in the room seemed to believe what Westfield had said, but only he, Michael, had any idea of what the truth could be—and he knew everything.

He kept his eyes on his plate through dinner, and afterward, upstairs, as he prepared for bed, he tried to hide Westfield from his mind as he had hid him from his sight. He was sure that he would receive another summons to the library. Westfield would not be afraid to speak to him in private in the way he dared not speak to him in public.

Or would he? As Michael lay in his bed, it came to him that Westfield would not speak at all. He had mentioned Kate Regan's name only once, back on Cherry Street. Now, if he had to, Westfield could deny that he had said it. There had been a witness, but he would say what Westfield wanted him to say. Westfield would not even have to prompt him.

But Michael could see that if he defied Westfield, there was nothing that Westfield could do about it—provided nothing ever passed between them concerning the real issue. Michael saw that if he was careful, as long as he was circumspect, he was free to do exactly as he pleased.

Why did he want to be free at all? At that moment he did not know. How could he—when to look inside himself meant quickening the agony that was tearing him apart? He had had a happy life and now nothing was left of it. He could not think of any part of it without feeling pain, and he cowered at the thought of his dreams, which were of that life, as if nothing had ever happened. He had begun to fear the early mornings as much as anything. It was spring, with a sweetness in the air. He could open his eyes, roll over and brush his lips against the pillowcase, in love again briefly with the beauty of the world. He could feel the pressure of his memory rising inside him without recognizing it for what it was, and then, having recognized it, he would struggle to hold it off like the evil thing it was.

It took him a week: he wanted to be free to go out and find the man who had killed his parents.

III

In those days New York was not yet the city its residents in the first half of the twentieth century would recognize, but there were signs of the beginning of the new age. The spinning of the cables between the towers of the bridge to Brooklyn went on day after day, week after week, month after month. There were telegraph lines strung above some of the streets. The construction of the first elevated railroads had begun downtown. Saint Patrick's Cathedral, its foundation dug before the Civil War but its spires still not completed, had opened its doors for worship. And from the jail on Ludlow Street came word that Bill Tweed was finished. It was no surprise a few months later when it was announced that he was dead.

If you travel today across the Verrazano-Narrows Bridge and look north over Upper New York Bay, the city rises out of its surrounding waters in walls of glass, steel, and stone. The city is at its most beautiful on a sunny morning, bright and shining against the dark northern sky, but what is truly breathtaking is the incredible verticality of its present state. One can see the Brooklyn, Manhattan, and Williamsburg bridges, and they are all dwarfed by the structures of Lower Manhattan. The smooth surfaces of the newest buildings create illusions of light weight and delicacy. There is a challenge to gravity and an oddly beguiling invitation to the viewer to do the same.

Farther north, beyond a low, dreary saddle of renewal and decay, is another stand of towers, no less spectacular individually but perhaps less effective in aggregate because their location denies them a relationship with the sky and the edge of the sea together. All around them and for as far as the eye can see, the landscape is black with the blackness of urban sprawl. Even the rivers are black. From the highest of the midtown buildings, Central Park is a tattered rectangle that cannot bear close inspection. The horizon disappears in dirt and soot. At twilight in the deepest recesses the haze is the color of dried blood.

A hundred years ago the tallest structures on the island were the church steeples, the dome over the post office, and the small tower atop City Hall. The masts of the biggest ships competed with most of the buildings for height. If you made your way to the top of any of these high places, you would have seen that the water surrounding the island was dark blue, not yet overwhelmed by the sewage being pumped into it, and its courses were wider than they are today. Landfill operations have been going on in New York since the Dutch possessed it, but not until our own era did they begin to seriously redefine the city's geography.

In 1877 the city was large even by today's standards, cobbled, paved, and developed as far north as Fifty-seventh Street. From there the gridiron of avenues and streets envisioned sixty years before faded into dirt tracks around Central Park and disappeared into the area known as The Territory. The park was thirty years old and still largely wild, but it was dotted with carefully tended formal plantings and appropriate and complementary public-garden structures. Surrounding the park, The Territory was littered with tiny farms, rough squatters' shacks, and, here and there, standing with the most astounding effrontery, clumps of row houses and even a mansion or two, waiting for the rest of the city to grow out of the ground around them. Farther north, along the Hudson, were some summerhouses, and in the center of the island, far from the northern edge of the park, was the village of Harlem. Most of Manhattan was covered with trees; there were streams, small game, dozens of kinds of birds, and several thousand acres of open space. It was a wonderful place for a boy to play.

From Thirty-eighth Street the journey north up Madison or Fifth Avenue was a long one for two boys, but as often as not Thomas had the fare for the horsecar. He was eager to pay it, for Michael had become a kind of asset to him. His standing with his chums was not that good, as Michael had guessed. By the time he met them they naturally had heard of how he had come to be in the Westfield household, and they wanted to see him for themselves, this boy who had lived through their wildest imaginings.

"You saw them get shot? You really saw them get shot?"

"Yes."

On Saturdays they passed the time on the corner of Fifth Avenue and Fifty-ninth Street. On passing horsecars they could see mothers and daughters headed downtown for shopping. If the boys looked too hard at the girls or stared too long, the girls would turn their heads away abruptly, as if they had been insulted. It made Michael laugh.

"How come you didn't see the guy who did it? If you saw them get shot, how come you didn't see the guy?"

"They were in the way. He didn't stay around afterward, either."

"That makes sense," young Thomas said. He had taken to supporting Michael, which made Michael feel even more sorry for him. Michael had seen that it would be no good to tell anyone that he had seen the man, and last of all Thomas's friends, who thought of the murder as nothing but high adventure. They wanted to hear about Lombard Street or they wanted to repeat what they had heard their parents say about Westfield, who was being praised in parlors and dining rooms all over Murray Hill for his benefaction. Michael had to wonder how many other fathers were like Westfield, and how many of them were lying and knew it when they praised him. When the boys' questioning became too intense, he could not help toying with the idea of hinting something, but he could see that without specific information about the other men, it reflected only on Westfield, and Thomas would feel the pain.

With Thomas and the others he had come around to being more himself, acting more his age. They thought it was Lombard Street that had made him so wise for eleven. Thomas suspected nothing, for all boys know things their parents never imagine. Thomas himself enjoyed a little stealing from time to time and tried to get Michael interested, and he took it for childishness when Michael said that he thought the risk was too great for him.

In fact he was exploring. They would go to Park Avenue and watch the New York Central trains, or they would climb to the top of the reservoir on Fifth Avenue and survey the city. He could see as far as the Palisades and the Sound and Brooklyn and, between the buildings downtown, the Upper Bay and the lovely colored shadow of Staten Island in the distance. All this was new to him; he had rarely been off Lombard Street or out of the congestion of the city. What had enchanted and distracted him was all the green to the north, east, and west: his heart could lose itself in it; and he could surround himself with Indians, self-reliance and magic. But for the most part he stuck to his decision and tried to memorize as much of the city as he could.

Thomas thought it was part of being eleven. Whenever he had the opportunity, Michael tried to convince Thomas that the real fun was in heading downtown—so he could learn the streets to be able to remember them at night. Thomas sensed nothing of Michael's real motives.

"Sometimes you're a real baby, you know that?"

If it seemed as if his masquerade needed bolstering, Michael would pretend to be hurt and force Thomas to go along with him. There was nothing for them to do in the shopping and commercial districts, and their journeys through them were as fatiguing for Michael as they were for Thomas. Once Michael saw a fat-faced man with a handlebar moustache and a bowler, and he made Thomas keep pace while he trailed the man for an hour, to one shop and then another, until he saw him clearly enough to recognize that he was not the killer. Thomas did not know that they were following anyone, and he thought that Michael had gone crazy. Thomas was nearly in tears when Michael turned to him and said he wanted to go home.

"Well, I'm taking the horsecar! You can walk. I'll wait for you at the corner!"

"You do and I'll tell your mother!"

"*Baby! Baby!*"

On the horsecar Thomas said that he would never go downtown with

Michael again. As depressed as he was, Michael could understand. He determined to let the exploring go for a week.

Thomas was basically a good boy, a little sad and certainly suffocating in his desire to have a true, lasting friend. He was one of those sweaty kids with hair like straw. He talked too much. He would go on about something that had happened to him at Saratoga or at a family reunion in Hartford and then poke at Michael and ask, "What do you think of that? What do you think, huh?"

He was not one who could keep a secret. Michael knew about his surprise birthday party two weeks before it took place.

"If you tell I told you, I'll give it to you, do you understand? I'll give it to you!"

Michael had too much on his mind to remember the party anyway.

It was not his birthday. He had been fourteen on November 5, and he saw that he could help himself if he saw to it that he was not a full three years younger than his true age. When they asked him when his birthday was, he said June 19, knowing that he would have no trouble remembering the date. It had been his mother's birthday.

When they had the party, with cake and candles and ice cream, he burst into tears. Murphy was there and Hannah was sitting at the corner of the table. Westfield was dumbfounded and the children did not know what to do. Suddenly Louise excused herself and Hannah chased after her. Murphy patted Michael on the shoulder, then impulsively patted him again.

It took Michael another week or more to complete his study of the house and its occupants. His own door squeaked when it was opened slowly, so he rubbed the hinge with candle wax. He was not worried about Hannah in the next room. She was asleep every night by ten o'clock, snoring. He knew where the noisy stairs were. There was a board in the hall outside Julie's room that gave way. When he opened the front door to the street, the suction caused the inner door to rattle so that he had to reach back across the six feet of the vestibule to hold it tight. And he had to do it when someone wasn't passing outside because it was something a thief would do.

In the evenings, after he was supposed to be asleep, he would open his door and sit on the floor and listen to the sounds from below and figure out what they meant. The nights Westfield was out seemed best, no matter how late he arrived home. If he stayed in for the evening, he tended to sit up longer; and when he finally went to bed, he tossed and turned for hours. When he was out seeing Kate, he might not come home until two o'clock but then he would go directly upstairs and hit his side of the bed like a felled tree. Then Michael would wait only a few minutes more before he would start to move downstairs.

It was impossible to get to Lombard Street. He could not risk staying out past four o'clock, and even if he had as much as three hours, he could not make his way down there and back quickly enough. He tried and twice policemen stopped him. What was a lad his age doing out at that time of night? If he said that he was working for a man, his clothes would give him away, for they were too fine and clean for that. His old clothes would have served, but they were gone. He said he was running an errand for his mother, who was ill. Did he need a doctor? Panic. "No, I'm going to get my aunt, her sister." He took to turning the corner if he saw a policeman three blocks away. Up here the gas lamps were so close together that they looked like lanterns strung at a political club's annual block party.

He refused to believe it was impossible. The man he was looking for was a night creature—he had to turn up. Michael moved from one street to the next as if the man could come around any corner. He could be anywhere, out of the city, far in the West, but Michael had decided not to think about that. He would never find the man if he did not look for him. He had to look for him.

He drifted toward those areas that were still awake in the late hours, Union Square, parts of the West Side. He could not get so far downtown as the Bowery. He fixed the locations of all the beer gardens and saloons and restaurants, and if he could see in their windows, he would pass over the crowd with his eyes in seconds. Michael had to be careful with the cellar stale-beer joints: the customers were bad eggs and were often wildly drunk. If a restaurant had a doorman, Michael would say that he was looking for his father and describe the man. Now that the weather had changed, Michael could not even guess what he would be wearing. With a laugh a doorman would tell Michael to go home.

The newsboys working the beer gardens suspected that Michael was trying to invade their territories. He told them the story he told the doormen, but without the description because he didn't trust them. He knew them too well. Some were ready to fight no matter what they heard. After a while he was more cautious with them than he was with the police.

There was nothing he could do about the sporting houses. They were easy enough to identify. In the early morning the city was so quiet he could hear people coughing in their beds or the sound of a horse and carriage many blocks away. The drapes were closed and the houses looked dark, but there is a kind of woman's laughter that pierces brick walls. At times he thought about Kate and wondered how she had changed. He was not even sure that he would recognize her, but that did not stop him from thinking that if he saw her, he would ask her what she knew about what had happened to his parents.

And then he would think for the hundredth time that if she knew anything at all, she would have passed it along to Westfield long ago.

When he was very tired, he would wonder if they had anything to do with it themselves, but it made no sense, for surely they would see that he would have to know; that if he did not find the answer this year, he would be out looking next year and the year after that. . . .

He would have to be even more quiet reentering the house. Once, when he cracked open the front door, he heard Westfield padding around upstairs. There was nothing to do but stand absolutely motionless until the bedroom door closed, and then continue to wait for a long time afterward. Michael did not get upstairs that night until the sky was lightening, and the next afternoon, out in the garden, he fell asleep under a tree. When he opened his eyes, the women of the house were gathered around him.

"The angel's awake!" Hannah cried.

Michael looked to Mrs. Westfield.

"We were just saying that you look like an angel when you're asleep."

He was still confused. He turned to Julie, who suddenly reddened deeply, spun away, and hid her face in her hands. He couldn't imagine why.

"Oh, pay no attention to her," Hannah said. "She said it, but we all thought it."

IV

If Louise was happy with Michael Monk, then Westfield himself was convinced that he had made a mistake of such magnitude that his only hope of surviving it was in closing his mind and shutting Michael Monk out. He loathed the boy. A strange and secretive child, full of wounded and miserable notions. Of course he favored Louise, and of course he remembered Kate and despised Westfield because of her. If he and Kate came to grief, Westfield knew that Michael would be at the center of it. And there was nothing to be done. No matter what happened, it was clear that Michael Monk would be in his life for years. *Monk!* The name was foul—it belonged to a beast. A waif from the slums. Westfield felt his throat tighten whenever he saw the boy. If they ventured too close to each other, Westfield did not even want to breathe.

He had stopped speaking of Michael to Kate, but not because of his feelings about him. Silence was part of a new approch he had taken with her. Once again he was a desperate man.

She had not responded to him through the spring as he had hoped. He had made no progress at all in his effort to get her out of Caroline's. Their domesticity had worked against him—it had eaten away at their most tender feelings.

She had discovered that he was vulnerable to a certain kind of cruel teasing. Perhaps their difficulty had started there. One warm afternoon when he went around to Caroline's, Kate pretended for many minutes not to know him at all. Tickled by her spirit, he went along with her, answering the deliberately mechanical questions she asked about how he made his living and so forth, as if he could only imagine what she would be like in a few minutes more. Absently she would stroke his neck with her finger, look over his shoulder at something on the other side of the sunny room, and then ask another question. She could do three things at once, she was saying; she did not pay attention to ordinary customers.

But in another moment her little theatrics took a turn. The questions continued but now they concerned his "appetites"—she meant that she made quick work of them, too, by giving them what they wanted. But that wasn't all. It was as if she wanted to go into detail, as if she wanted him to know how much she was willing to debase herself. He begged her to stop. He wanted to say that he needed no reminding of what her life was like and, further, that she had the opportunity to leave it with him, but he could see the scene that would follow. They went upstairs, but it was not over yet. She tried one more question, worse than all the rest. This time he reacted, and she saw how hurt he was. Couldn't she see that she could leave this whenever she wanted, if she went with him? She spent the rest of their hour together trying to make it up to him. He understood, but later, and the next day, he suffered with what she had opened up inside him.

They could not put it completely right, and he knew he was partly at fault. There was something ragged inside him, a fearful expectation, with which she had little patience. She wanted to continue to tease, and even if she could not tease him in the same way, the desire to do it, which was apparent, still hurt him. When she confessed in a whisper that she really wanted to play her game, he saw it for a moment as an opportunity to give her something no one else could. He tried, but almost from the start he knew it would be a failure. It was as if she believed that through their pretense they could find something fresh in themselves. He was afraid. He wanted to make love to her; he still believed in love, their love. He could feel the distance growing between them. Small as the distance was, it filled him with fear, for he was too old not to know what it meant.

In July he asked her to go to Saratoga. Originally he had planned it as a surprise, but his nervousness left no room for that. He had it all worked out, including a reservation in her name at the United States Hotel, but she never heard about that. She wanted to go, she said almost instantly, but she couldn't. She just couldn't. She had never been to Saratoga; she didn't know what would be expected of her. He knew she was fighting him—she didn't want to leave Caroline's even for a month—and he was sure she would yield. He kept after her.

One afternoon she suddenly twisted around and shouted no. They were in her room. She was sitting on the edge of the bed. She looked so wild and upset that he knew that if he stayed quiet, whatever she was hiding would choke her.

"All right," he whispered. "What is it?"

She paused. They had come to that point where everything they said had to be planned with the greatest care. He had just betrayed weakness, and she knew she had the advantage. Her back straightened, and by that mysterious process more readily available to the dishonest than others, she succeeded in gathering up her dignity.

"Don't come here tomorrow evening," she said quietly. She paused as if to check her malice, for what she said next sounded chastened, even sorrowful. "I won't be here."

"Where will you be?"

"A party. A private party. I'm going to get a thousand dollars."

He was almost in tears. His silence was not the result of confusion, for he understood it only too well. He could see the black sick thing it was; he could feel it, like a knife, like death. "Ah, Jesus Christ, Kate!"

"You have no right! This has nothing to do with you!"

"And this is why you really mean to stay in the city? In hopes of more?" He wanted to say, "You don't know what you're doing to yourself," but then he remembered her game. He got to his feet. "I think I'll be leaving."

"When will I see you?"

"I'm not certain."

He knew he was bullying her, but he believed he was right. Nevertheless, he went down the stairs as clumsily as a boy scalded with humiliation, and he felt as if it would take an hour to walk to the corner. He was helpless. He could not bear to think of her, and again in his life he felt like a fool.

He did not hear from her for almost a week, and then a note came around by messenger. Her heart was broken, she wrote; she had done a very bad thing and had lost him as one of the consequences. She knew now how much she loved him, and she did not know which hurt her more, how much she loved him or the pain of what she had done. She knew she was unworthy of him, but she hoped he was not so angry with her that he would not see her one more time. And then she repeated that her heart was broken.

He believed it. He knew too much about her not to take the letter seriously. She could hardly write, yet there could be no doubt that every line was carefully composed, revised, thought out again, and finally recopied painstakingly. She must have checked the spelling of every word. He guessed that her condition was so bad that Caroline had hold her to write the letter. Kate had her pride, as well as false pride, but perhaps the knowledge that she was so far gone that Caroline might be thinking of getting rid of her had given her a shock. And if it turned out that being dispossessed from Caroline's was her only motive for writing to him of her pain in such childishly beguiling phrases, he would find that out, too.

He could not get away immediately, and he sent the reply that he would see her at the end of the day, knowing full well that he would be even more useless until he saw her than he had been since he had gone down those stairs. And later, when a meeting at City Hall ended unexpectedly early, he saw the stupidity of arriving uptown too soon, and so he wandered down Broadway to the Battery in a heartsick daze for more than an hour.

She was waiting in the parlor for him, sitting stiffly and even primly in a dress he recognized, a dark blue dress with lace collar and cuffs, and when she saw him she got up and walked over slowly and whispered hello and headed for the stairs. Her face was like stone. In her room she turned to him and rested her cheek against his chest.

"Don't you have anything to say?"

"Thomas, I beg you—" She kissed the lapel of his jacket.

He held her lightly. "What do you want, Kate?"

"I want it to be the same," she said, so faintly that he barely heard her. He knew that what she wanted was gone forever, and for a moment he wondered if there was any use in pretending. She had changed, not because she had done a horrible thing but because the horrible thing had changed her, even if she wouldn't admit it to herself. If she had wanted to break down and purge herself, crying in his arms, he would have held more hope.

She sniffed. "Will you make love to me, Thomas?"

"Do you love me?"

She nodded. He had wanted her to say it. It was not a minor thing. He had come to her as she had asked, in the expectation of hearing something from her or seeing something—in any case, of *receiving* something—and now she seemed incapable of giving anything. She would say she was too hurt, but it was true simply in the sense that she wanted to be comforted. She did not want to reach for him again. Perhaps it really was too painful for her, but that did not change the fact that she was thinking of herself and not of his feelings.

He made love to her, and it was just as he had imagined. She withdrew into herself and responded to his thrusts with soft cries. She did not wrap herself around him. He wanted to believe that she had been hurt that badly, but he couldn't. There was only one way to establish what she was really feeling, and he had to wait until they were finished and she was quiet beside him. Again he had to be careful because he still wanted her so much. He obscured the testing question with another and some precisely chosen words.

"Do you love me as much as ever?"

She rubbed her nose against his nipple. "Yes."

"Can you come to Saratoga?"

"I really am scared, Thomas."

There it was. Even if he could convince himself that she was telling the whole truth, he did not have the time to bring her around again, for he was planning to leave in less than ten days.

Saratoga

I

NOTHING THE WESTFIELDS COULD HAVE SAID WOULD HAVE prepared Michael for Saratoga.

Twentieth-century America has yet to produce a resort as fabulous as Saratoga Springs in its heyday. Vulgar, garish, ostentatious, unrestrained, *excessive*—no matter: anybody who wanted to be somebody went there. Playboys with private trains equipped with their own bands; titans of industry with their mistresses (sometimes as many as six of them); mothers with daughters of marriageable age (traveling with so many clothes that the rope fire escapes in the hotel rooms became emergency wardrobes, strung out like clotheslines); gamblers, sports, and families, thousands of families, poured into Saratoga during the month of August. They came not only from New York, but from Boston, Philadelphia, Washington, Cleveland, Cincinnati. There were other resorts on the East Coast and in the New England mountains, but none could compete with Saratoga Springs. Mark Twain loved it. Henry James hated it. General Grant went there year after year, even at the end of his life when he was in agony with cancer. The place was a reflection and microcosm of America's giddiest aspirations, and because this was the common understanding, one found there an energy and excitement that infected young and old alike.

The chief attractions were the natural waters, reputedly therapeutic and available at a score of springs; horse racing (the custom of an August meeting at Saratoga continues to this day); other forms of gambling, then as now, illegal in New York State; the vices that usually trail in gambling's wake; the food, service, and accommodations at the great hotels, but most notably the food; the amenities and shopping that rise up around a great resort; and logically enough the atmosphere, the ubiquitous, heady release from the oppression of Calvinism into that blue air of possibility where secret dreams come true, whethere in fact they do or not.

For Michael it was more complicated than that. He would return to Saratoga every summer for the rest of his life, almost thirty-five years, and it would never fail to open him to a joy and a quickening of life inside him—a feeling that began before he saw the place, on a side-wheeler on the Hudson River Day Line, in the middle of the river that many claim to be the most beautiful in the world. He was standing forward on the top deck; because he could not remember having been on a vessel so large before, he wanted to see the shining white bow plowing through the dark blue Hudson flowing past them. The tension generated by this first long journey with the Westfields had him thinking again that he would be found out, and he wanted to create inside himself an experience worth preserving, substantial enough, beautiful enough. In his mind, too, was his history, his mother's story that he had been born on a ship, and in a way that he knew was foolish, he wanted to construct a memory that would serve that as well. Trying to fix the place in his mind so carefully made him remember that in the spring he had stood atop the Forty-second Street reservoir and had cast his imagination northward to this spot. The visions of wildness and magic he had sensed whispered through him again as he raised his eyes timidly to the broad highlands around him. The paddle wheels of the steamboat thrashed the water with a continuous, repetitive churning. Somewhere aft a band of blackface minstrels entertained the passengers, banjos and voices carrying a contrapuntal and frivolous beat. The sounds of the paddles and the music and the dank smell of the river and the sight of a cloud casting a shadow on a silent mountain on which a lone house stood froze suddenly in his consciousness. He wanted his parents to see how happy he was as their delegate to the future. It was a foolish, stupid, painful thought. In the years ahead, every August, he repeated the experience, standing in the same place, remembering and thinking the same thoughts, reflecting on the terror he had felt that was finally unwarranted. And inside himself, so that his wife, Emily, could not see it, for his face would be hardened, his mouth grim, and his eyes narrowed, he would cry. He would break down inside and cry.

For the Westfields, the first summer that Michael accompanied them to Saratoga began altogether happily. Like many another Victorian father, Westfield, in spite of his problems with Kate Regan, wanted to spend money lavishly on his family. Over Louise's objections, he bought the children more food than they could eat; and although the journey on the river took just a single day, he had rented a cabin below where all of them could take their rest. At the beginning of the day the thought seemed bizarre, but by the time fresh air had drained them and the paddle wheels splashing hour after hour had ground them down, the carefully organized little room was a heaven. Young Thomas did not even make it down there, sleepiness overtook him so quickly. He was found curled up in a deck chair, his face and neck badly sunburned. And it was still only the middle of the afternoon, the middle of the voyage. The boat would not dock at Albany until six; the passengers, hundreds of them, with their luggage and celebrated Saratoga trunks, would have to transfer to a Delaware and Hudson Special that would not chuff into the Springs, which everybody called the Village, until the middle of the evening.

So Michael did not see where they had brought him until the next morning. They were at the Grand Union, which they called the Union, because that had been its name before Stewart, the department store magnate, had taken it over. The Westfields knew him; Louise had known him all her life. Their rooms usually overlooked the interior court, and this year they had taken three, side by side, facing the Opera House at the other end of the long lines of elms. All the rooms had twin beds. Michael and young Thomas were on one side, farthest from the toilet, and the parents were on the other. It made sense, for Hannah, who shared the center room with Julie, could attend them all with ease. She was with them day and night, like an aunt, but she took her meals at a special servants' table at the end of the large dining hall, which accommodated a thousand people at a sitting. The Westfields ate in the small dining room, which seated four hundred but had the advantage of being somewhat quieter. At their first breakfast, their choice irked Michael, who had never seen a room as large as the other dining room, and who did not know what any kind of vacation was about or, for that matter, what was expected of him. Westfield had been able to get a table near a window, which allowed the fresh mountain breeze to pour through. The Negro waiters hurried to keep their food hot—cereal, eggs, bacon, steaks, chops, pastries, coffee, hot chocolate—a typical Saratoga breakfast, Michael was assured, completely paid for in the price of the rooms. He was supposed to eat as much as he could, and he was ravenously hungry, but he could not help pausing between the last mouthfuls, turning to the window, and drifting in that sated, dreamy state that good plain food and country air can cause and wondering what was to come in the following days and nights. It was all so impossibly good that he could not believe that something incredibly evil would come along to sweep it away.

It was an odd moment, and he remembered it years later. Long after the time when Louise's offering of maternal love had faded to a stepping-stone in his life, fixed and dead in their long relationship of substitute mother and real head of the family, this first breakfast continued to reverberate through his summers, these precious Augusts. In a quarter of a century, after Westfield was dead and only Emily (and Kate Regan Johnson) would know the lie about his age (forty-four then, but still pacing himself to the strides of younger men, and so weary of it he had begun to believe it was killing him) he found himself looking back across the courtyard from the porch of the cottage they had rented to the window that had enchanted him in his youth. He had lost it, forgotten which one it had been. He did not care. It was the sensation that was his connection with himself. After so many years he could not remember all the things that had happened to him, but he did not care about that either. He could still feel the fourteen-year-old's frightened assertion of his childhood, the first since his parents had died, and, although he did not know it at the time, the last he was ever to have.

He and Emily were facing each other, her back to the wind-tossed elms, and there were two small children between them, shoveling oatmeal into their mouths with spoons that were still too large for them. There would be two more children, and one of the two alive now would die young. Emily and Michael were still at the start of their marriage, and this was the first summer in two years they had gotten free of his family. Louise was in Long Branch, trying to convince Julie to stay with her second husband, an oily real estate agent she should have never married; and Thomas, finally prosperous but still in debt to Michael, had taken his family to Maine. If there was anyone who had given more to Michael than he had taken, Emily did not know him. She included women in that assessment, Louise, Julie, Kate Johnson, whom she thought she knew well but, in fact, did not know at all, and especially herself. It was the way he was, or the way he had become, after all that had happened to him. At one time she had not wanted to marry him, but she had been wrong; and now she could not imagine another life that could have made her happy at all.

He had become more remote after forty, but she could have expected that. His confidence had given way to something haunted, something broken and mended together. She never told him, but when he explained to her where he had come from and what had happened to his parents, she cried for a week for the tortured child he had been. .When she agreed to marry him, she believed with all her heart that she was making a conscious decision, but now she no more believed that than she believed in the man in the moon. The truth was, it was as he said, that it had happened to them forever two years before, the first time he entered his mother's parlor and saw her looking at him.

The fabulous Saratoga breakfasts had their purpose, for practically all of the men, and a good many of the women and children, too, spent the day at the racetrack. Westfield, although he was not a serious horseplayer, was one of these. He could not enjoy racing anywhere else, but at Saratoga he enjoyed it immensely. It was a spectacle and tradition, as new as it was, and Westfield liked nothing better than to wheel his rented carriage into the long parade of rich, fashionable, and celebrated people heading out to the track. Sometimes he took Louise or the family; just as often he was with politicians or journalists. In the parade he could find William H. Vanderbilt in front of him, John Morrissey behind. A telegraph clerk named Twombly had accosted Vanderbilt earlier in the summer, seeking permission to marry his daughter. The wedding had been announced for November and was still the talk of the resort. Morrissey, former bare-knuckle boxer, former congressman, had started racing at Saratoga during the Civil War. His health was gone and he would be dead in less than a year. While in Congress, he had operated Saratoga's largest casino, and because he had been a fighter and a hoodlum, the newspapers and especially the cartoonists had had a field day with him. Westfield knew them both, to tip his hat to, to bid a hello, and to exchange a pleasantry. In the parade or out at the track, more than anything, Westfield liked to direct Louise's or the children's attention to one notable or another, and tell a story about him, a surprising but appropriate intimacy. For Julie it would be a story about some fat man's eating habits; for Louise, how a newcomer had acquired his wealth. Thomas had told Michael to expect bold, shocking stories, but there were none. No stories at all. The truth was that Westfield wanted to talk, but Michael's knowledge of Kate inhibited him. Michael kept his eye on Westfield, caught a few frowning glances, and guessed why he was so silent. Thomas was baffled and disappointed, but Michael did not offer the obvious, expurgated explanation, that his father was still uncomfortable with him. Thomas was not less spoiled than Julie. If something else went wrong, Thomas could turn against Michael on both counts.

The betting frightened Michael. Westfield described himself as cautious, but he consistently bet more than Michael's father had seen after two week's work. Once in a while Westfield would let the boys choose their own horses, and then he would put a small bet down for them. Michael thought that choosing a horse was an unfathomable problem, but then by luck he had a winner and collected twenty-six dollars, more money than he had ever had in his life. Westfield seemed amused.

"What are you going to do with it all?"

"What can I do with it?"

"You can bet another horse, if you want."

In the next race he bet five dollars on a gelding that ran dead last.

"Let that be a lesson to you," Westfield said with a laugh. Miserable and bitter, Michael wondered what he got out of such cruelty. He could not see that it was as close as Westfield could come to being at ease with him.

For the family there were picnics, berry picking, excursions, boat races on Lake Saratoga. Louise made sure to point out Frank Leslie's estate, Interlaken, and, in the village, the grand brick-and-stone mansions of the Vanderbilts. Michael was still having trouble understanding so much wealth, that one man's home could inflate to such an enterprise that dozens of servants were required to run it. Even in the hotels the money spent on luxuries staggered him. His parents had told him that the rich lived in a style that was beyond his imagination, and they had told the truth. The Westfields seemed to have no opinion one way or the other. When his own boys were old enough to ask him what he thought, Michael told them that each man had to make his peace with his conscience, which meant that he had never done it. For each new rich man he met in his youth, Michael felt a part of himself slip away, compromised, lost. In his maturity he could not recoup, for it required hatred and by then he had had enough of hatred for one life. He knew that, too. When he could step back from himself in that way, the burden of what had been thrust on him was intolerable.

Thomas knew his way around Saratoga as if it were a playground. There was a swimming hole near the jockeys' quarters, and on hot days boys from all over the village met there to swim. If the mothers ever guessed how they stayed so clean, they said nothing or played innocent. When the sky was overcast or a wind was up, there was baseball or croquet or badminton or games of chase in the nearby woods.

In rainy weather they explored the village itself, shops, arcades, hotels. Before a week was out Michael had learned every floor and hallway in both the United States and the Union. He and Thomas would pass swimming-hole acquaintances who would tell them that something good was going on in a room down the hall or up the stairs, but usually the noise had stopped by the time they got there. Occasionally they would hear an argument, and one afternoon a couple was making love. Thomas wanted to disturb them, his eyes glittering malevolently. It made no sense to Michael, who had heard his parents together many times. He started to walk away when he heard Thomas pound on the door with his fist, and then they both had to run.

I I

For the first two weeks Westfield did a good job of keeping his chin up, thinking of Kate as little as possible, resisting the temptation to sneak off and write her a letter. He kept himself busy. When he was not on a family outing or at the track, he was with Louise shopping, or taking the children for ice cream, or at Indian Spring drinking the water. He was all right while he was alone. If the children started prattling or if Louise wanted to look in one more shop, his boredom would overwhelm him, his defenses would break down, and he would see Kate with such clarity that he thought he would be sick with his horror.

The night before the Travers Stakes, he made a mistake. He fell in with some sports reporters he had known for years, and he got drunk. One of them knew something of the story of how Westfield had taken a boy into his home, and he tried to praise Westfield for his compassion and understanding. Unfortunately, at that moment Westfield was thinking of Kate.

"I'm no saint. Never have been. I have my share of good times."

"We all do, Alderman," said a reporter who did not know him well. When Westfield turned to him, the man was smiling in a way that Westfield thought was lewd.

"You want to hear about it, don't you?"

He was still smiling. Westfield thought there was a hidden meaning, as if he knew one of Westfield's secrets. "I don't want to hear about it, Alderman," the man said, "unless, of course, you want to talk about it."

"Ah, you're a sniveling son of a bitch!"

"I don't have to take that, even from you!"

"I'm wise to you! You're one of those vermin who wait around for a man to fall—do you want to fight? Do you want to put your hands up like a man?"

The reporter, who was smaller and more sober than Westfield, backed away. He shook his head, affecting a satisfied smirk. "They're going to love hearing about this one down in the city."

Westfield was so drunk that he could focus only on the accuracy of his judgment of the man. When one of his friends put a restraining hand on his shoulder, Westfield pulled away. "Don't tell me I've had enough! I'm right about him and you know it." He didn't look around but heaved himself up and headed toward the door. "To hell with all of you sons of bitches."

"Leave him alone, he's drunk" were the last words he heard as he sailed out into the night.

And approximately the first thing he remembered that next morning. Somehow Louise had managed to get out of bed and dress without disturbing him. He didn't know where he was supposed to find her—the Travers, they were all to go. With the world coming clear, he remembered how he had left the reporters.

He buried his face in his hands. The depression of his hangover was working on him more than he realized. He had witnessed many scenes like last night's, and the result was never more than a few days' gossip and laughter, but as well as he knew all that, he could not hold onto it or shake the feeling that he had disgraced himself. He could rationalize that it was not as serious as he wanted to make it, but the miserable feeling kept surging up inside him. He could recognize that if he let go of himself a little more, it would run wild. He felt so sick and full of woe, he almost wanted the worst to happen.

It took him forty-five minutes to get downstairs. He was shaky, ragged, and sore. It was much too late for breakfast—the food would probably go right through him. Just the thought was enough to make his insides ooze alarmingly. He concentrated on getting his rubbery legs to bear him across the lobby floor with something like dignity. Louise was sitting on a banquette, with Julie beside her. Julie was wearing a dress that had been bought yesterday. If Westfield understood the situation correctly, the boys were somewhere nearby, dressed like little gentlemen. The thought was a stupid one—no: it helped him understand the seriousness of his predicament.

"We were going to wait as long as we could," Louise said.

"The least you could do is say good morning." In the corner of his eye he could see Julie looking at him as if he had just been arrested. "Go find your brother and Michael," he said to her.

"What for?" Louise asked suddenly. "You'll want a cup of coffee. At least. Go ahead, Julie. Tell your brother to stay close." She waited until Julie could not hear. "I tried for twenty minutes to wake you," she whispered fiercely. "You *stank* of whiskey. I can still smell it. Is this your idea of giving your family a vacation?"

"Do you want to say this here?"

"I am not arguing. I am stating facts and asking what is surely a reasonable question."

"For which you'll get no answer from me. Now I don't know if I can get a cup of coffee or not—"

"They are now serving lunch."

"Thank you. My watch stopped. I'll have the carriage brought around, and while we wait, we can all have lunch right here."

"They won't do that. They won't hold a carriage that long."

She was right. He sighed, or pretended to: the whole business seemed to be happening under water. "What do *you* want to do?"

"I suggest we go directly to the track. The fresh air might do you good."

It was hopeless. He told her to get the children, and while she was gone, he set his watch. He did not want to think or talk, and, most of all, he did not want to hear from her. Going back upstairs to bed would only make everything, especially living with himself, much worse later on. If he were alone, his remorse would plunge him into thoughts of Kate. Damn her! There was a slithering in his lower belly again, and he could see that for the rest of the day he would have to pay almost exclusive attention to himself. All the better, but damn her anyway.

As soon as he had the family seated in the box in the clubhouse he went downstairs for a drink. The dusty ride had made him think of it, but once the thought was in his mind, he grasped the wisdom of the expression "hair of the dog." He had known heavy drinkers all his life. They were not taking half the risk he had thought. In a way, they even understood their internal processes.

He returned to the box feeling a good deal steadier. He twisted around in his seat to face the children.

"I trust you're all right back there?"

"Yes, Daddy."

"Yes, sir."

Now Thomas was the one who looked stricken. Only Michael had any presence of mind, and maybe he had too much. He was looking the other way, toward a horse exercising on the first turn.

"Are you all right, Michael?"

"Yes, sir."

"Look at me when I'm speaking to you."

"Yes, sir. Sorry, sir."

"Stop picking on the boy," Louise whispered through her teeth.

"I'm not—" He stood up, feeling a little dizzy. "I'm going down to the paddock. Who'd like to join me? Michael? Come on, boy."

"Thank you."

"Come along, Thomas."

"Julie will stay with me," Louise said.

"Fine." He thought he would make her look as foolish as she was acting. "The boys will come with me," he chirped in sarcastic singsong. As he wobbled up the stairs, he couldn't help smiling.

Michael was in front. Without warning, the boy stopped still. It was so sudden that Thomas stepped into him, lost his balance, and nearly fell.

"Watch where you're goin'!" He pushed him, but nothing happened.

"Stop it, both of you!"

Thomas started to turn to complain, but Michael's head came around faster. For Westfield, who had already begun to regret getting out of his seat at all, Michael's expression was a shock. His eyes were wide— Westfield could see at once that it had nothing to do with what had passed between Louise and him. Something else had happened.

"Tell him to—"

Westfield's belly worked again. "Be *quiet,* Thomas! Michael! What is it, boy?"

His lip trembled. The blood had drained from his face. For a moment he looked years older than he was—there was the destruction around his eyes that comes with age; but then, slowly, as if the weight of whatever it was could not be resisted, as if the thing reached deeper inside him than any experience Westfield had ever known, Michael's face relaxed. He looked like a little boy, with the same submissiveness Westfield had seen in his father-in-law, wasted with cancer, in his last moments on his deathbed. In the slow, hideous interval in which this took place, Westfield realized that he had seen this expression on Michael's face before—in January on Cherry Street. He looked beyond Michael to the traffic in the aisle above him. Men and women were passing in both directions. The movement of Westfield's eyes made Michael turn around again. His head twisted one way and the other, and then suddenly he pushed past a man and a woman and started running.

"Michael!" He had to get around Thomas. He took him by the shoulders and all but lifted him aside. "Go back to your mother, boy!"

Michael was down the stairs. A crowd was coming up. When Westfield got below, Michael was struggling in the arms of a policeman.

"I've got him right here, sir. Tried to steal something, did he?"

"No, but hold onto him. Michael? Look at me. Who did you see?"

"You know—you know."

Westfield felt sick again. He cursed himself. "Are you sure?"

"Yes!"

"Then you can see that there's nothing you can do alone." He spoke faster and louder to give the ring of authority to his voice. He did not believe it himself. "He's not going to let go of you until you come to your senses!"

Michael cast his eyes behind him, indicating that he had nothing to say in the policeman's presence.

"We'll go out to the paddock," Westfield said.

Michael nodded. Westfield directed him to an old elm away from the walking circle. The midday sunshine made his head ache, and when he spoke again, his voice was thick. "Michael, I was told that he was dead—"

"He isn't!"

"I know, I can see. I believe you. Michael, there are thousands of people here. If you want, we can tell the police and they can look for him."

"He saw me. He didn't see me the first time, but he saw now that I know him."

Westfield had to decipher the meaning of "the first time." "There's something else," he said. "If they catch him, it will be very hard to make a jury believe the testimony of a twelve-year-old boy."

"I'm not twelve," he blurted. He stared, defiant and blank, as if he could not understand what he had done. He could see the confusion on Westfield's face. "I'm not," he insisted softly.

Westfield felt a blackness descend on him. "How old are you?"

"I'll be fifteen on November fifth. I could have gone to the workhouse if I hadn't lied; my mother told me."

"She told you the truth. Then you know Kate Regan well." He was beginning to see implications. "At your age, there's a lot that you know."

Michael told him exactly how he knew Kate. Westfield shook his head. "You'll be pleased to know she can read—" The implications kept unfolding. "Michael, if you think, you will see that the situation is much more complicated than we've already said."

He seemed to understand. The sun was in his eyes as he squinted up at Westfield. He looked like every child ever betrayed by adult compromise. "I don't want any help from you."

"Be that as it may, you'll see that you have no choice but to go back upstairs and tell Mrs. Westfield that something upset your stomach. You've used that excuse before, haven't you? And then you'll proceed as if I don't know that you're fourteen and should be in the workhouse no matter what happens to the man you saw."

"What else do you know about my parents?"

"I've told you everything I know. I will help you—"

"I don't want you to!"

"Michael! Neither of us can act against the other without destroying himself!"

His eyes were beginning to redden. "How can I go up there and sit quietly while that man is here?"

"What do you mean to do?"

"What do *you* care?"

"If it's bad enough—" He wanted to say, "And the police catch you—" He peered at Michael. "What will you do if you find him again?"

"Here? I don't know."

"Michael, if you ever do anything to hurt my family—"

He curled his lip. What could he do that was not the finish to something Westfield himself had started? "Tell them I saw someone I used to know."

"I can't trust you—"

"And you could trust Kate Regan? Don't worry, I'll be at the hotel when you get there."

"If it's any consolation to you, I don't think I'll be seeing much more of Kate Regan."

"I thought so."

How did he know so much? Westfield saw his eyes wander, as if he understood that he had won the argument and was not willing to wait to look for the man again. As for Westfield, he was beginning to realize that his stomach was sicker than it had ever been, and he was about to lose that argument, too. "Don't let Mrs. Westfield or the children see you walking around here by yourself."

"If they do, I'll just say that I've already said good-bye to my friend."

As he went away, Westfield could recognize that he had lost everything with the boy. He had just spoken to him as if he were an adult. He wanted to believe he had gained an ally, but against whom? For what purpose?

When he returned upstairs, chilled with a sick sweat, Westfield was unable to prevent his recollections of his affair with Kate and the romantic illusions he had felt last fall from mixing with this new situation. This was his comeuppance—to have lost control of his life. He had reached his limit, and children had made this happen to him. Kate, sixteen, and Michael, fourteen. Children had stopped him cold. Louise was waiting for his explanation. He repeated Michael's lie.

"A friend? From Lombard Street? Did you see him?

"He introduced himself. Some acquaintance of Michael's father. He knew the whole story.'

"You'll have to speak to Michael about running off like that."

"I already have."

"It's a wonder you thought of it, with the example you set."

There was no point in giving an answer. He looked back at Thomas and Julie. They had been staring at him right along. Thomas knew that he had lied; the knowledge was on Julie's face, too. Westfield could only hope that they would not be able to see just what the lie was or where it could lead.

III

The man had been wearing a tight-fitting, lightweight suit and an ordinary boater, and there were thousands of such outfits here, and hundreds of fat men wearing them. Michael still did not know what he was going to do if he found him. The best he could hope for was to learn his name.

Westfield was right about what would happen in a court. Even if he told the truth all the way down the line, and even if he and Westfield agreed in advance to leave Kate Regan out of it, there was still the chance that a skillful defense lawyer would learn of her and see that the connection was established in the record. Michael wanted to think that he didn't care about the workhouse, but the truth was that if he allowed everything to come apart in the way Westfield had described, there would be nothing left of his parents' dreams. He could not take the chance of bringing the man into court only to lose. There would never be another opportunity. Worse, the man would have the information he needed to come searching for Michael.

There was no doubt in Michael's mind that the man had seen something, too. Maybe he had even guessed who Michael was, for he had disappeared. No sign of him anywhere. It raised questions. He had not seen Michael last December. If he had, he would have shot him. Certainly he had read the papers and learned that a boy had survived. There was still no connection. Had he recognized Michael? How? Did he know Westfield? If so, then he knew that Michael was living in Westfield's house—but only because someone had told him. Who?

In the middle of the afternoon Michael gave up the search. The Travers had not been run yet, and if he did not see it, he would have to invent a more complicated story to satisfy Louise and the children. He could not be sure that Westfield would be able to keep up with it, even though he thought that the most striking thing about Westfield was his skill as a liar. Still, Michael was too agitated to sit down as if nothing had happened. Everything kept going over in his mind. It was clear that he could expect no help from Westfield. No matter what they said to each other in private, Westfield had his public position to protect.

He was almost beginning to feel sorry for Westfield. He had guessed the reason for the hangover, but what else but his situation with Kate could have brought it on? He had seen too much of it on Lombard Street, heard too much about it in school. His parents would have called Kate a whore and Westfield a fool. That would have been the end of it. As kind as they had been to him, what else were they?

He was outside the track, trying to get a ride back to the village, when he realized that the man he was looking for might already be looking for him. He stood his ground, studying the wagons and carriages as they passed. He could not walk back to the village; there were too many deserted stretches along the way. He was beginning to wonder if he was seeing his situation clearly for the first time. There was nothing he could do, nothing, absolutely nothing, without thinking it through and being as wary as a rabbit in a wood.

A farmer with a wagonload of peaches stopped for him. All the way into the village, while he kept his eyes open, Michael listened to an impromptu lecture on the disadvantages to health and morals of being the son of a rich city fellow.

He was asleep on the bed when Thomas entered the room.

"Hey! Wake up! What happened to you?"

"Didn't your father tell you?" Michael recited the lie he and Westfield had agreed upon.

"That's really what happened? What did you come back here for?"

"Oh, well he had to catch a train back to Albany."

"There's no train to Albany this time of day!"

"That's what he told me! If you don't believe me, go ask him!"

"You better get dressed, Michael. It's almost time for dinner."

He stayed seated on the bed, trying to shake off a hot, ugly feeling. The afternoon had been too much for him. It was stifling in the room. Before he had come upstairs, he had asked at the desk here and over at the United States for a fat-faced man with puffy eyes, but the clerks had recollected no one looking like that. As he sat trying to wake up, Michael wondered if he could sneak out at night here in Saratoga—from this room, while Thomas slept.

Thomas was at the door, his jacket on. "You better hurry, Michael. My mom was plenty mad already today, and you didn't help."

It took Michael another minute to stir himself. His pants were dusty from the long ride in the wagon. If he changed his clothes, Louise might be pleased. He was in his shirt and underwear, trying to button his cuffs, when the door opened again. It was Julie.

"Oh! I thought—"

"You're supposed to knock."

"I came up to get you. Everybody's waiting."

"I'm going as fast as I can." He looked up. She was staring at him, below the shirt. The shirt did not cover him, and his underwear fit him snugly enough to outline his privates. She did not see that he was watching her.

"Are you all right?" she asked.

"Sure. Is something wrong with you?"

"You have a lot of hair on your legs."

"You shouldn't be looking."

"I wasn't looking!"

"You'd better wait outside."

"My mother told me to wait for you." She stuck out her tongue, but then her eyes dropped again. He felt the pleasure of it; if she wanted, he would show her what he had. But even if she asked, he could not be sure of her. He reached for his collar, not daring to glance at her, but then, afraid of what she might say to her mother and the more immediate possibility of an erection, he picked up his pants instead.

She continued staring, he noticed. The pants were cut tightly. He had another change of mind and buttoned the top button before any of the others. His underwear bulged through his open fly. He tucked in his shirt—in the front, to give her the best possible view—and then he carefully arranged his genitals inside his pants. He waited a moment before he glanced at her. She looked as though she were going to faint.

Downstairs at dinner, Louise had a dozen questions about what had happened in the afternoon. Michael didn't know what Westfield had told her, and he stalled, hoping for a clue, but Westfield kept quiet. Finally, Michael said that the man *had* lived on Lombard Street but had made good and moved away.

"I thought he was a friend of your father's."

"He was."

"If he doesn't live down there anymore, how did he come to know of your parents?"

Michael was careful not to look at Westfield. "He told me that he learned of it only last spring, when he came around again."

"I see. Then how did he know that you were with us?"

"Everybody knows it." He remembered to shrug. "Whenever anything happens down there, they talk about it for a long time."

Her eyes went to Westfield, who looked unhappy. If Michael had contradicted him, he couldn't imagine how. "Is there anything wrong, sir?"

"No, Michael, there isn't."

But his expression stayed the same. "Mr. Westfield? Would it be all right if I took a walk this evening? By myself, I mean. I didn't have such a nice day."

Louise said, "I don't think that's such a good idea."

Westfield leaned forward. "I'm afraid I'm going to have to overrule you, my dear. I'm sure the boy had some unhappy memories stirred up this afternoon. Some people feel better after a walk." As he turned to Michael, he assumed a benign expression. "It's a good habit to develop. I just want you to be careful. And don't stay out too late. Do you have the key to your room?"

"Yes, sir."

"Where do you think you'll go?" Thomas asked.

"I don't know. I just want to be by myself."

"Stay out of this, Thomas," Westfield said. "This is beyond your understanding—yours, mine, any of us, except his."

Something made Michael look at Julie: she was sitting up straight, staring again, her eyes large, and when his eyes met hers, she colored faintly. He knew that if he held her gaze, she would blush so deeply that no one would fail to see it. He reached for his milk.

After dinner, promenading on Broadway under the elms, Westfield kept his eyes open for Michael but did not see him. Louise remained in as sour a mood as he could remember, but he was not going to allow himself to think about her. His deepest hope, naturally, was that the boy would simply disappear. He wished Michael no harm, but it would be pleasant, say, in twenty years, to receive a letter from California or Australia, full of regret for the pain he had caused the Westfields so long ago. They would be pleased to learn that he was married—but Westfield did not really believe that anything like that was going to come to pass.

As a more realistic alternative, he could give the boy enough rope. If Michael got into sufficient trouble, Westfield could back away and let the law take its course. Louise would never hear the boy's ravings about a Kate Regan or anyone else. It would take great delicacy, if it was to work. He could see additional problems: it was an about-face, coming so soon after bringing the boy in, after his own outburst last night. His liar's imagination envisioned that he could explain one with the other to Louise, and plausibly. He had gotten drunk because he had begun to think unhappy things about the boy. The whole thing would be cleared away in a single stroke.

He wanted to believe that he was going to stay alert for the opportunity. And he wanted to believe that he was so angry with Kate that he did not care what she thought. That was true, in fact. He knew what she was, unintelligent, narrow-minded, but even when he had been most deeply intoxicated with her, he had paid little attention to her views and opinions. He had always been touched by her, her situation, her condition. And now, although he hated what she was doing, he could not completely hate *her*. Perhaps what was most vulnerable and lovable in her was the thing that had driven her to inflict this cruelty upon him. But he had another example of her work that gave the lie to that hypothesis: Michael, who was as cunning as they come. If the police ever stopped by with a story about Michael, Westfield would think things through and make his decisions then.

"I'm ready to go upstairs, Thomas."

It was dark overhead. The crowd was still heavy—there would be people out walking for hours.

"The children will want to stay outside a bit longer," he said.

"Let them. I'm still quite upset and now I'm very tired. I do not understand what happened to you today."

"Last night. Last night I drank too much."

"You don't know what it was like, trying to wake you. And that business today in the clubhouse. I don't think I believed you for a minute."

"Are you saying that I lied and that Michael lied, too?"

"I love that child. If I learn that something happened between you and him and that you used your position over him, I'll never forgive you."

"Is that the way he acted at dinner? Did he do or say anything that could give a fair-minded person that opinion?"

"I don't want to argue. I'm going upstairs. You're staying down here, aren't you? Let me know where you'll be, so I can tell the children."

"I think I'll sit on the veranda a while."

After the children went upstairs, too, Westfield strolled into the bar for a brandy. He signed his name to the check, a bold step for one so secretive about his personal moments. It was late now, after eleven, and Michael still had not come along. Westfield was surprised to find himself seriously concerned about him.

If he did not return, Westfield supposed that he would have to initiate a search for him. He caught himself thinking that he would be doing it for Louise's sake, and he saw the lie in the thought. He had become attached to the boy, for just those very qualities that threatened him most. Westfield wanted to think that he had those same qualities himself, but that they were harder to see. He couldn't be sure. That his feelings were being drawn upon in an unwanted way dismayed him. He had too much on his mind, he decided, and resolved to turn his attention elsewhere.

Physically, Westfield felt fine, perhaps a little tired. His hangover had cleared up substantially during dinner, and, inexperienced heavy drinker that he was, he was pleased with his body's recuperative powers. However, the lack of any sensation at all, even negative, after so many hours of physical abuse and mental confusion, left him feeling peculiarly empty. When it was close to midnight, he remembered what time he had finally given up the night before, and from that thought it was easy to imagine what Kate had been doing at that hour, and not very much more difficult than that to wonder what she was doing now. For the sort of thing she was pursuing, it was still early in the evening.

He disliked being alone when he had so much on his mind. He could see that it was even possible that he had lived his certain kind of life just to be spared nights like this. But he had no choice tonight; he had to stay downstairs. If he went up to the rooms and Louise was awake or he wakened her and she asked if Michael had got in safely, he would have to say that he didn't know, and then she would make him go down the hall to see. Westfield could not imagine what she would want to do if Michael were not in his bed. If he were? The boy had been laughing at him all along. He was almost Kate's age. Westfield could see that she was laughing, too. His own children? Under everything, he thought they were worthless.

Westfield felt prepared for a late hour, but because he was drinking alone, with his head full of serious thoughts, he did not feel all the cumulative effects of five snifters of brandy, which were different, more leaden and, say, majestic, than the effects of the whiskey he had been drinking the night before. His legs were wobbly when he left the bar—it was two-thirty—and he honestly believed that he was sober.

I V

To the end of her life, Louise wished that she had pretended to be asleep.

It was a cool night, hinting of autumn, and she had the windows pulled almost fully down. There was light in the room, from the lamps in the court below; as the wind swept up, the shadows of the leaves lashed and swayed across the ceiling. But the room was quiet: the hall outside had been quiet for hours, and the lowered windows baffled to a murmuring the infrequent voices rising from under the trees in the court.

So when Westfield bashed his shin against the chair, Louise sat right up in her bed.

"Thomas? Is it you?"

"Yes, dear." His skin was killing him. It was cracked open, running blood, but he didn't know, and because of the brandy, he didn't much care.

"Is Michael in his room?"

"Yes." He didn't know that either and cared still less. Getting out of his jacket and vest was not the easiest thing in the world. She saw him weaving but did not know what to make of it.

"What time is it?"

"After one." That amused him. His collar button fell on the floor. He muttered something. She half heard it and knew what was wrong. She reacted involuntarily: her body stiffened. She was hardly aware of it, and if she had been asked what she felt, she would have answered, "Anger." That was not completely true, at least by our terms: we would have said she was terrified. She could see that she might not be able to control him, and in the process of trying to she forgot about Michael.

Westfield decided to ignore the collar button. Louise was sitting up, her hair under a cap. It had been years since he had seen it falling free down her back. He felt exceptionally brave, perhaps foolhardy. With Kate involved in a wild escapade in New York, he saw himself as defrauded, at least shortchanged. But he had no one to blame but himself. He could be as reckless as he chose. He was sick of deferring to everyone on absolutely everything.

"Are you all right?"

"Yes, dear."

She heard the exasperation. She miscalculated. "Thomas, I want you to go right to bed."

He was silent a moment. "I'm tired of you telling me what to do!" There was more silence. "When did you ever do what I wanted you to do?"

"Lower your voice, Thomas. You're drunk again and you know it."

He was struggling to get out of his pants. He lost his balance and banged noisily against the dresser. There was a spreading numbness, far duller than the pain in his shin. He perceived this as progress. His skin was sheathed in prickly perspiration and his body odor was strong. He headed for the window. She watched him, having moved up on her bed a bit. She was unconscious of the act, but she was beginning to realize that it would be foolish to oppose him strongly. She did not see yet what he wanted.

For that matter, neither could he. His resentments had been held in for so long that he was afraid to think of what he could do with her. Pleased with himself for opening the window wide, he thought she looked rather defenseless, drawn up as she was toward the top of the bed. He was silhouetted against the window, and the underwear clinging to his body allowed her to see the contours of his body as she had never seen them before.

Couldn't he see that he was ugly? Surely he knew what he was doing; his disgusting display made her hate him fiercely. She was fully awake, and the unpleasantness of her emotion made her uncomfortable—for that, she hated him more.

He stepped toward her. "Take off that damned cap!"

"*Lower your voice!*" she stage-whispered.

"*Take off that damned cap!*"

Her voice leveled. "If it will make you happy." She shook her hair out—a mistake. He was grinning fiendishly. She looked away from him. "Go to bed, Thomas," she said.

"Don't tell me what to do. Do you understand? Don't tell me what to do anymore."

"Yes, Thomas." She was staring at the wall, waiting for him to be finished with this madness, whatever it was.

He felt victorious. He had to urinate, and there was a chilly, crippling pressure on his testicles. He contemplated making use of the window. There was a path below. He stumbled back to his pants, dropped them, saw he was getting drunker by the minute, decided it didn't matter, and then failed in two tries to bend over far enough to pick up the pants. As inexperienced as she was in these situations, Louise intuited the real danger he was in and got out of bed to assist him. She stood by his side, holding the waist of his pants like the top of a peach basket, while he used her shoulder to bear his weight. She could smell him—her face had never been so close to his lower abdomen before. She thought she would be sick, and automatically she closed her eyes. His damp, underwear-clad body swayed forward so that his partially swollen penis pressed firmly against her wrist. She wanted to kill him! He crooned, drunk enough to believe he could be as casually obscene with her as with one of his whores. She understood his meaning, and as he got his feet in the legs of the pants, she tried to pull them up so high that the seam of the crotch would injure him. She was so timid in the attempt that he construed it for something else, and with his free hand, he reached under her arm and squeezed her hanging breast as if it were an apple.

"Ow! You *pig!*"

"Uh, lower your voice, Louise." He stood up straight, unbuttoned, again triumphant. He rested his arm heavily on her shoulder. She felt degraded; she cowered inside herself, awaiting what he chose to do next. He caressed her breast, studiously comparing her softness and relative smallness to Kate's resilient young melons. Louise was too frightened to move. Convinced that she had learned the lesson well, he gather together the front of his pants and sauntered unsteadily to the door. She expected him to stop and say something. The opening of the door showed him in a wedge of dim yellow light. He looked haggard, not all-conquering, and bloated, sick with himself. She remembered the last time he had looked this way, after he had been gone for days. She wondered if they would have to cut their vacation short. She would have to tell the children that their father was sick. She did not like the thought of having to face Hannah.

In the bathroom, Westfield's head orbited over the bowl like a balloon on a stick. He peed all over the seat, which chastened him. Still, he felt at the threshold of a great new experience, and the size and weight of his penis in his hand confirmed it. He felt guilty about the toilet seat and attacked the problem accordingly, doing a perfect job. He washed his hands, keeping his pants up by leaning against the sink. Praising himself for his adroitness, he took a long admiring look at himself in the mirror. He was not an ugly man, he determined. Gripping his pants, he trooped back to the room, caroming off both walls in the process.

The door was not locked. It had occurred to him that she would lock the door, and he had decided he would batter it down.

Louise was sitting on her bed, facing the window, which she had closed again, and she was stifling her emotions. In the time he had been gone, she had seen that this was going to be the worst night of her life. There was Hannah just next door, but she couldn't stand the shame of calling her. She would rather have him murder her in her bed; the thought of his inevitable punishment almost made her wish for it. She heard the door close, and she could hear him breathing.

"Louise?"

"Yes, Thomas."

"You know what I want."

It was worse than she had imagined. She was paralyzed. Her ears burned. Her tongue felt so thick in her throat that she thought she could strangle.

He found her modesty very fetching. He lurched to her side and sat down heavily. In his eagerness to congratulate himself in the bathroom for the exhibition for rudimentary skills, he had forgotten to tuck his penis back into his underwear. She could see it, and she couldn't believe it. It was not quite so erect now but in this context certainly not less effective. It passed in front of the window not a yard from her face, and when he sat down, his clothing bunched around and supported it so that it emerged from his pants, underpants, and finally its own foreskin like a flower from hell. If the devil had created man, she thought, he could not have done a better job. She cringed as she felt his hand on her knee. She wanted to die. If she had had the means within reach, she thought she would have killed herself.

She went into involuntary spasms, like the waves of shudders one gets with an onslaught of flu. She had withdrawn so far into herself that she hardly noticed. Her elbows were pulled in against the front of her rib cage; her knees were tight together. Even her eyeballs were immobilized; she could not close them or bring them into focus.

Westfield was seriously feeling what he could, given the circumstances. Normally when they made love, it was the result of some frenzy seizing him from dinner onward. If he thought enough time had passed so that she could have no objection, he would give her a word or two.

"I'd like to go to bed early."

"What time?"

He would tell her, and she would be ready. The lights would be out, the drapes drawn, and the covers would be pulled up around her. She would be on her back, her legs parted as little as she thought she could risk without getting him angry. Two or three degrees of angle were at issue. It would be up to him to get her nightgown up, another battle and

more complicated. She could discreetly tuck the gown under her legs to
make the untangling more difficult; he could try to get the hem up over
her breasts. If the warfare became too intense or the fantasies about Kate
that sustained his erection suddenly failed him, he would quit. If not, she
would turn her head to the side and adjust herself for his entry. She
never permitted more than his glans in her vagina. She did not know
what those organs were, much less the names for them. It was what felt
right to her; he was accommodated and her sense of decency was
preserved. When he ejaculated, which was always quickly, she waited for
him to subside, and then she wiped herself as dry as she could on the hem
of her nightgown, which she washed herself before breakfast the next
day.

Westfield's decision that this would be different had resolved itself to
specificities. The delicious possibilities had aroused him, even if Louise,
had she looked, would not have noticed. He did not know it, but his
body was completely numb and would remain that way for the rest of the
night.

"This isn't so bad, is it?"

"No." She could hardly talk. She didn't know why she had answered,
except to get it done.

"I love you, you know. Do you love me?"

"Yes."

"Have you been faithful to me?"

"Hateful, awful question—"

"That Italian," he moaned. "The piano teacher."

It was the same! That was when he had run away. She saw it at once.
He was going to be insane again. They would have to go back to the city.
Perhaps she had to get Hannah now.

"Give me an answer. Have you?"

"Have I what?"

"Have you been faithful?"

"Yes!" She tried to pull away, but he held her. In the movement back
and forth, his pants opened wider, and at last he saw that his penis was
out.

"Do you like to look at it?"

"It's horrible!" She turned in his arm, as if she could crawl away from
him over the bed. He held her fast.

"I suppose I can understand that a woman would feel that way about a
man, but a man doesn't feel that way about a woman. I would like to look
at you, for instance. You've never let me, not once."

"No!"

"Do it. Let me look at you once in my life. I'm not going to my grave
not knowing."

"You're depraved—depraved."

"Do it."

She saw that it was lost, and as she stopped talking, the full horror of the act welled up in her. She stood up. When she tried to pass him to get to the dark center of the room, he blocked her with his leg.

"The window, Thomas. Please."

He nodded, satisfied with his fairness. He had to turn to see her. She squeezed her eyes shut. She hated herself utterly and did not want to see his reaction, no matter what it was. She could not imagine it; nothing he had done so far was even faintly comprehensible. Out of all control herself, as terrified as she would have been stepping up for her final judgment she raised her nightgown above her breasts and stood perfectly motionless. It was disgusting. She could *feel* the filth of his gaze.

As for him, he was well and truly pleased with everything save his own failure to respond. He got out of his pants. She opened her eyes, saw what he was doing, and shut them quickly. She felt his hand take her wrist and pull her toward the bed. He sat her down, leaned her back, and arranged her gown.

"Don't touch me, Thomas. Please don't touch me."

"Don't *touch* you? How the hell am I supposed to—"

"With your hand. Don't touch me."

He had nothing to enter her with, but he got on her nevertheless, as if resolution alone could make a man of him. He really knew better, he could feel failure dissolving his bones; and as if that idea were true, he allowed them to give up the burden of his weight. Instantly she pushed at him to give herself room to breathe. His hips began to slap feebly at hers, and even she knew that it was useless. Now she believed she truly hated him, felt a hatred she recognized as enduring. It was as if everything he had ever been to her had come clear in this debasement and near-suffocation. He would never know it, but he was not living with someone who hated him so deeply that it made her fear for her salvation—*that* was what his lust had dragged her down to.

He was no longer conscious, not in any legal sense. He was crooning "I love you" over and over, but he did not know whom he was talking to. He was passing into that alcoholic and sexual dreamland that may have given our primitive ancestors their first thought of the possibility of a hereafter. His motions stopped. As soon as she sensed that he was asleep, she pushed against him violently and started him talking again.

"Ya love me?"

"Yes, Thomas, get off."

"Ya hafta say it."

"I love you. You're hurting me, Thomas."

"I'm a good husban'! I brought that boy in!"

"Yes, that was good." She hated him anew for mentioning Michael.

"Very difficul'—see? I was right."

"About what?"

"About *him*. You din' want him. That's not how you feel now, is it?"

"No, it isn't."

"Ha! Come on, give us a kiss."

She could have resisted, for she sensed correctly that he would not have been able to move his arms and hands well enough to force her to do it. He pressed his lips to hers, hard, so hard that she could feel his teeth through his flesh. Not knowing why, she retreated into thoughts of Michael. She had been happier this year than she had been in more time than she could remember. Michael, his pain and his need, had given her life substance. It was true. And she hated her husband more for having been responsible for it, holding that over her and threatening to take Michael away.

Now it occurred to her that he might have lied about Michael being in his room.

"Wake up! Is Michael in his room?"

Outside the door, that was all Michael needed to hear. He had been passing down the hall when he heard their voices, and when Westfield bellowed "I brought that boy in!" the words stopped him. The hours of going from hotel to hotel had fatigued, exhilarated, and finally confused him. He had found his man, or rather, had had success. At a cheap hotel near the railroad station, the clerk had told him that a man fitting the description he had given had checked out in the middle of the afternoon. Michael had told the clerk that Alderman Westfield of New York had had a business conversation with the man but had misplaced his card. The clerk was only too eager to give Michael the man's home address. John J. Moran of the Bedford Hotel on West Seventeenth Street. And now that Michael knew all he needed to know—provided the man had not lied or planned not to return to his former address, or, for that matter, the city itself. Michael did not know what he could do next.

He hurried down the hall. He had heard enough of the Westfields together to hope that he would never hear another word. Julie would have been no surprise, if he had been thinking. In the room he got out of his jacket and kicked off his shoes. If Louise was coming, he wouldn't have time to undress more. He got into bed and pulled the blanket up about his neck. He closed his eyes. He didn't even know which door she would be coming through.

He heard a knob turn.

"Michael?" A whisper. He figured it was better to engage her attention than to let her discover that his clothes were not on the chair. He sat up, holding the blanket to his neck.

"What is it?"

"Were you asleep?"

"Yes."

"Are you all right? What time did you get in?"

"I've been in a long while now." He dropped his eyelids as an indication of sleepiness, uncertain that she could see it. She stepped toward him, as if she wanted to kiss him good-night, but then stepped back.

"I'll see you at breakfast. Sleep well."

When he heard her door close, Michael threw back the covers and sat up. So did Thomas.

"That was close. Where were you?"

"It told you before. I wanted to go for a walk."

"All this time? Aw, now you tell me the truth, or I'll tell my mother what time you really came in."

Michael stood up and undressed carefully, stalling. There was only one thing he could think of. It could get him in trouble, but he had to keep the other thing secret.

"Julie walked in on me this afternoon when I was changing my clothes. She looked at me in my underwear—"

Thomas fell back on his bed, holding his sides as if in hysterical laughter. "Is *that* all?" he whispered, his eyes wide. "I *knew* she was going to do that when she said she'd come up for you. Boy, I wanted to see what you'd say. She's done it to me lots of times—"

"Oh."

"Hey, don't get mad! Shit, I seen her peekin' at a horse today!"

Revenge

I

EMILY REESE WAS JUST TWENTY WHEN MICHAEL WESTFIELD FIRST set eyes on her. The year was 1895. Like everyone else save Kate Regan, Emily thought Michael was twenty-nine. He was a tall, lean man, almost six feet two, less than one hundred seventy-five pounds. The round dark eyes that had been so beautiful in his youth had weathered like ship's wood. In 1895 moustaches were once again in style, and he was a man who looked good with one, full and precisely trimmed. By then he was known as a difficult man, shrewd, merciless at times; but his clothing was at once conservative and carefully tailored, as if he were betraying a desire for social execution or, a few thought, a sense of style, or even—this was thought, too—an inner courtliness. For instance, he had had his moustache for years, shaped as it was now, perfectly trimmed. His manners were exquisite; there wasn't a woman alive who claimed she had been insulted or offended by him: at least, there were none who dared say so. Michael Westfield was a careful man in addition to everything else.

The twenty-year-old Emily Reese reacted to this intense and formidable figure as would any young lady who read only the best literature, was rightfully proud of her sewing, who was his equal in intelligence for her age, as highly thought of in the part of the world that was open to her as he was in his, and who devoutly believed that her father was the finest man she had ever known. There was more to her, but these things should be mentioned first; she was seen by friends and family alike as a young lady of good character. She reacted to Michael Westfield with confusion and a certain shyness, yes, but because she had been surrounded for so long by people who bored her, which is to say that they had nothing behind their eyes, she reacted to him so quickly that it rather startled her.

The girl he saw was of medium height, slender with light-brown straight hair, a smooth complexion, and gray eyes. Her sight was poor and she wore glasses—round wire-rimmed glasses that had the effect of slightly magnifying her eyes. It was early summer when they met, and she had some color, faint, so faint it could scarcely be called a tan. Her hair showed the effects of the sun to the same degree so that the entire impression she made on him was that of a fragile creature blessed with the most subtle golden color. The occasion of their meeting was some charity meeting that Louise had organized; Louise had become a kind of *grande dame* of genteel good works. Michael's first impression was that Emily Reese, although not pretty in the conventional sense, was the most beautiful young woman he had ever seen.

But like other sensitive and intelligent young women who are not pretty in the conventional sense, Emily Reese focused on what was wrong with her rather than what was right. Her lips were too full, her teeth too prominent, her ears so large that she kept them covered with her hair all her life. She was trim-figured, not curvaceous or fleshy in the style of the day, and she had thin wrists and fine small hands. Because she was not vigorous or outgoing and because her coloring was generally pale throughout the year save for the summer, she was thought of as frail, in spite of the overwhelming evidence of her interests and activities to the contrary. There was support for the notion that she was sickly, however: given as she was to bronchial trouble, postnasal drip, and sinus headaches. It was believed that she had weak lungs and would not live long. Emily Westfield lived to be eighty years old, learning late in life from radio and television commercials that she was allergic, hypersensitive to dust, pollen, leaf mold, and the rest, producing the year round those symptoms that made her parents and friends fear that she was incapable of anything but the most restricted existence.

Michael heard about all her ailments soon enough after he began to show an interest in her, but he dismissed their seriousness as another example of the stupidity of "these people"—the way he thought of the stratum of society into which Westfield's impulse had thrust him almost twenty years before. He was thirty-two, of course, old enough to have quit trying to reconcile himself to his situation several years before. At times he felt disgust for them or pity, but mostly he just felt apart. Not estranged. He had never been one of them. They had fooled him into believing it more than once, but now he hoped that it was impossible to fool him again.

What he saw of Emily's character was a peculiar mixture of wit, sensitivity, and self-knowledge. She was moody, sometimes direct, sometimes so withdrawn as to seem in flight from him. For instance, like everyone else, she knew something of his background, and when it came time to tell her the truth, that his parents had been murdered and that Westfield had taken him in, Michael watched her recoil physically, pull herself up in a series of small almost imperceptible gestures that made him think of a victim of a beating.

It was the way she was; as he came to learn, people knew as little about her as they knew about him.

The Westfields returned to the city in September 1877, without further apparent incident. In fact, though Michael did not know it, everything had changed drastically for the worse.

The day after his drunken assault of Louise, Westfield was much too sick to venture downstairs. Louise was so tense and distracted that she was on the edge of hysteria. She wanted the children to stay away from the hotel. It made no sense, but Michael decided to keep his mouth shut and obey. Thomas suspected something, but he knew too little and felt too left out to do anything but make the day unpleasant for Julie and Michael, eyeing them furtively, making obscure remarks. It suited Michael. This latest dislocation, coming so soon after her episode in his room, had Julie enchanted. Michael had to keep his distance from her. His guard was down—he was too curious about what was happening back at the hotel.

Nothing could have helped him.

If he could have told Emily any of it, he would have said that the beginning was that afternoon in the hotel room with the Westfields.

When Louise went back upstairs after breakfast she found Westfield not asleep, as she had expected, but sitting on the edge of the bed, his head in his hands. "Go away," he breathed. "Get away from me."

"We have to talk, Thomas."

"Not now."

"You have to talk to me. You have to listen to me. Look at me. Look at me—I insist!"

He had to rush to the bathroom.

It was all confusion to him. The memory he had of the night before was fragmentary. He could not remember where he had been when he had done certain things; he could not remember if he had said other things or only thought them. Remorse held him fast. He remembered something he had done here in the bathroom and he felt sick again. It was as if all·the laughter was out of him forever.

"I'm sorry," he whispered when he returned to the room.

"You disgraced yourself again! You shamed and injured your own wife! What's wrong with you?"

If she expected an answer, he could not provide it. He retreated into his torment. There was nothing he could say that could turn her around to him. He had hurt her too deeply, and she was too stupid to understand why. He wanted to believe that Kate would understand, but he couldn't believe anything about her either, not now. The illusions were gone with the laughter: he had done it to himself, he knew, but he didn't know how or, even more terrifyingly, why. What was the point of telling either of them that for the first time in his life, he really wished he was dead?

"Thomas? Are you listening to me, Thomas?"

"Yes."

"If you ever repeat your behavior, you will have to leave. I will ruin you, is that clear?"

It didn't matter, it didn't matter at all.

"Is it clear? You have to answer me."

"Yes, it's clear."

"You will be downstairs for dinner. You will begin to show your children and especially that boy what a vacation really is."

She swept out, beaming with triumph, but in fairness to her, it must be said that she thought that they were on the threshold of a new life. Her imagination warmed with a vision of all of them, the entire family, enjoying not just this Sunday dinner but Sunday dinners for years to come.

So they passed the rest of their stay in Saratoga in the year 1877 as if nothing had happened. Louise was still unnerved by her degradation but happy with what she had wrested from it—happy, in fact, with her husband, who was subdued, restrained, and even considerate of her and the children. Nothing passed between Westfield and her privately, but that was not unusual. As far as she could see, he had come to his senses at last.

He knew what he had lost. He would have to leave. There was no fight in him. He wandered through the rest of his vacation weakly, trying to hold himself together. He had never been so alone in his life. He forgot about Michael and the man Michael had seen at the track—what could that lead to? Westfield longed to be back in the city, and the hours and minutes dragged. By the beginning of September he was desperate to see Kate again. His need outweighed everything. He hoped there was something there he could salvage, no matter how clearly he could see that she would be surprised to see him again at all.

But it started that afternoon in the hotel, when Westfield yielded to Louise without a struggle. It was her view of Michael that prevailed from then on, and because it encompassed nothing of Michael's real situation, he was free to do as he pleased, and soon enough he came to realize it. Thus the trap for him was set and was ready to be sprung.

It took him years to piece it all together, that afternoon, what was said and what wasn't; but by that time none of it mattered, for he had been living so long with what he had done and its consequences that he couldn't imagine life without it.

II

As soon as she saw Westfield, Kate knew she had no use for him. That was what she told herself, utterly forgetting that she had not thought of him once for most of the last half of the preceding month. Earlier, she had fallen in love again, with a handsome and dissipated young sport, one of the organizers of the parties she had attended. The battle she had fought with her conscience over the parties had fatigued her, and she found that she was in no mood to surrender herself to the young man's escalating and single-minded demands. Because he was the kind of man he was, no amount of guile could get rid of him; she had to tell him to go away, risking his anger and capacity to damage her reputation, and when she saw Westfield so beaten and contrite, she felt thoroughly drained and sour. She tolerated his humble, despicable murmurings for only a few minutes when she realized that she was sick of men.

He could see that she had changed, and it was not difficult to imagine what she had been through. He knew that they could not go back to what they had been. Yet his pain was so terrible and his belief that she could save him so deep that he did not care. Like him, she could be sentimental about the memories they shared. He would settle for that.

But not less. She was friendly, talkative, full of questions about Saratoga, but she was guarded to the point of being rude about herself. He thought that she suspected he was curious about what she had done, when in reality he wanted to know how she had *been*—an important difference, and her disregard for the way he had treated her in the past angered him. She would not change or yield no matter how the conversation turned. They were in Caroline's parlor, and it was late in the afternoon, after four o'clock.

"Can I come by and see you this evening?"

"No, I'm sorry, but I'm busy."

"How about tomorrow evening?"

"No."

"You don't want to see me at all, do you?"

"I can't stop you from coming here, Thomas."

His rage was instantaneous. How had he ever felt anything for such a creature? He got to his feet. She was smiling, frightened, the immature dolt that she was, a simpleton.

"Good-bye," he said.

"Good-bye," she said cheerily, as if it were nothing.

Going away, he was so furious and disgusted with himself that he wished that he had pulled her down with him, taking her upstairs and paying for her like the whore she was. He fueled his rage for as long as he could with malicious fantasy, as if he could convince himself that he could keep himself buoyed above the abyss indefinitely. He knew better, and he hurried home.

As it turned out, Kate was not so busy that evening as she had thought. When her gentlemen came around, they were told that she was indisposed. It had taken her until seven o'clock to see that Westfield had not mentioned Michael even once. She had acted like a whore and Westfield had treated her accordingly. But what else was she? With Michael taken away from her, she could not claim even a portion of his victory for herself. She broke down and wept. She was sixteen years old. She wept all night.

Michael Monk watched all these events from the middle distance the way a fox watches the doings inside a hen house. Whether Louise knew it or not, Westfield had begun to drink steadily. He was out of the house as before, returning when she was asleep, but the sounds he made at night were different—louder, more sudden—and not infrequently he could be heard talking to himself. Michael had heard those sounds outside his window on Lombard Street for more years than he could remember, men talking garrulously to themselves, crashing into ashcans, and he feared for Westfield; he feared for them all, including himself, because he knew where Westfield was going.

He was back in school in the seventh grade on Murphy's recommendation, and he was applying himself in the hope of gaining further recognition of his "gifts" and being moved ahead again. In that connection he manipulated Louise's affection for him to obtain some relief from Julie, who pursued him the way one puppy sniffs after another. He would wait on the second floor landing, listening to them arguing. "Where are you going, Julie?" "Only to my room. I want to read." "You leave that boy alone, you hear me?" "*Yes,* Mama!"

But ten minutes after that, Julie was tapping on his door. He was ready for her, mathematics textbook on his knees. She wanted to sit on the edge of his bed and stare at him. He dared not look at her. She was the prettiest girl he knew. If she asked him a question, he would pretend not to hear it. "Huh? Whadja say?" Once he tried a wild parody of the antics of the most immature boy in his class, but she saw through it, better than she realized. "You're acting silly, that's all. You're just acting." For a while after that he was nicer to her, afraid of what she suspected.

When she was out of the room he went back to his real project, *Daniel Deronda* by George Eliot. His mother had told him to read all of George Eliot, and *Daniel Deronda,* according to the title page, had been published just the previous year. He wanted to know how the Westfields had acquired the four volumes, for they had come all the way from Edinburgh or London, and why, since the pages were still uncut. Michael could only ask Westfield, but he had not had a word with him privately since the Saturday of the Travers in Saratoga. And just as well, given what Westfield was doing to himself.

Daniel Deronda was too difficult for Michael, but he kept at it. Under his mother's supervision he had read *Adam Bede* and *The Mill on the Floss,* and had loved them. His mother had told him to save *Middlemarch* for his maturity, and he supposed that this latest novel was in that category. Still, he wanted to read the book, as unhappy as it made him, and when he floundered, his attention would drift to the dresser on the other side of the room. Months before, when waking up in the morning had been more horrible than any torture he could imagine, he had buried her comb deep in the bottom drawer. Now, if he did not finish the book, he would have to get the comb out again; he did not know if he would be able to think of her without feeling despair, the despair of failure. In that way he came to push himself harder.

The works of George Eliot arose in conversation one evening when Michael and Emily were newlyweds, married little more than a year; again there were spiteful stories about them, but now they were about Emily's inability to conceive. At the center of the action of *Adam Bede* is an unwanted pregnancy and the subsequent death of the child, and when Michael saw Emily reading the book, he had to wonder if some advance knowledge of the plot had whetted her appetite for self-recrimination. He asked if she knew the story.

"Oh, yes, I read it years ago. You know I love a good cry."

That was true, and she seemed so happy about it that he did not believe she was hiding anything. "I read it when I was a child," he said. His meaning was clear: he had read it before he had gone to the Westfields'. "My mother said that it confirmed her notion that young girls are cruel and not to be trusted."

Emily leaned forward excitedly. That he was better read than she had been was one of her happiest discoveries about him. "The same author offers that evidence about young men in *The Mill on the Floss.*"

"That's true," he said. "They're insincere vapid louts." He grinned; she had used the same language in their courtship when he had asked why a young woman with her beauty and talents was not surrounded by suitors.

"You were not like that," she said. "You were never like that."

"I was never young," he answered with a smile. He let his smile broaden and she understood that he was only playing with words; she went back to her book.

Weeks passed before Michael ventured out of the house on Thirty-eighth Street. Westfield's new, erratic habits were only one factor in his hestiation. The fourteen-year-old told himself that he did not want to be caught outside at night for fear of being sent back to Cherry Street, but he really knew he was safe from that. Although he did not want to admit it to himself, he knew he did not want to leave the Westfields' standard of living. There was something worse. At night he would lie awake listening to the rhythms of the house, checking each sound with his memories of what he had heard before, waiting for Westfield, measuring the man's pace into bed. He hated Westfield more than ever but not for what he was doing, just as he knew he was awake not because he wanted to listen but because he could not sleep. He hated the Westfields and everyone he knew more than he could stand. He would not let himself think of his parents. Once he caught himself thinking that if he could understand *Daniel Deronda,* somehow everything would lift and his life would return to normal. It was insanity and he knew it, but he could not think his way through. He did not know what he meant. What would happen if he went down to Seventeenth Street and the Bedford Hotel and found that John J. Moran still lived there? Westfield had been right about the responses of the law, but that was not a reason why Michael hated him. He needed no reasons: he hated Westfield because he was full of hate. Michael had the rest of his life to think about it, and he came full circle two or three or four times, to the thought he had had—when? That night his father and then his mother had been murdered, with no warning whatever, in a room full of smoke? He *had* to find that man and *kill him!*

The Bedford was an old wooden structure several doors down from Seventh Avenue. The entrance was a long flight up from the street. The desk was in view on the right, and beyond it was another long staircase rising into the darkness above. The windows facing the street were so dull and dirty that the rare light inside shined so dimly that Michael could see it only out of the corner of his eye. He was across the street in a doorway or up on the corner. The nights kept getting colder. For a while there was little Michael could do but pull himself deep into his jacket and shiver. He had a winter coat, but it was brand-new, hanging straight and clean in his closet. The weather during the daytime wasn't cold enough to warrant his wearing it, and he was afraid to do anything that would be noticed or questioned. So he stood there shivering, hoping that Moran would come along, afraid that he *would* come. In that way he was paralyzed, his helplessness complete. *If Moran came along . . .*

III

"My mother was a complicated individual, I realize now," he told Emily. "She had a sense of humor about herself. When she told me that young girls were not to be trusted, she made it clear that she was talking about herself as well. All I can deduce from that is that she had her suitors and liked being the center of attention as much as anyone else in the same circumstances. My father came along later, when she was more mature."

She leaned forward, her hands in her lap. "Is it easy for you to talk about them now? Is it really?"

"Oh, yes."

A paralysis of will, because somewhere inside him, somewhere he could not see or understand, he had come to the conclusion that he would not be able to live while Moran went about his own vile, selfish business unpunished; but at the same time he could not imagine it, he could not bring his mind forward into that event, that punishment—from an even less accessible place came dark visions of violence, wild exertions . . . he did not know what they meant, but he loved them; they filled him up.

"When I was very young, my father and I would walk ɔwn to South Street and watch the mail boats heading out, bound for Boston, the Carolinas, or Cuba. The clouds come down low over the sea," he said. "You can almost reach up and touch them." What he loved most about the sea was the privacy and solitude. "The world isn't big out there, it's small, and most of the time you feel very safe and protected."

"It's a wonder you didn't go to sea yourself."

"I never thought of it. His stories are part of my memories of him. I didn't want to spoil them."

"With your own experience?"

"Yes, with what I had become."

This time she thought he was talking about the effects of his life with the Westfields.

Weeks more in the cold before anything happened, before Moran himself emerged from the darkness at the far end of the street, his overcoat stretched across his round gut, his hands dipped halfway in his pockets. He had an oddly sprightly walk for so large a man. There was a newspaper under his arm, as if he were every man who had ever lived, every man who had ever gone to work and come home again. The thought flew from Michael's mind as he stood trembling in a doorway on the other side of the street, his heart pounding so fiercely he could feel it against his ribs. He had no plan. There was nothing he could do. He watched Moran ascend the stairs, pass the lamp at the desk, and climb on into the darkness. A gust of cold, wet wind came up from the river. There had been snow some mornings before, the first thin snow of the winter. Michael did not wait to see if a light came on in one of the windows looking down on Seventeenth Street. He started away, and then he ran; as if he could run from the fate that awaited him, he ran for blocks.

"One of the things I remember most clearly about my father," he told Emily, "was the contrast between his hands and his face. He had large square hands, long fingers, and nails like horns, thick and striated. The calluses on his palms were so broad and deep that at times they cracked open. It was very painful, I remember. Yet with those hands my father could take two pieces of wood and fit them together so that you couldn't feel the place where they joined. You could see it, of course, but you couldn't touch it, no matter how sensitive your own fingertips were. I never could understand how he did it. I never had the chance to learn.

"But his face was delicate and pale, thin, soft, and he had dark, sensitive eyes. He could come home with sawdust ground into his skin and creosote staining his shirt, and I could still see the gentleness in his expression. I suspect he was a happy man. He was quiet, and it appeared that it would be many more years than he had originally planned before he would achieve what he had set out to do, but I think he was a happy man."

By December the hatred that had fallen upon him several months before had come again: he felt so bleak and helpless that one night while he stood across the street from the Bedford Hotel he allowed a policeman to step up to him out of the thickly falling snow and demand that he give a good account of himself. When he couldn't, the policeman motioned him out of the doorway, took his arm, and began to march him up toward Eighth Avenue. The snow was more than three inches deep. It had begun to fall while he had been walking down from Thirty-eighth Street, and he had underestimated it. Perhaps he had been thinking of ways to hide the wetness of his shoes and the new winter coat when the policeman had seen him in the doorway. He was in much more trouble than that now, terrible trouble, but the depression and hatred were so deep in him that he could hardly think of it. The snow was too thick to allow him to see Eighth Avenue, only a dim, sallow yellow glow. He trudged along, staring numbly. There was a shadow suddenly, small and growing larger, a man coming toward them. Michael nearly guessed who it was before he reached them. The shadow grew larger still and then became a man—Moran. He looked at the policeman first, then down at Michael. He recognized him. There was no question of it, for after he passed, he spoke. He said one word, and the policeman heard it, even if he did not understand it. Under his breath, but loudly, so it could be heard, Moran said Michael's name.

"Monk!"

The policeman's hand tightened on Michael's arm, but there was a hesitation in his stride, and he turned his head back. Michael was frightened witless. Everything was gone, everything—and now Moran would track him to the workhouse. Westfield would not listen. This was the opportunity he had been waiting for. Michael and the policeman were nearing the corner. Michael wanted to look back, but he did not dare. Even if the policeman called Moran back, where would it lead?

They stepped under the lamplight. There was a noise behind them, so sudden that there was an interval of time before they understood it, a window being broken. The policeman wrenched around—Michael was nearly thrown to the sidewalk.

"Help! Help, police! Oh my God, help me!"

It was Moran. It was years before Michael realized that he knew the voice, that he remembered the only other thing he had ever heard Moran say, "Here's one for you, Missus." He thought it within the next five minutes, but he had to grow to be an adult before he pieced it all together properly.

The policeman stared at Michael for a second, muttered something, let go of his arm, and started running back down Seventeenth Street. The series of shocks was too much for Michael, and for a moment he just stood there, watching—as if there could be something to see. When at last he realized that he was free, he started running, too, north on Eighth Avenue.

He turned east on Eighteenth, figuring that he would be better off out of sight if the policeman returned to Eighth Avenue too quickly. The snow was probably falling thickly enough, but there was no point in taking an unnecessary risk. He would turn north on Seventh for a few blocks, then east again. Even in the snow, he could run all the way. Why had Moran done it? Was he so stupid as to not understand the meaning of Michael in the custody of the police? He could know about Michael's connection with the Westfields, but still it made no sense.

It was clear in another minute. A figure stepped out of a doorway halfway up the block. A man, a big man. For too long Michael would not believe his eyes or obey his instincts, and he kept running straight toward him—Moran, who stood there stiffly as if Michael were blind. At the last moment Michael tried to change direction, but he felt his balance going; and finally, stupidly, he thought he could push Moran away as he ran by. He tried it, stumbling, and in a movement so quick that it made Michael feel a stab of pure terror, Moran reached out and snatched Michael's wrist, his grip like iron, so that for an instant Michael was in the air, his feet out in front of him. Michael hoped that his momentum would pull Moran down with him, forward; but Moran was big and had braced himself: his other hand came around and clamped itself over Michael's mouth at the same time that it occurred to Michael that he could yell for help. Moran held him so tightly that Michael could not even squirm, so tightly that he could feel Moran's breath against his ear.

"You thought I was a mug, didn't you? I'd have killed you too, if I'd known you was there. Now, you see how easy we're going to settle it? I knew where you was living these days, and I knew you'd come around the block this way if I gave you the chance. I came through the cellars and alleys. I knew they were there, you understand? Yeah, I bet you understand now. Now you do." He was breathing harder. He wrenched Michael's head back and let go of his wrist. "Now I'm going to slit your throat like a chicken's."

He was going for his coat pocket. With his free hand Michael swung back again and again, thrashing from side to side; he could feel his wrist banging against Moran's arm, his hand, the knife in his pocket. Moran cursed and tried to twist Michael in the other direction, and instead of resisting, Michael threw his weight that way, too. Suddenly he was headed down, as Moran's feet went out from under him. He tried to hold Michael while he moved to brace himself with his free hand, and the knife came flying out of his pocket. Michael saw it as he went down under Moran, an old butcher knife, small and thin, honed to a concave edge, sailing darkly through the settling snow.

"My mother liked to laugh," he told Emily. "Laughter came readily to her. She dwelled on the things of her own life, her husband, her child. I know she waited a very long time to marry, and perhaps she despaired of ever having a child. My clearest memories of her are from my early childhood, just after the war. Possibly her laughter was only her way of talking to me. But she had a good brain, I remember that. I remember that very well."

If he paused or lost his focus, his memory would slide into the darkness of her death—their deaths. Emily knew about that night and his mother's instructions to him. She thought that such a thing was beyond her, that she did not have the shrewdness and animal cunning. Michael thought she was wrong, but it did not matter. More than anything he had to have it all in perspective, even if Emily would never know the reason why. He talked on, easily, casually, quickly, but watching himself, watching Emily, lest he give a sign, however small, that she would remember, think about: that he was more evil than anything people had said to her years ago, that probably his soul was lost, that he had become a murderer in his youth—after a year of searching and tracking Moran down, he had killed him at the first opportunity, carefully and with relish, in the certain knowledge that he had wanted it more deeply than he had ever wanted anything, every day and every night, for the better part of a year.

Emily didn't even know Moran's name.

There was blood, his from his hand, appearing on the snow and probably spilling on their clothes. Michael thought he could feel something hot and wet on his neck, thick like blood. He couldn't move. For the moment Moran was inert on top of him, not as if he were stunned but as if he knew he had Michael trapped and was trying to regain his bearings or locate the knife. Michael was the one in a dream, curious about how he could recognize the blood so quickly. He wanted to touch it, but then suddenly he didn't, it revolted him, he started thrashing, yelling—but not words, sounds, long, continuous wavering sounds that grew louder and higher-pitched with every breath. He was still in that dream, not afraid. His bladder and bowels were open, but he had not soiled himself, a pleasant and obscure oddity. He could understand nothing now except that his noises had Moran confused—he did not know whether to go for the knife or to try to stop Michael's cries. He lost his balance, and his cut hand skidded into the snow. He felt it, for he let out a shout of his own and tried to pull back and lost his balance even more. Michael's arm was free. He punched Moran, solidly, behind the ear. It stung him; his body arched back. Michael hesitated, more frightened than before, and in that hesitation Moran turned toward him. At the same time Michael found the courage to punch at him again. His fist broke Moran's nose; Michael could feel it giving way. All the while there was still that same sound, that eerie crying. Michael knew where it was coming from, but he almost felt that he wasn't doing it, that it was coming from somewhere else. Moran was pouring blood now, and he lunged for Michael's face, grabbing with his fingers. He was snarling something; Michael couldn't make it out. He punched at Moran again, but Moran's arms blocked the blows. His thumb slipped into Michael's mouth. Michael bit at it, but Moran pulled it away. Not completely. Michael's front teeth came down on Moran's thumbnail. Somehow there was a powerful exhilaration in him, and he bit down hard and through the nail. Moran tried to pull back, but for just long enough, it was impossible. There was blood in Michael's mouth, and he could feel Moran's nail stuck in his teeth. He was going to win; he knew it now. Moran clawed at Michael's face, trying to get free. If he was crying out, Michael couldn't hear it. When he felt Moran pulling hardest, Michael released him—and pushed away simultaneously. Moran went back, landing in the snow on the base of his spine. Michael, his mouth full of blood, could see Moran wince. He kicked out at him quickly and scrambled to his feet. He was wetting his pants now. He could still taste Moran's blood. Moran started to get up, and Michael punched at him again, from too great a distance, and his fist merely brushed Moran's nose. It hurt him. Michael swung again, with his left hand. Moran tried to get back, but he had to put his hand behind him. He was open, and Michael kicked at him another time. Moran moved faster this time and got out of the way, but he slipped and landed flush on his back. The snow seemed to be filled with blood. Moran's eyes were glazed and sad, as if he could not believe that so much had happened to him. Michael leaned forward and punched him again in the nose. It wasn't a hard punch, but Michael could feel Moran's cheekbones on his knuckles. The nose was crushed flat. Moran was breathing through his mouth, the lower half of his face covered with blood. Michael hit him again as he sat there. Moran's eyes rolled back in agony and despair. He rocked forward unsteadily, his tongue out, his body in the position in which it would have been if he had just been rudely and comically unseated by a horse. He seemed to be paying no attention to Michael. Blood ran from his thumb as if from a spigot.

"You killed them," Michael said. "You were going to kill me."

Moran turned his head upward, and Michael hit him again. This time Moran went flat on his back, blood from his face spraying above him in an arc. Moran had looked confused when Michael had spoken, and now Michael almost felt sorry for the man. Now he had to finish it—he had to. Finding the knife took only a moment. Moran was unconscious. There was no one on the street. The snow was still falling heavily. If anyone had raised a window, it would not matter. Michael thought of the policeman they had left on Seventeenth Street. What could Moran say if the policeman came upon them now? Could he say that the knife was Michael's, when the policeman had last seen them both on the other block? To this point, Michael was perfectly safe. Perhaps not with the Westfields, but that wasn't important.

Moran remained motionless. Looking at him, Michael suddenly did not care about anything. He stepped toward him.

He straddled the man, the knife in his right hand, and then he lowered himself onto Moran's belly. He could feel him breathing. Without looking, Michael positioned the knife over Moran's chest and, with both hands and using all of his weight, pushed the knife down through his coat and as far into his body as the hilt would allow. Moran bucked once, and then the air went out of him in a single protracted sigh.

Michael began to cry. He wiped at his nose with his hand, saw that he had smeared himself with blood, and backed away, trembling. He let out another wail, and then he began to run. He crossed to the north side of the street, running. When he reached Seventh Avenue, he would be safe. He could not think about the policeman. He kept running. He had done it, but he felt no different inside. As if running itself made him safe, he ran on, slipping and stumbling, running to what he hoped was safety.

Michael had told Emily of the flat on Lombard Street, describing it in careful detail. In her innocence and exuberance, she asked him if he had ever heard his parents together—in such confined quarters, it only seemed natural. Her own parents were highly respected members of the community, old-line Calvinists, pious, believing that the changes in the larger world heralded the coming victory of Christianity. The two of them—rigid, boring, but nevertheless real beneficiaries of the conventional wisdom of the time about human character—had left their daughter not only as frightened and curious about life as Michael had found her but, because they were so locked up inside themselves, without an understanding of the dynamics of the human mind. What she really wanted to know, and what she was too steeped in a sense of sin to ask, was, *Are we normal?* Because he had heard the question in a half dozen different guises before, he knew that she needed to be answered.

He told her that his parents had been the same, that he had heard them trying to be quiet for his sake, that often they had sent him down to the street so they could be alone. Then it ran in the family, she said, cuddling against him. He knew he had given her what she had wanted to hear, the assurance that somehow she wasn't completely responsible for her feelings and behavior.

After she was asleep, he slipped out of bed and stood silently by the window, looking uptown. They had an apartment off Irving Place, and they could see over the rooftops Gramercy to Madison Square Garden a half mile to the north. He had told her so little of the truth that he might as well have told a lie. He had heard his parents, and they had sent him down into the street once or twice, perhaps more when he had been a small child and unable to understand. What he had not told was how infrequently they had made love in their fear of another pregnancy, or their attempts to silence themselves in their fear of having him hear them, or his mother leaving looking in on him afterward to be certain that he was all right. He could remember his father arguing with his mother for sex, and his mother pleading that it was the wrong time. It had been part of the nightmare of the Sixth Ward. The Monks had not been there long enough to have been degraded completely. They had been there for more than a dozen years, which was a measure of the kind of people they had been. A dozen years: he had seen others disintegrate in months. *Monk:* the name rarely passed through his thoughts anymore.

He could not imagine the person he would have become if his name had stayed Michael Monk—which was a measure of the kind of person Westfield had been, finally. Emily had never met him, but to her he was a god. And the reason for her feeling was simple enough: when she had asked Michael about him, Michael had said that Westfield was one of the finest men he had ever known. After so many years, and from his particular perspective, Michael had meant every word.

I V

By December Westfield was out almost every night. Louise knew something was horribly wrong, but she did not know what it was, much less how to deal with it. Her husband had accommodated himself to his hangovers. He was foul-tempered in the mornings and, if one ventured close enough, foul-smelling; but he knew it, so as much as he could, he kept to himself. He had big things on his mind. He hardly thought of Kate, and he did not miss her. His drinking was so regular and consistent that he had begun to see that he had organized a second life that somehow ran parallel to the first. In the past he would turn from his desk in his office downtown to gaze into the street to contemplate the evening he would have with Kate, or, before her, some other young girl for whom he felt a limited, even peculiar passion; now he would wonder where the drift of his drinking would take him, what odd realms of contemplation, perhaps some new delicious imaginings. He was always alone. He was acutely depressed and deeply confused. He knew it. But he could not stop drinking—he did not care to stop. He believed that it was helping him: indeed, as he felt the first flush of intoxication, he perceived in himself the occult moral superiority of the philosophic explorer. It would be only minutes before he was diving deep into the mysteries of his existence. He would be sitting in the corner of a saloon somewhere: he would study faces. Most men were accepting, submissive fools, but because he was obviously a fool himself, he was disposed to be forgiving. There was no solution that he could see. Life's real possibilities were far narrower than most men thought. There was no future, for nothing ever really changed; and life itself was the wily deceiver, concealing what was only the faster and faster fall into the abyss of death.

So he went on that way, night after night, until his body was so heavy and unresponsive that he had no choice but to gather himself together and stagger homeward. He was self-conscious but not guilty, never quarrelsome, his attention focused as it was on the final translucence of human folly, and as a result he was always a gentleman. And there was no talk. He had always been a good fellow anyway. His mornings were ruins, some painful, some sick, others punctuated by strange physical burbles and twinges that terrified him until he decided to dismiss them. He never drank alone during the day and he held himself to sherry at lunch with his friends, but he was glad to get it, relieved to get it. He had lunch with friends more often. Oddly, in spite of his ugly new addiction, he was better liked. The sly, self-deprecating sense of humor he had reserved for his mistresses appeared at opportune times, and once someone said that a remark of his was worthy of Mark Twain. Ah, well. By midafternoon he would succumb to moments of distraction, long moments if he did not fight his way back; in his office he would turn to the window and wonder why he was doing this, why it was happening to him, but he was too eager to see where it all led to think seriously about quitting.

Sometime in the latter half of November he discovered that Michael was slipping out of the house. Need it be said he could not be sure exactly when? He had come home one night in a sentimental and melancholy mood, with the result that he padded up and down the stairs looking in on the children, his children, his responsibilities. He was genuinely surprised to find Michael's bed empty, but since the discovery raised new questions about Michael and since a drunk likes to have a secret anyway, he simply went downstairs to his room to wait. And fell asleep. It was not until dinner the next evening when he was looking directly at Michael that he remembered it, having it dawn on him chillingly—but then it escaped him again. When he thought of it later that evening, he could not muster the memory of what had happened at Saratoga, could not make that connection, seeing instead a continuation of his former powerlessness in the situation, and he decided to do nothing about it. He told himself that he wanted to see what the boy was up to.

He was not thinking of that at all that night in December when the snow drove him home early—late enough for everyone else to be asleep, or so he thought. He was restless and clearheaded, not sober but not drunk either, the occasional inexplicable consequence of so much drinking, and it left him anxious and frightened for himself. Sitting in the parlor in the dark so that he could see the torrent of snow whirling in front of the streetlamp, a bottle of whiskey and a kitchen glass on the table beside him, he was, when he thought of it, trying to calm himself, but mostly he was letting his thoughts range where they would. He was thirty-nine years old, no longer a young man, and if he felt that he had little to show for it, the evidence around him clearly said otherwise. Something inside him insisted that he deserved only the most profound discontent, but these days he was numb, becalmed. He could not think of the future. There was nothing there, nothing more he could attain publicly, no private hope he could whisper into life inside the safety of his imagination. It was as if he could not find his way through himself to the place where dreams grew or the terrors of life lashed a man into action. He wanted to believe that if he died next month or next year, he would not be frightened; but that sense of failure nagging at him held him back. There was more to life. Had he missed something along the way, or had he reached for it so awfully hard that it had eluded him, perhaps forever? He knew he was incomplete, yet he did not want anything. The worst of it seemed to be that there was no honesty in the world. Men deluded themselves, and women, all the women he had ever met, had no interests other than men or the children men gave them. How could he have known when he left Hartford that he was beginning a trek that would lead to such emptiness? He could remember what he had felt for Kate—he was fully aware that he had loved the feeling; but when he summoned it up, as he could, it was as heavy as lead. He could close his eyes and look into her eyes and see the impossible: she was the same, happy and laughing, but it was like looking at death.

Michael at the front door startled him, naturally, but quickly enough Westfield regained his composure. More, he recognized the opportunity for a bit of amusement.

"Michael?"

"Huh?"

"Come over here, boy."

He was covered with snow; no amount of brushing had been able to get it off. Now Westfield heard his breathing: the boy was gasping for air. Westfield thought of the carpet getting wet. "Step back. You shouldn't be surprised that I'm here. I've known for some time that you've been sneaking out. What do you have to say for yourself? What do you have to say? Is this the way you repay me for taking you in?"

Westfield peered more carefully into the darkness, pausing sufficiently to allow Michael to answer, but there was nothing but the heaving.

"I—I—"

Westfield rose. "Maybe we ought to go downstairs before we wake everybody in the house." Taking his drink, he let Michael follow him. In the kitchen Westfield carried a match from one gas lamp to the other, and then he turned to Michael. He saw at once. The snow on Michael's coat was stained brown with dried and frozen blood. There was blood on his chin, dried there, frozen; it was down his neck. Yet the boy did not look hurt, only frightened and winded.

"What have you done?"

"Moran—" Now he started to tremble.

"Who?"

"The man at the track in Saratoga. The man—"

"All right, I know who you mean. Where is he?"

His voice quavering, Michael told Westfield that he had learned in Saratoga who the man was, and where he was staying in New York.

"You're sure, absolutely sure, that this was the man?"

Michael nodded. His lip was fluttering uncontrollably. But then he told Westfield about the policeman, Moran's trick to get Michael free, and Moran waiting on West Eighteenth Street. Michael's eyes were desperate, as if he thought he would not be believed. "He had a knife. He was going to kill me."

"And?"

"I killed him."

Westfield reeled. The silence seemed to roll around him. "You're sure he's dead?"

Michael started talking again, closing his eyes as if it could help him remember it better. Westfield seemed to step back inside himself—he was surprised to discover that he was not horrified by Michael; and although he could not help seeing what it would mean to his family and him if Michael was tracked down and arrested, his first thoughts were of the terrible thing it was that someone so young should have had to live through so much violence. Westfield could see that the boy had had no choice—in part, because of him. He had ignored the boy, with the result that the violence that had destroyed his earlier life had pursued him into the present—and now there was blood in the house.

"Then I ran," Michael finished. "I ran all the way home."

Westfield looked into his glass, which was empty now. "This is your home?"

Michael was silent. He was so pale he was yellow. "I'm getting another drink," Westfield said. "Put those clothes in a pile by the cellar door and clean yourself up. The clothes will have to be burned, but I don't know that we'll tell Mrs. Westfield."

"You're going to help me?"

"I don't know what else to do," Westfield said, and he headed for the stairs.

Up in the parlor, he realized that he had spoken the precise truth. He had to conceal this as well as he could. If Michael was caught, it would mean disgrace and ruin for everyone. Ah, damn, if Michael was arrested, Westfield would be pressed to explain how he had come to be interested in him in the first place. *Alderman Westfield's sixteen-year-old mistress.* People would be talking about it for years. Westfield poured a stiff drink. His body was heavy again, in spite of his clearheadedness—always a bad sign. He wanted to be more clearheaded than he was, for he really knew that the alcohol he was consuming night after night was having long-range and possibly permanent effects. Not that it mattered really. He had brains to spare to handle the life he lived. For instance, he could already see the danger in making so much as the most casual, indirect inquiry about a killing on West Eighteenth. Someone somewhere would know that the policeman had just taken a youngster into custody and that Westfield had a boy from the Sixth Ward living in his home. It would not take long to follow the connection from the other end.

Suddenly Westfield wheeled about. There was something Michael didn't know! Moran had indeed been the hired killer that Jim Sullivan in his saloon had spoken of. Westfield had all the confirmation he needed of his suspicion that Sullivan knew more about the killings than he had been willing to admit—Westfield remembered Sullivan slobbering over a plate of pigs' knuckles while he calmly explained what life was like in the Sixth Ward. Sullivan would hear quickly of the death of Moran, and if Westfield suddenly reappeared in Sullivan's corner of the world, Sullivan would understand it easily enough.

If Westfield's assumptions about Sullivan were correct, then Sullivan was too guilty and ruthless to do anything but protect himself. There was no way to pursue it without putting them all in the gravest danger.

Westfield did not know what to think. Perhaps it was a measure of him that he could not imagine a circumstance that would force him to kill another man. If someone hurt Julie? Westfield saw that he was the sort of man who wanted to believe in the processes of the law, in spite of everything he had seen for himself. He became aware again of the glass in his hand. There were so many ways that he was a fool that he would never be anything else in a thousand years.

When Westfield arrived downstairs again, he saw the clothing that had to be disposed of piled neatly by the cellar door and beside it, in his underwear and flat on his back, his eyelids fluttering ominously, Michael himself, succumbing at last to the shock he had held off through the long run in the snow up from West Eighteenth Street—and the inquisition to which Westfield had subjected him.

For a moment Westfield was indecisive. Michael was heavy. If Westfield tried to carry him upstairs to his room before the clothing was completely burned in the furnace below, the chances were good that the noise in the stairwell would wake Louise, if not the entire family, and the clothing would be discovered. Westfield touched Michael's forehead: ice-cold. He covered him with his own jacket, then remembered that warm air poured into the kitchen if the cellar door was left open. He dragged Michael nearer the door. The boy did not stir.

It took a while to burn the wet clothing. Westfield went back up to the kitchen three or four times. Michael seemed the same. Women of the period fainted and swooned all the time, and although Westfield himself had never seen it happen, it was logical to assume that a boy who had just had Michael's experience would fall victim to a similar loss of control. Conscious or not, he had to be cleaned up. No lie they could concoct would work if Louise saw blood, even though her first suspicion would be that it was Michael's own. How would she react to the truth? That it was Moran's blood caked to Michael's skin and driven up under his fingernails? Westfield could not imagine what she would think of her beloved Michael. Stabbed a man to death! *Pushed the knife right into him!*

Thinking of her reaction to the murder, Westfield could only smile. He got Michael over his shoulder and started climbing the stairs. Climbing quietly took still more energy, and when he reached the second floor, Westfield was breathing heavily and his heart was thudding against the wall of his chest. He could not take the chance of resting. He went up the next flight slowly, surer with every step that his heart would give out. If he stopped, he might never want to start again. Never mind Louise—at this point he would hit her if that was what it took to keep her quiet.

The truth was that he did not know what to tell her even if he got Michael into bed. He could not leave the boy to wake up alone in any case, for there could be only one story. Westfield had no choice. He would have to sit with Michael until he could rouse him.

V

When Michael had not awakened by his regular time, Louise went up to his room. She was startled to see her husband sitting wearily on Michael's straight-backed chair. Westfield was ready for her. He was prepared to lie with everything he had in him, all the years of experience of lying to her focused on this one moment between them.

"Why didn't you wake me? I thought you were downstairs already. Is he ill? What's wrong?"

"I'll tell you in the hall." He barred her way to Michael's bed. "He's had enough for a night and a day," he whispered.

Louise glanced into Westfield's eyes. He nodded in the direction of the hall, his expression a mask of confident authority. Outside, he closed the door behind him.

"I found him unconscious in the gutter on Madison Avenue," he said quietly. "This was last night around eleven o'clock—" Long after he had come in, in fact, a time when she had been sound asleep. "I had to carry him most of the way home. Oh, he came to, all right, but he became hysterical. Don't be alarmed—he told me what happened to him." He saw her eyes go past him to the door, and he took her wrist fast to prevent her from moving. "Listen to me, Louise. It's nearly a year now since his parents were killed. He's had their death on his mind. He told me so."

He could see the anger in her, but he knew he could control it; he could control her completely if he led her to believe that the action he was preventing her from taking would lead to consequences far worse than the force he was using against her.

"He wept bitterly for an hour last night. Do you want to run the risk of having it happen again?"

He felt her quit resisting. He eased her toward the top of the stairs.

"It took time to get the story out. He wanted to go down there, to Lombard Street. He's been lying awake nights thinking about it. He'd made up his mind last night. He waited until everyone was asleep—"

"Didn't he see the weather? There's more than six inches of snow on the ground."

"You have to understand that he wasn't thinking clearly. You ought to be thankful that the weather was as bad as it was because it was the weather that stopped him, indirectly. He could have gotten down to the Sixth Ward, and, Louise, you have absolutely no idea what it's like down there. If the people down there saw him alone, given that they know that his parents are gone, anything might have happened. He could have been killed for the clothing on his back. Conditions down there are unspeakable. He told me that he was already in tears when he left the house. The snow was falling heavily. I was on a streetcar not more than a few blocks downtown, coming home. He started down Madison, intending to cross the street diagonally in the middle of the block. There was a horse and carriage. He saw it. He thought he could get across in time. He lost his footing and the horse bumped him—out of the way, fortunately. The wheels of the carriage didn't roll over him. He was stunned—I was able to deduce that much.

"Now, Louise, the next part humiliates him. He's in an excitable condition, and he takes this very seriously. I had to give in to him on it. He's ashamed of himself on top of everything. He believes he failed us, thinking about going down to Lombard Street and acting so furtively—"

"I hope you didn't say anything to make him feel worse, whatever it is."

He felt the tiny thrill that accompanies a first glimpse of success. He put on a tired and hapless expression. "Louise, all I can say is that I did the very best I could—"

"You should have called me."

"Louise! The boy was humiliated. He became hysterical. He wants no one else to know what happened to him. In all probability, you'll laugh when you hear what happened. It is a measure of how upset he was that he begged me not to tell you this. He wanted me to manufacture something to tell you. It's very simple. When he was knocked down, he went into some nuisance hidden in the snow. He got it all over his clothes. I discovered that as I picked him up out of the street. He could not have been there long, only a few seconds. He came around almost as soon as I moved him. The odor of his clothes was something awful."

"He's a *child*—" She caught herself, remembering the long, silent adjustment Michael had had to make to them at the start of the year, specifically that day he had run out of the kitchen and gotten sick in the yard. A year since his parents' deaths: the Westfields should have expected something like this.

"I think the reaction he had to it is the result of what he really had on his mind, if you get what I mean," Westfield said.

"Of course, Thomas. Anyone would understand that. May I see him now, please?"

He stepped in her way. "I haven't told you the last of it, the worst from one point of view, certainly the most expensive." He could feel her growing annoyance with him. She was such a gullible and stupid woman that he almost wanted to tell her in the next breath that her precious darling had committed a murder with his bare hands. He said, "He insisted that I burn the clothes—"

"Oh, Thomas, that's not important. Now step aside, please. I can see you're being a fool about this as you are about everything else."

He had her so completely convinced of this nonsense that he wanted to laugh, but instead he pretended to sigh. "Be that as it may. The last of it is that I promised him that I would explain it to you. He didn't want to face you until he knew that you understood how ashamed he was. Do you understand? I promised him. I'm going to go in there and wait until he wakes up, then tell him that everything is all right. If the streetcars are running, I'd like you to send Hannah downtown to tell them I won't be in today."

She sneered. "I haven't heard any streetcars, Thomas. I told you how deep the snow is. I'm not even sure the school will be open. Why have you suddenly decided to take charge again? Why is he sleeping so soundly after all that? How did you calm him down?"

"I gave him a couple of drinks of liquor—"

"You and your liquor!" she cried.

"I didn't ask you," he said through his teeth. "Now if you're smart, you'll go downstairs without waking the boy and letting him get the idea that he's caused trouble between us. Do you want him to think that after what he's been through?"

"You're taking advantage of this, Thomas." She turned toward the stairs.

He watched her go down, and he wanted to kick her in the spine. She had spoiled it, robbed him of the first good moment he had had in months. It had taken him hours to invent a maze of lies he could lead her through, and she had believed every one or at least had given every outward sign of believing. He rejected the suspicion that she knew he was lying and had struck back at him on that account. It had been because she believed, as she said, that he was taking advantage of the situation. She wanted to discuss *his* behavior? What did she want of him that he had not already given her? It was clear that she would not give him a moment's peace until he was dead. He stepped back into Michael's room, closing the door quietly. Exhaustion thrummed through Westfield's body, as if it had an energy of its own. They had a lot to talk about, he and Michael. Westfield had gone this far because there had been no choice, and he was satisfied that in this instance, anyway, justice and survival were one and the same; but now he saw that the whole fantastical business he had created for Michael's benefit could serve his own interests. Whenever Westfield sensed that Louise was going to give him trouble, Michael was going to remind her of this night, or her version of it. All Westfield had to do was wait for the little bastard to wake up.

Coming of Age

I

WESTFIELD'S LIE HELD, THOUGH NOT, BY HIS OWN STANDARDS, easily. At home Louise kept her distance for a while; and outside, where Westfield's contribution consisted of silence and a watchful eye, there was no unwanted attention directed toward any resident of the house on Thirty-eighth Street. After that morning when Westfield waited for Michael to wake up and learn what story had been invented for him, the two had no further conversation on the subject; but the following January, in a move that made Westfield uneasy, Louise suggested that he take Michael back to Lombard Street if Michael chose. Michael chose, and this caused Westfield to wonder if the boy had something more on his mind and had manipulated Louise for that purpose. He was afraid to ask, as if not seeing Michael's shrewdness could hold it at bay a bit longer. The result was that when they made the trip some days later, Westfield was obsessed with what Michael may have deduced about Moran and his place in the scheme of things in the Sixth Ward.

It was a bitter day, an icy arctic day. They were in a closed carriage and there was nothing to see. Michael was silent. People were indoors because of the cold, and the accumulating dirt of winter made the slum look even more gray than usual. Westfield was alert. He could not remember what he had told Michael in Saratoga about Moran—in fact, if he had told him anything at all.

Nothing like that was on Michael's mind. For one thing, he had not seen Lombard Street for more than a year, and he was disturbed by how pinched and narrow it seemed. Once it had been his whole universe. For another thing, Westfield had forgotten something else, what he had said to Michael the morning after Moran's death. Reflecting on something that had gone through his mind while he had been sitting up with him, that Michael was the gift of all the whores he had ever known, he had said, more to himself than to Michael, "Well, I suppose I really am your benefactor, after all." Michael had taken this not as a comment on Westfield's behavior but as a statement of commitment, even confession. Westfield had not heard his tone, distracted as he had been by the memories that had prompted the remark, and Michael had not been yielding to his own needs by imagining that the tone was there.

For him it had been an admission and not a grudging one either: that Michael's hard life had given him a hold on the sort of personal reserve and self-discipline that Westfield knew had always eluded him. In the circus, after all, the clowns always look up to the men on the trapeze. Michael understood it. In his estimation Westfield was a clown, all right but a wily one. He had given Michael a lesson in lying that Michael would never forget. A lie had to be clear, simple, and logical, but above everything else it had to make the burden of searching for the truth morally onerous. His mother had stumbled upon the edge of this; her lie about his age held together in spite of its faults because of his circumstance. Who would attack an orphan? This was what Michael heard from Westfield. As clever as he was, Westfield admired something in Michael, yet Westfield had his skills: if Michael learned them, where would it lead?

On Lombard Street, Michael was mulling this over. He was staring through the window at the tiny street and seeing with no sadness whatever that he had outgrown it. He was aware of the absence of emotion. If Westfield had said, "You're not the same person anymore," Michael would have seized it as the truth of his life, for he was thinking of his parents for the first time without a sense of loss. He thought it had to do with Moran, that he had expended his grief, pain, and rage in the battle in the snow. He no longer remembered how he had won, and in later years, without explaining how he knew, he would tell people, especially his sons, that human beings could do anything if they wanted to badly enough.

The hardness that had descended upon him after the deaths of his parents had never left. In that sense he had not changed but was looking at himself with new eyes. Lombard Street was behind him.

"Is there anyone you want to visit?" Westfield asked.

"No."

"Is there anything in the neighborhood that you would like to see?"

Michael shook his head. He had one thought but knew he could not express it. It meant trouble. He wanted to see Eighteenth Street. "No," he said after another moment. "I'm ready to go home now."

During the ride home he went over it all again. He hated the poverty of Lombard Street—he was separated from it now. He did not ask himself if he would have it all undone for a return to what his life had been. Last winter in the shelter on Cherry Street and those first days at the Westfields', he had not really forgotten. It was not that he was not thinking of it now. It was not preying on him; he could not feel it.

He did not wonder again about the urge to return to Eighteenth Street until later that evening; but in the afternoon, when they were passing Eighteenth on their way to Murray Hill, he kept his face turned to the window, to the east, and Westfield saw it. Westfield took it as still another sign that Michael was going through the most profound change. Making his peace with himself, Westfield might have said, if he had had someone to talk to, someone who might not have known that Westfield had no personal knowledge of the meaning of the phrase. That night while Michael was in bed, thinking about his impulse to see the place where he had killed Moran, Westfield and Louise were downstairs in the library, both of them thinking about Michael. Louise, who had heard only that Michael had declined to get out of the carriage on Lombard Street, was hoping that this marked the end of Michael's grieving. The image of him lying in the snow, the center of Westfield's lie to her, would not leave her. The emotions roused were so intense that she had moments when she feared for herself, but she felt a wild determination to continue. Somehow she had been given the challenge to guide this boy to the safety of adult life. It was God's will. She could not fail.

Westfield, on the other hand, viewed the future with much less resolve. Where was he to go now? What could life hold for him? Kate, Michael, everything that had happened in the past year, added up to some grand climax of his life. The evidence was unmistakable. He would be forty on his next birthday; he could see clearly to both ends of his life. He knew what the next years held in store. It was as if the events of these twelve months had taken something from Westfield and handed it to Michael. Westfield felt played out. He had no moral energy.

"He's just like you," Louise said.

"I beg your pardon?"

"He's almost exactly like you," she said, as happy as she would have been if she had just solved a puzzle. "More than either of your own children, Michael is like you."

"That's bizarre, Louise, and in very poor taste."

She was stung by his choice of words. "I'm sorry, but it's true. I can remember times when you behaved exactly as he did before Christmas. When you have something troubling you, you run off in the same way." Now she saw a chance. She gave a tight little smile. "Of course, your episodes are accompanied by a good deal of drinking."

"And that makes us similar?" He groaned. "I should have expected this. You're so pathetic, Louise. I should have expected you to see our journey down to the Sixth Ward as an opportunity to lecture me, just as you did the morning after he ran away!"

"I was talking about Michael!"

"The hell you were!"

"I won't have that language!"

"The hell, I say, and the hell again! If you were talking about Michael, why did you bring up the other? Or are you afraid that somehow your little darling realizes that *I'm* really his benefactor and not you?"

"Oh, this is absolutely insane." She stood up. "I don't know which is worse, when you choose to twist everything I say to your own miserable purposes or when you're so drunk that you're—" She let it trail off; she was not strong enough to say that much.

"That I'm what?" He was wild. "That I'm what? I *insist* that you speak your mind!"

She regarded the door. He might use force if she tried to leave. Yet when she turned back, she saw that his expression was anxious, actually fearful. Sniveling and contemptible creature, he knew the truth and still wanted to be told. He had lost all dignity. Did he really wish to hear what she thought of him? "Leave me alone!" she cried, and tried to get past him. He seized her wrist, but she pulled herself free with such violence that she hurt herself. She had to fight back the tears as she moved away from him toward the door. "Does this mean that we can expect another occurrence of your antics?"

He had wanted to stop this before it went too far. He knew she hated him, but if nothing was said, they could go on as before. She could even be consoling and tender when she wanted to be, when he treated her well. "Go away, Louise. You wanted to be alone."

"You mumbled—are you going to feel sorry for yourself? Now you'll have an excuse to drink!"

He looked up at her. The best he could do with this, he supposed suddenly, was salvage some amusement from it. "Is this what your Michael is like, do you think? Do you suppose he'll show the traits you accuse me of? I do mean all of them—all my antics?"

"You're *disgusting!*"

The door slammed behind her, and Westfield sat staring at it, feeling a wry amusement. Perhaps he had wanted her to say something foul after all; in the process, at least she had showed some emotion. Now he wanted a drink, all right. He did not see how he would be able to get enough sleep tonight without the numbing effects of alcohol. He got out of the chair. There was no sense wasting time about it.

II

Louise's slamming of the door jolted Michael in his bed upstairs and made him realize that he had been hearing the undercurrent of the Westfields' voices for some time. He had been wondering why he had been tempted to return to Eighteenth Street today. He still felt the inclination and didn't know why, and it puzzled and alarmed him. It had occurred to him earlier to sneak out again, but he had decided against that. Michael still did not trust Westfield; he would turn on Michael in a moment if he was given the chance.

Michael got out of the bed and wrapped himself in the quilt and padded barefoot to the window. Where the carpet ended, the wooden floor was so cold it hurt. Clouds continued to hang over the city, dismal and threatening. There was a light in a window in a house across the barren garden. Was somebody sick? In the year he had been here Michael had come to know the neighbors and the shopkeepers on Madison Avenue and the policemen on their beats and the peddlers who went door to door. It was not different from Lombard Street, only more comfortable; and the fear and violence were missing, or at least not visible. It was one of the first things he had noticed: if there was a voice raised in anger, the next sound was that of a window being shut abruptly.

But he heard the Westfields. They were the same as people in the Sixth Ward. Most marriages were unhappy, his mother had told him, by way of explaining so much of Lombard Street. The Westfields' was an unhappy marriage, he understood that much, but he did not feel relieved. Their unhappiness gnawed at him.

He did not want to care about them, no matter what he told himself at odd times, or said to Louise when she asked, or showed her with a hug or kiss when the mood struck him. They had no mystery for him; but he was dependent on them, so while they sometimes filled his dreams and had become dream-symbols for him, he could not have a moment's satisfaction with any of them. Louise was always ready to dash to his aid, but because she knew nothing but lies about him, Michael had come to an understanding of Westfield's view of her, that she was someone to be looked after but not necessarily respected. He rejected the last part, because it was Westfield's lying, after all, that kept her so ignorant; but inasmuch as he had to live within the context of those lies and keep his distance, he saw that the situation was hopeless. Louise was stuffed with so many lies that her basic understandings were flawed. She believed things that simply weren't true, and the result was that there were too many times when she irritated him or when he felt he was suffocating.

He had no such problems with Julie. He disliked her intensely—fiercely. Thomas had told him stories about her that related to the episode in the hotel room in Saratoga, and although he didn't know if he should believe Thomas, the stories seemed to fit her character well enough. After Saratoga, when Michael hinted at some curiosity about her interest in him, Thomas had warned him away. "She'll tell on you if it suits her, just as soon as look at you, and make it seem like everything was your fault." And that did seem to be the case. She was a sneak. She shrieked, threw tantrums, lied, and when she was not acting like Astor's pet horse, as Hannah said, she was a brazen flirt. It was not worth the risk. At times Michael imagined that there would be trouble over her anyway, given the kind of girl she was, and there was every good reason for not giving that trouble, when it came, any basis in fact.

So far it had not seemed to have occurred to Westfield, the only one who knew Michael's true age, that Michael might know more about sex than he had let on so far, and Michael did not look forward with pleasure to the day when Westfield began to see things in their true light. Michael was not innocent. To be sure, his experience was limited to four encounters on a rooftop with a girl who had come around to Lombard Street the summer before his parents were killed, and during two of the encounters he was not alone with the girl, his friends watching and waiting their turns. But at least he knew the sex act and what it could do for a girl who enjoyed it. He had heard his parents, and the other boys reported what they had heard or, in many cases, seen. In thinking it through, Michael saw that people were all pretty much alike, even if they did have different ways of concealing it.

He suspected that he felt such a powerful emotion for Julie because she was becoming the prettiest girl he had ever seen. If he was not careful, the temptation became awful. Often enough he had to get out of bed to stand by the window to calm himself. His father had known about the girl on Lombard Street. He had seen Michael with her on the streetcorner, and he had assessed the situation correctly with a glance.

"The girls won't always be there, Michael," he had said later. "How you take care of yourself when you're lonely is as important as any other measure of a man. If a man can't control himself, he's no good for anything himself, and he disrupts everybody around him."

That seemed to be true. Thomas and his friends were having masturbation parties these days, when they could find the privacy. Once they invited Michael to watch—that was what they said—and when he said no, they became so insistent he began to believe they had something else on their minds. But he was trapped. There were three of them, all as big and fat as Thomas. They were going up to Thomas's room, on an afternoon when Louise and Julie were out shopping and only Hannah was left in the house. Still, Hannah was enough. If he could not get away from them, Michael could start screaming like a little kid.

It was revolting. Michael tried to stay by the door. The others were sitting on Thomas's bed and leaning against his desk. They couldn't decide who was to start first. Then they opened their pants.

Only one of them was as large as he, Michael was pleased to see, but that satisfaction was soon overwhelmed by the disgust he felt at the sight, sound, and even smell of them masturbating with such giddy glee. The smell of their flesh filled the room, and soon there were "oohs" and "ahs" and "who" as they reached their climaxes. One needed his eyes squeezed tightly shut, but the other two wanted to see. Their eyes glazed and crossed as their ejaculations splashed like soppy little fireworks onto the floor. Thomas had brought a rag for the purpose, and with his penis out and drooping, he kicked the rag through their splatters. One of the others moved toward Michael, his head back so he could look down his nose, his lips swept up in a dreamy smirk. "It's your turn," he said.

"That's right, Michael," Thomas said. "Let's see what *you've* got."

Even at Saratoga, Michael had been careful to conceal himself from Thomas. "You only said *watch!*"

"Listen to the baby!" snarled the third boy.

"I'll *yell!*"

"You do that," Thomas said, "and we'll fix you good."

Michael sensed that the boy near him was going to grab his arms. Michael punched him in the stomach, just under the rib cage. His fist went in as deeply as if it had hit a pillow, and for a moment the boy looked as if he were going to die. It was nothing to push him toward the others and get out of the room. With their penises hanging out, they couldn't very well chase him down the stairs.

Thomas hated Julie, perhaps most because she could not help him with his friends, who laughed at her snobbery and saw through her coquettishness. Of course, Thomas hadn't helped himself, telling his friends as readily as he had told Michael of Julie's sexual curiosity. In that way he was like his sister, desperate, even lunatic, when there was something he wanted, such as friendship, and brutishly unconcerned once it was his. For that reason Michael was not worried about another encounter with the boy he had punched in Thomas's room: Thomas's friends came and went quickly. And if the boy wanted to confront him in the schoolyard or on a streetcorner, Michael knew he could avoid showing how well he could fight by suggesting that he would tell anyone around just what the fight was about in the first place.

But that was not what disturbed Michael most. It was the first time he had hit anyone since his fight with Moran, and instead of his becoming sick, as he had expected, he had enjoyed it—enjoyed it so much, in truth, that it was some minutes before Moran even entered his thoughts.

It disturbed him, and he felt himself slipping into a torpor of confusion and guilt. The next afternoon he wanted to stay by himself, but Thomas was in too foul a mood to risk it. Michael took the book he was reading, a dime novel about cowboys, down to the kitchen, although being in the kitchen usually resulted in his being pressed into some service for Hannah. Something happened upstairs, there was a shout and a crash, and Louise went running; and later at dinner, the head of the household heard a full report—explanations and counterarguments—and made a decision. It was for Julie and against Thomas, who went up to bed at once, glaring, his face red, the sweaty hairs on the back of his neck sticking straight out. If he paused at the stairs to glower at Michael, Michael did not see it, because he was staring directly in front of him. In another moment, just as Thomas was slipping out of his thoughts completely, there was a slamming of a door far upstairs.

Throughout the discussion Michael had sat looking as if he were pretending he was not in the room. He had to wonder if he were not in a madhouse. He was sure Thomas could not see the connection between what had happened in Julie's room today and in his own room yesterday. He had hit Julie or pushed her; he had hit her before, so that was not important in itself. It did not change Michael's perception of Thomas as the saddest person in the household. If Thomas could not think or see, it was because he had no character, but how could he develop character in a place like this? None of them had any character, and Westfield himself was the worst of all, the real lunatic who chased after people. It was always going to be this way. As if he could glimpse the future, Michael saw that they would always be the same as they were now, no matter how old they became. He would always have to maneuver and negotiate his way through their suffocating pettiness and discord. Westfield was what he was, but he had given Michael a home. Michael would never have a moment's satisfaction with any of them, but he was dependent on them all.

So when he stood at his window with the quilt wrapped around him while Westfield was downstairs drinking himself into a stupor and Louise was trying to forget the ache in her twisted wrist that was keeping her awake, Michael's curiosity about his impulse to return to Eighteenth Street brought his thoughts around to the incident of two weeks before, when he had punched Thomas's friend. Moments afterward in the kitchen, when Hannah's back was turned, he felt his body yielding to the odd purely *physical* desire to throw that magically fulfilling punch again. He could remember it still, or his body could. If he had enjoyed it so much, why was it that he did not know how he had won against Moran? He could remember some of it, some of the punching. Why did he want to return to the place?

He was still afraid to think of that night. The first time it had come back to him, almost by accident, the memory of the taste of Moran's blood had made his stomach heave. Remembering that his teeth had cut into Moran's flesh was the beginning, that Moran's blood had spread through his mouth; what he remembered following it was worse, terrible, the long run away, the nonstop mile-long run through the snow, his heart smashing in his chest, the snow freezing on his face and hands, the air spreading the cold from his lungs downward into the rest of his body, the agony, the punishment, serving only as the setting for what was happening inside him, which was worse.

In those first moments of what should have been freedom from his obsession with Moran, instead of the burden being lifted forever, it locked itself upon him again with a fury that was doubled, the feeling, the memory, the awful, empty, ravenous horror, things remembered, the gun firing, his mother falling backward into the room, the glass breaking behind him, the sight of his father in the other room with his head split open. There had been the wet bits in the air after that second shot, bits of wetness flying into his room, his mother's blood, a spray on his face. Running through the snow with Moran's blood freezing on his face, even on his lips, Michael screamed so hard that he felt his throat tear itself open inside. He kept running until he reached Thirty-eighth Street, until he climbed the steps up to the door of the Westfields' house, guessing that he would be alone, that they would be asleep inside, but hoping, oddly, *wishing in the way a child wishes that Santa Claus would bring him a certain toy* that there would be someone awake upon whom he could throw himself for protection, not against the police or anyone else from outside but against himself. In the minutes it took to run from Moran's dead body to the Westfields' house through the falling snow, winter vaulted summer and merged with winter, the year between collapsed into a blur, he was back with his parents, the blood was on him again, he could taste and smell the blood as he had tasted and smelled it in his room when he looked down from his bed and watched his mother die. The horror was on him with all its force in those last steps on Thirty-eighth Street and as he stood at the top of the stoop trying to get the incriminating snow off his clothing, as if the human blood frozen to his skin were of less consequence. It went on ravaging and destroying him inside even while he sustained the oddly mild shock of seeing Westfield: *it's him,* he thought, with a distinct sensation of anticlimax. He could feel it going on inside him in the safety of the lighted kitchen while he told Westfield that he had betrayed him, that he had done murder, that he felt no remorse or even regret about having been caught. It struck Michael at the time as curious, for there seemed to be something else rising in him from under or beyond the storm, a warmth, tingling and hushed, strange; he could feel it in the pit of his stomach and his bowels and the palms of his hands, a warm, hissing, tingling sensation that made him think of the odor of a sun-shower, the odor of the country after a sweet sudden rain. He wondered about his sanity, for he *thought* those things; they came into his mind whole and alive as the sensation grew inside him—what was it? Without trying to formulate an answer, he asked himself what was to come next, what *could* come: was there more that he could endure? And as he realized that it was all a blankness in front of him, the sun-shower brightened, glittering spangles, and he was so blinded inside that he felt lightheaded, the room rolled, he seemed to be pitched off his feet, and he had another split second before he lost consciousness to contemplate with amusement the sight of the floor flying up to meet him. . . .

He knew now that whatever had sustained him from winter to winter had gone down with a crash inside him. If he thought of Moran, he would feel and taste his blood, and then, because it was confused in his mind, he would feel his mother's blood—yet he had to cling consciously to his memories of his parents. He could feel them slipping away; he did not want to think of them so much anymore. If he went too far, he would come to the long winter inside him of killings, to the winter and the murder that had been in his heart for the whole of the year he had been with the Westfields. He had had enough of it, so there was a deadness settling down between his parents and him. A year had passed, and the deadness was like the deadness surrounding a scar.

He could see that he had to confirm the feeling he had had today on Lombard Street that what he had here was better than what he had had down there. He liked this view, for instance, the yards and gardens behind these houses. He could not change anything that had happened, and there was no point in lying to himself about what he felt. He did not want to fight the other thing that was happening to him anymore. In the year he had been with the Westfields, he had become a different person. This life had taken him over, step-by-step, slowly, over the span of a year. The hardness was still in him, the hardness of knowing that dependence and a developing appetite for comfort was binding him to the Westfields and not anything in his heart.

Now he had the problem of getting to sleep, like Westfield downstairs. And like Westfield, Michael saw that he could let himself be caught up for hours more with the turning over of thoughts in his mind. He dared not think of Julie, or he would finish like Thomas, a drooling jabbering servant to his own pleasures. For that matter, he could not think of Thomas either, lest he fire himself up with still another reliving of the fight in Thomas's room, with perhaps a few more punches for the first boy, one or two for the other, and a roundhouse right for Thomas. Oh, he would fight again if he had to; he would use his fists. And he would go to Eighteenth Street—eventually.

What lulled him to sleep were memories of Saratoga. He liked the feeling of the air, the look of the trees when they thrashed in the wind, the brightness of the long warm days. A vision appeared, he could plunge into it; if he relaxed and concentrated, it could be another afternoon in August, at the track, with the horses going by the clubhouse into the first turn. He could always hear the horses' hoofs through the roar of the crowd. He liked everything about racing. The horses were in the backstretch when the good feeling penetrated his body and allowed it to settle at last into the best bed he had ever slept in; and because that last notion was far from his mind, sleep came.

III

In the spring the Westfields went up to Hartford to a reunion, Westfield's two brothers having decided that their father had grown frail and was liable to slip away at any moment. Louise had never liked her father-in-law, in his old age a gnarled, nasty man, but she was pleased to see how well Michael got along with him. The old man questioned Michael closely, with painful bluntness, but Michael stood up to it, telling the elder Westfield where his parents had come from and what his father's trade had been. Louise learned things she had not known before, that apparently his mother had been an educated woman, and that his father had been to sea as a young man. Madagascar, the South China Sea, the Society Islands—names evocative of exotic places rolled easily from Michael's lips. Louise was in love with Michael then. She could not have been prouder of him if he had been her own. He was in the midst of another cycle of growth, and now he was almost taller than Thomas. Louise worried that Michael would grow too tall, to become a string bean like Lincoln, whose memory she wanted to despise out of respect for her father. Michael had relatively broad shoulders, and he stood straight. His face was losing more of its childish plumpness, and he was beginning to look handsome in a mature sense. It was too bad for Julie, Louise thought, that Michael was so many years her junior. At the end of the visit old Westfield went so far as to acknowledge Michael's promise. "You study hard and stick to your own business. *You* could make something of yourself." His emphasis was so strong and clear that it was shocking, but since there were no other males in the room, the women who were present, Louise and Thomas's brothers' wives, simply turned away in embarrassment. Later she saw that he could have been comparing

Michael to anyone, including the Yankee louts that were Thomas's brothers. In any event, it was undeniable praise for Michael, and the sense of victory it gave her swamped any other dismal anxieties she may have begun to feel.

She had been concerned that her husband's drinking or, not less seriously, the loose morality that accompanied it, would come to the attention of the elder Westfield, and she watched all concerned very carefully. But nothing happened. Rather, she saw nothing. With his attitude of defiance, her husband could easily attempt some piece of childishness with his father, but perhaps Hartford itself served to chasten him. He hated Hartford and he was on his guard continuously with his father, and his brothers, too, whom he described as fawning and hypocritical villains. But not during the visit: just being with his family ran him down; he had no energy for making his own trouble.

When they left for home, Louise felt relieved, in fact, that it went so well. It occurred to her that her willingness to settle for so meager a reward was evidence of how far down Thomas had dragged them. She felt she was seeing it clearly. It was an odd moment, with odd resonances. She was sitting in the compartment of the train, looking out the window at the tobacco farms of the Connecticut River Valley, and the plants were small and bright green in the flat dusty fields passing before her. She was so deep in her thoughts that it was as if she were alone. Her realization that their lives would probably not get better made her feel almost glad, which interested her; but then she remembered, "And the truth shall set you free." She decided that this was what it meant, this strange feeling. There was a timelessness on the other side of the window: the people working the fields lived essentially in the same manner as the farmers and fishermen of Christ's era. The Westfields had not come far; and alcoholism would keep this branch rooted in the common clay for the rest of their lives. She knew she was looking into the worst of thoughts, that they were not going to be different from others no matter what they had hoped, but she could not make herself feel unhappy. *The truth shall set you free,* she repeated, and for a long time after she could be seen moving her lips to the words. They helped her to understand herself, she would have said.

When old man Westfield did die in July, the New York Westfields went back to Hartford, then returned to the city immediately after the funeral. Thomas wanted it that way, and Louise understood, or was beginning to understand. He intended in his own way to rid himself of whatever grief he felt. It was, objectively, ridiculous because her father-in-law had been over eighty and had died in his sleep, a gentle death if there ever had been one; but it was all the excuse Thomas needed to disgrace himself and wallow in dirt. Louise understood it perfectly now. Within an hour of their arrival home, Thomas announced that he was going out in the evening, and Louise took it to mean that he intended to be gone for days. It was the first time she had been bold enough for such a thought, and it turned out that she was right. He was back early in the afternoon of the third day, dirty, unshaven, smelling of vomit, and so drunk that he could hardly stand. She and Hannah got him to bed. Louise was beyond shame with him, and her lack of shame made her fierce. She told Hannah to help her get him down to his underwear. If it enraged him, so be it. Hannah fetched a basin, but no amount of scrubbing would get the dirt off him. He seemed to foul the bedclothing. Hannah thought so, too; Louise could see it on her face.

They were downstairs a half hour when he suddenly shouted from the bedroom. They went running. He was sitting up in the bed, shouting "Louise! Louise!" as if she were not there or as if he couldn't see. Hannah's face was a mask of alarm and pity, but Louise felt only disgust. She was standing right in front of him, and he went on calling her as if she were lost at sea. She told Hannah to get a glass and his whiskey.

"It might make him sick, Missus."

Quiet, too. Louise did not want him raving all over the house when the children were home from school. They did not have to see the spectacle he had made of himself.

In August they went up to Saratoga as they had originally planned, at her insistence. If Thomas had chosen to mourn a father he had not really loved in a more acceptable fashion, she would have been inclined to submit to his feelings on the matter; but as long as he could indulge himself as he had, there was no reason for the rest of the family to put themselves out so much as an inch. It let her see what a low creature a common drunk could be. Outwardly, nothing happened, but he went on drinking at night after the children were in their rooms, and he did not stop until late, after they were asleep and would not hear him stumbling into bed. In that way he was sneaky about himself, and she saw that his arrival home after his last excursion had been timed for midday, when the children were off to school. He was using the children against her because he saw that she would go to any length to keep them from knowing how precarious their situation had become. She saw what he was inflicting on her. An accident, or even just being found out by the wrong people, and he would be ruined anyway and his family along with him. So it was torture, waiting for the inevitable. But the revelation of his cleverness toughened her. She saw that she had to watch him constantly now, everything he did, because she would not know when something was happening simply for effect, to prepare her for something else further down the line.

Even with so much realized, it took her weeks to see how much she did not know. The true state of the family finances, for instance. It had been years since they had sat down and discussed money, possibly because he had not made the kind of gains he had made as a young man year after year. Now she knew that she could not be sure that he had not made money and hidden it from her. But for what purpose? There was none that she could think of that did not reveal pursuits that made her shrink in shame. Her position was hopeless. She could not go to the banks or to his clubs without alerting him or, just as bad, casting herself in the role of spying wife. A wife could spy with honor only if she intended to divorce her husband, and Louise could not think of that. Lawyers, a courtroom proceeding, and evidence of grounds for divorce, which meant adultery—the whole business horrified her. No, she had to stay vigilant against him.

The following spring, then, when Julie began to receive invitations to parties and dances as a matter of course, Louise argued her case before her father and carried the day. He was easier to deal with than Louise had thought, asking her if Julie needed clothes, phrasing only a few mild questions about the girl's new friends and making sure that Louise had it on good authority that these people actually were what they represented themselves to be. It was the sort of thing that a man would ask of his wife if their six-year-old had been invited to a little chum's birthday party.

Westfield was in a docile phase anyway. After a bad Christmas, during which he missed a day's work, and a week in February, when he tried to go to work but had to come back because he was so sick, he seemed to want to moderate his habits, holding back from his first drink of the night for as long as he could. When he took out his watch, it meant that he was beginning to yield to his desire or need or whatever it was, and that it would be another minute or two before he trooped down to the kitchen for his whiskey and his glass. Louise couldn't decide if he knew that he went through the same ritual night after night at exactly the same quarter hour, or that when he went down the stairs, his footsteps had a different, heavier sound than normal. When she realized that his demeanor bore a perfect resemblance to that of a sulking child, a miserable, whiny child who knows how to get around his mother, she lost the last shred of respect she may have had for him. He was threatening their lives, and he had no redeeming qualities or virtues; day in and day out, he was just an unpleasant and often sickening nuisance.

As for Julie, her reaction to her mother's efforts on her behalf was disdain. Louise should have expected it. Julie was a positively stunning young girl, very tall and straight-backed, with flowing light-brown hair and large dark-brown eyes. She was almost too tall and thin, her bosom too small and her bottom, which was not wide, too prominent; but her best feature, her mother knew, outshined all her flaws and drew the young men to her as if they had been mesmerized: her smile. She had perfect, white, shining teeth, and when she smiled at a man, she looked directly into his eyes—directly: *this is for you.* It was brazen; at times Louise wanted to speak to her about it. That she did not was in the nature of a punishment because Julie was all too aware of her own emergence as a young beauty. She had become secretive and scheming, and it was clear that she believed she could have her way in any situation if she continued to imply a young girl's promises in her gestures and movements, in her eyes and especially her smile. The promises were false, of course, and Louise often heard young men's voices mewling in disappointment. Once at a party Julie paid too little attention to her escort and too much to another young man; another time in Central Park, she refused to talk to a beau for more than an hour because he had bought her the wrong flavor ice cream. It was just a phase, Hannah said, urging Louise to be patient; but Louise felt that her patience had been expended already. The situation between mother and daugher had reached the point where neither could do anything right—even a small act of kindness was viewed with suspicion.

IV

If Louise thought that Julie was out of control, Julie herself thought that she was on the threshold of achieving a standing in the community on her own. It was what she had dreamed of; she could feel the dream coming true. When she entered a room, people turned to see who she was. She had to smile in order to feel comfortable; to put herself at ease, she focused her attention on something very small that she liked, her brooch, for example, or she gave herself a task, like finding the best-looking suit or the baldest man. Sometimes she looked for the prettiest dress. She was not afraid of women. They had begun to dislike her. She knew what it was. She could always have her way with men. None of the other women was as clever. Julie could even describe this delicious first victory over the world. *I can make them do anything I want and then make them glad that I let them.* She would feel a shiver, a delightful little stirring inside that left her cheeks flushed and her eyes dewy. Sometimes it would even hurt, it felt so good.

But oddly, in spite of the excitement, she did not meet anyone in whom she could have as much as a passing interest. She was bored with all of them within hours, if not minutes. It could be something simply unacceptable, his hair, the sound of his voice, the way he held his knife and fork. It could be his conversation, which took longer to uncover, or his character, which took longer still. All of them wanted what they knew they could not have. She saw them gazing at her hair and neck and shoulders. She loathed the ones who could not control themselves and laughed at the ones who tried to prove that they were above it all. Fortunately or unfortunately—she could not decide which—she knew what she was supposed to feel when she met someone who interested her, and she had not yet felt a glimmer. She was going to press on with her new freedom; for the while, the excitement and attention were enough.

She hated to think about how infatuated she had been with Michael in that first year. She had told no one of it, and the thought still gave her chills, for there had been times when she had been ready to tell anyone. She had wanted to write letters to him or go up to his room after everyone else was asleep to wake him and talk. She had been so in love with him that she had almost broken down and cried at the dinner table.

Now she did not know how she could have even liked him. The more they went along, the more she could not tolerate him. He was barely polite to her. If she entered a room, she would have to make a noise in order to get him to look up from his book. "Oh, hullo." He never said her name. And it seemed as if he deliberately glazed his eyes. She tried it herself, in front of a mirror, duplicating the expression on his face. He couldn't *see!* What was the point of that? He was always reading, hardly talking to anybody. She knew that he didn't have to be that way, that he was doing it deliberately. He had become a bookworm; they had skipped him a year at school, and she hated him for that, too. He was such a stick, such a bore, such a *child!*

She learned the truth of her father's drinking that next summer at Saratoga. The Westfields had taken their usual rooms overlooking the courtyard of the Union. A few months earlier, Edison had introduced the first practical incandescent lamp, and that summer, that sultry August of Julie's sixteenth year, the Union courtyard blazed nightly with great swaying strings of the lamps, and while the orchestra played, there was dancing, elegant and beautiful dancing, under the dazzling blue-white brilliance of Edison's magical device. It was dangerous to look too long directly at the lamps, people said, but for Julie that presented no problem, for she was much too busy looking at the faces that whirled in and out of her view.

It was her best summer ever. She could write a half-dozen letters a day, most of them to young men who burned with fever to know the truth beyond her delicately restrained selection of words, and even then she had adventures left to tell, moments of social success and romance. After a half-dozen letters she still felt fresh, and she could lie awake in her bed with Hannah's snoring ratcheting off the walls, thinking about the wonder and richness of life. Julie would hardly hear the snoring as the orchestra played on in her imagination, usually a waltz; she would hold herself and pretend to be moving gracefully, lightly, and swiftly in perfect three-quarter time.

The end came so quickly that in later years she could not remember what she had been doing only moments before; it was just *there,* like news of a death. It happened in the courtyard away from the lights, under the trees. She was wearing a pink dress with puff sleeves and a square-cut neck. There was a boy talking with her when her father appeared in the middle distance, coming toward her. At first he looked so little like himself that she thought she was trying to imagine that she was seeing him in someone else's strong resemblance to him; but it was him, and when he saw that he had her eye, he beckoned to her. Then he turned his back and folded his arms.

When she reached his side, she saw that he had his mouth twisted in an almost pouting snarl, his nostrils were glaring as he breathed, his eyes were red, and his straw hat was almost unnoticeably askew.

"First, have you seen your mother?"

"No, Daddy, I haven't."

"Do you know where she is?"

"No, I—"

He turned to her, glaring. "Second, do you have any idea what time it is?"

"It's a little after ten—"

"It's after ten-*thirty!* Do you know what's going on here? Do you know who these people are?"

"I don't know what you mean, Daddy. Mommy says I can come here. There's nothing wrong in it—" She could smell his breath. It had taken her a moment to recognize the odor of stale whiskey. He smelled like a bum—she was on the edge of tears. He pulled himself up.

"For your information, young lady, I saw a couple back there doing things that, if I described them to you, you wouldn't be able to understand. Or shouldn't. But I wouldn't be surprised if you did understand, in that getup. Did your mother see that dress? Does she know the way it shows you off?"

"It doesn't show me off! She helped me buy it. She picked it for me—"

He lowered his eyelids until he was squinting. "I want you to go to your room and stay there. You better hope to hell that I never catch you out looking like this again."

"Looking like what? I won't go to my room, I won't!"

His lips turned white. "Another word and I'll slap your face in front of all these people. You look like a whore. Does that satisfy you?"

She let out a noise as if in fact he had struck her. She took a step back. He wavered—her step back left him wavering, he was so drunk. It was as if someone had reached up under her rib cage, taken her heart, and squeezed it hard. She turned away and ran to her room.

That was not the end. Later that night, when she was lying awake trying to make sense of what had happened, she began to hear noises in her parent's room. She had lost track of time and could not remember if she had heard the rest of the family come in for the night. Not that she cared. She was terrified and heartbroken, which would have pleased the romantic in her but for the desolate reality of the matter. What was going to happen to her life? She felt overwhelmed, crushed.

Her parents were arguing. Julie listened to the nearer sound of Hannah's snoring before she got out of bed. Years ago Hannah had caught her listening at a door and had fetched her away by the ear. It was the only time Hannah had ever touched her, but for Julie it had been enough; it had felt as if her ear had been about to tear loose from her head. Julie tiptoed to the connecting door.

There was silence in the other room now. No, her father was talking quietly, almost muttering. It was impossible to make out the words.

"When did this happen?" her mother asked suddenly.

"A couple of hours ago," her father said. They were talking about her.

"Ah, now I understand," her mother said, her voice louder still. "All your complaints just now about the terrible time you're having were just a preamble to this disgusting confession. You called your daughter that name? Who do you think has used the word in her presence? If someone did, you'd huff and puff in your disgusting way—"

"I've heard that word enough for tonight, Louise," her father said.

"Disgusting? You *are* disgusting, you filthy, common drunk— *disgusting!* You don't like it? Change your ways, you despicable, *disgusting PIG!*

The last word, loudest of all, signaled some change in the room. Even Julie, on the wrong side of the door, could feel it, but Hannah, who had been roused by the voices and who understood these things better, knew exactly what was coming. Julie heard Hannah whisper her name at the same time that she heard her father use a word she had never heard before at all, but whose meaning she believed she understood at once.

"You goddamned cunt!" her father shouted. "You're the pissy-faced cause of it all! You're the one who ruined my life!"

Then there was a sound, a thump, flat, small, followed immediately by a mournful rush of air. "Pig!" her mother cried—she *was* crying.

"Step away from the door, child," Hannah said. She took Julie's wrist and pulled her back. With her hand on the doorknob, Hannah whispered, "Sit on your bed. Don't make a sound." She waited until Julie obeyed. Through her agitation Julie could feel a new pulse of excitement. Hannah opened the door. "Did you call me, Missus?"

For a moment there was no answer, then Julie heard her father say, "Are you nosy? Do you want to know what's going on here?"

"Be quiet, Thomas," her mother said. There was a pause. "Yes, Hannah, I did call you."

"She wants to commiserate," her father said. "You might as well have her." He was going out again. Hannah stepped into the room, closed the door behind her, and locked it. Julie heard the click.

Hannah returned in less than half an hour. Julie had been sitting up to stay awake—strange, because the excitement seemed to have drained all her strength.

"What happened, Hannah?"

"You should be asleep, young lady."

"No, I want to know. Tell me."

Hannah got into bed and rolled over. "You should be asleep. Like me."

Julie bit her lip. Whatever had happened in her parents' room had started because of her. Did Hannah and her mother *blame* her? Julie could not be sure, and that was enough to keep her awake for hours more.

In the morning, the children were given the message to have their breakfast by themselves. The boys had heard nothing the night before, but now their curiosity was aroused, Thomas's more than Michael's.

"Come on, if you heard anything last night, you have responsibility to tell us." Thomas's voice had grown husky, but Michael's was deeper, strangely enough, and sweeter to the ear.

"I was asleep," she said.

"Well, Hannah heard something, even if you didn't."

"There's nothing I can do about that."

Thomas made her cower. She could not remember how many months had passed since he had hit her, but he still looked capable of it. He was the sort of boy who would punch a girl in the breast if he could get away with it. And he had grown big, not tall like Michael but big and fat. She kept her eyes down, and then in another minute she put her napkin on the table and hurried out of the dining room.

She had wanted to get back upstairs anyway. If Hannah would not tell her what happened last night, perhaps her mother would. Julie believed that she would be willing to wait all day if necessary. And as if the possibility existed that her mother would try to escape rather than endure a confrontation, Julie stationed herself on her bed, her pillows propped up, so she could see the door to her parent's room while she waited for the first sound in there.

Hannah came up from breakfast a few minutes later. "I think you should find something to do, Miss, I really do."

"I don't feel well."

"Don't start that now. There's enough problems—"

Julie snapped her head around and glared. "I don't feel well, I said. I don't like being called a liar."

Hannah started for the boys' room. "I'm sorry to hear that, Miss."

After a while Julie began to hear movement in the other room, and in another fifteen minutes, the door opened a bit and her mother looked in. There were circles under her eyes and her skin looked ashen.

"Mama?"

"What are you doing up here?"

"Will you talk to me?"

Louise closed the door. "Of course I'll talk to you. You looked lovely last night."

"It *was* my fault!"

"What was?"

"I heard it! In your room!"

"That was between a husband and wife, Julie. There are some things that are no one's business."

"Oh, *no,* Mama! I heard him. You know what he called me. I know he was drunk, but why did he do it? What did he do to you?"

"I don't want you ever to be disrespectful to your father—"

"I wasn't disrespectful. I know what I saw. Now I know it's my fault—"

Louise took her hand. "If I promise to tell you the truth, the whole truth, as ugly as it may be, will you please believe it and not that what happened was any fault of yours? If I promise? Say yes."

"Yes."

"Then I promise. What happened was not because of you, but because, as you saw, he was drunk. It all happened because he was drunk, including that foul name he called you. You looked perfect last night, perfect. Julie, your father was drunk because he drinks. He drinks quite a bit these days, and I think you had better accustom yourself to it."

"Why? Why does he drink?"

"He blames me."

"Why?"

"Because it suits him. If he blames me, he doesn't have to listen to me when I tell him to stop. He has all sorts of excuses for everything he does now. He's not in there now. When Hannah looked in last night he used that as an excuse to run out. I'm not worried about him. He's drinking. When he's finished, he'll come home. His father was a teetotaler and his brothers have never done this, but I'm beginning to suspect that it goes back a long way with your father, back to the days when we thought he enjoyed his clubs and his cards and his friends."

Julie had stopped crying, but not because she was being allowed in on the secret. That much was true, but beyond that, deep inside her, she felt sick with a sickness that made her want to clench her fists and scream. Was she supposed to hate her father? She wanted to, but her own unnameable pain was too much. "What did he do to you?"

"I told you, Julie, that's between a husband and wife."

"You promised to tell me the whole truth. You said it, the *whole* truth."

Louise's eyes wandered unhappily, then, as tired as they were, fixed Julie so coldly that the girl almost wanted to squirm away. "If you ever let your father know I told you, I'll punish you, Julie. Do you understand? I *will* punish you."

"I understand."

"Your father punched me in the stomach."

Julie screamed.

V

She wanted to keep her distance from her father after that morning, regarding him from one day to the next as if through a glass. A miserable spirit had come over him, but she didn't feel sorry for him. She never wore the dress again; as if it had been a gift from him, she did not mourn the loss. She decided not to dwell on any of it. For the rest of August, and then in September and October in New York, although she may have wanted to stay close to herself and nurse her wounds, she found herself yielding more and more to the clamor of her new life outside the house. When one young man said he thought her month in Saratoga had done her wonders, she felt she understood what he meant and believed it herself even before she remembered the truth. It was one of those strange, splendidly vivid moments that one remembers, however vaguely, the rest of one's life. In time she would forget what the young man looked like, and then his name, until finally there was nothing left but the disembodied words, and that whatever she had been through had made her more mature, sophisticated, mysterious, and attractive. She knew she was less happy, but she came to accept it, after a fashion. At home alone, in her room or sitting in the front parlor watching the passersby on Thirty-eighth Street, so close to the window she could sense the vibrations of the glass when an occasional heavy wagon rolled by, she felt empty, just empty. Hours could pass, and nothing would happen. She would stare at her fingers and pick at her cuticles. A flow in the weave of the drapes would hold her attention. She would rise out of her chair to follow the progress of two women walking to the corner, and then feel gratified when they came back into view again. She wondered about them but did not make up stories. At the start of 1879 she had decided she was too old for that. She remembered the fairy tale of the children leaving crumbs in the woods so that they would be found, and she imagined a world in which people's trails could be followed in the same way, forever, all their lives. The thought and others like it came and went in the hours that she was alone. She slept too, and sometimes she assigned herself small tasks, like sewing a ribbon or a button. Not more. When she read, she kept to the periodicals. Once she thought she wanted to read some romantic verse, but it left her feeling oppressed.

The boy intrigued by the effect of Saratoga kissed her, but she forgot that; the young man she had seen the day before had kissed her, too, and the one after him was so bold as to touch her lips with the tip of his tongue. She was still thinking about that. She wanted to be kissed, and if she was not in love with this one and that one week after week, she did feel intense and, yes, *mysterious,* as the boy had said. She felt different from other girls, estranged from her girl friends, who noticed no real change in her. Possibly because she determined not to be curious about her father taking her brother out in the evenings once or twice a month, young men ventured compliments on her womanliness.

With the coming of Christmas her spirits quickened. The crowds on Broadway between Twenty-third Street and Fourteenth sharpened her appetite for the parties of the holiday week, and soon she was thinking again as she had the year before that this could be the time she would be invited to Delmonico's or some other place that only the best people went to—she felt the stirring of hope for adventure.

But she was frightened as well. Her mother was growing more tense and unhappy with every new day; it had a meaning so clear that Julie was actually not surprised when her father sat down to the dinner table unsteadily two nights before Christmas Eve. Still, she kept her mind closed and her fantasies alive. The days were as clear as diamonds and the nights were as cheery and warm as the faces reddening in the cold.

Her father held off until the day after Christmas. He chose to skip work. Julie understood what it meant, but somehow she had forgotten what the results could be. Her mother's anger annoyed her, and not because she wanted her mother to deal with her father differently but because the anger was adding to the household unpleasantness that was making it difficult for Julie to keep her holiday hopes exciting and fresh. The harder she ran after her dreams of Delmonico's, the more elusive they became. No matter that she had a party that same night. It was as if she had escaped into her fantasies so much in recent weeks that the process had lost its potency.

When she arrived home after midnight, the first-floor lights were on, but the front room was deserted. Her father had started drinking at eleven that morning and had sequestered himself in his library at two in the afternoon. He had not come down for dinner and had refused a tray Hannah had taken up to him. Julie had forgotten everything at the party, a marvelous party. The carriage that had taken her home had been full of happy young people; as it had wound through Murray Hill, stopping here and there to let the passengers out, they had sung carols. There was still a couple singing as Julie stared at the emptiness inside the house from the vestibule. Her escort asked her if something was wrong.

"No. But you'd better go."

"Will I see you Thursday?"

She was suddenly so depressed and anxious to get inside that she almost wanted to tell him no. With her back to him she could hardly imagine what he looked like. She said yes and hurried inside, not sure at all that she would remember when Thursday came around.

The house was dead silent. At the foot of the stairs she thought of calling up, but Hannah leaned over the balustrade on the second floor and motioned to her. She waited on the landing while Julie ascended the stairs.

"There's been some trouble, Julie. Your father and brother are out, and your mother's in her room with Michael—"

"Did he hit her again? Did my father hit my mother?"

"No, he didn't. No one hit anybody. Your mother's been upset. She's had a very bad evening, but she's asleep now. And she should stay that way."

"What happened here?"

"I'm afraid I can't tell you that, Miss. It's not my place."

"The last time you wouldn't talk, I found out anyway, so you might as well tell me."

"Please, Miss. Please."

Hannah actually seemed to be begging, but Julie could not help growing angrier. "Well? Can I see her at least?"

"Please don't wake her—"

Julie was headed toward the bedroom. The door was not latched, and she pushed it open slowly. The lights were turned down low, and it took her eyes a moment to adjust to the darkness. Her mother, dressed as she had been at dinner, was sprawled across the bed. On the side where her head was Michael sat in shirt and pants, his hair awry. He was staring back at Julie, as if there were something she still did not see. She gasped. Her mother's head rested in Michael's lap and her hand was near her chin, so that she looked like a little girl—or his lover. Michael put his finger to his lips and pointed behind her.

Hannah beckoned to her again. She closed the door behind them. "Your mother and father had an argument before he went out. When he was gone your mother started crying. We were in the kitchen. She couldn't stop. Michael was the only other person in the house, so I called him. He took her up here and quieted her down."

"I don't think my father would like to see him in there like that."

Hannah's eyes narrowed for a second, then she nodded, acquiescing. "Yes, I saw that, but you don't know what that argument was like, Miss."

"Don't worry, I'm not taking my father's part. How long has she been asleep?"

"More than an hour now. That's how long Michael's been sitting there like that. I just now came up to tell him and to see if there was anything he wanted."

"You'd better do that."

While she waited, Julie realized that she didn't know what the argument was like because Hannah would not tell her. Julie would say that—it would break her down. Hannah came out again.

"He says he's going to try to move her. I told him where the extra blanket was—"

"Hannah, I want you to tell me what the argument was about!"

"If you'd let me finish, Miss. Michael asked me to tell you that he would knock on your door."

"Oh, he's just like all the rest of you!"

Hannah's face grew hard. "If you won't be satisfied, Miss, your mother and father were arguing about your father going out tonight." She went down the stairs.

Up in her room, Julie saw that what Hannah had told her made no sense, in the light of her mother's reaction. She prepared herself for bed and put on her robe and slippers. By the time she heard Michael on the stairs, she had come to the conclusion that it had been something her father had said. If he would hit a woman, he was capable of *saying* anything.

Michael waited until she closed the door behind him. "I'm sorry I took so long, but she woke up again."

"Will you please, *please,* tell me what happened here?"

"I told your mother that you had come in and that you would want to know. She wants you to hear about it. She wants me to tell you."

She sat on her bed. "That's a relief."

"I will do it, but only because if I don't, she will, and I think I want to spare her—"

"Spare her what?" Will you make sense?"

He pushed his hands in his pockets. "Do you know where your father has been taking Thomas the times they've been out this fall?"

"To one of his clubs, I thought."

"Julie, do you know what a whorehouse is?"

"*Ow!* That's *filthy!* You're a *liar!*" She came off the bed, swinging her hands. He grabbed her wrists and held her fast. "This is what I wanted to spare your mother. I'm sorry, but it's true."

She gasped for air. Michael pushed her back toward the bed until she sat down.

"*He* told her, and not tonight, either. He told her after the first time, after she wanted the reason for his sudden interest in Thomas. She's been holding that back for months. I knew; Thomas told me. After your father has had enough to drink, he doesn't care what he does. He has no respect for anyone or anything. I saw this on Lombard Street—"

"Don't compare my father with those people!"

"You little bitch, *I* am those people!"

"How dare you speak to me that way?" She sneered. "Oh, yes, I saw you with my mother. That's how you dare."

"Now you're being filthy!"

"Why shouldn't I be, when all the rest of you—"

"*All* the rest of us? Do you *really* believe that? If you do, tell me, so I can get out of here. I'll be better off back on Lombard Street. I'll put it to you bluntly, young lady. If I go, if you're lucky, you'll wind up a shopgirl in your grandfather's old department store."

She had to stifle a smile. "Young lady? Why, you're three years my junior—"

There was a noise on the stairs. Michael said "Wise up" as he went to the door. "They're home. Your father's saying good-night to Thomas, who should be coming right up. Now there are things your mother wants me to tell you, so I want to continue this conversation after Thomas has satisfied his curiosity about the voices in here."

"What did you mean, 'wise up'?"

He put his finger to his lips as he had done downstairs. Thomas came into the room. He was sleepy-looking and disheveled. "I didn't think I had to knock," he said. "What's going on in here?"

"Get out!" Julie snarled. "Get out of my room!"

He blinked. "What?" He looked at Michael. "Say, what *is* going on? What are you doing in my sister's room?"

"Get out of here, Thomas!" Julie repeated, her voice rising. Michael stepped between them.

"We're having a conversation, Thomas. Your mother had a very bad time after you left tonight, and I'm just telling Julie why. That's why she wants you to leave her room. Now you do it before I beat hell out of you. You know I can do it even when you're not as tired as you are now."

"I'm not afraid of you, Michael."

"You'd eat my shit if I told you to. Now get the hell out of here."

"This isn't the time and the place," Thomas said, backing out. He peered around Michael's shoulder. "I'm not done with you either, Julie."

"Oh, yes you are," Michael said. "Do you understand that? Your mother knows what you've been doing because your father told her. I can't do anything about your father, but I sure can do something about you. And if you had any decency, you'd see who had responsibility for your father."

Michael pushed the door shut after Thomas had left, then stood there for a moment.

"How old are you, Michael?"

"What I meant before was only that I've seen a lot more than you have and the actual years don't count so much."

"Can you look at me and say that?"

Now he turned. "What's the point? I'm a male. That counts for something. This summer at Saratoga while you were dancing every night I was having my own adventures—"

She giggled. "You're a *terrible* liar!"

"If I'm a terrible liar, how have I been able to tell the same lie so well all these months? I'm smarter than you, Julie."

She was smiling. "Oh, yes. You certainly had the best of Thomas. Would he really do that thing you told him?"

"I'm sorry about the language."

"I enjoyed every bit of it."

"Your mother wants you to go about your business as if nothing has happened. She doesn't want your father to know that you know anything about his business. It would make him worse, she says, and although that's true enough, what's more important is that he'd blame her instead of the one responsible for the situation in the first place."

"What would happen if I turned out like my brother?"

"Weren't you listening?"

"I heard you. It's what I would have done, anyway. Answer my question."

"You'd break your mother's heart."

"If she found out about it. If you told her."

"I wouldn't tell her, if I knew. How would I know? All I can tell you is that if I ever learned anything, I'd try to stop you before you did do something that would hurt her."

"You wouldn't let me get away with anything, would you?"

"I don't want to play games with you, Julie. I'd be much happier if I never thought about the subject."

She stood up. "What would you do if I kissed you?"

"I'd kiss you back, I think."

"No, a real kiss. Do you know anything about kissing?"

"Do you?"

"Challenging me?"

He grinned. "Well, I protected you from your evil brother, I suppose."

"And told me that my father was with—those women." Whores. It bubbled up to the surface suddenly; he had used the same word on her at Saratoga. What was he doing right now? Staggering around his room, trying to get ready for bed, terrifying her mother. After what she had learned about him this evening, that his daughter was directly upstairs only kissing the boy he had brought in seemed not strong enough. She kissed Michael now, pressing her lips gently to his. She felt his hands on her waist. It was a rather nice kiss; she brought her head back and opened her eyes. He touched his lips to her cheek. "Relax," he whispered. She wanted to laugh—he *was* going to kiss her back. She closed her eyes and felt his lips on hers again; only this time his lips were parted, and he seemed to be encouraging her to do the same. His tongue touched her lips in the way she had had done to her in the fall, but his tongue *moved*. He was tasting her—he *liked* it. She moved back and again his eyes were open first, as if they had not been closed at all. He was looking at her mouth. "Open," he said, in the same soft voice, and kissed her again, not giving her time to think about it. His tongue touched hers, the wetness passed between them. He kissed her cheek and then the side of her neck.

"You *are* a liar."

He kissed her nose. "A good one or a bad one?"

"If you lie like you kiss—" She could not finish; she flushed with embarrassment.

"I'd better go upstairs," he said.

"Are you ever going to tell me the truth?"

"You can have one thing or the other, but not both."

"Oh! Arrogant, conceited—"

"Julie, do you know how much I've dreamed of kissing you?" He did not want an answer; he was gone, climbing to his room on the floor above.

VI

Westfield was home the next day, too, extending his holiday a little, he explained calmly to the children, and his presence settled a stillness upon the household that made it impossible for Michael to risk as much as a glance at Julie. He felt her attention, her expectation, but he was afraid of her and what he had loosed inside himself. In fact, he had not thought of her in months. He had not lied when he had told her that he had been having adventures of his own, disappearing for meetings with girls the Westfields knew knothing about. If Julie thought he had meant by the context of his remark that his activities so far had been restricted to Saratoga, all the better. It had started in Saratoga, but when the girl asked his age, a new way to organize his life came clear to him in an instant: this part of his life necessarily had to stay separate from the Westfields anyway, so why could he not say what he pleased? For one girl he was seventeen; for another, eighteen. Since he ran the risk of being found out, it was wiser to give out differing and even conflicting stories. What could they be, but lies told to please the girls? Westfield would not oppose Louise on him, Michael was sure, except of course if he was caught with Julie, and even then he could not be certain how Louise would respond. Michael knew that he was the fox among the chickens— if he was in Westfield's position, he would be more careful and observant.

When Westfield returned to work the following day, the atmosphere in the house brightened considerably, and when Michael and Julie were called downstairs for lunch, they found themselves alone together in the hall on the second floor. She was in front of him, and he told her to stop. He did not know what he wanted to say. She turned around, and, without thinking, he moved closer to her and kissed her again, lightly, on the lips. She smiled. They were only inches apart. She smiled, then blushed and hurried down the stairs.

In the afternoon she came to his room, and they sat on the edge of his bed, kissing, for almost an hour. She gave him no indication that she wanted more or even knew how to proceed from kissing, and he understood what could happen if he moved too quickly. He did not know how far he wanted to take this; he was frightened of everything about it. He could see how much he was controlled by her feelings. If he angered her in any way, there could be no end to the trouble she could make for him. But none of this seemed to be going through her mind. She was happy, she said. She had questions she wanted to ask him. She had never done this before. She had been kissed but never so much. She had never gone to a boy to be kissed. She felt shameless, she said. They ended with her head on his shoulder.

She had a party that evening, but when she returned, she went almost directly to his room. He knew because he had been waiting for her. "I missed you," she whispered. "I thought about you constantly." He pressed himself against her and she sighed. She held him tighter with her face pressed against his neck. "I love you, Michael," she said.

"I love you, too," he heard himself answer, as his desire and pity consumed him.

They met outside the house after school, telling Louise that they needed to go to the library or a friend's house. The stories were always different, and had them heading in opposite directions. He had been using the device occasionally in the fall, to continue his necessarily hobbled pursuit of one of the girls he had met at Saratoga, and when Julie found out about her, a pretty blonde with soft lips, she cried. When did he plan to see her again? Did he tell her he loved her, too? He reminded Julie that he had not complained about the boys who came to see her. That was different, she said. Why? She had not been a sneak about it. They were in a little restaurant off Longacre Square, having coffee and cake, and Michael was eating both portions of cake. "I'm not your pet," he said.

"I beg your pardon?"

"I'm not your pet," he said. "You can't do as you want and expect me to do as you want as well. If you have to have it that way, we might as well stop."

"Do you want to stop?"

"No, of course not, but you want to make it impossible for me to go on. Do *you* want to stop?"

"No, but why do you want to see other girls if you can't take them out? I know you. You probably have them wrapped around your little finger."

"Like I have you, I suppose."

"You do and I hate you for it."

"I know that."

"I *don't* hate you!" She stopped, realizing that she had trapped herself. "I don't hate you," she said quietly.

It was not as she said. She was in control. They were not lovers. She could not even talk about lovemaking. She came to his room as often as she wanted, often boldly, with her parents still moving about two floors below or with Hannah awake and hacking with a cold. Julie would not bother with a robe, dashing barefoot up the carpeted stairs, stepping into his room, closing the door silently behind her. He would be up on his elbow in his bed, over to one side, the bedclothing turned down for her. She would get in beside him and they would lie together kissing. If their bodies could touch through their nightclothes, she would not let him touch her with his hands. It drove him crazy. She knew what was happening, but she would not acknowledge it. Her body heaved and shook against his; sometimes he had to put his hand on her mouth to stifle her moans, and when she left his room, she knew she was leaving him to clean up a mess in his pajamas. But none of that mattered to her as much as the belief that they were still not doing anything improper. He wanted to feel and kiss her breasts, rub her bottom, see the hair he could feel crinkling against his thigh or his belly, or even his penis itself, but she would have none of it. He could whisper what he wanted to do if he did not take it too far, for a little of it excited her just as clearly as too much upset her. He could see that she could not imagine the rest of it, that as little as the thought of him sucking her nipples excited her as much as she could stand. They were having a kind of intercourse except for their nightclothes, but he never told her that their positions and motions copied those of real lovemaking. He could not believe that she thought anything else, for no one could be that stupid, but he could understand her self-deceptions. For his part, he felt relieved to have her. He liked her well enough, she held his attention, and her body inflamed him, but most of all he felt relieved. His sexual capacity seemed so immense that he was afraid he was abnormal. He could have sex whenever he wanted it, for as long as he wanted. He had found that out at Saratoga, when for a few days during which a pair of vacation schedules overlapped, he was seeing two girls, of whom one offered herself completely, and the other expected him to perform too. Absolutely raving, afraid of getting caught, afraid of what he might be doing to himself, he had left himself wondering if he had not been cursed somehow; he had come around to wanting a normal life, a career if he could have it, and the love of a woman he loved at least as much as she loved him. He wanted to love, to be in love. He imagined his desire and capacity growing out of control until it destroyed him, until he could not have a decent life. So Julie gave him some peace. She was the same as the girls at Saratoga and he was the same as any boy she had ever seen. She would never understand that, that they only needed each other in a fundamental way; and because she could never understand it, the pity welled up in him again, and it made him cherish her. Even when she made him so angry that he wanted to tell her how stupid she was, he took care to cherish her. He never forgot how genuinely innocent she was.

So when she came up to his room one warm, damp night in April to tell him how unhappy she had become, how tense and ashamed, he had to play the part of the wounded but still generous and loving lover. He had been prepared for months, perhaps from the beginning. There was another fellow, whether or not she would admit it. Michael suspected that she could not admit it to herself. He had been prepared for that, too. She loved romance and the attention given to a pretty girl. Her new suitor was a young man in his twenties, a college graduate and fledgling sportsman who belonged to the New York Yacht Club and raced his horses weekday mornings on Seventh Avenue on his way to work—in all, a prize for a girl not yet eighteen. But it was more than just moving to the top of her circle of friends that impelled her, for what she wanted to stop with Michael was the intimacy lovers have. The pain was more intense than he could have imagined, and it was not that she was lying that was the worst of it. Her lies had always managed to tell him the truth anyway. There had been just too much between them for him to be able to shrug it off.

The window was open. It had rained during the evening and the air was heavy with the perfume of the moisture. They could hear carriages on the streets. The conversation was over. She sat on the edge of the bed, her head down, her fingers picking at a loose button on her robe.

"I'm never going to find out about you, am I?"

"You weren't going to in any case, I told you that."

She sniffed. "Am I making a mistake?"

"Yes."

She brought her head around. "I didn't expect you to *say* it!"

"You were happy with me. Do you want me to believe that it was a lie?"

She clenched her fists. "I couldn't stand not knowing!"

"Now you're lying, and you know it."

"Yes. See? I can do it as well as you can." She stood up. "I got tired of losing with you. I lost at everything."

"At least you think you're telling the truth. No, the truth is that you only lost the battles. You won everything that was important to me."

"Good." She was at the door. "I can do it every bit as well as you." She hesitated now, and he wanted to tell her that he did not want her angry with him. He almost believed that if he could tell her, it could be the beginning of bringing her back to him. But he continued to stare at her in the way she was staring at him. Her lips pursed—she looked furious for a moment—and then she closed the door.

VII

The pattern emerged in the next year. Her young sportsman was gone before the start of the summer; she came back to Michael unhappier than before. She had nothing to say, nothing she wanted to tell him, not at the start: she wanted to be held, consoled, and then loved, gently, according to some arrangement in her imagination. He did not believe her for a moment. He watched her, but she seemed to see nothing. She wanted the consolation first. She wanted it even though it couldn't help her. She was so miserable inside that he felt no guilt, feeling nothing himself and giving her what she wanted. Her sportsman had taught her how to handle men—she told Michael in the way she could never tell the truth about anything, accidentally brushing him with her hand, pressing her hand against him with her pelvis, finally reaching inside his pajamas to stroke him, as if she thought she could make him believe that she was learning it with him as they went along. He thought he could sustain the charade for her sake, or the sake of what he could learn of what made her so dishonest; but it became unpleasant for him, and they finished with her in tears over disappointing him and him consoling her again, telling her that the failure was on his account. After she had gone, he was awake for hours, in a frenzy—was this what she felt? Was this the burden she had brought in with her?

He was her one true friend, she told him the next night. He understood her, she said. "If I take care of you, you'll take care of me, won't you? If I make you special in my life, will you let me be special in yours?" She wanted to make Michael her knight, a protector pledged to her. Before the sportsman had come along, she had called him her Scottish prince. She thought his name, Monk, was unsuitable for some-one so handsome and regal. He could see it clearly: she had left him a less satisfactory man, and now the dream had shrunk so small that he could almost imagine himself able to fit it.

But somehow it seemed harmless to try, if he could keep it amusing for her, entertaining, engaging. If he could not love her for herself, he could love her for being a woman. It gave him a breathtaking pleasure to assert himself with a woman, to step out of the role he had to play and find himself in the secret moments all men had with women. It was having to play a role that made him want women so much, of course, that made him work at being charming and firm and gentle; it was what made him watch them so carefully for clues to what to do next; and it was what made him so daring. He was sure it was what made him feel the impulse to respond to Julie, as unhappy as she was, made him push aside his own fears and objections: that she was getting worse, not better; that she would drag him back into something he had already done and had outgrown; that, not unlike her father, oddly enough, she was headed for disaster and could drag Michael down with her.

There was more. She was fighting with her father openly now—she hated him; she could not hide it. When he spoke to her, she would pretend not to hear, and when he repeated himself, she would answer curtly; and when she was sure that he had begun to turn away, just *begun,* she would sneer, twist the corner of her mouth, so that he would see it in the periphery of his vision, where he might logically conclude that the gaslight and the liquor in him were doing a mischief. But she was taking a risk. The timing of it had to be perfect—less than a twentieth of a second, Michael calculated.

He told her one night what he could see in the dining room and that he thought it was a bad idea.

"I do not sneer!"

"I saw you."

"I don't. I won't let you speak to me that way. I absolutely do not sneer."

"Maybe I was wrong," he said, but he kept alert for the next situation. Two weeks later it happened, and when the split second came for her to twist her mouth, she actually stopped herself in the midst of it, considered glancing at Michael, then stopped herself from doing that, too. All this while Michael was paying attention to something Louise was saying. He noticed that she had picked her opportunity, too.

He had known something about himself for a while now: he could see better than other people. It had come to him last August at Saratoga when he began to test his recollection of the previous day's races with what the sports reporters had written. In one case Michael could remember that the jockey had only shown the horse the whip, while the reporter had written that the jockey had hit the horse; and in another, Michael had the distances between the first three horses of a race closer than the reporter had had them. Michael was sure, and he went to the stewards and asked. The conversation there led Michael to ask Westfield how the judges did their jobs. There had to be tricks to it. Westfield said that he really didn't know anything about it but that he knew someone who did.

It was a correspondent for one of the New York newspapers who told him that there were tricks, tricks of memory, knowing little things about horses, but mostly having a good pair of eyes and knowing how to use them. If Michael thought he was so good, he might as well give it a try. The sooner a boy learned he was no good at it, the sooner he would stop filling his mind with thoughts about horses and racing.

Michael had seven of eight at the half-mile pole and eight of eight at the finish. The reporter was very impressed. "I think you found yourself some real trouble, boy," he said.

But he was curious about the problem of reporting, too. He thought he could do it as well as most of the correspondents he read, and at times he thought he could do it better. He tested himself as he committed the moment of a finish of a race to his memory, like a photograph, composing the sentence that said what he saw, and when he was back in his room, he would set his collection of sentences down and put the paper away so he could open the newspapers the next morning and compare his work with that of the professionals. He was nearly as good as some of them, and why not? He was only a few years their junior, and his mother, as he had come to recognize, had been an excellent teacher. At those moments it was easy for him to fall into despair, almost panic. He was years behind. Would she have told him to lie about his age if she could have foreseen what it would do to him?

It was his panic that made him look again at the world immediately around him. He thought that some might say he was spying on his family, but if he could see so well in the one context, what could he learn if he watched the people around him in the other? It was not an accident that he was paying attention to Louise when Julie decided not to sneer, for all the immediately preceding conversation had pointed toward such a moment; and he was not surprised when Julie did not come up to his room later: an hour after dinner, she had had a chance to exchange a glance with him, and she had kept her eyes busy elsewhere.

That night he went down to her room to tell her to come up to him. There was no way she could defend herself. As long as he pretended he had seen nothing, she could not claim to be angry with him because he *had* seen. Even worse for her, when he had been figuring out how to respond to her, had had an original crazy thought, and it had taken him over.

After he was back in his room, she made him wait five minutes before she came upstairs. He was not fooled.

"All right," she whispered, "what was so important?"

"I love you."

"What?"

"I love you. I want you to run out to the West and be a cowboy with me. No one will know. You can cut your hair and put on rough clothes. I read in one of the weeklies that it's going on all the time."

"Michael, your're a *madman!*"

He had her smiling. "I do love you, you know."

"Can I go downstairs again? I really didn't have such a good day."

"Go ahead. I said what I had to—but I'll be awake a while longer, if you want to come back to talk."

He heard her stop on the stairs. He moved quietly to his bed so she would not think that he had been waiting.

If it so much as crossed her mind that he had been manipulating her, it would take him a week to get her to speak to him again. He was sitting down when she opened the door.

"Michael? Are you all right?"

"I missed you."

"Do you want me to come in with you?"

"I was hoping you would."

He kissed her and held her close to him and comforted her, and what had started as a game with no point to it became real and he allowed his desire for her to fill him again. She was confused, distressed, and he could see that she knew he had caught her at dinner, so why this? He *wanted* to love her. She was cruel and dishonest, and he knew he would never be able to live with those things, but when she was happy because she felt loved or admired, it didn't matter, it poured over into him. He loved letting her sense his desire, loved the way it warmed and sweetened her; the sweetness was what poured into him, and as he went on kissing her, holding her, he wanted to taste and know her. The more he let her see it, the happier he became.

The following weekend she had a party and did not come home until nearly two. He had waited up for her, and after there had been silence for several minutes, he went downstairs to her door. He rapped softly.

There was no answer. He rapped again.

Her voice came from the other side of the room, where her bed was. "Go away, Michael. I don't want to see you tonight."

It took him a moment to understand, and then he went away. He did not get to sleep until there was light in the sky.

She avoided being alone with him that day, and at seven o'clock in the evening she hurried out. An appointment, he was told. He made sure he was asleep before she came in.

She had met someone else, she told him on Sunday afternoon. She was sorry—but he knew it could happen, didn't he? It wasn't fair of him to expect more. He had trouble looking at her. He had expected this sooner or later. He got up to leave; his eyes passed over hers. She was on the edge of tears. He was almost relieved to be reminded of how stupid she was. At the bottom of a stupid situation were stupid emotions.

"Enjoy yourself," he said.

They kept away from each other for the rest of July and up in Saratoga in August. He had a good holiday, coming out a little ahead on the horses and winning over four hundred dollars at poker—he'd latched onto a floating game catering to young men who had difficulty getting into the casinos. Poker was a chance to study people, manage his money, and wait for the right opportunity all at the same time. He was not afraid of the big bet, and the combination of silent, watching patience and explosive betting gave him many more pots than he had a right to win. He liked to let new players catch him bluffing early in the evening; if the cards fell right, it was like a key to the vault.

He had less luck with girls. It was a bad year, his pals said, a very bad year. If they had difficulty getting into casinos, they had no trouble gaining access to the whorehouses, but Michael was the one who declined to go along. He wanted to, but his father had once bragged that he had never paid for a woman even during all the years at sea. He had little else with which to remember his father at this stage of his life, and often he thought that it was not what he would have chosen, but he felt that he had to live with it.

He kept on with his writing, but he had no way of learning if it was getting better. He considered and rejected the idea of having Westfield introduce him to more of the correspondents. What could he do? He was too big to run errands, too young—they would think—for anything more serious. The whole business of his age had him going in circles. He was all right as long as he filled his mind with other things. Like doping horses. Poker. Girls.

VIII

One evening in October Julie was in a giddy mood and reached behind her on the staircase and grasped his penis firmly. He caught her wrist but not quickly enough to hold her hand in place.

"Come upstairs tonight."

"Oh, no, I'm not starting that again."

"Then why so friendly?"

She turned and he let go of her wrist. She was in a happy mood. "I just wanted you to know that I'm thinking about you. Is that okay?"

"Not too often or you'll have me thinking about you."

She tilted her head. "I want us to be friends. That's really what I want."

He smiled. "We're friends."

"That makes me happy." And she went down the stairs.

He forgot about that quickly enough, and there was a private kiss at Christmas, but nothing substantial passed between them until the spring. It was April, a year since she had first broken off with him. It crossed his thoughts once or twice, but his mind was on other things. He was reading one Saturday night when she suddenly opened the door.

"Oh! I thought you'd be asleep."

She looked terrible, her face blotched and her eyes filled up. Michael swung his feet onto the floor.

"No, stay there. I'm sorry. I thought you'd be asleep."

"Wait a minute. What were you going to do if I had been asleep?"

She stared. Whatever it was, she could not say it. Michael turned down the lamp. "Do it anyway," he said. "If you thought you could trust me asleep, then please trust me when I'm awake."

"Could you pretend you're asleep? Get under the blanket the way you do and close your eyes."

He did it. He felt her move nearer the bed, and then the dull color on his eyelids faded as she turned the lamp off completely. She undressed. The rustle of her clothing and the soft pop of buttons being undone caused his heart to pound and his palms to sweat, as if her connection to his heart had never unraveled. She got into the bed beside him, her body not touching his but close enough for him to feel her warmth. After a moment she brushed his chest with her fingertips. His skin was still smooth and hairless there, and she explored it expertly, touching his nipple and then his navel. She kissed his lips. As if he were really asleep and she were intruding on a dream, he moved a bit. He could smell wine on her breath. She pressed her lips to his cheek and whispered, "You'd be awake now. You'd be waking up."

He went through the pretense. "Oh, hey, what are you doing?"

She got up on her elbow. "Hello, sleepyhead. What do you think I'm doing?"

He could see her eyes in the pale light of the window, and they were different from anything she had ever showed him before. She did not want an answer to her question. Her anticipation was a kind of submission to something inside her, not anything that had to do with him. She did not want to answer his questions, not because she did not want him to know why she had decided to do this, but because she did not want to be bothered with him seriously. She wanted to use him again, and for that she was willing to be used.

After she went downstairs again, after the insubstantial and not-quite self-deceiving little love-acts that people who have indulged themselves sexually will offer each other—kisses, brief smiles, quick hugs, and conspiratorial winks in the acknowledgment of new, shared secrets—he cried. The ache in his chest was immense. She was not a virgin; she was doing what she had threatened so many months ago, after she had learned where her father and Thomas had gone. If she had had an insane look in her eyes tonight, it was because the act had been insane, part of a round of vengeance in which both the weapon and the victim were herself. Michael could remember how she had once thought of the things she was doing. What did she call herself in secret, where no one knew her? The wound her father had inflicted was that deep. Michael was not sure that she even remembered what drove her. He could see her future so clearly it made him shudder. Her future and her brother's. And West-field, who had given Michael more future than his own parents could have offered, had done it to them both. Because he was still outside their family, Michael could see the beginning and the end. He had met West-field's own father, and he had been able to feel that connection between father and son. After plunging the knife into Moran's heart and after try-ing to seduce his benefactor's daughter, Michael felt he had no right to judge anybody. That his was the worst sin of all only clarified the issue. They were all sinners now—Julie, Thomas, and he—when just months ago, when he had first arrived at the Westfield household, they had played Blind Man in the rear garden. The worst they had done then was knock each other down. Was this what growing up meant? They had joined the rest of the race, shouldering their share of the burden of the guilt of the world. He could see their futures, Julie's and Thomas's, but not his own. He had been forced by circumstance to invent his life—did that make a difference? There was nothing he would ever have to do that would not be his own choice, yet he could not help but conclude that he would nearly always be lonely. There would be more Julies, just as there would be Julie herself, but he would be alone. He could see that it was necessary if he was to save himself. He was outside of life, and there he would have to stay.

Young Manhood

I

FROM THE PERSPECTIVE OF APPROXIMATELY A HUNDRED YEARS, IT would appear that the rebuilding that began in New York after the Civil War and led to the city that many of us alive today would recognize took place in a twinkling of an eye, with little effort and less sacrifice. In point of fact, the bridge to Brooklyn was first proposed in the 1840s and the New York Bridge Company was not organized until 1867. Still, the bridge took another sixteen years to finish, and in the construction twenty men lost their lives, a fact concealed as carefully as possible from the public for fear the outcry would stop the project permanently.

The Brooklyn Bridge was built to develop commerce and to avert a potential disaster in the commuter ferry crossings in midwinter, when in the colder nineteenth century the East River was often jammed with ice; but soon after the bridge opened there was a panic and stampede, and a dozen people were crushed to death or thrown into the river. It happened on Memorial Day, 1883, six days after the opening; newspapers' scare stories that soldiers' marching would cause destructive vibrations infected enough of the crowd to send them suddenly running for their lives.

In the same way, the electric light that was to free humanity from the danger and unpleasantness of gas illumination killed people instantly and started deadlier fires; the elevated lines built to relieve the congestion of the streets and speed traffic were nerve-shattering eyesores that depressed property values all along their routes; the telephone destroyed the social grace of letter writing; and the steel-skeletoned skyscraper obliterated God's last gift to the poor, the sunshine.

For the most of the population, the changes wrought by man's inventiveness were only promises of a better future—promises that turned out to be empty. The distance between the rich and poor widened throughout the Gilded Age. The slavery of the working class continued into the twentieth century, slavery that was in the main unchanged from the beginnings of America's industrial revolution. Workers still lived in hovels. One could not walk on any street in New York without seeing the effects of the desperate poverty, if not the desperately poor themselves.

Michael lived surrounded by what his life could have been if Westfield had not rescued him—which is to say, as he realized, if his parents had lived. For instance, his relationship with Julie had sunk in a round of loathing and self-loathing—they had learned to despise each other without ever letting go of, or admitting to, the sex between them. They had not touched each other in years. He suspected that she had had more affairs than she could remember, but he knew that she would probably let him kill her (he had thought of it) before she would tell him anything. Learning this small thing about her, he knew, bit by slow bit over the years, was as much as part of the landscape of his maturing as the changes in the city around them, the optimism the changes made everybody feel, the poverty that haunted him, the lives he could have led—and the Bridge, *naturally* the Bridge, the place he took the young ladies when he wanted to convince them that he was the sort of young man they had always dreamed would take down their pants. He had found that the easiest way to do it was to look pleasantly and intently into their eyes and let them talk themselves into it.

His name was Michael Westfield. The previous September, after more than a year at the City College on Twenty-third Street and Lexington Avenue, Michael had gone down to see Westfield in his printing office behind Park Row. He had had enough of school; he wanted to get on with his life. And Westfield was in a condition to be approached with a new idea.

Westfield had been sober for months. It was not the first time he had quit drinking, but in the past he had done it almost on the sly, waving off suggestions of predinner drinks, calling for coffee with his meal, bringing in camomile tea for his bedtime. The family watched him, hoping but unconvinced and fearful, and eventually there would be the smell of whiskey in the house again, the sound of his rantings, and the crash of the furniture. At other times it was clear he had convinced himself that he had alcohol under control, a glass or two of claret at dinner, carefully measured and timed dosages of liquor through the evenings. Inevitably his schemes would dissolve in drunkenness and degradation. Once Thomas found him unconscious on the steps outside their house, his face covered with the dirt of the street. His hands were black, the dirt in whorls, his fingernails chipped and broken down to the quick, his knuckles so lined with dirt that it had to be ground away with pumice. Louise and Michael did the actual work. Thomas could not resist reviling his father, and Julie locked herself in her room. In her way Louise had given up on both of them. She and Michael cleaned Westfield together, never saying aloud what they knew, that he was the dirtiest human being they had ever seen.

Even being found on his own doorstep was not enough for him. He was no longer an alderman, refusing to run for yet another term for what he said were personal reasons—really, as he readily acknowledged to himself, so he could continue drinking without worrying about the added disgrace of being found out while in public office. Not that other aldermen weren't hopeless alcoholics, with faces ravaged by drinking. He expected disaster; he thought he could see it coming, so he knew he was courting it.

But in the spring of '86 he had had enough. It was a little thing that triggered it, a twisting of the lip of a bartender he had regarded as a friend. This time there was no blather, no hollow challenges. He simply let the thing sink in, and it kept cutting deeper, deeper into his accommodations with himself, until he could see what he was, what he had done to himself, and what he had thrown away. He was a drunk who had destroyed his family's life and had denied his own need for self-respect. Without another word to the bartender he settled his bill and went outside to take the next streetcar home. He was still drunk: he had gone so far that one drink made him as sick as a normal man would feel after making a night of it. He thought of walking the last half mile or so to work some of it out of his system, but he was afraid he would lose his momentum. When he arrived home, he told Louise to get rid of all the liquor in the house, even the wines and medicines. She hid the medicines but poured out the rest, and when she went upstairs again he was asleep in their bed, his nightshirt pulled down properly and all his clothes put away—something he had never done before.

He had been sober more than half a year when Michael arrived downtown that September afternoon. Julie was to be married the following month to the son of one of the Wall Street boys, and about that Westfield had to be glad. After all this time sober he had not yet regained his strength, and the message was clear: he had ruined his health.

He had shortened his life, or cut the heart out of it; he thought that if he had his choice, it would be the former. He had examined his life enough to know that he had done something wrong, that there was something wrong, that there was something that he had missed (Kate Regan was one of the people he thought of most, along with the young Louise Lowe and the young Westfield who had gone away from their first meeting as if poleaxed), but he was determined to live out the rest of his time with something approaching dignity. So when Michael stepped into Westfield's office and closed the door behind him, Westfield was prepared to listen to what he had to say. Westfield had thought about Michael, too, and knew exactly what he had not given the boy. Everything else, including the offer of a better education than the one Michael had accepted, had been only substitutes.

Michael had reached his full growth and had begun to fill out. Although he kept his head bowed when he walked, as many very tall men do, he had nothing of their awkward, giraffelike head-bobbing gait, as if he had seen it in others his size and had consciously rejected it as unpleasant and unsuitable for him. He walked carefully, and nearly always slowly indoors, as if aware of tighter confines than others recognized; and out on the street Westfield had seen him precisely unbutton his jacket so he could put his arm behind his back, deliberately inhibiting his stride so that the much-shorter young man in his company would not have to work at keeping up with him. Michael seemed to have sensed and accepted the fact that he was living in a slower world than he would have wanted. He even measured his words, gazing directly into the eyes of his listener as if he was making sure he was being truly understood. It was a perceptive tactic, Westfield thought; he had seen it work at a dinner party Louise had organized for Julie's fiancé's family, which included a girl of seventeen. She had to be in love with Michael yet, two months later, a dark-skinned, dark-haired shy little girl with high cheekbones and saucerlike brown eyes. Westfield thought he knew Michael rather well, perhaps better than Michael knew himself. Westfield had seen that sort of girl in Michael's presence several times, fresh, good-natured, and shy, who had cared for kittens in her childhood and kept her own scrapbook, neat and up-to-date—he had illusions, Michael had, that there were still some people he had not met who would turn out to be different from all the people he had met so far.

He had dressed for their meeting, wearing a bright gray checkered suit Westfield had never seen before. His dark wavy hair was neatly trimmed, parted on the side so sharply that Louise could have done it for him, and plastered down perfectly all around. Westfield had seen him more than once over the past several summers after ten or eleven hours at cards with his hair in its natural state, sticking up like wire in all directions. Last summer, drunk, yielding to impulse, Westfield had grabbed a hunk of it.

He had disguised his curiosity in a kind of rough, silent wish of good luck, and the boy had taken it that way—it was a delight to fool him once in a while. Michael was one of those dark-haired, dark-skinned Scots grown enormously tall, and Westfield could see where Michael's hair had already begun to recede at the temples. No one else, not the women, not even Michael himself, had noticed the change in his hairline from his childhood.

Michael took the wooden armchair on the other side of Westfield's desk and crossed his legs and got out his little black cigars. After a moment he remembered to offer one to Westfield, who declined.

"That's a handsome suit you have there," he said.

Michael smiled and fingered the lapel, admiring it himself. "I won this last week. I'm glad you like it."

"Was that at cards or at Sheepshead Bay?"

"A fellow named Hamilton bet a pair of tens into my nines. I raised him a little, he raised me, and then I bet a hundred dollars and he called me anyway."

"You took a big chance, even with the third nine."

"No, I know Hamilton. He plays a money-management game and would like to clean me out some night. I was playing to his feelings more than his accounting. I hesitated on my first raise, but he didn't raise again with authority. I thought it was worth a hundred."

"You're a heartless bastard. What does your little book read now?"

Michael got the book from his jacket pocket. "More heartless than you think. If Hamilton had folded, I had already decided to show him the nine. To set him up for next time."

The book had been Westfield's idea. Michael gambled the way Thomas visited whorehouses, with a lust that ordered his life; and since, as usual, Michael was so much more adept at his vice than Thomas was at his, it was a simple thing for Westfield, at the start of this period when he wanted to make amends, to suggest to Michael that he think of his gambling as a little business that had to show a profit like any other. Certainly it was nice to get the best of Michael once in a while: he took to the encouragement like a puppy, and almost immediately he appeared with his little leather-bound book immaculately organized into accounts for his cards and racing.

"I had a bad night last night," he said as he turned the pages. "I lost forty-seven dollars, so on the year, starting from April, I'm ahead twenty-seven hundred. A little more than that."

"How much do you have put away now?"

"Almost six thousand."

"You should have some of it in the market."

"I prefer to gamble on myself and my own brain, thank you."

Westfield had made the suggestion only to goad Michael.

He was very strong now—he didn't hesitate to tell you what he thought. Westfield knew perfectly well how he felt about the Wall Street crowd—as far as that went, about anyone who did not work at a real job for his money. Of course, Michael did not reckon himself into that opinion, perhaps because he was a student, but more likely it was because of his view of his own situation.

"How are you doing with your studies?"

"That's what I've come to speak with you about."

Westfield hesitated. Thomas had come down from Bowdoin in the spring to announce that he wanted to leave college and head West. It had taken Westfield all of twenty minutes to point out to Thomas that he had absolutely no qualifications to be a cowboy. Utter nonsense—he of all people had not even thought of the problems of prolonged sexual abstinence. This was more serious, for the least of it was that Michael usually thought of everything in advance. He never bet a race when he could not make up his mind, and there were very few men who had the honesty, never mind the discipline, for that sort of trick. Westfield leaned back. Out of the corner of his eye he could see through the window down to the streetcorner, and standing there were two young ladies, brunettes, happily gabbling to each other. Their youth and self-absorption made Westfield wince miserably. He said to Michael, "Did you dress in the hope of a free lunch?"

"Actually, I was going to take you to the place of your choice, if you'll let me."

Westfield looked out the window again. From his position Michael could not see the objects of his attention. It was silly, for Michael knew him. The girls moved on, then the horses drawing a streetcar blocked the view. "Let's go over to the Astor House. I had lunch there the day I got you out of the shelter on Cherry Street. This *is* that sort of day, isn't it? You wouldn't offer to pay if it didn't mean something to you."

Michael smiled.

II

For Westfield their special friendship had begun one night at dinner, after he had been on one of his binges. He was very shaky at the table, his eyes burning and his kidneys killing him, when Thomas suddenly spoke up.

"You really did it to yourself this time, didn't you?"

Westfield couldn't respond; not that he was too shocked—he was simply too sick. He had come to the table only to make a showing.

"*Your father,* Thomas," Michael said, "succeeds at everything he tries, which is more than he can say about you."

"I'd like to know what you mean by that!"

"I'll be happy to go into it in private if you wish, but I won't sit here and watch a sick man being attacked at his own table. You've been in that condition yourself and everyone at this table knows it, and for what it's worth, so have I—"

"Michael!" Louise cried.

"I'd like to hear about this myself," Westfield croaked.

"I'll explain. What I wanted to say, sir, is that anyone who has ever felt what you're feeling, anyone who has eyes to see it, should be inclined to be charitable." He turned to Louise. This was some time ago, when he was supposed to be eighteen. Westfield loved his language; he wanted to hear the cock-and-bull story he was going to hand her. "I'm sorry, but it was last summer at Saratoga—"

"But when?"

"I'm explaining. It's time you knew that we all have our bad habits, including me. It was late one night when I left my room after you were asleep to sit in on a poker game. I got drunk because it was the first time I'd ever won more than a thousand dollars at one sitting. I said the first time."

"Oh, my God!" Louise was up from the table, her hand to her mouth. Westfield was dizzy with disbelief: he had known about Michael's gambling for years, but this was the first she had ever heard about it. What was he up to? She had great hopes for him, that he would turn out to be something wonderful, like a surgeon. Michael was on his feet to rush to her aid—Westfield knew how much he loved her, enough to help her get her husband to bed night after night, when his own children would or could not help. What Michael had just said had taken place in this context, too: everyone at the table knew everything. There was a line they never crossed in conversation . . .

Ah, Westfield saw at last: first Thomas had breached it, then Michael. But then Michael had brought them back again, shifting the burden to himself, drawing attention away from Thomas, who could not tolerate so much as a hint that his sexual woes were common knowledge. Of course the whores talked: he liked to snuggle up close to them and have them tell him stories about their business with other customers. All this had come to pass recently, after he had attained his majority and come into an inheritance from his maternal grandfather's estate. This was a new activity; it had nothing to do with Westfield, for it had been years since those few times they had gone together to a brothel. Thomas had given no sign then of having enjoyed it, either, for that matter.

No, what had happened to Thomas was that he had become enor-mously fat, like his maternal grandfather. At times he reached almost three hundred pounds, Westfield judged. There wasn't anything that could be done about it, it seemed; it was in the blood. His weight had varied as much as a hundred pounds, but Thomas was doomed to be repulsively fat, a big pink thing. The truth of his situation ballooned before him in the mirror every morning and he could not stand a word of criticism from anyone; and now he entertained notions of going West. All this was in Westfield's mind when he was able to speak to Michael later. "Thanks, boy."

"It was on my conscience. She had to find out sooner or later, and better from me."

It took Westfield a moment to realize that he was speaking of his gambling.

A month later, on a tour of sporting houses and gambling clubs, Westfield happened to spy Michael at a poker table. By the number of chips in front of the players, it appeared to be at least a busy game. Westfield was a little drunk, his head spinning, his legs heavy. Michael was sitting with his back to him. Westfield moved out of the main saloon into the poker room and stood behind the young man, the youngest at the table by possibly ten years. Westfield leaned over.

"How're you doing, boy?"

Michael was smoking a small cigar. Westfield had never seen him with tobacco before. "I'm all right. I'm up a little."

"Do you know who you're talking to?"

Michael put the cigar in his teeth while he gathered his cards. The game was five-card draw, and the deal had just passed because no one had been able to open. There was a good pile of chips in the pot. "Yes, sir," Michael said as he fanned his cards. "I hope you've had a pleasant evening." He had four cards to a flush, four to a low straight. The man on the dealer's left tossed in two blues. The next man folded.

"Raise ten dollars," Michael said, dropping in three blues. Now Westfield had the stakes, and he could see that there was more than one hundred and fifty dollars in the pot. The man on Michael's left called, but then the man on the dealer's right counted out eight chips. "Fifty more," he said.

"Too rich for me," the dealer said.

The man who opened called, but his lips were pursed.

"Fifty," Michael said, "and another hundred."

The man on his left threw in his cards, the man who had raised fifty called, and the opener folded. Michael indicated that he wanted one card. The other stayed pat.

"Up to you," he said.

Michael glanced at his card quickly. "Let's see how confident *you* are. Twenty dollars."

The man's eyes gleamed. "Another hundred."

"A hundred," Michael said, "and raise you three hundred."

He would have killed Michael if he could have gotten away with it. It took him a moment to count his chips. "Call. What do you have?"

"Flush."

The other man threw his cards face down on the table.

"Figured him for two pair," someone said. "Three of a kind at the most."

"I'm going to take a rest for a few minutes," Michael said, stuffing his pockets with his chips.

"You *will* be back?" the loser asked.

Michael paused. "That's what I said." He led Westfield out of the room. "I have to stop for a minute. I've been waiting all evening for that chance, and it took the wind out of me. I don't like having my word challenged either."

"I don't see why you were waiting for the chance to raise on a four-flush."

"That wasn't it." They were at the bar. Michael said, "I'll buy. It would be my pleasure." Westfield wanted a double whiskey, neat, over ice. Michael asked for a Grand Marnier. "Sitting like that doesn't do my stomach a bit of good," he said. "No, the chance I was waiting for had to do with the other fellow. He takes advantage of his position in relation to the dealer. Thinks it's clever. He gave himself away when he first looked at his cards. His finger moved. Some people have to count up their cards to convince themselves they have a straight. If you listen carefully, you can even hear them, down here." He touched his throat. "I raised on the opening because I wanted to test him. When he didn't raise again, I knew that he didn't have a straight flush or even as much as a flush. With that much in the pot, my raise seemed like a good bet."

"Still, you took a chance on the draw."

Michael grinned. "Yes, but if I drew the club, I could pick him clean. Arrogant bastard's been asking for it for hours."

"You're letting your emotions get the better of you. That's never a good idea for someone who spends his time as you do." The whiskey tasted very good; there had been a time years ago when he couldn't stand the taste of the stuff. Michael raised his tiny glass in brief salute.

"No, he *is* an arrogant bastard. You heard him question what I said. The others were putting up with it because they think that's the way he is, when actually all it is is his way of getting them to do what he wants, including giving him their money. It's a crude way of doing it, but it works for him."

"I take it that you've studied all this for your own reasons," Westfield said.

Michael smiled again. "You just saw me use it on him. I kept indicating that I was in a weak position, and he kept trying to take advantage of it, bully that he is. I did it to him twice and I don't think he realizes it yet." He took another sip. "Are you just having a night out?"

"I suppose so. I never think of it in any particular way. When it's time and I feel like it, I just get up and go. I don't really think much about where I'm going until I get there. I'm pretty much lost in my own thoughts, if you know what I mean."

"I suspected it was something like that," Michael said.

Westfield's collar felt a little tight. "That's a pretty nervy thing you do there, prying into people's minds like that, getting them to talk to you. You're pretty slick about it, too."

"I confess," he said pleasantly.

"All charm," Westfield muttered.

Michael saluted again. "That's part of it."

"I suspected as much. I've been watching you. You know, you can't criticize anybody else's morality."

"You never hear me do that," Michael said.

"You went after Thomas the other night."

"I lost my temper."

"What would you say to me if you lost it now? Have you studied yourself as well as others?"

Michael was silent.

"How *do* you feel about me? I have my feelings about you, you know."

Michael looked distressed. "I don't know how to answer. How I feel about you seems to be bound up in what I am. You asked if I studied myself—that's my answer. I wouldn't ever do anything to hurt you, but I can't help what I feel about the way you live. What were you like when you were my age? Can you remember yourself? You must have had hopes. You must have thought you were a decent man—"

Westfield smiled. "Never." The image of Michael in front of him was blurry. Perhaps it was merely the taste of the whiskey that got him drunk now or the tiny piece of business of holding a drink in his hand. "I never thought I was a decent man, Michael. It took me a long time to realize it, but it's the truth. I always thought of myself as somehow *below* other men. I was the youngest of three brothers; I always looked up to the older two. It's always been that way, even though the older brothers have been long gone from my life. I even left Hartford because of them."

Michael bowed his head. "I'm sorry."

"Don't be silly. We both know I'm drunk—let's have our conversation."

"I don't want to hurt you."

"You won't. It comes with age. You get used to things, like the idea of dying. I'll bet it still scares the piss out of you."

"Not since my parents died. I'll be thinking of them the day I die."

"I don't doubt it." Westfield raised his glass. The notion of one's thoughts at the time of one's death vaguely irritated him. Michael was studying him.

"Why do you go on living with your wife?"

Westfield smiled. "You do know how to get to people, don't you? Well, you don't abandon a woman. She has money, but she couldn't manage it. I'd be abandoning her to destitution, finally."

"You know you could still support her. It's a poor excuse."

Westfield looked at his glass. "The scandal, too. I couldn't live with it."

"You're a scandal already, if you look around you."

"No. By now this is what they expect of me. It's very comfortable for everybody. I'm not too bad most of the time, which is to say that I usually make it home before the last stages of an evening that has gotten out of hand. There's been more and more of them lately, and I've begun to think about that. You've seen enough. You've always been a gentleman; I want you to know that I've been aware of that." He waved his hand. "But all these people never see me at my worst, and I don't know yet if it has to do with my incredible stamina, my understanding of the functions of my body, or plain dumb luck. So the answer to that is no, I am not a scandal."

Michael gazed at him with an expression of the most profound wonder and disbelief. Westfield rapped his glass on the bar.

"You want to hear it?" His voice was raised; he wanted to see if he could frighten Michael. It was impossible to tell. "You're good for another," he said in a lower tone, and pushed his glass at the bartender. "You want to know if I love her," he whispered. "I'm not sure I know what love is. She loves me, I love her; we say it and believe it. Once, years ago, I had a very strong feeling for her. But I've had that for other women since. Kate Regan, your friend, was one of them. I couldn't help myself—ah, the truth is, I went looking for it. Then I'd lose my nerve. The girls expected nothing from me. They were all girls, very young either in years or in what they knew of life. We'd get to a crisis point together, and then I'd lose my nerve. One day we wouldn't be able to see enough of each other; the next, I was glad to be done with her. That's what happened with Kate, as far as that goes. Others didn't have her verve; they'd whine and complain and be frightened, or I would see little things they did that put me off. Not at the beginning, mind you. I would see them later, when we reached that crisis point. I was always looking for something. Half of them, the ones for whom I felt something for a day or a week, I wouldn't have tolerated for a moment if I had not been in the grip of this thing I've known all my life. This cowardliness. It's why I said I never thought of myself as a decent man. Yet I was always afraid of that next step. It was there for me to take with Louise, I'm sure, but I was very young at the time and probably wasn't able to recognize it when it came. One of the advantages of growing older is that you come to recognize things as they happen, even in yourself. You've seen them so many times before. I was always afraid of that step; I was always afraid to throw off that mantle of respectability and be whatever I wanted to be—"

"I don't think I understand what you mean by 'a step.' I'm sorry, but I really don't understand."

"You will. Michael, I know about you the same way I know about Thomas, because people talk, and I still have friends, yes I do, and right now you're too caught up in playing at love and romancing girls and making them fall in love with you to see that eventually you'll tire of it and want to get to more serious matters. You're leading a common, frivolous life right now, but you don't know it because it's so entertaining. Unless what you're doing is actually changing the direction of your life, it's all nothing but play. You can drop it any time and walk away and remain the same man. No one suspects that you're a fool, that you're really doing it for some gnawing reason inside yourself, that you're looking for some relief from yourself. You won't feel that until you tire of the entertainment of making nice girls submit to your will. People talk about you, Michael. So far I'd say that only a certain lack of imagination is keeping you from being bored with your life." He took a breath. "In any case, eventually you'll want to change your life, and if you put it off, or weaken, or let yourself be distracted, you'll see that you're a fool. Other men won't know, but you will."

"I'm sorry," Michael said. "I'm really sorry."

"The only reason none of these things have happened to you yet is that you're young. You'll make your mistakes and you'll wind up in the same pickle as the rest of us. I don't know a man who's not in it, who wouldn't rather be someplace else, be some*one* else. Most of them don't see it as clearly as I do, I admit, but that doesn't absolve them from being fools. There are two kinds of fools, Michael, those who don't know it and those who do."

"I can see plenty of the former," Michael said.

"And you're talking to one of the latter."

"Why don't you quit? Why don't you change?"

Westfield looked into his glass. "I enjoy things too much. I haven't really tested myself in more years than I can remember. I don't know if I ever did." He took a drink; suddenly he felt uncomfortable. "I think I told you all this because you've earned it. You've put me to bed so many times that you have a right to know that you're dealing with a sentient being."

"You don't have to say that. You've picked me up, too, I remember."

"Are you enjoying this?" Westfield asked. "I'd like to talk a little more."

"I would like that very much," Michael said, looking him straight in the eye.

For a moment Westfield stood there. Was Michael patronizing him? "All right," Westfield said abruptly, "we'll arrange to meet for lunch or something. But stay a few minutes longer."

"I meant to," Michael said.

There was something about him that rubbed Westfield the wrong way. "You said that I picked you up, too. More than once, in fact, but we needn't go into the details. I have to tell you that on the second occasion, I don't know why. Save avoiding the scandal. God knew what would come out if you had been caught."

"I knew that at the time."

"But you warmed to me. You treated me better."

"Regardless of what I thought of you as a man, or whatever your motives were on either occasion, you saved my life twice. I've learned that I owe you my loyalty. You've done many things that I despise, but I can't let them matter. I don't know if I could change my feelings, but I do know that I don't want to."

Westfield felt better. It could not be untrue; no man would say such a thing unless he meant it. "I want to clear the air. The first time was for Kate."

"I knew that when you said her name the first time you saw me."

Westfield's glass was empty again, but he knew that he had had enough. One or two more, if Michael could abandon the card game and help him home, but Westfield could not dare impose. He put the glass on the bar carefully, in the bar well, to indicate that he wanted nothing more. "The truth is, when I look back on things, you're the only good thing I've ever done. I wanted Kate, but I wound up with you. She and I were very caught up with each other, I'll tell you that much. I stuck with it because it's what's left of—just say, it's what's left. Time to say good-night. I'll see you at breakfast in the morning, if I make it downstairs in time, if I leave now without having another drink."

"You must have wanted her very much."

"Hell, I want her still. To one degree or another, I want them all."

III

When Michael saw Kate Regan the following week, he related the conversation to Westfield's next-to-last line, and Kate said she thought she understood. Michael had thought it would be better to keep the last line to himself, and now he was not sure he had done the right thing. She said that she did not think that Westfield was being overly sentimental because she felt it herself, a sort of fond remembrance of what they had been together and could not be again because so much had changed. There was a peculiar flatness in her tone that aroused Michael's curiosity, and he wondered if his deception had uncovered something she would have preferred to leave concealed.

They were in her new home in Flatbush, an elaborate, three-story affair that could have housed nine, instead of Kate, her maid, and her cook. The houses on every street in every direction were just as new, on the same order, gleaming white and twice as tall as the new trees that lined the curbs. It was her step toward respectability, she said, but the neighbors were suspicious of her and she had to keep to herself. She was thinking of moving back to the city and taking one of the new apartments.

"I would have thought you would be more upset than this," he said.

"You have to understand what I know about love." She stood up, her skirts rustling. "You want a drink?"

"A very light whiskey and soda, please."

"You should lay off the soda if your stomach bothers you," she said.

"I've found that it clears it right out."

"Suit yourself." She stopped at the entrance to the dining room and called into the kitchen, "Hay, Gert! Let's have some setups out here!"

"Say please!" came the voice from the kitchen.

"Ah, shit—*please!*" Kate turned to Michael. "That's an old whore for you. You know what she said to me once? 'You give me too much lip, I'm going to slap you right in the puss.' She knows who you are now, so she won't hold back in front of you. 'Oh, like us,' she said. 'No, *not* like us,' I said. So this is her way of saying she likes you."

Gert brought out the tray. Michael had not told Kate that he had had lunch with Westfield two days after their chance meeting at the poker table, and at this point he planned to stay quiet about it. The conversation had concerned her, or Westfield's relationship with her: on the pretext of assuming that Michael wanted to know, Westfield had told everything—everything, shamelessly. Michael *had* wanted to know, but there had been details that Westfield could have left out. Apparently he remembered exactly the sort of thing most people hoped were forgotten after moments of intimacy: one result was that Michael knew the location of Kate's birthmarks without having seen them. But what really struck him was the contrast between the Kate Westfield had described and the Kate Michael had known for the last three months, even to her physical appearance. Westfield had described a plump young girl with rosy cheeks and full breasts, and the Kate Regan now carefully preparing Michael's drink was slender and small-bosomed, almost tall, seemingly delicate, with thin wrists and fine fragile hands. There was a vein close to her skin at the temple, a darkish streak covered with soft blonde down, and her cheekbones were prominent. Her mouth had stayed as small as Westfield had described, and that was all of it because she was not the person Westfield remembered, not in any way Michael could recognize.

It had been easy enough to find her, once he had come of age. He had to be able to walk in and out of the casinos and brothels, to ask questions and chase down clues. It had taken only weeks, although nearly a decade had passed; nevertheless, she had seemed content, fulfilled: she said that she had known he would find her eventually.

She spoke several separate voices, he thought, not simply the expected variants of New York English, and he was sure he heard in each a separate and fully developed array of feelings. The first was a carefully elegant construction of arch phrases and slow enunciations that she used when she wanted to talk about ideas—and ladies and gentlemen, as if their lives and feelings floated in the same pure air, as free and seemingly benign. She was more comfortable with the second, the brassy hardness of the streets, her confession of her place in the social order—but at the same time a claim to the rights and privileges thereof: if she had to be a whore (more a courtesan, actually, one of the wealthiest in the city), then she could raise her voice, curse if she chose, and drink like a man without giving it a thought. Michael believed he could hear a third voice, too, the speech of their common childhood evolved and transformed into a complex, emotional assertion of some kind of kinship. Her voice went soft and seemed to reach him; it made her vulnerable to him. He could almost imagine he was listening to a shy little girl of ten or twelve rather than one of the most beautiful and celebrated young women in New York.

But now she wanted to talk ideas. "Michael, what I know about love has to do with what I've learned about what I've really been selling to men all these years. Oh, they get sex, so let's not have any jokes about it, and that's what they think they want, but it isn't at all. People can think they want one thing, buy and pay for it and even be satisfied, but not because it's what they want, but because it helps them realize what they really want, which is their dreams. Michael, I've gotten five thousand dollars for spending one night with a man. Think of it, five thousand dollars, when he could have gone out in the street and gotten a younger, prettier, plumper girl for fifty cents or a dollar. I've been thinking about this for years. For this particular man the dream happened to be the company of a proper young lady who could cry real tears at the right time. He wanted to feel that I was giving in to him against my better nature. I had to make him forget that he had bought and paid for it, but I know I succeeded, and not because I was able to cry when I was supposed to—it's easy, you know; all I had to do was think of things that make me unhappy, my sister being murdered, a man named O'Rourke I used to know—but because that man with his five thousand dollars was *in love* with me when it was over. I find that if you give a man his dream, whatever it is, he'll fall in love with you and give you anything you want."

"You can only hurt yourself, thinking that way."

"And it's only because I'm a whore, I know. But that's not all of it, because I've also found that when a man comes along and offers me *my* dream, even if he's a customer, I fall in love with him. As often as not I see it happening, possibly because the dream is small and only a passing fancy, and I just laugh; but sometimes it's something important to me, like respect, and then I really fall in love. I fall in love, Michael. I fall in love a lot, and I fall hard."

"If you want respect, why do you call yourself a whore?"

"Because that's what I am. I can entertain all sorts of foolish notions and get mad at the people who keep me down to earth, like Gert. I almost lost Gert because of it. I was acting up something awful, and she tried to get me to see the light. I wouldn't, and then she said, 'Would you kindly remember that you became a whore to keep yourself alive?' And finally I've begun to understand that. Does that answer your question?"

"Yes."

"Do you know how many men in this city have the dream of youth, Michael? Do you know how many men have wanted me to be young for them? Oh, it takes many forms, but it's always the same. One man wants to be told that I've never felt anything so intensely before, and another wants me to actually *be* a little girl, not only wearing the clothes, but playing the part. I'm thinking of one fellow who imagines that I'm being me when I was little. I wear a frilly dress and sit very properly while he convinces me to let him do things to me. If he knew what my life was really like when I was a child, he'd be crushed. You know that they could have girls almost as young as they want me to pretend to be. They come to me instead. A younger girl, a less skilled girl is too much a danger for them; they want no accidents or mistakes. I wish you could hear them, Michael."

She was sitting on the edge of the sofa, her hands in her lap. She had not touched her whiskey. He thought he was going mad, for she was saying that men wanted her to pretend to be innocent, and here she was the picture of innocence itself. If men wanted the representation of perfect youth, could it be because that was her own best aspect? Could it be that she really was offering her innocence, that it had never been lost, that she had the power to draw it back to herself once a love affair had failed? "So what does this have to do with Westfield?"

"In his own way he's another one like the rest, off in search of something that can never be recaptured. Their lives have gone wrong and more than anything they would like to start over, but they can't and they know it, so they come to me for their dreams. Westfield reached for it with me when I was actually young. He wanted to set me up in a place of my own, and I believe he eventually would have left his wife for me, but I was afraid and there were other things I wanted to do—I know now that if I had had faith in him, our lives would have been different, but he was not a brave man, as he said." She sat back. "With you we tried to do something together, he and I, you mustn't forget that."

He shook his head. "Oh, no, you and I deceived him. Let's not deceive ourselves now." He had never said a word to her about Moran and never would. "Westfield found out, but by that time it was too late."

"I was trying to do something decent, Michael. So was he."

Westfield had hinted at the reason for their breakup—those "other things" she had wanted to do. She had been a girl, and as he knew, her feelings could turn around. He got to his feet. "I'm sorry, Kate, I really am."

"Sit down, sit down, I'm not bothered. Tell me the latest about sister Julie. When I think of her, I almost feel like an honest woman."

"Westfield has to answer for some of that," he said.

She sat back and crossed her legs. "Someday you're going to get wise to her. Then maybe you'll think about coming around to see me."

"I know what a self-serving little bitch she is."

"You keep saying that—but while you wouldn't dream of being another Westfield for me, it's exactly what you're being to her? She comes to you only when she thinks she can use you."

"I'm not there at her beck and call. Besides, I don't want to fall in love. You keep talking about love."

"Oh, Michael, I only want to go to bed with you to see what it's like. You're someone I've known all my life."

"I don't believe it would be that simple."

She shrugged. "Don't delude yourself."

IV

Months later, in 1886, that September when Michael went down to see Westfield in the shop behind Park Row, he had been Kate's intimate, but not her lover, for some time.

Westfield wanted to stay in the sunshine as they crossed City Hall Park. He had to shout to be heard over the din of the wagons and carriages rolling on their steel-rimmed wheels all around them.

"Did you see those two brunettes across the street from the office when we came out? I saw them from the window when they were up on the corner. I wanted to have another look at them."

Michael nodded noncommittally. Once he had you in his confidence, Westfield would indulge himself in moments of the most base lechery. Michael suspected that if he were ever challenged on it, he would sink into the floor with embarrassment.

"You know who I met in the month of September?" he asked.

"Ah, you noticed the weather, too."

"September in New York is not to be missed, is it, boy? There's the energy and anticipation. All the seasons save summer are wonderful in New York. I suppose even the Indians went north. No, I met Kate in September."

"The Indians had crops to raise, in all probability."

"You didn't hear me. I said, 'I met Kate in September.' "

"Oh, I heard that," Michael said.

Westfield waited until they were on the other side of Broadway. Out of the crowd stepped a little girl selling large orange flowers. Westfield went into his pocket and brought out two pennies. "Don't tell anybody you have these," he told the little girl, whose hair was tangled in dirty knots around her head. "You don't want anybody taking them away from you. You buy yourself some candy."

She offered a flower.

"No, no. You keep the flower and spend the money on yourself."

She stepped back and turned away, but Michael saw no sign that she understood. He had an unpleasant thought about Westfield's motive. "Did you do that for my amusement?"

"Oh, no. She might have something to do with my conversation. Come inside."

As they passed through the lobby, Michael realized with a pang that they might not get to his business at all. In the dining room they were shown to a small table near a pillar.

"How about some oysters? They're back in season."

"I'd rather wait a while longer. You never know."

"We'll have caviar." The waiter came up with the menus. "Let us have some caviar right away," Westfield said. "Do you want some champagne?" he asked Michael. "We might as well do this properly." To the waiter, he said, "Bring my young friend a split of champagne." He turned to Michael. "Is there anything nonalcoholic that goes with caviar?"

Michael shrugged.

"All right," Westfield said to the waiter, "nothing at all for me to drink. Don't even bring a glass for me to taste his champagne. Is that clear to you?" The waiter indicated that it was and he backed away. Westfield leaned toward the table and lowered his voice. "You had something on your mind, something about your studies."

"That can wait. You're my guest."

Westfield eyed him with mock suspicion. "You're not going to spoil my lunch, are you?"

"I don't know. Are you going to spoil mine?"

Westfield threw up his hands. "There's never any dealing with you. I'll begin, if that's what you want. Until you walked into my office today, I thought that I was just about as happy as I have ever been in my life." He saw the waiter coming with the small bottle of champagne and a single glass. "I envy you," he said to Michael. "I'll be almost able to taste every drop. I say almost because I want you to know that I understand that if I get the real taste in my mouth, if that happens somehow, I'll want to drink my way to the bottom, then the bottom of every bottle I can get my hands on, until I'm as close to death as I dare get. That is the basic structure of my life, day-to-day, hour-to-hour, minute-to-minute, reminding myself that that first drink will propel me directly into the gutter. It's that first drink, Michael, not the last or everything after the first two or three, but the first itself. That's the way to think of it."

The waiter came with the serving cart, and the two men sat back to let him do his work. Michael intended to tell Westfield that he wanted to give up his studies and go to work; but now he did not know if he would have the chance to speak of anything that was on his mind. Westfield helped himself to a piece of bread and popped it into his mouth, dry. "Still, for all that, and some other things that I'd prefer not to go into right now, I'm as happy as I've ever been, as I say. Persaps part of it is September, which is always so beautiful, and being back in the city. The beautiful things of life enliven me, but I feel more, that splendid contentment that comes with understanding. And it's not so much that I understand as that I see. I don't know how to explain it to you."

Westfield motioned to Michael to start eating. Michael thought he would try some of the fish eggs with the chopped egg yolk first. Just thinking about the champagne made his tongue work in his mouth. Westfield was right; the thought of never having this experience again was a terrible thing to have to live with.

"Let me see if I can explain myself," Westfield said. "In a very little while the leaves are going to fall off the trees and in a very little while more we'll be in our heavy clothes again and fighting every minute we're out of doors to keep ourselves warm. It seems like a dementedly simple thing with which to take up your time, but there are secrets within secrets in this. Life will go on. I know all I need to know about it. I tested myself and found myself wanting. Life hammered me down to size, and what I feared most, that I would not be able to live with my weakness, isn't true at all. I've been more profoundly comfortable with each day's doings than I have been in my whole life. I don't mind a bit. Do you understand?"

"I'm not sure." To Michael it was the saddest thing he had ever heard Westfield say, but he didn't know why.

"Let me try something closer to your own interests. Do you know what will happen to Thomas?"

"I have a fair idea."

"Is there anything you can do about it?"

"I wish there were."

"Now comes the important part," Westfield said. "What you wish and what is there for every man to see are two separate things. Can you draw any comfort from that?"

"Comfort? No, I can't draw any comfort from another man's misery."

"There's nothing you can do about his misery; you just said that. His misery's going to be there no matter what you feel. First, I think you *can* draw comfort from your desire to help him, as frustrated as it is, because your heart is in the right place. That's no small thing, Michael. The older you get, the more you see how weak, selfish, and small the great mass of humanity actually is. Take comfort in not being one of the herd.

"As for the other element, I wonder if you can see that Thomas and people like him are part of the great, unchanging, mysterious formula that governs our lives on this planet. Don't ask me what it is because I couldn't hope to give it to you. All I know is that life has its limitations. The leaves will fall from the trees and in the spring new ones will grow. There is no more that can be done about Thomas than can be done about the changing of the seasons. I have to accept it. I have no choice but to accept it. I don't know why, but accepting things just as they are has given me the kind of peace that allows me to feel the joy in small things—so many small things, in fact, that more often than not I'm filled with wonder."

Michael thought he was not finished, and reached for his champagne. When he looked over his glass, Westfield was staring at him, waiting for a reply. Michael had nothing to say—there was nothing he *could* say, still struck as he was by the incredible sadness, and sad smallness, of what had made Westfield quicken with such urgency and pride.

"You *are* in a good mood," Michael said. "Take that into account."

"Oh, I do," said Westfield. "I've had moments of very deep unhappiness lately, yet I still seem to remember all this. I draw comfort from it even then."

Michael finished the last of his caviar, wondering for not the first time how much of the stuff a man could eat before he exploded. "Let me think about it," he said, and wiped his mouth.

Westfield smiled the kind of twisted mysterious smile Michael had not seen since Westfield had quit drinking. Drunk in a bar, after some long discourse or other on the nature of the soul and the failure of the organized religions to honestly deal with it, not immediately after but long enough for one's thoughts to have moved on to something else, Westfield would break out into one of these smiles, half dreamy, half sour, and gaze off across the room or, more unnerving, directly into his companion's eyes. On such nights his own eyes would be vacant, haunted little caves. This smile, though fleeting, recalled all of it for Michael, and then the busboy and the waiter were at the table again, and the moment was gone.

Suddenly Michael wasn't so hungry. There was roast chicken and lamb on the menu the waiter opened for him. He chose a trout.

"You might as well order more champagne," Westfield said.

Michael indicated to the waiter that that was what he wanted to do. Westfield ordered a large rare steak and a pot of coffee.

"Now what was it that you had on your mind?"

"I've come to the conclusion that I would be better off if I gave up my studies and went now into the work that I want to do. I know you want me to have my degree, but in spite of that I have to ask you to help me."

"What do you have, another year? You could count the number of months on your hands, I'll bet. Oh, stay with it, Michael, please."

"I'll be twenty-four on November fifth."

"You're not having a decent life? You don't have enough money in your pocket? You're not doing the things you like?

"All but one. I want to be a journalist. I want to write for the newspapers."

"A mug's game," Westfield said flatly.

"I want to do it. It's the only thing I care about."

"Why can't you wait until you're finished at the college?"

"I've waited long enough. Even now, if I started without some kind of help from you, I'd be running errands for a year while they made sure I had the hang of things. I'm very impatient. I have to get my life under way."

"And you want me to use my influence, such as it is now, to short-cut some of the normal procedures?"

"If that's possible, yes, sir."

"You're adamant, aren't you? You won't change you mind?"

"I'm determined. I had a very bad time at Saratoga this year watching men my age do work that I do better without training."

"You want to be a *sports* correspondent?" Westfield laughed. "You're really determined to get into a mug's game."

"I think I have to look at my life as a whole. I'm a gambler. I have a certain view of people. Suppose I went on to become, oh, a lawyer? Can you imagine me getting any satisfaction helping one commercial thief sue another? You know how much happier I'd be cleaning them both out over a card table."

"Your luck could change. A dozen things could happen."

"I want to do the thing that suits me. I want to be near a certain kind of man."

"You're determined to be that kind of man yourself, everything my own father feared and despised, and you want my help." Westfield sighed. "Now I think we had better have the conversation that I would have preferred to put off forever. I only want to speak of these things one time, do you understand?"

"Yes, sir."

"You *are* determined, so that settles that. I'll see what I can do. I know some people at the *World.* If that fails, I'll go on to some others I know. When I was your age I was married, a father once and about to become a father again. But when I was younger than you are now, I was very eager to leave Hartford, so I do understand your impulse."

"Thank you."

"I'm afraid this conversation is going to be more than you bargained for. Don't be alarmed. Have you thought of what will happen to you when I die?"

Michael was silent. He had not thought about Westfield's death at all, and now he felt himself cringing from the idea of it. His uneasiness must have showed in his expression.

"Thank you," Westfield said. "It's good to know that someone cares whether you live or die." He waved to keep Michael quiet. "You know who will be head of the family," he said. "How do you think you'll make out under those conditions?"

"Thomas will be fair."

"You're deluding yourself—or lying to me. Either way, you're asking for trouble. The pie isn't that big, Michael. With half for Mrs. Westfield, what do you think your chances are of sharing in the remaining half?"

"I have no right to any of it," Michael said.

"*I* decide that, and if I decide that you do, then you have a right. No, I'm afraid that if I put you down in my will, even for as little as five thousand, you'd have no end of trouble trying to collect it. I've really gone over this. Given what will be left, there's no amount too small for him to overlook. You'd have to retain lawyers. And I wouldn't want to bet on your chances in a judicial procedure. Thomas is no fool. He knows my habits. I can see him putting two and two together over my open coffin. He'd laugh out loud."

"I think you're being very severe," Michael said. The waiter was coming with the serving cart again, crowded with covered silver serving dishes. The men sat back and stayed silent until he was gone.

"Michael, think on it: nobody in the world hates anybody else the way Thomas hates you."

"I would have guessed that he hated you more."

Westfield stopped eating and stared, honestly surprised. Michael drew his breath. "I'm sorry. I see it that way."

A shadow of misery crossed Westfield's face. Michael knew he had said too much, but he had thought that Westfield understood what was at the bottom of the bickering and arguments between Thomas and him the past several years; that his understanding was the source of Westfield's patience with his son. Somehow all the Westfields still harbored expectations of one another, as if they were still a family, when Michael could remember thinking that first winter he lived with them that they were a poor substitute for a family.

"I'll get to the heart of it," Westfield said, as if he had lost interest in the subject. "I've provided for you. It's outside the will, which means that the transfer would have to be effected before I die—"

"I don't need anything! You know how much I have put away. I could live on it for years!"

Westfield waved him silent again. "And your luck could change, too. I've never been a bold man with money—and do you know something? I've never wanted for anything either. Perhaps there's a lesson there." He leaned forward. "Let me tell you something. I'm not going to say this too loudly, so if you can't hear me, get a bit closer. Not all my money is accounted for. In various banks around town I have another forty-six thousand dollars. I've never needed it. It's yours. Free and clear. Outright. I suppose you can have it any time, now that you know about it."

Michael was flabbergasted. "I can't take it. Where did it come from?" He shook his head; it was like that day in the shelter in Cherry Street.

"You *have* to take it!" Westfield snarled. "No one knows I have it. I have the passbooks hidden where no one will find them. The banks will know I've died. When no one comes around to claim the money for the estate, they'll steal it. You know they will."

"Where did the money come from?"

"Politics. I never had a hand in anything. It was always just my share."

Michael nodded. It was like Westfield; he had enjoyed being an alderman too much to have wanted to give it up over a matter of conscience. Michael said, "I don't want the money now. There's more that I haven't told you. It's time I was out on my own completely. I want to take an apartment."

"You want—or you *plan?*"

Michael smiled sheepishly. "Plan."

"All right. I didn't think of that, but of course. The sooner you pick up the money, I suppose, the better."

"Why?"

"You'll be out of touch, for one thing. What if I died in an accident?"

"You've been speaking of your death since the beginning of the meal."

"No, I haven't."

"You have. You've brought it up in several contexts."

Westfield put down his knife and fork. "This is the second of the things I didn't want to bring up. I mean to tell you, but I want to be assured that you believe what I've already said about myself, the way I've been feeling these days."

"I believe you."

"I'm not right, Michael. I drank too much. I don't spring back the way I used to."

"Come on now. You're not a young man anymore. You could hardly expect to spring back under any circumstances. You've never been healthier. Look around the room at other men in their forties. You weigh just what you did ten years ago, maybe even less."

"That was the drinking, Michael. It emaciated me. I know what I'm talking about. I don't feel right. I don't feel the same. There's nothing wrong with me, as near as I can tell, but I wouldn't give a plugged nickel for my chances."

"I think you're wrong, and I wish you wouldn't talk like that."

"I can see that you don't understand," said Westfield. He had his knife and fork in his hands again. "I will add this: I'm more afraid of being sick and an invalid than I am of dying. Well, we'll see. Let's finish what we have here; I thought I saw strawberries listed among the desserts. Tell me what you really think of Julie's fiancé. Your opinion, your *true* opinion of Roger Fleming, should be very interesting."

V

It took Michael only a month to change his life completely. He was out of school for the first time since the weeks on Cherry Street, out of the house on Thirty-eighth Street, only the second home he could remember. He had an apartment on Fifteenth Street near Irving Place in a new building with central heat, two rooms, a small kitchen, and a bath. A woman came in twice a week to clean up, but mostly he chased after the place himself. He had Westfield's forty-six thousand banked and was resolved not to touch it, but its presence had helped him to see that it would be a mistake if he did not spend his own money to furnish the apartment nicely. He gave the appearance of a wealthy-young-man-about-town. He was concerned with Westfield, he wanted to keep an eye on him, but he was caught up in his own business, indulging himself, installing a telephone, walking one evening down Third Avenue and the Bowery to the old neighborhood and Lombard Street, and finally going out to Flatbush to call again on Kate. He did not tell her about the forty-six thousand, but as he was leaving he yielded to an impulse and kissed her on the lips. It caught her by surprise, made her blush, and that gave him moments of delight all the way home.

Westfield had got him the job at the *World*. Michael was enchanted with it, and so busy the first week shuttling between the office on Park Row and the church uptown where Julie's wedding was to take place that he was exhausted. He was an usher, along with Thomas and the Flemings' two brothers—the usual dubious honor; and the afternoon before the wedding when she called, his first reaction was to sigh, for he was sure she wanted still another "small" favor. He was to see her fiancé at a bachelor dinner that evening, and when she said that she wanted to stop at Michael's apartment, Michael actually felt relieved, guessing that she wanted him to be the bearer of a gift from her or a note. Before an hour had passed, however, his suspicions had stirred; and by the time she was due, his defenses were as ready as they would have been for a fight.

It had turned out that Westfield, too, had serious reservations about Roger Fleming. Michael did not want to be around him, and of course Westfield had seen that. Fleming was a bore, a prig, a stick—Westfield's words. He had taken Michael's sudden frozen silence for good manners or a desire not to cause trouble.

For himself, really. He had to remember that Westfield, like so many fathers, did not know his daughter and probably did not want to—a daughter was a woman, after all. If Westfield perceived that Michael's reservations were based on what Fleming's alleged surface vices might mean, then eventually Westfield would come around to ask himself how Michael could have such a specific understanding of Julie in the matter.

Nothing else would be clear, either, because Michael did not know how to explain what was bothering him about Fleming. Westfield had not gotten it right. Michael supposed that Fleming was as stuffy and self-righteous as Westfield had implied, to someone as indifferent to him as Westfield happened to be; but exactly because Michael has such a specific understanding of Julie, he felt he would have reached for language that more clearly expressed the absence of qualities in Fleming—he was colorless, humorless, lifeless.

Fleming was twenty-five, prematurely gray, with a smooth pale complexion. He had regular even features and hazel eyes, and there were always girls who thought such men were handsome—eyes turned when Fleming entered a room, there was no question of it. He had a wonderful situation in his father's brokerage. He dressed well, conservatively, in well-cut clothes, perhaps a little too old for his age. He was too correct in the Westfield household, too polite, too thoughtful, speaking when spoken to, and then only quietly. He had a *soft* smile, but his eyes worked behind it and it did not seem shy. He rarely attempted a joke, and when he laughed, he blushed as if he were afraid he was giving away a secret about himself. Sometimes he was, for often the occasions for laughter when he was present came out of stories Julie told or situations in which she had become involved. She dominated their relationship. She teased him and was not afraid to criticize him—gently, to be sure, chidingly—in front of her family. Michael watched Fleming's eyes working, studying his chances. He wanted Julie, there was no question of that either. At times Michael thought that Fleming was trying to see how much of her domination he could take before he disqualified himself with the rest of the family. It was like that in other areas, too, this attempt to figure out in the reactions of others how he was to behave. It seemed to be all there was to him, as far as Michael was concerned. Fleming wanted Julie very much, and because he was willing to let others think there was nothing else inside him when it was there to be seen in those moving, working eyes, Michael was concerned for Julie's sake.

So why did she want to marry the man? She had told Michael once that she was beginning to frighten herself, and Michael had understood what she meant because three or four other girls had told him the same thing, one way or another—an artful arrangement of bitter truth and feminine wiles: sex interested them and they were afraid for their own reputations (but most certainly sex interested them). Michael could handle the wiliness of it easily enough, but the bitterness had made him feel sorry for one or two of them in the past, too much for his own good. He found himself wondering if he could live with the girl—and then it would be time to write that letter: *In the light of our recent conversations I have come to believe that as a gentleman I would be serving your interests best if I suggested that you terminate our friendship as it is presently constituted. I would like to remain your friend; however . . .* and so on. It was the sort of letter that hardened as time passed. Michael knew that young women had a language that described young men every bit as vividly as the language young men had for them, but he doubted that his letters would ever get around. When a girl got past her confusion and managed to see that her gambit had failed and that he had gently but effectively booted her out of his life, his letter would probably be torn into a thousand tiny pieces.

Julie was not different from girls like these, but what astonished Michael was that she saw herself as capable of no better than a Roger Fleming. It was as· if she had stopped thinking or forgotten everything she knew about herself—or, worst of all, she had discovered a wound inside her and now the pain of it dominated her completely.

Westfield's attitude was interesting. Michael indicated that he thought that Fleming was a terrible bore, but there was nothing to be done, since Julie knew what she wanted. Westfield laughed out loud. She didn't know what she wanted, he said. She was as silly as any girl her age he had ever known. Fleming was a prize in her set, and she had made up her mind to have him.

As a father, Westfield thought that it was an awful match that would evolve into an awful marriage, but Michael was right, even if he had the reason wrong: there was nothing that could be done. Westfield put his hands flat on the table. "Even if our situation, hers and mine, were better, I'd have to stay out of it. I'd only create more unhappiness. She has the bit in her teeth—she wants to be married, she wants to have a wedding. We have to accommodate ourselves to it." Now Westfield laughed. "I'm waiting to see the girl you bring around, you know."

"Why does that amuse you?"

"You so obviously want perfection." Westfield pointed a finger at him, his face red with merriment. "Confess! The student of human nature has the effrontery to want perfection in his own life."

Michael blushed. For the past hour he had been thinking of Westfield and Julie. Westfield had caught him by surprise. Of course it was true; he did want perfection. But the idea stood out boldly against the background of the rest of the conversation, and he could see how carefully he had separated that part of his life from that of the Westfields.

Westfield waved for the check. The meal was over.

VI

In the autumn, and in October especially, twilight falls on the city with a crystalline clarity. The temperature drops rapidly, the wind comes up, and the clouds darkening overhead blow across the sky quickly. People huddle into their coats, but they breathe deeply because the air is invigorating. Lights are on everywhere and people looking down into the street from warm rooms above feel the cold on the windowpanes, see the darkness and ominous clouds in the yellow sky over the rooftops, and feel a presentiment of winter. The months of ice and cold stretch out bleakly; the euphoria of September vanishes for good in the first anxious longing for spring. Michael was standing at the window when he saw Julie coming along—with his suspicions aroused as they were, he nearly jumped in the air.

It took her a moment to get up the stairs. He left the door ajar and went to the kitchen to put on some water for tea. He heard her come inside. "Michael?"

"In here."

"Where? This is my first time here, you know."

He stepped out of the kitchen. "Your last, too. This was a mistake. Suppose someone saw you? It could cause you terrible trouble."

"I don't think the word will get around fast enough to ruin my wedding, do you?" She was unpinning her hat. She looked tired and her hair was beginning to come undone. There were faint circles under her eyes.

"A month from now," he said. "A year. Would you like some tea? You don't want to catch cold the night before your big day."

Perhaps he was not supposed to be as flippant about it as she was, for she waited a moment before answering. "All right, but I can't stay long. I have a lot to do this evening."

"You'll have time. I have to be at dinner at eight o'clock. Give me your coat."

She did, then moved tonight's newspaper off the sofa so she could sit down. "The bachelor dinner—isn't that your last chance to talk the groom out of it?"

"Traditionally."

"What are you going to do?"

"Enjoy my meal as well as I can. Take my leave at a reasonable hour. Sit down to a couple of hours of cards before I come back here."

"Will you be thinking about me?"

"Only if I learn something new right now."

"Do you want to know why I came down here this evening? You don't sound as if you do."

The teakettle started. "Excuse me." He had to get his wits about him. He had expected something, after the wedding, probably, an ugly word or look, presumably the real finish, but nothing like this. He could see that he did not have to hear her out if he did not want to—hat, coat, and to the door, good night, Julie, I'll see you at the church—so why permit her to stay? He drew a deep breath, and then picked up the tray bearing the brewing tea.

"Your gambler friends should see you. All you need is an apron."

"I have it. Your mother gave me one. Now what is it, Julie? What do you want?"

"Do you know why I'm getting married tomorrow?"

"You told me."

"Oh, I remember," she said. "That was true enough, as far as it went. It made no mention of us. You've made no mention of us. I thought you would want to see me."

"What was there to see you about?"

She brushed at her purse with the palm of her hand. "I thought you would want to have a little talk." She looked up again. "I'm sorry, I thought you'd like to have a talk, that's all. I wanted to know that we were friends."

"I thought we were." He had to take a small padded chair opposite the sofa.

"You don't approve of this marriage, do you?"

"I think you're making a mistake."

"Why?"

"I know you better than your parents do. I can't phrase it any more delicately than that. And I don't think you're going to be happy with that man."

"That's so self-centered it's loathsome."

"My opinion of myself has nothing to do with it. I know what I know."

"Have you ever wondered what it would have been like if you had grown up in a different household?"

"If my parents had lived, Julie, I would have left New York eventually. You would have never known me."

"You know what I mean," she said.

"I know what you mean."

"I love you, Michael," she said softly. "Ive always loved you. I always will."

"You don't know what love is."

She clenched her fists. "I know that you don't love me."

"I loved you and you know it."

"That's what I mean! If we had grown up in different households, all those things would never have happened!"

"You mean, I wouldn't have seen you as you really were."

"Those things wouldn't have happened if you hadn't been there to smother me. I fell in love with you first, you were the first one—was that supposed to be all there was for me? Was I supposed to wait for you? You wouldn't ever tell me the truth."

"I never trusted you, Julie. You never had any patience. What you're doing tomorrow proves that you haven't changed."

"I wouldn't be doing any of it if it weren't for you."

He got out of the chair. "You're a liar."

"I'm not! Try me—test me. All those things you never liked? You'll never see them. I'll change."

"You tell me what you want me to do, Julie."

"Tell me," she whispered.

"You're still a liar," he said.

"Test me, Michael. I'm begging you—aren't I begging you?"

He looked out the window. Across the street on an upper floor a stout grim-faced woman was putting dishes on a table. If he stared long enough, he would see what she and her husband would be eating for dinner. Michael took out one of his cigars. "You'd throw it all over for me? The wedding, the honeymoon on Lake George?"

"Yes."

"Why?"

"I don't want to lose you, Michael. I don't want to lose you."

"And you'd be faithful to me," he said. "You'd be faithful to me for the first time in your life?"

"Yes."

He peered at her. "You'd make love to me now? You'd make love to me even if I promise you nothing—if I send you down the stairs afterward?"

"I couldn't do anything about that." She tried a small smile. "You could deceive me, if you want."

The smile enraged him; he hardly heard the last thing she said. Something about deception: she had the gall to speak to him about deception. "I want you to leave, Julie," he whispered. "I want to forget that I saw you this evening."

She nearly screamed it. *"Why?"*

"I don't believe you." He thought he was going to be sick. "I don't believe you'd stop the wedding. I don't believe that you'd do anything but try to convince me that you were going to do it. I'd be at the church, staring at you, and you might go so far as to wink at me to make me think that you intended to do it at any second. At the altar, if necessary—" She glared and moved to get up; he reached across the table, took her wrist, and held her still. He leaned over close to her face and blinked to clear his eyes. "I'd stand there and watch you get married no matter what happened here tonight because that's really what you intend to do. You might even wink at me coming down from the altar. Everybody would see, but that wouldn't matter. I'm almost your brother, aren't I? Do you tell people that? And when you came back from Lake George, after a month, maybe two, after we saw each other at a party or at dinner, you'd send around a little note. *When can I see you?* It was all a mistake, you'd say—when you woke up in the morning, all the confusion and people made you afraid, and then finally you saw that you couldn't hurt Roger, not Roger, everybody can see how weak he is—but couldn't we go on as before, couldn't we be special to each other again?"

"I hate you now, Michael," she cried. "I'll see you dead before I let you touch me again." She tried to wrench her wrist away, but he held it fast.

"I'm not finished. You came down here for adventure, and now you're having it. All that I just said would be just what you had in mind right along."

There were tears in her eyes and he could feel himself yield a little. She saw it and pulled herself free. "Get out of my way. Let me up. I told you the truth." She got out her handkerchief, a tiny thing fringed with an inch of lace. "I've always loved you. Maybe this explains why we were never happy together. You were full of hate for me."

"You only *believe* you'll do the things you say, Julie. All the time I've known you, you've never done anything that wasn't expected of you. You like to have people look at you but only to admire you. You'll do anything to keep them from *inspecting* you."

"Are you finished? There's no reason why I shouldn't tell you this now. Maybe you'll think about it tomorrow. I always had a dream about us. I did wait for you. I'm not marrying young and you know it. They were even starting to talk about me. 'Look at Julie Westfield, already twenty-three and not married yet. I wonder what's wrong with her.' They did wonder, too, Michael. I never told you this. I was afraid to come near you because I could always see how you were suffering. Do I have to tell you what they were thinking about me, Michael? Are you going to make me have to say it?"

"What do you mean, 'suffering'?"

"There was always something on your face. I used to think it was because you were thinking about your parents. It's on your face right now. You don't even know it. Now do you understand? This wouldn't be happening if it weren't for you."

"So you do intend to go through with it," he said.

"I do now. I've made my peace with myself. I never knew you had so much hate for me. Let me have my coat and hat."

"Gladly."

"Don't get married, Michael," she said as she dressed. "You're not mature enough. You do say you're twenty-one, don't you?"

"Hurry up. Just get out of here."

She had her gloves in her left hand. "I told you the truth before. You had your chance. You'll have to get used to me the way I am now."

"Julie, I've always been used to you the way you are now. No matter what you think, you've never treated me any differently."

He saw it coming and did not recognize it for what it was. He had never been slapped by a woman before and he seemed to understand almost at once that she was hitting him as hard as she could, with all her force, and she was not a little girl; that she knew, in fact, how big she was. She could not hurt him enough with words, or he had hurt her back once too often and too well; in any case, he understood almost at once that she was trying to do him physical injury.

And she did. It was like an explosion. He was actually blinded for a moment. He pushed at her, his ear ringing. "Get out of here!" He had her by the sleeve, and he was pushing her so fast that she could not get her footing, and then she was out in the hall.

"You planned it!" he gasped. "You had your gloves in your other hand!"

"Because I told you the truth!"

"*You* think so. I could love you, but God in heaven, you don't know how to love at all!" He shut the door and locked it. She pounded on it once, perhaps not so much an attempt to gain admittance as a last act of rage, but then almost immediately he heard her footsteps on the stairs. Touching his cheek gingerly, he went to the window. Out on the sidewalk, she made no secret of looking back up. She could see him clearly. They stared at each other. Just before he was about to move, she turned and walked away, moving fast. The sky was almost black, and in a moment she had disappeared in the darkness.

The side of his head ached as if he had been struck by a fence post. He did not have to look in the mirror to know that his skin was imprinted with the outline of her hand. He would go late to the dinner, if necessary.

He could even have the welt tomorrow—he was tempted to let everyone see it. Let them be curious.

Petty, ludicrous . . . he belonged to the Westfields as much as she did; at least, he seemed determined to prove it.

Talc covered the marks on his face that evening; in any event, no one asked about them; and the next day there were no marks at all. She did not look at him at the church or later at the reception, and when the men lined up to kiss the bride, he found something else to do, someplace else to be. He was thinking about cards, in fact; he had not played the night before after the bachelor party because their scene had upset him so much, and he had to wonder how soon he might make his escape from what was developing into a fairly commonplace afternoon.

The reception was over by seven o'clock, but by then Louise had gotten the word around that she wanted to entertain the immediate families with a small dinner on Thirty-eighth Street. Thomas was in a sour mood; not even the prospect of more food could stir his interest. No wonder. All the Flemings were there—the palsied senior Mr. Fleming; his wife, a large-breasted woman of fifty who could have passed for Louise's mother, she was so jowly; Grandmother Johnson, Mrs. Fleming's mother; the groom's married older sister Polly, who with three children was rapidly losing the bloom of her youth; his unmarried older sister Leah, who looked like the other but was thin and a foot too tall; a cousin; Polly's husband and children; the cousin's husband and children. Representing the Westfield side was Louise's mother, still sturdy at sixty-eight; her mother's sister, sturdier still; her mother's sister's husband, who was another man who wished he were elsewhere; Westfield's two brothers from Hartford and their families, down to the grandchildren, who were as wild as their parents were sullen. Downstairs was Louise's mother's dog, a fat, yapping male spaniel that could not be left alone. The house was filled. The adults were tired and the children ran loose up and down the stairs. Thomas was the first to give up, climbing to his room; later Michael heard the children at his door, giggling at his snoring.

The groom's parents left soon after, and the party ended. Most of the food remained uneaten; the children had only mauled their cake. Louise had put too much into it, perhaps because the wedding had not been that popular, sparking no one's imagination. After Westfield's brothers had left for their hotel, and after Louise's mother had gone upstairs to Julie's room, with the table cleared away and set again for breakfast, and Hannah still rattling distantly in the kitchen below, Michael and the Westfields settled for a moment in the parlor.

"If I were still drinking," said Westfield, "I'd want a brandy about now. Do you want a brandy, Michael?"

"No, thank you."

"Louise?"

"No, Thomas."

"It was a good wedding, though, wasn't it? Nothing to be ashamed of. People had a good time."

"I think so," Michael said. "I think it was an excellent wedding."

"You were bored all day," Westfield said.

"That doesn't mean it wasn't an excellent wedding."

"Smoke a cigar, Michael. Feel at home." Westfield stood up and raised his arms. "Excuse me, if you don't mind. I want to go to bed. If I stay up any later, I'll start to get nervous. Now I go to bed when it's good for me. It only took me fifty years to learn that lesson."

"You're not fifty yet," Louise said. "You've got most of three years." She offered her cheek to be kissed. "He does this, Michael. He's decided to act his age, but his trouble is that he doesn't know what his age is. He doesn't know how a forty-seven-year-old behaves, so every once in a while he'll try something to see if it suits him."

Perhaps Westfield was too tired to feel any indignation. "I'm going to bed," he said to her.

She sat still until they heard the door close above.

"Well?" she asked. "What did you think of that?"

"I suppose he's feeling his age because his daugher was married today."

"I don't feel that," she said.

"He's a different kind of person."

"He's so sad all the time now," she said. "Will you listen to me? May I speak to you?"

"You don't have to ask. Do me the honor of never asking again, please."

"I'll remember. He was very unhappy when you left. He didn't expect it. He had hoped you would finish your studies. It would have made him very proud."

"I know, but I couldn't do it. I wasn't cut out for it."

"You're not like him, are you?"

Her fear was charming. "No, I don't believe I am."

"There's something I'd like you to think about very carefully, Michael. It's something that we should have done a long time ago. We should have discussed it." She leaned forward, her hands on her knees. "For his sake, because I think it will do him good, I want you to think about taking his name."

He stared at her. Later that night he dreamed he was an infant again, or something like it, something helpless, on its back. His eyes were open, but he couldn't see, and when he tried to scream, no sound would come. The effort awakened him, and staring at Louise after she had asked him to change his name was the first thing he thought of. Without a hesitation he got out of bed because he knew he would be awake for hours. "I'll think about it," he said softly.

"I can ask for no more than that."

She had more to say, about not being completely sure that Westfield had won his battle with himself, but Michael wasn't paying attention, not really. He had never thought she would ask him. She loved him; she would not have asked it if she had not thought she had a good reason. He had to think about it too; he had no choice. Perhaps she was feeling her age as much as her husband did: in less than a month two of the children had moved away. It was as if she were asking him flat out: *How much do you love me?*

It stayed with him in the days that followed, but then he saw that he was making sure that he did not see her, and in that way he recognized what he wanted to do. Michael dropped in on Westfield, who seemed fair enough, a little quiet and not as good-humored as he could be, but Michael was satisfied, all things considered. Michael could not help being distracted by what Westfield might know about her request, but after a while, possibly because he had stopped thinking about it for other reasons, Michael concluded that Westfield didn't have a clue, and that it was all her idea.

He saw her at Thanksgiving and Christmas and a couple of weekday dinners, too, and for all he knew, she thought he still had it under consideration. It made him feel terrible, but he never got around to telling her that he had already decided. It was a bad, unhappy winter anyway; it went on too long. For him, some of the unhappiness had to do with the fact that Julie was married. He missed her. He couldn't deny it: he felt a sense of loss.

VII

After the first of the year Louise telephoned him to announce that Westfield had started drinking again. Michael heard the misery in her voice in the way she said his name, asking if it was truly he—"Michael?" so dead and flat and small; the tone came through the distant, tinny sound of the telephone. Westfield had been gone for two days already. There was nothing to be done. He could be anywhere, in this weather, even dead. She knew it. She broke down and cried. Michael asked where Thomas was, but she didn't seem to hear him. She really had had her hopes up, Michael thought. He asked again for Thomas. She had heard him the first time, she said. Thomas was out for the evening. He had seen no reason to change his plans.

Michael telephoned her the next day and again that evening, as he worked his way from one brother to another in search of the great man himself. The great man turned up the next day voluntarily, a little disheveled but not bad. The only problem that remained, as Michael saw it that night, was that Westfield had not drunk his way down to the bottom: he was at a delicate stage, coy and belligerent by turns. Michael stayed with him as late as he could, and then he went downtown again. Thomas was home and Hannah was in the house. It would be all right.

Westfield tapered off the next day and the next, spacing his drinks ever further apart; the process seemed to ravage him, his face twisted continuously in a mask of self-hatred and pain. He wanted to sober up as fast as possible and forget that this had happened. His profound unhappiness was obvious, and in his own guilt Michael didn't dare look at Louise.

The next month Michael instructed a lawyer to proceed with the steps necessary for a change of name. He wanted Monk to remain in his signature, no matter how few would recognize it. "I want to sign my name Michael M. Westfield," he told the lawyer. "I'm sure you understand." The lawyer said he was sure he did, and Michael never had to see him again. All their business thereafter was done through the mails. That same night Michael took the Westfields to Delmonico's and told them what he had instructed the lawyer to do. It could be stopped if they thought it was wrong, he assured them; it was just that he wanted them to know how he felt. "I don't want to be adopted," he said. "I've been given to understand that that can be done at any age. No, I want this to be from me to you."

Westfield sat staring at Michael for a long time, his eyelids blinking. "Thank you, Michael," he said quietly.

And that was all. Westfield had thought about it, that was clear, but if there was any visible change in any of them, it was in Louise, who seemed to relax. Westfield saw it. Six weeks later, on a mild night in early spring, he leaned over to Michael and whispered as she left the room, "You made her happy, boy. Thank you."

In that way the Westfields continued to pass the year. By the fall of 1887, then, by September, something had settled upon them, some permanent gloom—not dread, for there was no rebellion; it had settled down upon them all so gently that none of them really felt it. Michael had begun to write for the paper, mostly revising the sports dispatches that came in on the telegraph. Little of it was printed. During the summer he had covered some baseball, traveling up to Yonkers or down to St. George or over to Long Island City. Those were long, long days. The life was interesting, but his reputation as a gambler had preceded him, and although the men wanted to know him, they held something back. They had never had any money, and they could not believe his seriousness. So he kept to himself—it did not make him unhappy.

He had been able to get up to Saratoga for only a week. No cards: the mood of the family had him too tense to be willing to bet on himself. Fleming was there with Julie, at Westfield's invitation; they had a separate room, but in private Westfield grumbled about the expense. He didn't say it, but Michael was sure that he didn't think he was getting value for his money. Perhaps he had looked for a kind of reunion, because the year before they had all been living on Thirty-eighth Street and Saratoga had been a normal extension of their lives together. If anyone knew that something special was expected of him, he gave no sign. While Michael was there, they took breakfasts and dinners as a family, but then they went their separate ways. Michael stayed with the Westfields; he was their guest and felt like one. In the beginning of the week, after Louise retired, Westfield suggested that they tour the casinos, but it was clear that he was patronizing Michael. His own plans had not worked out and he was trying to be amiable. But he was too docile, quiet, and turned in on himself. It was not so much an unhappiness as a lack of emotion. Michael could see it, a stolidity, an internal distance. Whether they sensed it or not, the others expected something to happen and they were resigned to it: they sat down to the meals as if assembling for a last portrait together.

Westfield was in his death throes, although he did not know it. In other cultures individuals are prepared by the examples of their elders at least to recognize the coming of death and to resign themselves to it. In our time we say that a man has lost the will to live and let it go at that, but there is more to it because there are unconscious forces at work that we do not understand and cannot control. In Westfield's case he had been so unhappy with life for so long that his hopelessness had grown into him more deeply than he knew. Its roots had entwined themselves around the organs he had abused with his drinking. He was not right, he understood that correctly; he had lived with a physical tenderness for so long that he was terrified of himself. He thought he was afraid of life. Each day took too much out of him. Since his last fall from grace, he had come to realize again that he would never be rid of his drinking problem, not ever in his life. There were things to smile about all through that year 1887, but Westfield could not smile without still feeling the full burden of all the wrong turns and small mistakes, the things unsaid and undone, lapses of intelligence and nerve clear back to his childhood, more than he could hope to remember, that added up to the failure of his life.

When he returned to the city in September, he slipped easily into his routine again. He could buy the *World* from the boy on the corner to find anything Michael had written. He could recognize the style now, spare, flat sentences, as if the job were already too easy for him. Westfield knew that Michael was not perfectly happy, as quickly as he was advancing. When Sheepshead Bay opened for the fall, Michael was forty miles away, covering a baseball game between Yonkers and Nyack. His story ran seventy-five words under accounts of the Giants and Metropolitans. Westfield didn't follow baseball, but he was coming to know why the Mets were hitting and the Giants weren't. He wouldn't read the Sheepshead Bay story, which ran two full wide columns.

He had stopped going out. In the evenings he would retire to the library and read the papers, first the *World,* all of it, and then the morning's *Times.* When Louise came in to say she was going to bed, often she would find him standing by the window, looking down into the street. She knew he was struggling with something, the expression in his eyes was so unhappy; but she didn't know how to ask him what he was thinking. For his part, he could not look at her without thinking that he had ruined her life as well as his own.

As much as he stayed home, he itched to get out—outside, anywhere. He was afraid of himself. It was not just the drinking. The city was opening up wider than ever, there were many new places he had heard about, but he simply could not see that for himself anymore. He was afraid of even seeing another Kate. Whenever he felt tempted now, he reminded himself of her. He had lost track of her completely, but only because he did not have the energy to search for her. He knew that, too.

When the nights began to cool, he took to walking himself tired, pushing himself until he was exhausted. He saw it as pleasant exercise. He wanted to keep his spirits up. He knew he was lonely, but he saw no honorable solution to that either. Louise was too wary, too deeply frightened, to be able to resume any kind of marriage. If he had taken better care of her, he could look forward to a happier old age.

When streetwalkers passed him, he so scarcely noticed them that they ignored him completely. He thought about it and remembered his youth when he had first come to New York, when the hissing of the prostitutes had promised adventures beyond all imagining. When had he learned that it was not true? How many years ago? How hard had he tried to resist the lesson?

The weather turned colder still. Thomas was away at school this last year, and, not so oddly, Westfield did not relish the notion of Thomas home again next year. It was a matter of having his nose rubbed in still another failure. He did not know how much Louise had had to do with what had happened to Thomas, but he didn't care. He hoped he was beyond blaming her for anything. Michael came up to dinner once or twice a week, and sometimes he called Westfield on the telephone to come out for lunch. The *World* was right around the corner on Park Row. There was a quietness that was coming out in Michael, a kind of courtly reserve. He was flawlessly polite and patient with Louise, but Westfield suspected that the visits and lunches were a bore for him, that he attended to them because no one else bothered. That much was already clear with Julie. She resisted seeing them. She came on the holidays and the Sundays she thought her mother had fussed about. Westfield had been to her apartment on upper Broadway only once, in the spring. There was a view of the river and little white houses on the other side. Louise had been there on several afternoons, before and after shopping jaunts. Westfield did not know why he was surprised to discover that Julie was interested in money. He had begun to believe that all things he liked in girls when they were young developed into traits he abhorred in women as they matured. When he had thoughts like these, he wondered if he had ever learned anything in his life.

One night in November he rented a room on Third Avenue. He had no idea why he did it, but at the end of the evening he tapped on the old woman's door and pressed into her hand another two weeks's rent in advance. "I'll be in and out," he said to her. "You may not see me."

It gave him a feeling of independence, he decided as he walked back across town. The window opened directly on the elevated tracks, and when the train chugged past, steam blasted against the windowpane. There was a bed, a chair, and a dresser with a washbasin on it, all so snugly packed in the room that it was impossible to take two full steps in the same direction. He liked it. He had started in a furnished room, but he had been different then, a tortured, desperate young man. He remembered fighting lustful thoughts of a moustached Irish housemaid. He could not look at any woman now without feeling a hideous sense of failure. On the second evening he brought in his newspapers and read them. Then he stayed away most of a week. It was enough to know that the place was there.

He tried to be kinder to Louise, not so much to make amends as to show that he cared for her. He patted her hand and squeezed her shoulders, and when she came into the library to say good-night, he stood up and kissed her cheek. She turned toward him and he pressed his lips to her lips. They had not made love in so long that he had put it out of his thoughts. He would not inflict himself on her. He could not remember the last time he had been with a woman. It did not disturb him or alter how he viewed himself. He had wallowed in everything he had ever wanted years ago, and he had had his blackouts in recent times. So it made no difference. He knew what he was. He looked at Louise and felt ashamed.

In December he bought a gun and put it in the furnished room with the other things he had collected—the newspapers, a few books, periodicals. Aside from those things the room was the same as he had found it. Buying the gun and bringing it to the room was merely an act of honesty. He had been thinking of killing himself for months. He could see that the idea has been with him all his life, most of the time so far in the background that he had not been able to see it. What a human being was inside did not change like the weather. He wanted to be honest at last. The thought of killing himself came looking for him like death itself—every day it found him. He never thought about being dead. It was the thought of killing himself that had begun to consume him.

Thanksgiving was a disaster. Thomas was down, and although he looked no worse, Westfield supposed, his behavior was intolerable—superior, sullen: he seemed unable to look any of them directly in the eye. He twisted his lips whenever he tired of the conversation. It was as if he could not even pass the bowls of vegetables decently. He was contemptuous; it showed in the way he did everything. Westfield had to stop looking at him; he made him so sick.

And all the while Julie chattered on about her new life among the truly privileged. She was going to dances and parties; the Flemings were introducing her to all sorts of new people—artists, writers, millionaires, titled people from Europe. She was put off when Westfield told her that her mother had had artists, sculptors, and musicians in their own house years ago—quite put off, in fact. "Oh, yes, but this is different, Daddy. These people are *famous.*" He said he understood, but his mirth got the better of him and he shook with silent laughter. She saw, let out a long sigh, and turned away. It was all he could do to control himself. He wanted to slap her face—he had to remind himself that she belonged to her husband now. Michael was looking the other way, but he had seen; he never missed anything. It was too embarrassing for Westfield. He kept his head down for the rest of the meal.

After they had gone, after Thomas had clumped up to his room, Louise found Westfield in the library. Although he tried to obscure it in her mind over the next ten days, she remembered their few minutes together for the rest of her life. He thought she would be so unhappy with the holiday that she would cry, but she had come in to say how sorry she was that the day had been so bad for him. He stared at her, his heart breaking. Had she seen what Julie had done to him? Or had she seen it all, the whole hopeless travesty their family had become? "I'm all right," he said. "The food was delicious. Do you see how Michael has grown? Do you see what he is these days?"

"More than *my* equal," she said.

"Mine, too," he said suddenly. It surprised him. He had not thought of it before, but he said it so quickly that it had to be true. She regarded him carefully—did she want him to say something good about their own two children? There was nothing he could think of that would not make them seem dismal by comparison. Cautiously he peered into her eyes again. He had no idea what she thought, what she knew. In any case, he had no right to subject her to his feelings. He reached for her, squeezed her wrist, held her hand. She bent over and pressed her cheek against his bald head.

"I do worry about him," she said.

Did she want to assure him that Michael was far from perfect, too? His curiosity almost drew him to her, but he resisted. He would just be punishing her at this stage. He patted her arm and turned away.

VIII

He never looked at the gun he had bought, an old .44 revolver. It was up on the shelf of the wardrobe, back out of the landlady's sight. No, all the next week he lay on the narrow bed and looked across the gleaming elevated tracks at the tenement on the opposite corner. One evening snow fell and the room became bitterly cold. He covered himself with his coat and studied the faint lights in the windows through the falling snow. Now and again he could see a figure with dark hair. He pretended he could see her face in spite of the distance, a handsome woman but a little grim. He really could not imagine what her life was like or what she thought and felt. At times in his life he had been curious about others, but his motives had been selfish. He had had Kate tell him about her childhood because he had wanted more of her than one human being could give another. He could remember hoping that it would bring her around to him. He had never brought anyone around like that, not the way he had wanted love to be.

At times he stared at the wardrobe where he had hidden the gun. One evening after the snowfall he closed the draperies and lay in the dark staring at the shadow of the wardrobe. His hands were clasped behind his head and he was perfectly comfortable. It was, in fact, the position in which he stretched himself after a day's racing at Saratoga, in the hour before dinner. He had been as happy then as he had ever been in his life; why hadn't he seen it? It had not filled him the way falling in love had filled him. How many women had he had? How many could he remember? It had been a stupid exercise thoughout. Faces and names were gone; what he retained were fragments of memory. He could begin again this evening if he wanted, but he could not be bothered investing the energy. How long had it been since he had indulged in what people called the solitary vice? He could remember when *that* had been his consuming passion, instead of women, liquor—or this. So he lay still in the dark under a dream of how he had lived his life. He knew he was no worse than many others. No matter.

He had waited long enough. Thanksgiving had slowed him down. If he had done anything then, they would have thought it had to do with them and what had happened over the table. They had to understand that they were not responsible. He was doing this on his own.

By the first week in December he had it worked out. He had to wait through the Monday. He made a last tour of his old places. What better time? The girls were as young and pretty as ever, but they were all different, and he recognized few men, as well. Young sports. He was old enough to be the father of most of them, but life seemed the same, which was exactly what he had learned in his own life—that life itself was unchangeable, unbreakable. Everything would be here a year from now, or ten or twenty. He thought of drinking, of having a few drinks, but he had no taste for the stuff, no taste for the feeling it would give him. He thought of the woman in the tenement on the opposite corner. There was no night life for her, probably never had been. He could stay sober one more night. He was in the bar of a brothel, and he distracted himself by looking at one of the prettier girls, a round-faced, tiny-mouthed blonde. When she thought he was interested in her and moved toward him, he shook his head and got up to leave.

He spent the next day staring at his desk. He thought he might have something to put down on paper, but not a damned thing came. Michael called for lunch, but Westfield said no. "Some other time," Michael said, and Westfield grunted. He felt like a fool. He wanted to tell the truth, but he kept quiet. It was not that he was ashamed of what he was going to do. He had lived enough of a life.

Suicide is the last moment of a natural death. The organism succumbs as if to disease. The point of no return has been crossed long before. Death itself is only the last step.

During dinner Westfield's heart began to pound so fiercely that he had to get up from the table. Louise asked him what was wrong, but he said nothing. He wanted air, but he knew that if he stepped outside, she would think he was ill and try to make him stay home. In the parlor he calmed himself by imagining that he would be going to work tomorrow the same as always. There would even be Saratoga again in August. He returned to the table with a smile. "Something caught between my teeth," he said. She nodded.

Before he left, he kissed her cheek as he usually did. He had considered it, and he didn't want to do anything she would think unusual. When he reached Third Avenue, he bought a pint of whiskey; when he got under the el, he calmly poured half of it onto the cobblestones. If passersby noticed him, he did not see them. So far, so good.

In the room he did not bother with the lamp and took off his coat and hat and put them on the chair. He sat on the edge of the bed and faced the window. After a moment he thought of the dark-haired woman, and peered out to see if her lights were on. They were. It was a clear night; a few small clouds were edged with moonlight. A strong wind blew the city smoke away and made the window hum. The dark-haired women would hear about this in the street tomorrow. It would be in the newspapers. Probably Michael would be the first to hear about it. Westfield tried to close his mind to the next days and weeks. In a year, in a matter of months, life for Louise would be better. Life itself would be unchanged. Young sports would be lifting glasses to folly the same as ever. Would Louise remarry? A train was coming. He thought of having a drink, but instead he went for the gun.

The train rumbled by, the lights inside the passing cars flickering on the walls. There was a shimmering gleam on the blued steel of the revolver. Heavy thing. He returned to the bed and kept his eyes down until the train had gone. He did not want to see people, and the faces were quite clear. He remembered the bottle still in his coat. His plan was to leave the bottle where it could be seen so that people would conclude that he had been drinking again and had killed himself because of it. He did not know if he had to drink any of it. He could spill it on his neck and shoulders and get the same effect, although he could not imagine anyone getting that close to him. But he had to be sure. He really did not want to drink any of it.

He opened the bottle and sprinkled about half the remaining contents down the front of his shirt. The smell hit him. Now even if he stopped, he would have to explain it. The smell filled his nose and his throat and his lungs, almost as if he actually had had a drink. He turned the pistol toward himself. In trying to see how he would do this, he had not taken into account the weight of the thing. But it was right, the weight, as it should be. He wondered if it could stop him. He had never done anything in his life. For as long as he could remember he had asked himself if he really was going to do one thing or another, and the answer had always been no.

He turned the gun on himself, brought the barrel closer to his face, and finally allowed the steel to touch his lips as gently as a kiss. He did not have his thumb on the trigger. He could still stop. It was going to make a terrible noise. He had another vision of the woman on the opposite corner. He did not want to be found right away. He would wait for a train. He would do it when the next train passed. For some reason the idea seemed to tickle him.

The noise would not be so loud if he had the window open. Maybe he had to move the bed closer, too. The sound would carry out better. He did not want to be found until the daytime if he could possibly help it. He had no reason, except that he did not want to be found at night.

A train was coming. He was sitting up to the window, leaning forward. The cold wind tore into the room. He wanted a drink now. Why shouldn't he? The stuff was cheap and raw and burned his throat on the way down. He felt sick with himself. The train was coming. He had never been able to resist anything in his life. He saw the lights in the windows on the other corner. Maybe she would hear it after all. He could see the locomotive up the tracks, the smoke whipping into the night. He could see the rails yielding under the advancing weight, the rails turning from blue to yellow by the light of the locomotive's lamp. It was a crisp, clear, beautiful night, a wonderful winter night.

The train was almost upon him. He sat back and brought the revolver up again. He put it to his mouth, not allowing it to touch him. Now he knew what had tickled him a moment ago. He had been waiting for the train so he could end his life in the way a child plucks at petals of a flower. Decisions were made like that. He stank of alcohol; the drink made his stomach twist. He had never learned anything. The locomotive rolled by, louder than the last because of the open window. He wanted to see the lights of the cars. For a second he thought he would let the train pass. He made a noise in his throat that burned like the alcohol. The woman across the street should see him, ending a life too rich for her to imagine. He shivered. The room grew brighter with the lights of the first car. He was still afraid that he would fail, and his fear mixed with a sudden chilling fear of death. His penis squeezed into his belly. He jammed the gun into his mouth and clamped his teeth down on it. There was a taste of blood. His eyes were bulging. People would see.

The first windows were steamed, but then out of the corner of his eye he could see one that had been wiped clean. A woman was peering out at the tenements, a fat woman with a great pile of orange-red hair, with red lips and rouged cheeks and painted eyes. She stared at Westfield. They were looking into each other's eyes and she almost seemed to understand what she was seeing. He had his thumb on the trigger. She was directly in front of him staring in horror when he growled again, growled at her, pushing the gun in farther and pulled the trigger simultaneously. Her widening eyes were the last things he saw as he felt his head blowing apart.

IX

The funeral was on Saturday, with the burial in Brooklyn. So many people had come to pay their respects that by the day of the funeral Louise wanted to open her house to them afterward. There were a few people at the service—enough, Michael thought—but almost all declined to make the journey to Brooklyn. Part of it was embarrassment; there was nothing one could say to the widow of a suicide.

So it was Louise, Thomas, Michael, Julie and Julie's husband, Westfield's brothers and their wives, Louise's mother, and two men from Westfield's office who made the trip to Brooklyn. Louise invited the two men to join the family back at the house on Thirty-eighth Street, and when they declined, Michael was grateful. Louise was in agony, and the sooner she was free of any sort of burden, the faster she would begin to think of herself.

She had been told that the police had found liquor, and she believed what Westfield had wanted her to believe. Michael was determined to keep his own opinion to himself. No one knew that he had talked to Westfield on Tuesday. If he told that much, he might be drawn into telling what he thought, too. Westfield had sounded like nothing he had ever heard before. The liquor had only been part of it, if Westfield had been drinking at all. In the end the effect was the same as he had wanted, even if Michael was seeing it on his own terms: it had to do with Westfield alone, as if he had been overwhelmed by some hidden force and carried away.

In the early evening Westfield's brothers returned to their hotel. Louise's mother was going to stay on a few days in Julie's room. The house had been hushed; now it fell completely silent. Someone, probably Hannah, whom Michael had seen crying quietly two or three times in the past three days, had turned down the lamps. From the parlor one could see the black wreath hanging on the other side of the glass front door. Michael sat facing the other way; there was a pot of coffee on the table. He was smoking a cigar. Julie was downstairs in the kitchen with Hannah, putting away the food, and Fleming was upstairs with Thomas. Louise was upstairs, too, helping her mother get settled in Julie's room. Michael heard Thomas's footsteps on the stairs.

"Michael? Will you come upstairs a minute?"

"Certainly." Until he heard the tone of Thomas's voice, it hadn't occurred to him that they would have anything to discuss, but something began to come clear. Fleming was going to side with Thomas.

Thomas was waiting at the library door. "In here." He closed the door behind him. "Sit down, Michael." Thomas hustled around to the other side of the desk. Fleming had been standing at the windows; now he positioned himself beside Thomas's chair. Together they looked as if they were posing for a photograph, like little boys in their fathers' clothing. As he sat down, Michael almost smiled.

Thomas said, "I found my father's will the other day, Michael, and to tell you the truth, I was in a bit of a quandary over whether to give you some news that I knew was going to shock you then, when I found it, or later, after my father's funeral. I know you cared for him and probably will come around to care for him again after the shock wears off. At least, I hope you will, because it was on that notion that I made my decision to wait until now. I think you understand." He glanced down at the desk, where some papers were unfolded. "If this is a true copy of my father's last will, Michael, I'm afraid that it was his intention to leave you only a token amount. He has some things to say about his affection for you, but nothing by way of an explanation for the size of the bequest." He paused, a pudgy finger tapping the papers before him. "Ah, he wants you to have a thousand dollars."

"It's more than I expected."

Thomas eyed him. "Expected? Did my father discuss this with you?"

"Oh, yes."

"Would you mind telling me what he said to you?"

"It was a private conversation."

Thomas put his elbows on the desk. "Michael, I'm trying to discern my father's intentions. He has very little to say in his will. Any help you can give me—"

"Sorry."

"Don't interrupt me—please. There are critical decisions that have to be made. Obviously if my father had a conversation with you about his last requests, perhaps it will shed some light on what he did to himself this week."

"I'm afraid it won't."

Fleming rocked on his heels, his hands clasped behind him. "I don't think that's an answer the family will accept, Monk."

Michael narrowed his eyes. "I no longer use that name, and I don't want to ever hear you use it. Do *you* presume to speak for the family?"

"I believe I have a more legitimate right to speak for it than you do, as a matter of fact, yes."

Michael smiled. "You sound as if I scared you to death." He turned to Thomas. "Let's put our cards on the table. What do you want?"

"I think we can forget about any conversation that you say took place, Michael," he said. "We have only your word for it. My father's bequest to you speaks clearly enough. We can discern his intention. You'll have your thousand as soon after probate as possible, as the distributions for debts and so forth permit, if you'll go to the trouble of keeping my father's attorney informed of your whereabouts."

"That shouldn't be any trouble. I'll be seeing plenty of your mother."

Thomas poked a lumpy finger at him. "I'm afraid you still don't have the idea. I had you forced on me originally. I don't plan to have you forced on me any longer."

The door opened. Louise stood there with the handkerchief in her hands, wringing the handkerchief, trying to tear it apart. Her mouth worked, but no sound came out. She stepped over the threshold, never taking her eyes from Thomas.

"Your father's body hasn't been in the ground a day!"

"Mother, father's will is clear! He left Michael only a thousand!"

"I don't care about that! You don't have the decency—" As if she had enough talking suddenly, she swept across the room to the desk, her black skirt rustling. She stood over Thomas. "Get out! Get out of this room!" she shouted, her tiny fists shaking. "I decide my life now! You decide nothing! I decide! I decide! You get out of this room!"

Thomas pushed out of the chair, watching her as if she were about to hit him. He clambered around the desk like a child trying to stay out of her reach. Michael was on his feet, heading toward Louise. Fleming moved back, then sidestepped around him. If Louise hadn't turned her attention to Fleming, Michael might have laughed in his face, but her shock and pain were too immediate, too transparent. Michael reached for her, tried to move himself around to block her view of Fleming. He heard the door close. They were gone, Fleming and Thomas.

"A thousand dollars! Oh, Michael! He knew this was going to happen!"

He took her arms. "Don't upset yourself. He provided for me quite a while ago. I never expected anything. He provided for me amply."

"How? I heard you say something to them about a conversation. I was in the bedroom with my mother and we could hear you plainly."

"The conversation we had concerned my future. He had some money put away. It came from his politics. He wasn't a thief. The money came his way. It gave him no pleasure. He wanted me to have it. You heard Thomas. His father suspected that something like this would happen. He wanted to be sure I had money."

"Did he say anything to you about himself?"

"No, nothing. I've wracked my brain, and I can't remember a thing. He was an unhappy man. He could find no peace with himself."

"I think he realized that he was going to drink himself to death. We know he resisted it as much as he could. He knew what was going to happen to him. He had his pride, too."

"I know."

"Promise me you won't drink, Michael. Don't drink again, ever, please. I want to know that some good will come of this. I can't ask Thomas to promise me anything."

"I promise." He meant it, but he was distracted by her reference to Westfield's drinking. Michael had not been thinking of it. Westfield had been an unhappy man all his life. The drinking had not come first.

"I want to know that you really are provided for, Michael. How much did he give you?"

Michael told her. "He said it would be less than what Thomas and Julie would get, but that it would be enough. I never expected anything, I said, and I meant it."

Her face hardened. "It's good to hear that sort of talk for a change. I knew what Thomas was like, but I hoped for more from Roger. I suppose Julie is like her brother. I blinded myself to both of them long enough."

"She's not like her brother," Michael said. "Don't talk like that."

"*He* brought this on with his stupid will," she said bitterly. "*He* created this situation."

"It would have come out anyway," Michael said. "The feelings existed long before this. He said it would be worse if I were in the will."

"He thought *that* little of them? I'm sorry, I would have a happier memory of him if he had shown his children that he loved and trusted them. I know how he felt about me!"

"He loved you very much," Michael said, and put his arms around her.

When Louise was asleep that night, Michael went back to Brooklyn. He took the el down Third Avenue and the Bowery to the Bridge. The night was damp and overcast, but the temperature was mild. Westfield had not realized how much he had held the family together. Now Michael had only Louise, when last Saturday at this time he had had a whole family.

The horsecars were still running out to Flatbush. He had told Louise that he would call her tomorrow and look in on her in a few days. He could feel himself wanting to keep his promise to her, having Westfield with him as he had his father. What had he done with himself for his mother? He had lied about his age, but he had done that to save himself.

He was still adrift. He did not know what he would have been. From time to time he would wonder how Moran came to knock on their door in the first place, who had sent him there, but it was fruitless, desperate stuff. He had never asked Westfield what *he* had known. The school records had disappeared—how had that happened? No matter what Michael turned over in his mind, everything remained a mystery.

He was the last passenger on the horsecar as it reached the end of the line. The streets were empty and the wind made the car rock. He took out his watch. It was almost eleven o'clock.

Kate had heard the bad news about Westfield from him. He had called her on the telephone. She had let out a shriek, a *"No!"* that still sounded in his ears. She had wanted to come to the funeral. He had discouraged her, but in fact it had not taken much. It was just a reaction to the shock, she said. His interpretation of the presence of the whiskey satisfied her. She could remember nothing that Michael had told her that sounded as if Westfield had been getting ready to start drinking again. She would ask around, in case someone had seen anything. Michael called her every day but never asked what she had learned. He could hear how badly she was really taking it, and when he was not able to call her, he worried about her.

She opened her door right away—she had been sitting in the front parlor. Gert was asleep. Was he ready for a drink? He had to tell her about the promise to Louise, then how it had come about. She said that he should have expected no less of Thomas and Fleming.

With a sigh, Michael settled on hot chocolate. He followed Kate out to the kitchen, opening his collar and loosening his tie as he went. It had been arranged yesterday that he would spend the night. She wanted it—she wanted to keep an eye on him. She expected him to sleep with her. Through the long day today it had slowly and bizarrely filled his thoughts. He had watched Westfield going into the ground through a haze of visions of the girl Westfield had loved best. It had wrung him out or the episode with Thomas and Fleming had made him sour; he did not know how he felt about anything.

It was very warm in the house, the hot air coming up through the brand-new, brightly polished brass grates in the floor. Kate liked to be warm in the winter and cool in the summer, she had told him once. She had odd ideas of what constituted luxury. Her larder was stuffed, for instance; there was more cash in the house than he considered wise.

Yet oddly there was a plainness about her, a plainness more subtle and private than her love for Gert. Michael could see it in the openness of her eyes, feel it in the gentle way she touched his hand and the tentative pressure of her lips on his cheek. She wanted to be herself with him. Her hair might be uncombed, and often she walked around barefoot. "Tell me what you've been doing," she would say eagerly, because he was doing interesting things and because between them they knew the best gossip, all the secrets worth knowing in the entire city.

She had kissed him amorously one evening after he had kissed her, putting her tongue in his mouth, laughing and saying that she only wanted to know what it was like; and after Julie's wedding, the following weekend, he had gotten drunk and made a pest of himself. She had not made him feel embarrassed, and he loved her for it.

But in the long time since, he had never felt that he could make love to her honestly. "Let's preserve the mystery" was the closest they had come to telling the truth about themselves. She had said it, and he guessed that she had found the words because she was more experienced in matters concerning these feelings.

Yesterday had been very rough for her—she had not been out of the house since Michael's first call. "This is one of the times I don't like being a whore, and I want you with me. You shouldn't be alone, either. Please. I'm asking you." Because he had never heard a woman so honest about herself, his curiosity about her had ignited at last.

He told her how strong Louise had been when she had sent Thomas scurrying.

"I once hated her as I never hated anyone. I don't now. It's ten years ago. We're different people. She's alone and not young and I'm very sorry for her."

He had his hot chocolate in the kitchen. He felt so tired his body was leaden. His life had been remade again, and again it had taken a year. It was whirling inside him, and then she saw something in his eyes. It was as if she knew where his thoughts were going, and she took the cup out of his hands.

Her bedroom was warmer than the rooms downstairs. She lit the lamp by the bed and opened the window. He sat on the bed and unbuttoned his shirt. He started to cry for Westfield. Why had he thought no one cared for him? Michael tried to catch himself, but when he stood up and turned around, Kate was staring at him, crying as he was crying, her eyes red and her cheeks smeared with tears. After a moment, and then hesitantly, she turned the lamp out.

They lay together naked. She kissed him and stroked his body, and he kissed her breast, but then they stopped. He let her rest her head on his shoulder. He could feel her breasts and her soft belly against him; there was a warm, milky odor to her body, and the rhythm of her breathing soothed him. He thought of Westfield one more time, and then his thoughts scattered in every direction as he drifted, passive and benign, toward intimations of eternity.

He awakened near dawn so disoriented and excited that he rolled toward her without knowing who she was. He realized as he kissed her, and laughed. She woke up. "Huh?" Her breath was bad. She reached for his penis: "Ah, that's nice." She stroked him and he kissed her and got over her. She was smiling, and it made him think of what he had been seeing in his mind through so much of the day before. He had not doubted that she would be as experienced as she was, but he thought he could see that she was surprised and pleased. He let her guide him into her, and he entered her quickly and she wrapped her legs around him.

It took them another moment to find their way with each other. They were beautifully matched. He held her, kissed her, and fucked her hard. He wanted to—surrendered to it. That she could hold him tighter only excited him more, and when he came, she bucked her legs in the air and yelled in astonishment more than passion. For her sake he had to go on; she growled suddenly and her convulsions nearly lifted him in the air. It took them a long time to calm down, kissing each other, the rhythm of their fucking subsiding like a storm.

"This doesn't have to do with Westfield," he said.

"No."

"I don't want to give it up."

"Don't lie, Michael."

"I'm not lying."

"I'll fall in love with you, Michael."

"I won't say you can't."

She kissed him. He began to fuck her again and they laughed. He had another thought of Westfield and it chilled him like a premonition of disaster, but he looked down into her eyes and she was smiling as if she were in love with him already. He fucked her as if she were, and tried to surrender again.

THE TURN
OF THE CENTURY

I

"Were you and Kate Johnson ever in love?"
"No.

II

By 1895 the marriage of past and present is more evident in the streets
of the city. The air rattles with the roar of passing trains; electric light
stabs out of the darkness. Consolidation is coming, the newspapers say,
and most people believe it, in spite of fierce opposition with deep
historical roots. In the city, a substantial portion of the population is
committed to a memory of "Little Old New York." Across the river, the
towns of Flatbush, Gravesend, and New Utrecht have been part of the
city of Brooklyn for less than a year—the fact is, villages and farms cover
eighty percent of the area about to become the city of New York, and the
pace of life is decidedly slower and simpler than in the international port
and pirates' den its shakers and movers will soon call Manhattan. The
New York of 1895 is the most corrupt of cities, wilder, more brutal, and
downright disgusting than anything Westfield could have possibly conceived. We can consign him to history, though even now the city still
glitters with fires that started in his imagination, among others. The
opponents of consolidation did not see that they were being drowned in
the dreams of their contemporaries. Like any other human enterprise,

the city is a metaphor for the dreams spinning out of the unconscious while the race puzzles over its destiny. The dreams of a Michael and a Kate, outcasts of the streets, are no more fantastical than the dreams of the reformers who believe an enlarged city represents a greater opportunity to serve God. From either side, from all sides, the city is heaped up. Dreams are dreams; who knows what they mean?

But while some men may be crushed by the burden of their imaginations, like Westfield, the process goes on. History explains our condition, but we know the past is dead. The suggestion of a wedding between past and present is really a bit of sleight of hand. There is only the present, the imposition of other men's dreams, and the struggle to realize one's own. There is no marriage between the outcasts and the reformers, either, and the city is not a union of two forces. Dreams are dreams, and the watching and waiting and counting of chances at the poker table have taught Michael how mad men's dreams can be. Times are bad and he is weathering them well. So is Kate—she is doing better than ever, in spite of the reformers and a depression. Kate knows how mad men are; she is thirty-four years old. For her, the city is built of the lies men tell each other. The lies they tell themselves shimmer in the air she breathes.

III

Emily Reese first saw Michael Westfield in April 1895. It was two months after her twentieth birthday, at the end of the long, cold waiting-for-spring. There were buds on the trees, still small but at the beginning of their swelling, which cheered her spirits. She was one of those people enslaved by weather, exhilarated with the change of the seasons, content in the summer, oppressed by the winter. She was physically vulnerable, almost always ill with some small thing or other. And although the beginning of spring certainly meant the end of one of the few intervals in the year when she was free of complaint, the evidence on the trees on upper Broadway that the world was about to be reborn delighted her sufficiently to distract her from the prospect of the boredom of yet-another edifying afternoon at Mrs. Westfield's.

Emily had received a note. The lecture today was to be on the future of the city, and once again the few dollars raised would proceed to the Orphan Asylum Society. Mrs. Westfield liked people to know that her interest in the Society dated from her arrival in the neighborhood three years before. Emily's instinct was to be cautious. Her father said that no one knew if she had any money (why did she sell the house on Thirty-eighth Street? he wanted to know), and there was her continuous pretense that she never knew anything (about another lecturer she had once written on the invitation that she wouldn't know if he would be telling the truth—typical) so Emily had allowed herself to come to the conclusion that there was more to Mrs. Westfield than met the eye. Possibly something sinister, she fancied romantically. Wise to herself in this instance, Emily nevertheless kept her eyes open. But all that did not mean the afternoon was not going to be a bore. Emily dreaded going, not so much because of the announced business, for a lecture was a pleasant enough way to pass an afternoon, but because of the real agenda of the ladies assembled: gossip. Emily wanted to think she had been living with it for too long to be anything but bored with it, but she knew she was still capable of feeling pain over something almost any one of them could say—some new way of uttering what was essentially the same jape she had heard as a schoolgirl.

As far as the rest of them were concerned, there was something wrong with her. She didn't know what it was. It wasn't the endless sickness, or that her eyesight was so poor that she almost always had to wear glasses, or her basic plainness (although in truth she was one of those plain girls who are also beautiful women, and Michael was far from the first to recognize it), or her intelligence or shyness about her feelings, or all those things working together in different ways at different times. She was ill at ease with people, and although she was no more inept in dealing with others than anyone else, when she made a mistake with someone, she felt agonies of remorse and never seemed able to forget what she had done. The smallest *faux pas* was an irrecoverable loss, for there was something she didn't know, some profound ignorance about people still inside her. It was true; she could *feel* it. She was *outside;* whatever happened to people in life was not happening to her, and she knew it.

And other people knew it. At best, they simply gave up on her. She had never had a close friend for long. It had taken her years to recognize this. People in the middle distance treated her well enough. If they began to seek out her company, eventually they let her drop. Nothing happened; there were never any bad feelings. She was allowed to fall out of their lives. Emily was no longer even bewildered when it happened.

She had never had a real suitor. There was her plainness first and then her shyness. And then there was the something else. Men were never very interested in her. Occasionally one would come around and try to look at her the way men were supposed to look at women, but it never worked. It made her feel uncomfortable, and he would stop before he grew angry. The girls who had their fun with her seemed to know that so well that they might have been sitting in the room when it happened. She could see it in their eyes after every failure. For a while she had assumed that one or two of the men had felt the need to explain to others why they had lost interest, but that wasn't it. The girls who disliked her knew what her life was like just as easily as they knew how to make men look at them in that special way. And because they really were petty, vicious people, they reveled in it.

"Are you going down to the Jersey shore again this year, Emily?"

She would nod apologetically. She would always start in the belief there would be no malice.

"Well, I suppose that's all right," the girl would say. "That is, if you like that sort of thing. I myself prefer Saratoga—as so many people do these days, apparently."

At twenty, Emily had the sense to walk away.

Happily, the young ladies and their gossip and charity afternoons at Mrs. Westfield's were only a small part of Emily's life. She had her volunteer work at the settlement house downtown three afternoons a week. She read, wrote, and painted. She saw herself as a person who was happy to be alone pursuing her talents, provided she had the opportunity to reach out to others as well. She could not sing and she danced poorly—which confused her, really, for at the settlement she had no difficulty reading to the small children or leading poetry discussions with the older girls.

Perhaps it was the situation that gave her release, confirming in a way that was beyond her understanding her belief that she needed useful work. The poor and hopeless did not torment her. She was only one person and there was just so much she could do. The people she saw, Jews and Italians mostly, had been worse off in Europe. They had come to this country to better themselves, and eventually, inevitably, they would. The forces that had brought thousands upon thousands of immigrants to the New World were too immense for the understanding of an Emily Reese, she was sure. But when she thought of those people, she saw that she was right in not admitting to be any more than bored by the remarks of the foolish girls she usually found gabbling and fluttering at an afternoon at Mrs. Westfield's.

She loved long romantic novels, especially the great stories of adventure and sadness and love. Before she was twelve she had read *The Leatherstocking Tales* four times. She still painted outdoor scenes, even though she had gone from watercolors to oils, from bright, sunlit meadows and flowers to shadowed woodland glens and hollows, the greens deeper and darker until they were almost black. As a child she had tried to imagine the sound of Natty Bumpo striding through the woods, and one afternnon years later—it was the first autumn in the new house uptown, and a breeze had suddenly rushed up from the river—she remembered. The wilderness of her childhood imagination rose up again as if she had never forgotten it; and she realized with an unpleasant shock that the little girl may have thought she had wanted to hear Natty Bumpo coming her way, but in fact she had wanted to fill her nose with the sharp smell of his deerskin clothing. The next morning as she sat down to her easel she felt unpleasant again, even upset, and with the unhappy memory of the previous afternoon pressing her, she thought that she didn't want people to see her paintings anymore, that the visions of woodland pools, mountain ravines, and great firs and hemlocks that she tried to commit to canvas were really too personal to share with anybody. (Later she saw that her father's certain hurt feelings and her mother's probable anger were more trouble than her privacy was worth, and so she compromised: when either of them wanted to see her work, she made sure she was in another part of the house.)

It was the best she could do. She could no more hurt her father than she could avoid displeasing her mother. Emily was the third child, the last, the only daughter, a Daddy's girl. She knew it, knew she had been a spoiled child; but more clearly she could see she was now a different person, one who looked back on her childhood from a distance.

Her father was the most successful man she knew, president of two banks, a stockbroker and trader in real estate, but he yielded to his wife in all things concerning the household and the raising of the children. It made for a system, he said, and consequently there was no appeal, once Emily's mother had made a decision. He was a shrewd, rigid, pious man who was not afraid to denounce Saratoga as "that hell on earth," and he was suspicious of people who tried to make life easy for themselves, even his own children. He had a big voice, one that filled the room, and inevitably he could be heard over all others in church. He worked hard and he was as proud of his accomplishments as he was of his family, home, and possessions.

Emily's mother ran her home with approximately the same shrewd rigidity her father employed at the bank, where it was more appropriate. Her mother was a cold, severe woman, and the fact was, and Emily knew it, that Emily literally did not want to be in the same room with the woman. There was only the most tense, tightly controlled interaction between daughter and mother. Emily could feel her mother's presence behind her shoulder at every step of her childhood; homework, piano lessons, sewing—suddenly her mother's hand would dart into view to seize Emily's wrist: "No! Do it *this* way!" Emily could remember too clearly the hot, uncomfortable sensation of her mother's breath against her ear, the pressure of her mother's other hand on Emily's back as she leaned over to guide Emily through still one more correction.

Emily's brothers were twenty-three and twenty-six, unmarried and living at home. They were clerks at the bank working their way up. The younger had little aptitude. It was not that Anthony kept doing something wrong, it appeared, but a kind of lack of interest so all-pervasive that it passed for incompetence. Nothing was ever discussed at home, but some days were worse than others, and often there was little conversation at dinner.

Jerome was no better. He was still so eager for games and sports and prizes and trophies that he hardly realized that he was within sight of thirty. Emily had come to the conclusion that both of them were children, with none of their father's ambition or judgment. They did not seem to care very much about her, and they had even less influence on the household than their father—for Emily, a hopeless situation.

There was no evidence of him anywhere in the house. "That's her department," he would say, and the result was that everything was the way Emily's mother wanted, from the food on the table to the pattern of the paper on the walls. The men outnumbered the women, but the house was still a woman's, a woman who was so cold and unremittingly peevish that the house itself felt the same whenever Emily entered it.

So Emily kept to herself. For the past six months she had been able to have her settlement work, traveling on the el far downtown and back three times a week, mixing for the first time in her life with all elements of the city. Her mother had opposed her independence, naturally, her opposition so apparent in advance that Emily had waited eighteen months until her twentieth birthday approached before daring to raise the subject.

So she ascended the steps of Mrs. Westfield's brownstone just off Broadway with a specific, deep-rooted nervousness, and gave her sweater to Mrs. Westfield's white-haired, overweight maid with her usual polite, shy smile, and passed into the front parlor in that momentary heightening of expectation and equanimity that is the legacy and curse of all timid people at the threshold of even the most insignificant social event. It was spring, after all, and sunshine and fresh air flooded Mrs. Westfield's front room, where more than a score of women and girls in the brightest frocks stood chattering. There were giant sprays of vivid chrome-yellow forsythia on tables in the corners and, by the movement of the crowd, punch and cookies in the dining room beyond. It was one of those awkward moments when she could catch the eye of no one she cared to talk to, and so she stood there not quite out of the room but by no means in it either. She saw Mrs. Westfield near the windows and her daughter-in-law stationed at the dining room. Her husband, Mrs. Westfield's son Thomas, who certainly was the only fatter person in the room, stood beside her, his collar crushed under the weight of his chins. Emily disliked them both enough to figure that she would have to do without punch for the afternoon, if it meant having to get past them. She did not know them well, having met them only twice previously, but they were the sort of self-possessed people who left clear, permanent memories wherever they went. Near the mantel stood Mrs. Westfield's daughter, the tall, glamorous, and utterly composed

Mrs. Fleming. Emily had met her before only once; her presence at this occasion Emily offered to herself as evidence of the importance of this afternoon's event or speaker. Mrs. Fleming was very social, in Emily's estimation, *very* social. And of course she was with the man Emily at once took to be the afternoon's speaker, a very tall, dark-haired man with a full moustache. He was leaning back against the mantel. He appeared to be about thirty, his wavy hair receded at the temples, his eyes dark and expressive in a distracted way. It was strange, for Emily felt that she could read what he was thinking instantly. He was amused with Mrs. Fleming—but wary, too. Suddenly she reached out and touched his hand, a gesture so startling to Emily that she actually caught her breath. Across the room, he sensed it. He took Mrs. Fleming's hand and, listening to whatever she had to say, tried to turn his attention around. Emily felt like a child, vulnerable as she waited for his gaze. Inspection, actually: she felt her anger rising. He knew he was holding her. He carried himself with such languid self-assurance that Emily thought if he were the speaker and not a friend of Mrs. Fleming, some intimate, even a lover, she would hate him. A glimpse of an unpleasant, uncomfortable afternoon passed through her thoughts as he began to establish in fact that he was not Mrs. Fleming's lover, definitely not her lover. Time had slowed: something downright peculiar was happening. There was a smile playing about his lips; Emily could not tell if it had to do with his conversation with Mrs. Fleming or with what was suddenly going on between them. Now she remembered having heard something about a younger brother, but this man was too old. And too unlike the other brother. Emily did not sense what she sensed in the rest of the family, a strange purposelessness or redundancy that left them morally suspect. The younger brother was the worst, Emily had heard; there were stories that the men would not tell the women. She realized she was staring at him. He knew it. He was smiling at her, not laughing because he had caught her staring but smiling as if in recognition, as if he knew her. He was so sure of himself that it confused her—no, it was different from that, more serious. It had to do with the time slowing down. She had never felt anything like it before, yet she believed she knew exactly what it was. He was still smiling at her—impossible. Impossible. She could feel herself struggling against it, although it was certainly too late for that, like stepping through a door and seeing everything—the room, the people, the forsythia-colored light—*everything* simply melt away and disappear.

IV

As for his part, Michael had been on his way uptown to see a certain Colonel Robert G. Latham, a seventy-year-old relic of the Civil War, to give the colonel a horse. Not a whole horse, merely the horse's name, which was all the good colonel wanted. Not that he was really a good colonel either, having been so obsessed with racing and becoming a successful gambler that he had turned himself into a snarling little crookback, filthy and half starved. He had plenty of money, frayed tens and twenties that emerged from tattered envelopes to pay for the racing information that Michael sold him. Normally Michael sent Andy Fletcher up from the newspaper, for the old man liked to talk, ask questions, compare systems, pulling people into the rancid hotel room piled high with newspapers and magazines—his *sanctum sanctorum,* the prison from which he was trying to free himself. He was not a man who could be told that fifty dollars a horse did not buy private consultations, but he was too regular a customer, worth two or three hundred a week, to be allowed to get away.

So Michael usually sent Andy, who was twenty and eager to learn, and could carry a "confidential message from Mr. Westfield" with something like conviction. The information that certain good horses were coming up from New Orleans would bring a smile to the old colonel's dry lips, and he would give the boy the money and take Michael's carefully sealed, fresh white envelope with gratitude.

An old fool's money was going to go somewhere, and Michael was as good as any other handicapper, losing no more on paper than any of the rest, losing because the customers wanted action more than winners. Michael himself played fewer than ten percent of the horses he recommended; but he could never teach the patience and self-scrutiny real gambling required to his "selected customers," or the subscribers to *Westfield's Private Wire,* or the readers of his reports in the *World.* They were the same men whose money he took at cards, and although they hated him, they admired him, too. They wanted to know his secrets; they could not see that they did not have the capacity to learn them, having come to gambling from the wrong direction and for the wrong reasons. At odd times in the past he had tried to teach them that patience, counting one's chances, understanding the desire to win, and having to wait while others around them seemed to be winning were all part of a discipline that could *build* their characters, not destroy them in the way gambling was supposed to do. But it was impossible, and he could see that it was because of what they were inside. They weren't called chumps for nothing: what drove them seemed as common to the human race as larceny. He had come to the point where he could see the sense of not thinking too much about it, and he was able to accomplish that by exercising some restraint with the chumps themselves. Perhaps that was where he had the edge: he *knew* he could take things only so far. So he bled them, little by little. He had quit wondering what he would have become if his parents had lived, because they hadn't. The chumps seemed willing to bet against the wind—Michael thought of it that way because it reminded him of his father's stories of the sea. "You make your peace with them or you die," he had said about the forces that moved the wind and the waves, adding, "and that's the sweet beauty of it." It had come to Michael that Westfield had been saying the same thing.

Michael was uptown on a second errand, as well. Kate had asked him to look over a brownstone that had just come on the market. Operating out of the Tenderloin had its disadvantages with the clientele Kate catered to, older men who needed comforting more than eroticism. They were frightened to begin with, being seen entering the Tenderloin frightened them more, and the rowdyness of the district had them terrified. Setting up in a quieter neighborhood made sense, provided the location was not overly quiet lest the customers begin to feel on display for the biddies peeking from behind their curtains. Michael had no patience for any of it, but Kate had asked him, and for the time being he was the only man she trusted who had the brains to do the job properly. There was more to it than inspecting a building, but that would come later, if Michael approved the deal. The broker representing the seller would not have Kate's signature until he agreed that the salesman's commission would revert to her designee, who was Michael. It was just Kate's way—she never missed an opportunity. Once, annoyed with another similarly cheap trick, Michael accused Kate of still having the first dollar she had ever made. She laughed and admitted that she probably did have it, and she added, because she understood his meaning and because she knew him as well as he knew her, "If you made yours the way I made mine, you'd have it, too."

And there it stood, and had stood, for more than five years; and if the finagling or her love life or her too-frequent pose as an ignoramus bothered him, it was because he had forgotten that they had been in love with each other once and that she had backed away as well as she could under the circumstances and had held the friendship together for longer than he cared to think.

He had come to a crisis after Westfield's death; perhaps it had taken six months to come out fully and another six months for him to realize that instead of loving her as he had wanted, he had been using her mercilessly. Part of it had been the way she had wanted to love him, the way she had loved every man perhaps, from Westfield to the latest, a lunatic silver king out of Colorado named Johnson. How many times had Michael seen it? He had lost count. She would stare up into the man's eyes dreamily, moonily, self-sacrificing: when she loved, she thought there should be nothing left of Kate Regan the whore, madam, and wealthy young woman, and she became infantile, devoted as a puppy. A man would learn soon enough that she would suffer indignities, and a man full of anger and irresolvable hatreds would learn in his course that she had no limit. Johnson had cornered Michael not long ago, and his conversation, or rather the conversation he'd wanted, had drifted toward that very subject, reminding Michael miserably of his own experience with her. Johnson had been assured long before that Michael and Kate had never been lovers. It was a late winter afternoon, and the two men were sitting in her parlor.

"It's a strange thing for a gal of her background, but I think she'll do anything I want."

Michael stared at him evenly. "I'm not completely at ease with this sort of talk, Mr. Johnson, particularly in the lady's own house."

"Yeah, I know what you mean." Johnson's big mitt seized his drink. "Sorry. Ah, women are different from us," he said lamely.

Michael gave him a reassuring smile. Johnson was a beefy man with small eyes and a fringe of curly yellow hair; he was twenty years Kate's senior. Although Kate insisted it was not true, he looked like a man who could enjoy a bit of cruelty now and then. The suggestion made Michael unhappy, and not completely for her sake: after Westfield's death he had used everything he had known to make her love him and had taken advantage of her to absorb his rage. After six months of filling her life with himself, he disappeared, huddling in his apartment, bitter and hurt. One afternoon he began to weep and, for the next month, almost nightly, he cried like a baby.

The following fall he was almost over it, still ashamed of himself, afraid to call her, when she found him. She understood, she said; he was right to break it off. She was calm, she insisted, but she was really under tight control, stumbling over words, her hands shaking. She wanted to be friends; it was important to her. What had happened between them had had to do with Westfield and she wanted them to get over it. But first she wanted them to be friends—did he understand?

He said yes, but he thought the truth was that they had gotten past Westfield and their grief and in the last months they had been trying to hold it together when in too many ways they were just sick of each other. He had wanted her to read really good books and she had fought him. There were too many differences between them. He didn't like too many of the things he felt, and finally he didn't like himself. He said nothing, and got out of the chair to make a cup of tea, not even bothering to indicate that the conversation had somehow ended—the last cruelty; really, the ultimate indignity. In that way they abandoned it forever, and it was a shameful moment for him, but before the next year was out he saw that dumb look in her eyes again, when she introduced him to her new lover. This one knew the truth about them, and he gloated a bit, strutting his stuff—it was all Michael needed to see to be convinced that this new one was punishing her, taking her over, leaving nothing left. It made Michael's skin crawl, but he had to see that it was what she understood by love, or wanted to understand, in the way she understood what she wanted about business or the books he read.

But out of that sad little epilogue they began to become real friends. She told him her secrets, secrets within secrets: she entertained the fathers of the girls he pursued—when she warned him off and he ignored her, he inevitably learned that he should have paid attention. She called him with Wall Street information, which was never wrong. There were real estate deals and, as often, chances to buy things that had disappeared from the docks.

From his side there were the horses, and when he couldn't reach her, he put her bet down anyway; if the horse ran out, he didn't bother to mention it. He used her place when he wanted to get a game together for some visiting fireman, collecting a fee for her, and when he had an exceptionally good night, he would send part of his winnings around to her. He told her to think of it as insurance; as long as he had her on his side, he would not worry about going bust. He had never come near it, never even falling behind for long, but he meant what he said. Because she was there he felt he had reserves, a feeling he did not get with any of the Westfields. In fact, she was the only one he knew who could tend to business as well as he could, and the more he thought of it, the more important to him she became.

But one Christmas she sent around as a present one of the prettiest girls he had ever seen, and when he called Kate to say thank you, but no, thank you, she fell back on coarseness and stupidity and he accused her of not understanding him; but on another occasion, after hearing of a girl he was interested in, a schoolteacher who wore eyeglasses and liked picnics, she exclaimed, "Do you know what you really want, you dumb son of a bitch? You want a goddamned *old maid!*"

He had heard something like that before, from Westfield.

Having to see the colonel and running for Kate what was hardly more than a boy's errand would have been enough for him to dismiss the day as a waste, but the fact was that he himself had been at sixes and sevens for months, a kind of doldrums of the spirit. He had become a man who needed goals, or, at least, a plan, to bring pleasure from life. He had assets approaching two hundred thousand in cash, real estate, and some stock, and a basic income of more than seven hundred a month, which, with reasonable luck, often went over a thousand—enough, anyway, to keep Louise from spending capital. That he was there to help her when her own children could not gave him only the satisfaction of having proved himself. He felt sorry for all of them, Julie, Roger, Thomas, and Ethel: they were going down to disaster like so many others. They could do no more than stand by helplessly while Louise's security disappeared like snow blown away by the wind. They really didn't care. They were all worse, as if it went beyond economics and they had lost the last shred of their youth—or had tried to hold it too long. Thomas owed him five thousand dollars; Michael never expected to see it again. Fleming had changed jobs three times in the past three years. Julie kept up appearances by saying he was doing as well as ever, but Michael, asking a question here and there, had learned the reality, which was terrible. They were living on half of what he had made as recently as two years ago. Julie lived behind so many façades that Michael was curious to see if she would ever tell the truth again. He supposed he wanted some kind of petty revenge, thinking like that, but she had not spoken a genuinely civil word to him since the night before her wedding.

With Ethel in the family Julie could have relaxed a bit, or let the matter drop entirely. Thomas had needed money within two years of his father's death, and he had decided, in the flush of his newly acquired power and wisdom, to marry it; but his girth and inexperience had put him at a disadvantage. From Michael's viewpoint Ethel seemed acceptable enough for someone with as little to offer as Thomas, but from the start Louise had had her suspicions.

"Michael, he's making a mistake! The girl has absolutely *no* breeding!"

He couldn't help laughing out loud. "And you want *me* to tell him that?"

It took her a moment to realize what she had said. "Michael, the truth of the matter is that you're the first real gentleman in the family since my father died, and as much as I respect his memory, I honestly believe that you outdo him."

He had come to the conclusion that she was a woman whose life seemed to have gone along well enough but who knew that it had gone from bad to worse. What he admired about her was that she had carried herself through it all with unflagging dignity, exactly the sort of behavior she described as gentlemanly in men. She never seemed to think of it, but whatever her limitations, she was her own best example of what she wanted to see in others. Michael suspected that she would have made her choices in life differently, and she now saw herself as what she needed to be. But he wondered if she would be willing to impose the precarious balances of her inner life on others if she could be brought to understand how much they were a part of the conduct she seemed to admire so much.

Whatever her limitations, she had been able to see as no other in the family what Ethel would become in less than a year after the wedding. (She had not been able to see that Ethel's father would be one of the first of the new rich to feel the pressure of the hard times or that it would determine the direction Ethel would take. Thomas had no luck at all: there was only enough money to keep him going bankrupt slowly, instead of with a thud.) In any event, Ethel brayed.

"Michael has all the money in this family! Don't you, Michael? How much are you worth now? When are you getting married? You're going to be some catch once you make up your mind. I'd like to see what you bring home."

She could have said every word with her mouth full. Thomas was doomed: his own stupendous size had been all the excuse she needed to stuff herself thirty pounds' worth in that first year alone. Now she nearly matched him, a woman as big as a horsecar—as Michael had once said to Julie so that the description had stuck, a joke among the Westfields. But as much as her proximity provided a continuing source of laughter in their family life, Ethel's actual presence was still an ordeal for all of them. Julie's two children kept away from her, her own three simply cowered, and at the end of any family gathering all five were just impossible. She bellowed and whooped and never noticed a thing. Mostly Michael was embarrassed for Thomas, for out of Ethel's mouth seemed to come all the resentments and hatreds Michael could see behind Thomas's eyes. Thomas was already brought low: it was not enough that his physical condition hinted how badly life had whipped him; his wife's mouth seemed to strip him naked for everyone to see.

"Michael? You're not going to be a racetrack judge after all? Well, it only proves you're human—you have to learn to take the bad with the good, just like the rest of us. Besides, what was the honor of going to Canada?"

That had been last year, and it had stung; he had wanted the judgeship very much, from the moment he had heard he was being considered for it. By the end of six weeks, when he learned that he had been passed over in favor of an older man from Boston, he had managed to convince himself that he wanted very much to spend June and July of every year in Toronto. The judgeship would have taken him out of New York for most of the hot weather, he would not have missed Saratoga, and the appointment would have signaled his emergence as one of the first-rank sports journalists.

By the fall he had gotten it behind him, but with the start of the year he found himself wondering what he would have done if he had been chosen. What would he have reached for next? The recognition would come eventually, for he was certainly good enough to warrant it; but how really important to him was it? Because he recognized that he would have turned his attention elsewhere quickly enough, he was able to see that the thing itself had no value for him, that it was just a suddenly foresee-able next step in some mysterious climb upward—just upward. Why? He saw it as so much pointless thrashing. Where was he going? Was he going anywhere at all?

Or was it that he was still trying to move away from his parents' deaths? He had never been able to learn anything about Moran, and through the years he supposed he had tried everything. One of the crime reporters on the paper had a friend on the force check the records, and there was nothing. Michael had even gone to the hotel on Seventeenth Street, but the registers for 1877—and '78 and '79, for that matter—had been lost or destroyed years before. It was all foolishness, but because he was still not satisfied with what he knew of that night in December of 1876, it pursued him, dogged him—and gave him nightmares yet.

He could not remember the nightmares, but he wanted to think they were dreams of running. He was running with his parents; they were running together. In life they had run away from Liverpool, and they were planning to run away from New York. The violence had caught up with them, and he was running still, probably because he did not know any other way to organize his existence. He had been running ever since he could remember. He had been running all his life.

V

Doldrums of the spirit. He would be carried out of them by precisely what had carried him in, something to engage his attention. He knew it. By April he had smiled over it a dozen times, and on the afternoon he had decided to stop off at his mother's to postpone scouting the location of Kate's new whorehouse and seeing the colonel, the proposition—that the cure of his illness was another, stronger dose of the disease—was necessarily in the forefront of his mind. (He had begun introducing Louise as his mother years ago, a natural and logical solution to the problem of dealing with people who had no need to know their business; the word had fallen into his conversation that way, and finally he had begun addressing her as "Mother," trying not to think of it and hoping she wouldn't speak of it: she hadn't, ever. Not to him.) Stepping into the house and discovering that she had given it over to another of her cultural afternoons and that Julie, Thomas, and Ethel were in attendance had caused him to laugh aloud. There was really no way to win today, and there was nothing he could do but cut his losses. Louise was pleased to see him, grateful with that gratitude she had been showing him of late that made him so unhappy, that feeling that she believed he was too busy or important for her. Did he want to meet their guest of honor, the speaker for the afternoon? Absolutely not—in the past they had proved to be little peacocks strutting in even littler moments of glory. Figuring to beat his retreat before the lecture began, Michael stationed himself by the fireplace where he would be away from Thomas and Ethel and still see and be seen by the young ladies. Soon enough Julie came through, bearing for him in her left hand a glass of a punch he recognized and which he would as soon have avoided. Perhaps she knew it because as she handed it to him she gave him the sweetest smile.

"Don't you get tired of putting yourself on display, brother dear?"

He arched his brow. "Really?"

"Oh? Am I about to get a glimpse of the real you?"

"You're feeling playful," he said.

Now she peeked over her own glass. She did not know how predictable she had become, a travesty of her younger self. She thought that his vexation with her had to do with some deep emotion she still aroused, but what he felt with her was annoyance. Putting himself on display? She had no idea how far he could take it. He yawned and stretched his arms out with a deliberate indolence and propped his elbows on the mantel. His unbuttoned jacket swung open wide to give an unobstructed view of his vest so that the entire effect was the same as if he had been in his shirt-sleeves, dress that was jarringly inappropriate in such polite mixed company. "Tired? Julie, I get *very* tired."

She understood. "I don't think obviously lewd tactics will work in this gathering. These girls won't understand what you're doing."

He smiled. "Oh, yes, they will."

"And they'll come running up to you? Is that what happens?"

"They give themselves away. There's something in their eyes."

She sneered. "Gamblers' tricks. Is that why you're here, to test your skill? Oh, Michael, surely you have something better to do with your time."

"I don't know that that's so. I'm uptown on business, and I thought I'd look in. I didn't know that anything was happening this afternoon." Perhaps she was listening; it didn't matter. He was telling her the truth. Taking a look at the life on a streetcorner? Trying to elude the hoary clutches of the depraved colonel? Michael was being obscure mostly because of Kate, of whom the Westfields, after so many years, still knew nothing. The time when any of them could have made the connection with Westfield had passed long since, but Michael remained on his guard. The woman chatting by the window loved him, and as much as he loved Westfield, understood him, wept for him, he was not going to permit him to reach from beyond the grave to hurt her. It was all pointless anyway, running a whore's errand; given the way he felt about it, it would almost be fitting if Louise discovered through such stupidity that he was the living proof of her late husband's deceit. If Julie learned of Kate, she would see that it got to her mother. While Julie's eyes were elsewhere, Michael looked at her. She was not the only young married woman to indicate to him that she thought there was something *immature* about remaining unmarried. He made them nervous; until his case was settled, all was not right with their world. More than their proselytizing put him off; they did it themselves with their nervousness. They had married too young, too early in their lives, and only partly for love, no matter what they thought. Fashion, a fit of personal pique—Julie was not original or even rare. She had never been anything but commonplace. She had descended to an uncertain parody of her own girlhood, and she wanted his endorsement through a marriage to a girl like her.

"What is so amusing?"

"According to a friend, my lewd tactics, as you call them, would be wasted on the girl I'm really looking for."

"And who is that?"

"The opinion is that I'm searching for an old maid—"

"That's right!" She grasped his arm. "The last time Thomas asked if you had seen any more of your schoolteacher friend, Mother and I saw something on your face and we argued about it later. While I was still angry with her, I thought it would serve you both right if you married an Emily Reese."

"And who is Emily Reese?" He was amused; he wanted to know how her mind worked.

"Oh, she'll be here. Is she already? She might have heard me. No. Good. Well, she fits the description, but you wouldn't like her. She's intelligent, incredibly rich, but terribly stuck-up! Every time she opens her mouth she just shouts that she knows she's better than you are."

"Is she pretty?"

"God, no. She wears eyeglasses. So plain and washed-out—" Julie moved close and whispered, "See for yourself. She's out in the hall right now, giving Hannah her sweater."

He laughed. "I think she's rather handsome."

"You're probably thinking of unpinning her hair. You see her as a nice little trophy—"

Perhaps, but not with her hair unpinned; he wanted to know her, but more slowly than that, more carefully. She was not happy, but there was a clarity and innocence of intention. Didn't his sister and the other young ladies see it? The combination of his own thoughts and Julie's remarks suddenly caught him, and he imagined kissing Emily Reese. He looked away from her as she stepped toward the wide doorway to the room, and as quietly as he could, so Julie would not hear, he drew his breath.

But she heard. She had difficulty concealing a smile as she searched his eyes. "I really don't think I'm going to let you forget this."

"Are you going to tell your friends—her friends?" He was having trouble keeping his eyes from the door.

"Oh, I might. You're making a mistake. No one can get close to her."

She was staring at him—not Julie, the girl: Emily Reese? Well, Emily Reese was standing in the doorway staring at him. Could she know they were talking about her? He took Julie's wrist before she could see what was happening—*she* would embarrass the girl. Julie was still willing to study him like a schoolgirl being entertained, just *enchanted* by the turn of events. "You're wrong about her," he said. "You're being very unfair."

"Oh, no, I'm not. She thinks she's better than everybody else—you're not the only one who can play that game. You're going to suffer, believe me. Is that the kind of man you are? Do you enjoy suffering?"

"No, I don't. And I'm so certain that I'm not going to be treated that way by her that I think I'll talk with her for the time remaining before the lecture."

"And leave me here alone? You deserve everything you're going to get."

He started to turn away from her. "You've forgotten who taught me what I know about the kind of suffering you mean. Now smile, no matter what you say—you don't want this girl thinking badly of you." He had been trying to put her in her place, but as he looked to the girl and saw in the next split second that Emily Reese was not really anyone Julie had to fear, even when she suspected she was trespassed upon, something strange happened: Emily Reese gave herself away, like all the others he had ever seen, and with a force so astonishing he could feel it himself. How did anyone believe she thought she was better than everybody else? The unhappiness in her eyes was that of someone utterly defenseless. It was twelve feet across the room, and he raised his hand, as if she wanted to run and he had to make her wait. As he moved he kept his eyes on her, afraid to do otherwise, not because he knew he might make a fool of himself if he looked to see that he was not stumbling over his own feet, but because he realized that something done wrong, badly or not bravely enough could break the spell. It *was* a spell, a small, precious moment extending itself—how long could it last? How long did it have to last? When he was in front of her, he stood very stiffly, his hands at his sides.

"Miss Reese? My name is Michael Westfield. I asked my sister to tell me your name—"

"Why?"

Since he had lied, he had no reply. She seemed to want to understand him instantly; she was studying him so closely. "Frankly, my sister wants me to get married, and she suggested you."

"Your sister doesn't like you. She doesn't like me. Is this a game, Mr. Westfield?"

"No, it most certainly is not."

"Then is it a proposal?"

He hesitated: had she been unfair? Had he said anything that warranted less? Now she smiled—*smiled!* So he said yes.

"Very well, I'll consider it. Now what about your sister? I know how she feels about me. Why did she suggest me?"

"My sister has nothing to do with this. You're right in what you said, and I would like very much to let it go at that. I came by today to see my mother, not knowing that there was to be a lecture, and I can't stay. Even if I could, I wouldn't now, not being able to talk to you—"

"Blarney, Mr. Westfield? I thought you were talking marriage."

"The truth, Miss Reese. The point is, I'll have to leave soon, and I'd like to be able to call on you."

"Why?"

"What do you mean, why?"

"What will happen? Will you take me to dinner and tell me about yourself? And on the basis of what you tell me, shall I make up my mind? Oh, Mr. Westfield, you've already made me a better offer."

"Which you said you would consider."

"All right, then." She stood still, watching him, waiting to be invited into his life. He was absolutely shocked.

"Miss Reese, what I have to do will tell you all you need to know about the kind of man you seem to want to place so much trust in. Unless your interest in the lecture is keen, why don't you accompany me on my rounds?"

"Will you buy me tea?"

"I beg your pardon?"

"Will you buy me a cup of tea? I've just arrived and I haven't had any punch, and I'll be thirsty. I always am in the afternoons."

"Miss Reese, it will be my pleasure to buy you tea."

"Do you want to say good-bye to your mother?"

"I don't have to say good-bye if I tell Hannah I've left. My mother knows how I am and my sister will tell her what's happened between us."

"I'm sure she will, Mr. Westfield, but what do you mean, how you *are?*"

He grinned. "Isn't that what you wanted to find out? Do we have any other business here?"

"None that I can think of."

"If that's the case, let's get your sweater and leave. I don't think we should look back at my sister, do you?"

"Absolutely not, but she'll deny to the end of her life that she so much as noticed us."

On the steps they looked at each other and giggled like children. The sun was in Emily's eyes and she was squinting. He would remember forever. They were going to fall in love and they knew it.

VI

No spell ever lasts; the moment always passes. It is the present that continues, and moments, such as they are, one after another, reach toward the future through memory just briefly, then must capture the imagination. The past drifts into legend, and the legend of Michael and Emily falling in love at first sight that is given down to their children and grandchildren is necessarily revised and censored. For one thing, Louise saw them speaking their first words to each other, and it was everything that she thought perfect love to be, whatever it really was, the eye contact, the unconscious, almost-imperceptible movement toward each other, the flush suddenly appearing on Emily's cheeks. As an old lady Louise would say that she had been privileged to see their falling-in-love, that it had been one of the most beautiful events of her life.

A second factor was the absence of Julie, identified in the minds of the children, naturally enough, as their nasty old aunt and only playing at taking her rightful place in the tableau. This was Emily's doing, the result of Michael's asking her for more patience with Julie than she could really muster. Emily was wise to her future sister-in-law. Emily became one of those shrewd wives who knew what she had and trusted no woman. She kept all this to herself, for Michael thought it was a marvel that she was not petty or jealous; and as for his own memory of the afternoon, he lived long enough to laugh with his children about the antics of their aunt. The children knew everything, that Julie had told lie after stupid lie to their grandmother about what had happened between their parents— and then had denied everything, saying that none of it mattered to her. It had been part of the tale for so long that Michael had forgotten how it had come to be told in the first place. Emily was a very shrewd wife, and often when Michael felt he was being loved in a way he did not deserve, she was celebrating another kind of victory.

The third and by far the most important element in the development of the story the children came to know was the decision taken by one of the principals on that same afternoon, a decision that hinged on intuition and obscure reasons.

The invitation to accompany him on his errands tells everything about Michael, and not simply that he saw immediately that it would be smart to tell her as much about himself as he could, as quickly as possible; or that he trusted her that much on what he could see; or even that he knew he wanted her with him, just like that; but that his mental processes were instantaneous, perhaps even involuntary.

He wanted her. She was a beautiful woman, subtle, handsome, and shy. Her body was womanly with a full womanly roundness to her bosom and her hips. Yet she was small; she disappeared beneath him when she stood close enough. Her eyes moved constantly, darting back and forth as if she believed she could see more if she worked harder. And later, when he told her that he won at cards because he knew the other players better than they knew themselves, she said she understood, but when he attempted to engage her in a conversation about it, he had to see that her understanding was perhaps so rudimentary that she had no idea how much she had given herself away.

By then she had met the colonel and had heard of Michael's real parents and what had happened to them, and that Westfield had rescued him. She had been warned that the colonel was liable to say anything to her, and the colonel did not fail: "If you're seen in his company too much, young lady, people will think you're as depraved as he is."

What a thrill! She had had two hours of vicarious high adventure, and now the colonel was confirming that everything Michael had told her was true. She was looking up at Michael, studying him still again. He could not stop touching her. She seemed to take no notice of it, and he could not stop himself from taking her arm, caressing her back. She had grown so at ease with him that he could move her toward him at will; now when she had something she had to say, he brought her closer to him before she spoke.

"Are you depraved, Michael?"

"I suppose I am. I've thought about it. I am," he repeated. "Yes, I am."

She could see that he was serious, but she said, "Well, I'm glad." She glanced at the colonel. "You see? You were right."

The colonel scowled. "I'm beginning to form opinions about you, young lady."

"Good day. We must be going." She hooked Michael's arm. "Come on, you *promised*," she squealed.

Michael gave the colonel a shrug, as if he were helpless to do anything but obey, and headed with her toward the stairs.

Before they reached the next landing, after they heard the latch of the colonel's door, she stopped and he took her arms. He was one step below her so that he could look almost directly into her eyes.

"I'm sorry," she said. "It was all meant as comedy. I know you don't think you're depraved."

"I love you. I want to marry you."

"I'm afraid, Michael. I really am."

She had told him a little about her family; he could see that he would not be able to get her away from them in a straightforward manner. But this was the first either of them had spoken of real feelings—he suddenly realized it, realized that she had said it clearly, sure of herself, when it had burst out of him. He kissed her impulsively, gently, and she could have taken offense just as easily, but she let him taste her full soft lips. She did not resist him, but when he moved back and she saw that he was trying to see into her, she looked away nervously.

"I forgot myself," he thought he heard her say.

"Emily?"

"Nothing." She stepped in front of him to continue down the stairs. He took her arm.

"I shouldn't have done it."

Her eyes were wet. "No one has ever wanted anything from me before. How is it that I know exactly what you want? Why *does* it frighten me so?"

"I'll try not to be so obvious." He was bitterly unhappy with himself.

She touched his cheek with her hand. He took it and kissed it, but she was trembling. He wanted to reassure her, but now he was frightened himself, frightened of losing her. She still did not know about Kate, the role she had played in his rescue from the shelter and, worse, that she had been his only friend worthy of the name for most of his adult life. Would Emily realize that they had to have been lovers once? Even what she knew of life, it was unlikely. In any case, if asked, he would lie. Lie again. His first words to her had been a lie.

He used his intelligence. They could walk the few blocks downtown to the site of Kate's proposed new brothel. He talked about Saratoga and how the frenzy of the place actually restored him. His real parents had wanted to escape the city; Saratoga was all he knew of anyplace else. He had been to Canada, Maryland, and New Orleans for the racing, but he could not help looking at those places as if they were not quite real. He had always reckoned that Saratoga would be in the life he would construct for himself when he was given the chance.

"My father calls Saratoga a hellhole," she said.

"It's true. The people who give me my living can't take their pleasure at all unless they believe they've surrendered to the devil."

"You must never say that to him."

"Life is more dense than many Christians suspect."

"You're as good a Christian as any man."

"Don't think that. When a fool sits down to play cards with me, I figure that he has to take responsibility for himself." He looked down at her. "If you try to change that, I'll finish as if I had never left the shelter."

"Yes, but you must never say these things to my father. Please."

"I never will." Naturally. He planned to use them on him.

Her family loomed in his mind like a mountain. None of them would accept him if he presented himself straightforwardly. Michael didn't know how he was going to do it, but he was going to move her father into his territory so he could *steal* his daughter away from him.

"Now there's more," he said quietly. As he'd planned while he'd blathered about Saratoga, he told her first that Westfield had not executed his business alone, that he had been directed by someone else. Her curiosity piqued, he diverted her attention to the logic of it: there had been so many murders in that area in those days—how would Westfield know of his parents? Why would he care? Michael watched her; she was nodding to indicate that she understood what he was saying, but she was frowning, too, as if she were searching for the answer to his questions.

"Westfield wasn't a man like your father," he said. "Or mine, for that matter."

She looked blank. He was unsure of himself again. He made her face him. "Or me," he said. "Do you understand? I swear to you. He had a mistress, someone very young, who had known me on Lombard Street." He let her study his eyes. "Westfield saved me because he was in love with her, and she wanted it because she was a child. She read about my parents in the papers, and that I had seen them killed. She wanted to do something, and she reached for me in the only way she could. Now she's what I have left of that life. I'm the same for her, and none of the Westfields know it. I want you to know. You *have* to know. She's a prostitute and a madam, Emily. I'm sorry," he added in a whisper.

Although he had planned everything he had said as scrupulously as a burglar studies a darkened house, he found himself in complete disarray. She was staring at him in disbelief and near-terror. It had been too much for her. He had forced everything, and he was left with only the intensity of his need for consolation.

"Are you her lover?"

"Oh, no." It came out a moan, desperate—he had no doubt it would be believed. She had asked the question as if she had never said the words before, as if she had no real idea what a lover was, like a child. He realized that she had gotten it from a book: it was so clear, he almost said it aloud. "We're not lovers, she and I. Her lover is a miner from Colorado."

She paused. He would not have tried such an inept veiling of the truth with someone more sophisticated, and now he wondered if he had been too ingenuous. Suddenly she gave him an odd half-smile. "Do you have a mistress?"

A game? "There's a woman I love."

"Who?"

"You."

She blushed. He wanted to make love to her, and he thought that if there were moments like this when he could make love to her—he did not fail to see that that meant marriage or that he was really thinking of it just that quickly and just that way—he *would* make love to her. They were on Broadway near Eightieth Street, and there were crowds under the budding trees, but he felt her lean against him ever so gently. It was her way of yielding to him, and as shy as it was, it was also brazen for a young lady of her position—who had never done it before, he was sure. He could not touch her lest people suddenly turn their attention to them. "I love you, you know," he said quietly.

"Is there anything more? Is there anything more that you want to tell me, Michael?"

What he had feared about it being too much for her was true, and as he prepared to tell her no he thought of Moran lying dead with the knife in his chest and that saying no would swing the gate shut and lock it; but something of the memory clouded his eyes. "Westfield shot himself," he said. "The other family scandal. It was years later. Julie was already married. I'm the only one in the family who knows with certainty that the two events are connected. Louise suspects—"

"How are they connected?"

"He tried to tell me. I'm talking about what his affair with Kate meant to him. He wanted people to think that he was drinking again, but before that he talked to me about his life. My parents were people who tried to understand themselves, and for a long time I thought Westfield was a fool; but then I saw that he gave me something, too, something special. He believed in something that he discovered wasn't true, and then he wouldn't lie to himself about his mistake."

"I still don't understand."

He could see as much. "He thought he was a weak man and bound to be a burden eventually. He did what he thought was the honorable thing."

"Do you think it has anything to do with you?"

"No. No, I've never thought that."

He had not spoken of his parents or Westfield in years and because he was in her presence—he was that sure of her now—he felt a deep pang of grief. They would have rejoiced in this. He wished they could see her. He started crying and she saw it.

And made her decision, on intuition mostly and for obscure reasons having to do with the future she was beginning to see for herself, one which she wanted to protect. "Don't speak of any of it again to anybody, Michael. Promise me, please. Come to me if you must."

The people who had drawn such promises from him in the past had been already dead, and he felt a start of fear for *her*. "I'll think about it," he said.

"Please. I want you to promise."

More than anything he wanted to avoid those words. "I'll do what you want." Of course it was a promise just the same, and he never regretted it. After their wedding and after their children began to come, and then after David died and finally when he became ill himself, he thought of the promise and more importantly of the woman who had exacted it from him. On all those occasions he came to the conclusion—that is, the moral intersection where everything militates toward only one possible course—that confession would bring him back to the world he had left when his parents had died. And when he became ill and knew what it meant, how the illness would end, he wanted to remove this last element of his estrangement from his own moral center and make his peace with God. By then he had come to believe in God very deeply, the most primitive and profound kind of belief, that all things came from God, the deaths of parents, the death of a child, and that one could find his own peace only if he could accept the will of God. But he had come to understand what Westfield had meant, and his father, too. There was a limit to life itself. He was able to take Emily just so far, for instance. He freed her of her family, but she had never stopped being frightened in her heart. Casting her lot with Michael had cost Emily her family and friends, as little as they were worth, and when he was about to die he saw he was going to abandon her, too, at what was still, he judged, the beginning of her life. He loved her, he loved her; everything he had done from the first day had revolved around his loving her. The wound of David's death had never healed in either of them, and now because he was ill he could see terror in her eyes again. Michael could not imagine the terms on which she could survive his death.

The first afternoon finished on Riverside Drive. It was late, the air growing colder, the sky clouding over, and the river turning dark. They should have quit an hour before; they were so cold they couldn't sustain a conversation. He was walking her home, like a boy. They had already developed an odd little conflict: he wanted to take his pleasure from small things, patiently; she was curious about him and what he was teaching her about the world. Kate's proposed location was just off West End Avenue on Seventy-sixth Street, back downtown again from the colonel's, and it seemed right enough for Kate's purposes, a quiet neighborhood but sufficiently busy to obscure the necessarily abnormally heavy traffic in and out of her brownstone. Michael was prepared to give the problem only the few minutes it deserved, or even a walk-by, later making the details he would pick up anyway seem in Kate's mind like the harvest of a long observation. But Emily was curious—ah, very.

"Would my father visit a place like this?" she said.

"Why ask that?"

"Mr. Westfield—you said *his* family didn't know."

"About Kate. And yes, for a long time the family didn't know. Then he took Thomas to a brothel and everybody knew about that."

"Did he take you?"

"No."

"Why not? He loved *you*."

"He knew I wasn't interested. He took Thomas because he really wanted to hurt my mother—Mrs. Westfield—and show off in front of the boy. It made Thomas worse; it made him smug and cruel."

"Have you ever done it?"

She didn't give a damn about Thomas, which pleased him. "I decided early in my life that I didn't need it. My father didn't need it. He loved my mother."

She hesitated. "Would you tell me if you ever saw my father?"

"Never."

"Why?"

"Because it would only be making trouble for you, me, and him."

"But I'd want to know! You've told me so much already!"

"You don't really understand. I'm sorry, but that's true."

He had to tilt her chin up so he could see her eyes. "You've overwhelmed me," she whispered.

"I'll never do it again."

He meant it, but later, as they were stopped on Riverside Drive, the cold wind buffeting them, he wanted to hold her and kiss her. There were carriages passing and people on the sidewalk across the way, but the light was poor. He turned her around to him, gathered her closer, put his arms around her and kissed her. Their bodies were touching through the layers of their clothing, and he felt her shudder as she gave a tiny muffled squeak of pleasure. When they broke away, he could hear her moan softly.

"That's the second time today," she said. "It happened when I saw you the first time." She rested her head on his chest. "I used to read about it and I never once believed it."

He stroked her back gently and closed his eyes. She did not understand it, and he doubted she would believe him if he told her that it was not necessarily an emblem of love, and he could see how deeply she would be hurt if he took this opportunity to continue her education by explaining that it was precisely what Kate guaranteed her customers. In a little while he would become too afraid for her and the delicacy of her understandings to think of mentioning it again. The further along they went, the more clearly he would see what he meant to her, and without discussing it with her he would withdraw from the list of topics for their conversation how intricately he knew the ways in which people insinuated themselves into each other's hearts. Emily had her illusions about love, but they were illusions in which he could see his own lifelong dream. By kissing her in public he had taken advantage of her again, but he carried from it his sense of a fragile interdependence. He could have told her to keep as their secret her romantic "swoons"—it crossed his mind—but he did not want her ever thinking about the terms in which others might define the experience that she had decided would change her life.

His silence and the reasons for it colored the myth that grew up around their first afternoon—a lovely afternoon, the center of their lives. But it was what they had chosen to make of it as much as anything. The distance between them was more apparent to him later on, but he never forgot that it was what he had chosen because they would be better off for it, just as she had decided within two hours of meeting him that the children they would have would be better off in the world if his past were buried once and for all.

VII

Emily entered her house that late afternoon in a panic. She had left Michael on the corner, promising to see him the following week, putting him off that long for the same reason the panic had seized her. She had been able to see the pain in Michael's eyes, but that a beautiful afternoon should finish in such confusion had plunged her into a depression—she could not turn to him, not for this, not so soon. As suddenly as she had fallen in love, she felt ashamed of herself and unworthy of it.

How could she tell her family of him? She had told them she was going to a lecture. Now she was not even sure she had seen the lecturer. Her behavior had been disgraceful, and if Michael could not see it, he was as big a fool as she. He would be back in a week—*if* he came back—and she had no idea how she would introduce or explain him. She would never withstand the assault of her mother's questions. The thought that he might not come back almost pleased her. She knew what it meant, that she was slipping back into her old view of things. . . .

It was too late. At dinner, with her brothers sitting on the other side of the table, she almost put down her fork and announced, "I met a man today. Michael Westfield." But she didn't; the fork stayed in her hand.

She couldn't eat. She waited until she thought she could get away from the table, and then excused herself. In her room, she thought she would cry, but nothing happened. Whatever she felt, it was locked inside her.

Michael was there in the morning—in her thoughts. For her it was the most extraordinary thing, like the mornings of her birthday or Christmas in her childhood. She lay quietly in her bed for a long while, remembering his face as she had seen it yesterday. She had noticed handsome men before but had never been able to really remember them, not clearly; and this man *was* handsome, too, although others might not think so, deciding that he was too tall, too thin, or that his eyes were too dark or tired. She knew he was handsome with a conviction she had not held about a man before; she seemed to be working out how to argue the point if she had to, and she seemed to be languishing in the delight of it, like a kitten having her belly rubbed.

She saw him everywhere; he filled her thoughts. It was one of her mornings to go downtown to the settlement house, and she resolved to gain control of herself, but she fell into such a reverie on the el that the conductor closed the gates on her stop and she had to ride back north the five blocks from the next station down.

There was a note from him when she got home; it expressed the hope that she had found the previous afternoon as happy and promising as he had, and asked for confirmation of the invitation she had given him to call on her in a week.

How soon did he have to have an answer? "Mother, a gentleman is coming to see me next Tuesday at two o'clock"—would it be so difficult? She would be telling, not asking; if she were normal, she thought, an ordinary girl, all of it would have happened years ago. She replied to Michael that she expected to see him on Tuesday at two, but she said nothing about her feelings about the day before, and she did not speak to her mother. She was still frightened, and because of that more than anything else she was ashamed.

Because she was ashamed and frightened, and because she wanted to help herself and did not know what else to do, for the first time since her childhood she spied on her father. She tried to imagine him in places like Kate's and in the arms of other women. (Since she had no idea of what Kate's place looked like inside, she imagined rooms of red velvet merged indefinitely with lewd settees, and since she had never seen Kate—Kate, to be sure, no one else—she pictured a plump, bosomy woman with dark hair piled high on her head.) She could not imagine her father's behavior, and so the fantasies were still lifes, with her father and the semi-naked Kate close to each other—just close. Their proximity chilled Emily; somehow she felt in jeopardy.

She went through her father's desk, looking for confirmation of the things Michael had said—of Michael's world, really, for as the days passed he began to move away from her again. Presumably he had received her reply. She did not want to hear from him; in fact, she was afraid he would seize her failure to comment on their afternoon as a reason to cancel their appointment. More than anything she wanted *nothing to happen,* as if she had set in motion some complex plan, when in truth she had done nothing at all. She found nothing in her father's desk; he was exactly what he had always represented himself to be. She had to remember that she had been the one to speak of her father in this context, not Michael; it was as if she had wanted to find something wrong not with her father but with Michael himself.

So by Saturday she had fallen into a torpor of indecision, and when she awoke to find that she had to bring Michael back to her through force of will, she nearly cried; it was as if she had lost him already. She felt dead.

She went with her mother to call on her mother's aunt, a woman in her seventies enfeebled by arthritis. Aunt Jenny lived alone on the second floor of a brownstone on Ninth Street and had not negotiated the stairs in years, and calling on her really meant seeing that she was all right. Her daughters did her shopping, but Emily's mother almost invariably saw that something had been forgotten. At the end of the visit, then, the two women would go down to the Avenue and bring it back. Neither could do it alone in the middle of a visit, for that would be insulting. Aunt Jenny was not a woman who took offense easily; she liked to tease and laugh over gossip. Emily's mother felt duty-bound to visit the sick, but she was so grim about it that Emily had begun to wonder if old Aunt Jenny thought her niece a bore. Her niece's daughter, too.

Aunt Jenny had a surprise for Emily. She had heard about the episode at the Westfields'—that as soon as Emily had stepped into the room, young Michael Westfield had walked right up to her, taken her arm, and escorted her out again.

Emily could feel the blood rushing to her face. They were sitting in Aunt Jenny's parlor, the curtains drawn to keep out the afternoon sun. "It wasn't like that," she murmured. Her mother moved forward in the chair.

"You didn't mention this to me!"

"There was nothing to it. I've met him there before. He's a journalist. He wanted to ask me about the settlement house."

Aunt Jenny laughed and patted her lips with her handkerchief. "You can't fool me, young lady. I know that look on your face."

"You never told me about this," her mother said. "If you leave someone's home in the company of a young man, the least you can do is tell your mother so she knows why people are spreading tales."

"No one's spreading tales, Mother."

"No? What do you call this?"

"Now, Margaret," Aunt Jenny said. "I heard it from Katherine. Her daughter-in-law was there."

Emily was afraid to look up. Katherine was Aunt Jenny's daughter; her daughter-in-law was Emily's second cousin by marriage. Emily had not seen her, or worse, had not recognized her; they had not been in each other's company in two years. That she had talked about it meant that Emily and Michael had really caused a stir.

"A journalist?" her mother demanded. "For whom?"

"The *World.*"

"That terrible sheet! I wouldn't have it in the house."

"He's coming to call on Tuesday."

"Tuesday? When did you expect to tell me?"

"I just did." Emily glanced up. Aunt Jenny found the situation amusing.

"This is very improper, Emily," her mother said. "Is he coming in connection with a story he's writing?"

Aunt Jenny laughed silently, covering her mouth; her false teeth didn't fit her and sometimes they fell out. "Don't be a goose, Margaret! Emily has a *beau!*"

Her mother snorted.

There was a lecture on the el as they rode home, and a glare through dinner, but her mother said nothing more. On Monday Emily mailed a note to Michael explaining her lie. At dinner that night, the eve of his arrival, Emily expected that her father would have something to say, but he didn't, and she wondered if her mother had even told him anything. If she was playing a waiting game, Emily could not understand why. There was no question that what had happened was improper, and her mother could snuff it out any time, with the right word to her father.

But nothing; in the dining room Emily looked at them all as though through a stereopticon: her father was regaling her brothers with a story of some funny Texan who had come into the bank today, demanding to see the president; and her mother was attending to the maid's service of the meal. It was an odd and unnerving feeling; while Michael had moved away from her, she had moved away from her family. She was outside them now, and if he did not marry her, she would be as alone as Aunt Jenny down on Ninth Street.

Michael arrived at one minute after two the following afternoon, bearing candy and flowers. He was laughing as he gave them to her, and when the maid turned to put his hat away, he whispered, "I'm sorry, but I want you to have everything."

He could walk out with her again, on *her* mother this time, she was so pleased. "Why are you apologizing?"

"Because I want so much for you to understand me that I'm no longer sure how you'll receive what I do."

She closed her eyes and breathed the fragrance of the spring blossoms. She let the perfume fill her lungs, then looked up at him. She wanted to say, "I'll tell you when you've gone wrong, Michael," but nothing would come out, nothing witty or clever, and she smiled a little and turned away.

Her mother was waiting for them in the parlor, waiting. "I want to meet your young man," she had announced at noon. She knew that Michael was the youngest Westfield, and possibly she expected someone like her own second son or someone more nearly Emily's own age. Emily was holding her flowers and smiling when she introduced him. Her mother looked startled; her first words weren't clear. She had put on a severe-looking black dress and pulled her hair back into a perfect tight bun, as if the harsh picture of a mother would chasten a "young man." Michael smiled easily, as if she were his equal; he understood her completely.

"Emily tells me that you're a journalist."

"A sports journalist."

"Emily told me that you were writing a story about the settlement house. Sit down, sit down," she announced suddenly. "Please, Emily, why don't you take care of your lovely flowers and see about the tea? I thought I was going to stay, but I'm not." As Emily started toward the door, she saw her mother turn to Michael with the biggest, most polite smile Emily had seen in years.

"Actually, Mrs. Reese," she heard Michael begin, "the sort of story I've been researching can run in the newspaper at any time. It would be about the sports programs of the settlement houses." Emily stopped and looked back: Michael kept his eyes on her mother. "This morning I found myself reading what had already been written on the subject; very little has been done. You see, writing about sports, and specifically horse racing, has left me with the desire to do something more useful—"

Emily stepped from the room, hiding her grin until she was safely out of her mother's sight. He was *lovely,* veiling the most subtle of messages, sensing at once that he had an advantage over her mother. Why was he so cocky? It was as if he were playing a game with Emily. He knew how difficult it was going to be, but he had come in as if he owned the place.

When she returned with the flowers in a vase, her mother was gone. "The tea will be right along," she said.

"Your mother said she had to leave."

Emily went to the window. Her mother would be around the corner even if she had left only a minute ago. "She had nothing to do. I know that she got everything out of the way this morning."

"She seemed flustered."

"Why are you smiling? What did you say to her?"

"I told her how old I was and how much I made and how much I was worth."

"*Why?*"

"She asked. So help me. She said she expected me to be a younger man."

"I could see that."

"Then she asked me about my financial condition. I drew her into it. After I told her that I was twenty-nine, she said she thought I must be fairly well settled by now. I asked her if she meant my financial condition; she said, well, yes, and I told her. She said I was a wealthy young man and excused herself." He chuckled. "Does she have difficulty speaking?"

"No—no, you *fool!* You know perfectly well that you had the better of her the moment you walked through the door. How did you do it?"

"I kept remembering I was looking at a banker's wife. Do you think she was really interested in how much money I have, or was she being polite?"

She could feel herself blushing. "Stop *smirking!*"

"All right, it was all in the eyes. She seemed like a person used to staring other people down, so I gave her a dose of her own medicine. She never found me not looking at her. I do it in poker games all the time."

"Do you?"

"Sure. Ah, I missed you. Last Tuesday was the happiest afternoon of my life."

She stared at him, realizing he could manipulate her as easily as her mother. "How is the colonel?"

"I suppose he's managed to live another week. Never mind. If I may, I'd like to ask you to invite me to dinner tomorrow night." He was sitting on the sofa opposite her, and now he leaned forward, put his elbows on his knees, and clasped his hands. The movement brought him so much closer to her that she sat back straighter in her chair.

"Emily, I've thought about it all week, and there's nothing to be done but approach this directly, no matter what I do for a living. They have to see the kind of man I am."

She could not move her hands from her lap, she was so afraid they would start shaking. "all right. Unless I telephone or send a note."

"I'm not going to open my mail or answer the telephone," he said. "I'll be here tomorrow."

"Seven-thirty."

He was up from the sofa. He came around the table, leaned over and kissed her, pressing his lips to her lips. He was wearing a beautiful medium-blue suit; she wanted to reach up and touch the fabric, but then they heard the rattling of the tea service on the silver tray. Michael was just getting seated again when the maid entered. The girl saw, or could guess, what had been going on.

"You did send me to the morgue on settlement house sports," he said. "I thought I ought to be ready with more than you could have said."

"They're gabbling about us. My great-aunt knew all about it on Satur-day."

"I wasn't going to bring it up. My mother reported that we had them all buzzing."

"One more thing to live with," she said. "They've been buzzing about me for years."

"I don't care. Don't you understand these people? It's how they fill their lives. When they're out of my sight, I never give them a thought. If gossip bothers you, I'll try not to bring any more down on us."

"I've always said I didn't care." She smiled at him. "But I've never believed it myself. I've always been afraid."

"How do you think your father will respond now?"

"If she likes you too much, he may decide to be contrary. He does that every once in a while, but usually he backs down."

"How does he respond to unpleasant shocks in general?"

"That's an odd question."

"We'll do better if I knew what to expect. Any clue at all will help."

"We never have unpleasant shocks in the household. It's the way things are organized here. I'm sorry, but it's true."

He smiled. "It's all right. We can talk about something else."

He stayed another hour. She was surprised to find that, by her stan-dards, he was well read and knew the theater. They talked about the plays they had seen during the past season. He asked if she liked musical comedy.

"My father has his opinions," she said. "I would love to see Gilbert and Sullivan, though."

"Well, soon enough you'll be able to see for yourself just how good they are."

She sat back. It had not occurred to her in such specific terms that she would be able to determine her life for herself—or have a voice in it, at least. He sensed what she was thinking. "I mean what I say, Emily." He stood up. "It's late, and if tomorrow isn't a success, then all this is a dream best forgotten."

"I'm afraid of you, you know."

"It's because you want to be."

"I'm no bargain."

"I would have you believe the same of me. I really would."

"You're wrong about me. I have no courage. I'm ugly and sickly—look at me."

He kissed her forehead. "You don't know the truth about yourself."

"Suppose you lose? Suppose you lose?"

"Tomorrow? Oh, I'll win. You still don't understand what a gambler is."

VIII

He arrived on time the next evening and stepped into the scene Emily had prepared for him, although she would have denied it. It was more than their curiosity; Emily had asserted herself in ways she would not have recognized even if Michael had been able to call her attention to them. The Reese men understood that this dinner was important to the family's only girl. She had stopped them all at dinner the night before, letting her voice suddenly fill a lull in their conversation, the voice so carefully modulated that the dullest of them—(the older brother; neither of the boys having any real intelligence, taking after their mother as Emily took after her father: all this Michael puzzled out that night)—the dullest, then, knew at once that the words being spoken, announced, had been chosen with great care. "I have invited someone for dinner tomorrow. A gentleman. I would like everybody to meet him."

She was bleeding. She had been so frightened that she had torn away a fingernail clutching her napkin. As Michael had begun to learn, she had no sense of herself when she was frightened. Her father broke the silence.

"What time?"

"Seven-thirty."

"We'll all be here."

And they were, apprehensive for her, they thought, none of them seeing how effectively she had closed off discussion. Michael learned this, too, in due course, and it confirmed his suspicion about the strength of her will. But she was afraid of life and had to move on a thing slowly. She saw herself in terms of limitations—in that way as well as others she never understood what it meant to be a gambler.

She was on the edge of terror all night, having expected no less. Her father and brothers were polite, hesitant, perhaps intimidated by Michael's height and age. They were drinking sherry, the women nothing—sherry itself being a rarity in the Reese household. Her father fell into a conversational style that made Emily wonder if Michael would take offense—question after question, as if Michael had appeared at his bank for a loan. But Michael seemed comfortable, if a bit formal. Possibly because she was looking for it, she saw flashes of his humor that made her worry, for he made it clear that he was laughing not at what was being said but at the fact that it was being said at all. He was giving these strangers their due: all he wanted was her.

Her father shifted in his chair. "I must confess, Mr. Westfield, that I've never seen the attraction of horse racing."

"Well, we're all different, Mr. Reese, so I'm sure you can appreciate the fact that I'm just as unresponsive to banking."

Her father smiled. "My guess would have been that you would be interested at least in the venture-capital aspect of banking."

"Not at all. Too many variables, too many risks."

"Isn't that the situation in racing horses?"

"Within limits, horses can be read and understood on the basis of their lineage and past performance. You have to understand that in handicapping, the object is to minimize risk."

"Suppose you have two horses that are nearly equal in ability?"

"Pass the race."

"Doesn't that happen frequently?"

"Most of the time."

"But don't you select horses on a daily basis?"

"The readers insist. But if they read my column regularly, they know that I try to teach them to pick their opportunities."

"Some people think that gambling is a sin, you know," her father said.

"The way most people gamble, it is."

Her father laughed. "I like that. It doesn't address itself to the question, but I like it."

"It does. Most people throw their money away in everything, not just gambling. And that's a sin."

"And you don't mind taking that money. I mean, if you gamble on horse races yourself, then the money they lose comes to you in the form of winnings from the bookmakers, doesn't it? Where's the morality in that?"

"One can't identify morality unless one can identify the structure behind it. I'm still a young man, but I'm no longer a boy, and I've been studying this for some years. It seems to me that only a very few people are anything but slaves to their situations. They never use the intelligence God gave them in their lives, much less in what they do with their money."

"Do you believe in God, Mr. Westfield?"

"I'm not sure I know what belief is, Mr. Reese. I think a lot about God, and I ask myself why the world is the way it is."

"Perhaps the message there is to do more good in the world oneself."

"I'm afraid that the only thing I do would make you unhappy."

An eyebrow shot up. "Which is?"

"I make interest-free personal loans to friends."

"Why?"

"The reasons they needed the money were more important than the money itself. I'll get it back."

"How much do you have out?"

"Nine thousand."

Mr. Reese glanced at Emily. "Now that does make me unhappy." She looked down, afraid her father was going to laugh at Michael. She was a banker's daughter and knew what her father was thinking: to contemplate marriage to a man with nine thousand out in interest-free and probably unsecured personal notes was to court insanity, if not disaster. When Emily raised her eyes again, her father was shaking his head at Michael in amused disbelief, but she knew that his real feelings were not so benign. "Well, I suppose you know if you can afford it," he said.

"Yes, I do," Michael said.

There was no way of knowing what Mrs. Reese might have told him about the previous afternoon. She might have decided to tell her husband nothing. She was a devious woman, and there was no point in wondering why. Devious people often did devious things simply to keep the pot boiling.

Dinner was served. Michael was seated between Emily and her mother, and for a while his conversation was directed toward Mrs. Reese. Emily's brothers wanted to hear the latest from their father about the mad cowboy who had started coming into the bank on Monday, a Coloradan, it turned out, not a Texan. Emily was trying to listen to Michael telling her mother about Mrs. Westfield and how she had come to involve herself in volunteer work and fund-raising. Suddenly he stopped and snapped his head around to Emily's father. His eyes were dark and searching.

"Excuse me, Mr. Reese, I couldn't help overhearing your conversation. The man you're talking about—does he wear an emerald-and-diamond pinky ring?"

"Yes. Do you know him?"

"Well enough," Michael said.

"That doesn't sound enthusiastic." He was patronizing Michael.

"It isn't."

"Would you mind telling me why?"

"I would be *relieved* to tell you why, if I could have the opportunity," Michael said.

"Very good. Immediately after dinner."

Michael nodded and turned again to Mrs. Reese. Emily wanted to ask him how he had been able to identify the man from her father's conversation, but of course she couldn't. For a few minutes more she sifted through the things she could remember her father having said, but for the life of her she couldn't find a thing that would serve as an identifying characteristic of anybody.

After dinner Michael and her father went into the study, just the two of them, and closed the door behind them. In fifteen minutes Mr. Reese appeared—for sherry, he said with a quick tight smile—and then the door closed again.

An hour went by.

Her father came out and called her. "Mr. Westfield has something to tell you," he said grimly.

Michael was standing in the middle of the room. His eyes were on Mr. Reese, who closed the door behind them. Michael touched his moustache with his knuckle.

"Emily, your father has given me permission to speak to you because, as a result of the work I do, he questions my integrity." He was looking directly into her eyes; it was clear that he wanted her to be still until he could speak his piece. "You know enough about me from all the things I've told you to believe me when I say I can appreciate your father's position as if it were my own." There had been a sly emphasis on "*all* the things"— he wanted her to take his secrets into account. Had he told her father? Secrets upon secrets. She was convinced that Michael had not done badly with her father, but how? Who was he, that he could have brought her father around so quickly?

"Your father objects to me on two counts, the first being the shadow my employment would seem to cast on my character, and the second being my age. At twenty-nine I may be too old for you—"

"Oh, no." She put her hand to her mouth, her eyes popping wide. The words had jumped out. Michael was looking at the floor, all but frowning in the effort to keep his composure, but she could see the color coming to his cheeks.

"However, and provided I do not make a pest of myself in the process, he will allow me to call on you and escort you in public, if it pleases you."

She frowned and turned to her father. "If you disapprove of him, why will you let him see me?"

He studied Michael. "I am hoping your friend will tell you."

Michael smiled. "Our conversation began on the subject I raised at the table. It's enough to say that I believe that the gentleman from Colorado is in a situation that could cause your father serious embarrassment. As you saw earlier, your father is interested in what makes me tick, and in trying to explain how I had come to my belief about the Coloradan, I opened the door to a conversation about how I make my living. Your father thinks I take advantage of people. And that I give away my money, in his phrase, to salve a guilty conscience."

Yes, she thought, if you want to forget that his real parents were murdered and that he is still doing the thing forced on him by that event: fighting to stay alive. Beneath the graceful manners and the lovely conversation, the vanity that was finally charming and the arrogance that made him give away his money and made her really worry about him, he was only fighting to stay alive. The thing that would make her father understand him was the one thing that she would not tell him. *She* wanted it forgotten. She wanted it to stop filling Michael's eyes as it was doing this very moment.

"There's more," Michael said, "but right now I would like to ask you to be my guest at Luchow's this Sunday evening."

She smiled. "Yes. Now tell me the rest."

"Like you, I want to assure your parents that our friendship will not be bad for you. They don't know me, and I think you'll agree that you don't know me well—"

She disagreed violently—she wanted to shout it.

"Your father has asked me to proceed on the basis that there are no understandings between us and that I won't try to develop any for at least a year. It doesn't have to do with your age, but your father wants a year." Suddenly he seemed to be pleading with her, so much that his words didn't penetrate immediately. "I've given my word. This is the last conversation we'll have about ourselves for a year. It's the way it has to be."

A *year*—such a cruel, unnatural thing to impose on them! She had not begun to think of them in terms of time. She had not imagined herself married to Michael by Christmas, as she could have done; but now she was crushed by time, the long stretch of months—she would watch the seasons change!—during which they would not even be able to dream, much less talk. Her father seemed not just unaware of what he had done but positively numb. Since Wednesday, he had had nothing to say about Michael. He smiled and said good-morning at breakfast and good-evening at dinner, and in her anger with him she wanted to believe he was gloating, certain he had driven Michael off. She would see him Sunday; she was sure he would not fail her—the idea that he *could* fail her made her want to scream.

Her father had business on Saturday night, her brothers were out, she was alone in the house with her mother. Emily stayed in her room writing letters, and went to bed at ten o'clock. She was nearly asleep when there was a commotion downstairs. She sat up, but the noise stopped. Now someone was coming up the stairs. She was sitting in the middle of her bed when there was a knock on the door.

"Emily? It's Daddy. I need to speak with you."

"Just a minute." She lit a candle and put on her robe. She opened the door.

Her father looked wild and disheveled. "I'm sorry to disturb you. Your Mr. Westfield—do you know where he lives?"

"Off Irving Place. I don't know which street. Why?"

"I have to speak with him." He looked about impatiently; he had a problem he had to solve immediately, no time to waste.

"I remember that he told me he had a telephone," she offered. "What is it? Can I help?"

"No—no. This is a business matter. I just hope he's on our telephone company. You wouldn't know the number, would you?"

"He's had no reason to give it to me."

"No, of course not. I'm sorry." He stepped away. "Well, I'll give it a try. Go back to bed. There's nothing you can do. This isn't your business."

Nevertheless, she put on slippers and belted her robe properly. The telephone was on the wall in the downstairs hall. Her father was trying to get the operator to check his directories. Her mother, in her robe, too, stood beside him. Her father put his hand over the mouthpiece. "I think I woke him up." He took his hand away. "That's fine!" he shouted. "Will you try to put me through, please!"

Emily felt something go out of her. Her father wanted Michael for something—it could not be bad. He was going to be in their lives. He would see that he and Emily made the most of it.

"Mr. Westfield? Mr. Reese! I'm fine, fine. I'm afraid I need your help, if you will . . . Who? What's that name? . . .Yes, that's right. . . I have to speak with you as quickly as possible . . . Tonight . . . That's quite all right, I'll come to you . . . No sir, thank *you* . . . Good-bye, good-bye . . . That's right, in an hour!" He hung up and turned to the women. "You heard me. I have to go out. Margaret, I'll discuss this with you in private. Emily, do me the courtesy of not asking me about this. If your young man's a gentleman, you won't be able to learn anything from him either. Good night and go to bed."

She tried to stay awake until her father returned, but finally the hour and the darkness and her fear that tomorrow evening's journey to Luchow's would be canceled drove her into a fitful sleep. Michael would have to travel from downtown to the Reese house twice in the evening—he would tire of that before long. In her dream she was the one on the elevated train ratcheting along in the darkness looking for Michael; and the only man she saw, leering through every window, was her father.

IX

It took Mr. Reese until nearly midnight to get to Michael's apartment. Michael had brewed a pot of coffee. It was clear that Mr. Reese had not known what to expect of the place, and the combination of expensive pieces of furniture and the clutter of what was essentially a small editorial office had him visibly confused. He sat down on the brocaded sofa, facing the six-foot piles of old newspapers leaning precariously against the opposite wall. Under the windows was Michael's desk, three inches deep in correspondence and more newspapers. Michael was in his shirt-sleeves, and when he brought in the coffee, Mr. Reese actually stood up to help with the tray.

"I'll be brief," he said. "It's late and I see that you're a busy fellow. I have to say that you've engaged my curiosity. In any case, something happened with our mutual acquaintance, and it was worse than you had imagined. It could be worse, at least. Do you know many like him? I hope not. You were right, I did tire of him. Anyway, I'm beating around the bush—"

"If you'd rather not talk about it, Mr. Reese, I'm sure we can just have our coffee and forget it."

"I *have* to talk about it. I'm in *trouble,* man! Tonight I went up to his hotel suite to finish our business. I have a few individuals for whom I invest money. They have quite large accounts and I manage them all at my discretion for a fixed fee and a percentage of the profits. This man begged me to do the same for him. The other men are Easterners with breeding—I—"

"They're gentlemen, and he most certainly is not."

"That's it exactly, thank you. So I went up there, I thought for the signing of the papers and the delivery of the money, a draft on his bank in Denver—I would have gotten clearance on the check by telegraph at nine on Monday. Instead he had a table set in the parlor, champagne chilled—if it's any evidence of innocence, Mr. Westfield, I can prove that I'd already eaten dinner."

Reese seemed to want some kind of comforting. "Well, it might help, depending on what happened. You were there on business—"

"He had the table set for four," Reese blurted. "I didn't know it, but there were two girls in the bedroom, his mistress and another girl, a prostitute. Both girls are prostitutes, it turns out. He was opening the champagne and starting to tell me what kind of evening he had planned—I didn't know the girls were there, remember—and I was trying to figure out a way to tell him he had misjudged my character while still getting him to sign. I never liked the proposition, I never was sure of him. I wish I had followed my instincts—it's what you told me. It was on my mind when the door to the hall opened and in trooped four men and a woman. Two of the men had cameras with flash powder, and these things went off in my eyes while the woman started yelling the worst obscentities at the top of her lungs. That's when the two girls decided to come out of the bedroom to see what was going on. Two of the men had to hold the woman back from hitting his girl friend. 'Who is this man?' I heard her ask her husband—oh, they were exactly as you described them, Mr. Westfield. I appreciate your explanation for their behavior, but never in my wildest dreams did I anticipate something like this."

"If I had anticipated it, Mr. Reese, I would have told you."

"I wouldn't have listened to you. I've misjudged you on one count. You do know a lot of people."

"What did they say to you? What did the woman say?"

"Well, he told her who I was and she started with something about my respected position in the community. One of the men was busily writing everything down. He told me that I might be called to testify, along with the girls, in a divorce proceeding. Because our man has his strike-it-rich notoriety, it'll be in all the papers. I will ruin my family."

"Not necessarily. I told you that when I knew them in Saratoga they were known for their public battling. This may be just one more event in their lives that they'll allow to blow over like so many others."

"That's not much consolation, Mr. Westfield."

Michael leaned forward. "I certainly didn't mean to indicate that we should sit back waiting for that to occur to them. I can find the woman; I don't think there'll be any difficulty with that—"

"If you do, I authorize you to offer her any reasonable sum for the pictures they took."

"Oh, she wouldn't want money! Money would only offend her. You have to understand that with people like these two, who've never had anything in their lives, the money they've earned themselves is their one source of pride. This is the life they've wanted, and precisely because it's gotten the better of them, they're determined to prove that they haven't worked for something that will destroy whatever they'd had together beforehand. If you offer her money, she'll feel that you look upon her as the common trash she's always believed she isn't. Why do you think they've worked so hard? To prove themselves right about what they are."

"What do you propose?"

"They're coming to understand that the measure of the success of a man in our society is not the money he's earned but the money he can borrow and the size of the favors he can offer. *He* understands that, or he wouldn't have attempted to entertain you."

"You don't know how that revolts me, Mr. Westfield. I feel dirty. I'm not that kind of man."

"Neither am I, Mr. Reese. I surely do know how it revolts you."

"I apologize."

"Let me find the woman and tell her what I can do for her if she can find it in her heart to forget this particular episode. Something will come to me. And if she can't be reached through reason, we'll do something else."

"I have friends in politics, but I'd rather not use them."

"For good reason. With them, you'd never know how this will come back to you."

Reese stared at him.

"With me, Mr. Reese, you know exactly what I want, in addition to the fact that you have my word on the subject."

"That's not what I was thinking, Mr. Westfield. You're an interesting man. You have your own way of looking at the world."

"Tomorrow's Sunday. I doubt that I'll accomplish much before the first of the week."

It had gone perfectly, and Michael didn't need the assurance of the participants to make him believe it. Johnson, Kate's girls, the old whore who had played Johnson's wife, and Andy Fletcher and the fellows from the newspaper who had been the photographers and the private detectives all had performed creditably, and Michael was not afraid that the secret would get out, in spite of the number of people who knew it. If they had to talk, they could talk to one another—or him, Michael. They understood that their vaudeville by no means had sealed the matter for him. It was still going to be a long time. They had done it because it seemed like a good thing to do to a banker and stuffed shirt, or because they were romantics who wanted to celebrate Michael's bewildering surrender. The girl had to be really something, they agreed. A high old time as well as a stunningly executed little bluff, but Michael felt far from elated: something left him uneasy.

He knew what it was. After he had left Emily that first Tuesday afternoon, he had gone down to Kate's, not so much to tell her what he had observed for her uptown as to celebrate what had happened to him—but just as much to think through what Emily had told him.

Johnson had been there, Kate, a couple of her girls, and then somebody remembered Andy Fletcher, since it was a party that was getting started, and when Andy showed up he had another of the young reporters for the second of Kate's girls. While Michael sat in the corner with his feet up on an ottoman, coffee at his side, and a cigar in his teeth, the others got the drinks in them they needed. No one had ever heard of the Reeses, and all had their own peculiar ideas about how to deal with the situation. One of the girls, less than bright, suggested abduction. At that point Michael was still thinking in terms of both of Emily's parents, and his guess, on the basis of what she had told him, was that his only chance stood with her father. There was nothing Michael could do for him, no way he could ingratiate himself with the man. The next morning he would be in the *World*'s morgue, reading what he could about Reese, but he had the basic idea that first evening, and he was sure it would work. The next-to-last thing Reese would expect was daring. The least was a sense of humor.

But then the situation changed. Mrs. Reese seemed to be a pushover, although Michael was sure he would hear more from her later; and Reese himself proved to be substantially harder than the man Emily had described. Perhaps it was Michael's own presence that made the difference, causing the man to fall back on the pose of banker—Michael had no more use for bankers than he had for politicians. Bankers had the advantage of not having to conceal their motives the way politicians were forced to do. They sold money for double and three times what they paid for it. Michael was prepared to set his scheme into motion to gain an entrée into the Reese household; if Reese intended to argue that Michael had no value in society, then Michael would demonstrate just how valuable he was. That's all. When the two of them finished talking about Johnson that first night after dinner in Reese's library, and turned to Michael's business with Emily, Reese's first *seeming* acceptance of Michael made Michael capitulate inside. He thought he could live with Reese's terms. But he had forgotten that Reese knew his daughter, and when she came into the room, he saw in her stricken expression what her father really meant to do. She could not be held back like that, and if Michael really acceded to Reese's terms, she would lose respect for him forever. Just looking at her, he knew that Reese had understood all this in advance. Michael decided to let the scheme proceed as he had arranged. If Reese did not come around this time, Michael would give him another chance, and another. Michael intended to cheerfully hammer Reese into the ground until he gave up what Michael wanted.

It had gone too smoothly. Reese was not that stupid. Michael did not believe that he would go for long without asking himself questions. Michael went over it repeatedly, looking for something that could go wrong. Normally when he ran a little bluff like this, he was prepared to shrug and walk away, and later in his life when he was running a few horses of his own, his sons saw him take a five-thousand-dollar bath because he had been found out, and he never blinked. You always have to be prepared to lose, he told them. This was different. He wanted her. She knew very little of the way the world was. Strangely enough, he loved it; he even wished it for himself somehow, although it meant going back, which was impossible, and not being the same man. For her, though, the result was that she was more civilized, in the sense that civilization is an art. A natural art for her, to be sure, for she was gentle in her movements and with her eyes, and everything seemed to reach her. She was awfully vulnerable, but it seemed to him that she could not be otherwise. He had never wanted anything to do with a woman who could seal herself off. He saw that he would have to protect her all her life, but from what he had seen of the two households he had lived in, it was what a man did if he wanted to make a woman happy. He thought he could see what it could lead to between them, that if she became more afraid as time went on instead of less, she would turn to him for everything. But he thought he understood it; in any case, he was prepared to take the risk.

X

In the summer of 1916, when Mike was fifteen and Tommy was six, he took the two of them, the oldest and youngest, up to New Hampshire where he was campaigning three cheap horses including a mare named Mary Jenkins who had had speed in her youth but had developed a certain tenderness since. It was only a matter of time before she broke down completely, and he had been hiding her in New England, running her in claimers with no intention of winning. At last her workouts—the real workouts, that no one recorded—showed that she was coming around, ready to win.

The boys were with him for two reasons, for the adventure and to provide him with an acceptable explanation for his presence at a little track in New Hampshire. People knew that he liked to travel with his children when he could because he wanted them to live with each other as they never did at home. Brothers were forced on each other, he sometimes said, and the least he could do for his sons was to try to get them off to a good start with each other. Fair enough. Meanwhile, the mare had begun to favor a foreleg, and it was too late to stop his friends in New York from spreading around among the bookmakers the five thousand Michael had left with them.

She was a little mare, chestnut, with no special markings. Michael, the boys, and the trainer, an old ex-slave named Bill, were in her stall at dawn on the day she was entered in the race she was supposed to win, a seven-furlong sprint for fillies and mares. It was a race buried in a program of small purses at a minor track, the perfect setting for a ten-to-one shot to run the last good race of her career. Bill had arthritis, and his skin looked cracked like the leather of an old shoe. Tommy had

had very little experience with black people, and every time he looked up at Bill he took a step backward, as if to get a better perspective of this strange-looking but withered and delicate creature. Bill had a gravelly voice and slurred everything. He knew that part of the five thousand (at ten-to-one) had been earmarked for him, Michael's automatic participation in the generous traditions of racing, and when he said that he figured that the horse wasn't going to live long anyway, Michael was sure he heard the pain of a man who could not protect his interest unless he could find a collaborator for the larceny in his heart.

So they gave it a try; they tubbed Mary Jenkins. Mike knew what they were doing, and he was the one who made it clear to Tommy as Tommy grew old enough to understand the seriousness of it, what the five thousand paying ten-to-one would have meant to them all, that, among many other things, their father would have been banned from racing if he had been caught, that they had come as close to being caught as possible, that the track officials put a guard outside Mary Jenkins's stall to make sure that the horse in it ran the seven furlongs. It was not Mary Jenkins, of course, but another mare that looked like her, while Mary Jenkins stood with her foreleg in a bucket of ice in a stall at the far end of the track. As nearly as their father had ever been able to figure out, one of the bookmakers in New York had gotten wise to one of the men he had put on the betting, and the bookmaker had tipped the agency that policed the track. The horse that ran in Mary Jenkins's place finished dead last, and as Mike said to Tommy after each retelling, after each new amazing fragment of information expanded the meaning of the image, "He never flinched. He never batted an eye."

He had been burned.

But their father had been burned before. He had had things blow up in his face.

10

More Miscalculations

I

In the first rush of confidence Michael thought he would wait until midweek before contacting Reese again, but before Sunday evening was done he was feeling again that it was going too easily. The Reeses were in the parlor when he arrived to pick up Emily, and there were smiles all around and the usual strained conversation. To avoid letting Mrs. Reese see that the business between them was still pending, Michael kept his eyes away from the banker completely. Perhaps it was a mistake. As he looked around when Emily entered the room, he thought he saw more than the glassy-eyed sort of smile Reese's predicament should have evoked; yes, something more: the frozen quality that goes with a man thinking something else altogether. Could he have learned anything?

So when Emily was ready to talk about what she had seen of the previous evening's excitement, Michael began wondering if he could question her closely if the need arose, or if she would be able to see into him well enough to know that something was in the air. In any case, it distracted him from her sufficiently for him to see that his inattentiveness hurt her at least once, and finally to alter the course of their evening. At the end of it, after all the German food, oompah music, singing, and entertainment, he wanted to have his arms around her, but his mind had wandered too often, and it was clear that she was a girl who wanted to be courted. She wanted to be courted, she said, adding suddenly that she had never been courted before. The admission made her unhappy. Riding home—he had hired a carriage—she was silent and withdrawn. Later he realized that he understood nothing about the evening. By the week's end he thought he understood it, but at the end of his life he saw that he was still learning from it.

"We were nervous tonight." A harmless glossing over, one Westfield would have been proud of.

"Yes." She had her hands in her lap. She was wearing her glasses. The carriage squeaked slowly uptown.

"If we had not been nervous, I would be kissing you now."

"Beggar." She looked up. "I believe that we'll be married, don't you?" She was absolutely serious.

"I want to think so, yes."

She wanted to be kissed, so he kissed her. They made themselves more comfortable and went on kissing and growing excited and trying to be discreet about it until he noticed that they were only two blocks from her home, and then he moved away. "Do I have to explain this?"

"Do I have to answer?"

They were in love.

But on the way back downtown again, he was thinking of Reese, and the next morning when Andy called to report that someone had come up to the office to inquire about him, Michael was not surprised. He even thought he had expected it. At the time the incident seemed funny; later, when Michael had to think about it, what seemed funny that Monday morning was engraved more clearly in his memory than the events of the night before.

"I'm looking for Mr. Westfield."

"Sports. Over in the corner."

No one took notice of him. When Michael had to go back over every step and ask everyone who possibly could have seen or heard anything for any crumb of information he could gather, ten days had passed and minds were blank. According to Andy, who still had not seen him by then, the man made his way through the welter of cluttered desks toward the cluster of young reporters standing at the window near the sports desk. The presses were running and nothing on the sports pages would have to be changed until the scores started coming in later in the afternoon. Michael had an impression that the young men were watching the girls down on Park Row; he was not sure if Andy actually told him that or if he had simply fitted in the detail from everything else he knew about that room and the people in it. As soon as the warm weather came, the young men passed their free moments at the windows watching the girls. When the presses were running, the floors vibrated, and it was Michael's observation that the men planted their feet differently, as if to try to feel the humming that said that something important was happening down below, and that they were still a part of it.

"Any of you here Westfield?"

They turned to him, a squat, wide man of about forty, in a close-fitting black pinstripe suit and a black bowler. He had not lost the youthful habit of standing on the balls of his feet; he had been a streetfighter, and all the young men at the window could see it at once—a cold, bloodless man who, old as he was, might challenge and whip any one of them. He had fierce eyes; there was enough hate in him to raise the question of how much he would enjoy using his fists. They cowered, all of them, but because they were together, it did not take very much for one—not Andy—to bait him.

"Who wants to know?"

"I'll tell Westfield."

"The way you're conducting yourself," Andy said, "even if Westfield were here, he might not be willing to talk to you."

The man turned to him. "Are *you* Westfield?"

"I'm not saying I am, and I'm not saying I'm not. Why don't you just tell me your name, and I'll see that he gets your message."

"Well, just tell him it was Mr. Smith," the man muttered, and started away.

He was on the other side of the room when one of the boys hooted, "We'll give him your message, Mr. *Smith!*" They could see him stiffen with anger, but he never looked around and disappeared through the doors while the boys whooped with laughter.

The conjecture of the others was that the man was a disgruntled user of one of Michael's touting services, but Andy thought otherwise. It was not just that Andy was more familiar with Michael's customers than the others; it was the menace of the man himself. Michael made it his business to keep away from madmen, and Andy knew it. Andy thought the visitor might be a private detective, hired by Reese, but Michael doubted it. A private detective wouldn't learn much by storming into a man's place of business. Could Reese have hired a tough? Michael did not believe what Reese had shown him so far, but surely hoodlumism was beyond him. In any case, to indicate that this apparently irrelevant episode had an influence on what was supposed to be a "normal course of events"—the recovery of the photographs and their delivery to Reese—would be catastrophic to Michael, if not fatal. Under no circumstances could he show Reese that he was a wary man, studying events for their meaning. He had planned to give the photographs to Reese on Wednesday night. Wednesday night it would be.

II

If he had been asked by a listener to describe himself in those last days of April 1895, Michael would have characterized a man some people considered arrogant, even contemptuous. He was aware of the comment about him. For one thing, he found the problem of making a living not a very difficult one to solve. A few years later he would have explained it as a matter of wanting it badly enough. If one wants a thing badly enough, the saying goes, one usually gets it. In 1895 he would have said that he applied his intelligence to his life, a thing few people ever do. But it was more than that and he knew it. He wanted it *seen* that success came easily for him, that he looked over his situations and ran his little bluffs exactly as if life itself were a game he had mastered, like all the others he had tried.

But he was as thin as he was because his stomach gave him trouble. He had to eat sparingly and carefully, and fried and fatty foods as well as certain vegetables were difficult for him to digest. Doctors and others warned him long ago about his coffee and black cigars, but he enjoyed them too much to give them up. He knew from observing himself and others that there was a connection between the emotions and the problems people had with their stomachs, but he had to conclude that there was a limited amount he or anyone else could do about it, given the lives they were living. He would stay awake for hours after an intense evening of cards. He drank coffee to maintain the concentration he needed at the table, and it kept him awake and jumpy for hours afterward. He accepted the trade-off. He saw it as a thing that worked two ways: the coffee in his stomach made him nervous, and when he was nervous, he upset his stomach. Some nights he fell alseep in his clothing, after lying awake for hours, not reliving what he had done with the cards earlier so much as trying to relax, letting his mind run free. At such times he could not muster enough attention to read anything but casual entertainment—in those days the newsstands were awash with periodicals of all descriptions. Once in a while, when he thought of it and could bear the taste, he would brew a cup of camomile tea. But in too many ways he was a slave to his weaknesses. Like Westfield. The older he became, the more he understood how much his dead benefactor had struggled with himself.

He was too tense to subject himself too frequently to small unpleasantnesses. He reached for what he liked, and only the best of that. He was impeccably tailored, traveled only first class, and accepted only the best accommodations. He would cut a man dead for creating an embarrassing scene. A year before he had punched a man in a restaurant for loudly cursing a woman—word of the action buzzed around town. Before that he had emptied a bottle of soda water on a man whose drunkenness had disrupted a poker game. Two summers ago at the Spa: the gossips had buzzed about that, too.

He could see that he gave less and less time to the simplest parts of his life. All through his apartment was the evidence that he lived in something close to chaos, and he learned long ago that it took him real effort to introduce to his life even the most rudimentary improvements of habit. Instead of nightmares and conscious, accidental recollections of what had happened years before, he was subject to fits of depression, more frequent and intense as he grew older. He had come nearly full circle: at first he had shrunk in terror from what Westfield had done to himself; later he had come to feel the seductiveness of Westfield's act as a solution for any unhappy, lonely human being. By 1895 he was still curious about life, but he could see its limitations, too. It was his sense of humor that pulled him through much of the time. Like Westfield, from whom he had consciously copied the practice, he created situations for his own amusement, and they went beyond practical jokes and what he called his bluffs.

His clothes entertained him. When faced with the decision between a conservative fabric and something daring, he instructed his tailor to make up the daring because something in him begged for the conservative and the chance to disappear back into the crowd. It was a bad, unhappy feeling for him, akin to a failure of nerve, and when he felt it coming, he struggled like a fish caught in a net.

By 1895 he had replaced the original furniture in his apartment with costlier pieces—another elaborate message to himself. In fact, it had taken him his first two years on his own to realize that he could replace everything, and as a result he laughed at what he had to show for his efforts as often as he took them seriously. Once every six weeks or so he managed to get the apartment looking as he imagined it in his more expansive, buoyant moments; but because he knew it would all be buried again under armloads of newspapers and books, he could not help looking at the whole business as more of his secret foolishness.

He had similar difficulty with the art of conversation. He wanted it to amuse him, but people told him too much and he was reminded too often of how little there was to most things and how quickly life was moving by. Laughter, memorable phrases, moments of companionship, only rippled through the dark, somber music of life like the sweet insistent singing of small birds—indeed, when he went to Saratoga, he rose early no matter how late he had been up the night before, because the morning birdsong was a soothing thing, pretty, harmonious in the most subtle, complex, and elusive ways. Often when he had such feelings he was left with a satisfying sense of himself as a creature like others, that there was a balance he was striving for even if he could not understand it.

He would have wanted to end it there, his description of himself, even if it hinted—however falsely—of self-accusation. That was hindsight. By

1895, by any standard of measurement, he had made a success of himself. His reputation as a judge of horses was nationwide. Strangers stopped him for conversation, as if he had known them for years. They gave him horses, volunteered information. Part of it had to do with his generosity with other horseplayers, including bookmakers; there were as many stories of his openhandedness as of his ruthlessness at the card table. If he never lent money to poker players, it was because invariably he would find himself playing against his own money, although often coming out of the pockets of a third party. People watched him play, sitting well back—he concealed his cards so carefully and studied them so quickly that none but him could see them.

For all that, and people knew it, he kept his circle of true friends small. It was not that he judged people harshly; he thought he was in as good a position as any man to understand that no human being was perfect. He did not like to be used, and he sensed something hidden behind too many eyes. He wanted to be loyal, and he prized loyalty in others. Gert was still with Kate, and he loved Kate for keeping her there even if Gert liked to act as if she had no use for Michael. When he was at the door, Gert would yell over her shoulder, "Hey, kid! The Prince of Wales is here!"

III

Michael remained in the apartment the rest of that Monday, working on performance charts and answering mail. From time to time he thought of the man who had stormed into the city room, but more often, naturally, he thought of Emily. He was still surrounded by her perfumes and scents, and occasionally he would remember her soft, full body against his in a way that made him tingle. He tried to keep his business with her father as far from his thoughts as possible. There was nothing he could do—nothing could be permitted to give the impression that something had rushed him.

He met Andy Fletcher for dinner at a chop house downtown. Andy had nothing more to tell about Mr. Smith, but he wanted to speculate about who he was. Michael's attention drifted. This was an ordinary night for him; he planned to go up to Canfield's in search of a game of stud, and soon he would begin to ply himself with coffee. But as he tried to prepare himself mentally, he felt little stabs of alarm. If Andy noticed something, he kept quiet about it. He had seen other women pass through Michael's life. This was a different kind of distraction, and if Andy noticed the difference, as Michael looked out the window and watched passersby shivering in the chill of the spring night, it wasn't in Andy's eyes in his reflection in the glass. Later Michael realized that his focus on Andy's reflection on the window was the one moment during all the days it would have mattered that he had a clear idea that he was out of control. But the message wasn't clear enough, and Michael went on trying to turn himself toward a night of poker.

He said good-night to Andy at nine o'clock and headed for the elevated uptown. On the platform at Chatham Square, while he and a half dozen other men watched the train coming up Park Row, he thought of Mr. Smith again and realized for the first time that someone might be following him. And if Reese was behind it, something Michael was beginning to expect, it might have started days ago. Perhaps Smith was not as smart as he needed to be, but Michael could just as readily assume, if in fact this was a game of cat and mouse, that Reese had put others besides him on the job. No matter. Michael had kept away from Kate's, where he might have run into Johnson—Reese would have had him followed, too. The reporters who had been at the hotel didn't figure into it; Reese wouldn't be able to remember what any of them looked like. So Michael was safe. He remembered that he had nothing to worry about.

In his first hand of cards he was dealt a pair of fours, two fives, and another four; around the table there appeared aces up, a possible straight, and a possible flush, in that order. He was up against good players who saw immediately, once the last card appeared, that he had almost certainly made a full house, but by that time the aces up had built the pot. The others checked to him, and Michael had no choice but to bet the limit, a thousand; aces up folded, the straight called, and the flush hesitated before deciding the price was too high. The pot netted twenty-five hundred, and it was the last good thing to happen to him for the rest of the evening. He understood this as well as any other part of the game, a miraculous first hand and then busting out for hours, having to hold on, winning a small pot here and there. He managed to get away with seven hundred, more than enough to make it worthwhile, but better than that, he thought at the time, the game had engaged his attention and drawn off some of his energy. Before he went to bed he replayed some of the hands he had seen earlier, and then he wrote a note to Emily, a love note:

> *I should have asked to see you again sooner than Friday. I miss you terribly. Life is full of twists and turns. If I had been told two weeks ago that I was about to meet the woman I had been waiting for all my adult life, I doubt I would have really understood, because I knew nothing about what was involved. That is the*

truth. My education, as I understand it now, seems to have started
with you. . . .

It wasn't all he knew or felt about the two of them; he wanted her to
know how deep and tender the emotions she stirred in him actually were.
She saved the letter, and he saw it again years later when it fell out of
their Bible. He had forgotten it, and his own fading handwriting trans-
ported him back over the years so that he was in this room again, the
blinded, zealous lover. The envelope was gone, but he could remember
sealing it and putting it on the table by the door. Then he went to bed.
He never gave Mr. Smith or Andy Fletcher a thought.

Michael telephoned Reese late Tuesday and told him that his errand
would be completed the following morning and that a package would be
available any time after noon. It was a bad connection and Reese sounded
impatient, but Michael decided not to draw inferences. In any case, he
had come to the conclusion that he had Reese locked in, and that there
was nothing Reese could do about him no matter what he knew.

He called Reese again the next afternoon, when a stormy rain fell on
the city out of a yellow, leaden sky. The connection was better. Michael
had prepared himself—he wanted to control the conversation. He told
Reese he had the package and wanted to close out the matter at once.

"Come by my office at four o'clock," Reese said.

"I have the address," Michael said, and hung up. There had been
nothing in Reese's tone. Michael was on edge again; the situation had
been too intense and had gone on too long. Planning a thing like this was
always more enjoyable than executing it. At the end, the loss of interest
eroded everything. Michael tried to remember that as he was ushered
straightaway into Reese's inner office. He wanted to take Reese's desire
to get on with it as a good sign. Michael was wet from the rain, and more
than anything he wanted to get home and dry off, with this business
finished for good.

Michael was settled in a chair facing the desk when Reese strode in
from a side room.

"Is that it? Let me have it."

Michael handed him the soaked paper package containing the photo-
graphic plates. Reese tore at the string with his letter opener, then, held
the plates up to the light. "So this is what these things look like. It's
difficult to tell what I'm looking at. These people could have been posed
to resemble us." He was agitated. "I want to be sure that these are really
what they're supposed to be."

Michael found this annoying and unsettling. "I looked at them myself
this morning. I could recognize you and the other fellow."

Reese eyed him.

"You've forgotten that I met him last summer in Saratoga."

"Yes, of course." He stared at the plates again for a long moment. "You *are* absolutely sure that I'll hear no more about this?"

Michael did not like his inflection at all. "That's what they told me. The lady understands that you were an innocent bystander."

"And there are no copies?"

"That's what they said. We can only wait and see. The detectives gave me no reason to believe that they needed to commit blackmail. There's a good living to be made just gathering evidence of adultery. They seemed like old hands at it. Remember, they'd been paid in advance by the wife."

"Well, I hope it's settled. I don't want to see them around here."

"Or at your home," Michael said. He thought Reese deserved it. Reese's expression was cold as he waved the plates at Michael.

"What do you propose I do with these?"

"Break them."

Reese nodded, but in another second it was clear that he did not know how to go about it. Michael took the plates and wrapped them in the wet paper, moved the blotter to the edge of the desk, then brought the wrapped plates down on the blotter smartly. Michael dropped the broken glass in the wastebasket and restored the blotter to its original position.

Reese pushed his hands in his pockets. "What do you think of a man who does a thing like this, Westfield?"

"I don't think I understand."

"A man who cheats on his wife, who has no respect for fundamental values."

"I try not to judge people, Mr. Reese."

Reese rocked on his heels. He was half a foot shorter than Michael, and it was as if he were trying to get up to Michael's level. "You know, there are always men who will do absolutely anything to get what they want."

Michael was silent.

"It's a bad business to get mixed up in. There's always someone around the corner more debased and ruthless than you. Gambling and taking chances are really small potatoes, and I think you know it, too. Small potatoes or not, it *always* comes to trouble. I've seen it all my life. Do you think I'm not ever tempted, that I'm not offered opportunities? I think you know more about banking than that. But I keep to the straight and narrow because all my experience has shown me that anything else always come to grief." He filled his lungs. "That's my objection to you, Westfield, I told you that. Everything I know tells me that if I allow Emily to continue with you, it will end in grief. I'm hoping for your sake and hers that you'll come to your senses."

Michael hesitated, staring at him. Reese's stupid lecture had made him so hot that for a moment he forgot the reality of his situation and contemplated accusing Reese of ingratitude and bad manners. Whose fat had been pulled out of the fire, and by whom? *Now* he came to his senses and straightened up to end the conversation. "I'll think about what you said, Mr. Reese. I have to be getting along. As you can see, I'm wet from the rain."

He allowed a sour expression to twist his face as he reached the door. He had looked forward to a sense of relief, perhaps even a relaxation of the tensions between them. All he had gotten for the exercise was a soaking, and he would have to wait to see if he was going to catch a cold. He had hoped that he would feel good enough to want to play cards in the evening, and now he could see that he might be home with hot tea, lemon, and honey. And like a banker, Reese had not even remembered to say thank-you.

IV

Thursday was a much better day—he remembered thinking that, too, later.

The weather had cleared. And he had not caught a cold. His mother called. And there was a note from Emily. It was dated Wednesday.

> *Dearest—*
> *Could I possibly see you before the end of the week? My mother wants to leave on Monday for Deal. It will be at least a week, and of course she wants me with her. I was unhappy so much of Sunday evening and I awakened unhappy on Monday, but then yesterday afternoon your note arrived. Thank you—it was so lovely and kind. I want to see you so much.*
>
> > *Love,*
> > *Emily*

He had the note an hour when his mother was on the telephone to invite him to dinner on Saturday night. When he said he couldn't be sure if he would be available, she asked him straightaway if he was trying to see Emily before her mother took her away to the Jersey shore.

"What do you know about it?"

"More than you, I think. Her father objects violently to you. He was in a rage after you left on Sunday. Since then he's worn her mother down, questioning your character. Two mornings ago she was asking a friend of mine—never mind who—what *she* knew about you. Naturally my friend reported to me. Oh, Michael, I saw the two of you together, but I don't want you to be hurt. I know that her father is showing you a false face. Mrs. Reese said as much to my friend. This man is a tiny little sneak. He's been checking on you."

"I know."

"I don't know how you know. I got it through Mrs. Reese."

He was thinking of the man who had come to the *World* office. Now Michael saw into the event a bit better. Early Monday morning. Reese had started working against him on Sunday. The lunatic scheme with the photographers had backfired. Michael could remember the state of Reese's mind on Saturday night too clearly not to wonder what had gone wrong, but he couldn't allow that to occupy his attention. Louise asked him to telephone her after the first day of the following week. With Emily out of town, she could keep him out of trouble on at least one night if she forced him to take her to dinner. She liked to pretend that he had an insatiable appetite for women. The thing with which Westfield had finally crushed her now gave her an uneasy pleasure when she saw it in Michael. She teased him, but he thought she was really afraid to know much about the reality of his personal life. Once he had asked her why she had never remarried, and she had replied in a dull, thoughtless way, "I wouldn't know why I would want to." It gave him something to think about, and later he saw what truth the remark held, and that made him feel even sadder for her. She had never given remarriage a thought. Michael had realized long since that she had gone into a spiritual decline years before Westfield's death, that she had been making her peace with her life all that time, and that when he had gone into the ground she had resigned herself, as if something inside her had decided that it had had enough. She kept busy. Her grandchildren gave her joy and she teased Michael, but mostly she kept busy. He told her that he would take her to dinner on the assumption that her conversation would be interesting enough to keep him from talking about other women. She took that as the challenge he had intended, but when he hung up he felt uneasy again.

He did not want to fail. Later, when he had the opportunity to live it over and over again, he saw that his panic infected everything he did from that point on, but at the time he saw it only as a desire to protect the small advantage he had gained. Something had soured Reese on him after Saturday, but whatever it was, his own position—or behavior—had prevented him from taking it directly to Emily. He would have done that by Wednesday afternoon. Michael could remember thinking that trying to corner Reese had been the stupidest thing he had ever tried, and having to remind himself that he would have been no better off if he had done nothing. He did not wait very much longer before he telephoned Emily.

"I was wondering when you received your mail," she said.

"I wanted to read your note a dozen times before I talked with you, that's true. But then my mother telephoned me and she knew all about your trip to Deal. Your mother's been asking about me, and according to her, your father's been checking on me." There was no point in mentioning the man in the office; Mr. Smith would make it too real for her, and she might confront her father.

"Michael, I don't want to wait a year. I've made up my mind."

In the years that followed, Michael had many occasions to reflect on the state of his mind during these events, and for a long time he thought that he might have been able to approach it differently if Louise had chosen to do her shopping that morning instead of picking up the telephone. It had to do with the panic her information had brought on, to be sure, but it also had to do with the way she had left him feeling about himself. And her—the city was full of women like her. He had not lied to Emily; he had read her letter a dozen times, but *after* he had talked to his mother. Like so many other girls, Emily wanted him to save her from her parents. But unlike all the others he had ever met, she was asking to be taken on face value. Louise had brought all the old woes down on him—he was thinking of Westfield again, knowing what the old rogue would have thought of an Emily Reese: "She meant what she said, but did she know what she meant?"

Westfield had shown him that there were two kinds of fools, those who knew they were fools and those who didn't. By 1895 Michael had expanded the lesson enough to let him see that the first usually told too much about themselves and the second told too little; but of the first there was a special group who told most of all when they discussed the people who had failed them.

And it seemed to him that fully half the young women he had ever known complained of fathers who were too weak and mothers who were too strong. In recent years he had been able to sense it coming and predict what would follow. Inevitably the girl would begin to want more of him than he could possibly give. The smiles and fluttering eyelashes would give way to sniffling tears if he happened to be unavailable for some function or other. But if he yielded, he knew, the issue would never be raised again, for she would assume that he would do anything to prevent her tears.

But if he forced her to tears a second time, she would be angry with him for making her resort to them. "You're cruel and insensitive, Michael! You know how delicate my feelings are!"

These were things he had lived through and seen in the lives of others, and when people started telling their secrets, he saw into their lives the way he saw into his own; and when a woman started complaining about the very things that had made her who she was, Michael could read the future like a clairvoyant.

Never mind that he thought that her dance or family party was absolutely the worst thing he could do with his time, and never mind that she really wanted him there to display like a prize goose. Neither had anything to do with the issue at hand, which was her tears. If he tried to break it off at that point, she would beg and plead her way back until she was strong enough again in her position to lead him by the nose to the next concert or cotillion or charity ball. She would have him do her bidding; she would battle him with sulking and tears until he learned to obey her. He had lived through it, seen it in others, heard the lunatic confessions of desperate young men only to watch them go out and do exactly the wrong thing all over again.

And one fine morning the poor devil would wake up married to her, to discover that the two of them had become the very people she had professed to hate when she had been most interested in him, back at the beginning, before everything between them had begun to curdle like milk in a bucket.

Half the young women he had ever known, living in the best of all possible worlds, within sight if not reach of the top of New York Society, pretty young princesses playing the game as they found it, as well as they could understand it. And why not? After all, they were among its prizes, almost more sought-after than the money it cost to afford them, a subtlety lost on very few. They filled the air with their perfume and the rustle of their skirts and the chirruping of their voices. They were society's prizes—the Arabs had their heaven filled with virgins and, heaven help him, Michael thought he understood why.

His working life was spent in a man's world, and he did not have access to the young women of other levels of society. Occasionally he would strike up a conversation in a library or bookstore, but the girl would always know someone who knew Julie, for instance, or had been at so-and-so's party. If he caught the eye of a shopgirl, if he thought he saw something intelligent in her eyes, he was just as likely to discover afterward—that is, if she didn't turn up her nose on his first word—that she put on airs, or was cowed into silence, or tried to wheedle presents. He was a gentleman, he had money, and they were as nervous and eager

to grab their chances as they would have been if they had been called to
the stage as a volunteer in a vaudeville show.

The result was that in recent years he had drifted toward harder types,
those who were spoiled rotten, adventuresses, adulteresses. He was not
shy with other men's wives. He believed he was free to do as he pleased
with those who were already looking for trouble. It was a matter of
necessity, for without them there were very few women available to him.

He had plenty of time before Saturday night to think about all these
things and more; the truth was, by Friday afternoon he was so deeply
caught up in these reveries that he thought nothing of it when he called
Andy Fletcher down at the office and learned that he had not come back
from lunch. Michael was so out of control that it did not occur to him
even once that something, somewhere, was going completely wrong.

<h1 style="text-align:center">V</h1>

He had not been wrong about one thing anyway. Two, actually. When
he arrived at the Reese home, Emily opened the door for him and kissed
him on the lips in view of anybody who might have been passing on the
street. Her parents were occupied elsewhere in the house, so he kissed
her again.

And she put her hands up to his face as she had last Sunday and kissed
him in return. She had been looking into his eyes from the moment the
door opened. She was shaking with fear, but he could see how much she
was reaching for him. He asked if she was ready, and she said she wanted
to leave as quickly as possible—was she properly dressed? A pale-green
silk suit, a white blouse, and a tiny dark-green hat. He said yes, and then
they seemed to be rushing outside again. It was twilight; the sky over
New Jersey was red, but the streets were dark. The wind from the river
made the gas lamps flicker. He said he would take her anywhere she
wanted to go. It didn't matter, she said; she merely wanted to be with
him. She was searching for the carriage. He had been afraid that she
would find it ludicrous the second time, but then he had hired one
anyway because he had been just as afraid that there would be no room
for that kind of laughter—that they would need their privacy. He had
made up his mind that he would make love to her if that was what she
wanted; he did not intend to be fainthearted either. She did not want
that, not if she wanted to be taken at face value. He had many years to
think of this, and he was not wrong in what he thought she was saying to
him about herself. Events bore him out on that. He told her that he had
left the carriage up on the corner. Her father had not taken her into his
confidence, she said. Presumably he was having Michael investigated on

her behalf, but he didn't have the common sense or decency to discuss it with her. Insinuations at the start of the week, that he had discovered that he and Michael had mutual friends. It had taken Michael's telephone call to help her understand just that much. Did her father think she had no character? In the carriage she turned into Michael's arms and kissed him, but then in another moment she was sobbing. The driver set a steady, rapid gait down Broadway, and they were being pitched forward and back in the carriage. She had Michael's handkerchief, and when the light caught her, she was laughing because she had smeared her glasses.

I Corinthians 13 has always been one of the more popular passages of the New Testament; in our time it is read at weddings and funerals and generally is taken to be a reflection on the necessity of Christian love. In the King James version, love, translated from the original Greek as charity, is compared with other Christian virtues, and the conclusion of the author, Saint Paul, once a soldier, is that charity—love, modest and enduring—is most important, greater even than faith or hope.

Later in his life, when Michael felt compelled to find his way back to the lessons of his mother and father, he returned to the book his father told him sailors read when they were long at sea. Michael paid particular attention to Ecclesiastes and Job, but because his mother had made it clear that he was to think of himself as a Christian, he was drawn to the lessons that appear in the second half of the New Testament. The first ten verses of I Corinthians 13 are soaring poetry but relatively straightforward, uncomplicated declarations of the indispensability of Christian love, perfect love; but with the eleventh verse the chapter takes a sudden ironic and chilling turn: the voice changes, the tone becomes muted. *When I was a child, I spake as a child*—after ten verses of absolutes, the reader is bidden to think upon the ambiguities of the development of human understanding. By the end of his life, Michael had come around in his vision of himself to something like Emily's original sense of the sophisticated, too-clever thirty-two-year-old who had first presented himself to her: a human being struggling to stay alive, nothing more.

One forgives oneself last of all.

The carriages entered the mythology of their life together, like the story of their first meeting—in the two years of their courtship, he had always come for her in a carriage. Finally the story of the carriages became another of the ways most of her family measured the length of her life, the clop-clop of the horses' hoofs on the cobblestones, the gentle rocking of the ride, the shadowed elms on Broadway passing by at a good pace, the moist air of the night entering through a lowered window. . . .

Michael and Emily made love. She wanted to be taken at face value, but what could he tell her about himself? When he thought of telling her the truth of his business with her father, he remembered that there was another, bigger secret that he had already decided she would never learn. What could he have said? *When I was fourteen, I found the man who killed my parents and I killed him?* He was in love with her. He thought he would win the way she wanted him to win. There was nothing else on his mind.

He had to get to I Corinthians 13 before he discovered for himself that he could not be held responsible for what he did not know, no matter how the knowledge was hidden from him. The fact of the matter was that if they had not been interfered with, the story of the two-year courtship might not have been the lie it was; there would not have been any two-year courtship at all. He would have had her forever from that very night.

Michael knew what he wanted. He wanted to close his eyes and forget Moran's footstep on the stair. He had it in his grasp. She wanted it settled quickly. He took her to dinner, a little chop house with curtained booths off Longacre Square and afterward down to his apartment. They fell into a silence in the restaurant. He thought they would be married in a matter of months—in August, at Saratoga again; he thought of it constantly. He let it torture him. When he kissed her he thought it was like a wedding night. He wanted to tell her, but he already knew that she was happier with the unsaid. She looked into his eyes as if she were reading his mind. How had this happened to them? Part of it was the terror of everything that drove her. "I never felt anything before," she told him later. "Anything. Ever." She had been afraid to let go of it. She had been afraid it would stop.

But they were not completely without their wits. In the restaurant, she said, "My father's attitude toward you changed dramatically for the worse after Saturday night. I was asleep when he came home and he was out again in the morning when I woke up, but when I saw him again he was in a fury. He missed church, which is very important to him."

It was Michael's first thought that there was somebody else involved, that Reese saw someone on Sunday morning, someone who might have known that the scene in the hotel the night before had been only a performance. Someone who would have told Reese that he was about to be blackmailed. It would explain the visitor so soon at the paper, on Monday, and the relentlessness with which Reese must have worked on Emily's mother at the same time; and finally, Reese's conversation while the rain came down on Wednesday afternoon. But why was he leaving Emily out of it? If Reese was so sure of his suspicions, he would have told her. If he wanted to kill their romance, he could have done it this week. What would hold him back?

"On Saturday night your father asked me to do him a favor, and I said I would try. I did, and accomplished what he asked me to do on Wednesday afternoon."

"Would you tell what that favor was, please?"

He reminded her of the conversation in her dining room the previous Tuesday and that he had spoken to her father alone in his study afterward. Then he told her of the events of Saturday evening that impelled her father to call him so late *that* night."

"And you were able to recover the photographs," Emily said.

"Of course. They were my friends."

"Well, that's what you told him."

"No, I'm afraid you don't understand." He was looking into her eyes. "They were my *friends.* After I saw my chances on Tuesday night, I decided to go ahead with my plan. So he would ask me to get him out of trouble."

"All of it? You arranged all of it?" She put down her fork. He thought he was dead. She wiped her mouth carefully with her napkin, and her eyes were averted from him for a moment. "You did that? To him?" She looked at him. "I don't know if I'm more afraid of this or—"

"What? Do you want to tell me?"

"It's not important."

"After Tuesday, it was a gamble I thought I had to take."

"Would you do it again?"

"I dislike your father just that much. I have to tell you, I made him suffer."

"You're the one who lends money to friends and he sits in judgment of you, so perhaps he deserves it. I made some decisions on Tuesday night, too."

"In the process," Michael said, "I was able to establish that your father isn't the sort of man who knows much about the girls he met Saturday night."

Her eyes were bright. "I suppose not, if he suffered. I was concerned. It's strange, because now that I know *you,* I can see how preposterous it was for me to think about him in that context. You would know about them because you know more about life than he does. He should know you have more character than he has." Then, as she looked away, she held his eyes for a moment, as if he needed to be told that she never wanted to raise the question of his character again. Later, when he wanted to remind himself that he had allowed his "confession" to work to his advantage, he had difficulty seeing that he had not known that in advance.

He had difficulty seeing that she had made up her own mind, or that she was testing him. When they left the restaurant and entered the carriage and he told the driver he wanted Fifteenth Street and Irving Place, she stepped in and made herself comfortable with the most extraordinary calm; and after an interminable starting-away from the entrance and into the protective darkness, he turned to kiss her, and she was far more ready to be kissed than he had thought.

He was without artifice. He told her he wanted to marry her as quickly as possible. In the apartment she was able to see how he lived. He had cleaned the place but now he realized that it still looked like half a newspaper office. He made tea.

He told her that he wanted to take her to Saratoga this year as his bride, and she said she wanted to go. She had taken off her jacket. He kissed her and she put her arms around him and they leaned back on the sofa. They were lovers. She told him that he could have had her there the week before, and he said that he knew but that it had taken him until Wednesday to understand it. "Do you see why?" she asked. "They saw that I had made up my mind and that I know I'm right, but they want to fight with me anyway. I am so frightened—that they will win because it has been so hard to win anything from them. You don't know how I feel—I've been trying to tell you. I want to be with you more and more. I don't want it to stop."

At that moment it occured to him that there was a fair share of his terrible reputation that was richly deserved. She meant what she said, and *he* knew what she meant. He had thought that would be a situation that he would control, but now it was clear that he could not take another step unless he committed himself on the same terms. Forever—saying good-bye to everything else. It *was* a wedding, whether he had been able to see it or not. In her way, she understood it better than he did; she had already made the decision.

"If your father felt he could send investigators after me, then perhaps I should feel released from the promise I made him."

"He did that?"

"Seems so."

He stood up, taking her hand. She seemed surprised, then moved from behind the table and walked with him to the bedroom. More than anything in his life, he did not want to hurt this girl.

The bedroom of his love nest was no better than the parlor, a heavy dark bed crowded by two huge dark wardrobes—there were more newspapers on top of them. The building had not been electrified yet, and the gaslight in the other room cast only a faint glow on the wall. He could not help feeling shy with her. He brought her along slowly. She was beautiful, full and womanly. She knew nothing about herself. With her jacket off he still had to contend with her blouse and skirt, her shoes, a slip, a chemise. And then his own clothes. The light inhibited her, and he closed the door. He told her he loved her. He kissed and praised her and talked gently, and when he sensed she was afraid, he stopped. The darkness calmed her. It took him an hour to undress her and bring her into his arms. She could feel his body against hers and she had more confidence, but he held her in his arms and kissed her, their bodies touching, for a long time more. Their bodies had warmed the air in the room. She held him tightly as he rolled her onto her back on the bed, but as tightly as she held him she wanted to look into his eyes. He could see her, darkly, and she was frightened. She was drawing her breath through her mouth. Now she was very wet. She was very soft and her hair was soft there, and when the wetness came outside so she could feel it on her skin, she relaxed, surrendered; he opened her lges and raised her knees. He had told her he would do it and that it would probably hurt her, and she watched him now apprehensively. He could see she had not expected to be so open or exposed to him. She was afraid to look away from his eyes and he wanted her to see him smile; he told her again that he loved her and he entered her, feeling her tear open slowly before him, slowly but not so slowly that he was not surprised with how quickly it went. She saw his surprise and felt the pain he had warned her of at the same time, and in that moment of astonishment, pain, penetration, envelopment, with their eyes locked together, he ejaculated, his contractions coming suddenly, one after the other. He was afraid to look away from her, and she could see what was happening to him and feel it hammering and flooding inside her and see it on his face so that she could feel her legs going around him before she realized what was happening and her body gathering him closer to itself, and there was an intensity to the mounting sensations that made her think that something else was tearing inside her and her eyes closed and she cried out so loudly that she thought he should have told her about that, too, but she heard his voice, as well, and it made her feel complete in her joy.

It was not yet ten o'clock, and they had hours more ahead of them. The room grew warm and he reached over and flung open the door. She covered them with a sheet, and they held each other, cuddling. She felt playful, and proud and sure of herself. He made love to her again. She was sore but she wanted to do it, and with the room so warm even with the door open he was thankful when the sheet slipped off his back. He could see her clearly and she could see him, and when he smiled she lost the rest of her fear. Her skin glowed with perspiration. She was absolutely beautiful and he told her so. He raised himself up on his hands to look at them together, and he told her to look, too, and he was thrilled when she did. He watched her looking down at their bodies moving together and he kissed her cheek and neck, and she put her head back on the pillow and said it was beautiful—*he* was beautiful. They made love, sweating, both of them aware of the pain she was experiencing but knowing, too, that she understood it now and wanted what was coming, wanted it enough to steady herself and keep her legs up in spite of the pain. When she asked him if he loved her, he came so suddenly that he shouted. She was a deep, soft woman and he was deep inside her; when his semen surged out of him, it frightened him. He had been afraid of impregnating her, but he had not wanted to expose her to the paraphernalia of contraception the first time. She was looking into his eyes. "I'm going to marry you," he said. "You know that—you do know that, don't you?"

"Yes." But her voice was different, distant. "In any case, it's too late to worry about tonight."

"Do you want more?"

"If you want to."

When they made love again later, it was as if they had been making love for years. He had kept the sheet off them until the room had grown cool again and they had explored each other, and then when they had brought the sheet up again, they had curled in each other's arms for nearly an hour. It was what she had wanted, what she had hoped for, she said, the feeling of peace and joy . . . she had been right to trust him. He had never been wrong with her—for her. She understood what he had done to her father. "I was desperate, too," she said. "I decided this. I never wanted anyone before. I suppose that if they had been better about it, I would have fought with my conscience in a respectable way and you would have waited for me. Yes, I think you would have. I never felt anything before, but I knew what it was and I didn't think anyone else had the right to decide this for me. When you came to the house and the two of you spoke, I wanted to accommodate him, but I could feel something going sick and dying in me, too. Now I see why society doesn't want this, and why he tried to prevent it. I went too far. Now you have me and he doesn't. And he can't push me toward someone who suited him, as if anyone would have wanted me."

"They're all wrong about you, you know."

"Yes, I do know now. You made me feel it about myself the first time I saw you. You made me feel good about myself. This is natural. Tonight was natural."

So when they made love again it was a continuation of their love talk. She was quite sore, and in trying to make her more comfortable, he showed her that there was more than what they had done so far. She giggled, she was so pleased. She relaxed and made love with him, and when they finished, they were both exhausted, wet with perspiration, and laughing at the prospect of getting themselves together for the trip uptown.

"We're a scandal," he said.

"We're going to be, you can be sure of it."

"If we continue to lose control like this."

"Yes. I'm serious, though. People are talking about us, and my parents have stirred things up even more by going around asking questions."

"What are people saying about us?"

"That you've seduced me."

"Well, are they lying?"

"Yes. I seduced you. This *is* serious, Michael. My parents really have stirred things up. I told you my father knew someone who knew you, too. That person knew you before you went to the Westfields, and he told my father the whole story, including the fact that your school records were taken out of the school—"

"I didn't tell you that!"

"I know. This man told my father—*he* told me. What's wrong?"

He had to be careful! His heart was thudding in his chest. He sat up, put his feet on the floor. "It was all dead and buried for years." She couldn't see his face. "You're right, and I was thinking that I wanted it that way myself, forgotten completely. Now it will be dragged out again."

"I'll ask my parents not to discuss it with people. It's in their interest to forget it, too."

"Yes, it is." *It was as if someone had him by the throat!* His hands were shaking. It was as if someone had begun screaming in his ears. "Do you know that man's name, by the way?"

"Sullivan. He's a politician. Do you know him?"

He had had to look at her directly when he'd asked his question. Otherwise, she would have known that something was wrong. He was still looking at her, seeing that she was believing everything he said. "No," he lied. "I never heard of him."

VI

He was calmer by the time he was taking her home. He was even capable of thinking about something other than the shock he had just sustained. He had two years to think of this and the events of the next three days, and he was able to remember everything that happened, everything revealed to him, everything he thought. It was a useful exercise, because later in his life he would have to do it all over again.

Emily saw that something had gone wrong, and she thought he was being unduly upset, considering the reason he gave. It seemed to her that he was brooding, but he was really being carried away, drawn to think about what he knew—that Sullivan had been the alderman in the Sixth Ward, that neither Westfield nor Kate knew anything about the lost school records. Westfield had thought he knew what Michael was thinking, warning him away from pursuing it further. Westfield must have been in his midforties by then, the circles under his eyes more and more obvious all the time, his head shining blad—not the imposing figure he had been a few years before. "It won't get you anyplace, kid. Be thankful for what you were allowed to survive. The next time might be the death of you." And Kate, his forlorn, long-suffering lover, before they broke up, before he broke down, seeing how serious he was, saying, "It's the ugliest thing I ever saw in you, Michael!" Her voice went up an octave when she was angry; she could be as shrill as anyone he had ever heard on Lombard Street. "Don't you see what you're doing to yourself? You're poisoning yourself just like Westfield, who was a goddamned drunk!"

All of that had come and gone by the time he and Emily were in the carriage rolling uptown. It was after one o'clock, and there was a wet mist in the air. He told her he would call her tomorrow at five o'clock in the afternoon. Later he could not remember walking with her up the stairs, but he must have done so because he could remember kissing her good-night outside her door. He could not remember going down the stairs either, but he remembered waking up in the carriage outside the entrance of his building on East Fifteenth Street. The color of the night sky was changing, and over on Third Avenue drunks were singing out of key.

It took him another two hours to fall back to sleep again. Climbing the stairs, being startled by the sudden recollection of the information about Sullivan, and remembering what had gone on in these rooms just hours before were all bad enough in themselves, but then he discovered that the pillows smelled of her powder and perfume, and without another thought he took a book into the parlor to read until he was groggy again.

So he slept until twelve-thirty, and she telephoned at one o'clock. They had a good connection. He asked if she was well.

"Yes, very well, thank you. It's just been decided that my mother and I are leaving for Deal this afternoon instead of tomorrow. I wanted to say good-bye. I'll write to you as often as I can."

"I love you, Emily."

"Thank you." She was silent.

"Can someone hear you?"

"Yes."

"Do you love me?"

"Yes. Well, I have to say good-bye now."

"I love you. Send me your address as quickly as you can. I'll write to you every day."

"Yes, I'll do the same."

He said good-bye. Her voice had been wonderful, a girl-in-love, marvelous. He did not realize right away that he did not know when she would return, but when he did, he felt a deep pang. But he was awake. And there was something he wanted to do.

He went down to the office and, before he made his selections for the next day, found himself a comfortable corner of the morgue and read everything he could find about James P. Sullivan. The natural successor to a member of the Tweed gang who had preceded him, a member of the Board of Aldermen for more than twenty years, now a member of the Real Estate Commission. There were sketches, a couple of cartoons in which he was depicted as a pig, and an editorial decrying his position in a zoning squabble. It appeared that he was very much on the side of moneyed interests. The sketches showed an enormous potbellied man with a gold chain stretched across his vest, a diamond stickpin, and an apparent penchant for striped suits.

That evening he tried to telephone Emily's father, but the operator reported there was no one home. He wrote a letter to Emily, taking a long time for such a short letter, and turned to his reading. The letter took into account the fact that he knew nothing about the condition of her privacy, but he thought it conveyed his sentiments. It was not the sort of letter he wanted to write, however, not clever or fresh or rich with wit. For reasons that had nothing to do with her, her did not feel very resourceful or gifted.

Mr. Reese's secretary had the message that Mr. Westfield had called, and when the telephone rang a few minutes later, Michael thought it was Reese getting back to him, but it was someone at the sports desk at the *World.* Andy Fletcher had been found with his throat slit in a doorway in the Sixth Ward. Michael asked if they had the exact address, but no, it was still coming in. "I'd better tell his parents," Michael said. He realized he was going to cry. It had been like being hit in the chest with a bat.

"Don't worry about telling them," the guy said. "It's being done. When I get that information, I'll give you a call."

When Reese called in another hour, Michael still had not cried, and he had not heard from the paper either, but he had thought his way far enough into it to have been able to change his plan a little.

"Mr. Reese? I'm so happy you called. With your family out of town, I thought you might be free to be my guest for dinner this evening. There are some new developments that I'd like to discuss with you."

"New developments? What do you mean?"

"Something that happened over the weekend. Say, would you like me to call you later today?"

"That would be better, Westfield. Let me see how my day goes."

A little while later the sports desk called and then the second delivery had a postcard from Emily. He put the postcard in his pocket. He had to spend the next several hours in the office looking over Tuesday's entries. He did the best he could, going as fast as he could. He was sick to his stomach, sicker than he had ever been; he had cried, and he was going to cry again. It reminded him of Westfield's death more than anything. He had Westfield's gun and when the second call from the paper came in, he took the gun out from the back of the closet and held it and cried like a squalling infant. So when he went downtown to the office, he could not help thinking of Westfield, and he had the gun with him in a paper bag, cleaned, oiled, and ready to fire. People came over to talk to him about Andy, but he discouraged them as much as he could. The paper bag was under the desk, and once in a while he had to touch it with his foot for reassurance. He wanted to stay in control of himself; he wanted to keep his wits about him. At two o'clock he rolled an envelope and a piece of paper into his typewriter, then put the paper in the envelope and sealed it. He found a kid in the office who had always seemed pretty smart and told him what to do. When the kid had the idea, Michael gave him ten bucks and the kid understood what else it was for and took off. These kids were sharp. He would run all the way downtown and forget what he had done forever.

At two-thirty he called Reese.

"Mr. Reese, I was wondering if you'd like to try the Waldorf-Astoria tonight."

"Ah, not tonight, Westfield. Something's come up. Would you mind letting it go for a couple of days? There are some things I have to attend to." He did not want to bother saying good-bye.

Ten minutes later Michael was on Broadway in the shadow of a storefront watching uptown streetcars. It was a crisp, clear, blustery day, and where the sunshine struck the wool of his trousers he felt grateful for the warmth. Soon enough the kid came along on the streetcar, waving his arm and pointing to Reese sitting two benches in front of him, and Michael hopped on and the kid hopped off and disappeared into the crowd.

Reese got off at his stop and Michael rode another two blocks under the elms and then walked back and found a corner on Broadway that let him see down the block to the Reese household. There was nothing he could do as the afternoon light faded and the wind turned bitter and raw. He tried to think about Emily, but he was too sick with himself. He had thought of tucking the .44 Remington inside his belt, but it was a big damned thing and he didn't want to feel it against his body that way. Louise had given it to him two months after Westfield's death, and for much too long after that Michael had sat in his room staring at the thing. When he failed with Kate sexually and burst into tears over Westfield's death, he wept and before the night was out he vomited blood.

It was easier to think of those things than of Emily as it grew dark and became so cold that Michael's teeth rattled in his head. Finally it was seven-thirty and Reese came out of his house again. He came up to Broadway and got in a hansom and started downtown. Michael crossed Broadway and hailed the next cab. He had ten dollars ready for the driver and called up his instructions as quickly as he could. It took the driver a moment to understand all of it, but then Michael was able to get in. The air inside was still and so it seemed warmer, but Michael was shivering down to his bones. He waited as long as he dared, and then he took off his coat, folded it, took the gun from the paper bag and slipped it under the coat. There was a newspaper in the bag, too, and now he tucked that under his arm. He leaned out of the cab and told the driver he was ready.

The driver pulled the cab up to the other. Michael waited until the drivers were talking and the cabs were slowing, and then he leaned forward and waved and hailed Reese. The cabs were coming to a stop.

"Hullo! Good evening!" He stepped out and took the handle of the other door. "We're going to the same place. Let me ride with you. There's something in the paper I want you to see." Reese was gaping, but Michael raised his coat enough to let him see the gun. "Let me ride along, Reese."

"Get in."

Michael sat beside him. "Tell the driver we're going to the Waldorf."

Reese did it. Michael watched the driver of the other hansom, who was conferring with his counterpart on this. He reined back until Michael had drawn even with him, and then he leaned over. "Say boss? Boss?" It was developing into a guileless performance; he was an old driver with a yellow moustache curling into a nearly toothless mouth, and rum-stunned eyes bulging out over sunken, reddened cheeks—he was no actor. "Boss? You changed your mind about Three-fourteen East Sixty-seventh?"

"Yes, thank you. We're going to have something to eat first."

And as he pulled away, the old man nodded gravely and closed one eye.

Reese tried to move away. "For God's sake, I hope you know what you're doing with that thing. My first thought about you was that you were a madman. All these people are going to remember who you are."

"No, they won't."

"Well, at least you're no thief. He told me you were a thief. He didn't want someone to have me in a position of compromise. He wanted to protect his own interest. He said that. He's a stupid, stupid man. Worried about a thief. What does he think he is?"

"Thief is the least of it," Michael said.

"I don't know what you plan," Reese said nervously, "but you won't get away with it. These people are going to remember you."

"No, they won't. We're going to the Waldorf-Astoria on Thirty-fourth Street. I don't want you to think about what I've planned. Just proceed on the assumption that you're going to be all right. You will be, too. But I want you to tell me how you got mixed up with Sullivan in the first place."

"He came to me. When consolidation comes a lot of money will be made. It's been decided that there will be another big bridge across the East River, this one at Blackwells Island, going out to Queens. It's all farms over there now, but with the bridge will be an elevated railroad running all the way up Flushing Avenue to North Beach. There will be country clubs and resorts—the well-to-do are going to live there far from the city noise and dirt."

Michael was seeing a banker up close, revealed to his essentials. As Reese's visions of country properties grew in his head, his eyes widened, his lips whitened.

"We're acquiring properties. It's a speculation. We intend to be in and out. I'm innocent of any wrongdoing. I'm lending money for my clients—"

"You're forgetting what you did for Andy Fletcher this weekend."

"I did nothing! Sullivan called me on Saturday afternoon and told me that you had been caught on Friday trying to follow someone. I didn't know what he was talking about—"

"What did you do, hang up?"

"I said good-bye, yes—what was I supposed to do? He told me you were trying to blackmail me. He didn't believe that you gave me the genuine plates. When he said he had you, it seemed to me to confirm what he'd been saying about you."

"But when I arrived for Emily, you called Sullivan right away. Did you see the paper today?"

"Yes, I know what happened. If anything, I was trying to help your friend. I didn't know anything like this would happen. Do you think I'm a murderer?"

"It doesn't matter what I think. That boy was twenty-two years old. Before the night is over, you'll thank God that I was here to help you."

"Look, I know you helped me before—it's clear that he was all wrong about you—but I don't want you to do anything. Please."

"Sit back and be quiet," Michael said.

Before they reached the Waldorf, Michael tucked the gun into his belt and maneuvered the newspaper to cover the bulge in his jacket, and when they stepped into the lobby, Michael told Reese that he wanted them to check their coats. There were no tables in the dining room. Inside they could hear a string quartet. The headwaiter told them that there would be no tables for at least an hour. "We'll wait in the bar," Michael said.

He ordered a whiskey for Reese and a bottle of Saratoga water for himself. "I don't drink whiskey," Reese protested.

"This will be good for you," Michael said. "I've been told that you know something about me. The gun I have is the one my father used on himself." He motioned to the bartender for another round.

Reese watched the bartender. "Westfield, you mean. Well, I knew about that when it happened."

Michael said, "Drink only a little of this and leave it at the bar." He waved to the bartender again. "We'll be back in a few minutes."

"Certainly, sir."

"Come on," Michael said to Reese, "we'll go out the Fifth Avenue door." He had him by the elbow. "I'm sorry I confused you. Westfield killed himself; my real father was murdered."

"I know."

Michael steered him to another empty hansom waiting at the curb. "Three-fourteen East Sixty-seventh," he said to the driver. As they pulled away, Michael asked, "Do you know anything about my real parents?"

"Not really."

"Their money ran out and they were trapped here."

"Sullivan wouldn't have known that part."

"No, he wouldn't."

There were other things Michael needed to be told. Sullivan lived alone, according to the file; his wife had died and his daughters had moved away, one of them to a convent. Were there servants? The times Reese had been there, there had been a man. Reese described him and Michael relaxed.

It was as if Sullivan wanted to keep an eye on operations, for at the top of the steps of his brownstone was a view down to the river, Blackwells Island, and the summer mansions on Astoria Hill on the other side. Now it was Reese who was freezing, and he glared at Michael as Sullivan's man opened the door and bathed the stoop in the naked glare of electric light. He saw Michael first, and scowled.

"I have a message," Reese said. "This is a friend of mine."

The man matched the description Andy had given. As the man opened the door wide, Michael pushed Reese in before him. He took the newspaper off the gun and turned the lock on the door. "Let's have it quiet," Michael said. The man was ready to lunge, like a dog. "Mr. Reese, help him take off his suit coat." The man was wearing a shoulder holster. Michael took the gun. It fit in his pocket. He draped the man's coat over his own gun. "Lead the way."

Sullivan, looking as he did in his sketches and, oddly, in his caricatures, was in his library on the second floor. The house seemed empty otherwise. Still, Michael pushed the door closed behind them. Sullivan was on his feet. "Sit down," Michael said. "And keep your hands on your desk."

"*This* is Mr. Westfield," Reese said.

Sullivan started to get up. "Oh, I'm not to blame for that. See him," he said, pointing to his man. "*He* roughhoused him; *he* brought him here—"

"But you thought he was me," Michael said. "I told you to sit down. You, too." He waggled the gun at the hoodlum. "Mr. Reese, you sit down next to him."

He hesitated. "This doesn't concern me. I don't know what's going on between you two—"

"What did he tell you about Andy Fletcher?"

"Your friend? They were going to let him go, but he wasn't going to listen to reason. He was going to tell the police what they had done with him the moment he got out of here."

"So they cut his throat."

"They told me that he was unconscious when they did that. I told you, I had nothing to do with it!"

"And you don't read the papers.'" He looked at Sullivan. "Well? Are you going to tell him or shall I?"

"Listen to me, Westfield. It was the way he said. The kid got upset and Pete here let it get the better of him."

Michael turned to Pete. "He told you where to dump the body. Did he tell you what that address was?"

"No—no."

"Maybe it got out of control with Andy, but your boss made sure he got his use out of it. He told you to drop the body where I used to live with my parents almost nineteen years ago. He wanted to make sure *I* understood. He's not as smart as he wants you to think he is. If Fletcher's body had been found anywhere else, I might never have connected it with anything to do with me—and that even after Mr. Reese's daughter told me more about myself than anybody has the business to know—or remember. I would have gotten here eventually, but I wouldn't have been certain of myself. He might have been able to talk his way out of it, saying that an alderman would have remembered my situation. But he remembers my address as well; *somebody* does, I thought this morning. Mr. Reese led me here. Were you expecting him?"

Sullivan was nervous. "What the hell are you doing here?" he asked.

Michael said, "I sent him a note signed 'S.' and he automatically thought it was you. What you told him yesterday made him get his wife and daughter out of town a day early. If he hadn't panicked yesterday, I wouldn't have known that he could be had today."

"He's a stupid son of a bitch anyway," Sullivan said. "If he was smarter, I would have kept my nose out of your caper."

"Get him a drink."

"What?"

There was a bar in front of the bookshelves. "Mr. Reese wants a little whiskey in a glass. Get it for him."

Sullivan moved. "I don't know what your game is. You had a nice little con working on this one here, but then you let it go. And now this— gunplay. I kept an eye out for you, you know. When I heard that Westfield thought you were eleven, I thought, the kid's got moxie." He had the whiskey poured. Michael was watching him carefully. "Yeah, I figured out that your school records would give your right age." He gave the glass to Reese and turned to Michael. "I didn't see why you had to get it in the neck any worse than you were. You were payin' enough for your old man's mistake."

Michael froze. "Get back to your seat. Keep your hands on the desk. Drink up, Mr. Reese. I want you to drink it all. What mistake was that, Mr. Sullivan?"

"*He had money of mine!*" He was still standing, his face red. "*People saw him take it!* He was given every chance to return it, then I heard that he'd bought three tickets on a Paquet boat—"

Michael looked away. "Mr. Reese, you haven't finished your whiskey."

"It's—it's a bit strong, young man."

"Are you lightheaded?"

"Yes. Yes, I am."

"This man murdered my parents years ago."

"I understand that."

"For years he let me believe it was a case of mistaken identity—"

"I took care o' you!" Sullivan bellowed. "You were a kid off the streets, and you wouldn't have gotten anywhere if I hadn't helped you. I've known who you were all these years—you never heard from me. I heard o' you! Do you know how many times I seen you cleaning the chumps in Canfield's?"

"Pete? Pete, do you see that you're in the presence of a pair of fools?"

"I ain't too sure about you, too, mister."

"Well, if you're curious about your own role in this, ask your boss about John J. Moran."

Sullivan tried to get around the desk. "You? Jesus Christ, man, don't—"
He was trying to reach for Pete as if he could stop what was going to
happen there, before it touched him, but Michael had the gun barrel well
wrapped in the suit coat and he reached over and pressed the coat up
against Pete's belly and at the same time pulled the trigger. The muffled
report sounded like a heavy book being slammed to the floor, but that
was loud enough. Reese was staring, his glass still in his hand, his mouth
wide open. The room was filled with smoke and Michael's ears rang.
Sullivan was falling back over his chair when Michael fired at him, hitting
him first in the chest, and then after a pause, firing again, hitting him right
in the middle of the forehead. In his last glimpse Michael saw his head
split wide open. "Like Westfield," Michael thought first, and then, "like
my father." He sensed something wrong inside him, something going
wrong—he knew it. Reese was rising from the sofa, still silent, his mouth
open. Pete's dead body, spilling blood, slipped over onto Reese's seat.
The smoke was as thick as a fire. Michael took his elbow.

"Mr. Reese, if you're thinking clearly you'll see that the only place we
can go is back to the Waldorf-Astoria."

VII

They were around the corner when Michael heard the first doors
slamming and people coming into the street, and they were reaching the
next corner when they both heard a man's bellowing shout, followed by a
woman's scream. Reese shuddered, and Michael took this as a good sign.
Michael had Reese by the arm, exerting a firm, steady pressure forward.
When they reached the stairs up to the elevated, Reese said in a clear,
strong voice, "I'll be all right now," and Michael let go.

There was a potbellied stove below the stairs to the platforms, and
after the northbound train came along, the two men were alone warming
their hands over it. Michael had the gun wrapped in the newspaper
tucked under his arm.

"You can throw that thing in the fire," Reese said.

"No, they'll find it. That's what they do. And then if they find the
driver who took us up here, they'll fit the two pieces together."

"You thought of all this in advance?"

"I had all day."

"You think you'll get away with it?"

Michael looked at him. "With what? We heard them admit to killing
Andy to protect their interest in your business. The police might mis-
construe our relationship and insist that we killed them to defend
ourselves—that killing Andy was their attempt to muscle in on this.

There are a lot of ways to see this thing. No, go about your affairs in your normal way. If your business with Sullivan is really legitimate, the police won't get around to you in weeks."

"You *used* me!"

The train was coming. "Mr. Reese, what do you think they would have done to you if I hadn't come along?"

Reese sneered and turned for the stairs.

Michael insisted that they go down to Thirty-third Street before crossing to Fifth Avenue. The cold assailed them, but the extra effort seemed worth it. If they were seen approaching the hotel at all, it would be from the south—they could even say that they had walked down to Michael's house. His energy was leaving him quickly now and he was weary of thinking ahead. The string quartet was still playing in the dining room, and the bartender leaned over to tell them that they shouldn't have any trouble getting a table now. That meant the headwaiter had been looking for them, and if the bartender had an odd way of saying so, it was only his way of looking for something extra. A little something: no sense calling undue attention. Reese stiffened at the thought of eating, but Michael pointed out how they had been noticed. "Well, we'll be quick about it," Reese said.

The dining room was filled with music, the murmur of voices, and the rattle of plates; there were the odors of food and perfume; and Michael could see even Reese's narrow banker's eyes darting to the beautiful women. Michael was thinking of what Sullivan had told him, that his father had taken—or found—some of Sullivan's money. The records of the Paquet Company might still be available, but his first thought was to forget them—not so much because Michael was afraid he would find his family's names registered, as he was afraid that he would *not* find them. It would be better for him if he tried to relax and enjoy his surroundings. The headwaiter asked about Michael's newspaper, and Michael said that he would just as soon put it on an empty chair at his table, thank you. The tabloids were right in playing up the contrasts of the city: LUST-CRAZED GUNMAN DINES ELEGANTLY AFTER DOUBLE KILLING!

After he let Reese go home, he walked over to the river and threw the gun as far as he could past the rocks on the shoreline, and then he walked back to Third Avenue to take the el downtown. It was late again for the third night in a row and he still wasn't tired. He wasn't comfortable with Reese, but he could not second-guess himself. He had not been able to see any other way of getting to Sullivan. And he had not been able to see anything else to do about it but what he'd done. The man who had murdered his parents by mistake had killed Andy as a warning. Michael would have been in grave danger as long as Sullivan was alive. That Sullivan had been after his father because of money was beside the point. That he had assumed that Michael was a thief or that he could be frightened away by what had been done to Andy, *was*—he could decide any time that Michael was a threat to him or even merely an annoyance. All of that was rationalization, too. Michael thought he would have killed Sullivan if he had found him helpless on his deathbed. With Andy alive.

But he was not afraid of Reese. He was not happy with him, he was not comfortable, but he was not afraid.

The final editions of the morning papers had the story on the front pages with banner headlines. Sullivan and a business associate murdered in Sullivan's home by two men seen leaving by a woman peeping around her curtain. Michael thought he should have expected that and warned Reese in advance. He called Reese after eleven o'clock. Reese wanted to meet for lunch; there was a little seafood place down near his office. Michael wanted to say something, but it wouldn't help matters, and Reese's tone was too suspiciously self-controlled for Michael not to take it into account.

After Reese suggested seafood, Michael wanted to say that he had been curious about what Reese would eat today. Last night in the dining room of the Waldorf, Reese had put away a steak with Béarnaise sauce, potatoes, and a flaming dessert, and although he had hardly calmed down, he had gone at his food like a dockworker. Whether he had known it or not, Reese had given all the signs of a man celebrating an escape, and for that reason Michael did not think he would place himself in jeopardy again. No matter how Reese wrestled with his conscience or agonized, he was a man who liked his safety too much. He was not a brave man. He had never done a brave thing in his life.

At lunch Reese seemed merely to have come to grips with his terror. He ate silently and quickly, but determinedly, as if whatever the fates had visited upon him would not be allowed to interfere with the proceeds of a life justly lived. He had oysters and Maryland crab. The restaurant was filled with a lunchtime crowd. Michael had eaten nothing the night before, and settled for a piece of sole today. Before the waiter took the plates away, Reese mopped up the last of the broth with a chunk of bread. The bread made a knot in his cheek as he wiped his fingers carefully on his napkin.

"Didn't sleep last night," he said and swallowed. "I had a long time to think about the difference between a man like you and a man like me. The difference between the things we're *willing* to do is obvious, and I won't waste your time." Reese dropped his napkin on the center of the table. "I wanted to understand the difference in *how* we're willing to do things. From the moment I saw you last night, you were doing things that I'd normally never dream of doing, bribing this one and that, using force—do you see what I mean?"

"Normally I don't come out for lunch, Mr. Reese."

"Yes, yes, I know you're busy. I know now how busy you are. Well, I decided that that was the secret of your success. So I wanted to see if I could continue to give you a dose of your own medicine."

Michael sat back and stared. Reese had screwed himself up for this, and if Michael gave him an argument, it would only make this easier.

"You're a very clever young man. Not so young, in fact. You lied your way into the Westfield household. If I understood your remarks last night correctly, there was a man named Moran with whom you had similar dealings years ago. If I had the context right, that came *after* you took up residence with the Westfields. Astonishing. I knew him, you know." Reese was picking at his nails now, and from time to time he would look up to engage Michael's eyes. "Westfield. I knew him. We used to live in Murray Hill, too, on Thirty-fifth Street. Occasionally we had business. I'd see him on the streetcar. A sad man who liked to talk, I remember." Reese looked up. "Did he know about you? You didn't deceive him, too, did you?"

"Yes, he knew about me, and no, I didn't deceive him."

"I'm glad you regard the question as an affront because I don't intend to ask any more like it." He smiled. "For instance, I'm not going to ask you what my daughter knows about you because I don't want to hear it. I don't want to know the answer."

Reese leaned forward. "I asked about Westfield because I wanted to know if you had any awareness of how much a father can know about his child. I've watched you now, and I have to believe that you were less than candid with Westfield—that he found you out."

Michael felt uneasy. If Sullivan had had him wrong out of stupidity, then Reese was less wrong for more sinister reasons. He was bending his facts and his own shrewd guesses to conform to something else on his mind. The dismissal of Westfield as a sad man who liked to talk had given Michael a glimpse of a very cold-blooded man—the same man Michael had seen getting out of Sullivan's library so quickly last night. If he didn't want to hear what his daughter knew—Michael would have declined to tell him—it was because he already had all the information necessary to make him satisfied with the course his fears required him to take. He was a frightened man all the time, Michael realized, frightened of everything; when such men lost heavily at cards, they were liable to do anything to save themselves.

"To be truthful with you, Westfield, I was hoping that you would go away, just disappear of your own accord. Perhaps Emily would have come to her senses somewhere along the way, though I doubt it. She's led a very sheltered kind of existence. You're the first man who's ever paid any real attention to her. What do you want with her anyway? I knew that sooner or later men would come around, junior officers from the bank, at the worst one of her Jews from her settlement house, but not you. Do you know what people say about you? You're the cleverest cardplayer in New York. Among the people closest to you is a notorious prostitute and madam. What does a man like you want with a girl as plain and frail as my daughter? I know her, you see. I know what she is. And why shouldn't she feel swept off her feet, as they say? Well, it didn't make sense to me from the start, and when Sullivan said he knew you and that you were probably trying to blackmail me, I made up my mind. I don't know if she's gone mad or what, but I do know that you're mad. Mad as a hatter. Oh, I don't care what your grievances and complaints are, young man—"

"You said you made up your mind before you knew what they were."

"And I had. I don't like people like you, Westfield. I don't like the people you know. I don't like the way you think. I don't like your motives. Whether you think so with your gentleman's manners and dress, to me you're one of that whole mob, prostitutes, madams, thieves—"

"Which thieves?"

"Sullivan! Do you think I didn't know what he was? He told me who you were. He was the one who said you were trying to blackmail me, and out of respect for my daughter I wanted to believe your version. As late as last night, in fact, I did."

"Emily knows all about it."

Reese glared. "That's all the confirmation I need." He breathed through his teeth. "That's how far you've dragged her down already. Well, I'm going to protect that girl, Mr. Westfield or whatever-your-name-is. I didn't want her with a gambler; I don't want her with a common criminal and murderer. I'm going to keep you away from my family. You're not going to drag anyone in my care down to your depths. But I'm wary of you, Mr. Westfield; I want you to know that, too. I'm not going to tell you what I'm going to do to keep you away from her, and I'm not going to tell you what I will do if you manage to get close, but it will be something, I promise you. You're not going to see her again, Mr. Westfield, and I'm warning you not to try." He stood up. "My recollection is that you paid for dinner last night." He crumpled a five-dollar bill and dropped it on the table. "Good-bye, Mr. Westfield. Good-bye to you." Michael did not watch him go. Crumpling the money had been some kind of insult. Michael wanted to compose himself before he got up from the table, and he was beginning to see that it was going to take a bit of time.

There was a postcard from her from Deal, dated Monday, in his mailbox when he got home later in the afternoon, and in the evening he tried to telephone Reese, but there was no answer. The postcard bore the information that the weather was raw and that she missed him terribly already. If her father really did have a plan, she had not been aware of it Monday morning. Michael spent part of the evening writing a reply. He saw no point in telling her about her father's ultimatum. At this moment he still could not imagine what her father could do that would not bring it all down on top of him, as well as running the risk of losing his daughter completely. The tactic of silence suited his mood anyway; something was going out of him—he was beginning to get some perspective on what he had done.

The next day was Andy's funeral, and he and Kate rode up the Harlem Valley branch of the New York Central to Millerton, Andy's hometown, and walked up the hill from the railroad station to the church where the funeral was held. Kate had wanted to come, and they had met at Grand Central early in the morning. He had not slept again and he could see her concern; so he bought her a couple of newspapers so that he could snooze undisturbed on the train. She found the stories about the double murder and asked if he knew about Sullivan, and without opening his eyes he said he had seen it in yesterday's late edition. It was a cardplayer's moment and he could not look to see how he was doing, but after a silence he heard the rattle of the newspaper as she turned the page.

The coffin was closed and the church was cold and smelled damp. The minister spoke of the deceased as if he could not exactly remember who he was, and then the coffin was carried out by six beer-bellied farmers—one of them Andy's father, it turned out. The coffin was put in a hearse, but before the procession formed people talked to one another and a woman introduced herself as Andy's mother and said she could guess who they were, and then she called one of the pallbearers and introduced him as her husband. He was more suspicious than his wife, but he warmed when Michael and Kate expressed their sorrow. It was an icy, clear day and the procession formed, twenty or twenty-five people marching down the hill behind the shining hearse, across the railroad track and up wagon-rutted roads through the fields for another half mile. There was a burial group up there, around a knoll where the land began to rise. Kate wept and Michael held her, but he was thinking that Andy and Emily would never know each other. Normally he did not go to funerals and there was the emptiness that had begun to spread through him yesterday. After Westfield died, Michael had had a lawyer find out what would be involved in having his parents reburied, but then when he thought it through again, he let it go and told the lawyer to send him a bill for his troubles.

They caught the early train back to the city. The family wanted them to come back to the house, but Michael thought that he and Kate would be too much the objects of attention for that. On the way down to the city he looked out the window at the poor farms and the hard land this far from the Hudson and asked himself if Andy's parents would have felt comforted if they had been told that their son's death had already been avenged. He thought not. He could not take the paddle boat up the Hudson without thinking of his parents and the part of his life they had never seen. He thought of Westfield in the same way.

It was dark when the train reached the station, and they had to go up the ramps against the rush of commuters. She waited until they were on the sidewalk before she asked if he wanted something to eat. He said no. She asked if there was anything else bothering him and he said no. She took his arm. "I want you to get your rest."

"I'll call you."

She kissed his cheek and turned for the line of cabs.

He walked around for a while. When he realized how much easier this would be for him if he knew Emily was all right, he turned around and went home.

There was nothing in the mailbox from her, and the letter he wrote was short, hardly more than a note, but by the time he finished, it was too late to telephone Reese. Michael went out to mail his letter, and when the air hit him he felt awake again, so he went down to Fourteenth Street to pick up the papers. The real theater had moved uptown years ago, but there was still the Academy of Music and, on the other side of Third Avenue, the Jefferson. The el rumbled by and the traffic noise filled the street and the lights poured out from under the el and past the square all the way down to Eighth Avenue and beyond. If you were willing to walk that far, you were rewarded with the best steaks available anywhere on earth. And coming back, full-bellied and ready for bed, you could look up Broadway to the lights at Madison Square, thinking that there wouldn't be enough nights in a lifetime for what was there to be had. It was a wonderful city, a marvelous city, small enough to walk around in, various enough, mysterious enough. Michael was by no means the man Reese thought he was. He was still learning and exploring; he knew

Indian curry and Italian veal, Theodore Roosevelt and Gyp the Blood. In the context of all this, the brightness and the activity, the newspapers reporting nothing more on the Sullivan killings, Michael missed Emily, as much as she said she missed him.

In the morning he telephoned Reese at his bank, and Reese's secretary responded gruffly, "Well, I'll see that he gets your message." Michael had the more important message at once, that Reese had told his mug of a secretary to discourage any and all calls from a young man named Westfield. It was Thursday and Michael had not tended to business seriously for days. If he thought it would do any good, he would go downtown and stand outside her father's bank, waiting for the man to come out. There was nothing new on the Sullivan case, and in the afternoon detectives set up shop in the office of the religion editor to question people who knew Andy. As a matter of routine, Michael was asked to account for himself and he told them he was home, not alone, and when he was asked whom he was with, he saw the connection that would not be dismissed as coincidence for long: Emily *Reese!* He was with Emily *Reese!* Reese's name would appear all through Sullivan's papers. Someone would see that the man who had given Andy Fletcher all kinds of work for extra money had spent the Saturday night of Andy's death with the daughter of Sullivan's banker. The description of the visitor to the *World* the previous Monday fit that of the other dead man. *Miss Reese, did you happen to mention a man named Sullivan to Mr. Westfield?*

To the police, Michael said, "I was with a young lady. In deference to her family, I'd like to leave her name out of it."

The detectives exchanged glances. "You may have to give it to us eventually."

"We had dinner off Longacre Square. I rented a carriage in the early part of the evening."

The detective took off his bowler and showed his partner and Michael the sweat-rotted lining. "Look at this thing. I was thinking last week that I got to replace it." He put it back on his head. "Dinner off Longacre Square, a nice ride in a carriage down to your apartment. Now you want to protect her good name. You really know how to do it, don't you?"

"I get by."

"Hey, you're not one of those guys who's going to get his cock in a knot if I treat myself to a good-lookin' hat, are you?"

"I think everybody should have a nice hat."

"I'll bet you do," the detective said, and waved him out. They could see his desk from where they were, and he had difficulty keeping his fingers moving over the typewriter keys while he sorted things out. They thought he was a dandy and wouldn't have any interest in him in connection with Andy—unless he drew more attention to the other ways he could establish his whereabouts Saturday night, or how much he wanted to protect the girl. He had not told them the name of the restaurant, but now that seemed more right than wrong. He had to leave it as it was.

There was no letter from her that evening, and later on he went up to Canfield's to shake off his lethargy. He sat down at a draw poker game; one of the players who knew him well had read about Andy and offered his regrets. Michael had been thinking of Emily and he felt a shock, but then after a moment he saw that he shouldn't have been thinking of anyone at all.

Trying to pay attention didn't help the cards. He couldn't play for two dozen hands and then lost with two pair to someone who bettered a pair he should have folded. He won two small pots, and held on with no confidence in his cards in one that was larger. Betting against him was the man who had beaten him earlier with the cheap three of a kind, and this time he showed a flush to the ten while Michael's flush ran on to the queen. An hour later Michael lost an opportunity when the man opened strongly and then leaned back from the table to draw two. Then the man bet two hundred dollars, a large bet, with a sweeping toss that didn't quite get the chips to the center of the table. The last of the four tangled up in his fingers somehow and he brushed at it quickly, as if it had given his game away. Michael knew he was lying, but he didn't want to believe his own instincts. He folded his two pair, and the man showed aces as openers and kept the other three cards down. He was radiating relief as he raked in the chips, no matter how he tried to set his face. Michael decided that he needed two more hands to commit the man's style to memory for possible future use, and then he picked up his own chips and went home.

The next morning's mail brought the news that he had been anticipating for most of the past two days. It was his Tuesday night letter to Emily, delivered to Deal and properly marked and scribbled on—and returned. ADDRESSEE UNKNOWN stamped on both sides by some thorough soul. It was possible to trace the letter's progress from the city to the Jersey shore through all the dated stamps and cancellations. It allowed him to see that the letter had reached there and not found her. Before he threw it away he opened it, as if by some mysterious process it had acquired a clue to her disappearance, but it contained only his letter, his Tuesday night, which he saw differently now. He had had some hope, still not awake from the insane dream into which he had been plunged—he had dream-walked through it, he knew that now. He saw it differently. Andy would not have followed Sullivan's hoodlum if Michael had not wanted it, if Michael had chosen another way of dealing with Andy. And around on the other side, the position in the world Sullivan had attained was nothing like a matter of chance. No, Michael now had a different view. That he and Sullivan had arrived in the same room a scant thirty-six hours after Sullivan's third threat against him was more a demonstration of Sullivan's view that what they had in common was finally more important than all the other considerations; and more certainly still it matched Reese's preconception of him. More than he wanted to admit, he was what people thought he was. Sometimes a man pleading for his life can build an elegant little gallows for his executioner. Michael believed he would have been thinking these things even if his letter had not been returned. But he was not sure what the situation would have been if he had been receiving *her* letters or if he was expecting her to return Sunday or Monday. More than anything, he had emerged from the insanity. None of this had happened by accident. He had had to kill Sullivan and he could have protected himself from Reese only by implicating him in the act itself—and somehow he had convinced himself that it would work just long enough to finish the job. Even by Friday the shock was still wearing off. He had responded to insanity with insanity, but he could not see that it could have gone any other way.

VIII

In the next days the rest of his letters came back, and on Saturday he telephoned the Reese home a dozen times, and on Sunday he went up there and knocked on the door even though he could see that the house was closed.

In the morning he called Reese's office and asked the secretary if his employer was in the city, but the secretary said that he was not at liberty to say.

"Is this at Mr. Reese's direction?"

The secretary said that he was not at liberty to say that either, and when Michael tried to find out if Mr. Reese was receiving his messages, the secretary said good-day and hung up. That night Michael went uptown and walked past the house, but the windows were dark, as if the family had gone away. Michael was afraid that Reese was courting police attention, but Michael did not see how he could do anything about it under the circumstances. He was more concerned with Emily anyway. With each passing day he was safer from the police, he knew; but, just as important, he was growing impatient with their inability to find him. He wanted to get on with his life—if he could figure out how.

The two detectives who had questioned him in the office came around to his apartment on Thursday morning. The one had not bought a hat, and the other, who was older and had a pocked complexion, was interested in seeing the inside of the apartment. Michael was in his pajamas and robe.

"Couple more things to talk to you about, Mr. Westfield," the man with the hat said. Michael showed them in and closed the door. If they wanted to use the few seconds in the parlor alone to snoop around, he could establish that he had nothing to hide.

"Ah, Mr. Westfield, we have a report of a man coming to see you a week ago last Monday and gettin' into an argument with Fletcher. Why didn't you tell us about it?"

"I wasn't there. I thought somebody else already told you."

"Who was this guy?"

The other detective was looking around the apartment.

"I never found out. He never came back and he never telephoned."

"Yeah, well, did Fletcher tell you what kind of lookin' guy this fella was?"

"Short, stocky, around forty, a hard face, looked like a hoodlum."

"You remember all that, do ya?"

"I'm a trained observer, like you. I thought you had all this."

"We did, no thanks to you."

The one with the pocked face was staring at Michael. "I think you ought to watch your ass, Mr. Westfield."

"I don't understand."

" 'I'm a trained observer.' Who do you think you're fucking with, the suckers who play the horses? What do you mean, you thought we had the story? Who was going to give the story if you didn't?"

"I thought you heard it Wednesday. I was out of town."

"Where were you?" the man with the hat asked.

"I went to the funeral. It was upstate."

"Why didn't you go back to the house?"

The man with the pocked face stood up.

"I don't like that stuff," Michael said. "I don't like funerals."

"Yet you went to this one," the man with the hat said.

"He worked for me. I liked him."

"But you wouldn't go back to the house. You didn't tell us about the argument the kid was in. And now you tell us that he worked for you. When are you going to start coming clean with us?"

The pockmarked one said, "You know what I think, you son of a bitch? I think you got something to hide. I catch you fucking around, I'm going to fuck you right back!" He moved around the table. "Where's the bedroom?"

"In there."

The other said, "You better give us the name of the young lady you were with the other night, Mr. Westfield. I gotta check everybody's alibi."

Michael told him. "She's out of town. You can get in touch with her through her father." He told the detective how. "Look, you want me to be honest with you. I don't know how to get in touch with her directly because that is the way her father wants it."

The detective laughed. "And you wanted to protect her reputation? Oh, Mr. Westfield, I am surprised. Did you hear that, Herman?"

"I heard it," the other called. "He better not make any mistakes or he'll get the fucking of his life." He came back to the parlor. "Let me hear that you been usin' drugs on young girls, I'll fix ya'! You know what I mean? I'll fix ya'!"

The man with the hat was on his feet. "We'll check this out, Westfield. Don't go makin' trouble for yourself."

He waited only until he heard them on the stairs before he went to the desk to start writing to Emily. He expected to get this letter back, too, and as much for the evidence as the belief that he was actually communicating with her, he wrote what he could of what had happened to Andy and that he had gone to the funeral with his friend Kate, and so forth—as straightforward a recitation of the facts as he had a right to. He kept on going, planning each sentence in advance, leaving no wastepaper behind, finishing with an apology for the betrayal of her trust that made him aware again of his ultimate readers. And thinking of them, he delayed mailing the letter until late that evening so that it would bear an appropriate postmark.

He never heard from the police again. He felt them behind him for weeks, months, but he never saw them again. His letter to Emily was returned from Deal the following Tuesday, and he put it away. On the weekend he took the ferry to Weehawken and then the train down to the shore, but he couldn't muster the courage to go all the way to Deal. If he learned anything at all, it would be only bad news, the worst being that she had decided she had made a mistake. He rode back to the city in the middle of the night.

The gossip had started. Louise telephoned him in the middle of the week to report that she had heard the most loathsome story, that the Reeses had spirited Emily out of the city to get her away from him. He asked her if she knew any more, and she said that she had only been told that he had been exerting an evil influence over the girl. She started to laugh before she realized that his question confirmed the story she had heard, and then she said she was sorry. She said she would say nothing to

Julie and Thomas, and then, because she felt helpless, she invited him to dinner. He accepted.

Kate telephoned him the next week. She had thought she would hear from him before this. At once she sensed that something else was wrong, and without inquiring further, she invited him to come over. "Gert says the place is a dump without you."

He accepted that invitation, too.

He was trying to hold himself together. He was disintegrating inside, so sick in his soul he thought his body would die. He wandered through the days, trying to remember what he was supposed to be doing, and when he had to go out of his normal routine, up to see the colonel, for instance, it became an ordeal that left him exhausted. Yet he understood that he could not try to close himself off from other people—he wanted to do it so much that he had to start getting up earlier and earlier to make sure that he got to the office at a reasonable time. He had no energy. He had been through it before, and as the weeks went on, he remembered the other times more clearly, but nothing helped. He had been this way after his parents' deaths and then after Moran's and again after Westfield's. In his youth when he had gone after Moran he had hoped for some kind of reward, a state of grace, a lifting of the misery that had brought him down. He could remember shivering in the doorway across from the Bedford on West Seventeenth Street, thinking that he was going to bring it all to an end. Michael could remember feeling a terrible fear for Westfield in the last months, but it had not prepared him for the shock of his death. It was the kind of blow that echoed and reverberated for months afterward. The night of Westfield's death he rode uptown on the el and felt the pain even as he stood on the platform waiting for the train uptown, but then the train went by the rooming house and he could see the people and commotion in what must have been the room—from the train Michael could see Westfield's body on the bed and the gore spattered on the wall behind him. Michael was standing and he could feel his strength leave him so suddenly that his knees gave way. He was arriving to identify the body. In another few minutes he would be looking down at Westfield's corpse with the gun still in the mouth, the eyes open, the two incongruous trickles of blood from the nose in a face that was otherwise spotless, though misshapen. His face was clean, but the bed—that whole side of the room—was covered with blood, brains, and bits of bone. Michael stood over Westfield and looked down into the dead eyes that seemed frozen in a moment of acute disappointment, thinking that if he endured this he would have earned at least some kind of peace—but before many more months had passed he was thinking that everything had fallen apart again, that the winter itself was the one in which his parents had died, the way the winter he had killed Moran had become one with the first.

Michael wrote to Emily once more in Deal, and when the letter was returned, he sent it to the uptown address. It did not come back. It was June now and he took the ride up Broadway. There were different curtains in the windows, and when he got closer, he could see a different name over the bell.

A maid answered, and while she was saying that she didn't have the information he wanted, the lady of the house came down the stairs.

"The Callahans live here now, young man."

"Did the Reeses leave a forwarding address?"

"All I have is their lawyer's name. I'll get it for you."

The maid stared at him.

"How long have you been here?"

"Two weeks."

"She seems to be tickled to be here," Michael said quietly. The maid was a big, dark-haired girl with tiny blue eyes. She looked over her shoulder.

"New money," she whispered. "Braggin' to their friends about the money they saved on this place."

"All they've been talking about for two weeks, eh?"

"Right. They're in politics—"

Mrs. Callahan heard something. She looked at the maid as she came up, then gave Michael the paper. She looked as if she wanted it back. Michael said, "I've been out of town. Do you have any information about the Reeses?"

"I suggest you contact him," she said, pointing to the paper. She closed the door. As he went down the stairs, Michael could hear her shriek at the maid.

The lawyer was the last person Michael intended to contact. If Reese was so frightened that he felt he had to run, he could be panicked into anything. Michael had been following the case. A police reporter had told him, "They're hoping people will forget about it. They thought it was gang work, but nobody knows a thing. Now they're saying a paid killer came in from out of town, which is their way of saying they know they don't have a chance." Now Michael did not turn around to look back at the Reese/Callahan house. The Callahans were in politics, and they had gotten the house at a bargain—if there was a connection between the sale and the bafflement of the police, Reese had paid a heavy price indeed.

And the gossip seemed to confirm it. Louise reported the stories, the worst of which was that Emily was pregnant. Since the story was in circulation within two weeks of her disappearance, he dismissed the possibility of validity at once, but the idea of such malicious gabbling upset him deeply. Louise told him he should have expected no less. "It wasn't that you defied conventions, it was that you appeared to defy them. Everybody expected it of you, but nobody expected it of her. They're angry with her for unsettling their world, and they'll be free to talk about her the rest of their lives."

He asked her what she thought.

"I only know what I've seen and what you've been willing to tell me, but I would say that you went too far. Somehow you went too far."

By then they had heard that Reese was ill, but the person passing the story along could not say if it had originated in New Jersey or Europe. It was the middle of July, and he was thinking about Saratoga—and what Saratoga might have been.

He was back a month when Louise telephoned him one afternoon at the office. She never did that, and for a moment, after what may have been weeks of peace, he thought she had learned something about Emily. It was his sister. Louise was crying more out of shock than anything else, for Julie was unhurt. Her marriage was definitely over, however, and her eye was blackened, and she was in an embarrassing predicament. But she was unhurt.

Not completely. By evening, when he saw her, the swelling had puffed up the side of her face to frightening proportions. She was ambulatory. Thomas and Ethel were present, but their children were not. They were at home. Julie's children were home, too, with Roger, which was Julie's embarrassing predicament. Michael had not eaten, and the others were waiting for Hannah to bring him a plate of cold beef and potato salad. Hannah had been in the family for more than thirty years. Hannah was an old woman now and growing frail, but when Michael had attempted to talk to Louise about her, Louise had said, and shyly, as if she did not want to call attention to her good works, "Hannah has a home with me as long as she wants one."

When Hannah was gone, Michael paid attention to his food. Ethel and Louise were tending to Julie's cold compresses while Thomas drummed his fingers on his knee. "He ruined a beautiful face," Thomas said. "Look at her face. He doesn't have the right to do that."

"We don't know that she'll be marked," Louise said.

"I want to kill the son of a birth," Thomas said.

Julie coughed, spat blood and drooled a little. Louise was there with a cloth. She listened to Julie mumble. She kissed her on the forehead.

"Yes, I understand. I will." To the others, she said, "Julie wants to be sure all of you know the truth as I understand it and as Julie has told it to me—"

Then, as if she wanted to preside over the telling of her "truth," Julie rose, pushed herself up to a sitting position and, like a little girl caught with her skirt up for the neighborhood boys behind the garage, tried to smile—*Wait! There's an explanation for this!*

IX

As Julie sat up, smiling, idiotic, glassy-eyed, the child rising phoenix-like from the adult, the smile freezing into an act of child's defiance, and Michael heard the dreary recitation of Fleming's drinking and violence as well as a mercifully short lie about her adultery (she was caught *flagrante delicto* and some explanation was required)—he thought he saw that human beings, himself included, moved within a narrow range indeed. It was a bitter moment. He was not half as incensed as Thomas about Fleming; he had been watching Fleming staring out of those tiny eyes at everyone else for years, and it had occurred to him long ago that Fleming wanted to stop staring and start punching. And if Julie wanted to continue the battle that seemed to have begun so many years ago in Saratoga with her father, then she would find another fool like Fleming, and it would come to this again, or something like it, eventually, in the future.

He was thinking of what Sullivan had said about his father. Michael was too old now and knew too much about people, and remembered too much of what his parents had wanted, to dismiss the accusation as untrue. While he had no reason to believe Sullivan, he was not going to lie to himself. He did not owe that to anyone. What Sullivan had said conformed to what Michael knew of people, including himself, just as Michael could see that there was no point in lying to himself any more about Emily Reese. They had met in April and this was September, and what had made her different from all the others of her social class was becoming more and more difficult for him to discern. He had been told he wanted an innocent young girl who would love him. Now no one could say he had not found her.

Julie needed money, which was the real reason Louise had called them together. Having to manage her own affairs and watching her children squander their inheritances had made Louise crafty with money and more respectful than ever of those who knew how to make it, so Michael felt that the problem was in good hands. Presumably Julie would be able to take possession of the house again, but she had no cash for running expenses and she needed a lawyer. If Michael gave Louise two thousand, she would pay it out to Julie so that it would last until the end of the year.

It was a very bitter moment for Michael. If Julie was still caught up in the battle that had begun at Saratoga, then Michael himself was still fighting to get free of Westfield, too, the man who thought he was a clown, who wanted romantic adventure, and a great love. A son easily achieves his father's most secret dreams, and then must pay his own price for them.

He had been over everything. Reese had fled New York for only one reason: he was afraid that Michael was going to kill him. From that first Sunday morning meeting with Sullivan, Reese had known that Sullivan had killed Michael's parents, but his first thought had been to protect his investment, his deal with Sullivan—never mind his daughter, or her suitor. Reese was afraid that Michael would see his behavior for the disgrace that it was and want to come after him as he had gone after Sullivan. Michael was still tangled up with Westfield? Emily had been spirited away from New York—and a boy named Andy Fletcher was dead and buried with his throat slit at the age of twenty-two.

A long winter. Hannah died and then Gert; and Julie found, after everything, that she did not want to change her life; but Louise made her change and finally so did Kate.

Not long after the meeting called to announce the end of Julie's marriage to Roger Fleming, it was discovered that Hannah had a massive stomach cancer, and within days she went into a rapid decline. By Christmas morning the stout woman was something fragile, yellow and waxen, muttering the vowels of the Nicene Creed; and died two nights later, unconscious and drooling. There was an odd cough and she was gone. Michael was by the bed. They were all there, Julie, Thomas, and Ethel, whom Hannah had despised, crying the loudest.

They saw each other again a few days later at the funeral, but mostly Michael kept to himself. Julie was giving Louise a bad time and Louise reported to Michael that she was seeing the man Roger had caught her with, a real estate slicker she had met the previous summer in Atlantic City. When Michael tried to tell her that it would all blow over, Louise cried, "No! No! Her husband came home roaring drunk and found her—notorious! Living like pigs! Pigs!"

The day after Hannah's funeral, on New Year's Eve, at four-thirty in the afternoon, Gert, not quite sober, slipped and fell on a patch of ice and broke her hip. Kate found Michael later that evening at Louise's; she identified herself first as Katherine, and it startled hell out of him when he took the earpiece and heard her voice. Yesterday at the cemetery he had asked Louise if she had wanted company this evening, and she had said yes. Thomas was with Ethel's family and Louise didn't know where Julie was, but she guessed that she was with her real estate man. Kate knew about Hannah's death, but when she said she would wait for him later, she started to cry.

Louise was looking up from the foot of the stairs. "You don't have to stay."

"The maid of a friend of mine broke her hip. There's nothing I can do and my friend doesn't expect to see me."

"Has she ever called here before?"

"Once."

"Oh." She thought she was on to something. "I wish I knew your secrets, Michael."

"If you knew my secrets, you wouldn't love me as much as you do."

At midnight they went for a walk, up to Broadway where the Christmas lights were strung, down to Seventy-second Street, where the construction site of the Ansonia Hotel a block to the south shadowed over everything. Michael knew that the elms sheltering Broadway would be gone soon enough and that buildings as tall as the Ansonia would line the street for as far as the eye could see. It took no great prophet. New York was already the rival of London or Paris, and what had happened downtown would happen up here—there were already brownstones in Harlem.

New Year's Eve, 1895. The horns blew and people cheered, and he kissed Louise on the cheek and wished her a Happy New Year, and she hugged him and said she hoped 1896 would be better for him, too.

He got to Kate's at one-thirty, and by then Gert was dead from internal bleeding. Johnson was out in Colorado tending to his mines, and Kate had a couple of the girls with her. The girls were crying and the bartender looked terrible; Kate was lying on the sofa with a towel over her eyes. Michael kissed her on the mouth. Without moving the towel she kissed him back. She knew his lips.

"I wasn't asleep, but I didn't hear you come in the room. That's some trick." She sat up.

"I'm sorry I took so long getting here."

"Well, it didn't matter. The doctors told us we could leave. She was in pain and they gave her opium to knock her out, but they said she was all right. I guess they wanted us out of there."

The bartender snapped his fingers. "Just like that. It's funny how they go sometimes."

"Let me have a little shot," Kate said to him. "I sent Johnson a telegram. I put at the end, 'Happy New Year.'"

One of the girls asked Michael if he wanted anything and he said no.

The bartender brought the drink around and Kate knocked it back. After a pause, Kate announced, "The rest of you can get out of here now."

The girls got their coats on and waited for the bartender while he straightened things up a bit. Kate did not get up to allow any of them to kiss her good-bye, so it was a bleaker scene than it needed to be, but not more bleak than Louise being alone in a house just emptied of death. As if she had been waiting for the passage of a suitable interval, Kate suddenly got up and locked the door.

"You know what Gert said about Hannah, don't you? 'I don't want to go like that.' She said that this week. Doesn't that beat everything?"

"Are you all right, Kate?"

She brought her arms in against her chest and her eyes closed and small furrows appeared in her brow. He was on his feet, reached for her and she opened her eyes again to see that he understood, and she let out a wail.

"You're going to stay with me, aren't you? I want your company."

"Sure."

"I'm going to have another. You know, I think about you. Look at me. You don't have a better friend than me, Michael."

"I know that." Kate could get wobbly from booze once in a while, and he was afraid that something unhappy might be starting. She came back with a real drink and sat down again. For years she had been sitting like a man in his presence, putting her ankle on her knee and pulling up her skirt to scratch her shin. Johnson thought it was wild. "Did you ever see a *lady* sit like that?" Now she put her feet up on the coffee table and took a sip of her drink.

"I've been thinking anyway that I got to make some changes. There's nothing to tell you now, but when there is, you'll hear it. It's the way you've always been with me, isn't it?"

At the end of his life he could remember that he thought this was the first clue he had that she was thinking of marrying Johnson. "Oh, you know I don't tell you everything, Kate."

"Sure." She raised her glass, but he realized that he had just hurt her badly. He was sitting forward in the chair as she suddenly began to cry. She waved him off. "Stay there, you bastard. Remind me to tell you sometime what I see in Johnson."

"I think you just did."

She blew her nose. "Well, I'm an old whore. That's one of the things Gert taught me. 'Please yourself, honey.' Oh, boy, have I always! I could tell you the things I've done in *my* life—well, we all have stories to tell. She did. Gert." She gazed at him. "She did a lot of things. Stole a lot. She told me a man gave her a diamond and she sold it in an hour for a hundred dollars. You know why? She asked me that. Because she thought the party would last forever. That's what she told me. Old people know strange things. She was right. Nothing lasts forever."

If she was angry about something beyond his careless remark, he didn't know what it was. He decided to let it go—he couldn't even tell if she was drunk or sober, he was so tired. And to cap it all, when he looked up, she was smiling.

They had not been together in years. Westfield had told him that she had been a chubby thing at sixteen, and almost ten years later when Westfield died she was a softer, slimmer, quieter woman. Now she was nearly thirty-six, and as Michael watched her undress and get into bed, she was another woman still. She knew that he had not been with a woman since Emily. They made love, or she tended to him—she was so expert he couldn't be sure which—and they fell asleep, their backs against each other as if they had been sleeping together forever.

In the morning he found her already awake, waiting for him. It was cold, with frost on the window, and they could see their breath on the air in the stillness of the room.

She wanted to make love again. For months he had been awakening to gather up yesterday's woes one by one, and today was no different. Hannah and Gert were dead, and here were Michael and Kate again as they had been after Westfield's death, but something had changed and it was more than their ages. Now she was thinking about marrying Johnson.

He saw her at Gert's wake and then the funeral, but if she had something to say she held it in. Two weeks later, however, she telephoned to say that she wanted to see him.

"I'm going to close up," she said. "Counting the real estate, I've got a million bucks—what the hell do I want to keep working for? But I'm staying in the city. Years ago I wanted to go to California, but I didn't have the nerve. I'd a been a fish out of water. There's only so much you can do in one lifetime. Johnson has to go back and forth to Colorado, and that suits us both just fine. I'd get sick of having anybody around all the time, and he says it's a different world out there, and there's something he gets out of it. He doesn't care if I'm faithful to him, but he doesn't want to be made a fool of. I know you're not crazy about him, but he thinks more of you than he's ever wanted you to know. 'That guy's so smooth,' he says, 'he could do your woman for years and you'd never know it.' "

"He didn't say that because he thinks a lot of me."

"He say's we're two of a kind. He never met people like us before and I told him there was nothing between us, but he only *wants* to believe, if you know what I mean."

"You knew all this two weeks ago."

"And now I'm telling you." She looked unhappy. "Listen, Michael, I know you think he's a dumb, bald, old cowboy, but you know me and you know the way I like things." She stopped; there was more, and she was afraid to say it. If he suggested she was holding something back, she might grow angry—but as soon as that was clear, she started crying. "I got to think of myself, Michael."

She had been seeing Johnson for years and he was the kind of man she enjoyed most, there was no question of it. She wanted to laugh and stay up all night drinking; if she slept all the next day, she did not feel a sense of loss. Johnson had told Michael that he had given up in despair many times out West and had gone on because he had had no other choice, and now he wanted to enjoy the time he had left. There were men who thought the rich life was their due, or they tried to pretend that they thought so—she could do worse. Michael knew her, and another kind of man would victimize her.

So he listened to her in that kind of daze, kissed her good-bye, and told her that he was her friend for life. In the hall she started crying, and he held her in his arms while her sobs echoed in the stairwell. He didn't know if he was ever going to see her again. For all he knew she was out of his life for good.

In March Louise put the house on the market and moved into a new five-room apartment near the park, and in April Kate was married, with Michael as best man and one of her oldest customers giving her away. The bride's business affairs having been concluded, the happy couple left at once for a honeymoon in the Colorado Rockies. Michael paid out another five thousand for Julie's divorce. No gratitude—not even a word. She had the detectives on Fleming, and Michael was just as glad not to hear from her. He went to Saratoga in an uneasy mood and had his worst season ever, losing seven thousand before the end of the meeting. 1896 was the first year Michael showed a loss, and in spite of a flurry of hope in December, the hemorrhage of money did not end. In December Julie's detectives found Fleming performing an unnatural act with another man, and now Fleming was covering her expenses while the lawyers rounded up the hotel room and the girl for the "evidence" in a New York divorce. For her silence and a complete suppression of evidence, Julie was going to get everything she wanted, including her real estate operator. He was an older man with pomade-flattened hair who wore a diamond pinkie ring—Julie knew the family hated him but did nothing to keep him in check. He was a man who believed he had an instant grasp of all situations, including Michael's "adoption," as he called it, and Thomas's bankruptcy after the first of the year. His name was Hafner and he thought Westfield "must have been some old boy" and that the way to deal with Thomas was to step in and take over his affairs. Hafner was asserting the position he had gained as a result of Fleming's indiscretion (even though he jeopardized Julie's settlement, whispering to all who wanted to hear how Fleming had been found—fully detailed); he was an outlander who had decided that his early successes with Julie had made him superior to them all. No matter: who and what he was costing Michael an additional five thousand, because of the delays caused by his advice to Julie to put the squeeze on Fleming. Julie was reasserting herself, too, the emerging *grande dame*—Michael liked to think that she was going to be legit again. When Kate wrote that she was coming into town, he looked forward to her visit so much that he wondered if he had fallen in love with her, although he knew what was really bothering him. He was sick of everything and everybody. In March he caught a real sucker of a rich man's son and cut into him for almost twenty-two thousand dollars. It made him believe that he was coming out of his misery. It was 1897; he was almost thirty-four years old.

X

The telegram arrived in the morning on a Tuesday in June. He received telegrams all the time as part of his business, and often he put them aside while he shaved or finished making his coffee. He actually did it with this telegram, dropping it on the pile of old letters on the table in the hall. He picked it up on the way out and had it in his hand when he locked the door. It seemed like a bright day, fresh, clear, and he finally got his thumbnail under the flap of the envelope as he went down the stairs.

> "MICHAEL—
> ARRIVING TODAY IN NEW YORK FOR THE FIRST TIME IN TWO YEARS AT 2:20 PM. PLEASE ADVISE IF YOU CAN MEET ME AT GRAND CENTRAL.
>
> EMILY REESE"

It was dated early afternoon the day before, in Portsmouth, New Hampshire. A train arriving at two-twenty would have just left, figuring a stop in Boston. He read the telegram again, but he could see no clue to what it meant. The sight of her name had stopped him cold, and when he became aware of himself again, his heart was racing in his chest. He wasn't sure he knew what she looked like. And when he thought twice, he wasn't sure that he wanted to be at the train.

Deep in his thoughts, he could imagine a police trap. Perhaps Reese had confessed—Michael knew it was madness, but he thought it: something in him fought against everything. He did not want to go through it all with her again.

But he was going to be there. He had hours before the train and he went down to the office, but before he arrived he knew he was not going to accomplish anything. In a way it was almost a relief because at least he had an answer to himself and perhaps—at last—an answer to her. She had been out of the city for two years. The last he had heard, she had gone to Europe with her family. For all he knew, she had led the way.

He had to struggle with his work and he was late getting up to the station, and she was out on the sidewalk with four pieces of luggage when he came along. He almost didn't recognize her. She was wearing black. He had to stop and call her name, and it wasn't until she started to turn around that he realized that she had changed as much as any of them. He had been right about the weather and the street was crowded, but as she turned he thought he heard her say his name. She was wearing her glasses and she seemed to search for him among the faces for a long time, but then she saw him. Her hand came up to her mouth, and he walked into somebody as he tried to get to her. She looked frightened. He felt as if he were going to his execution. He took her arm.

"Are you all right? I missed you so much. I couldn't find you."

She looked at him. She had lost weight and there were circles under her eyes. He wanted to kiss her, but he didn't know what he could do—he still didn't know what to think.

"We buried my mother yesterday," she said. "She was in poor health this past year. On Friday morning my father woke up to find her dead beside him."

"I'm sorry."

"Did you write to me?"

"Yes. I'm still in love with you, as much as ever."

"I wrote to you every day, Michael. Finally I had to stop."

"Where are you staying?"

"The Fifth Avenue. I sent them a telegram."

"Emily, every letter I wrote to you came back to me. I wrote for months."

"I was ill. I was ill for months."

"One of the stories that came back to New York was that you were pregnant. I didn't believe it. You would have come back."

"I heard the stories. People will say anything if it suits them."

"Are you ready, Miss?" The driver was back in his seat, leaning over to hold the door open.

"The Fifth Avenue." She looked at Michael. "When no telegram came, and you weren't at the arrivals gate, I was so afraid that my father was right about you."

Michael waited until they were in the hanson. "Your father did it all. I went over to Jersey once, but I was afraid you didn't want to see me. I went to your house twice. The second time there were new people there."

"When I became ill, they took me to Maryland for the sunshine. My father swore he had given you the address, that you had just taken advantage of me, for a long while I was too sick to write, and after that I gave up. When I got better we went to Europe. I didn't learn for months that my father had liquidated his holdings here. My mother told me he had had trouble, but by then I wasn't thinking of you. I was trying to forget you. Michael, I told her about us. I wanted someone to talk to about you."

"Then you weren't sure about me when you sent the telegram."

"No, but I couldn't stay there. Saturday morning, my father blamed me for my mother's death and her stroke in Europe."

It still wasn't clear. He started to ask a question, but she stopped him, saying that she had waited two years to see him. She kissed him on the mouth, moving toward him so suddenly that her tooth hit his lip and he was sure that he was cut and bleeding.

"Well, I love you," he said. "I've always loved you, and I'll do anything you want to make this up to you."

She kissed him on the cheek, shyly, like a little girl.

That evening after she had rested he went around to the Fifth Avenue with a carriage and had the driver take them over the river into Brooklyn and down Flatbush Avenue to Lundy's on Sheepshead Bay. The weather had been perfect all day, and by eight o'clock the air was chilly again. The moon was up, huge, a dark, fiery orange flashing through the trees as the carriage sped along. Emily was still in black. He had chosen Lundy's far out in Brooklyn because of the problem of her mourning—utter foolishness; her presence alone in the city so soon after her mother's death was scandal enough. She understood it as well as he did. "I don't *intend* any disrespect," she said, explaining her choice of dress. He took her tone as confirmation that she was prepared to break with everything, if she had to. He had had time to think. If there was more than she had already said, he did not need to know it. He has seen her now, and he knew that what he had thought the night they had together two years ago was true. He had married her. He had been married to her all this time.

She wanted to know what had happened while she was gone. There was no point in telling her about Andy. He told her that Kate was married, and he told her about the wedding and the party that had gone on for two days. He told her about Louise moving and the deaths of the servants, saving the choicest bit, Julie's escapades, for last. He wanted to hear her laugh. She was spellbound, seizing his wrist. She wanted to know all about "Julie's Mr. Hafner," as Louise insisted on calling him. And she wanted to know exactly what Julie's private detectives had caught Rober Fleming doing. Michael told her. Her eyes bulged. He kissed her. In another moment her embarrassment had her crying, her face hidden on his shoulder.

They went on. In the restaurant she told him more of what her father had said to her. He had turned on her, hysterical. Michael listened carefully. When he asked her what she thought of her father's reasoning, she said that he had changed for the worse in the past two years and had become insane after her mother's stroke. If anything, she said, her father's behavior had shortened her mother's life.

Now Michael wanted to let it go. Perhaps in his terror her father had done a perfect job of concealing the connection between her relationship with Michael and his own alleged business reverses, but perhaps he hadn't, and Emily understood that something her lover had done had precipitated everything—in any event, she had made her decision, and Michael felt in no position to question it.

Neither of them ate heavily—broiled fillets of fish and salad. She wanted to tell him how her father had moved them from New Jersey to Maryland and then to Europe while making everything seem newly invented. "When we were in Maryland and I was sick, I heard them fighting. First I thought they were fighting about me, but they weren't. It was the only time I ever heard them shriek at each other."

"What did your mother say to you when you told her about us?"

"She said she was being punished for her sins."

He smiled, "What do you think Roger Fleming has in store?"

She was goggle-eyed. "I never thought of that before in my life."

"Don't think about it now." In the two years he had been without her, in all the things he thought about her, he had forgotten how young she was. "I love you, Emily."

"Do you?"

"Yes."

They were ready to go. She was very tired, and they were quiet during the ride back to New York. She was asleep in his arms when they crossed the bridge, and the moon, higher now, small and white, cast a swaying patch of light into the carriage. From time to time he could see her hand, her fingers curled like a child's, but her nails perfectly shaped and buffed, a woman's. But he could see the child and he wanted to go on holding her.

She was still not awake when the carriage stopped in front of the Fifth Avenue Hotel. He told the driver to go on.

He awakened her as they approached Fourteenth Street. It was not yet eleven-thirty.

He sent the driver home and they went up the stairs. He would go down to Third Avenue to get a cab when she was ready to leave. He wanted the extra time with her, and she seemed to want it with him.

But they were both tired, and while he was getting tea she fell asleep on the sofa. He took off her shoes and put a blanket around her shoulders. Then he fell asleep in the chair.

At four they were awake again, and when he said he would get a cab she told him she did not want to leave. She started to tremble, and before he could reach her she was crying again. She had come to New York with only the hope that he had not married someone else, and the sound of his voice calling her in front of Grand Central had ended a despair that had threatened to carry her away.

She cried for a long time. There was more to tell, and when that was done he helped her to bed and then returned to the living room for one of his small cigars.

He slept on top of the covers that night, and the next day he went with her around to the Fifth Avenue to get her things. The manager of the hotel wanted to lecture her for being out all night—while she was in mourning—and Michael threatened to use his fists on him, and by the weekend the tongues were wagging again. But on the following Tuesday at City Hall, with only Louise in attendance, and the bride in a gray suit trimmed with black velvet, Emily Reese became Mrs. Michael Westfield.

11

Secrets

I

"Does Mike know any of this?"
"I never had cause to tell him," the old woman said.
"Good. Let's keep it that way, at least for a while longer."

II

Louise was put off by not being told what had happened to Emily up to the week before the wedding, but she made a far better adjustment to the marriage itself. Her curiosity was softened by the delight she took in Emily, whom she judged, against the evidence of the sudden marriage and the testimony of the gossips, as a "nice girl." In the light of that, Louise had an explanation for everything she heard. "Michael, the gossip is just terrible. I can see what's going on behind their eyes. You're a fiend and you've done something to that girl and ruined her."

Thomas thought so, or something like it, judging by the hearty welcome to the family he gave Emily and the glances that followed when he thought she wasn't looking his way. It was more than mentally undressing her. Thomas had had a dirty curiosity about other people all his life, but the intensity of this indicated that it had been inflamed by conversations he had been privy to. Louise had already conveyed Ethel's message that she felt "insulted" by Michael's assumption that they would have opposed him. It was one of those times Ethel chose to feel insulted; with her own marriage the oldest and apparently the most durable in the family, perhaps she saw an opportunity to claim a louder voice in the family's affairs. Michael had ignored her ploys in the past and he planned to do the same this time.

That was the beginning. Eventually Ethel forgot what she had on her mind and came around, even though she caught Thomas ogling his sister-in-law more than once. "My, that's a pretty dress she's wearing," Ethel would say to him loudly enough for the others to hear, and Thomas would grunt and get his attention on something else.

Julie kept her distance. Michael could see how well Emily remembered her—her voice would shrink to a murmur when she was speaking to Julie, so that Julie would strain to hear and then give up trying to communicate with the girl, to the point of appearing rude. But Michael could see that it was Emily who had Julie fixed in a careful glare, like a cat intimidating an inquisitive dog.

She was less successful with "Julie's Mr. Hafner," as she and Michael had taken to calling him. He was a lout and bully who made her skin crawl when he asked her how she had been, looking her over like something in a shop window while she answered. That the man was such a presumptuous bore made Emily want to see Julie more sympathetically, but it was as if Julie had deliberately closed her eyes to Hafner for the purpose of tormenting her family. She could see what they thought of him. It was as if Julie had no respect for herself or anyone else, much less him. When Emily concluded that that was in fact the case, she sealed herself off from her sister-in-law for good.

It was through Louise's suffering with Julie that Emily learned the rest of the family's secrets. Louise spilled everything, glad to have someone to fuss over again. For her part, Emily wanted Louise's attention; she needed a friend and she was trying to turn Michael's apartment into a home. Two afternoons a week the two women were off shopping, moving the furniture around, arguing with paperhangers; and when Michael came home he found the drapes down, the furniture covered with boxes and wrappings, and once, the women sitting in the parlor waiting for him, both giggling drunk, new hats askew on their heads. If he wanted to fight with anyone, Louise said, he would have to fight with her.

He didn't want to fight with anyone. He was happier than he had ever been in his life. In some ways he felt as if all the misery in the world had been lifted from his shoulders. Emily had changed everything. Whenever Louise was there, Michael assumed she would be joining them for dinner, and the night she was drunk was no exception. Even she had changed, and if she intended to giggle through dinner, it was the first such opportunity offered to her in many, many years. But Louise had her suspicions. "Is she all right, Michael? Is she really all right?"

Yes. Yes, she was. Without having said it aloud, Emily had made it clear that she meant to live as if the two years had never happened. She was back at the settlement house Mondays and Thursdays; on those evenings he would meet her on the sidewalk outside, and they would walk across Grand Street to Little Italy for cannelloni, or they would go straight home, up Clinton Street and through Tompkins Square Park. The streets were crowded all the way, the air heavy with the odors of horses, rotting vegetables, stale beer, cooking, and human sweat. It was not unusual to hear five different languages in as many blocks. The Italians, Jews, and Slavs had pushed the Irish and Germans westward and uptown. There had always been Chinese with their tongs and opium dens at the foot of the Bowery, and lately, a second neighborhood of Negroes in the sixties to the west of the Park—they had been far downtown on the West Side for years. Because she had been away, there was a lot she had to discover and learn, and it made her talk about her girlhood in Murray Hill and walking with her mother to shop along the Miracle Mile on Broadway. The city was too big now to walk around in that way anymore. It had been too big in that sense for some years, but not in the minds of those who had grown up under a bluer sky, with the reassurance of a natural horizon in all directions. She was painting again; she went up to Central Park a couple of times, bringing back some attractive watercolors of the stone bridge over the duck pond. But she wasn't happy with her work. She wanted to paint something else, and after a while she realized what it was. For the first time in her life she wanted to paint herself. She wanted to put a full-length mirror on the wall and paint a formal portrait, studying the way she placed her hands and composed her expression. She wanted to examine her character, she said.

But perhaps because she said it, she never bothered to try to do it. Michael was disappointed; he wanted to see her believing she could do herself justice with craftsmanship; she undervalued herself, and he thought she would discover in her work that she was a beautiful woman.

He was willing to believe she had chosen him because he was a man to whom not very much ever had to be said, and she was a woman who offered her deepest feelings in only the most timid and silent ways. She bought him gifts, books and jewelry, and surprised him one evening by telling him she had been down to Lombard Street that day and had walked along the docks. It was no use telling her how dangerous it had been; she had known that. It was something she had wanted to do, she said, and he could see that she really didn't want to go into it any more than that.

When it came to apparently less consequential matters, on the other hand, she was nothing like quiet. He knew all about her childhood pets, what her brothers had done at various ages, and how all her grandparents had died, as well as their ages, and how her Uncle Frank, who died before she was born, aged nineteen, choked to death on a chicken bone. But Michael was the same, talking too much about Saratoga, recounting the turn of every card in a hand of poker played seven years before only to find that she didn't know that a full house beat a straight. And if he had been slower than he was willing to admit, sorting one brother from the other, then she gave him more of a shock than she realized when he tried to show her the mathematical formulae he used for rating horses, and she threw up her hands and cried, "My God! It's like mortgages!"

What was most unsettling about it was that the last thing he wanted to do was remind her of what she had left behind. She never spoke of her father, she never spoke of the two years, and for the most part he was glad; but he had his suspicions, like Louise, and he looked at Emily while she was reading or painting and he wondered if she really was as well as she wanted him to believe. Again, it came down to her reluctance to confide her deepest feelings. He was determined not to pry. Although she had not said this either, it was clear to him that she wanted to be taken at her word.

That was their first summer in Saratoga, the year they met the Johnsons there and spent so much money, she thought. Michael rented a cabin on the Dayliner and made love to her while kids ran by in the passageway and there was a distant, thinning sound of violins playing "Tales from the Vienna Woods." She laughed at him when he kept pace with the sound of the engines for a while, and the surfacing of their absurdity, the two of them doing what so many others must have done and were probably doing elsewhere on the boat—that made her open for him. It was a summer of lovemaking, deep in the season of their honeymoon, and the lovemaking on the tiny bunk of the cabin with most of their clothes still on was the fulfillment of a promise he had made to her before they left the apartment that morning, his hand rubbing her bottom. He knew how she liked to have her bottom rubbed. She had read somewhere that snakes hypnotized their prey so they couldn't move, and she equated it with the way she felt when he stroked her gently there, her knees dissolved into her shoes. He had been gentle with her in the beginning, but now he was very strong. There was a lot she knew about him now. He liked to make love in the daytime. He said he liked to watch her face, but just as much he liked to watch what they were doing. He was shy about it, as he was about many things, shy and boyish about approaching her sometimes, strong as he was. Once he called her up from a sketch she was doing and fairly marched her into the bedroom, put her down on the bed, lifted her legs up and pulled off her drawers in one near-acrobatic gesture—and only unbuttoned his trousers. She was not ready for him and he was done in about a minute, but even with his trousers just unbuttoned, she felt it happen to her, a little, that thing that at its best she imagined as a profound, mysterious opening inside her. That afternoon he was up from before he had gotten completely soft again, and she watched him tuck himself in and button himself up again. Even with the gray light from the window behind him she could see him clearly, and his smile was exactly like a boy's, as wide as his rosy cheeks would allow.

She liked Kate—it was a summer for bawdiness. She asked Michael again if he had ever made love to Kate and did not completely believe his answer, understanding that he was a liar long before she ever caught him in even a small, innocent lie. He had told her as much two years before—he had told her that he knew how to live a lie. But Kate was straightforward and obviously, not elaborately, in love with Johnson, her charming bald drunken coot of a husband, and Emily liked and trusted her. The three of them, Michael expected, were drunk several times before the season was over, and one evening when the men were off gambling, Emily and Kate drank some whiskey Kate had in her room. Whatever the truth about Kate and him, Michael had not discouraged Emily from seeing Kate; that afternoon when Emily had told him that Kate had threatened to get her drunk, Michael had answered calmly that he was going to see the whole card at the track whether or not women were sleeping it off at the hotel. Perhaps he had not taken her seriously, but at least he had nothing to fear from Kate. In any case, Emily had already made up her mind: she intended to let Kate get her drunk. It was a summer of bawdiness and there were secrets in the air.

Kate was thirty-six and Emily twenty-two, and while Emily may have been the relatively highborn young lady and Kate the old whore, Kate had seen and done things Emily could not imagine, and Kate could hold her liquor. Emily knew that Kate was Michael's oldest and most precious friend, but that summer in Saratoga she could not help thinking about Kate's secrets, the secrets of a whore—but when she was drunk enough, she asked Kate the other thing she had on her mind, the more important thing. They were sitting on the bed in Kate's room, the window open, and a crowd in the courtyard was waiting for the orchestra to start playing. The clamor of voices penetrated Emily's stupor, and she had to shake her head to hear Kate's voice clearly through all the noise. Emily was swimmingly drunk, but she remembered clearly the next morning: she has asked Kate if she had ever made love to Michael. By morning Emily had her face pressed against Michael's back, her legs wrapped around his thigh. Her head throbbed. She had managed to stay awake until he had come in, and although he had seen that she was drunk, he hadn't realized how drunk she was. He had won money and wanted to make love. She was almost too drunk to feel it, and then it left her dizzy and unsatisfied. He was asleep, curled up like a baby, facing away. She promised herself that she would never get drunk again, and it took the rest of that summer to keep the promise in that atmosphere of celebration, but that morning she was afraid she had lost him. Kate had said, "What the hell would I want to do that for?" and then had gone on to enumerate her own specific requirements and know well her lovable old coot met them; Emily could see that Kate was telling the truth, but there was something s-l-o-w about it, not real, not her drunkenness, but what she said—and the next morning, her lips pressed to Michael's back, her head throbbing, her legs wrapped around his thigh, Emily remembered: he had slept with Kate and had lied to her about it. He was sleeping the sleep of a man who had seen a flush coming against an unimprovable two pair, and thus had covered the entire holiday, his young wife afraid that he would discover that she had checked on him, never mind his lie, and he would rise up in wrath against her. She was twenty-two, and that morning, before he woke up and made love to her so carelessly that she cried after he withdrew from her and clumped naked into the bathroom, she was afraid that God would strike her dead.

Finally she decided that he had not really lied, that Kate had been trying to conceal something long dead—Emily was not going to let it become important. She was in love with Michael, and if she had shamed him in Saratoga by getting drunk, he did not say so. He did not hold back from her; it was as if he expected her to be unpredictable. But her experience with Kate in Saratoga frightened her, and she felt happier responding to him, seeing after his needs.

Louise asked her if they were trying to have a child and it was true, they were, although neither of them spoke of it. Emily knew that there were things he could do to prevent a baby, but he wasn't doing them. She knew why; he was on top of her pushing in and holding on while she held onto him, as if afraid he might accidentally kill her if he didn't, and he knew she was in a kind of prison with this. He knew now that she had difficulty with her menstrual period—they both knew her pattern by heart: the first sign of tiredness, the first cramp, and they were sentenced to another month of waiting. But he would not speak of it—was he afraid that she would think he was disappointed in her? There were times she resented him for thinking so little of her, for not believing in her just a bit longer; she thought about him making love to Kate, whom she loved as she did Louise—Emily felt so ashamed, it was as if she had raped herself. She wanted to snarl it in his ear: *you still don't know how much I love you!* when all she wanted, as she knew when she had calmed down, was for him to make her pregnant.

He was softer, gentler, older than the memory she had carried for two years. She had not recognized him in those first moments on Forty-second Street, he looked so tired. His hair had receded more at the temples, and there was gray on one side of his moustache. That first afternoon she was afraid she would never see him as he had been two years before—she remembered thinking that; she remembered thinking that he looked as if he already knew what she really wanted to tell him. Later he said it was over and they never had to discuss it again, which was what she wanted. But it wasn't working—everything inside her was too different. She looked at her charges at the settlement house and thought of the sinful world they were growing into; she sat at her easel and wondered if she could paint herself in heaven and hell at the same time. She wondered what Michael would think if she painted herself in the throes of her passion. There was an agony inside her that she could get out, she believed, if only she dared. She had finally told him the truth late that first Saturday night of her return to the city, the last thing she told him before he told her to forget it forever and sleep—that she had evaded his question about her having been pregnant because there had been other things that had needed saying first. She had been pregnant. She had gone five months in seclusion and humiliation before she had miscarried. "I didn't do anything, Michael! They even accused me of that!"

"You were not responsible. You know it. Now forget it."

There were times when she thought that what her parents had said was right, that in giving herself to Michael she had surrendered only to her own lust. She imagined him with other women; she suspected him of planning to corrupt her. When they made love, she asked him questions that even he thought were lewd—he was amused anyway. On those rare occasions when she could see the frenzy she was in, she thought of the mess of blood, fluid, and tissue in her bed that gray, sick morning in Maryland more than a year and a half before. She thought of that when the pleasure of their lovemaking was most intense. Perhaps she would never be able to give him a child because she had lost the first. If she had not surrendered to her own sin, why was she so tortured? She was not sure that she would have lost the child under conditions different from those created by her father's deceptions. And she could not understand why returning to Michael and marrying him had not put things right.

They went on. If she ever wondered if there was more to her father's interventions than she already knew, she never spoke of it to Michael. From what she had said, it was clear to him that both of her parents had had more to fear from an investigation into Sullivan's business than Reese had let on to Michael that Tuesday night Sullivan died. Whatever the case, important people had come to the Reeses' aid, relieving them of the burden of their property in New York, among other things. The Reeses' terror must have been immense, and it went a long way toward explaining what they had done to Emily. He supposed he should be sorry about her mother's death, but he didn't care any more than he felt any remorse for Reese, who had obviously become deranged. He had been living on capital for more than two years, and although Emily said that he had plenty of money, Michael understood how her father's circumstances had to curdle his old banker's heart. He still had his sons to bully, and Emily hoped that they would escape, too, but they had not written to her, and Michael took that as a sign that they had been let in on rather more of the truth about the Reese family business than their sister. Michael had come to appreciate how genuinely naïve Emily was: as cleverly as she could see into people in their dealings with her, she had no idea how far they would go for money—or love. If she never had a second thought about her father, she never expressed a reservation about Michael either. Sometimes he saw that she was frightened, but just as often she said that he was being too patient with her. He thought that if he lost her now, he would not want to live.

She took on more important work at the settlement, drew Louise into a separate project uptown, put away the easel, and set up a sewing machine and a mannequin in the living room. They had given up on the apartment. He knew they had to move, but he had lived here the longest portion of his life, and he wanted to hang on a while longer. She did not complain; she was apologetic about the space she took, but took it anyway. From this and other things he inferred that she was happier. She had new favorites at the theater, including Gilbert and Sullivan. She was looking forward to the coming season at Saratoga.

It was in this context that a new wave of gossip started, that she could not have children because of the complications of an earlier pregnancy. Michael heard it before she did. Louise took him aside to warn him what was going around about them. It could have started anywhere, Portsmouth, Maryland—a useless speculation. They were going to Canada for the racing at the end of the month, and he thought that that was not too much luck to hope for, but the following Tuesday he found Emily sitting in the dark, trembling, the color so drained from her face that her lips had turned blue. He never did hear who had talked to

her—there were more important things to think about—but he had had
enough of these people.

When they returned from Saratoga later in the season, they began to
look in earnest for a larger apartment; and in October Emily found one,
off Grand Army Plaza in Brooklyn, five really large airy rooms in a new
four-story building with a marble entry and halls. There was steam heat
instead of hot air, hot water, and the electrical wiring was embedded in
the walls. He had a room to work in, and there was space enough in the
bedroom for her things. But they had been together for so many months
that they missed each other's presence, and in the end they both moved
back to the living room, settled down in the mess as they had on Irving
Place.

That winter was a white winter, cold, with the rivers frozen solid so
that people could walk across them. He had already learned how much
she liked the snow. Her nose turned red and ran like a child's and her
glasses misted over, but she wanted to be outside day and night to look at
the way the snow changed the world.

When they came home, they made love. The snow on the street
outside reflected so much light into their room that they could see each
other plainly. The cold weather invigorated her, and she was sure enough
of herself now to be aggressive, even demanding. It was the winter she
became pregnant again, and later when she went through much the same
cycle after David died, Michael had to wonder about this winter and if
she could have had a successful preganacy any time earlier. The aggres-
siveness was part of it. Louise had asked him once if he was being gentle
with Emily and he had said yes, of course; but Kate, who had told him she
thought Emily at least had possibilities, knew better. That winter, in the
oddly vivid, chilly bedroom, they moved like performers in a shadow
play, their noises magnified by the silence created by the snow outside.
Mostly it was the rustle of bedclothing, her gown and his pajamas and the
crisp sheets under the weight of the blankets and the quilt, that rustling
and their faces dark in the brightness, the two of them pacing themselves
until they generated sufficient body heat to throw the covers back. She
would be holding his arms then, kneading them like bread dough. She
had strong hands and she walked miles every day; she had great strength,
fierce strength; and if he finished before her, or she felt it coming again,
she would grab his arms tighter, looking into his eyes and making a sound
as if she wanted to say, "More," but could not actually utter the word, not
asking but insistent, the sound moving deeper in her throat, her teeth
clenched, her eyes still on him, filling with strange, wonderful expec-
tancy: then her head back, her spine arched, the room ringing with a

convulsive animal cry. She carried the baby easily and was in labor only an hour; and ten years later when she was recovering from something worse, he understood her better, he understood life better, and he was better able to go with her in the necessary surrender to life's own deepest needs.

III

The letters, the few there were, are gone; and the other artifacts, like theater ticket stubs and postcards, have similarly vanished. She wanted her telegram to him destroyed and was relieved when a search established that it was really lost for good. There is a photograph of him, yellowed and rapidly fading, a tall, thin, oddly graceful man. He is in a dark, lightweight, single-breasted suit, white shirt with a rounded celluloid collar, dark tie, and a straw skimmer perched rakishly on the side of his head. His weight is on one leg and his hands are clasped behind him. It is a posed photograph and he is following the photographer's instructions, looking out toward an imagined horizon, and the result is that his dark eyes have a dreamy look his friends would not have recognized. There are no pictures of her from the period, but she is remembered as a beauty with unusually smooth clear skin, lovely golden hair, and perfect teeth.

The jewelry is scattered, a diamond ring he gave her after they had been married a month, the earrings she found on her pillow one New Year's Eve, an emerald brooch he saw in a shop in the village at Saratoga. She was with him when he bought it, pointing it out to her in the window and then ducking inside when she said she liked it. She stayed on the sidewalk while he counted out the cash, the clerk's head swiveling to get a look at her. Before it was done the clerk was outside to help Michael with the pin, saying "Lovely, lovely" over and over—the memory can always fix an image more clearly than a photograph. Gone now, down to the last of it, the tin candy-boxes full of ribbons and dried flowers and even more obscure mementos, indecipherable final scraps left of the heart of a family, secrets of a lifetime.

Mike was born in the Brooklyn apartment, and when they left it a year later, they were about to be five, with Mike, David, and Mary Frances, the new, young, dull-witted Irish maid; and before they left the house in Flatbush for the big home in Mountain Lakes, having added Amy and Maureen, Mary Frances's equally dull-witted younger sister, helping with all three children, they were seven, an entourage that required a suite on the boat on the annual summer pilgrimage northward.

The house in Flatbush had three bedrooms and two baths, fireplaces in the parlor, dining room, and master bedroom, to which was also attached a sleeping porch overlooking the spacious rear yard. The maid's quarters and the children's playroom were on the third floor. Milk, bread, ice, and newspapers were delivered every day; a man came regularly to sharpen scissors and knives; another to clean the chimneys; and still another to carry off the rags. The grocer had a man who had been kicked by a horse to push a cart around the neighborhood with the orders that had been called in by telephone; the man had no sense left and talked with his tongue hanging out of his mouth. The butcher had a boy with a bicycle, the white, string-tied packages riding in a basket out over the small front wheel; the boy picked his nose and always stared at you as if he were trying to learn your business. And the shoemaker up on the avenue rarely spoke and Michael and Emily presumed he was deaf and shouted at him, but they never knew for sure. He glowered at them, his mouth full of tacks, and then made strange chalk glyphs on the sole of the shoes. "Friday," he would grunt, and nothing more.

Emily was visibly pregnant for Julie's wedding, and pregnant again for the baptism of the baby Julie had by Carl Hafner. Julie's marriage meant the end of the family, Louise warned, if only because Julie's removal to New Jersey meant the end of family holiday gatherings. For Michael it seemed to be true, for it was more and more of a strain to travel the distances involved. At the baptism Thomas told him that he had decided to go in with Hafner, which necessitated selling his house in the city and moving to Jersey, and Michael saw that as the true end of it, for Louise would not be able to resist following them for long.

It turned out not to be the case. Thomas was out to Brooklyn one evening the following spring, staying far into the night. He still owed Michael ten thousand and Louise fifteen, but he was doing well with Hafner in real estate turnovers and new house construction. He had a business proposition that would get them even and return a profit besides, involving a parcel of industrial property in Newark and the usual privileged information. Thomas had already been to his mother, and as Michael heard later, Louise thought it was the solution to Thomas's problems. Michael saw he could not be perceived as backing away from the deal on his own account—why, he would be kicking Thomas when he was down. Michael didn't like being sandbagged, but as he explained to Emily, at least he would be in a position to look after Louise's interests.

It was one of the few financial matters he discussed with Emily in those years. She had said early that she had no reason to question his judgment; but even if, as he thought, she had only found another way to turn her back on her father, this deal fell beyond the range of "judgment." Michael was doing it for Louise, and Emily had no objection. A night or two later Emily kissed him on the cheek, and when he asked what he had done to deserve it, she said that it had to do with how he spent his money; her father would have moaned and carried on and probably kept his money in his purse.

But Michael was wrong about the Newark investment, and over the next three years Thomas delivered, in odd amounts at random intervals, a total of thirty thousand dollars.

Still, it could have been a near thing. A month after the papers were signed and the money turned over, Julie goaded Hafner into slapping her and she threw him out of the house. He proved to be stronger stuff than Fleming and brought her to heel, cutting off her money and using Louise to carry the terms of the new "proposition" to Julie. It was the summer Louise chased back and forth between them for six weeks. "They're very cynical people" was all she would say about it afterward.

That would have been the end of it except for Michael's own stupidity. Thomas had assured him that it was going to be business as usual no matter how Julie's situation changed—after all, this *was* business. Michael thought he saw a hard, ugly person emerging in Julie, and he told Thomas that he did not want to be in the position of having to come to her aid again over something like this—in the whole dreary saga, Michael's biggest mistake, because Ethel made sure that Julie heard what he had said. The last threads of friendship were broken there. Whatever else she had on her mind, Julie determined that that was sufficient grounds to break it off completely. Five years later, she could hardly bring herself to attend David's funeral, and then she did not go to the cemetery. That was Mountain Lakes, 1907.

We had a glimpse of Michael and Emily in 1902, that August at Saratoga, Mike and David played with their cereal, Mary Francis off having her breakfast with the other servants. Saratoga was her holiday, too, a month of gossip and romance while the family was away on a ride or the children asleep and the Mister and Missus out on the town. Louise was attending to Hafner and Julie—Julie the spoiled child, Julie the woman with marital problems. We know now that her mother would have called her cynical, but this far along we do not have to examine Julie's interior life to appreciate some of the processes Louise must have observed.

There are deeper mysteries, darker secrets. Seen from Michael's childhood, the summer breakfast in 1902 seemed an idyllic interlude, but our perceptions have been changed by events only the passage of time could have revealed. After twenty-five years Michael could still feel under the palms of his hands the butt of the knife that a fourteen-year-old had driven into Moran. Remembering that first summer, too, the ending of his childhood, Michael realized that the boy he had become by that fall was as beyond his comprehension as the man who had killed Sullivan and his other hoodlum in the presence of his lovely wife's father. The night Emily returned to the city and told him what had happened to her, Michael could see how plainly she was offering herself to him, how much trust she was placing in him after all the pain she had already felt; and if that frightened him, then his shame brought him to the nub of his fear: she wanted him to believe her; she wanted him to believe in her. She was offering herself to him, but in return she wanted his true belief.

In the carriage on the Brooklyn Bridge he realized that she had already made the gift of her belief in him.

And in the apartment when she told him that she had been pregnant and had lost the child, when he could see all the things she had thought and felt in the two years but was concealing, he saw that if he had any love in him at all, he was going to give her what she wanted. He could not bear to think of how she had already suffered because of him. That night he put a cover over her on the bed and kissed her and went out to the parlor to wait for her to calm down. He wanted her to understand her life was going to be different now, that she would be able to mark the beginning of the difference, that he meant to take care of her. What amazed him was not that he could make such a decision but that she was willing to submit to it. He did not know what she knew about him—he did not know why she loved him.

When she had been quiet a while, he returned to the bedroom, sat beside her, and brushed her hair back from her cheek. Her eyes opened and he told her that he wanted them to be married as quickly as possible. She closed her eyes again and pressed her lips against the back of his hand.

The tin candy-boxes are all the evidence most of us have of people like these. The rest of what we know is inside ourselves, who we are, what we have been taught, perhaps some shred of family gossip. Given the circumstances, Michael would have remembered what Westfield had told him about being a fool with women, of being afraid to take the final step. And given the promise he made to himself the night Emily returned, Michael would have told her, to please her, to try to win her even more. After what she had been through, he wanted her to feel loved—he wanted her to have everything.

That she could see what he was doing did not make it less effective. From her point of view he could have forgotten her after that first spring and moved on; he could have married someone else; but she had found that he had loved her all along, almost as if he had waited for her, as if he had not been able to help himself. He wanted to make her happy, and in return she wanted him to have the home and family that were his right as much as any man's. If she had originally challenged him to accept her surrender, then she never stopped. She adored him; and on that August morning in 1902 when he was thinking of what she didn't know about him, he saw that she had really submitted to not ever learning it. The ways she anticipated and waited on him by day and yielded to him at night were parts of the same submission—she wanted him to love her with the force inside him that had nearly ruined her life, the thing about himself he couldn't understand. No matter. She wanted to feel his *need*.

And without it, she would have drawn into herself, hurt and alone. She was a genuinely modest human being, and more than with others he had to reach for her and lead her to him. She gave up her settlement work when she was carrying Mike, and she put away her easel, brushes, and paints when David was born. Michael wanted her to go on, but she said that the children took too much of her time. It was true, but it was by her own choice—a part of her wanted to be a child with them, and after a while he expected to find her down on the floor playing with them when he came home. One night in the house in Flatbush when the babies were still small enough for her to carry them both at once she brought them to him and said they all wanted a kiss good-night. He arched a brow at her and asked, "How old are *you*, little girl?"

Later she said, "I'm spoiling them, I know, but I can't help myself."

"I can't complain," he said. "I've spoiled you rotten."

"Yes, you have. That's exactly what you've done."

It is easy to see Michael on the porch in Flatbush on a September evening in 1905, say, his collar off and suspenders loosened. The handsome, dreamy-eyed man in the photograph is forty-three, still reed-thin, perhaps a little soft in the stomach, and his hair has receded more at the temples and there is gray showing all through it. Mellower, more a creature of habit, he would be on the porch after dinner often, standing with a last cup of coffee, one more cigar. The neighbors would know enough of his business to be slightly wary of him, and their hellos are terse as they pass beyond his ragged hedge. Although he loves the house like a man who has never owned one before, he has spent the previous month at Saratoga and is lazy about looking after things. As for the neighbors, Michael likes his distance—he likes being free of them. Maintaining good relations with the neighbors is one of the burdens Emily shoulders for them both.

It is easy to imagine her, too: she is upstairs with Maureen, preparing

the children for bed. When they are in their gowns, Emily will read them
a story, and then she will summon Michael for the ceremonial saying of
prayers and kiss good-night. In those days it was customary to keep
children in infants' clothes for as long as possible and a good health practice was to keep them as fat as possible all through the same period, with
the result that Mike and David, at six and five respectively, have been out
of dresses, long curls, and baby fat for less than a year. Emily has had
three children since 1899, nursing all of them, and she has lost the bloom
of her youth. She remains a quiet person, but her shyness has been
relieved by the assurance she has gained through motherhood and the
management of a complex, efficient household. The children are the joy
in all her hard work, and she has showered them with attention and
indulgence.

Emily knew there was something wrong with David. Mike was a
vigorous, squalling infant with quick, watchful eyes, but David was
lethargic almost from birth, colicky and mewling. A woman learns her
children first at her breast, and Mike had been a scrappy, demanding cub
of a nurser; and while she was carrying David she remembered the way
Mike had gone at her, scratching, chewing her flesh, and kicking, but
when David came, she could feel a silence inside him, something chilling.
She had to help him too much, and when he looked up at her, it was as if
he knew, sadly, that she was something superior, something he would
never be.

She tested Michael, asking him what he thought, and he admitted that
he could see a difference, but he wouldn't allow that it necessarily meant
anything serious, much less abnormal. She knew it was his way of trying
to protect her, but he did not see—or want to see—that she felt the pain
of it already. The doctor said the child's reflexes were slow, but inasmuch
as there was nothing else of note, the doctor was inclined to take an
attitude of wait-and-see. As for the child's occasionally vacant expres-
sions, the doctor wanted to assure Emily that he had treated many, many
other babies that would have alarmed her more. The doctor's name was
Ferguson, a dark, dried-up Scot of fifty who tended to be brusque with
his patients. He had an automobile for house calls, one of the first in the
neighborhood, and you could hear it blocks away. Michael disliked
automobiles, he said that riding in one was like sitting on a printing press;
but he admired Dr. Ferguson's combination of shrewd business sense
and professional responsibility in having one for himself. Emily told
Michael what the doctor said, and Michael said he thought the doctor
knew what he was doing; but Emily was not cowed or convinced—she
knew that Michael could see that there was something wrong, and she

knew that he did not lie to himself. And later, when David showed such poor balance as he was learning to walk, Michael told Emily to speak to the doctor about it; she did, and again the doctor said that he could not see anything that required investigation.

So there it was, and by the time David was three, they had learned to live with his problems. They expected less of him and praised him perhaps too much for his accomplishments. The moments of listlessness were gone, and he and Mike played as equals. Mike was the leader and David the follower, but Mike was the leader outside with the neighbors' children—a natural leader. When Emily was pregnant again, he marched around the neighborhood announcing that he was going to have another brother, and cried bitterly when his father told him the new child was a girl. Michael sat up with both boys in his arms that night, Mike unhappy and David trying to console him. Emily heard about it later, David holding Mike's hand and telling him not to cry, Mike's lower lip puffed out and his brow furrowed down.

Louise was the one who called Mike headstrong, but Emily thought that her mother-in-law was unfair, because Mike was not willful like Thomas's children, or selfish like Julie's; he was a little general, organizing the play, making the rules. He was a Daddy's boy, and wanted long pants almost a year before he got his first pair, to go with his shorts and knickers, but because David was so close in age, their father decided—and told them together—that they would have long pants at the same time. Emily thought that Mike was a little man about the decision; but on the other hand Michael saw that it was an awkward position for the child to be in, so close to his younger brother in age, obliged so much of the time to restrain himself until David caught up, with David so slow. Still, Mike was good about it, looking to his father for approval at almost every turn.

Most of the time he got it. It was a time Michael was working hard, having changed jobs twice, trying to put together enough to carry the five of them in case something happened to him. From 1895, when he met Emily until 1900, when David was born, Michael had added nothing to his savings, the energy he had been able or willing to devote to his business having been so low right through that half decade that he had to force himself to do any work at all. After Thomas came to him with the Newark offer, Michael had begun to make money again, so that by 1905 he was worth four hundred thousand dollars, and he could see approximately when he would get to a million—and if he kept going, he would be able to leave all three children a million apiece. A million sustained itself; with care, it could last forever. Michael had all these things on his mind through his older boy's young childhood, and sometimes he did not pay attention. It was Mike, most of the time, who grabbed at his jacket as he came up the walk, with the *World* and then the *Journal* under his arm.

"Daddy! Daddy! We built a fort!"

It might be a circle of rocks or a blanket over a clothesline, and in the dusty sunshine of the late afternoon at the ebb of his energy Michael would not have the patience for it, and then Emily would come out through the kitchen door and intercede. She was plumper then, fuller figured, heavier in the bosom, and she had circles under her eyes. She wore her hair in a bun, and some strand or other would be hanging loose over the wire frame of her eyeglasses. Michael's back ached and his feet hurt, and he would look up at her on the kitchen steps with such an expression of weariness that she would rush down to his rescue. "Your father is tired! Let him catch his breath!" Stopping for a kiss and a hug, pressing her full soft belly against his groin—it was so automatic that neither of them thought of it anymore; what he loved was the smell of her: he wanted to fill his lungs with it. And the boys, and then the three children, would be looking up at them, waiting. "Let your Daddy catch his breath! My goodness, you two, and Amy, it's as if you haven't seen him in a whole year!" She did that to them, threw herself at them, playing to him. She thought she was fat and her breasts sagged and the marks on her stomach made him unhappy, but in the backyard just before sunset, with their toddlers in attendance, she would let him see her joy so that what she thought of herself would melt away—melt away: and then Michael would remember the candy or surprises he had brought for their tiny audience.

The maids knew how they were, and in the darkness of their bedroom, Michael and Emily wondered what their children heard. Emily told him how the maids giggled and blushed the mornings after he made love to her, after they had heard her, in her own words, "bleating like a goat"— their lovemaking was a lot quieter in the warm weather with the windows open. To tease him she would make him work for her; as often as not he took it as a signal to be more forceful—more than once, with the windows open, he wrestled her down, getting her the way animals did it. It made him feel alive. She loved it; she would bury her face into a pillow to stifle her noise. When he was over her like that, able to see himself sliding in and out of her, he wondered if other men dared feast on their wives this way. He would pound at her harder, giving her, she made clear, exactly what she wanted.

She liked to dance—specifically, to waltz. Louise and Julie had taught him to dance years before, whirling around in the parlor with one to the clapping hands of the other, spinning in the long afternoons; and now, with their popeyed, giggling children peeking from behind the drape, he and Emily would whirl around the parlor to the tinny strains of violins reproduced by their windup phonograph. He tried to bring something home every afternoon, if not candy or trinkets for the children, then a new cylinder for the phonograph, some saltwater taffy direct from Atlantic City, the latest novel for Emily. There were old men with shopping bags full of new and used books who made the rounds of the newspaper offices, and they came to know the tastes of the reporters' wives better than the reporters themselves knew them; and when Michael appeared with a new Tarkington or Winston Churchill, he knew her reaction would go beyond anything *he* thought the book deserved.

The phonograph was something he brought home the same way. He wanted them to have the chance to live well. He initiated the dinners out and trips to Coney Island and Sheepshead Bay; he bought the fireworks for the Fourth of July—though she always chose the Christmas trees and had them brought around while he was at work, great monsters, spreading out into fully a third of the parlor, spruces always, blue spruces when she could get them. The children would spend all day Christmas Eve decorating the tree and hanging their stockings. Christmas had always been her holiday, and she devoted herself to making it beautiful and satisfying for the children; and in the last two years in Brooklyn he made a spectacular of Independence Day. There were fireworks displays on every block in those days, and every year the sky flashed and the air shook with the concussion of a hundred thousand explosions. Michael liked the rockets and Roman candles best of all, and he would set them off in the street while the children watched from the lawn, the rockets whooshing up and lighting their faces. It was her reaction he wanted, that he would look for, and before long she saw how vulnerable he was at such moments. She made sure he saw her smiling or raising Amy's hand in a wave.

It is easy enough to imagine them. After all, someone like Kate could see right through Emily, past her fears and timidity into the nature of her sexuality and see it clearly enough to assure her husband that the girl had "possibilities." Emily's moments of uncertainty had changed with the changing of their circumstance, and those last years in Flatbush, when it was clear at least that something was wrong with David, they were back with her again. As a bride she had been afraid that what her father had said somehow mirrored the truth—that by returning to Michael she would surrender to her own lust, and in ways others could not suspect, she would be punished for it. She wanted to believe that David had outgrown his problem, whatever it had been; but at the same time she expected something more to happen. Michael was the lighter sleeper, but over the years he never once realized that she was awake and out of bed in the small hours as often as he was, that she often stood by the window or went downstairs and sat in the kitchen, where the silence was punctuated by the ticking of the mechanical clock.

There were times when her nervousness did not let her respond to him, though he did not know that either. It was as if she could feel herself slipping further into some kind of secret prison, for she wanted to respond to him so much that she drove herself toward him, giving herself even more to exactly what her father had said, surrendering to her fantasies of Michael, pretending things about them both. There was no end to it, which was what frightened her most. When she was alone, she sometimes thought that it was the natural punishment for having given in to herself in the first place, for having lost the first child, that there was a set of natural balances that she had disturbed forever—but all of it, the whole cycle of worry and failure and sense of condemnation happened only rarely: in any case, she could not tell him. He deserved more from her and nothing ever happened, not in Flatbush; the children had their diseases, and when he was six, Mike tripped and fell into Amy and cut her head open so that he cried that his father would beat him, something he had picked up from the other children on the block, but nothing happened. Michael never beat his children. It was a time of holidays and routine and children growing up, and aside from the effect on the children, what remains are the tin candy-boxes collected by a woman—like so many others; the reasons are finally unimportant—determined to be able to convince herself sometime in the future that all of this was real.

IV

In those years Michael was known as The Broad Street Turf Exchange and The Southern Shores Horsemen's Syndicate. He had an office in a building at Broad and Wall, and he used both addresses in advertising his turf counseling services in racing publications as far south as New Orleans. Service under his own name was still available, but he never advertised that. He had resigned from the *World* in 1903, after chafing under the job for months—he had given himself an unnecessary bad time, afraid to get out on his own but suddenly too successful to do anything else. He made the rounds of the poker games again and let it be known that he had investment capital available. It was as if he had been away for years, although it was not the case; it was just that he had not been *serious* for years. Thomas's Newark proposition had unnerved him sufficiently to make him reconsider his entire situation—he never discussed it with Emily—and he decided he was young enough to take some risks. There was a whole new criminal element moving through the ranks of gamblers in New York—Germans, Jews, and Italians, tough-talking killers some of them—Emily didn't have to know about them either. So many men said hello to him in restaurants and theater lobbies that he did not have to identify them all. She was not surprised when he came home to tell her that he had quit the *World*. He had gone down to Havre de Grace the week before to play a horse, and he had already been told that he had been pursuing his own interests too much lately.

What surprised her more was that he went over to Hearst—he thought he needed to have a job. He was out of there in six weeks. It was not that he hated Hearst more than before, if indeed that was even possible; it was that he was done working for anyone else for good.

He bought some horses and raced them in Maryland, but while he made money, he was away from home half the time and didn't like it. He couldn't fall asleep without her beside him, and made no secret of it. She asked him if he ever thought of getting someone else and he said he never did, which was true. He got rid of the Maryland horses because of the separations, and the next time he bought horses he made sure he had a trainer who would stay sober more than two or three days at a time.

In the off-season he wrote racing articles for the mass market magazines, and occasionally one of his poker experiences converted readily into a Western, but fiction editors wanted surprise or trick endings, which eluded him. After a long summer he would feel that he wanted to write, but by the middle of February the following year he would have had enough of it and would spend more time looking at the snow in the yard than at the typewriter trying to bring in a check. The size of the check was a factor in his lethargy: he could spend all day on an article on the new three-year-olds for a net of forty-five or fifty dollars, and it simply wasn't worth his time.

In the spring of '04 he opened the Broad Street office, and by the end of June he had a man working for him, an old-timer from the *World* who knew every dodge in the game. They had mail and telegraph services, telephone numbers, private wires, special offers (three horses for twenty dollars; a three-horse parlay for fifty dollars), charts, systems, subscriptions, and, finally, the throne before which only the ripest chumps were ever ushered, the opportunity to become Judge Westfield's Private Client. There were men who made money with him, to be sure, but Michael made most, sometimes as much as a thousand a week, and in those days before the income tax it was all his to keep.

After the Newark deal Thomas got him into a pair of subdivisions in East and South Orange, New Jersey. Thomas was giving him stock market information, too. Michael had other sources, but Thomas's tips were by far the best. It was Carl Hafner again: Thomas had let it be understood that Hafner was well connected in Trenton and the New Jersey State Democratic machine. Hafner now had a big house in Asbury Park, and Julie was planning a summer in Europe just as soon as they could all get away. And in the spring of '06, Thomas had still another proposition for Michael.

That was the season Kate came back to New York for good. She came out to Flatbush alone on a Saturday afternoon late in March, and within an hour of her arrival a late winter snow began to fall. They knew at once that she was in for the night. They had not seen her in years, and suddenly they were thrown together while the snow piled up outside. She looked older, and tired. It was the traveling, she said readily, and getting away from Johnson, and before that, the drinking that had really finished everything. She was still drinking too much, she said, acknowledging the whiskey she had been sipping since her arrival. The boys were in awe of her, this thin, pale, redheaded woman who drank whiskey and cursed, who whispered things to their baby sister Amy that made their mother blush. She knew cowboys and Indians, men who had been in shoot-outs, grizzly old prospectors who had been scalped. . . .

And when the children went up to bed, she said there were toys for them back at the hotel but that she had forgotten them. Michael thought she was understating her distress—she had been surprised when she had seen Amy; she had forgotten that Emily had been pregnant again and that she had even sent a present from Colorado. . . .

They had come to the time of night Mary Frances went upstairs, and she wanted to be sure that she had left everything to Emily's satisfaction. The breakfast table was set, for instance, and Mary Frances had assumed that the guest would be eating with the family. Michael knew that Emily was preparing a tray for Kate—ice, water, and the whiskey bottle. There was a fire in the parlor fireplace; the wood had gotten wet under the fallen snow, and the fire popped and spat against the screen.

"I'm trying to figure out what I'm going to do," Kate said.

"You can take your time with that. You aren't even out of the hotel yet."

"I'm not going back into the business. I don't want to be bothered. Everything's changed, but I wouldn't even want to go back to the way it was."

Emily rolled open the dining room door. "It looks like it's going to go until morning." She put the tray on the table next to Kate's chair. "Michael, I'm going to go to bed. Is there anything you want?"

"No." He stood up to kiss her good-night. "Are you all right?"

"I'm tired." She asked Kate if she thought she would be able to find everything in Amy's room. Kate nodded, and suddenly Emily leaned over and kissed her on the cheek. "I'm glad you're here. I'm sorry for your trouble, but I'm glad you're home."

Kate touched her arm and murmured something Michael didn't hear. Emily turned to kiss him good-night and said she would leave the lights on upstairs. "Make sure the fire is down," she said. Then, as she pulled the door closed after her, when she was out of Kate's line of vision, she gave Michael a little smile.

There was still a draft in the room. Outside, the snow whirled around the lamppost, crowned the hedge, and rushed against the window. He pulled the drape. When he turned around, she was pouring herself another drink.

"You didn't see Westfield at the end the way I did," Michael said gently.

"I was waiting for you to say something. It isn't as bad as it looks. I'm having my moments, but I remember him and a whole bunch you don't know anything about. Remember what I told you about them and their dreams?"

Michael nodded.

"Well, we all have them." She raised her glass. "Whenever I see a drunk now, I think he's sitting in front of his dreams like a kid over spilt milk. That's what I learned—that's what I got out of the whole damned marriage."

"I never understood why you married him in the first place."

"It seemed like the next thing to do. I'd known him for years. We had good times together. I got to the point where I felt I had to go on to the next thing. Gert was dead and you were no good to anybody. Johnson kept me going. I began to think that if it went on indefinitely, I would wake up one morning and the rest of it would be there—"

"The rest of what?"

"I know you think I'm drunk, but I'm not that far gone. The rest of what I wanted for myself, the rest of the thing inside me. I look at her, Emily"—she motioned upstairs again—"I can actually see the thing I mean. Maybe it's just a drunk's long way of getting around to the point, but what I'm saying to you, what I'm trying to say to you, Michael, is that in my life I've had the chance to know people—I know things and I've done things I've never discussed with you. I don't want to chase anything anymore. But I have to get myself established again and let people know that I'm back in town."

She turned to the side table. "Last one. I want to sleep tonight. You don't know it, but I'm taking it easy tonight. I was going to say to you that I might feel something for some man again, I might feel it, but Jesus Christ, I'm not going to be fooled by it. You know why people drink this stuff? They want to be fooled again and they're afraid they won't be."

"Westfield told me something like that."

She sat back. "I'm your friend. I can say what I want to you. I know you better than you think I know you." She paused, waiting until she had him smiling at the way she was manipulating his tension. "You know people the way I know people. You were like this—I remember it. How are you fooled now?"

"I'm not. I know her as well as I know you, as well as you know me."

"You don't really believe I know you, but I do. It's not important. The important thing is, she's not like us, and you can't say she is."

"Why is that the important thing?"

"Look, you know her. Before I knew you, I knew girls like her. Girls like her wind up in my profession just like any other kind of girl. Girls like her never lasted long, but that's something else. I know what they're like, backwards and forwards—you don't want to know how I know? I'd rather tell you about my abortions, and I don't even remember how many of them there were. Ah, you see, I'm drinking because I don't want to live with what I know—that I'm not going to be fooled again. It's true. I have to learn to live with it."

"I don't know any secrets, Kate."

"Sometimes I think of the abortions, but what kind of a mother would I have been? Maybe it's simply a matter of facing who you are. *She* did—Emily. That's why she came back. That's how I know her as well as I do."

"I was very lucky," he said.

"She was just as lucky as you. Remember when I used to live around here? I had my dreams then, too. It tells you how young I was. I wanted to fit in, can you believe it? But I like this house better than the one I had."

"We've just decided to move," Michael said. He got up to push the logs in the fire back from the screen. "We're going over to Jersey. There's a twenty-seven-acre parcel on a hillside running down to a lake. The house has fifty-four windows. I haven't seen it yet, but it's a very attractive proposition." He turned around. "I'd have to make a heavy commitment—"

"Fifty-four windows?"

He laughed. "That's about all I've been told, in fact."

"But you're impressed," she said.

He was—he told her the truth. Thomas had said it was a beautiful piece of property, facing westward, with stands of mature evergreens, maples, and elms. Kate was surprised to hear that he would go in with Thomas, and he had to tell her about the other deals. She was suspicious—she was suspicious of all the Westfields, including Louise, who was now over sixty years old. Kate reached for the whiskey again. "People have something inside them that either gets stronger when they get older or just breaks to pieces. In all those people it's broken, including Louise—*especially* Louise. I know what I'm talking about. You've always been there for her, covering Thomas, covering Julie, but what is she going to do the first time you have to let her down? You're not stupid, you've thought about this. How do you think she'd feel about you if you let one of her beloved monsters go to the poorhouse? We don't even have to discuss them. You know I said before that I knew girls like Emily because the girls I knew were like the girls you'd find anywhere—"

"I understood that."

"Well, I knew girls like Julie, too. A girl like Julie will do anything. Believe me."

She had had enough. She wanted to talk about Johnson; she wanted Michael to understand that what had finished the marriage had been something inside her, something that had gone stale. "We went every place and got thrown out of hotels together, and once in a while we got into the kind of trouble I wouldn't tell you about, but one morning instead of waking up to find that I had the best of it, I came to thinking that I wan't going to lie to myself another day about how goddamned lonely I still was, how goddamned lonely I'd been all along."

In another moment she was standing, and then she leaned over and kissed him on the forehead, drained her glass, and put out the lights in the room. The fire had broken down to a bright pile of orange coals, and outside the window the snow swept inward, tinkling faintly against the pane. "I love you," Kate said at the door. "I love you both." He turned away, listening to the door roll shut behind him. When he noticed that she had not asked him about his dreams, he tried to find the language to answer the nonexistent question. He could see that he wanted good things for his children; he had begun to hope that this property that Thomas was going to show him would somehow be able to contain what he wanted for the children.

The fire darkened to a small cluttered glow. He got up, took Kate's tray to the kitchen, and rinsed out her glass. There was a gazebo in the backyard, a set of swings, and a seesaw; now the snow lay democratically over everything. Earlier in the week there had been a pair of sunny days and the ground had thawed, and now everything was buried under the winter again.

It was late enough to shake the furnace down and throw more coal on the fire. The cellar was the warmest place in the house, warm enough to make him sweat. He liked to work by the firelight, even when he was only shoveling out the ash. He did not do that tonight and just covered the firebed with fresh black coal, temporarily blanketing the heat and filling the cellar with shadow. He opened vents in the layer of new coal with the poker. He liked the sound of the new coal catching fire, and the heat rising again somehow felt fresh and new.

He went straight upstairs, turning out the lights along the way. The air was chillier on the second floor and the hiss of the snow around the house was louder, but he could feel the heat rising. The light was out in Amy's room—Kate was settled. Michael felt sorry for Kate, but her torment made him nervous. He looked in on the boys and wished that their room was not as cold as it was, but he and Emily had had a plumber in who had said that there was nothing he could do. Another reason to sell the house. According to Thomas, there would be rooms to spare in the house in Mountain Lakes. In spite of Kate's warning, Michael had Louise in mind, and Emily agreed and approved. Sometimes Louise went for weeks without seeing anyone in the family. The subways made the trip to Brooklyn easiest of all—just an hour, from Central Park West to Flatbush—but she felt she was imposing on them if she visited more frequently. If Michael and Emily moved to New Jersey, they would need a house large enough for her, too; if she wanted to continue on her own, that could be arranged—but both Michael and Emily thought she wanted to give it up and was just waiting for an acceptable invitation.

Emily was facing the window when he entered the bedroom. She rolled onto her back. "Did you hear her when you were in the cellar?"

"No."

"I heard a thump. It sounded as if she went down on her backside. It woke me up and so I just lay here listening for more, but she didn't seem to need help."

"Her light was out." He was undressing quickly in the dark. In the winter they had the doors to the sleeping porch lined with paper, but the cold came through anyway. He wore a nightshirt that came down to his knees. She watched his progress, and then at the appropriate moment she raised her hips beneath the covers and pulled her nightgown up. She had the bed warm enough for her bare legs. She kept her hands under the covers, and when he approached the bed, she lifted the covers so he could slip in quickly, letting his nightshirt come up to his waist as she brought the covers up to his neck. She wrapped her legs around his to warm them, slipping almost beneath the covers to press her face against his chest. She liked to hold his penis in her hand, and once in a while she was able to masturbate him. When his own hands were warm, he slid his hand into the slick softness of her pubic hair. She worked herself against his fingers until she was comfortable, and then she fell asleep. When he fell asleep himself he was thinking about the Mountain Lakes property again, and his cheek had found a cool, fresh part of the pillow. The wetness of the snow was in the room, and he could feel it against his skin.

Kate stayed until Tuesday. On Sunday they had her out in the snow in a rented sleigh, Michael, Emily, Kate, and the children pounding down Flatbush Avenue, the horses' hoofs thumping solidly, the bells on their collars ringing. You could hear the horses snorting and the runners of the sleigh slicing through the hard-packed snow. The children's noses were running, the adults' noses were red; all of them could smell the sweat of the driver frozen on his woolen coat. He was drunk, a bottle-in-disguise beside him. "A little medicine, m'am," he whispered to Emily, who nodded politely, merrily. Michael had made love to her earlier in the bright light of the sunny morning. She had to douche afterward in the cold bathroom, and to make it up to her he went downstairs to help her with the breakfast while Maureen and Mary Frances were at Mass. Kate staggered down last, hung over, sallow, moaning. The sleigh had already been called. She protested, but Michael had put whiskey in her coffee and told her to taste it. She licked her lips and allowed a contented smile. "I suppose it's the only way," she said. Michael and Emily had already made the day's plans, and they insisted that she take part. She said she thought they were merciless, but she gave in. Emily's clothes fit her well enough. They had a leg of lamb in the house that could feed them for days—there was no reason not to surrender to the festive atmosphere. Mary Frances had steaming clam chowder for them after the sleigh ride, and in the late afternoon the children built a snowman in the yard. Dinner was a sleepy affair, with the children barely making their way through it, and Kate went upstairs hardly an hour after.

The next day was warmer, but Kate slept through the morning and Michael went into the city without her; and when he telephoned later, Emily told him that she had invited Kate to stay still another night, and that Kate had said yes.

The children were upstairs when he got home, and Kate was sitting by herself in the parlor, the lights out, the fading twilight pressing into the darkened room. "I tried to make a fire, but I failed," Emily said in the hall. She told him to say good-night to the children, her eyes assuring him that his confusion, such as it was, would be cleared away when he got upstairs.

In their bedroom Emily told Michael that Kate had been watching the children playing in the yard and Maureen chasing after them and Emily shouting out the window—Kate had been talking of traveling through the West by train—when her voice quit so suddenly it made Emily turn: Kate was sitting at the table, her hand to her neck, her eyes wide. She waved Emily off, whispering that it wasn't anything stuck in her throat, just a feeling that had started to come over her. She stood up, asking if it would be all right if she lay down, not really waiting for the answer, not that she needed one; and in a while, with the children still outside squealing in the wet, blustery air, their voices carrying into the house and up the stairwell, Emily climbed the stairs, heard Kate crying, and entered Amy's room without knocking. Kate was sitting on the bed like a child, simply crying, Emily told Michael; he was getting out of his collar and tie and putting on his sweater. "She said it was something that women like her sometimes went through and that it hadn't happened to her in years. Then she told me to get out because it was contagious. It was—I don't even want to talk about it now."

"Then don't."

"She came downstairs a few minutes ago and she's better, but for a few minutes I didn't know what was going to happen next. I tried to make a fire. She's been talking about all the places she's been."

"She must be better."

"I told Mary Frances just to heat something for us. We'll eat in the parlor. Make a real fire. If you want more to eat, I'll fix it for you later."

The sky was black when he got downstairs again and he had to put on the lamp in the corner in order to work around the fireplace. Kate put her hand up to her eyes.

"I'm a sight. I don't mean to be sitting here like death, but I don't want to frighten people either."

"How are you feeling?"

"I'm all right. I had a crying jag. I was trying to explain to Emily. I used to have them all the time. Sometimes you'd get three or four girls crying together. I suppose it was coming home."

Emily and Mary Frances came out with the trays, and when they were set, Mary Frances excused herself for the night. The fire was up, and with the lamp in the corner there was plenty of light for the meal, yesterday's lamb and gravy, creamed carrots and onions, and some old bread pudding in heavy cream. And coffee—the aroma of brewing coffee suddenly gushed out of the kitchen.

The talked the rest of the night. Kate wanted to apologize for having been such a bad guest, drunk one night, exhausted the next, and finally breaking down completely on the third day, but the truth was, she said, that she should have seen it coming. They told her they needed no apologies, but she wanted to go on. She had held everything in all the way back from Denver, having had to hold it in for months before. Now she was not sure that she would go back even if there was no drinking problem. She knew she would wake up feeling as dead inside tomorrow no matter what she did.

She had had to come home anyway. She had had to go away to have the chance to come home, if that made any sense to them. She had been scared to death the first time she left the city, but now she could see that it wasn't different from her first trip to Saratoga. The fear had been the same—now she knew that she turned into a frightened rabbit whenever she tried something new.

The coffee came out, and whiskey for her. She accused Emily of trying to get her drunk again, and Emily threatened to take the bottle away. Kate asked her if she had ever been in a fistfight with another woman, and Emily laughed and blushed.

Kate said she had known how far Saratoga was, Atlantic City and Newport; and she had been looking at maps all her life; but even though Johnson had said when they left for Denver that they would be traveling for the best part of a week, she'd no idea how big and empty the country was. She knew that Michael went down to New Orleans and up to Canada all the time, and that Emily had been to Europe—she thought she would never cross the ocean, now that she had some idea how big it was.

Kate had more than traveling on her mind. She wanted to talk about the distances in the West and how it had taken her years to make sense of them. Johnson had said she would be looking at the waving yellow grass of the plains from Chicago to Denver, but she hadn't believed him. They traveled across flat land for two days. Michael and Emily had seen sketches and photographs of what she wanted to describe; to Michael, the West had seemed a bleak and empty place, hot, dry—a hard life. Here was Kate saying that it was true but that it was also beautiful and her best memory of all the years with Johnson. In Colorado it was not unusual to travel for hours to an isolated valley as big as the island of Manhattan and find one family living there in a hut that was smaller and lower to the ground than this parlor.

She had been all over the West, down into the desert and up into the mountains of Wyoming, Montana, and Idaho. There was still practically nothing there, a few rough towns, ranches that were mostly wild land—every bit of it could be carted off in a single season, or blown away in one bad storm.

Two summers ago she and Johnson had gone West across the desert to the California mountains and San Francisco, then north on the coastal steamer to Alaska. In the summer months Alaska was as hot as anyplace else, swarming with mosquitoes. On the way back, she had an odd moment. They were drinking too much—they could have been off the coast of Canada or south of Seattle. It was sundown, and she was up on deck on the portside watching the darkness gather over the mainland. She knew port from starboard; she said she had been listening to men for so many years that she knew more about their business than they did.

She'd heard things about Anchorage twenty-five years before she'd arrived there, and then she learned that she knew more of its history than most of its citizens. Michael believed it. The lines under her eyes were not from exhaustion or drinking. She had been out in the sunshine for years—all over the country.

"I was by myself," she said. "We were only a couple of miles offshore, and I could see the lights of a settlement flickering down at the waterline. It could have been a town or a lumber camp. There were Indians living there ten or fifteen years ago, real Indians living free, off the reservations, making the same kind of wood fires. The mountains run right down into the sea there, mountains to the north and south for miles. I could see the fires and the smudge of blue smoke down at the water and I started thinking about myself and how I grew up and what I grew up into, or what I became, and I thought how small and insignificant and far away it really is—not just from way out there but from everything else, and for all time. I had to go back and forth across the country and then out to the Pacific and up to Alaska before I saw how small we are. While I was standing on the deck of that steamer, I thought my way all the way back to here, over every hill, across the plains, over every mile. What I loved most about the mountains was the silence, but I've seen our progress West. Chicago is smaller than New York, but it has the same buildings and streetcars; and when you get to Omaha and then to Denver, things are so much smaller a scale that they aren't really the same—but I'm just the right age to be able to remember when New York was like those places, different because this part of the country is different, not that many years ago. I remember people talking about the Civil War; I saw men in uniform. The silence out there makes you realize how much time passed before any of us ever got here. And what the hell are we? I've seen it now; I've really seen it. I've been back and forth and up and down and I've seen people, the way we live our lives. I started thinking about it back there on the steamer, but I had to get home before I really started thinking about it again.

"The valley as big as Manhattan is a real place, and there's a real hut there, by itself, and there isn't one full set of teeth among the three adults living in it. I don't want to talk about the children—you don't want to hear about the children. They were his friends, Johnson's, and we went out to visit them, grandfather, father, mother, and four children. We went out in the summertime, when the thunderheads gather every day over the mountains. I wish you could see this place, a long rising meadow that goes on and on, covered with wildflowers. The people had the smallest corner under cultivation. From their house, which was what they called it, you could see the whole garden, because it was on rising land, all fenced and partitioned. They had cattle up at the other end of the valley, and pigs, goats, and chickens. They were from Tennessee; you could hardly understand a word they said, but they all knew what they needed to survive, even the twelve-year-old. The woman didn't think anything of touching my dress—she wanted to feel the material. That happens on an Indian reservation. The girls and young women would come up and paw you; some of them wanted to know what you felt like underneath, too. They'd think nothing of squeezing your breasts, Emily. An Indian camp is a beautiful thing once you understand all the things that happen there. Oh, it smells like hell. When I was in that valley, I heard the women yell after the little children, and at the time I remembered thinking that I heard the same sound in the Indian camp, a mother with her children. At the time I thought that the people there—Johnson's friends—weren't that much different from the Indians who had been there before them. When I was coming back East, I couldn't help thinking that I'll never see any of that again—and I won't, I don't want to—but that I'm always going to feel it. I felt it when I came back to visit. You come back East and see the slums and misery when there's so much open land, but I know that that's why people originally came *here*. I've seen the movement of civilization West, and I know that Denver will become a Chicago, and Chicago, New York, and that someday there will be electric lights everywhere. I've seen smoke rising, but it's a dream that's going to disappear. But I felt something good out there in so many places that I'd never felt here, something I almost felt part of. My life with Johnson wasn't that different from what it was here, not really part of anything, but for a while I thought that what was good out there for me had something to do with Johnson. It didn't, not really. All he could do for me was take me to the places that made me feel it, and I could do that for myself.

"It all came back to me out in the kitchen when I heard you, Emily, shouting out to the kids in the yard. I've heard that sound all my life—my own mother, before she drank herself to death, used to shout at me years ago on Lombard Street." She tilted her glass to Michael; she was starting to cry again. "You see?" she said to him. "I have lots of reasons to go easy on this stuff." She turned to Emily. "Coming back here, I didn't know if I'd feel what was important to me ever again. Some of it was in the corner of my mind, it must have been." She leaned forward, reaching for Emily's hand. "When I heard your voice, I heard hers, too, the woman out in Colorado. I heard it deep inside, and then I saw that place again—it all happened so fast I can't really describe it—because it was as if I were there. I would swear that I even got a whiff of that summer air." Still holding Emily's hand, she turned to Michael again. "I could even remember what I was thinking when I was there. It was as if I'd made the whole thing happen for me again."

"You don't know what's liable to happen when you've been through all you have."

"Yes, that's true. In Colorado I thought that she wasn't different from the Indian women I'd seen earlier. That was wrong. She was different, just as you're different. It's the thing itself that's the same. I'd forgotten that it was here in the East, so dirty and ugly and inhuman. I'm sorry, but it's the way I feel; I've seen the wave of ugliness moving West. I'd forgotten you and I'd forgotten my own mother. I grew up in a family. I don't think I could have ever found any peace in myself if I had not gone out there and come back, but just as important I had to come here." She held Emily's hand close, with both of her hands. "This is the only family I know now," she cried. "I need you a lot more than you need me, and don't you forget it!"

"Kate, you will always be welcome in my home," Michael said. "If you didn't want to come here, I'd change things so you would."

"Thank you."

"And if you cry again, I will join you," Emily said. "I don't ever want to hear you crying again."

V

Kate left the next morning with Michael and they rode into the city together, sharing the newspaper. She was still pulling herself together—and would be for some time, Michael guessed. He had asked her on the walk to the train if she had begun to make any plans and she said no; what she still wanted more than anything else was sleep and rest, in that order, and more of the same.

They parted at Broadway. She came out onto the platform. It was after rush hour and they could feel the cold air rushing down from the street. He kissed her good-bye. He had her telephone number at the hotel, but he wanted her to give him her new number when it changed. She said sure. She smiled.

"You're a marvelous man, Michael. You don't know the half of it."

"I love you, too." He did; he wanted her to know how much he felt for her. "Promise me you'll call us at least twice a week. Call Em at home or me at the office—please yourself, but call us."

"Aren't you going to call me?"

He grinned. "You'll hear from me every day about horses, if you want to go partners again."

"Oh, you sweetheart! Get my bets down, will you, until I say hello to folks? Start our account with a thousand. I'll send you a check."

"You're covered."

She nuzzled his cheek. "You see? You don't know the half of it. You can go on, if you want. I'll wait for the next train."

Emily heard from her before the end of the week. Kate was still in the hotel, but she had begun to look at apartments. She had made some calls and would be going up to Rye for the weekend. She needed a maid, but that would have to wait until Monday or Tuesday—in all, Emily reported, she sounded rested and in better spirits.

Early on Sunday morning they met Louise on Twenty-third Street on the west side of Manhattan and took the ferry over to New Jersey and the train out to Boonton, where Thomas met them at the station shortly before noon. With Louise they were a party of six, the maids having been left in Brooklyn, and Michael, Emily, and the children had been traveling since eight-thirty. It was a mild, damp, overcast day, true March; the snow was mostly gone, cinder-covered piles of it in the city, drifts still clinging in the shadowed pockets out here in the country. Thomas had an automobile, a Winton fitted with brass lamps and tufted upholstery, but it could not carry all the adults and children at once. As they had done on previous visits, Michael and Emily chose to remain behind for Thomas's second trip; but after a few minutes' strolling on the platform, they were driven into the waiting room by the wind. The hard, sparsely furnished room smelled of kerosene and the windows were grimy, but it was a country place and the view outside was of trees thrashing ominously under the boiling sky. Michael had known that he would be tense, but in fact he was a little frightened. He was already prepared to like the house that Thomas planned to show him before dinner, and he wanted the land as an investment or even a last hedge against ever going completely broke; but the weather and the length of the trip made him worry about the isolation and their own strangeness to the area. He knew the sort of people who lived out here, and he anticipated involving himself with them no more than what was required to keep up the family reputation. Being understood as a man who minded his own business had suited him in Flatbush and would suit him here; it was Emily who concerned him: the friends she had made in the neighborhood in Brooklyn were simpler people than those she had grown up among—and a long way from the probably showy new rich established out here.

So far, it seemed that she liked what she was seeing. They had come through miles of bare, misty farmland, not as pretty as the highland around Saratoga but pleasant in its own way. She wanted to know about the school and the shops in the village. The maids would have to be able to get to the city on their Thursday nights off or at least, to a large town nearby. If Michael and Emily decided to buy this house, there would be a lot of work for her that he really could not help her with, calling upon all of her knowledge of homemaking—she was already drifting into making imaginary lists, drawing tentative schedules.

Thomas was back for them in twelve minutes. Michael had timed the round trip before, but now it had more meaning. The property Thomas meant to show was fifteen minutes from his own. Fifteen minutes farther out of town?

He wanted them to see the place right away. It was beyond his house, twenty-five minutes from the station. Thomas knew how to drive, all right, maneuvering the wheels past the worst ruts in the country road. Michael was up front with him, his long legs far to the right to avoid the levers and pedals rising like madcap flowers from the floorboards; Thomas stomped and wrung them with stolid, godlike authority, and the Winton, writhing over the mudruts like a lust-riddled salmon, clumsily did his bidding and carried them all out into lovely rolling countryside.

Thomas tried to tell them about the property as he drove, shouting over his shoulder to Emily sitting behind them. Michael had no idea what she heard; he intended to make Thomas repeat every bit of it. The heat, smell, and vibration of the automobile had Michael sick to his stomach. The canvas top was erected but not the side curtains; the wind blew in, carrying with it still more noise. The thing gnashed and gnarled, bouncing them up and down; at times their heads hit the canvas, and twice Michael thought they were going to tip over. But Thomas was sure of himself and laughed out loud.

"You don't know what you're getting into, coming out here. There's a fellow on the other side of Mountain Lakes who's trying to build his own aeroplane."

"He can go to hell," Michael said.

Emily leaned forward. "How will Michael get to the railroad station?"

"There's a taxicab company in Boonton that comes day or night. But he'll get the hang of it out here. Either you're going to keep horses or buy an automobile, and horses are on their way out."

"Not for years," Emily said.

"Can't make money with horses," Thomas said.

"Of course you can," Emily said. "What do you mean?"

"He means that you can't make a new fortune with horses, but you can with automobiles."

"And everything that goes with them," Thomas said happily. Having made money had made him confident about practically everything. He liked to talk about a future filled with perfected new inventions, like absolutely painless dentistry. He was as fat as ever, and his life with Ethel and the children seemed as chaotic and overwrought as always, but somehow the changes he had made in the past few years had made him feel like a new man; and if he was still not scintillating company, at least he was no longer sulking and oppressive. Michael remembered Thomas's youth in the whorehouses with two or three girls at a time arranged in tableaux he had orchestrated, but which made him moan like a mourner at graveside. Michael had heard all about it from Westfield—and Kate, because it had gone around town. Perhaps Thomas's fever had simply disappeared from his consciousness under the avalanche of life with Ethel. If anything, he had become a bit of a prude, as if he thought Michael had forgotten the antics of twenty years before or, more likely, as if he had actually forgotten them himself.

They went deeper into the country, following a march of T-shaped telephone poles. The narrow road was straight, and the trees hung over it from both sides. Michael knew he was unhappy, but he wanted his family to reach for more out of life than he ever had. He wanted them at a distance from most of the people with whom he had to do business. The children saw plenty at Saratoga, but Saratoga lent his enterprises an elegance they often did not have in the city.

They began to see more houses, three- and four-story homes, small estates. Smoke rose from the chimneys, and electric lights could be seen in the windows. There was a telephone line to every house. It was more wooded through here; the evergreens were as tall as anything Michael had ever seen. Thomas brought the automobile to a noisy stop and switched off the engine. In the silence he pointed to the house directly in front of them.

It was twice the size of the house in Brooklyn, much wider, with a porch that ran around all four sides. It had three floors, the third the size of the bungalow they rented in Saratoga. The whole thing had the beauty of a ship, the trim in a natural wood finish, the shingles stained dark brown. It was empty. Thomas had the keys.

As they walked up the hill, the view to the left side of the house opened up, and they could see down the tailored slope to a metallic sheet of water. A twenty-acre pond, Thomas said, really a lake. The lawn was bordered with mountain laurel and rhododendron, and there were spruce and pine among the tall elms running down to the water. Behind the house the raw woods continued on up the hill for another several hundred feet. Thomas had the history of the house, a horrible tale of a stockbroker's butchered dream; there were oil men out here, he was quick to add, railroad executives—substantial and important men.

They walked around the porch before they went inside. There was a stable that could be converted into a garage, two other smaller buildings, and the beginnings of a formal garden, a trellis and some marble benches, at the edge of the woods. They saw enough of the downstairs rooms through the large windows facing the porch. The kitchen was enormous, gleaming with white tile. Emily noticed the height of the ceilings—more than twelve feet, Thomas said, for better cooling in the summer.

Emily wanted to go through the house twice, upstairs and down; she had pencil and paper for sketches and measurements. The house had been closed all winter, and the air inside was colder than the weather outdoors. Good insulation, Thomas said. It was obvious that the furniture they owned would disappear in this place: the parlor was twenty-five feet long, and so was the master bedroom above it. The front staircase going up to the second floor was six feet wide, and the back stairs were completely enclosed all the way to the top of the house.

Thomas was flushed from climbing up and down. He gave Emily the key and told her to be sure that the front door was locked; he was going to go down to the car where it was warm. Michael was satisfied with what he had seen; if Emily wanted the house, if he saw that it made her happy, she could have it.

The engine compartment of the automobile radiated heat like a stove. The wind jostled the vehicle so that it squeaked and flapped from all directions. Thomas was still breathing hard, his chin pressed against his chest, his nostrils flaring.

"It's up to her," Michael said. "It's a good deal for me, but I won't like the traveling."

"It'll be a wonderful deal for you." Thomas puffed. "In twenty years it will make you rich."

"This is for the children," Michael said. "In twenty years I'll be an old man. Money doesn't matter that much to me now."

"Well, it matters to me," Thomas said. He shifted, rocking the boat, as it were. "If I had the money, I'd buy this property myself. I *know* how much money this is going to turn over someday."

"Do you want to be rich?" Michael asked. "Is it that important to you?"

"I'm *getting* rich," Thomas said. "Five more years and I'll be able to retire, if I want. I'll have my children provided for." His cheeks puffed as he stifled a belch, and he was still in the throes of some digestive inconvenience when Emily appeared on the porch. She waved, and Michael saw a girlishness in her movement. She was smiling as she started down the stairs. Michael was going to tell Thomas what it meant when Thomas suddenly opened his mouth to release a long and resonant burp. He had to crank the engine. "Ethel's putting on the dog," he said as he climbed down. "I made the mistake of going light on breakfast, and boy, am I hungry."

The cold had everybody indoors: the seven adults, Julie's two teen-
agers by her marriage to Roger Fleming, Thomas's three children between the ages of six and twelve, Michael and Emily's three, and Julie's
two babies by Hafner. Also in the house were the two resident servants
and Julie's babies' nurse, a heavy woman of fifty-five who spoke with a
German accent. Ethel had indeed put on the dog, with a fire roaring up
the chimney in the parlor, the table in the dining room extended so that
all but the youngest children would be with their parents. Because of the
heat in the house there was much adjusting of the windows, with Ethel
telling the children playing upstairs to raise this window or that in one
or another of the bedrooms. Occasionally a cold gust would whip through
the warmth and noise and conversation, the girl struggling through the
crowd to serve drinks and hors d'oeuvres or to clean up something a
child had spilled; and out of the clamor would rise another complaint
about a draft, and people would be sent running to the windows again.
The boys got at it and there was a terrifying, house-rattling thump from
somewhere upstairs; they said it was nothing, and when they were called
down to dinner, no one seemed damaged.

Thomas had his mother on his right and Emily on his left; Ethel was at
the other end of the table with Michael near her. Hafner was in the
middle of the table on the opposite side. He had revealed himself as a
disciplinarian with children, and he had Julie's older boy and girl
cowed—Louise had the boy next to her. Michael did not know what the
boy knew of his father's disgrace, but he acted as if he were aware of
something, a silent child who stayed by himself. Neither he nor his sister
had their parents' good looks, not as if the parents had been a bad mix
but as if the strains had spent themselves one generation too soon. Their
father lived in Boston now; he was married again—Louise knew the
details. Her face hardened when Fleming's name was mentioned; she
once told Michael that a man like him belonged to the devil because he
genuinely *loved* sin. No matter; it was clear that she thought the wound to
the boy was the worse. The girl was a blank to Michael. Her features
were thick and unpleasant compared to her mother's, a plight so desperate that everyone could see it, including Ethel, who tended to fawn over
her to an extent that was embarrassing. Whatever the girl thought,
Michael was sure that someone had told her that her grandmother
favored her grandsons over her granddaughters, because that was true,
too. All by herself, by mismanaging her role as grandmother to all these
children, Louise had succeeded in creating a mess of resentments among
them that Michael imagined was the equal of the long-simmering stew
among the adults. Michael wondered if Thomas or Julie ever saw it in
those terms—that their children in their turn had lives of their own, and

even that the oldest might have secrets as sophisticated as anything that ever occurred upstairs on East Thirty-eighth Street.

It was the sort of day that led to thoughts like that. If Hafner was a disciplinarian, Thomas and Ethel were not, and by the end of the meal the shrieks and spillages had everybody's nerves ragged. Ethel had had something else in mind—Thomas and Hafner wanted Michael to buy the property, but they had tried to put the best face on it, a family party, a family reunion. If there was more, Ethel wasn't in on it; she wanted to know right away if Michael and Emily were going to buy. Hafner at least was able to wait until after dinner. He and Thomas took Michael into the library where they spelled it out for him. Thomas said that much; Hafner did the rest. He was fifty now and had grown heavy and gray. He colored his moustache, which had grown thinner through the years. His eyes were beginning to go; they let you see that he was probing for your weaknesses. His wife had become harsh in her own way now that she was past forty, and together they seemed to have so little love in them that you had to wonder how they dealt with each other during sex. It crossed Michael's mind when he was looking at her at the table; and later in the library it occurred to him that Hafner was older than her father had ever been. All the secrets of Thirty-eighth Street had been running through Michael's thoughts today; for all he knew, she had told Hafner about the two of them. Whatever the case, Hafner had all the figures for Michael—exactly how much profit there would be in living like a king. He wanted a quick answer, and finally Michael realized that the Hafners' passion was money. Cynical people, Louise had called them. Money before everything. Michael told Hafner that the proposition seemed attractive but that he wanted to know Emily's feelings about the house itself—when they were alone and she could express herself freely.

Louise accompanied them on the long, grim trek back to Brooklyn. The children were asleep ten minutes after the train left Boonton, and the sputtering journey in the taxicab down Broadway toward the bridge seemed to take forever. Michael had had enough of automobiles today to last him the rest of his life. But Thomas was right about the automobile, and he and Hafner were right about the property in Mountain Lakes. Somewhere on the way to New Jersey this morning Michael had remembered what Kate had told them earlier in the week about the look of things across the country. In his own boyhood Michael had been able to stand on the top of the Forty-second Street reservoir and be able to see to the horizon a full three hundred and sixty degrees. Brooklyn had been mostly open country. But even then the bridge had been under construction, and the elevated lines had started their march uptown. The future had been there for anyone to see. Now there were three bridges to

Brooklyn, the bridge to Queens was under construction, and they were going to tunnel under the Hudson. Kate knew where such dreams began, and she had warned him against the Westfields—Michael could not help remembering it. She had never met Carl Hafner, but Michael doubted that she could tell him anything about Hafner that Michael could not guess. It did not matter. Michael would have title to the land. Hafner wanted to develop it later, but long before that came to pass, Michael would have learned what Hafner's competitors were offering. That was all in the far future. Hafner and Thomas were short of capital and wanted to tie up the land. If Michael wanted, Hafner would show him other parcels. In the future.

It was the future itself that was the real problem. It was becoming something Michael couldn't recognize, but he could see that it was his business to try to find a way to live with it. If he did not start making changes, others would make them before him, and someone else's children would reap the profit.

That night Emily told him that she wanted the house. They were in the kitchen, where she was brewing him a cup of camomile tea. Louise was upstairs now, too, getting settled; she had said she would be coming down again.

The sky had cleared. The wind had come up and a full moon had begun to race through the clouds, and when the taxi had pulled up to the house, Emily had let the girls and Louise get inside before she started up the walk. She had wanted to have another look at this house; silent in the moonlight, it offered Michael no clue to the future. It looked only small. He had come all the way from the west side of Manhattan in the taxi sitting on the small rearward-facing folding seat, Amy curled under his arm. The moon had come out as they had chugged across the bridge, and he had been able to see the mostly blackened towers of lower Manhattan facing the water like a solid wall. In his youth the tallest structure had been the spire of Trinity Church, and now there were office buildings looking down on it from every side. Michael was still thinking about what Kate had told them about the people living in the Colorado valley as big as Manhattan. Kate had tried to think her way from there to here. He had seen enough of the country; the train to New Orleans took almost two days. And now the city lay spread before him, as big as a valley in Colorado. . . .

For a tired moment in the kitchen he wanted to entertain the thought that he had only these few seconds to make the decision of a lifetime. There was a bit of truth to it; Emily and Louise were waiting to hear what he had to say. Could he explain to them the ways he thought the decision had already been made? While he had been looking at the city from the bridge, he had seen a train coming up out of the tunnel, a great, shining iron serpent that would have terrified the savages living in Kate's Colorado valley until a few years ago. Did that explain how history had much of the decision for him? Something Kate had said glimmered beyond his capacity to recall, something about what the hell we were or what the hell we thought we were. He had to look at the situation plainly. He had to make the best decision for everybody.

He called Thomas the next afternoon, and by Wednesday the preliminary papers were ready for his signature. The closing took place in another month, and in June, with the house in Flatbush not yet sold, they moved. Louise arrived in July. The smell of paint was still in the upstairs rooms, and furniture would be coming for months. Michael took the boys to Canada with him and was waiting for Emily, Amy, and the girls in Saratoga for the start of the season there. Louise wanted to stay in Mountain Lakes. While they had their vacation from her, she said, she could get around to see her other grandchildren.

Michael had a good August. Some horses he had spotted in New Orleans ran well on the faster Saratoga track, and he had luck with the jumpers. He held his own at the card tables; players came from all over the country now, and some of the private games in the hotels ran for days at a time. Michael had his selections and newsletters to get out, which kept him away from the family and he did not like the idea of sitting at a card table all night. The afternoons at the tables in the clubhouse of the track were the best of all. Between races a band would strike up, or some other entertainment would begin, and people would be hurrying below to see the odds chalked on the bookmakers' blackboards. There was a murmur and bustle up and down the grandstand, the odor of food everywhere, and the air brisk in the dark shade of the long green roof.

Thomas got sick on the twenty-first. Louise's telegram offered no details save that he had been hospitalized. There was no answer at Mountain Lakes, and the girl at Thomas's house knew only that he was in Saint somebody's in Newark. The second telegram arrived that evening and resolved the ambiguities: it gave the name of the hospital and the information that Thomas was dying.

Michael took the night boat from Albany. He would send Emily a long telegram just as soon as he had more information. He was awake all night, and when the boat put in to Forty-second Street, he was up on deck watching the ferries gliding back and forth to Jersey on the still water of the early morning.

Hafner had taken charge. He had rented rooms at a hotel, and servants were on their way from Boonton and the shore with changes of clothes for everyone. A specialist had been brought in but had pronounced the case hopeless. Thomas's heart had given out. He had had two massive attacks already, and the doctors did not expect him to last the week. He was in terrible pain. They had him doped up, but when Michael asked if it helped, Thomas shook his head. He was elevated so he could see people. His eyes gaped with fear. Ethel was there, and Julie and Louise. Hafner was down the hall seeing about another room. The curtain was open for the sunshine, but the window was stuck and now the room was becoming too warm. Michael asked Thomas if there was anything he could do.

"Nothing can be done," he gasped. "I know what's going to happen."

"You don't know anything of the sort—"

Thomas waved his hand to stop him. "I want to talk to you. Get out of here, Ethel. Everybody get out of here. I want to talk to Michael."

"I'll be in the hall, Thomas," Ethel said.

"If I start to die, I'll call you. Shut the door," he said to Michael.

Michael closed the window curtain, too. "Try to go easy on her, Thomas."

"She understands. Listen, I want you to look after her. Carl's too far away. I don't know what she's doing to do."

"If it comes to that, we'll do the best we can. I promise you. Don't worry about it."

"I'm going to die, Michael. There's no point in lying to ourselves." He stopped and waited, as if the energy to talk had temporarily left him. "There's a little cash. The deal I have with Carl has him paying Ethel fifty thousand over the next two years. She doesn't know how to handle money. Will you take care of her affairs? I want my boys to go to college."

"I'll see to it. Get your rest, Thomas."

"No—what for? Look, I didn't get you to come out to Jersey for this. I didn't know it was going to happen. You're going to have to take care of my mother, too. It isn't just that Carl is too far away. I know you know Julie.

"I don't hate you, Michael. I want you to know that. When I was a kid I hated you, but you would have felt the same in my position. You know what my problem was. The only times I ever got anything from him was when he was too ashamed to look me in the eye otherwise. He'll be dead twenty years next December, and I still can't think of him without hating him. I know you thought he was a wonderful man, but you know as well as I do that he ruined my life. I made enough mistakes of my own, but I didn't do to my children what he did to me."

"I'll remember that, Thomas."

"Tell them. Maybe it will help them understand the bad things. I'm scared, Michael. What the hell did I live for?"

"I don't want you to worry about anything. What needs doing will be done. You know I don't hate you either. I'm grateful to you for what you've done for me."

"You might as well let them back in. I always liked Emily. I don't want her coming down here. It's too much for her. When she came back, I knew I had been out of line about you. You kept a lot to yourself, Michael."

"I had to."

"Well, don't worry about it." His chest heaved. Alarmed, Michael opened the door. Hafner had returned. They were doing what they could about the room, he said. He eyed Michael briefly, but the very little that Michael cared to tell him, that Thomas was concerned with his family, could wait until later.

The nurses moved Thomas to another room that was a bit better, and he died before dinnertime. Michael was at the hotel, having sent Emily the telegram and napped fitfully for a couple of hours. Hafner telephoned with the news, saying, "He's gone. He slipped away quietly," and Michael replying, "I'm sorry," having heard in Hafner's tone that the two men had become close. There was no reason to say anything to Hafner about Thomas's conversation. Michael himself had another telegram to send, but now at least Emily expected it. After this, she would be waiting to learn the funeral arrangements. Michael could see the grim procession of the days ahead. And there was nothing he could do, presumably, but make himself useful, help with the arrangements and try to cover his own work.

The funeral was in Boonton, and the interment in a cemetery more than twenty miles up the old Morristown–West Point Road. Ethel did not want to be so close to the cemetery that she would be passing the grave every other day. Louise was not bitter; it was she who first raised the question of pallbearers. "I saw the way those nurses struggled with him," she told Michael and Hafner. "You tell the undertaker to take care of that. If he wanted pallbearers, he shouldn't have stuffed his face the way he did." By then everyone knew what had brought on the original attacks, a violent seizure of vomiting brought on by some bad seafood. He had been on his way to the bathroom again when the first pains hit him, and he grabbed the door with such violence that he tore it off the hinges. Michael did not find the whole business as funny as some people did, and when callers at the house wanted to discuss the indirect cause of Thomas's death, Michael made sure that they heard about what had been done to the bathroom door.

He found himself truly grieving and, more than that, judging himself harshly. Even when the man was putting money in his pocket, and worse still, over these past five months, Michael had been unwilling to give Thomas a second thought. He had always been able to outwit him; he could have done better than I *don't hate you either.* He felt what he thought he deserved. He had put nothing into the relationship, and at the end Thomas had been treating him like a true brother.

Michael had to say that aloud. They did not return to Saratoga but let the girls pack the last of the trunks and come down alone with Amy. The boys had come for the funeral. In Mountain Lakes, then, in the huge parlor, after the boys had gone to bed, he said it aloud to Emily: "You know, at the end, he was treating me like a brother."

"I think so," she said, and then looked up to see that he was weeping real tears.

VI

That was the beginning of a dark season, and for months it seemed that they could not move about the neirhborhood, or even walk through their own house, without somehow thinking of Thomas. They indulged themselves with a little talk about selling and returning to the city, but they really knew that they were committed at least until Ethel's position clarified. Hafner had started making the scheduled payments, but he let it be known that he felt the pressure. Michael heard it from Louise, who had heard it from Julie—Michael took that aspect seriously: Hafner wanted a new arrangement badly enough to manipulate Louise's fears for it. Thomas may have asked Michael to look after his family, but it did not seem that he had mentioned it to Ethel. She had her own family, and of Thomas's she continued to favor Julie and her husband. Things appeared so cozy among them, in fact, that Michael thought it would be insane, if not suicidal, to sound any sour notes. Ethel had never been all that fond of him anyway. And Louise did not want trouble.

Just as well: it was a dark season. He had a siege of sleeplessness and then, because he had pushed himself too hard, the worst influenza of his life. He was in bed for two weeks and home for a month—people worried about *him* for a while.

With the end of winter came the announcement that the Hafners and Ethel and all the children were off for a three months' tour through Germany, Switzerland, and Austria-Hungary—all German-speaking countries, Louise noted miserably. When it went badly for her, Louise thought Carl Hafner was Attila the Hun. They were taking Ethel for a rest and a holiday, Julie assured her, but Louise was not fooled. More miserable business—no matter how they cheated and lied to each other, Louise was more and more dependent on the family as she grew older. For years her daughter had manipulated stituations for chances to settle old accounts. She could have taken her mother to Europe just as easily as her sister-in-law—unless, of course, it was the sister-in-law's deferred payment that was taking them in the first place. In any event, Louise felt every bit of it, but she kept her peace to have access to the grandchildren. She went down to the pier to see them off, and after ten days, when there was no telegram indicating their safe arrival, she had to be assured that, in the absence of news reports to the contrary, it was appropriate to proceed on the assumption that the ship had docked safely. Michael could see that it was only going to get worse, and he resolved that they were not going to be drawn into a pattern of placating her. During his illness he had decided to take Emily with him on his annual trip to New Orleans, and although he had not discussed it with anyone, he saw no reason to make any changes. The fact of the matter was that Louise had money of her own and could do anything she wanted. He told her of his plans straight out. She took the occasion to praise him for thinking of her as much as he did; but the next day she was waiting to know what was in the mail, as dismal as ever.

Kate joined them—they got on the train in Newark, and she and her companion, having boarded earlier in Hoboken, were in the parlor car waiting for them. Her companion was a bit of a surprise. She had told them she would be traveling with her lawyer, who was a married man and required discretion. Michael and Emily had never met him, although Kate had known him for almost a year. Only in the past month had their flirtation come to anything. He was in love with her, she had told Emily on the telephone, and the idea was beginning to fascinate her.

He was thirty years old, with black hair and blue eyes, big athletic—as handsome a man as Michael had ever seen. He could feel Emily gasp as she realized who he was, and after the introductions were made, she did not know what to do with herself.

"We never know what you're going to do next Kate," Michael said.

"That's what I like about her," her friend, Charles Duran, said.

"He's a pretty persuasive fellow," Kate said adoringly. "Don't let him kid you." She looped her arm in Duran's. Married or not, he was in love with her, all right. And whatever their second thoughts about his wife and kiddies, Duran did not seem to be a bad fellow. He had seen Emily's first reaction to him as clearly as everyone else, and in the next seconds he turned his attention carefully and completely to Michael. Kate was glowing—she was in love, too, whether she knew it or not. Duran concealed his feelings better, but when they all sat down, his hand moved to take hers. At thirty there was a lot to him. He may have blundered into more trouble than he had ever known in his life, but he looked as if he had accepted the fact that the blunders had emerged from his own character. He said that Kate had told him a good deal about them—polite talk, but it was a way of saying he wanted to be friends.

The rest of his conversation said the same. He didn't know much about racing, he said, and if he couldn't learn, he would stay out of their way. On the other hand, he had been to New Orleans many times in the past on business and knew the restaurants. Michael said he thought it sounded fair enough; he could see Emily out of the corner of his eye, and she was having difficulty keeping her attention off Duran.

"Charles plays a little poker," Kate said.

"These people can skin you alive," Michael said.

"Kate says that you're the best of the bunch."

Michael would adjust his game. "I don't play much anymore."

Duran grinned. "That sounds like a come-on."

It did, but the grin made Michael think that he would adjust his game upward, if necessary. Figuring what he knew about Kate, he should not have expected less. Cardplaying was the least of Duran's gifts, as far as she was concerned. You could feel the sex between them—they had probably nearly missed the train. When a man and a woman were really making love, everyone around them somehow sensed it; and with Duran so much the sort of man she was drawn to naturally, Emily sensed it very clearly indeed. Kate was watching Michael. He held her in his eyes a moment, and she smiled. She wanted him to be happy for her. He had a pleasant thought about her and promised himself that he would pass it along to her as soon as the opportunity allowed.

Later, when lunch was over, the two couples retired to their compartments. The porter had made the beds, trafficking with the deepest human secrets. They were south of Philadelphia, bound for Wilmington, Delaware, and then Baltimore and Washington. There they were hooked up to the rest of the overnight to Memphis, and late the following night they would be in New Orleans. It was an arduous journey no matter how people tried to make a party of it, and a porter who knew his business had to trust his instincts.

"Duran's a handsome bastard," Michael said when the door was closed.

"He knows it." Her back was to him. There was little room when the beds were down, and if the two of them wanted to undress together, they had to keep clear of each other's hips and elbows. They had been married long enough to have reached understandings concerning their idiosyncrasies even in railroad compartments. They slept together, no matter how they had to cling to the edges of a bed. The shades were up, and he watched her undress while they rushed by a landscape of dried reeds and telegraph poles. In the daylight her skin had a bluish tint. The air was cool so that when she turned around to him, her nipples were erect. He undressed her the rest of the way, undressed himself, and put his arms around her. His heart was pounding.

"Whether he knows it or not, he's still a handsome bastard," he whispered.

"I'm so *ashamed.*"

"You have nothing to be ashamed of. He caught us both by surprise. The last time that happened to you was the afternoon you met me."

"Do you think it's that simple?" she whispered.

"No."

She shook in his arms. "I *am* ashamed!"

"I brought you back here to make love to you. I love you. I don't care about anything."

"You don't mean that."

"You don't want me to mean it, but I do, more than you know."

"And you tell me now," she said and held him tightly.

"He's interested in her anyway."

She moved away. "He had a look."

"Are you feeling brazen?"

"Here, now—with *you,* yes."

As it turned out, Duran had his own points of vulnerability. At dinner he could see a change in Emily, and it seemed to challenge him; and later, when he and Michael found a game to their liking in a forward compartment, he played erratically, pressing his luck, and finished winning twenty-five dollars when he should have won five or six hundred, given his cards. Michael had won a hundred and a half. They went back to the parlor car, and the steward offered to find them some hot chocolate. It was after two., but there were a dozen men up talking. The train was filled with gamblers who followed the horses. Duran said that he thought he reserved Michael's kind of concentration for business hours, pouring over lawbooks.

"You play for the pleasure," Michael said. "You like to bet a lot and draw to the big hand. Whenever you make it, you forget about all the times you don't."

"I've been thinking about that lately. There's enough recklessness in my life."

"Have you made plans?"

"None. My wife will get everything, so I'm as good as wiped out. I'm not even sure I want to practice law. The firm thought it would be in its best interest if I resigned. Anything I do will be a clean break."

"Well, you're not alone."

"No, I'm not. I've never had such a good friend as her. *You* know that. She loves you—I admit that it made a monkey of me at times. I was tense about meeting you. She was right. I've already seen your generosity and intelligence. Lately, I've been thinking that I've just stopped being a child."

"I think the trick is to recognize that you remain a child forever and that it takes only the right set of circumstances to bring it out." He was thinking of this afternoon with Emily "which is the way I play cards."

Michael studied him. Cardplaying? Duran had moments when he feared his soul was lost. What would he be like if his panic eased? Would it occur to him that the delicate and beautiful Kate Johnson was a fast-fading forty-six-year-old? Michael remembered the little attentions he had paid to Emily at dinner when he saw that she was much more interested in her husband than she had been earlier. Duran had learned that Michael was shrewder than he'd thought—and generous yes, that, too—but what had he learned about himself? He was on the edge and could go either way. "I think you ought to use this time to find out what you want out of life. You might even want to remember what you originally wanted years ago, when you really were a child."

They were already in Tennessee. It was the darkest time of night and there was nothing at all to see, but for a long while Duran stared at the window. "When I was a child I didn't know that I could feel anything like the thing I feel for Kate. I wanted something fine for myself. I don't know if I have it now or if I've just thrown away any chance of ever having it. Kate says I'm too young for her, and neither of us knows if she's right or even what it means."

And so it went through their stay in New Orleans and on the train back north. Emily was alternately attracted and repelled by Duran, although he pretty much minded his own business, and finally she came to the conclusion that, regardless of what Kate thought, Duran and his problems were too young for *her* Before that, however, Kate had her own fun with Emily—Emily told Michael about it later. The men had gone off somewhere, and after telling Emily how happy she had been since she had begun to feel something for Duran, Kate suddenly smiled and said, "He took *your* breath away."

"And what did you say?" Michael asked.

"I said, 'He certainly did.' "

By then it was a game, the whole thing settling into a trifling erotic interlude; but it had them intoxicated with each other again. Emily was blushing. "You have no idea. Then Kate said, 'He's every bit as good as he looks.' Michael, I thought I was going to faint!"

"She loves you, you know."

"I know. And I love her. Michael, I've been shameless. She told me all their secrets, all *his* secrets. Do you hate me?"

He thought it was hilarious. "No, but I'm watching you."

"Are you?"

"I don't want to lose you," he said

"You won't." She put her head on his chest. "You're stuck with me."

They were home a week when Kate called Michael downtown to tell him that Duran's wife had hired private detectives and they had burst in on the two of them the night before. "She wants her pound of flesh," Kate said. "She knows about the New Orleans trip and I'm sorry, but when it gets into court that might come out and you and Emily might be named."

"If he fights his legal battles the way he plays poker, we will be," Michael said. "Under the circumstances, I'd be very annoyed if he did anything but fold his cards."

"That's what he's going to do. He wants you to understand that he's going to do everything he can to keep you and Emily out of it. I think you taught him something, Michael. He's been talking about you ever since we got back."

After the prospect of scandal, the notion left Michael feeling disagreeable. The image of private detectives crashing into a flat with their cameras popping had given him a real jolt, he realized—he could have reserved his comment until she had finished telling what she knew. He asked her how she was doing.

"A woman twenty-one years younger than me can't wait to tell the world that I took her big, handsome, juicy husband away from her, that's how I'm doing. I'm thinking of going into business or putting money into a business. He's a better man than you saw. I got to have something besides myself to think about or I'm going to go crazy."

From his office he had a view of another building across the street, and the shadows of afternoon were so deep that the lights were on over there. He could see people working, curled over typewriters, hurrying back and forth. Michael watched them for half an hour before he realized he was through for the day. He wanted no trouble with anyone, and if he had to duck process servers in order to get into his office, he might even close it altogether. For the time being he would say nothing to Emily; it was the sort of thing that just as easily came to nothing.

It was a cool spring day, and it seemed to him that he was not alone leaving the city early. On the ferry he went up to the top deck, where, in spite of the wind, the sun felt warm. The wind was strong, but there was always someone to forget to hold onto his hat, and on almost every trip you could see a homburg or bowler bouncing aft and floating away in the wake. Sometimes there would be a cheer to send it off. It was a day like that, with people in a good mood. There were big ships tied up at the piers, and the river traffic was heavy. Holding his hat, newspaper under his arm, Michael walked around the top deck. There was a group of women far aft, almost out of the breeze, but he could smell their perfumes curling back on the air. He could hardly look at a woman without eventually thinking of Westfield, but he looked at this bunch anyway, cautiously, because he really did not like to see one who made his knees buckle. While he had the one he wanted, he still liked the same type, and once a year he saw one in her midtwenties or so, fairly pretty, with good eyes, intelligent eyes, usually light-haired. He saw one today. She was taller than Emily, with the same straight blonde hair, her nose longer and narrower, and her lips thinner. The more he looked at this girl, in fact, the better Emily seemed; he liked Emily's plumpness. He liked the smell at the nape of her neck. It was spring, and he was not surprised with himself. Westfield had been wrong in his understanding of male sexual desire, too: at forty-four Michael was still as interested as often as he chose, and Kate had told him years ago that she had customers as old as he was now who were as good as men half their age. It was the mind, not the body. Michael knew that if he looked at a tender slip of a girl like the tall, slim maiden here and imagined her yielding to him, it was Emily's cries he really heard, her big soft bottom he held in his hands. This one, like Emily, could be curious about men—Michael caught her trying to get a look at him. The ferry was in the middle of the river, and to the north you could see all the way up the Palisades, past the little lighthouse on the New York side. Beyond that the river widened a little, creating the illusion of a lake or another bay. Michael turned back to the girl, found her eyes locked to his, smiled and winked. She reddened, smiled back, and turned away.

It was noticeably cooler by the time the train reached Boonton. There were leaves on the trees now, but the sun still weakened in the late afternoon. Two of the taxis were out, and Michael rode home in the third, a touring car, with the youngest brother in the family driving, a slack-jawed fifteen-year-old who had been fetched out of the back yard by his mother. Driving was just another chore for him, and he took out his adolescent rage on the machine. With the canvas top down, they whipped along at twenty or twenty-five miles per hour, even faster downhill. The cool air was heavy with spring; he and Emily had been waiting for spring, waiting to rediscover the beauty they had moved into last year.

The house, he learned after a few minutes' investigation, was empty. No one, not even Maureen hiding upstairs with one of her love magazines. He went back downstairs. The sun was setting, slanting in under the porch. He had his jacket open, so he buttoned it again and stepped outside. The surface of the big pond was dark and the wind had it looking rough. He had thought that he would walk around the porch, but now he changed his mind and went back inside. He was in the kitchen when he heard the automobile draw up out front. He had water coming to a boil for coffee, and it needed his attention. He was at the back of the hall drying his hands when Louise came in the front door. She stopped when she saw him, but then dropped her eyes suddenly. There was something wrong. The others were coming up the steps behind her, Emily and the girls, and the children behind them. Emily saw him as she stepped into the house.

He had not moved. Now he could not even attempt a step forward. The girls came in behind her and one of them waited before closing the door, but he was looking at Emily while she bent her head to remove her hat and then raise her eyes to him again. When she tried to speak, her lips spread across her teeth in a grimace of agony he had not seen since she had come back to New York years ago, and she told him of the miscarriage. He was going toward her when it was Louise who spoke, her arms reaching for him, too.

"Michael my dear baby, David died this afternoon."

It was his cry that filled the house.

VII

It would have happened sooner or later, the doctor had reported. He told Emily to have Michael call him as soon as it was convenient. As he found out, there was more to it than she knew. They had let her believe that they had tried to save the child, but there never had been any hope. "You could say that it was a cerebral hemorrhage," the doctor drawled. "A blood vessel in the head weakens. Your boy was done hemorrhaging when he got here, and I think you can understand that we just can't go inside there and stop the bleeding in any case.

"You have to understand, Mr. Westfield, that there's a good deal we don't understand. As of now, we suspect that it was something defective from the beginning. Things like this happen more frequently than most people know. We want to learn more about your son, Mr. Westfield, We want to do an autopsy—"

"Did you speak to my wife about this?"

"I thought you would want me to speak to you first."

Emily had been in the kitchen. Now she stood in the doorway, her hands at her sides. Michael beckoned to her. Into the telephone, he said, "I'm sure my wife will go along if you can tell us what happened."

"What is that?"

"They want to see what happened."

"Did you see his bedroom?"

The door upstairs had been closed.

"They think there was something defective from birth. Wouldn't you rather know that?"

"A little boy bled to death here this afternoon—*I don't care about me!*"

"Well, I do." Into the telephone, he said, "Go ahead. I'll be waiting to hear from you. There are arrangements that have to be made."

"I understand."

Michael hung up the earpiece, and when he tuned around, Emily was glaring at him. She looked as if she wanted to go for his eyes. *"How could you do that to your helpless little boy?"*

"Emily, if you think I'm going to leave any question about this unanswered, then you don't know me at all." He wanted to say something about his parents. "I would have wanted him to do it for me. If you had asked me yesterday, that's what I would have said."

"They're mutilating him! I don't want him bothered anymore!"

Louise came out of the kitchen, then Mary Frances with a bucket and rags. Louise cried, "Please! Please!" Michael stopped Mary Frances.

"Where are you going?"

"To clean up."

"No, you don't." He took the things. Emily was staring at him. He was crying again. "Do you really want *her* to do this?" She was silent. "He would have had to do this for me. His brother *will* do it someday."

She turned away. Louise waved him off. She was right. They were both too upset to make any sense.

He was afraid that she thought he blamed her. No one was responsible. In the middle of the afternoon David had complained that his head hurt and Maureen had taken him upstairs and put him on his bed. In fifteen minutes Emily had gone up to check on him and found David unconscious and the pillow covered with blood. A neighbor had driven them to the hospital—the neighbor's automobile needed cleaning, too—and Louise and the maids had followed when Emily had called, thinking the boy still alive, though in dire straits.

The bedroom told the story. There was nothing to do but throw out everything with blood on it, right down to the mattress. He would have to hire a cart to take it down to the dump. He knew he was in shock, but what could he do? She was in shock herself, and he felt more alone in her presence than he did away from her.

He bound the linens and blankets up into a sack and carried it down the front stairs and out onto the lawn so he wouldn't be heard at the back of the house. When he returned, Emily was on the telephone. A neighbor, Louise whispered. He could see that people were going to start visiting. Louise had composed a cable to send to the tourists in Europe. Michael groaned, attracting Emily's attention. She turned back to the telephone, speaking more gently to acquaintances than she had to him earlier. He could feel himself losing control again, and he went upstairs.

He waited for her to finish the telephone call before he carried the mattress down the stairs and up the hill to the smaller of the sheds. The exertion was good for him, and when he came down the hill, the breeze cooled his skin. The shadow of the house filled the darkening sky; he suddenly wished he could sweep it all away with the back of his hand. He thought of David sleepily bleeding to death on his embroidered pillow and remembered something he had thought while his baby boy was alive, that he had not given to him the way he had given to Mike because fatherhood had lost its novelty. If he cried out now, he would only be cursing himself and he knew it. He let the pain enter and fill him—he let the pain fill him up.

There was the undertaker in Boonton to call, and then the doctor to wait for. The undertaker said he would contact the hospital and make the preliminary arrangements—later he would have to talk further with Michael. Michael understood. The first of the neighbors were arriving, and Louise was busy in the kitchen supervising the making of sandwiches; Emily was upstairs. He had to tell her that people were in the house.

She was sitting on the bed, facing the fireplace, her shoulders curled over; for a moment, he thought she looked like Louise. She did not raise her eyes to him, and he had to stand there looking at her a few seconds to realize that she was rocking, slowly, back and forth.

"I didn't mean to hurt you. You took him to the hospital. I had to clean up—I couldn't let anyone else. It was my blood as much as yours."

"You don't have to say anything."

"Yes, I do." He waited until she looked up at last. Her face was blotched; there were dark circles under her eyes. "I want you to know how much I love you."

She bit her lip.

"I was coming back from the shed and I looked at the house and had a horrible moment—" He moved closer. He wanted to be next to her; everything he was about to say was a lie. He had come into the house in a rage, and it had been the need to compose himself for the undertaker that had calmed him down. He improvised as he went along, going slowly. "The week before we were married," he whispered. It *hurt*—just as quickly as he was thinking of it, the lie was becoming the truth. "Do you remember what we did? Do you remember where we went?" He paused, but not for a response from her. He had lost David, and now it seemed that he was going to lose her, too, to her grief. "What I remembered clearest is that we went dancing. Do you remember how we looked at each other? There was music—after all we had been through. I promise you that we will survive this."

"My little boy," she whispered.

"Before Thomas died he told me how much he still hated his father, but his father told me before he died that there was more to life that was out of our control than we were ever willing to admit. You know that that is true—you know it in your heart better than he ever did. In spite of what he did to himself, I believe that man had found some inner consolation. You can, too."

"Do you know what I was doing today?"

"I've thought of that myself. I will remember everything about this day for the rest of my life."

" 'Pride goeth before a fall,' " she said. "I spent the morning in the sun down by the lake with Amy. I wanted to go through the magazines for things I want to take—oh, Michael. Oh, dear God!"

He had his arms around her. "Stop. Things aren't going to look like this later on—you know that."

"Amy had so many questions this morning that I told her she was a pest."

"You're punishing yourself—"

"No," she said bleakly. She pulled free of him. "I'm not sure what I believe. I've been living with this all my life."

"I want to pray, Michael."

He thought of his first spring on Thirty-eighth Street, lying in bed remembering his dead parents. He could even see the window and its view of the back yards. In his condition, he would not be surprised with anything that came into his mind. He wanted to go downstairs. "Em, I want you to pray or anything else you want to do."

She was looking at him, her eyes so red they would have looked fierce if her mouth were not pulled down so much that her lower teeth were bared. "What if God hates us?"

He took her arms. "Don't you ever say that to me again. You don't even have the right to think it."

"I'm sorry!" she wailed. "God takes my babies! He hates me!"

"He doesn't! Stop it!"

Louise was behind him. "I heard her. You don't understand, Michael. Let us help."

There was another woman, one of the neighbors. He yielded. Emily looked up at him as if she were beyond his reach, slipping further away. He didn't understand, but he suspected that Louise and the neighbor understood no better because they were women. Whatever it was, Emily was determined to lock it in her own heart. It was the first time he did not know what she was thinking, and he could see that she wanted it that way, no matter how much it hurt him.

Other neighbors had arrived, and for a few moments the parlor filled with the murmuring of condolences before the questions began. Because David had been their playmate, the neighbors had brought their children, and now there were five little ones, including his own, slumped unhappily in chairs around the room. Two more women went upstairs, and then the doctor telephoned.

"Normally these things take a bit longer than this, Mr. Westfield, but I know that you want to get on with your business, and I can tell you now, so I will." Michael turned away from the eyes watching him from the parlor. "Ah, Mr. Westfield. The thing I said about a defect turns out to be true, but not the way I originally thought it would. Sir, I'm sorry to say that your son had an abnormal brain. A whole portion of it wasn't developed at all. It's surprising that he lived as long as he did. You can come down if you want to, but I don't recommend it."

Michael was chilled to his soul. "I can get on with it now, can I?"

"Yes, you can."

"We'll discuss this further at another time, if that suits you, Doctor."

"Oh, I'll be out to see you. He was a nice-looking little fellow. I make it a point to call Mr. Westfield, if you don't mind. Have you worked out your arrangements?"

"We'll have to have the burial Friday. There are old friends and neighbors in Brooklyn who have to be told. Now, my wife is very distraught—"

"Sleep," the doctor said. "Let her have some laudanum to sleep tonight and tomorrow. These things take time, you know. Women suffer. Well, good night."

Michael went directly upstairs. The women had Emily on the bed, a compress over her eyes. The laudanum was already on the night table. Michael sat beside her and she pulled the compress away and blinked at him.

"I spoke to the doctor. He said you should sleep."

"He's as mad as your mother. Is he done? Is the doctor done?"

"Yes. It could have happened any time. There was something wrong."

She squeezed her eyes shut.

"Let me make the arrangements," he whispered.

She nodded.

"It has to be done. I'm not heartless."

"It's not your fault." But she was drifting away.

"I love you, Em," he pressed. "I've always loved you."

"I've never understood why. No one else ever has."

It was like a sledgehammer. "That's not true," he whispered. He had hesitated, and now even he could hear the agony in his voice. There was a hand on his shoulder, Louise's, and when he resisted, she pulled on him firmly. She took him out to the hall.

"She's so very unhappy, Michael. Her heart is broken."

"It could have happened to anyone!" he cried.

"She doesn't know that. She blames herself. She feels she betrayed you."

"Never—"

"You don't know your wife, Michael. She wanted to be perfect for you."

That was not it; he stopped at the head of the stairs and let out his breath. He still had to telephone the undertaker. The next hours, days, weeks, and months opened up before him—he knew everything he was going to feel.

The undertaker came out the next afternoon, and while the family sat in the library, he closed the doors of the parlor and finished his work. The four-foot closed coffin was at the end of the room under the windows, surrounded by flowers. Neighbors called that evening and the next day, and the old neighbors in Brooklyn came out for the funeral on Friday, as well as people from Boonton, who were virtual strangers, and a few of their friends from the New York-and-Saratoga racing crowd. And Kate. It was the first time she and Louise had ever been under the same roof. She had Duran with her, and the two of them blended in with the other city people and left with them on the afternoon train.

Michael had called her the morning after David's death, figuring that that would be easier on her than hearing the news at night. Emily was asleep and Kate asked him to learn if Emily wanted her to come out. Louise didn't matter; so many years had passed that they could tell her anything.

When she awakened near noon, Emily said she really didn't want to see anybody, and when Michael talked to Kate later, he could hear a disappointment in her voice. She had wanted to see him, too, she said. But something made him suspect that she knew Emily was taking it badly. He had no evidence, but the feeling was so strong that he would have taken notice of it if he had been sitting at a poker table. She was deeply hurt, and there was nothing he could do about it.

But just as well. Late Friday evening, after everyone had gone and the rest of the family was preparing for bed, Louise asked Michael about Kate.

"She's the friend you've had for so many years, isn't she?"

"Yes."

"And the young man?"

"Her friend."

Louise had been told years ago by way of explanation that he had known Kate on Lombard Street and had met her again when he had moved down to the apartment off Irving Place. Louise knew that Kate had been married to a rich man from Colorado.

"She carries herself so gracefully and is so well spoken. Was she in the theater?"

"No."

"She didn't go to a ladies' college."

"No, she didn't."

"I'm not a fool, Michael."

He smiled. "I know. You've known for years that I have friends and acquaintances from all walks of life. I don't discuss their business, not because I think you don't know about such things but because they prefer that I keep quiet."

"How old is she?"

"A year or two older than I am."

Louise shook her head. "That's what she's told you. She's closer to fifty."

"I don't think so," Michael said. "I remember when she was a girl."

That seemed to convince her. He had not lied, of course. While she thought otherwise, he was going to be forty-five on his next birthday, and Kate was less than two years his senior. But he had made Louise quit thinking about the possibility of Kate having known Westfield—she had done the arithmetic of Kate's age against the calendar much earlier in the day. She got up from her chair. The smell of the flowers was still heavy in the house. Louise stopped at the foot of the stairs. "I'm sorry, Michael, but I think your friend offended your wife today by bringing her young man here at this time."

"Did you see something?"

"I believe I did."

Two weeks later Kate telephoned him at his office. Since her return to the city, Kate had become Emily's friend more than his; for the past year the two women had talked with each other at least once a week and sometimes twice. Before she called Michael, Kate had telephoned Emily, and it had been like talking to a child who expected a scolding. It took him a moment to remember what Louise had told him about what she had seen two weeks before. Two weeks: in two weeks, confirmation of Louise's perceptions had become important to him. Kate told him that she had seen Emily staring at her at the funeral. "Listen, Michael, I don't know what you think, but what I heard today bothers me more."

"I'm interested in everything you have to say, Kate."

"It took her a long time to feel at ease with me. Today she sounded like she did when I first met her. She sounded ashamed of herself again. Are you going to tell me what's going on?"

"She's having a lot of trouble."

"What about you?"

"I'm all right most of the time. I know how to take care of myself." He wanted to surround himself with silence. She understood; she said she would call him again the following week.

It was shirt-sleeve weather, bright and sunny, and even the air on the river was warm against his skin. There was no doubt that it was going to be a brilliant summer. He had told Kate the truth; most of the time he could go about his business without feeling the cutting edge of his sorrow. At his age he understood himself well enough to resist the notion—it was not a desire, far from it—to open the door to David's room, for example, or to ask himself again if he had treated the child badly. He had not. They had known from the beginning that there was something wrong with him, something special about him; if anything, because of it, they had learned how different all their children were going to be one from another.

And Michael was old enough to know that once he had thought all these things, he would be doing himself a favor if he did not go over them again. The pain he felt was not punishment, and he did not have to look for a reason why he continued to feel it. The trick was to recognize what you could not control. Westfield had been right, and better than ever Michael could see how Westfield had been swallowed up by his judgment of himself—David would not have cursed his father on his deathbed. A certain number of these thoughts could not be helped, but Michael tried to go about his business. There were mornings when it was the first thing in his mind, so heavy on him that he did not want to move.

There was still the wind on the river, the flapping of flying pennants, the flashing smiles of pretty girls. Perhaps his greatest comfort was that he had known for years that he was no longer young. Emily still had to come to that inside herself, that distance, that perspective. This week at dinner Mike had asked him if they were going to Saratoga this year, and Michael had had the answer for him at once. Looking at Mike, he had addressed himself to everyone at the table. "Grandma will be able to tell you that

Saratoga has been good for me ever since I was a boy. We're all going to Saratoga this year, and we're going to have a good time of it, too."

A moment later he tried to engage Emily's eyes, but she looked away. It had come to that, and it ripped through him more savagely than his mourning of David: more than having moved away from him, she had come to regard him with fear and maybe even hate.

They went to Saratoga; by August all of them felt better. It was the summer Mike fell in love with his father, watching his movements, studying his gestures. Mike was eight, and if it had not been for his father, he might have broken apart inside. The death of his fat Uncle Thomas had taught him that death came to humans as it came to birds in the yard, and squirrels and skunks curled up in the woods. So Mike had known what it meant when he was told that David was dead. He saw the blood, and he was able to remember the conversation of his chums, that usually when something got killed there was a lot of blood. In fact, his first thought was that David had been killed and that people would want to know who or what had killed him. Mike was innocent, but it was not until David's coffin was actually in the ground that he began to believe that there really wasn't any question in anybody's mind about it. It was his father who actually told him that there had been something wrong with David that happened to very, very few children and had to do with the way he had fallen down so much when he had been little. Until then Mike had always been intimidated by his father, and he even thought that the explanation about David was some kind of trick to make him tell something that he did not know. But later he thought it through and realized that his father had been telling him that there was nothing wrong with his brain, reminding him that he had not been the one who had fallen down as a baby. It was the first time Mike was able to see that there was more to his father than the power to make the women in the house bend to his will. Now Mike saw that there was a reason they did it—he was wise. So Mike was paying attention when his father answered his question about Saratoga. In a way, the question was a test: Mike had grown tired of having to be quiet in the house because of David when David's body was in the ground miles away and his soul up in heaven. It made no sense, and Mike wanted to know where he stood in the world.

By August he knew. His father had sensed his plight and taken the boy with him up to Canada, and in Saratoga he had Mike accompany him to the track as often as he cared to go. As for Mike, at his age it was not the racing that interested him or his father's patient, solicitous company or, for that matter, the hearty greetings of his father's friends. It was the introduction to the larger world of men and his discovery of the importance of his father's place in it. So many people came to his father that he never had to get up from his table in the clubhouse. Everyone had heard about David, but they seemed glad to be introduced to Mike. Late in the afternoons he would ask his father if he could wander around, and by post time of the last race he might find himself far in the back, lost among the stables. One afternoon he did not get back to the clubhouse until long after the horses had passed under the wire. He was afraid his father was going to be angry with him.

"You missed it. The three horse caught the favorite at the wire. I didn't think she could do it. Sometimes you find a filly that can run with the colts, but not always."

It was a day they walked back from the track, the son running around the father like a dog.

They never talked about David. Mike did not like to think of him anymore. He missed David and was sorry he had died. Mike had been told that David had not suffered, but that was confusing—it seemed impossible to end up dead without having suffered. From time to time he looked up at his father and thought of asking him what the truth was, but while he was less frightened of his father, he was more in awe of him than ever.

It was the summer he saw his father fight with his fists. The family was together more that summer than ever, taking boat rides on the lake and touring the various springs. Grandma was with them, spending most of her time with Mike's mother; Mike had already sensed the change in his mother even if no one had spoken to him about it. When they sat down at the table, he tried to get as close to his father as he could. His mother rarely spoke now, and when she did, she was just as likely to say something unpleasant as not.

They went out to dinner often, the five of them usually getting a large round table in a restaurant, Mike between his father and grandmother, Amy and his mother around on the other side. One evening just after they had sat down, his mother turned to some men at another table and said loudly, "We didn't come here to listen to that kind of language!"

One of the men said something to his friends. There were three of them, and Mike heard them laughing. The sound of his mother's voice had already startled him, and the laughter made him understand even at his age that there was going to be some kind of trouble. He didn't know what it would be, but then he saw that it was going to be very bad when his father pushed his chair away from the table. His voice was so loud that Mike's bladder opened for a second, and as he winced in shame he realized that the entire restaurant had stopped still.

"You're *drunk!* Apologize to my wife and get out of here!"

The man got to his feet with such violence that his chair hit Mike's mother on the arm. Mike's father reached over his mother and plucked the man up by the collar. He was drunk; even Mike could see it, but Mike did not anticipate what happened next. Still drawing the man toward him, his father brought his right fist down on the bridge of the man's nose. It broke with a snap that everyone in the restaurant could hear, and the man's eyes rolled upward and he dropped like a load of wash to the floor. One of his friends was up and punched his father on the side of the forehead, but just as quickly his father had him by the collar and bent flat on his back over the chair and the table so that the man's head was almost in Mike's place setting. His father's face was so red it was almost purple. "Sit back, Mike!" he roared, and punched the man once, twice, three times, until the blood spread from his teeth onto his lips and onto the tablecloth. People were screaming now, and as suddenly as the fight had started, it stopped, as men grabbed his father's arms and pulled him back. Mike's chair with Mike in it was yanked away by somebody else, and the man on the table rolled onto his hands and knees on the floor. People were holding the third man, and men from the restaurant were taking charge and restoring order.

The men were quite drunk and the restaurant got them out quickly after some people at other tables said that they had heard the original obscenities as well as the insult to Mike's mother. His father's knuckles were cut, and the family had to go home. Mike and Amy ate in the kitchen with Grandma while his father put ice on his knuckles in the parlor. Mike was beginning to understand what he had seen his father do, but Grandma and their mother wanted both children to leave their father alone. He didn't want them talking to their friends about what had happened, either.

That would have been the end of it, although Mike itched so much to tell his friends that he thought he was going to get himself in trouble. It wasn't the end, though: late that night he heard his mother crying, and although it made him decide that he was going to keep quiet after all, more importantly he could see that life was going to change again and he felt afraid as he wondered how.

He found out less than a month later when they were all home again in Mountain Lakes. Not that much had actually changed for Mike; he was back at the Mountain Lakes School for Individual Instruction, which, with fewer than twenty students, met in a private home rented for the purpose. The teacher, who always had bad breath, and her young companion and assistant, who was pretty, lived upstairs. In the backyard was the garden the children had planted in the spring, and downstairs in the cellar were the jars of fruits and vegetables the teacher said they needed to get her and her friend through the winter.

The teacher's bad breath and her assistant's pretty face and bosom, as well as the lode of vegetables in the cold dripping cellar, were part of a whole experience Mike was having outside the household, the experience of childhood. He had his heroes besides his father, big kids who were tough in their own right, good ballplayers and graceful athletes; and from others he had come to understand that there were secrets to be learned about life. At eight Mike did not know where babies came from, but since David's death he had come to see that the connection between David, Amy, and himself was really something mysterious, and buried in the past. It was September and Mike was back in school surrounded by the heroes and magicians of childhood; and one warm night after something awakened him and then he heard the door downstairs close and his father's footsteps on the porch, Mike's heart began to pound and his head filled with the illicit whispers he had begun to hear again with the new fall term at the Mountain Lakes School for Individual Instruction. Children are always desperate to understand things, and there had been something wrong in the house since the fight in Saratoga, something strange this evening at dinner—in the midst of a silence, his father had gotten up from the table and walked out of the house. And now, in the middle of the night, he was out of the house again.

The moon was on the other side of the sky. The window was up and the summer screens still in place, but the night was so bright that Mike could see his father bare to the waist, striding down to the lake. Now Mike saw that his mother was at the water's edge. She did not turn around until his father was almost upon her.

He spoke to her. They were too far away for Mike to hear anything, but he could see clearly enough to know that she was answering. Suddenly his father took her wrist and drew her to him. She shook her head and tried to pull away, but he held her. She turned her head up to him again, and this time Mike heard her voice, if not her words. She was angry, crying. Mike was electrified. His father continued to hold her wrist, but he was not laughing or gloating. He seemed to be whispering to her. Mike had seen him sweet-talking her before—sweet-talking was what Mike's grandmother called it. Men hypnotized women sometimes, the kids said at school, but Mike didn't know how or why. He was frightened for his mother, but he was with his father—he wanted to see his father hypnotize her or whatever it was: he wanted to see his father make it work.

There was more. They sat down on the grass, close to each other. They talked longer, touching each other about the face and shoulders. He kissed her. He had her hypnotized, Mike saw—she was hypnotized already. Mike's heart pounded as the kissing went on. The two of them lay down on the grass then, next to each other, still kissing. Mike wanted to go downstairs to see better, but he was afraid that he would be heard or, almost worse, that whatever they were doing would be done by the time he was able to get them into view again.

It took longer than that, much longer, and Mike got down on his knees and put his chin on the windowsill while he watched. He knew he was seeing one of the world's important mysteries, but it was so startling to him that he was afraid that it was not real, that it was a dream like one in a fairy tale, so vivid that you believed it. His father had brought up his mother's skirts and lowered his pants and now they were joined together, their bodies moving rhythmically. Mike heard her cry out, but she liked it—it was part of it, for she was kissing and petting his father and holding onto him and then holding him with her legs, too. They were still for a long time, and now Mike was aware not so much of his heart pounding as the pleasure he felt, a warm glow all through his body; and as his parents separated and stood up, Mike ducked down below the windowsill; but he looked once more to be sure that they were coming up the hill, and they were, arm in arm, holding each other.

He got into bed and listened as they came into the house and climbed the stairs, talking, murmuring. Mike was facing the wall when his mother opened the door of his room. He had been trying to keep himself as still as possible for many seconds, and now when she came to his bed he was afraid that she was going to say that he had been seen watching them, and that an unimaginable punishment was going to take place; but instead she sat on the bed and brushed his hair. She had a wonderful perfume about her and he almost wanted to tell her that he was awake, but he was afraid, and she got up and went away. Mike fell asleep trying to draw the last of her scent into himself and somehow prouder of his father than he had been a month ago in Saratoga.

VIII

Louise sensed the change the next morning; the girls did, too. If they were not as encouraged as Mike, it was because they were older and understood such things better. Michael would have been glad the boy had the illusions he did, had he known of them. As it was, Michael was glad that Louise and the girls were as naïve as they were, thinking his assertions of the male prerogative untimely at best or, at worst, a capitulation to a frenzy of grief. Emily was subdued when she came downstairs; there were lines under her eyes, and her skin was puffy. She came down to his end of the table to kiss him, but he knew that she did not really want to engage his eyes. Mary Frances called the taxi, and when it was heard rolling up outside, Emily got up to walk with him to the porch.

They were more dead inside than ever. She had lied to him last night, the night before, and four weeks before that. Until last night, they had not made love since David had died—he had sat in the parlor a month ago in Saratoga for hours after everyone but the two of them had gone to bed, his hand numb and puckered in the ice water. She was sitting not six feet away from him. Every few minutes she would get up to chip some more. It was long past the time the ice would actually help, but she was so stunned, it seemed, that he thought she would keep getting ice until the sun was shining through the windows. He took his hand out of the water and looked at it. Where the skin was parted, the cold had turned it bluish-pink, like raw veal.

"You knew this was going to happen, didn't you?"

She stared at him.

"You know why it happened surely."

"You're not blaming me—you heard what they said."

"No, Emily, I'm talking about me and what I am. Can't you see why I hit them so hard? *I* instigated the violence."

"I don't understand, Michael. Really I don't." But she was pale and her lip was trembling again.

"You've closed me out. You can't expect me to go on waiting for you with the same *sang-froid* that would be appropriate for a streetcar. You knew what I was when you married me—better than most women, you know why I married you."

"Michael, that is cruel."

"Is it? You have thought of me so little since David died that I've gone mad enough to smash someone—what did he call you? Moonfaced? For God's sake, Emily, I broke his nose!"

"You're not asking me to do something I don't feel—"

He held his knuckles out so she could see how he had ripped them open on the teeth of the second man. "Emily, I did it on purpose! I was fourteen when I hit a man exactly the same way! I don't want to kill anybody because of you. David was my son, too. You owe me what I've been trying to give you."

"I'll try, Michael," she said, but he heard the defeat and sensed the lie, and the night before Mike saw them, in their room, he told her what had begun to steal into his thoughts.

"If it doesn't change, Em, I'm going to leave you."

He saw her tremble, but she still couldn't look at him.

The next evening, as it crossed his mind that she was willing to let their lives crash in ruins around them rather than answer him at all, and the prospect of being alone seemed more attractive than any more of this, he caught his breath and walked out of the house. When he came back an hour later Louise was waiting for him in the dining room in the chair she had occupied during dinner. If she was trying to convince him that she had not moved since he had got up from the table, he was willing to accept at least the spirit of the gesture.

"I suppose you're going to tell me I'm being cruel, too."

"You're not being fair."

"David died in April. She hasn't allowed me to hold her in my arms since. Don't tell me she blames herself. She's waiting for someone or something to come along and save her from what she feels."

"She's a woman, Michael."

"That does not give her the right to do this."

"I'm trying to counsel patience."

"You saw that my patience ran out a month ago. She saw it, too. It would not have come to that then, or this now, if I had been given the smallest indication that she's trying to come out of it. It's as if she believes I have no humanity of my own. She hasn't allowed me to put my arms around her in all this time, and in all this time I have been afraid to ask myself if she's ever thought of putting her arms around me."

"I will tell her," Louise said.

"I'm coming to the conclusion that she already knows, but doesn't care."

He worked late, and when he went upstairs, the bedroom was empty. He knew where Emily was. In the past he had felt her getting out of bed when she thought he was asleep, and he had stood by the window watching her on the lawn or down at the water's edge. He started to undress, but then changed his mind and went downstairs.

She heard him coming down the lawn behind her, but she kept her back to him.

"I'm desperate, Em."

"Your mother told me. I wish you had kept her out of it."

"If we go on this way, she'll have to find another place to live. But that wasn't why she was waiting for me this evening, and you and I both understand that. And we understand that we couldn't possibly keep our problems from someone living under the same roof with us. Let's not lose ourselves in a side issue. You haven't even said that you heard what I said to you last night."

She started away, but he took her wrist. "Why do you hate me for it? He was born with half a brain. Only God knows why. If his symptoms had been more apparent, neither of us would be suffering the way we are. We would have been prepared, but it wouldn't make him less dead."

"I would give anything to change places with him."

"And he would have lost his mother, like me. If you love him as much as I think you do, you wouldn't want him to change places with me, which is really what you're saying. Listen to me, Emmy. The night he died, I remembered the room I had when I first moved in with the Westfields. I don't know why I thought of it, except that I lost my parents when I was a child, and now that I'm a parent, I've lost my child, too. I've come full circle. There's nothing more of myself that I can give without being destroyed. I'm older than you are, Em, in more ways than years." She had not looked at him yet, but he suddenly realized that he was going to make love to her. "A month ago you heard that I broke a man's nose when I was fourteen," he said quietly. "You never heard it before because there never was any need." He took her by the shoulders. "Em? Please look at me. When I was in that room on Thirty-eighth Street I started to come out of the grief I felt for my parents. Maybe I was trying to remind myself that I would come out of this if I wanted to, if I wasn't willing to give in to it."

She looked up and blinked. "And be destroyed?"

"My mother says you blame yourself."

She shook her head. "Your mother only thinks she understands me. She understands part of me. Nobody understands all of me. My father thought he did. He cursed me when I left him for you. He said God would bring all these things down on me."

"Do you think God hates you?"

"My father said God would punish me for lusting after you like a whore." She shook her head again. He could feel her suddenly heavy in his hands, and he made her sit down. "He understood a very small part of me. It's true. I came back to you in the knowledge that I was surrendering to my lust. And later I saw that, just as he said, I was pursuing the pleasures of the flesh. These were things I thought of and put out of my mind, and now I have them back again."

"What does all this have to do with David?"

She was not willing to say it, whatever she believed—if she believed anything at all. He had his doubts.

"Do you remember when David was conceived?"

"Exactly? No, we never knew that."

"He was fourteen months younger than Mike, and in the first months after Mike was born, when David was conceived, we were happier and more in love with each other than we had ever been. When we made love then, we laughed and tickled each other. If that was lust, it was not a sin, and David was not our punishment for it."

"Do you believe that?"

"We are not being punished for your lust. We are not being punished—I refuse to believe it." For a moment he thought he had her, that he had moved her a little, and he took her arms again; but as he did, something else happened to him, an older torment revealed itself, and he saw more of what he felt about the things he was saying: and just that quickly, he was sobbing. "And if we are being punished, it doesn't matter. Not to me it doesn't. I promised to love you, and I love you still. I want you—Jesus Christ, Emmy, I need to. Me, Michael Monk, from Lombard Street!"

Her eyes came up, open wide. "Oh, dear God—what have I done?"

"I love you, Em. Be married to me."

He reached for her—it took her a moment to understand. They made love, watching each other, holding each other. His semen flowed out of him and filled her up so quickly that it startled her into crying out. They walked up to the house with their arms around each other, but he understood that they were only beginning again. But in the bedroom she initiated the lovemaking, and this time it seemed that she felt some pleasure, too. He knew her too well to expect more. It was the first time in months that he fell asleep with his arm around her.

There was daylight in the room when his eyes came open again. Her side of the bed was empty, and the bathroom door was closed. He got up.

"Em?"

"I'm here."

"Will you open the door?"

The door swung inward. She had the light out, and the dawn against white curtains beyond her let him see the silhouette of a woman who had slipped out of his reach again. She did not have to tell him; he could see it at once.

"I lied to you, Michael. I was pretending."

"It doesn't matter."

"It does. I pretend a lot. I have to think of things. That's what I meant when I said that I found myself pursuing the pleasures of the flesh. Not the things we have done together. If you could see what I have had in my mind, it would make you sick."

"No, it wouldn't. We all do things like that. I know that you love me."

She looked at him. "Duran?"

"You told me that. I knew it."

"Kate told me all his secrets. Do you see? I told myself that I was thinking of him so that you would have what you wanted, but I was really thinking of him because I wanted to."

"While you were with me? I knew it, Em. It was something that would pass."

"No, it was worse. I dreaded being in his presence."

"You told me that, too. He took your breath away."

"More than that."

"You know you're not being punished for it, not the way you've been trying to tell yourself. When my mother told me that you wanted to be perfect for me, I dismissed it out of hand. Now I'm not sure. One thing I do know: you want more from yourself than I could ever give you of me. I didn't know that these things troubled you. I'm not different. When you were taking David to the hospital, I was looking at a pretty girl on the ferry—just looking at her. I told you that I would remember everything I did that day. It wouldn't have helped you to hear it in detail, just as it doesn't help you now, not for its own sake. I thought you knew these things—I honestly thought you understood them."

"You make it sound so simple!"

"It *is!* Em, I won't be able to go on if I think you're still trying to find an explanation for David."

"You don't understand. You don't know what Kate told me."

"I know Kate. We'll keep away from them for a while."

"I encouraged her. I never wanted to see him again. I let myself think about doing things to him."

He knew what she meant, and it hurt. He held out his arms to her. "Come to bed. I know you love me."

She stepped back. "I've lost two babies, Michael."

"I won't touch you," he whispered, and backed away.

And the next morning, gray with exhaustion, he went into the city. When Kate called him later in the week, he told her that it was clear that Emily needed more time. She said she suspected as much. As for her, Duran's divorce was coming to court, and his wife was being more reasonable. There was an agreement, and they would be going through the legal steps as quickly as possible. "It sounds to me like she has a boyfriend," Kate said. "If he's as good as the last one, I'd say she has no complaints, considering what an iceberg she is."

Michael hung up thinking that even she would have said that he had not been patient enough with Emily.

The holidays were difficult—Halloween, Thanksgiving, Christmas— each a little worse than the one before. There had been no Westfield family gathering last year because of Thomas, and there was none this year because of David. Last year Louise had been with Ethel and Julie; this year she was with Michael and Emily. Louise's cable had caught up with the Hafners and Ethel in Braunau, Austria, from where they had sent a message of condolence that had arrived in New Jersey the day after the funeral. Emily received a letter from Ethel sometime later, and when they were back from Europe, the Hafners and Ethel made separate trips to Mountain Lakes. But none of it could reverse the natural drift away from the old center and into their own lives. Michael and Emily put themselves into the children's Christmas: if they were still not talking much, they had managed to find other ways of reaching each other. They began making love again, and finally, at the end of January, he asked her to go dancing, and she smiled and said yes.

Mike was fair like his mother; Amy, too; and when they had been babies with David, there had been talk about their hair and eyes turning dark like their father's as they grew older. But the talk had stopped long ago. Mike's hair was dirty blond now, but he had his mother's eyes. He was a stocky kid as well, like his mother's brothers. The hope now was that he would have his father's height, but that was a long way off. In any event, it was the sort of talk women indulged in, Michael suspected, to flatter their men.

Amy was even more like her mother. She was five when Tommy was born in July 1908, and she made Tommy her child, following her mother around the nursery, insisting on responsibilities. She had been the youngest in the family for so long that she was not happy until the rest of the household understood that Tommy was in another category and that she had as large a say in his upbringing as everyone else. She would be waiting for her father at the foot of the walk to report to him on her brother's activities—not to mention her own. "I changed him today! I changed him today! I wiped his heinie and everything!"

They could be in the parlor then, waiting for dinner, Mike slumped on the sofa, his hands to his face as he tried to hide from the conversation. Amy was in her father's lap, her feet pulled underneath her. She was still small enough to get inside his open newspaper and leave him room to read it. Mike would come over, too, and sit on the arm of the chair. It was a long, quiet year; as the weather warmed again the children followed Peary's dash to the Pole, and heard the story of Blériot's flight across the English Channel. Mike wanted adventure. Amy was harder to please; she wanted more of Michael's time, and there were afternoons when the best solution was to scoop her up in his arms and carry her everywhere.

Tommy was dark-haired, dark-eyed, compact, and vigorous. He looked like Michael's mother. Michael wanted to keep that thought to himself, but Emily sensed it almost at once; and later—within a month of the baby's birth—Louise took Michael aside conspiratorially to ask him if, as she thought, Tommy looked like his paternal grandmother. So she was happy for him, perhaps more purely happy than he was himself. Emily had submitted to his terms concerning the questions that had tormented her after David's death—if she still believed she was guilty of something, she knew better than to allow him to hear even a whisper of it. She never asked him about the reference he had made to breaking a man's nose at the age of fourteen. He did not know how he would have answered her. Possibly he was beyond lying, perhaps David's death had

had that kind of effect on him. Michael was so far from the boy who had
killed Moran, and the young man who killed Sullivan—he had imposed
his will on Emily, and it had left him with no other resources. He had
been right about himself; he had had nothing more to give.

Michael had lost money in 1907 and 1908, and in 1909 he started to
make it back again, and by 1912 he was back to where he had been in
1906. He was spending more, but he was living the way he wanted. He
ran a few horses for a while, gave them up, then bought some more.
Every year he took Emily to New Orleans, and Mike or Amy or both of
them up to Canada, and one year after the season in Saratoga the family
toured the Maritime Provinces, returning to New York from Halifax on a
luxury liner that had originally set sail from Liverpool—the route his
parents had taken a half century before, the year of his birth. The liner
came into New York in the early morning in a cold lashing rain, but
Michael was up in the lounge before dawn, alone at first, then surrounded by the returning tourists and titled Englishmen who had made
the voyage from the other side—a rich crowd: their conversation was of
other crossings and the changes they had seen. Michael's thoughts, which
he kept to himself, were not much different. At fifty he did not like what
he took to be the direction of the world, but he could see, too, that the
passage of time was very gradually relieving him of the capacity to do
very much about it. If there was to be a war—with the English involved,
judging by their arrogance—he might not be able to keep his sons out of
it. The events of his own lifetime had only served to make the individual
smaller, less significant, and easier to deal with. If he had not liked
Mountain Lakes when he had first arrived there, now he could see that it
had its uses. Mike's father may have taught his older son the three-finger
drag and how to cut a new deck of cards so that five players were dealt
full houses and the dealer a straight flush, but Mountain Lakes had taught
the boy the more respectable if not more practical skills of golf, tennis,
social dancing, and the French language. It was more than Michael had
imagined, and he had no idea where it was going to take the boy. Michael
loved him and rejoiced in his triumphs—a curled-up Shylock in a school
production of *The Merchant of Venice*—but the future he faced was
terrifying to Michael, more terrifying than anything he thought he had
had to face.

IX

In 1915 Kate had three restaurants around the city, one in the thirties
off Broadway, another out on Surf Avenue in Coney Island, and a third,
the smallest, at North Beach in Queens. She specialized in seafood.

Duran managed all three places, driving from Coney Island to Penny
Bridge at Newtown Creek and then up Eliot Avenue to Junction
Boulevard. From the bluff over North Beach you could see across Long
Island Sound all the way to City Island, and on a summer's afternoon the
sails of the yachts on the water mirrored the clouds floating above them.
Michael had not intended to do the entire circuit with Duran, but he had
had to see him; and he spent a lost six hours one Tuesday in Duran's
Packard, thundering around trolley cars at speeds of forty-five and fifty
miles per hour. In the afternoon they were on the Queensboro Bridge
over Blackwells Island, with the tenements of the east side of Manhattan
spreading below them. Kate and Duran lived in a new building on
Riverside Drive. The neighbors thought they were married, and the
truth was that their lives were conventional enough for them to maintain
a proper façade without difficulty. Duran was heavier and puffier, and
perhaps he was taking the gray out of his sideburns, but Michael liked
him more than ever. Emily said that she wouldn't be able to tolerate the
confusion that Kate and Duran brought to their lives, but that impressed
Michael far less than the work Duran did for Kate, seven days a week,
almost the year around. Michael had driven with him in the past down to
Coney Island and out to North Beach, but never before to both places on
the same day. Hard work, hard work under any circumstances, Michael
thought. As they rode up in the elevator at the end of the day, Michael
had generous thoughts about Duran and the life he had made for himself.
Kate was a fool, Duran said, if she didn't open a place in Seaside in
Rockaway Beach. The man actually wanted to work harder. Kate had told
Michael that Duran had his percentages all the way along and that he was
absolutely straight with her. So he had generous thoughts about Duran.
On this particular Tuesday in July 1915 he wanted to think he was in the
company of people who had their own fully developed metaphors for
love. Duran let them into the apartment. Kate was in the bedroom with
the Negro maid. For as long as Michael had known her, Kate had reminded him that a Negro had knifed her sister to death. Her first words
to explain Sissy had been, "As long as they don't have anything sharp to
wave at me, I ain't got too much to worry about," but Michael had seen
Kate opening herself to Sissy as she had to Gert: "You know what the
little bitch has on her mind, don't you? She wants to operate the elevator
operator. Up and down, up and down! Ha! How do you like that?" But
she gave the kid the night off as often as she could, saying Sissy was
young and needed the excitement.

Duran poured himself a drink. Michael sat down with his back to the
river. The windows were open and the awnings were extended all the
way down so that air swept into a room that was dark and cool and filled

with the singing of the birds carrying up from the trees on the other side of the Drive twelve floors below. When Kate came out of the bedroom Duran handed her a drink he had prepared for her. Michael hadn't seen that, and just as soon as Kate said, "Here's health," she looked from Duran to Michael, because there was something to be told. In her midfifties Kate was thinner than ever, reminding Michael of no one so much as Louise. After he had stopped wondering what Westfield would have thought of that, he wondered what the old boy would have had to say to Duran.

Nothing harsh. Duran was in tears. "Your old friend here wanted to find me today to talk over some little business that he thinks is going to inconvenience us. Look at him sitting there!"

"What is it, Michael? Is Emily all right?"

Michael nodded. His hand reached out for her. Her head turned to Duran, but in the same moment that something in his eyes told her that she was released to give Michael whatever is needed, she was in front of him, on her knees, gathering his hands in hers, her eyes widening. "What is it?"

"My stomach," Michael whispered. "I went to a doctor, and he sent me to a specialist. The specialist called me this morning and asked me to come over. He says it's a cancer." He let the blackness of the pupils of her eyes fill his vision. He had let down in front of Duran this afternoon; he had said that he wanted to curl up in Emily's cunt, if God would let him. But now he saw that he would give himself to Kate in the same way, to anyone who loved him, if it would wipe away what was to come. He could not stop looking into her eyes. "Kate. He says I'm going to die."

She kissed him on the mouth.

He had anywhere from two months to two years. Michael did not think it would be two years, but he did not think it would be two months either. That marked the beginning of the really significant part of the conversation in doctor's office, for the underlying fact had been clear enough for more than a month, something new going wrong, getting worse every day. It had been everything he could do to eat anything, and it was getting harder and harder to keep it down. He hadn't needed a specialist to tell him that it was not a tapeworm. Or an ulcer. He had doctored his stomach for so many years that he had become expert in sensing when he had gone too far, irritated his stomach too much—no, this was different.

But it was not his stomach after all; it was his liver. It would not be terribly uncomfortable for a while, even a long while, if he had luck; but then things would rapidly get worse. There could be periods of remission, but the symptoms he had now would intensify and finally overtake him. He would lose weight and energy until he needed a wheelchair; and at the end, which itself could last a long time, he would be unable to rise from the bed, emaciated, covered with sores, and incontinent. Michael told the doctor that he wanted to know everything he could; given the circumstances, the fewer surprises there were, the better off he would be.

"What happens at the end?"

"The cancer spreads everywhere, every organ—"

"No, the end."

"You hemorrhage. Something inside will rupture, and you will bleed to death. There will be many hemorrhages before the last. I'm sorry." The doctor sat back. "Mr. Westfield, you're an intelligent man. I don't expect that you'll take my opinion alone, and if you want, I'll give you the names of colleagues—the best in this country. I'm putting my professional reputation on the line with my diagnosis. I wish to God I were wrong. Mr. Westfield, there are men who will say they can save you, but they're charlatans who prey on those natural periods of remission. Don't be fooled. You're a fatally ill man."

Not even Kate was willing to believe it. Duran had predicted that. Like Michael, he knew that the doctor had told the truth; but Duran had told Michael that the women would not give up easily. Before it was over, he said, they would ply Michael with cure-alls and the names of quacks; it was not going to be as bad as the disease, but it was going to drive him to despair. Then Duran said he stood ready to help him in any way Michael saw fit—sentiments too similar to those Thomas had wanted to hear nine years ago to give Michael much comfort now. Ethel had turned to Hafner and that had been the end of all commitments to the dead man. Michael had not seen her children in so long that he could not be certain that he would recognize them on the street. And regardless of how deeply Duran felt what he was saying, life itself was too grindingly pitiless to allow him the luxury of his concern for long. He could see that Duran knew he was thinking these things, but there was no way for Michael to reach him. It was as if a wall had been brought down between him and everyone else. If the women were not going to give up easily, it was because they would not say what their eyes were telling them, what he could see for himself in the mirror. He was as good as dead.

There was talk of doctors and half-remembered stories of clinics and cures, what the doctor and Duran had warned him of, with Duran nevertheless participating to the full. Michael left after an hour. He was late getting to Mountain Lakes, and when he got home, only Emily was downstairs waiting for him. He ate a sandwich in the kitchen, guessing that the less he thought about food, the easier it would be for him. He told her that he was going to get another opinion and see if there were treatments he could take either to relieve the pain or prolong his life—he had to give her that much; Kate's behavior had made that clear. There was no point in telling the children or their grandmother or disrupting the routine of the household at this stage. He could see that she had her own ideas. "I want life to go on," he said. "I'll be all right with this if you respect my wishes. Please—do you understand what I'm saying?"

She said yes. She was not looking at him, and he did not want to force anything now. If he said straight out that he did not want to lose control of himself, it would begin to slip away from him in the same minute. Perhaps he would have other thoughts further along, but for now he felt thankful he had been given the chance to prepare himself and get his business in order, a chance he had not given three men in his life, but which had been denied by two of them to his parents. Thomas had had less than a day to get ready, David had not lived long enough to have been able to imagine death, and Westfield had walked into it willingly. The fact itself was so overwhelming that it did not matter, from Michael's changed point of view, how it came to pass. He sat in the parlor alone for a while; he wanted Em to come to her own peace with the inevitability of this, but just as clearly he could see that it was just one more thing over which he had no real influence. It was all going to slip out of his fingers in the near future anyway, and that was almost the hardest thing about it to accept.

She was sitting on the edge of the bed waiting for him. She had been crying; he had dreaded this as much as anything else.

"Em, we're going to do everything we can. You know that."

"I do—do you know how much I love you?"

"Yes, but we have to accept what we cannot change."

"I never will! Not for the rest of *my* life!"

"Then love me for the rest of mine."

In the next days he consulted another specialist and dutifully brought in the loathsome but revealing little specimens, but his body told him more than a doctor ever could. There were things that needed doing, and Michael used the interval before the second specialist's confirmation to make his plans and set his sights. Given the reaction of those who knew so far, he would have even less time to himself when the rest of the family and friends heard the word. He wanted privacy. He was beginning to think more of his parents, and if that meant that his own circle was nearing completion, he wanted to make use of the chance he had been given to come to some kind of understanding of it. He was not awfully afraid, and if a lack of fear was part of it, then he wanted to be able to tell Emily and the children what he could see. He wanted dignity; his feelings about his parents were part of that, too. He had to educate Emily to their finances. Michael did not know the details of Ethel's arrangement with Hafner; the woman preferred being under Hafner's wing. But that was exactly what Michael did not want for Emily, Mike, Amy, and Tommy: Michael thought the children would be better off for what Kate and Duran could give them. He wanted to set that in motion and go about his own business while he could—his own business being all he needed of a last look at the world.

Mike realized there was something seriously wrong the following November, when he heard his father in the bathroom late at night. Mike was sixteen, taller than his mother by half a foot, and the situation as it revealed itself made him wonder about his mother for the second time in his life. He asked her what was wrong with his father, and at first she lied, saying it was nothing, but when he asserted himself, she said it was his father's stomach and that the doctors had it under control. Mike could see how pale his father looked and how slowly he ate. Mike was older than his mother imagined, knowing more than the three-finger drag, and so he took his time, and one night when the old man was downstairs alone, Mike got out of bed to join him.

His father was reading the paper. He was in his robe, pajamas, and slippers. There had always been days when he did not dress, but now there was a difference in the way the robe hung on him, and his smell was different. When he saw Mike standing in the doorway, he put his paper down.

"Well, Sunny Jim, what can I do for you? Come on in and sit down. Your mother says you're concerned about me."

Mike thought his father had the most beautiful resonant voice in the world. He made you think it was rolling out from deep inside him. Mike knew it was a trick he did, because Mike had watched him slow it down until he had everybody ready to fall off their chairs, reaching for the next word. But he never tipped to it, the old man; he saw what he wanted to see—in every sense. If he wanted to know what you were made of, he had only to look at you to know. Mike was sitting on the couch, but he was not comfortable. The old man knew it, so he lit one of his cigars so slowly that the smoke itself seemed to hold still in the air, and then when he started to speak he drew Mike so tightly to the sound of his words that it took the boy more than a moment to remember the reason his father was speaking at all.

"It made me think of the time I wanted to quit college and go to work for a newspaper. I was older than you are now, and although nobody loved the old man more than I did, I was always a little on edge when I had to approach him. Anyway, you got me to thinking about him. He was a man who had trouble with himself all his life, and I could tell you stories of his episodes until the sun came through the trees out there, but out of all his inability to hold onto himself came the ability to look at himself plainly. He had thoughts about himself that no man should ever have, but he was honest with himself. Of all the things he taught me, he taught me that best. I learned it best from him.

"So I was thinking about that, and more than anything I would like you to understand the percentage you're giving yourself—"

"All the hoping in the world won't make you a winner," Mike said, quoting him.

"Exactly. You have to play the cards. So if I lied to myself now, I'd be missing my opportunities."

Mike understood at once, although he did not know it. It appeared inside him and went on rising while his father talked about his illness and what it meant, rearranging the world before his son's eyes, changing even the way the boy saw, the way his eyes worked. The father talked about money then, and what Uncle Carl had told him about the property— seventy acres now. "Listen to me, Mike. It's clear to me that you'll all be all right if you stay together. More may be asked of you at first because you're the oldest, but it will all come back to you. You must take care of Tommy. You'll feel this, but you'll know why. He won't because he's so young, but he'll feel it just the same, just the way you felt David. Do you see?"

"Yes. Yes, sir."

His father's eyes had reddened, but now he smiled. "My father used to insist on 'sir.' And he had to report by mail to his father. My father didn't like his father a damned bit and what my father got from me was what I wanted to give him—"

Mike was staring at his father. He could see the sickness in his father's face. He knew what his father wanted, but he could not help choking on his fear.

"It's all right," his father said. "You'll come around."

Mike started to weep. "You're going to live! You're going to get better!"

"I'd be disappointed in you if you went around quoting me while you're thinking like that. It's a sucker bet. All the hoping in the world isn't going to make this a winning hand."

"I'm not going to bet against you, sir."

It made the old man pause. "That's right, too," he cried. "You'll see."

A man can indulge in bravado with his son, but as Westfield before him had learned, it runs back again like a wave hisses down the beach into the sea. The summer's campaign for some kind of killing, including the loss with Mary Jenkins in New England, finished Michael, and in September, when he wanted to go into the city for the last time, he needed Mike's help. His skin was bad now, and he had so little energy that he could not be sure that he would make it home again by himself.

The office was closed. He had done that in the spring, as well as moving his case from the downtown specialist to the general practitioner in Boonton. "If something comes up, he won't hesitate to call me." The specialist held out his hand. "You're a fine gentleman. I'm sorrier than I can say." So Mike was taking him into the city to see Kate; she had wanted it, and Mike's mother had made the arrangements. The old man had not lost his sense of humor. He carried a slender black cane and his collar hung on the back of his neck, but he moved with a stately elegance that denied the pain he felt. "What I need is a top hat. I feel like a vaudeville star coming out for another turn."

They took a taxi up under the Ninth Avenue El through Hell's Kitchen and San Juan Hill to Riverside Drive. Mike liked the city; his father said it bore little resemblance to the city of his own youth, when most of the area from the foot of the park had been open land, but Mike believed he could see it still in the empty lots between the apartment buildings and tenements, and the long strip of land sloping between Riverside Drive and the river. He had no idea why they had come to the city, and he suspected that his father did not know the reason either, save his own desire to see the city again. To Mike, Mrs. Johnson was the same as an aunt, and he was afraid she was only trying his father as his aunts Ethel and Julie might have done if his father had given a damn about them. As far as Mike was concerned, his father was so much the best in the family that the rest, including Mrs. Johnson and Mr. Duran, if they were family, were hardly anything—and Mike was not sure that he excepted his mother from his judgment either.

No sooner had they arrived at the apartment than Mike found himself being escorted out by Mr. Duran, who said that he had to go down to Coney Island and wanted company. Even the old man was caught by surprise, but he gave Mike a smile and a salute good-bye, and then the door swung shut.

Kate looked very bad. When Michael could imagine people going on after he was gone, he wanted to put his arms around them and love them; they did not seem to understand that he felt no bitterness. What the hell was life anyway? He was going to be fifty-five years old, and in another fifteen—a twinkling of an eye at his age—he would have reached his three-score-and-ten. If this sickness was what it felt like, he was ready to say it wasn't worth it. He had not been willing to subject Emily to lovemaking for some time, given the condition he was in, but he still had desires—he was even capable of a fairly original thought. So when the door closed, he took advantage of his privileged state of condemned man and allowed himself to remember the way Kate's cheek had felt against his own when they had made love so many years ago (her cheek and the smell of her perfume not so much as the vuluptuous squeezings of her very deep vagina; now that he was where he was, he relished the thought of having loved her as he had never allowed himself to relish it before). In the same way she let herself relax, too, her tongue brushing his lips when she kissed him. It was as if she measured the time in their lives in a new way, too; and it was not so much that they had been lovers that was important as the idea that because their loving was once something real, it was real forever. The brushing of his lips was an acknowledgment that their kissing was a part of the lives they had already lived—because it had been, it always would be.

"How are you doing?" she asked.

"All right. I want to get the fire out of my gut, but I'm all right."

"Is Emily all right?"

Michael nodded. "Did you ever smell anything like me in your life?"

"Yeah, when Gert was in the hospital. The whole floor smelled like that. That isn't why I asked you to come down."

"I know."

He was smiling, and she was staring at him. He had no idea what was coming. He didn't know how many more times he was going to see her. He wanted to see the people he cared about; that was what was important to him.

"I want to talk to you about Sullivan," she said. "And Andy Fletcher."

"Ah, no, Kate. I don't want to go into all that—"

She sat on the sofa. "Michael, after Gert died, I tried to tell you that I knew, but you wanted to hide it. You know what I'm talking about. I knew it when we went up to that little town for Andy Fletcher's funeral. Then I thought that you understood that I knew. It took me a long while to realize that you thought you were safe and why. You knew who Sullivan was, but you tried to bluff your way through. I remember, Michael. Please. You never really asked me what I knew about your parents' deaths. I love you, Michael; you have to tell me the truth."

"For God's sake, Kate, why?"

"Because if you don't, I'll go to my own grave believing that the only person I ever loved my whole life long closed the door on me when I wanted to love him most."

"I don't want the children to know about any of that, and not because I promised Em. I want them to have a better life than I had—than we had, you and I and so many others. Neither of us knows who our grandparents were. It's as if we just came out of the caves. God knows what our people were. We've climbed out of all that, Kate. Let it go. Let it disappear."

"What do you think is going to become of Mike?"

"He'll be all right."

"As what? Tell me about Mike Westfield when he's as old as you are now."

"I don't know. Nobody knows a thing like that."

"I saw him last month at Saratoga, Michael. He's known about you for a long time; you told me so yourself. You remember us at his age."

"I know. And so?"

"Life goes on! *Life* goes on, just as it did with you. Oh, Michael, don't you understand yourself at all?"

"Don't say a thing like that to me, not now."

"Aw, no." She took his hand. "I've known you—I remember you on Lombard Street, the smartest kid in the class. Michael," she whispered, "I knew you when you were somebody else. And when you found me again I could see the change in you, but as hard as you'd become, I could still see the Michael you were on Lombard Street inside, carrying the weight of the world on his shoulders. I thought it was Westfield and what he was doing to himself, and after he died and you came to me for loving I was sure of it. I know men, Michael, and I never saw in anyone else, not even Westfield, the pain I saw in you. That's why we went on as we did and why it had to stop. At that age I didn't know I loved a man unless I could see that I was willing to absorb his pain, but what you were doing to yourself went on and on. No one was happier for you than me when you met Emily, because she actually made it stop. You knew what you needed. Then Sullivan killed Andy Fletcher and you killed Sullivan and Emily disappeared. It took me a long time to figure out that much, and I still don't know it all, but somehow her father knew about you and Sullivan—"

"Reese was there. I used him to get to Sullivan. Sullivan thought the thing we did to Reese with the photographers was an attempt to move in on his pigeon. I was absolutely insane. I destroyed my wife's family."

"Don't you understand that you couldn't help yourself? I watched you after David died. Your wife was in mourning, but you thought she was closing herself off from you—"

"She was."

"You *panicked!* You were very lucky that she was able to come out of it when she did. If she had not been as strong as she is, you could have compounded the tragedy."

"She needed a push."

"Possibly, It might have waited, too. Be honest with yourself, Michael, the way you think Westfield was. He might have been a bit more honest with himself than most men, but he was first, like you, a man. And not the only one we've known in our lives who's killed himself."

"I've thought of it myself in the past few months."

"Well, you can't, just as Westfield shouldn't have done it either. And for the same reason. Your life would have been easier if he had not made you feel that pain again. In all the things you had to say about him years ago when you were with me, you never let yourself think that his death reflected on his love for you."

"It didn't. He made that clear. He wasn't perfect. He helped me after I killed Moran. I was fourteen. As time went on, he loved me more than he loved his own family. He was a very flawed man, Kate."

"A *man,* Michael. Please, please, please, listen to me. When he was hurt, he drew into himself and suffered, and when you were hurt, you acted as if something had been stolen from you. When we were lovers you told me that the first girl you made love to on Lombard Street took something from you. You felt that way about Julie Westfield. You always felt that the love in you was being stolen. When we were young, you were the nice little boy who could always spell the words, and you've stayed the same all your life. You're Michael. As God is my witness, beloved, you're only the stuff that men are made of, and that has always been good enough for me."

He wanted to read. As he felt the need to stay closer and closer to home, he wanted to fill himself with all the books he had put off for years; at this stage the worst thing about the pain was that it would not let him think about any one thing for very long. You could think your way through pain, but only one nerve at a time, one series of throbs at a time. He loved Conrad and Hardy. At this point in his life he was almost afraid to find a good American writer; Crane, Norris, and now London were dead of tuberculosis, appendicitis, and suicide, in that order. One owed God a death, but literature was an uncomfortable, sinister business. Mark Twain was a more terrifying writer than Dostoevski, and what was wrong with Henry James was the most significant thing about him. His characters were the first emotional nomads of the industrial age, loveless and unloved, fragmented, without roots or direction. Michael had read that James had thought Mary Ann Evans the ugliest woman he had ever seen—Mary Ann Evans, who as George Eliot had poured so much passion into her novels that she had had to be carried from her desk. A man who would have it known that such a thought occupied his attention in the presence of a genius perhaps was best equipped of all to hold up a mirror to these times. In any event, Michael couldn't read the son of a bitch.

Michael had always been in love with Mary Ann Evans anyway. Emily knew it. In his more lunatic moments of their early marriage Michael liked to imagine he could read aloud, and one of his favorite passages for this fatuous exercise was the flood and Conclusion of *The Mill on the Floss*. He must have given it three or four different renderings in the attempt to find the voice inside the words—the great writers always let you hear their voices. Emily had asked him, "Would you make love to her if she were here?" And he had answered, "Not if she preferred to read from her new work."

Now the question of lovemaking had become more and less serious. He fell asleep early but could not sleep the night; and when he awakened in that static time that drifted sideways through the dark because the rest of the household slept, he would find Emily moved from the single bed they had set up on the other side of the room to beside him in their own large bed, her backside pressed against his hips. This was the final lovemaking; she was going to be with him until he died—or for as long as possible. He did not lie to himself. It was his need as much as hers. All she was giving him by waiting until he fell asleep before she moved was the privacy of his deepest mortification, the thing that was happening to his body. When he found her beside him, he would press his nose into the hairs at the nape of her neck, as if by plunging himself into the depths of her odor, he could disappear from himself. She did not want him leaving the room at night, and so he had his books in there with him, on the table by the chair at the window. The amount of pain the human body could generate was unbelievable. The Bible was best at that hour. He was thinking of his parents and the things Kate knew. She had shocked him, but she had promised to stay silent. Everything he had was in cash and this land. He had not made money in years, but if Emily followed the instructions he had given her, she could go another twelve or fifteen years, or until Tommy finished his education. It was beyond his control and he could not let himself think about it now. Kate had been right about him. So be it: all his mistakes and limitations stood out in bold relief—it was all in Saint Paul. At this point his only thought was that he could have seen Emily's limitations years ago as clearly as he now saw his own. What he was and what he had to show and how he had loved were all pretty much the same thing.

They had to bring in a nurse, but he was able to get downstairs for

Christmas. It was the last time. All the family was there, Louise coming up with Ethel and the Hafners. She had been down there for months, too old to endure the worst of this. She was in agony and the children, some of whom Michael didn't recognize, looked beset; after a suitable time, Michael asked to be taken upstairs, the women kissing him, and then Hafner, too, on the forehead. At fifty-five Julie was a tall, hard, angular woman, as fierce as her paternal grandfather; her husband was capable of greater tenderness.

Michael was glad to see them go, and that night he had a hemorrhage that had the women up cleaning the mess until daylight.

Around noon he felt well enough to take some soup and sit at the window while Amy pulled Tommy back and forth in his wagon in the street at the end of the walk. They waved to him. Mike visited briefly; and then, in the afternoon, late, while Emmy was resting, it came. He knew what it was and they barely got her in time. She came running in and got her arms around him. He knew it, but there was no way to tell her. He could hear the noise in his throat. He was going to drown in his own blood. In another moment it was as if a hand reached into his chest and wrapped itself tightly around his heart, one week short of the fortieth anniversary of the day Westfield had come for him at the children's shelter in Cherry Street. He was fifty-four years old.

X

The funeral was on Tuesday, a sunny, frigid day, and it was the last time Kate ever set foot in New Jersey. She was home before sundown. Louise was back in Mountain Lakes, and Emily really needed nothing anyway. Kate had wanted to be home early to watch the sun set. She had told Duran, but he had already anticipated her needs. Sissy waited until he excused her, and while Kate stood at the window, he mixed the drink she expected, Scotch, ice, and a little water. "I had Sissy call downtown for a couple of fresh sole. I'm going to do them with small boiled potatoes in parsely butter. And there's still some of that Kentucky lettuce left."

"Not yet."

"You tell me when."

"I'm not going to get so stinko that you'll have to put me to bed, I promise you that."

"When did that ever happen?" He gave her the Scotch. He was smiling. She had become hysterical after Michael had left fifteen months ago, and she had sat up drinking until five o'clock the last time he had been here in September. Duran was a man who had been dominated by women all his life, first by his mother, then by his wife, and now by Kate;

but this was the first time he had ever been happy, and it pleased him to tell outrageous lies that flattered her. She knew she dominated him, of course, but he had become more and more loving in ten years, and she was dependent upon him for more than merely managing her business. She had given up on the idea of a man who would dominate her when Michael had unwittingly abandoned her, after Emily had disappeared, when he could have made use of her and chose to keep everything sealed inside himself. For a few long weeks that spring so long ago, Kate had hoped for a flood of honesty between them; but then as he gave her the chance to see him at his worst, she realized she was past wanting what she perceived as his domination of her. So she married Johnson, a good egg, and had outgrown him. Duran was old enough to understand that at the center of her love for him was the aloneness that she took to be the fundamental situation of every human being. Because she knew there could be no miracles, she let Duran tell outrageous lies and cry defenselessly when *her* dearest friend died. He knew how intimate they had been. Oh, she never had to worry about what he was thinking. He was twenty pounds overweight and had built his life around her, and at night when she rubbed his stomach and told him how beautiful he was, he grinned like a schoolboy. He reminded her most of all of Westfield, but a sixteen-year-old does not trade her dreams for homey comforts. There was nothing she could have done any differently, and now that Michael was dead, she did not know why any of it had happened at all. He had told her that Mike had been instructed to stay in touch with her, but she had stopped thinking about his children long ago. She had her thoughts about what would happen to them. Duran's children remembered him once or twice a year, and as their father he had easier access to them. It was reduced to that, all the lifetimes of feverish running about—not the ideas or accomplishments or accumulations of wealth—it came down to the children and what they carried out of it into the future. When she had sat up so late three months ago, she had been thinking of all the things she had meant to tell Michael and didn't, or couldn't. She had always had to go back to a conversation a second time to assure herself that he had gotten her thinking, but this time there had been no second chance.

"Charlie, when I get so old and sour that nobody can stand me anymore, like old Louise, I want you to take me out in the yard and shoot me."

"What do you have on your mind?"

"Nothing. Not here." The sun was low enough to reflect on the ice on the top of the Palisades. There were wooden houses facing the river all along the top of the cliff; it was developed there, but from Manhattan the trees in the yards made it look like the country, and she enjoyed thinking that that was the way it really was. She turned to Duran. "Remember when you met Emily, Charlie, and you made her knees buckle?"

"We almost had a mess."

"Suppose you had made the change, the children had become your responsibility, and this had happened to you?"

"That's what made me pause ten years ago," he said. He was looking her straight in the eye. "I was pretty impressed with myself in those days—hell, I thought I'd conquered *you*. She was a lovely woman, and she still is in many ways after all she's been through, but I saw then what would have happened. The issue came up only because you're such a great woman, Kate. He was the gambler, but I made the better bet. I've realized it many times."

"I'm getting old now. Most of the people I've known in my lifetime are dead or getting ready to slide into the grave."

"I don't want you to talk like that. Don't even think like that."

"Yeah, well, you're right about him. There was so much I wanted to tell him. That was the one thing about him. He had an idea of what he wanted his wife to be like and, after her, their marriage and their family. It was a dream, and maybe it wasn't even his own. His real parents maybe or the two Westfields together, or all four of them combined. One of the things he said to me in September was that none of it had any value to him. We talked for a very long time while you were out with Mike. He told me that Sullivan claimed some responsibility for what he had become—not exactly the ravings of a man who knows he's about to be murdered. Murder is different from ordinary dying, and it was murder that made Michael not like you and me in a special way. It wasn't something he could run away from, but at the same time he thought he could keep it hidden. It isn't just her decision; it was his as well. Don't kid yourself. He never told his wife all about himself, and in that way he allowed her to become the kind of woman who wouldn't believe it now."

"What good would it do?"

"That's what he said, and I suppose it's right now, but he told me that he was ashamed of the things he had let Mike see him do this past summer. He tried to fix a race. In trying to show his boy that his father knew how to die, he let him see the way he had always lived. You know, Michael always took pride in his ability to separate the suckers from their money. 'I was showing off in front of him,' he said to me. And he was ashamed of himself."

"That's the saddest thing I ever heard. Nobody loved him as much as Mike does."

"He said the same thing about his own feelings about Westfield. A lot of what Michael did in his life had to do with the way he felt about that man. Michael wanted it both ways, Charlie. He had murder, larceny, and mischief in his heart, but he thought he could keep it out of his home, marriage, and family. He couldn't. At the end he wasn't even trying."

"I don't know why he bothered in the first place."

"Dreams are what make life real, Charlie. You know that."

In January there was a good deal of snow and the schools were closed for days at a time. The younger children stayed mainly in their rooms, but Mike had his chores that took him into contact with his grandmother, whom he had once loved very much but now despised routinely. He had been getting up at five o'clock every day for more than a year, shoveling coal and cutting wood; in October he had cut three cords into stove-sized pieces for this winter's cooking, and it had not been enough. His father had told him that his mother would be too distracted to take much notice of him, but she had, with a smile here and a touch there; his grandmother, on the other hand, had become even more of a cranky old fussbudget for whom he could do nothing right. One afternoon when he tried to build a fire to lift the gloom of winter from the parlor, she stood in the doorway and glared at him as if he were desecrating his father's grave. So when the thaw came at the end of the month and the story was told that the strain had been too much for her, Mike was glad to see his grandmother leave for Aunt Julie's. The next day was a school day. He had missed all of the previous week and seven of the ten days before that. In the classroom he lasted less than an hour. It was a two-mile walk back home, and his mother was in the kitchen when he came up the back steps. She did not seem surprised to see him, and he did his father's trick of making the other person speak first, but she had nothing to say. He went upstairs and changed his clothes. She was elsewhere when he came down again, but later, when he looked up from the chopping block in the back yard, she was standing at the kitchen window, watching him. She was not going to give him trouble. He smiled, and he saw the corner of her mouth come up a little before she turned away.

The next day he was out of bed at five o'clock and on the 6:09 when it left the Mountain Lakes Station for the city. He had written a note. He had figured all this out months ago. He was ready to go to the *World* or up to Mrs. Johnson and Duran, but he wanted to succeed on his own; he wanted to test himself. He was a boy. A neighbor had come to the door last summer with a guest to whom he wanted to show the house—not unusual in Mountain Lakes, where so many executives were building houses. Mike had showed them around, and the guest had had a few good words for Mike, who was a boy and wounded now.

That evening when he got home he told his mother he would be starting the following Monday at Gimbels for seven dollars a week. He wanted her to understand that he was not setting out on his own. He was going to give her money, but because it was so little in relation to what they spent, he had trouble saying it clearly; and his mother seemed only bewildered. He kept his disappointment to himself, thinking that it was the results that mattered. If he stayed on the job until eight-thirty at night, she would not have to hold dinner for him, and the store would pay him thirty-five cents meal money. The nine-fifteen train would get him home by ten-thirty, leaving time enough for the furnace and the kitchen firewood. His father had said that he would tell her to leave him to himself, but it was almost as if she had understood the message too well, for now Mike felt lonelier than ever.

Still, he went about his business. They belonged to the country club, but none of the family had been there in months. There were girls who were looking for him, and he knew he could find them at the club, but he didn't feel right about it yet. His father had told him about that, too, that he had to give himself time. Mike had no argument with it; the girls were so stupid that he had all but given up on them before last spring. He had gone around to see one girl who had promised to listen to reason, only to discover that she had shaved her cunt in anticipation of his visit. She was the worst, the craziest, but they were all crazy, gossiping geese. His father had told him not to go out of his way to hurt people for his own pleasure, but it was difficult not to see the advantages and opportunities. He was over six feet tall, one hundred and seventy pounds, and still growing. Girls were interested in him and he never hesitated to make use of the things he had learned from and through his father, and the combination of the two gave him the kind of reputation that made him angry enough to use his fists. He had had a bad temper ever since David died. He was better with his hands than his father had ever been, and he was beginning to realize it. One thing: the way they taught self-defense was wrong. You had to act when you sensed danger coming, and then you had to step into it, putting all your weight behind your arm, and you couldn't turn your wrist; if you kept it as stiff as you could, they dropped as if they had been hit with a ball bat. He had dropped two like that, a cheat in a card game in Saratoga and the brother of a girl Mike had talked into doing something he had first learned when Mrs. Johnson had made a joke about it when he was eight years old. It was tough getting the leverage with your pants around your ankles and the girl trying to crawl away between your legs, but the brother had been too busy trying to see too many things at once to notice Mike's fist about to crack him on the brow.

So he got into the habit of staying home weekends, even though the time there passed dead slow. Because he was gone all week Tommy wanted his company anyway. The things the kid was interested in just made Mike tired, but he couldn't help seeing that they were the things he had been interested in when he had been Tommy's age. And Tommy wanted to know what Mike's life was like now, standing in front of Mike's chair the way he had stood in front of their father a few months before. Mike felt sorrier for the little guy than anybody in the world. There were times on the job when Mike had the chance to think about his brother—the job was repetitious and made him sick with boredom, but he was trying to stay with it. They had him at the employees' entrance taking care of people's time cards and making sure they were punched right, and he knew for the rest of his life he would think of the smell of cold winter clothing as the smell of boredom. He was going to stay with it because the money was buying time for them all; and as time passed his own position would improve—so he sat on the stool they had given him and thought of his brother and wondered what kind of pleasure the kid felt in his play these days. The old man had said that Tommy would not understand everything that was happening, but the fact was that Mike could not see much of a change in Tommy's behavior at all.

On Saturday afternoons he was home by five-thirty, and when he came in he put his pay envelope, less what he needed for himself, on the kitchen table. This was the blackest moment of the week, for the envelope itself was not so much an affidavit of his integrity as a bit of persiflage to take the sting out of how little was inside it. By mid-March he had brought home barely more than twenty-five dollars. He had the consolation of knowing that he had made a contribution. His mother would be sitting up waiting for him no matter how late he worked in the back yard. She was not sleeping, but he thought that trying to accommodate him had something to do with it, too. She did not want to talk about his father. If Mike had nothing to say, she would have some anecdote about the neighborhood. He worried about her, but he did not know how to talk to her.

"I'd like to see you getting your rest, Ma."

"I'm all right. I don't want you to think you have to carry all this on your shoulders."

But he worried about money, too, and he wondered why they had to keep both Mary Frances and Maureen. They were sisters and they had no one but each other and Mike understood all that, but he could not see that the Westfields were required to keep them together when their own family did not see so much of one another.

"Do we have to spend so much money each month?" he asked his mother one night.

"I ran the household for your father, and that was good enough for him. I'm only following his instructions, and you know it."

She was referring to the fact that he had been able to go to work at all. His father had said that she had been told about their conversations. Mike had always thought school had been like being sent to jail, and at any point in his life he would rather have been exploring the world his father knew, and at last his father, who had battled with him from the beginning, had relented. Mike knew he wasn't ever going to be the kind of man his father was. His father would give him *The Open Boat* and Mike would reach for *The Red Badge of Courage.* He liked exciting stories that had to do with real life. When his father laughed and pointed out that *The Open Boat* had been a newspaper account and that the other had been whipped out of Crane's imagination like a soufflé, Mike had tried to explain what he meant. It was the doing itself that interested him; he was absorbed by the struggle and fight. His father stared, then said that he would eventually come around to an interest in all the work of Stephen Crane. Nevertheless, the message had been given to his mother that he was almost a man and was to be given his room.

The week after his "discussion" with his mother about Mary Frances and Maureen, Mike was fired by Gimbels.

He had an argument with a girl who showed up one morning ten minutes late and would not punch in and sign her card. Being late for work meant suspension or dismissal, and the girl knew it. Suddenly she cursed him and spat on his shirt and pushed her way past him. Ten minutes later he was in his boss's office answering the charge that he had wrenched her umbrella from her and struck her with it. The boss offered him a two-week suspension without pay, provided he apologized to the girl—he didn't even want to hear Mike's side, and Mike could see from the girl's expression that she had made a deal with the boss, so Mike spat in her face, shook his fist at the boss until the man was cowed, and then Mike spat on him, too. On the way out, with his knuckles wrapped in a handkerchief, Mike put his fist through the face of the time clock. He was in tears. Someone yelled after him, and Mike shouted an obscenity and forged out into the cold of Thirty-third Street.

He had a couple of bucks in his pocket, and when he called Mrs. Johnson at four o'clock from a hotel, he was blind drunk. Mrs. Johnson laughed and told him to come uptown. He took the Ninth Avenue El. The wind came up from the river so hard that he had to cover his face to catch his breath, and when he got upstairs, Duran, Sissy, and Mrs. Johnson herself just stepped back while he reeled in and fell, like a toppled tree, across the carpet.

As he realized later, they saw his situation in its entirety and made sure that he was fit to travel home at his regular time that night. Without explaining why, Mrs. Johnson told him to come to the city as usual the next day, to her place. "But kill a couple of hours first," she said. "We'll see you at nine o'clock."

His head hurt too much that night, but the next morning, his stomach still queasy, his hopes rising, he was at her apartment at the given time. As he had guessed, they were just starting their breakfast. Sissy set a place for him.

"What did you tell your mother?" Mrs. Johnson asked.

"Nothing. I just did what you told me."

"Yeah, well, okay. We'll work that out. Go to work for us. Learn the restaurant business. When you get home tonight, tell your mother you came up here during your lunch hour and sold yourself to us. You travel around with Charlie for a while, and we'll slot you in."

"I don't want you to make a job for me."

"You weren't listening, kid. Charlie is going to see that you learn this business. You're going to help us. Now have yourself some breakfast."

In truth, he was so eager to show them that he was not pushing for something that he forgot to ask what they were going to pay him. Charlie told him before the day was out. And that night, instead of telling his mother what Mrs. Johnson had said, he got himself into even more trouble. He asked his mother what she thought of the idea of him going to work for Mrs. Johnson and Mr. Duran.

"I don't want you to do that."

"Why not?"

"I don't, that's all."

"I can make twice as much money—"

"No!" She looked up from her mending. With her hair so close to the lamp, he could see how much gray there was in it. For as long as he'd known her she had parted her hair in the middle, and it had always made her look delicate and young. Now he could see how old she had become in the years of his growing up. He did not want to defy her. He did not want to cause her pain, and now that he had saddled himself with a lie, he did not know what to do next.

"Why don't you want me to see them?"

"Do you find the way they live so attractive?"

He sensed that he was on a dangerous ground. "Is it because they're not married? Is that what you have against them?"

"You have no right to speak to me like that! From what I heard last year about your tomcatting ways, you really don't need any instruction from them. You might think about *my* reputation now. I don't want to hear again that a boy blackened his sister's eye because of you."

"Aw, he should've minded his own business anyway."

"All very well and good for you, but I have to deal with these people. With your father gone, they'll say what they please about me."

"Not with me around," he said.

"Don't make these problems at the start!" she cried. "My brothers didn't do this to my parents!"

"Yeah, and—" He stopped and allowed his restraint to become a distance between them. He had been about to say that his father had called her brothers "a pair of soggy meatballs," and now he was seeing that she was not only vulnerable but limited. Mike had never had such a thought about his mother before, and he felt ashamed. And unfaithful. He stood up. "Daddy wasn't different from me."

"You will not speak that way of him. You will keep away from Mrs. Johnson."

He was in tears for the second time in two days. "I could make twice as much money! It doesn't make sense!"

"I didn't want you to quit school! If you're going to work, I want you to work for a respectable firm!"

Like the Southern Shores Horsemen's Syndicate, he thought, and left the room.

He took the 6:09 the next morning and had a cup of coffee in the Automat before taking the el uptown, but he didn't tell Charlie that anything had gone wrong the night before. Charlie told him that he had been thinking, and the sooner Mike learned to drive a car, the better off they were all going to be. He didn't want to put Mike in any of the kitchens until he understood the problems of opening and closing, stocking the bars, and dealing with the various purveyors. Restaurants weren't like other businesses, Duran said, and they had gotten their brains kicked out the first couple of years. Bartenders could bleed you, but kitchen thieves could put you out of business. Still, you had to take care of the chef. The chef at the Broadway store—restaurants were stores, as far as Duran was concerned—took more money out of the place than the manager—Charlie Duran, not incidentally. "The important thing in this business is liking people," Charlie said. "You can't pry too much into their business, and in spite of everything you really have to like them, and want to please them."

The thought of being in such a business gave Mike an indescribable pleasure.

It went on that way, with Mike keeping the hours he'd had before, his mother thinking he was at Gimbels while he learned the secrets of the restaurant business, the extra weekly sawbuck going into a sock in the corner of his drawer. Mrs. Johnson thought he was carrying her greetings home, and his mother was in awe of his stick-to-itiveness. He felt pretty tricky, but once he treated himself to a sirloin while killing time before the nine-thirty train and found that they had had hamburger at home. Through the newspapers he followed the developments in America's participation in the war. He knew that his grandfather had bought his way out of the Civil War and that his father had been almost thirty-five at the start of the Spanish-American War. When this war had started, his father had said that the outcome would depend on which side outsmarted the other, with his bet on the British, and Mike could not help wondering if America's entry signaled that the game was over. He read as many newspapers as he could in a day, and with more than a dozen to choose from, had a sense of being on the edge of events, only scant hours behind them. It was an exciting time and the city was an exciting place. It was almost May before Mrs. Johnson telephoned his mother, and when he stepped through the kitchen door that night, his mother slapped him across the face.

He was a big, strapping boy with good teeth, blue eyes, and blond hair, and her hand left a mark he bore until noon the next day.

"Liar! Liar!" She flailed at him with her fists. "You said you were at Gimbels! I don't want anybody's dirty charity!"

The next day, at noon, while the sergeant stared at the mark on his cheek, Mike signed himself into the army.

It was not finished. Emily telephoned Kate to tell her what Mike had done. In the first moments Kate lost her own control.

"Well, what the hell did you expect? He misses his father. Ah, you have to understand men, Emily. Of all the bad things that happen to them, the worst is when their fathers die."

"He should have come to me!"

"You don't understand. His father took care of him, not you. How could you have taken care of him when his father took care of you? No, Emily—and you know I have loved and respected you from the afternoon Michael met you—if Mike is going to survive at all, it is going to be on his terms."

Emily struck out at Kate the way she had swung at her son the night before.

"I hate you," she suddenly shouted, and hung up.

In two days there was a note from Kate, apologizing. "I would have said the same thing myself; it seems I knew everything this afternoon but the weight of the responsibility you carry." But Emily set the letter aside for the purpose of forgetting it. The next week Kate telephoned, but the conversation proved so unsuccessful that Kate did not call again. It was the last time the two women spoke to each other in their lives.

That month the weather changed, and Julie sent a girl up from the shore for the rest of Louise's things. She did not think any explanation was required, and the larger meaning was clear to Emily; that she would soon see the last of the Westfields. A part of her felt a gratitude that went beyond being relieved of the burden of Louise, who was over seventy-five—in recent years she had become stooped, slow-moving, and silent. Emily could not bring herself to think about what she had done to Kate, and she did not have the energy necessary for the woman who was not really her mother-in-law.

There was no mention of Saratoga that year, and in midsummer, with Mike still training at Camp Shanks, Pennsylvania, Emily's life settled into the comfortable patterns she had glimpsed when Louise was removed from her life. Running the household did not take much of her time. There was little for the girls to do, and Emily even gave thought to trying to place them elsewhere. They were hard-faced Irish girls with small mouths and faint moustaches, and now as they approached forty, they were both ten years past the possibility of marriage. They had their Thursday nights off and more if they wanted it, but they rarely went out. They kept to themselves in the evening, and after the children were in bed, Emily was done for the rest of the night.

She wrote to her son, and if she had other people to write to, she would have written to them. She sewed. She did not read, and when she prayed, either for the repose of her husband's soul or the safety of her son, she murmured the words of the Lord's Prayer or the Nicene Creed while her attention drifted.

The crying had not stopped—there were lengthening periods of quiet between the waves of the storm that assaulted and tormented her. She knew what it was doing to her, and she knew that it would not stop until the job was finished, until there was nothing left of what she had been as a girl. It was the same thing she had felt after the miscarriage, the thing that had started again after David's death. Now it was going to continue until she had no defenses left at all, until even her mind was invaded.

She could not help looking at the whole of her life and asking herself what she had to show—she could not help blaming Michael for her emptiness. She had borne his children and he had left her almost as soon as she was no longer young. Now the oldest child was gone, and because the process had started, she could see all the way to the end of it. Like Louise, she would spend her old age a victim of her children's charity, homeless and finally helpless.

Then it would come again, the storm, welling up and rolling over her.

She would cry in deep wracking sobs that came from deep inside her. At the worst, when she was completely degraded, she would whimper to him as if he were in the room, begging his forgiveness for her anger. She knew that if he had died within a year of their wedding, she would not have remarried. She could not imagine marriage with anyone else. If he had not been outside Grand Central Station, she would have gone looking for him. Now she knew how she had been in love with him. He could have done anything with her.

She did not sleep. She sat looking at his chair or she sat in the chair, watching the sun come up. She would walk down to the lake. She would be in the parlor when Mary Alice came down to start the breakfast fire.

"Good morning, Missus."

"Good morning."

"Would you like anything, Missus?"

"No, I don't think so. Maybe I'll be able to sleep now."

"I'll see that the house is kept quiet."

But she would be awake when the morning mail arrived, in case there was a letter from Mike. Although she had received more than one letter in a week from him only once, she had become so obsessed with the possibility of some surprise, some added token of his forgiveness and love—she had all his letters, standing up in their envelopes one after the other in the front of her top drawer, in front of the tin candy-boxes full of hairpins and the souvenirs of a woman's life. When Emily died at the age of eighty, it fell upon her daughter-in-law to go through the old woman's most precious possessions, and these letters were among them, the paper brittle, the ink almost like glass:

> ". . . so even tho' I know I made a mistake I am taking my medicine and doing my duty. I think of you often, along with everybody else. I think of Daddy, too. Please believe me when I tell you that I am conducting myself in a way that he would have been proud of. . . ."

Back to the first:

> ". . . and that time I shot Amy in the behind with the B-B gun, he didn't hit me, did he? Never! Never once did he raise his hand to me. . . ."

To the last in the packet:

> ". . . and so we are going directly from the camp here to Hoboken

and the route takes us thru Boonton, the Route of Phoebe Snow, the
Delaware, Lackawanna and Western, so I will be able to 'drop'
one last line, so as we pass the Boonton Station I will throw a letter
to you out the window I will wait until I pass under the
light. . . ."

That last one—the promised letter, to be thrown from the train—was
not in the collection. But presumably she was out there beside the tracks
in Boonton that night, looking for the piece of paper that flashed away
into the dark. It was part of the legend—even Tommy's children knew
the story. Mike said he let the letter go and she said that she was there
waiting for it, but it was a very long time before anyone realized that she
was out there searching in the weeds until the commuters started arriving
at the station long after dawn, or that she must have seen his face as he
later described it, grotesquely pressed against the window as the train
roared through Boonton, the effect almost circuslike, it was so bizarre,
his skin glued to the glass, the train roaring by. He had seen her and let
his letter go, watched it fluttering into oblivion, a few senseless scratches
on paper, nothing at all, leaving a broken woman pushing the weeds this
way and that until daylight and other human eyes shamed her into giving
it up, the letter torn open by the wind and tumbling in the breeze
hundreds of yards up the track, the pages rolling over and over as if they
were celebrating a life of their own.

Part Two

BROTHERS

For now we see through a glass, darkly:
but than face to face; now I know in part:
but than shall I know even as also I am known.

Book Four

TALES
OF MANHATTAN

12

Tough Guys

I

OUR STORY BEGAN IN 1877, AND NOW IT IS 1925.

Every generation invents its own definitions of love, and in the summer of '25, when he is twenty-six years old, Mike keeps a suitcase by the door of his flat on the second floor of a brownstone on East Forty-fourth Street. The suitcase contains three bricks for weight and two wrinkled double-sized sheets for bulk, and when Mike wants to make love to his latest conquest, he steps around to the Commodore where he meets her and they check into the hotel as man and wife. Mike's landlady on Forty-fourth Street does not like her tenants having women in, and the hotel does not accept guests without luggage.

Lillian Tracey was seventeen, a tall, leggy brunette fresh out of the Paulist Fathers' school in Hell's Kitchen; she lived with her Aunt Marge on West Fifty-sixth Street. She had come into Mike Westfield's Steak Cellar on Fifty-second Street last June looking for a job; her Uncle Johnny—another relative, not husband to Marge—occasionally supplied gin to Charlie Duran. Charlie, who had an idea of how Mike would respond to her, had passed her along. The girl's mother was dead, her father AWOL, and her family had more than its fair share of alcoholic uncles like Johnny and wild old women like Marge, but Lillian was a lively, wise-cracking kid. Mike liked her.

He had a Buick touring car, a big, fast machine he used for runs up to Peekskill or out to Montauk, and after he had let her cool her heels for a week, he had taken her out to Forest Park, given her some real Scotch, and, on a picnic table hidden by the night, led her through her initiation.

So now she was in love with him, but she knew what he was and sooner or later it would wear off. She even kidded him. He was meeting her outside the Commodore a couple of times a week, but on the afternoons she didn't see him and he drifted in after the lunch trade had cleared out, she would tell him he needed a nap, or to wipe the lipstick off his face. If she had the privacy to say that much, he would be able to grab her by the bottom and pull her against him. She fought him off and cursed him when he smelled of another woman, but there was still laughter in her eyes.

The Steak Cellar was Kate's; she had put up the money for the fixtures and the original inventory, and now she took a percentage of the net. There was a minimum guarantee involved, but Mike had been able to exceed that after the first two weeks—easy enough; Fifty-second Street was lined on both sides with speaks. Mike Westfield's Steak Cellar was better than most, with steak sandwiches and special sauce one of those features people remembered and came back for. There was a piano player and a blonde who sang; she had a guy drop her off and pick her up. His name was Iggy and he supplied cocaine to showfolks and stockbrokers; not much of a tough guy—he liked to carry a gun and put on airs. Kate didn't mind a little snow now and then, and if her supplier needed to believe he was a big-time gangster, it was all right with Mike.

Mike was six three and close to two hundred pounds. When people asked him why he had never gone into the ring, he told them the war, leaving it to them to figure out exactly what had or had not happened to him. Because he was so big, people in the store rarely acted up; but when they did, he merely had to step between them. He liked to be a peacemaker: in eighteen months, he had only had to eject one man, and he had been able to do that without actually touching him. But usually he was able to buy everyone a drink and get them started toward laughing it off.

Every other week or so he had to make the run to Peekskill or out to Long Island, but mostly the bootleggers got the stuff into the store themselves—in their overcoats, buried in the laundry, stashed in the sides of beef. Tough guys came around to sell him their booze, but he told them that he was part of Charlie's organization, and that was the end of it. People left Charlie alone. Charlie had silver-gray hair and a diamond pinkie ring these days, manicured nails, and another twenty pounds of paunch; his skin had so little color it made you think that he could not have been out in the sun in years, and sometimes he affected a silver-headed cane that he liked to lean on when he was sitting down. Given the nature of the city and the times as well as the business he was in, at first glance he could be taken for a gangster, but there was a kind of deep, waiting silence behind his eyes, and the circles under them were so purple they were terrible. Charlie listened to people and kept his word when he gave it, and the result was that he had more security than he would have had if he had surrounded himself with muscle. Of course, making sure the cops got theirs helped; he had told Mike that that was the first thing Kate had taught him. If he felt he was getting too much pressure to take one guy's beer or another's linens, and he couldn't get relief by passing the word to his friends, then he went to the cops and told them he was in danger of being closed down. More than once Charlie's speaks had cops manning the doors.

He and Kate had fifteen or twenty stores going constantly, opening and closing them as the law and business conditions demanded. They had brownstones and Chinese laundries, and an old stable on the East Side that served duck à l'orange and stuffed squab on the second floor, but their best places were in the skyscrapers downtown. After dark the customers rode up in service elevators, and if you were very quiet on Nassau Street after midnight, you could almost believe you were hearing a Dixieland jazz band from somewhere high overhead.

Kate had been ready to quit the business after the war, but stock losses in '19 and the opportunity created by the Volstead Act had persuaded her to hang on a little longer. She was the one in the combination who rarely went out. In cold weather she could be in great pain with her back, but no one could make her see a doctor. The cold did it, she said, and when the weather changed she always improved. In the meantime everyone was on guard against drafts in the apartment.

No one was going to argue with her anyway. Charlie waited on her hand and foot and saw that she had everything she wanted when he was out making the rounds. One afternoon he had Mike in tow when he went shopping for her underwear. She wanted a particular kind, and the two men were in three stores on Fifth Avenue before they found them. Kate had quit dyeing her hair, and it was as white as porcelain. Mike had remembered that she had once had a little more meat on her bones, too. He guessed she was in her sixties, but she was so thin and stood so straight, in spite of the trouble she had with her back, that when she passed in front of a sunlit window it was as if you could see the girl she must have been. Charlie said she had been heavy in her youth, but Mike could not imagine it. She was as much a mystery to him as ever.

Charlie knew all about her. She had been everywhere and done everything, out to the West, married to a crazy old miner. Mike was able to guess the rest, but Charlie told him: that she had been a whore, that she had come up out of the gutter. Mike was in awe. She had known his grandfather, Charlie said, and the old goat had told Mike's father to look her up. Here Charlie unraveled one of the mysteries of Mike's own past:

he told Mike that Kate and his father had never been lovers. His father had always known exactly what he wanted. Mike and Charlie were in a speak on Madison, in the basement of a brownstone; it was late afternoon, and Charlie had Kate's underwear firmly under his arm. The girls loved Charlie, and if he had not been in love with Kate, Mike thought that the two of them together could scoop them up in handfuls. But all that sort of conjecture ended with the fact that old Charlie was deeply in love with much older Kate Regan—she had dropped the name Johnson years ago.

Deep inside, Mike was stunned by the two of them. If one saw hints of the girl she had once been, she really was an old woman now. Sissy did everything she could for Kate, but there were nights when Kate was in her cups and Sissy had to take the most vicious abuse. Kate could be quiet, staring out the window for as long as half an hour, and when Sissy entered the room, Kate would start talking about her sister, who had been murdered. *How old would she be now?* Kate would ask out loud, almost as if she wanted to be heard across the river. *Look what she missed!* And so on. Mike would sit there looking for a clue to what to do next. The afternoon in the speak on Madison Charlie tried to set things straight. Kate was in a lot of pain. When he heard her crying in bed, he would try to turn her toward him, if she was willing to be turned. Charlie and Mike were pretty drunk by then; it was at the start of the summer Mike knocked over Lillian Tracey. Charlie told him that when Kate was able to respond to him, when she let him put his arms around her, she would look twenty-five or thirty years younger. Charlie was a philosopher; what she looked like wasn't important to him. He wanted Mike to understand how much there was to the woman, how much he saw in her. As far as he was concerned, she had given him more than the home he'd had in his marriage. She had given him himself.

"I've been with her almost twenty years," he said. "Every morning I feel better about myself, and every morning I'm just a little bit smarter. I can tell by looking at you that you don't understand me. Every morning when you wake up you're still the same dumb son of a bitch you were the day before." Charlie was very drunk. They were both very drunk, for Mike found this wildly amusing. "That's what Kate says about you, you know. She loves you like her own child, but you know what she calls you? 'That big goofy bastard'—right. She says you get it from your mother. Your father was a serious bastard."

The evening ended early, but required day-long recoveries anyway. When they saw each other at the end of the week, they winced and shook their heads. It was that kind of year. By September Mike was seeing Lillian Tracey two or three times a week and getting out to see his mother in Mountain Lakes every Sunday. Mike had a good season at Saratoga—Lillian Tracey came up one weekend, telling her Aunt Marge that she had gone to Asbury Park. A good year. He was on his feet.

Kate and Charlie had found him in a speak on West Forty-fourth in the fall of '22, drunk. If he had not been raising a ruckus, they might not have seen him. And after the awkward and drunken hellos, he might not have lasted another ten minutes with them if he had not passed out cold at their table.

They took him home. He had not seen the Riverside Drive apartment in five years, and it had been redecorated completely. They were older, and Sissy had changed. Sissy had been a girl five years before, but now she was getting thick through the middle.

Louise was dead. She went in 1920, in her sleep, probably of heart failure, leaving a puddle in the bed behind her. Ethel was dead, too. Influenza got her in '18; she had been so fat that her lungs had filled up in minutes. And Hafner was dead, the bastard, though not half soon enough, leaving Mike's Aunt Julie, the old iron-faced wooden Indian herself, the final beneficiary of most of the eventual profits from the sale of his father's land. It was all finished by the time Mike came home from the war in the spring of '19. His mother had needed cash, and Hafner had "generously" offered her an option on all but the four acres surrounding the house. Now Julie held the option, which had three more years to run. When Mike first heard about the deal, he had raged for days, but his mother still defended it. She had been short of cash, and the arrangement with Hafner allowed her to keep the house and land together for as long as she needed it, the time of Tommy's growing up. When he was ready to leave, she would have the rest of the money from the land and the proceeds from the sale of the house as well. This was what his father had in mind, she said; if she took care of what she had, it would last her the rest of her life. She did not want to see that the land was worth five times what she was going to get for it, or that she could have raised cash any number of other ways. When Mike wanted to go to the Hafners to rewrite the deal—this was when Hafner was alive—she wouldn't hear of it. "If they've cheated me, then they'll have to answer to their consciences for it" was what she said, as if she really wanted to be defenseless, as if she wanted people to take advantage of her.

Which was probably the case. The girls were gone, Mary Frances and Maureen. Mike checked their accounts against the prices in the Boonton stores, and it was clear that they had been taking ten to twenty percent almost from the day his father died.

He had to demand to see their books. He was still in uniform—he was in uniform that spring until the leaves were heavy on the trees—and while he worked on the bare dining room table, they were upstairs trying to hurry their packing. He knew what they were doing. His mother was in her room. She had not believed his accusation, and now she would not look at the proof, much less participate in what had to happen next. After a half hour he had seen so much evidence of theft that it occurred to him that the two girls could not be trusted in the house for another minute, and he went upstairs after them. Their luggage was on the beds, their clothing piled around.

"You're supposed to knock before you come in here!" Mary Frances screeched.

"And you're not supposed to steal from your employer either. That she's a widow with two little children only makes what you are that much worse."

"Don't give us that! He didn't leave us nothin'. We were only taking what was ours fair and square."

"He expected you to stay on. We've always taken care of you."

"Sure, sure. Just let us out of here."

He realized that the luggage was already closed and locked but that the clothing still unpacked seemed to be as much as could fit inside. He reached for one of the oversized carpetbags.

"Don't let him do it, Maureen!" Mary Frances shouted, and while Maureen tried to hold the bag, Mary Frances dug her nails into Mike's wrist. He needed no further confirmation of what he would find in the bag, so he pulled it free of the one while he shoved aside the other. He got just a glimpse of the silverware before Mary Frances slammed him on the top of the head with her framed picture of the Sacred Heart of Jesus. With glass sticking out of his scalp, Mike turned and gave her a short hook to the left eye, hoping to blacken it. Her sister tried to claw his face, and he pushed her down. He herded both of them toward the stairs, then down the two flights to the front door. When he got them to the porch steps, he tried to boot their behinds but missed. There were people walking down on the street, but he could feel the blood running down his neck and he didn't give a damn.

The sisters were back with the police in an hour, claiming assault and theft of their personal property, as well as wrongful withholding of earned wages, which was not a police problem. But by then his mother had seen the silverware and vases and her jewelry; and although she insisted that Mike was wrong in what he had done, she assured the police that his side of the story was the truth. The blook caked on his scalp clinched it, and the girls were permitted to take their possessions and get out. They wanted two weeks' pay. The police were still there. Mike told

them to sue him for it, but when his mother came out of the kitchen with
fifteen dollars, all that was in the house, no one moved to stop her.

He wanted to live there, but it was impossible, he could do nothing
right, and by the end of the year he was in a boardinghouse on the upper
West Side—within walking distance of Kate's place, in fact. He had a
succession of jobs as a telegrapher, trading his army training for really
good wages, but he lost them all for the same reason he missed Christmas
that first year he was home although he knew he was expected with the
family.

He was drunk.

He had spent his last year in the army drunk. He had not seen combat;
it was nothing like that. He had fallen into the habit of drinking to ease
his tension or to help him get to sleep or to celebrate some dubious
victory. He was not surprised with himself. His grandfather had been a
drunk and the men on his mother's side hadn't been much either. By the
spring of '22 he was out of the telegraphy business completely, and in the
fall, when Kate and Charlie found him, he had been working as manager
of a health club on upper Broadway. He had been fired when the boss
found him in a horse room after he had called in sick. Mike had marked
himself so lousy that the boss was even affectionate about it, clapping his
hand on Mike's shoulder. "Don't worry about it, kid," he said. "I was
going to let you go anyway."

Kate and Charlie straightened him out. He moved into the spare
room, took walks, ate right, and went to bed at regular hours. He left the
girls alone. It was the first time he really tried to take care of himself
since he had left the discipline of the army. Kate told him that his father
had had his bad times, that he had given up drinking in memory of his
own father. Mike could hardly bear to think of his father, he was so
ashamed of himself and what had happened to the family. Kate had
things to say about that, too. An awful lot was his mother's fault. She was
a woman who thought she had to suffer. Although Mike didn't quite
believe Kate, he was so sick himself about his mother that he wanted to
hear anything that would help him continue to question her judgment.
He knew she had not been her real self since his father's death, but he
had no way of reaching her and telling her what he could see. The more
he struggled with her, the harder it was for him to calm himself afterward. No matter what he wanted to discuss with her, if she did not want
to listen to him, she would respond with anything else that came into her
mind. The result was that the conversation made him think of trying to
rescue someone who was drowning but who had panicked: her thrashing
about was going to pull you under, too. And when it was done she would
sit there insisting that his torment was his own doing, that he was *wrong*

in the way he saw things, *wrong* in the way he acted on them. Once he told her that she would not have talked to his father the way she talked to him, and she replied, pulling herself up grandly, "You are not your father." He curled his lip at her. She was getting like his grandmother—he couldn't stand the sight of her. When Kate and Charlie found him, he was ready to follow their counsel whether he believed it or not. He would not have been able to make his rent in another ten days, and he would have been out on the street or back in Mountain Lakes. He had become a bum.

He still drank, but except for the occasional toot with Charlie, he watched himself carefully. He was a good drinker anyway, with a large capacity; when people commented on how much he could drink, he said it was because he was an old soldier. It wasn't his age that gave him authority, it was his size. He knew it. He tried to act as if he were not especially proud of his body's ability to absorb punishment, but the fact was that he thought it was buying him time until he got his life really straightened. He made sure he got to work every day; and on Sundays, no matter how much he was shaking, he made sure he was on the 11:37 for Mountain Lakes and Sunday dinner with his mother and Tommy.

Lillian Tracey's Uncle Johnny was not only a small-time bootlegger, adding juniper to potato alcohol in his bathroom and calling it gin, and drinking so much of it that his brain was baked; he was a fag, too, and Lillian had barged into his flat on West Fifty-eighth Street more than once to hear Johnny in the back bedroom getting his ass fucked, the bed jouncing and Johnny moaning in flesh-rending ecstasy. He wasn't the only looney she knew in Hell's Kitchen, drunks sleeping it off on the sidewalks, guys pissing under the el, perverts whacking off in doorways. Aunt Marge sent her down to the corner for beer and the bartender would leer at her while he filled the bucket, and the priest would question her closely about her sins. She expected every bit of it—men were all crazy. Little boys looked up her skirt when she went up the stairs, and when her mother had died five years ago, Lillian caught her father playing with himself through his pocket while he looked at her, sloppy drunk on beer. So much had happened to her by the age of thirteen that she expected something every day. Once she caught her younger brother trying to get their baby sister's pants down—ages eight and six. After their father disappeared, they went out to Astoria and Newark, respectively, to live with relatives while Lillian, as the oldest, stayed in the city with the least reliable or lovable member of all their family.

No one knew how old Aunt Marge was, or if she had ever been

married, or even if she actually was somebody's sister and merited the title "Aunt." She bragged that she had never been to a dentist in her life; her breath would stun a moose, and she chewed her steak, when she could get it, only on the right side of her mouth. She was a horseplayer, and when she heard that Lillian was involved with someone named Westfield, she remembered the handicapper and judge of the same name and told Lillian to ask, in case there was a connection. Lillian did, and there was—not that it mattered, she had the job anyway; but Marge was that far ahead of Lillian: although she kept it to herself, she thought Lillian was a whore.

Not that Lillian hadn't known what was involved, going to see Mike Westfield. Charlie Duran had asked her if she was ready to have an affair, and her Uncle Johnny knew Mike Westfield, too. "Too big for the likes of you, dearie. Say 'ah' "—the usual fag stuff.

But meeting Mike Westfield made it something different. She could see that he wasn't the brightest guy in the world, but on the other hand he wasn't intimidated by her either. He looked her straight in the eye, leaning in close, as if he wanted to tilt her head back and smell her skin where the blood pulsed close enough to the surface to let people see.

She had white skin and black straight hair, hair that was short and wispy around her ears and dark on her wrists so that she looked Spanish or Italian, and he told her so that night he drove her out to Forest Park in his Buick and got on her on the picnic table after making her wet with his tongue. He was heavy on top of her and big and rough. She didn't know what she was supposed to feel, but she felt vaguely familiar pleasure and pain. She would have been in love with Mike if he had never touched her, although in fact she was more than merely resigned to his touch, once she grew accustomed to it. She had dark eyes and a good figure— Mike, who knew, told her she would be beautiful all of her life. She had hardly been on East Forty-second Street when he started meeting her outside the Commodore. She loved it, being sprinted up in the elevator, waiting while the leering bellboy got his quarter, and then the door being locked and chained.

They made love. Whether he knew it or not, they made love to each other, holding, caressing, and sucking each other, fitting their bodies together, their sweat commingling—*that* was love, sweet, inconsequential fucking in a tiny room above the city's summer traffic. They would be falling asleep when some cabby far below leaned on his horn, making their hearts jump. Mike's belly was covered with hair, and when it was limp, his cock looked as if it were asleep, lying against his thigh. He had absolutely no idea that he was the sweetest man she had ever met. He was a drunk, but her mother had told her in her childhood not to concern herself about such a thing; she would marry a man like her father no matter what she thought she was doing—oh, but Lillian loved Mike; he was a pleasure.

They took showers together, chased each other around the room. It was all new to her and she understood that it was not new to him, but it was the way he gave himself to it that made her love him. He *played*—he tickled her and grabbed her pubic hair and squeezed her against him, but he never hurt her. One night, at a party down in the Village, the two of them drunk, he pushed her into a bedroom, tipped her back on the pile of coats, took off her underwear and stockings, and then held her feet together and sucked her toes, licked them all around. He was dead drunk—he said he wanted to marry her. She could not believe it. When she thought of the horrors she had been through, it did not seem possible that she could be so lucky; but the more she saw of Mike, in spite of the drinking and whoring around, the more she wanted to give it a try.

I I

Mike elected to take her home for Christmas. There were three of them on the train on the afternoon of the twenty-fourth, Amy deciding at the last minute not to make matters worse between her mother and herself. But she had arrived at the station with liquor on her breath, and a flask she claimed was filled with real bourbon. Mike was in good shape and give the stuff a taste in the men's room. It wasn't real, but it wasn't bad—the result was that both brother and sister were drunk when they arrived at the house, and their mother took an instant dislike to Lillian Tracey.

"Have you been a waitress long, Miss Tracey?"

This was at dinner, a gloomy, skimpy meal in a dark, unhappy room.

"No, except for summers, this is my first real job."

"I didn't know you had finished school."

"Why should you think I hadn't?"

"Mike hasn't," his mother said.

Lillian thought she understood her. Mike's mother could try to be as tough as she wanted, but underneath she was scared senseless. Lillian wasn't going to yield a thing. In any event, being able to meet the woman helped Lillian understand a lot. Kate had made her aware of Mike's mother, and when Lillian tried to get close to Amy, she found the girl to be a first-class bitch. Lillian had heard from both Kate and Mike about the grandmother and Aunt Julie, and when Amy asked Lillian what she saw in her "big jerk brother," Lillian had to wonder how much of a man Mike's father really had been, for he had been surrounded by roaring bitches. Kate had told her that she had thought for years that Mike's old man had married well but that as soon as he was dead, Emily had cut her off completely. This was what Kate wanted to warn Lillian about. Mike's mother had a dirty mind: deep down, the thought of surrendering herself to her own pleasure froze the marrow in her bones. All through their marriage, her husband had had her hypnotized.

Lillian told Kate that in his childhood Mike had seen them together and that he had used the same word to describe the effect his father had on his mother.

"Don't kid yourself," Kate said. "The old man knew what he was doing."

Looking at the woman who had been his wife, and thinking about the kind of people his older children were at the ages of twenty-six and twenty-two, Lillian could not help having her doubts about "the old man." Kate had said that he had made the most of his opportunities but, for Lillian, suggested that the son of an old-line New York politician who'd had his mitt in the tambourine, as her Uncle Johnny would say, would not have left his family so wounded and vulnerable.

Children came around singing carols, but it was a dark, quiet Christmas Eve in a house that seemed to Lillian to resist brightness and joy. Tommy was off to the country club to wait tables at a private party, and Mike wanted to show Lillian the family albums. The mother had her own stories to tell, and finally Amy slouched up to bed. There was a fire in the fireplace, but the light only sealed them off from the darkness. Lillian knew she was supposed to be impressed with it all because she was from Hell's Kitchen, but in her estimation the place was grayer and more deadly than a church. There was a radio, but when they tried to tune in one of the New York stations, all they could get was static and some distant voices and squeaks. It was typical of Mike's mother, Lillian thought: things could be disintegrating around her, but she would remain too proud, stupid, or both, to ask anyone for help. She said she thought it was one of the tubes, but even Lillian knew it was the antenna or the ground, and it was too dark and cold outside to do anything about it now. Lillian's Aunt Marge had a crystal set she kept in a bowl on the dining room table to amplify the sound, and it played better than the Westfields' fancy Atwater-Kent. Sitting in the hissing silence while the others tried to fiddle some sound out of the thing, Lillian longed for the stink and violence of the West Fifties, the cold of the streets and the Latin of Midnight Mass. Her mother had made sure that their stockings were filled with fruit, candy, and nuts, and there had been a toy for each of them even if she had had to make it herself. Lillian excused herself, kissed Mike on the cheek in front of his mother, and went upstairs. She was crying, of course, but she was thinking that it was better to be alone with her prayers for her mother and her dreams of Mike (she hoped there was an extra pillow; since she met him, she liked to sleep with a pillow between her legs) than in the presence of that woman and the ghosts swarming around her.

Mike had promised to come into her room in the morning, and so when she found herself fully awake at a quarter after two she felt a pang of guilt and betrayal; but after a few minutes more she was thinking of his crazy mother and this ruined Christmas and having to get out of bed in the frozen morning to clean herself out as Kate had taught her. She found her robe and slippers and worked her way through all the halls and rooms down to the kitchen to look for something substantial to eat and drink. If she was alseep when he came to her in the morning, he would just have to make the best of it.

The footsteps on the back porch startled her, but she remembered who it would be. The kid had a smile and a hello and a Merry Christmas for her before he had his cap off. She had met Tommy before, in New York; Mike saw that his brother got into the city about once a week.

Tommy wasn't like his brother, short and dark, with curly hair and small dark eyes and a pug nose. Mike said that the kid had their father's coloring but the build of their mother's brothers. He was hardly as tall as Lillian, but his shoulders were broad and had real meat on them. Mike said that if people thought he should have gone into the ring, they had not seen Tommy; Tommy had the compact, powerful body of a natural boxer. But it was clear to Lillian that Tommy was the one in the family who had inherited his father's celebrated intelligence; you saw it right away in the eyes, which were quick and showed a pleasure in what was happening.

He went at once to the refrigerator. "You didn't take the last of the pie, did you? With those drunks puking all over me tonight, it was what I started thinking of instead of my sex life." He found the fried chicken. Mike ate cold fried chicken like candy, sprinkling it with a concoction made of vinegar, spices and salt, and now it made her smile to see Tommy shaking a cruet of the same stuff. He could read her mind. "I can't do this." He grinned. "Your pal takes care of me."

"I know."

He had a way of talking out of the side of his mouth. At seventeen he tickled hell out of Mike, who hovered over him so admiringly that it might have been unpleasant if the kid had not had so much on the ball. Lillian felt it. He was a quick, sexy kid who was not spoiled. She watched him hustling about the kitchen preparing his snack—chicken, pie, and a glass of milk so big she would have had to hold it with both hands—and something gave her a thought.

"How often do you sneak into Manhattan, Tommy?"

He gave her the grin again. "How could you tell?"

"You're dealing with a native. What's the idea?"

"I've got plans," he said. "The old man always had plans—"

"Come on, you don't remember him that well."

"Sure I do. I was going on eight when he died. Don't get me wrong—I know he wasn't perfect. I was there when he got caught tubbing a horse. Did Mike tell you that one?"

She smiled. "Tell me about your plans."

"Yeah, I guess you have heard it all." He wiped his hands. "This place must have been a shock, huh? I'll say it for you: it's a dump. If you heard it all, you heard that part, too. She brought it all on herself and everybody else, too, letting people walk all over her. She wants to suffer. I could fix that damned radio, but she won't let me touch it. Well, I'm getting out. Mike doesn't know it yet, but I'm going in with him. We're going to be partners."

"Just like that," she smiled.

"Oh, I'm going to make him want me. He's going to ask me. You watch." He shook Mike's sauce on his chicken. "You can tell him, if you want. But you won't know if you're only doing what I want you to do."

"Suppose I tell him that, too?"

"Do you think that will change anything? Hey, I want you to like me. I know he's going to marry you."

"You have it all figured out."

"You wouldn't put up with this if you didn't have plans of your own. You wouldn't even put up with my sister."

"How do you know she isn't my friend?"

"We all know how girls are when they're friends. I haven't spent the last two years working at a country club for nothing."

"Do you know Kate Regan?"

"Oh, sure. I'm not supposed to, but I do. Mike took me up there a couple of times."

"I've heard from everybody, including her, what a wonderful man your father was, yet everything he seemed to try to do has come to nothing."

"You're blaming him for dying," he said.

He stared at her, but she kept quiet, waiting to hear what else he would say.

"Mike's been teaching you the family secrets," he said finally. "Okay, look, she wasn't like that when he was alive. He told her what to do before he died. Mike and I heard them when they were in the bedroom. She did what she wanted. She didn't want to have anything to do with what she thought was his. It took her two years to get rid of his clothes. Amy fought with her about that. 'What is Mike going to say when he comes home?' She had to use Mike to shame my mother into doing something about the old man's clothes. You don't know my mother."

"Kate says that your father had your mother hypnotized all through their marriage."

She expected him to defend his mother, but instead he said, "My mother hasn't had a coherent thought about that woman since my father died. She'd like you to believe that Kate was always jealous of her, but she gave the truth away a long time ago, as far as I'm concerned. I asked her about Kate—there were plenty of pictures of her in the albums at one time, when my father was alive—and my mother said she couldn't bear to look at the woman. When people are lying to you, that's when you have to start listening, because that's when they really begin to hint around the truth. She can't bear to look at Kate? The only time you can't look at somebody is when you think she has the goods on you." He got up from the table. "You know who taught me to think like that? My old man." He was very pleased with himself. "Mike doesn't have the heart for it and Amy didn't believe it, but I was little. When you're seven years old and your old man is dying and he looks you straight in the eye and tells you he's going to give you the key to the vault, you listen. You remember."

"He told you all his secrets?"

"He said I reminded him of himself."

"Mike said that you were the smart one."

He let her see the smile again—he let her see that he knew he had won her over to his side. "Oh, I have a lot to offer."

At dawn Mike came to her room, and when the bed started squeaking, he made her brace herself against the desk while he did it to her standing up. She thought of Tommy's remark about Mike not having the heart for the way the old man thought and she realized that, as big, rough, and even cruel as Mike could be, the judgment was probably correct. He could understand her only so well. This encounter was typical, for his pleasure. She was supposed to take her satisfaction from the fact that he wanted her so much as to take her against the desk in the cold light of Christmas dawn, and if she was dry at the start and he finished before her, she was supposed to be pleased that his fluids were gluing her thighs together.

The bed was cold when she got back into it, and for a long time she watched the daylight fill the room. She thought she knew what she was doing, but she was eighteen and had only her experience in her family and Hell's Kitchen to draw on. She knew the story of Michael Westfield backward and forward, of the tosspot alderman who had killed himself and the fine house in Murray Hill, and how the old man had walked away from a college education to go to work for the *World,* of how he had courted his wife in carriages (all this part of the tale through the mother, a madwoman, Lillian thought; two years of the clopping of horses' hoofs through the empty cobblestone streets of old New York: It made Lillian crazy! the two of them—what? holding hands?). The strange story oppressed the girl while the light filled the room and she weighed her chances. She loved Mike, Tommy was so smart she was ready to believe there was something unusual about him, and perhaps the old man had been the unflinching all-seeing wizard they wanted to believe; but she had put herself in the position of having to make a decision. She was eighteen. Mike was rough too often and sometimes so cruel in his stupidity about her or about life that she wanted to scream, but it was there: she had to do something. In the same way she did practically everything she was bringing them to a decision. She lay there with the light so bright against her eyelids that it almost forced them open, but she kept them shut, thinking of what she had grown up in and what, after all, this house and the land around it really were: she voted for it.

The person in the house for whom the move from the bed to the desk was designed was the one in the household who actually heard the creaking of the floorboards under her son's feet. She was awake not because she was spying on them but because she was always awake at dawn, just as she was always awake sometime in what she called the middle of the night and awake hours before that at midnight. And the thoughts Emily had about history repeating itself had to do not with the fact that this was the last of her children to smuggle a sexual partner into the house—it was true: Amy first, on her bed one October afternoon; then Tommy, scared to death and funny, in the parlor on a Saturday when she had told him she would be shopping in Boonton. Her thoughts had to do with what she believed in her soul was happening: that, like her three decades before, the girl was hoping for the "divine" intervention of a pregnancy; hoping, like her, for the man's mercy and a quick marriage. What she was afraid of was that the curse her sin of pride had brought down on her was going to be passed to Mike, the purest, sweetest, and most wronged of her children. She knew as soon as she saw the girl what she had in her heart, and as the evening went on Emily began to see that the girl would do to her son what she had done to her husband by forcing herself on him. She knew that this one was different from her, more experienced (one knew with a look; Emily had learned her husband's tricks, too) but just as naïve in her reasoning nevertheless, just as stupid—no, what had Emily breathless with dread was the idea that this curious, coarse reincarnation of her own sullied girlhood might just be the genuine divine instrument of the curse she had brought upon herself when she thought she could manipulate her lust to change her life.

She had felt the life go out of her husband, and in the same split second she was certain that it was the last conceivable punishment for destroying her parents' family, for her arrogance for presuming so much authority over herself. Her father's face, after so many years, still appeared unexpectedly before her. She had thought, even hoped, that mourning would be agony, but no, not at all: she lay in the bed night after night, half awake, not asleep, more physically beaten than she had ever been. No one knew that at the center of her existence was the darkness and isolation of the simple night when everyone in her reach, everyone she dared reach for, was asleep. She prayed, as she had taught her children to do, and which she still insisted was good for the soul, but she felt nothing. She could not read the Bible—she could not read anything. She could not sit through an evening at the theater.

And the thing, whatever it was, would not stop.

When he had gone down to New Orleans by himself or up to Canada, he had never known it, but she had spent nights on the bed fully clothed, only a robe over her. The girls had known; it was one of the secrets she had had to have with them and one of the weaknesses in her they had exploited after he was dead. She had neglected herself, and in the years since his death she could spend days at a time the same way, in the same clothes. She knew what she had become better than any other living thing on the face of the earth, and now, as if God Himself needed more human blood, He seemed to be extending His shadow over the first of her grandchildren.

And in the darkness of the middle of the night, in the hours between midnight and three, and three and six, when she would have insisted she was alseep but was still conscious enough to control herself, she allowed her imagination to recall Michael so vividly that she was ready to believe that what she was doing was real, that in her continuing sin she would not even allow his soul to rest. He came to her then, breathing heavily—it took her a long time to be able to imagine his breathing—and looking at her with his dark eyes. She kept her own eyes closed, as if to punish herself, and her body absolutely motionless. At times she could feel the hard, thin body of his young manhood against her body, in her body, filling her body. More than once she thought that if she could stop her heart, she would. In her motionlessness she tried to muffle every sound but that of him in the room, being there.

In the years since his death she had become so good at all her pretenses that she could not only open her eyes within seconds of six o'clock and begin the day's business as if she had really been asleep, but she had become so adept at pushing things out of her thoughts that she honestly believed she had been asleep. If someone asked her if she had gotten rest, she would reply, "Oh, yes, I slept soundly," and it would not even occur to her that she had not only lied, but she had moved herself beyond the reach of everyone around her.

III

For New Year's Eve they went out to an estate on the North Shore, the home of some stockbroker who had a taste for the wild life, and Lillian had it in her mind not to do anything to protect herself that night: but it was a dirtier, uglier party than Mike had thought, and they were lucky to find an unoccupied servant's room before Mike himself passed out. The people were terrible, and she would have fought with him the next morning if he had wanted to hang around. His head was killing him anyway. He let her drive the Buick back to Manhattan, and when she got out in front of her Aunt Marge's tenement, he realized that he was not going to get back across town. He got as far as the store, where he woke up at three in the morning on top of the bar, not knowing where he was or how he had gotten there or if the war was over or if Kate and Charlie had found him yet.

It made him think twice, he told her later. Actually, he told her twice, too, once before and once after she caught him with another woman, and she didn't believe him either time. However, she needed to believe him both times, and whatever he concluded from her behavior, she knew she was caught in the rush of events. If she still loved him, she knew better than to trust him. Men were men after all and only a fool would ever forget it.

As for him, he knew in January what was happening to him, that he was falling for her, but even though he had been frightened badly by his New Year's Eve bender, he was still young enough to believe he could bounce back from anything. He loved her; he hadn't thought he could feel such a gentle, happy attachment to any human being. Nevertheless, he was curious about different women, he liked to have fun, and he still wanted to prove himself. Whatever he wanted to do, he did, and then explained it to himself afterward. In that way he was like most other young men. He could cheat on his girl in the morning because he would be ready for her in the afternoon; and if she ran him aground in the afternoon, then a good dinner and a long, moderate evening would have him restored by midnight, or three—or six the next morning.

There was a woman who had worked the speaks for years, the rabbit-faced wife, now the widow, of a lawyer. Everyone on the street who had looked at her twice had had her; before and after her celebrated widowhood she had furnished vigorous, if toothy, oral sex. Mike had had her a couple of times in the office behind the kitchen; she liked to take care of the ownership or the bartender before sauntering out with the house's big spender, often tossing a wink behind her. The thinking on the street was that she imagined herself to be the instrument of some kind of cosmic Marxist irony: while their best customers probed her mouth with their tongues, the hired help were supposed to enjoy the knowledge that they had been there first, on far more advantageous terms. She was completely mad, and as she pitched Mike for another opportunity at him, she told him that one of her publisher friends had made her an offer for a book on her experiences as a widow. All Mike knew about literature was that contemporary authors didn't seem to be made of quite the stuff his father had admired. Fitzgerald and Red Lewis had been in the store at different times, roaring and staggering as if all eyes were on them, as they thought. However, if Mike could do something to advance a literary career—well: he bade her to follow him back to the little office, and as the lady got really busy, Lillian Tracey pushed her way through the door and kicked the widow smartly in the left kidney, giving Mike a moment of stark terror and the widow herself an uncomfortable sensation in the back of her throat. Lillian pointed to her own belly. "Do you know what's in here? You'll crawl before you see it! I might even kill it first!"

Kate thought Lillian had said exactly the right thing.

It took him a week to call Kate—to realize that she might know something. Sure, Lillian had relatives in Astoria, over in Queens, but maybe he ought to come uptown before he decided he was in the AEF again and was going to cross the water to save the world a second time.

She had guessed right, if one could call it a guess—he was lousy. He even smelled bad. What Lillian had told him had sunk in, and he was hideously ashamed.

"My father would have kicked my ass, wouldn't he?"

"No. You're different from him—and God knows Lil is different from your mother. He would have seen that. You know, he's been dead so long I don't know how he would have felt about her. I think he would have liked her. He liked me, but I was never much like Lillian. If you want to take that as a clue, go ahead. She's clear in her own mind about what she wants, and your father would have liked that. But he would have said that she knew what you were from the start—he wouldn't have said it with any pride, of course. The two of you have made your trouble together. He would have seen that. He was a gentleman, not a fool."

And she sat back, pleased with herself, buzzing on cocaine. He snorted coke once in a while, but it only made him think of sex. People said it revealed a flaw in his character. A woman like Kate could unravel the darkest mysteries, explaining them lucidly, her eyes clear, the silver box full of the tiny, sparkling crystals within inches of her elbow. Either he did not understand her, or he did not understand the effects of cocaine. He had tried it once on Charlie, who had replied, "Shit, you don't even understand booze!" Mike had threatened to pull him outside, but he had really understood. He wasn't much of anything, and what did he have to show for his life that had not been given to him?

He went out to Astoria. It was March, and the empty lots on both sides of Van Alst were yellow with last year's tall dried weeds. There were semiattached houses going up all around, and when he got to a broad street, like Grand Avenue, he could see through the branches of the elms and maples to the elevated BMT line that ran up Second Avenue to Ditmars Boulevard, which was the center of a new Greek community. There were shanty Irish and Italians in Astoria, lace curtain Irish in Jackson Heights, Germans in Elmhurst, Italians in Corona. It had taken hundreds of years for the towns and settlements of Manhattan to grow together into one city, and if Harlem had been a little farming community in Mike's father's childhood, and a middle-class neighborhood at the turn of the century, now it was filling with Negroes by the hundreds of thousands; but here in Queens, in the Bronx, and in the farther reaches of Brooklyn, too, the towns were becoming a city and developing into neighborhoods simultaneously. Mike's father had told him that he had known a madman who had been rock-solid certain that Queens would become the haven of the very rich. The Westfields had gone in the opposite direction not to live among the rich, or for the investment, but for the choice. In his own childhood almost in the middle of the last century, the old man had said, most people were penniless; if they arrived in New York during the Civil War, say, they might have had to stay there not because of the war but because of a lack of money. "I know what New York was like," his father had said. "I was there. I saw it myself. You and Tommy won't have to go through it."

Mike told Lillian about that conversation under extreme emotional duress. She recognized that she would never be able to express any opinion of her own about his father. Mike's eyes were wet, and he had to gulp for air. "And anyway, as far as he was able to take it, it's been true. My brother hasn't had the childhood I had, but at least he wasn't in the slums."

Where he wanted to be, Lillian thought. This was in the Buick, one of those March afternoons when Mike showed up with his hat in his hand

and a stupid expression on his face. She had him exactly where they wanted each other; she could see that much. She couldn't feel a thing, but because she had missed two periods, she believed she was pregnant. Well, one thing was clear: she was not going to marry Mike simply on belief. She had him doing anything she wanted, but that wasn't enough, not since the question of a child had been raised, and she had learned that Mike would always cheat on her. No, she had to have a *sign;* and it did not even matter that she controlled him so completely that he agreed with her. She knew better. She knew that she was in for trouble. If he would indulge himself after what he had said he felt for her, he would do anything he wanted whenever he pleased.

For weeks he showed up with candy and flowers, dressed right, and with the car polished. She would start by laughing at him, but the weight of what they were trying to resolve would have them both silent before they reached North Beach, if they were headed that way. Each day he had a new place to take her, and she could see how hard he was trying, but finally what brought them to a dead stop was the fact that she did not believe in herself. She did not believe her own feelings.

She told him she wanted to be alone, really alone, for a while. He took it calmly. She could see he was hurt, and she actually felt a little hope when he did not try to take it out on her. Still, before she left, she was not even sure she wanted to give him her address in Virginia. But because she had never been anywhere, and because after three months she knew she really was pregnant, and because she was eighteen, and lastly because she was so scared that she had no idea how she was going to live through this, she gave it, the address of a small private house in Richmond, the home of old neighbors of her Aunt Marge, people Lillian did not even know. When he saw her off at Pennsylvania Station, she cried on his shoulder as if she were being sent away. And he seemed more helpless—worse than that: she had to tell him that his mouth was hanging open.

He went back across town from the station destroyed inside. He had tried to begin a letter last night, intending to send it to Virginia this morning, but it had been a terrible letter. He had none of his father's gifts. He wanted to talk about his feelings and the things they had done together already, but all he could see was how badly he had treated her. He did not seem to have much of his father's character either. When he got to his room, he got down the bottle from the back of the closet and poured a good one. There were nights when he had done the job on himself so well that he was sure the landlady had heard him. It didn't matter; there were furnished rooms all over the city. He was going to get stinko as quickly as possible and get it out of his system, because more than anything he wanted to hold himself together for Lil and the kid. She was going to come around because she had no place else to go, but he wanted her to be happy about it, and he wanted her to be pleasantly surprised when she saw him again.

He wrote to her two and three times a day, even when he was drunk and weepy, but all of it made sense in spite of his lousy grammar. The handwriting didn't look that much different, and so he sent the stuff off to her anyway. He told her what he was feeling and doing, everything, the drinking, too. He thought he was in charge of himself. Whether he was or not, he knew that he was courting her truly now, and that his behavior made his feelings about her clear to anyone who cared to see.

Through the letters they made an appointment for a telephone call, and after two weeks and one day he took the Florida express south and got off at Richmond, where she was waiting for him, pink and glowing. He could see the change in her at once, and when he was close enough to touch her he took her arms and lifted her straight up, as if she weighed no more than a ten-year-old child.

They were married the next day, her Aunt Marge's old friends in attendance. The woman knew Lillian was pregnant, but it caused no difficulty. She gave the girl a blue garter, watching her put it on and praising Lillian's long curvy legs almost lasciviously; she was one of those old women who could make a filthy suggestion in a moment and the sign of the cross in the next. She thought Mike was a Catholic and Lillian did not want to have her thinking otherwise; but in her own self-consciousness she thought she heard the women telling her to dedicate her inner thighs to the greater glory of God.

But later, on the train heading north, when she tried to tell Mike what had happened, he looked at her in a funny way, one word led to another, and they spent the rest of the trip arguing about religion. He went crazy, accusing her of tricking him into the marriage for the purpose of converting him to Catholicism—well, he hadn't signed the child over to the Pope, as was usually the custom, as he understood it, and he wasn't going to. In fact, if she tried to have the baby baptized a Catholic, he would make her sorry she was ever born.

They had a reservation at the Hotel Pennsylvania, a beautiful two-room suite on a high floor looking north toward Broadway. It was raining in New York, and the lights from the streets filtered up the walls of the buildings while the raindrops ran down the windows in beads of twinkling gold. Mike didn't carry her over the threshold—the bellboy saw her distress before Mike did. She was wearing a light yellow dress that had been right for Richmond, and the rain, which they had first encountered as the train rolled into Newark, had been a surprise. She had a sweater, now wet, over her shoulders, and her hair was plastered to her forehead and the back of her neck.

Then Mike gave the kid a quarter and the kid closed the door on them. Mike had his back to her—he was trying to get his valise open. That was enough. She had had enough. She started for the door. Her movement made him look up.

"What's going on?"

She stopped. "That's what I'd like to know! All that crap in your letters about how much you love me and how much you miss me—well, you're full of shit, and I don't give a good goddamn what happens to me or this bastard of yours, I'm not going to let you do to me what my father did to my mother. Just as soon as you got me alone you started giving me this and that about the Church until you were a damned lunatic. I don't give a damn about the kid's religion and you know it. According to them, I'm already excommunicated—it would take too long for me to list all the sins I've committed for you. But you want to give me all that stuff that you don't give a damn about either. What's the matter, you scared? Are you scared of being married?"

"Now just a minute, bitch—"

He had stepped toward her, and now she slapped his face resoundingly. He grabbed her wrist. She bared her teeth. "Don't you hit me! You hit me and you'll never see me again! And let go of my goddamned wrist!" He let go. "You said you loved me! You haven't treated me right since we got on the train, and it's the same damned thing that it was before I went to Virginia, or before I went out to Astoria. I sat up late with your brother on Christmas Eve and I felt lousy about it because you were going to come into my room in the morning—where the hell were your feelings about me when that dame was sucking your dick? I'm married to you? Oh, you son of a bitch!" And with the best right cross he had ever seen, she cleanly broke his nose.

They had to get the hotel doctor up and the place was splattered with blood, but the management people were eager to go along with their story that he had stumbled during horseplay and had struck his nose on the dresser—it seemed to suggest to them that there would be no suit against the hotel. Mike bled for half an hour. The doctor was able to set the nose without difficulty, although Mike let out a yell when the doctor actually moved the bone. Lillian could not stop crying. The bellboy had to call room service for the steaks for Mike's blackening eyes, and before the doctor left he asked her if she wanted a sedative. She said no. She was prepared to run into the bathroom and lock the door just as soon as she was alone with him again.

Instead, she ventured closer to the bed. He was bare-chested; there had been so much blood on his shirt that she had thrown it in the wastebasket.

"Are you there?"

"Yes."

"Will you talk to me? It hurts me to talk."

"I'm sorry."

"I had it coming. I don't know what's wrong with me. You can go if you want. Get a lawyer. I'll pay for everything."

She didn't answer. He was on the flat of his back, and with his nose bandaged and the chunks of meat over his eyes, he looked as if he were already laid out in their parlor. It made her cry out again. On the train in her anger she had remembered that she had not been sure of this at all, but that she was going to fix it in her mind as her wedding day—she understood that even if she had to compromise herself so much as to marry again she would not feel it in the same way. But as bad as the moment on the train had been, it had been nothing compared to this. She had destroyed everything.

"Do you want to break it up?" she asked.

"Well—his hand reached toward her—"you don't want me hitting you, and that's okay. I don't care if you hit me again. I think I already took your best punch. But don't you call me those names. I can't take that. I know what kind of a guy I am."

She was crying again. "You want to make a try?"

"We owe it to the kid. I'm not going to be the guy who ran out on his kid because his mother sucker-punched him."

It wasn't what she wanted to hear, but this wasn't his kind of a night either. She sat on the bed and held his hand in hers for more than an hour, and then she fell asleep beside him.

They changed the story for their friends and families, saying that he had caught his toe in a wrinkle in the carpet and had pitched into the dresser. If anyone thought he had been drunk, there was Lillian's solicitousness and concern to be seen: she waited on him as if he were a visiting prince. It was obvious from her rosiness and five extra pounds that she was pregnant; but her attitude had most men envying him, and all the women envying her—a woman so selfless in public had to be truly in love. With the bandage over his nose and the discolorations fading under his eyes, Mike accepted her adoration gratefully, so helplessly that he almost gave the game away. So she kept kissing him. Oh, she loved him, loved him more than ever! If he had broken her nose, she would have been in a lawyer's office in a minute, looking for an annulment. She could see that it wasn't simply that she had something over him that had him so disarmed. She honestly believed that he was starting to love her. She knew it that first week, in spite of his broken nose, in spite of everything else that happened before that week was out.

Amy had fallen in love—that had been one of the tidbits that Mike had brought down to Richmond with him. The fellow's name was Georgie Howe. Mike knew more, but he wanted Lillian to see for herself. She took it that he was pleased with his sister's choice.

There was going to be a dinner out in Mountain Lakes that Sunday, but Amy wanted to have a party of her own for Lillian and Mike. Amy lived with her roommate Ruthie in an English basement apartment on Bank Street on the far west side of Greenwich Village, two rooms that smelled sickly sweet of Borax in the usual struggle to keep the roaches on the other side of the walls; Lillian knew all about it. Amy had a rare bunch there that night, cloak-and-suiters from the garment district where she modeled (and other things, Lillian suspected), burly sculptors from the neighborhood, a nice kid named Tommy Westfield, Charlie Duran, and the oldest person in the place, white-haired and elegant, Kate Regan. She and Charlie had brought a bottle of genuine twenty-five-year-old Ambassador, and some Negro musicians from Connie's Inn up on One Hundred and Thirty-first Street had brought some fresh boo—the place stank of it in no time at all.

It was a good crowd, and Amy—or, more likely, Ruthie—had managed to fill the empty spaces with pretty girls who loved a wedding, a good cry, and getting lost in a dark corner with some young boiler-room salesman. Lillian's Uncle Johnny got down to Wall Street once in a while on business, and he said it was like dealing with college boys. When Lillian looked at Mike, she had to be glad that none of that had ever touched her. He had his bandage over his nose and his eyes were still discolored; because he was so big, everybody in the place could see him. He stuck to the story, although he got drunk enough to hint at the truth. By then Lillian had begun to look for Tommy. He had come alone, and she felt that affection for him that made her want to see him leave with the prettiest girl at the party. He was at one end of the bar, a ramshackle construction nailed to the floor by a previous tenant. It was almost midnight, and there were seventy people jammed in the apartment. You could not see across the room for the smoke, and the noise of people shouting at each other was so loud that you had to put your mouth against the other person's ear, if you wanted to be heard. It was a wonderful party. Lillian started by asking Tommy if he was having a good time. He shouted for a repeat; he had heard her, he said, but he wanted to get a whiff of that perfume one more time.

"I said, are you having fun?"

"Not as much as you! When am I going to be an uncle?"

"Mike told you!"

"No."

In the far corner somebody went down of his own drunken dead weight; he took a standing lamp with him, and the resultant clatter drew applause, even a couple of whistles.

"Well, it's the end of the summer," she said to Tommy. "Are you sore at us?"

"Hell, no—"

"You should watch what you say where people can read your lips," a male voice purred behind her. She recognized it; it belonged to Georgie Howe, Amy's new flame. Lillian thought she already had an idea of the kind of self-important jerk he was. She didn't turn around to him. "I'm sure your mother didn't teach you to eavesdrop, Mr. Howe. You remember your mother, don't you?"

"Every year on her birthday," he said.

Now she looked at him. "Not Christmas?"

He was smiling, not showing any teeth. His lips came up in a V. He was a big guy like Mike, which was what Mike probably liked about him, and he had his black hair carefully glued in place. There was no question of what he thought of himself. "No," he said. "Not Christmas."

"If I want to find your mother in the phone book, what name do I look under?"

There was a flash of anger in his eyes. "That's my secret."

"Not really," she said. "I'm a Mick from Hell's Kitchen. Once a Mick, always a Mick, my mother used to say. By the same reasoning—you don't mind, do you?—once a Yid, always a Yid. What is your name anyway?"

"*My* name is Howe. It's all legal."

"Sure, but you used to be Jake Horowitz or something like that. Does your father still talk to you?"

"He's been dead a long time."

"What does your mother think of you changing your name?"

"I didn't tell her. You see," he said, trying to turn on the charm again, "I'm not a completely bad guy after all."

No, just a sneak. "Are we going to see you in Mountain Lakes tomorrow?"

"I'm looking forward to it, as a matter of fact."

"Well, we can tell that you've never been there before. Now listen, Jake, Mike and I want to deal with his mother on our own terms."

"Suits me, but my name is George."

She smiled. "I'll always think of you as Jake."

"You make your own trouble, kid," he growled.

"Keep your tongue in your head, wise guy," Tommy said suddenly.

"I'm not looking for trouble."

"You'll get it—"

Now he laughed and stepped back, raising his hands. "Sonny, I'm more afraid of her than I am of you. What did you hit your husband with?" he asked Lillian. "Your left or right? You're a big girl—"

"Why don't you ask him?" But he had her: he had kept his eyes on her, staring at her with amusement, and now she could feel the blood coming to her cheeks. *"Ah, get the hell out of here!"*

He brushed the end of her nose with his fingertip. "Don't you shit me, honey, and I won't shit you."

"Touch me again and you'll have Mike to deal with!"

"And me!" Tommy snarled.

Georgie Howe just laughed and walked away.

IV

She told Tommy to forget it. She knew he would: he had a terrific crush on her. He was less than two years younger than she, which made it no joke; but at the end of the evening, as she saw the pleasure in his eyes when they were saying good-night, she felt the impulse to kiss him. She did, on the mouth, quickly but firmly, and he beamed.

"I like you, too," he said.

The next day was mild, and in the late afternoon the sun came out. As usual the meal was dry and overcooked and the atmosphere at the table subdued. Lillian had the feeling that her new mother-in-law had not failed to see the changes in her. And later, when Emily said she wanted to show Mike something in the back yard, Lillian guessed with a start that it was a pretext created for the opportunity to twist the truth out of him. As it turned out, it was a pretext, but for an entirely different, more dramatic, purpose. In any event, Mike and then Tommy left the house, and when Amy went upstairs to get her bottle of rum for the coffee, Lillian was alone with Georgie Howe. He was trying to make a good impression, his double-breasted gray pinstripe so sharply pressed it looked as if it could stop bullets, and he had been so careful of the shine on his pointy roach-stomping shoes that he had come up the path as though it had been a minefield.

"I want to apologize for last night," he said.

"Don't worry about it."

"I don't want us to be enemies. I got off on the wrong foot with you."

"Look, I don't know what you're up to, but you said not to shit you, and in return you wouldn't shit me. We'll be all right if you stay on your side of the family. I have every intention of staying on mine."

He smiled. "I don't know why you don't like me."

"I don't like your eyes. You think you can get away with anything."

"I can. 'I'm going to live forever."

"What the hell are you talking about?"

"I'm not going to die," he said cheerfully. "I made up my mind."

"You belong in an asylum. How do you make your living?"

"That's for me to know and you to find out."

Amy was returning. "You never did a day's work in your life," Lillian said.

Later she saw that he had gotten the better of her again, if only in a sly, dirty way. By then she knew that he was a cheap rumrunner who ran a boat from outside the three-mile limit into the beaches on Long Island. What surprised her was that he had any kind of skill at all, but the story Mike had been given was that Georgie really knew how to handle a boat. The guy was getting on Mike's nerves, too, but there was nothing that could be done about it now. Amy wanted to act as if she had the situation under control, but Mike could see that she was wound tighter than usual. As much as it was possible, Mike supposed unhappily, Georgie Howe had Amy wrapped around his little finger.

Mike and Lillian were on the last train going back to the city, a local that made so many stops that it took a half hour longer than the earlier train Amy and Georgie had taken. Mike had arranged that—he and Lillian had too much to talk over.

His mother was going to put the house on the market and move back into the city. It was not their business unless they wanted it to be, he said, but he could see how much Tommy wanted to take this chance to make his own start. He did not want Tommy out on the streets alone. He knew the kid did not want to go to college and probably was serious about going in with him. Lillian saw that he wanted Tommy moving in with them, but she decided to let him tell her, instead of the other way around. He knew that Tommy was crazy about her; he didn't want to put her under any unnecessary pressure—or Tommy either, for that matter. It would be for only a few months, until the kid managed to get himself sorted out."I don't want him there when the baby comes," Mike said. "I'm looking forward to that. A few months is all he needs anyway."

"Tommy and I will be fine," she said.

"My mother's money isn't going to last. If she can save rent on a smaller apartment now, it will be easier for us all later."

For the first time Lillian could see that, one way or another, the old woman was going to occupy at least part of her husband's attention for the rest of her life—or his. Still, for the next few months, or until school ended, or the house was sold, their time, Mike and hers, would be their own. The baby would be along shortly after, and that would be the end of it. She curled her hand under his bicep and put her head on his shoulder.

"Do you love me?"

"Sure." He put his arm around her. "We're going to be all right. "You'll see." He squeezed her. "I'm going to take care of you."

She thought of Georgie Howe for an instant.

"I don't want to outlive you, Mike."

"The way I take care of myself? You're going to have to step in front of truck."

"I'm serious."

"So am I." He tilted her head back so he could kiss her. Sometimes he had a way of touching the insides of her lips with the tip of his tongue, and now when she knew he was going to do that she would open her mouth so his tongue could touch her exactly right. This time it set her nerves on fire, like the fuzz on a peach. They were sitting midway in the car, and the only person in front of them was a sleeping drunk. Mike looked over her shoulder and told her there was no one else.

"Should I look for myself or should I trust you?"

"I love your smile."

"That's not all you love." She opened her legs, "Come on, take care of me. Give me a good one."

He pushed her skirt up and pulled the crotch of her panties aside. She had her stockings up because of his mother, but normally she wore them rolled down a bit because he liked to look at her legs. He liked her hair. She had been afraid that she had too much hair, but he told her a funny story about something that had happened to him as a kid. She wrapped her arms around his neck in the expectation that he was only going to take care of her the way he did in movie theaters and once in a while behind the bar at the store, but he pushed her down on the seat and opened his pants. Her Uncle Johnny liked to make jokes about big cocks, and she had asked Mike if he had one and he had given her an answer about no complaints. It could get all the way to the back of her, but she liked to watch it sliding in, spreading her open, filling her up. This time because he had not been drinking it was as hard as a rock and he went all the way to the back while he stood over her, bracing himself against the back of the seat. She didn't realize right away that she had let out a scream that should have awakened the drunk, but Mike didn't give a damn; he held himself deep inside her, indulging himself. She could not stop looking at him; he was breathless, his eyes away from her, darting about, wild. She thought again about not wanting to outlive him, and the idea of being without him made her try to hold him inside her tighter, and that made her come, which made him come with a noise like something in a zoo, and it started her laughing. She was still laughing when he drew himself out of her.

"It wasn't that funny."

She put her head on his shoulder. She knew he was hurt—mildly—but she was sure she could kid him out of it. "But baby"—she giggled—"all I wanted was a little hug and kiss."

"The hell you did."

"Are you mad?"

"Nah. I had it on my mind all day. That's really why we took this train."

She snuggled him again. "Then you do love me."

"Sure"—he thought this was funny—"but not as much as I did ten minutes ago."

She closed her eyes. "Someday you're going to make me sore enough, and I'm going to bop you right on the beezer."

"Again?"

"I can beat hell out of you any time I want, and you known it," she said, getting his arm around her the way she wanted. She could feel him laughing, but when he brought his big fist to rub on her "button," the point of her chin, she quickly ducked her head down to kiss his knuckles. Then he put both arms around her.

Because there was a ring and Lillian acted like a bride, Mike's landlady allowed her to move in "for a little while—but I'll need more money." She was one of those old biddies who always thought there was something fishy going on, but Lillian knew what she was really looking for, her own ticket to Easy Street. The "more money" she needed came to nearly double Mike's former rent, so Lillian did not hesitate to tell the woman that they would be there at least two months—on Mike's instruction, she was out looking at two-bedroom apartments. He wanted a nice place on a high floor, with a view if possible. Lillian knew that he had Kate Regan's place in mind, but that wasn't much help. As for her, she didn't want a lot of noise. In Virginia she had experienced something like a relatively quiet world. She wanted a lot of sunshine, too, for the baby. If it was a girl, she was going to name it Irene after her mother.

At the end of the week she found a place in a four-year-old building in the East Eighties, two bedrooms, two baths, a kitchen with a dinette and a dumbwaiter, a dining room, a large foyer, and a delivery entrance off the kitchen. There was a doorman downstairs and a maintenance man living in the building; and Mike would be able to keep his touring car in a garage on the other side of Third Avenue, and somebody would deliver it when he called. The rent was more money than her family had ever seen in a month, but Mike said it was within their budget. Anyway, he said, he was tired of living like a bum. As long as his mother had kept the house in Mountain Lakes, he had always felt there was a place to go, if necessary, to remind himself that there was something left of him. All of it disgusted him now; he was glad it was over. He wanted Lillian to spend what she needed to give them a proper home.

They were getting along better than ever. Maybe because she had punched him out, she had gotten softer with him in private, curling up against him in bed, making herself small, calling him "Daddy" when she thought he wasn't listening. Maybe she had realized that most guys would have quit that first night, after beating hell out of her. There were times when it made him feel stupid, which made him feel angry, but those times rarely occurred when she was around and being sweet to him.

He saw that she was only a kid; aside from what the Paulists had taught her and what she had caught her Uncle Johnny doing, she really didn't know much. He had to teach her how to hold a knife and fork. She didn't know how to deal with the maintenance man or the doorman, and when he asked if she wanted someone to come in to help with the cleaning, she answered him so vaguely that he couldn't remember what she said.

She knew his work schedule and organized herself around it. She met him at the store for lunch and sometimes dinner, but the time of day he really wanted her was after nine-thirty, when the dinner rush was over. He loved the business, but he was such a worrier that he regarded a day without problems as a victory over the forces of chaos and evil; by nine-thirty he would want to celebrate. "Let's go uptown," he would say. "It wasn't such a bad day after all."

He liked Connie's Inn and the Saratoga Club, although he wanted the name "Saratoga for a place of his own downtown, a big place—he told her about it. He told her all his plans that spring, shouting them across a table in one loud, overheated dungeon or another. Prohibition wasn't going to last forever, and he wanted to be ready to open a legitimate store just as soon as the law allowed. People were making plenty of money and times were better. Now that they were married and going to have a kid, he had to figure out how they were going to live their lives, too. She knew then that he was really falling in love with her at last, but she was afraid that he wanted to go back to a place like Mountain Lakes. Oh, no, he said; the best time he had as a kid was in Brooklyn, where people were friendly and not interested in putting on the dog. He wasn't ready to think about owning a house anyway. They were just getting started and they were going to have plenty of responsibility soon enough. "I want to have a good time with you," he said one night, holding her hand. He was sober and she could see how frightened he was of letting her know how he felt about her, but she was happier than she had ever been in her life.

They finished that night in a little cellar club on 155th Street, one of those places that served fried chicken and hog jowls. There was a trio playing Duke Ellington tunes—a violin, guitar, and saxophone—and Mike and Lillian, the only white people in the place, were the only couple on the dance floor. They knew Mike in here; they knew him as well in Harlem as they did downtown. His father had taught him to treat black people with respect, and he had seen their bravery on the troopship that had taken him to Europe during the war. They were far down in the hold where they didn't have a chance if the ship was torpedoed, and out in the middle of the ocean, when men started dying of influenza, when there was panic and hysteria all over the ship and the crew started sliding bodies in the sea, the Negroes were the calmest men on board. Mike didn't know why, but it was true, and it was only right to say so.

She was paying careful attention to all this because he liked to tell people that he was drunk from one end of the war to the other, and now he was letting her see the things he kept deep inside him. "You're the first girl I ever met who wasn't at least a little afraid of these people," he said.

"Why should I be?"

"Well, the others are afraid something's going to happen to them."

They were in the middle of the dance floor. She put her head on his shoulder. "It already happened to me."

He stopped. "I've been thinking about us. I'm glad about it now. My mother likes to brag how my father used to take her dancing down at Sheepshead Bay—that that's the way they started. Here we are, you and I, and we're dancing. Maybe we hurried things a bit, but it comes down to the same thing. We're together, and that's what counts."

"I love you, Mike."

"I'm always going to love you, kid," he said. He kissed her, in front of everybody, and when she opened her eyes again, while people were whistling and cheering, she saw that he had tears in his eyes, like a big kid.

V

Tommy turned down their invitation to move in with them; he was too smart for that. He liked Lillian, all right, and it didn't make any difference whether she knew it or not; but he was going to do himself a favor and keep a safe distance until his feeling for her passed. Besides, the old lady couldn't get rid of the house until July, and they didn't actually move until mid-August. The baby came on the first of September, a boy they named David, after the long-lost original kid brother. Tommy should have expected it, and he didn't feel unhappy about it after the initial shock. Mike had always been soft for David after he had learned that there had been something wrong with the kid's brain. Mike probably had forgotten it, but he had told Tommy all about David and their Uncle Thomas and their grandfather on their father's side, the alderman. Tommy was one of those sharp, fast kids who never forgot anything. He wasn't crazy about being named after a fat guy and a drunk who had committed suicide, but at least he knew there was nothing the matter with his brain. He had been in and out of so many doctors' offices all over New Jersey, doctors staring into his eyes, pinching his belly, playing with his dick, making him wriggle his toes, that before he had been able to bring it to an end, before his father was even dead, he had had to threaten to shit his pants in a doctor's office in order to make her stop. Every doctor had told her, "Nothing wrong with him, Missus. The boy's all right." Not even Mike knew about any of that. Tommy remembered those tedious train rides to Newark, Jersey City, and New York, to see a dozen different "specialists," the expense concealed in the household money. When Mike had rolled down the stairs with two Irish witches trying to beat his brains out, Tommy had been the most surprised kid in the world. Hadn't Mike known that their mother had always been everybody's chump? Tommy had been nine and ten years old during the war when the girls had been smuggling men upstairs; before Mike came home, there were men in their room for days at a time. They had Amy in on their conspiracy, using Amy's fury with her mother to keep Tommy in line. Not necessary. In spite of everything—the doctors, her outright dopiness, her inability to face the truth, Tommy knew his mother too well to feel anything but sorry for her. He thought she was too far gone to be tormented with anything like the truth—she probably wouldn't have believed it anyway.

The very things his mother did that evoked Tommy's pity drove Amy to wilder rages. "Ah, the stupid bitch!" Amy would shriek. "How stupid can she be?" At times she would throw herself across the bed and weep bitterly; it had been going on for years. Their mother had tried to be as strict with Amy as she had been with him, with less success; Amy was seven years older than Tommy, almost a woman when their father died.

Amy wasted no time on their father, either; according to her, they wouldn't be in this fix if it had not been for him. "This fix" had been going since the day their father died. Amy had been ready to join the social whirl when the old man got sick, Mike said; Amy never got over it. Tommy paid no attention to that. Mike always tried to look on the bright side and it had taken Tommy years to realize that the old man had not been so generous in his opinions of people. There were all kinds of generosity, and there was a difference between being openhanded and being a fool. As far as Tommy could see, Amy was a pretty girl who thought her life owed her something, and who hated her mother because the woman was not what she wanted her to be. Amy never took into account what her mother actually was: she didn't really care.

And if her disposition hadn't changed all that much when she had gone into the city, it had since she had met Georgie Howe. Amy was a tall, slender, leggy blonde with a look of contempt in her eyes that not even the first blush of love could conceal. Georgie Howe thought he was slick, but he was having a rough time. Amy knew that she was the sort of girl who attracted men who liked to be seen with someone whose coloring or figure made other men turn around; and at twenty-three she knew that such men would always try to punish a woman for costing as much as they thought they had to spend, and she knew, too, that at her age, time was running out for her to work the best possible permanent deal for herself. So Georgie had his hands full. Amy had that smile, but he was going to have to pay plenty to continue to see it when he wanted.

Tommy didn't bother to tell his mother that he really wanted to live by himself. He watched her go through the house, all four stories including the attic and cellar, turning over in her hands every single piece of crap before letting him heft it out to the porch. The junkman backed his truck up the slope of the lawn and left ruts that cost another thirty dollars to repair. Mike came out two weekends to help push cartons around, but he knew that Tommy was bearing the brunt of more than simply the labor involved. Mike knew that their mother wanted to tell a story over everything she came across, that this final dissolution of the last fragment of their father's physical reality was tearing her apart as well. Why couldn't the woman stop grieving? As children they had been unable to imagine her marrying again, and maybe they were responsible just that much for what she was, but in their exasperation with her they could say out loud that they hoped that some pomaded sheik would carry her away. They were in the kitchen drinking gin Tommy had picked up at the undertaker's in Boonton, the sun down for hours and the view in the windows only the reflections of the butter-colored light of the incandescent fixture overhead. They knew all about her—her sleeplessness, the wanderings from room to room at night; sometimes she slept in her clothing on top of the bed, but Mike remembered seeing that in his childhood when the old man had been in Canada or down in New Orleans, and there were times they found her sitting in his chair by the window, her eyes open, her fingertips massaging her temple—they knew all about her. She rarely responded the first time she was called, and often she needed a prod on the shoulder. "Ma? Ma, are you all right?" It didn't matter which of them was talking; she would blink her eyes into focus as if she had trouble identifying who they were.

"Yes, I'm fine. Do you want anything? Are you hungry? Do you want me to fix you something?"

"No, Ma. Are you having headaches? Why don't you see a doctor?"

"It's just sinus. I don't want you to worry about me. I'll be all right."

They could only look at her helplessly. She had lost weight during their father's illness and more after his death. In her childbearing days she had weighed as much as one hundred and thirty pounds, and now she weighed less than one hundred. The lavender they smelled in her presence only partly concealed the less pleasant aspects of her self-neglect. The undertaker's gin gradually brought this back into their thoughts that Sunday evening in the kitchen, and it stopped their grumbling and mockery. Later they were able to realize that if they had not been so ashamed of themselves and so ridden with guilt, each might have seen how the problem was destroying the other.

Aunt Julie did not come to the party the Mike Westfields gave when David and his mother came home from the hospital, but no one was surprised. She had been invited as a courtesy and not expected to make the trip up from the Jersey shore; no one on this side of the family had any use for her, and Emily for one liked to say that she thought Julie was years older than the sixty-five she claimed to be. But, surprisingly, Aunt Julie telephoned with good wishes and asked the new mother to describe the child. Lillian understood that she wanted to know that David bore some resemblance to the late wizard, the baby's grandfather, Julie's younger brother; but the resemblance wasn't there and Lillian told her the truth. David was blond and blue-eyed, like his father and maternal grandfather. Lillian could hear the woman's disappointment, but the conversation ended cordially, with the old woman saying that she wanted to send the baby something.

Nothing came. When Lillian thought of it two weeks later, it made her question Mike's understanding of the ages of the older generation, for he was sure his mother was wrong about his aunt and that Julie's age was what she said it was. When they found Julie dead on the floor of her living room the following month, the first suprise offered confirmation of Emily's opinion. The heart attack that had killed Julie had sent her hurtling forward and downward with such force that she had struck the corner of a table hard enough to split the wood and shatter her jaw, sending her false teeth skittering into the far corner. No one in the family, not even Emily, who was later discredited anyway by the discovery of Julie's birth certificate and her own comments the night of the funeral, had known that Julie had had false teeth. "She always had beautiful teeth," Julie's son said over her coffin, which the family followed through a long, tiring day from the funeral parlor in Deal to the

Hafner plot farther inland. The others supposed that the son was expressing his confusion in the face of the enormity of death, but he brought smiles to their faces because already Emily had been heard to say, more than once, "Not a tooth in her head," so fixed on the revelation of toothlessness that she had changed Julie's name in the minds of the younger adults in their party. Tommy was the one with the wisecracks—it was as much a part of his posing as the fact that he heard more dirt about the family than any of the others—and when somebody got hold of the local paper containing Julie's obituary, he said to look under *N,* for Not a Tooth in Her Head, and when Lillian looked up at him at the grave, he crossed his eyes like Ben Turpin, pulled his lips over his teeth, and gummed away.

"I've got all *my* teeth," Emily said on the train going back up to the city. "They've always been dark, but at least they're my own."

"Ma," Amy said, "be quiet about the teeth, okay?"

Emily clenched her fists. "I will not! That woman never gave me a moment's peace while she was alive! She always looked down her nose at me as if she had a dirty secret over me! I knew what she was the moment I set eyes on her—she *smiled* at me over your father's grave! You didn't see it, any of you! She *laughed!*" They heard her voice catch; they were afraid she was going to have a stroke. This was the first they had heard of their aunt misbehaving at their father's funeral, and they didn't believe it. "I can't say I'm sorry she's dead!" their mother cried. "I'll sleep better tonight."

"Will you, Ma?" Amy asked. "Will you sleep better tonight?"

"I'm glad I outlived her. I'm sorry." Her rage boiled up again. "She was a monster whose heart was totally devoid of love!"

Lillian took her hand. "Ma, you don't believe that. Not really."

The slight, pale woman looked at her angrily, but her lip was trembling. "Don't you be a fool like me!"

"You're not a fool, Ma."

She pounded her fist into her knee. "I was! I was!"

The next morning Mike called Tommy to find out how she was doing, and Tommy told him that she had been up all night crying part of the time, praying the rest.

"Why don't you get out of there? You don't have to live with that stuff."

"It's better than cleaning shit off the rug. Look at it that way."

"All right, smart guy, let's hear it."

"If I moved out I'd get lonely at night, and if I bought a goldfish I'd only forget to feed it, so I'd get a puppy. You can see how I'd wind up, on my hands and knees."

"You can still live with us, if that's what you're afraid of."

"Nah, it would be the same thing. You and Lil would go out some night and the kid would get out of his diaper and I'd be down there scratching the rug again. No thanks."

Mike had been able to remember something their father had told them about their aunt. Her first husband, later arrested on a morals charge, had punched her in the mouth when he had caught her with Hafner, long before any of them had been born.

"Proving what?" Tommy asked. "I already know the toughest guy in the world gets so scared at night he always wakes up with his gun in his hand."

Mike laughed. "Toughest guy, eh? How do you know that?"

"I just told you."

Mike had started him in the kitchen, but having his hands in and out of water all day had driven him nuts. The work of a busboy wasn't much different and he was too young for anything else out front, no matter how good he was. Mike had him doing everything Mike didn't want to do, running downtown for supplies, making deliveries to special customers. Sometimes he ran an errand for Kate, and there were a couple of cathouses where he flirted with the girls after he dropped off steaks and "authentic" Johnny Walker. He was getting around and learning a lot. His mother thought he was becoming a restaurateur, like his brother; she had never set foot in Mike's store, as if even she knew she would not be able to lie to herself after she saw the place. Mike wanted to succeed in the business, but he was like Tommy in that he cared more about turning a buck, and in that way they were more like their father than their mother would ever be willing to acknowledge.

Tommy adored the city. When he had time of his own, he would duck into one of the big theaters on Broadway for a picture and eight acts of vaudeville. Mike's friends had passes to legitimate shows, and Tommy got to see Eddie Cantor and the Lunts that way. There were guys from the *World* who remembered the old man, and from them he got Annie Oakleys to fights and the six-day bicycle races at the new Garden on Eighth Avenue. One night some wiseapple brought a pro into the store and left her there, slipping out through the kitchen, and when she caught on she tried to set herself up at the bar, where Mike waved her down to the end where he and Tommy were sitting.

"You wouldn't be trying to get us in trouble with the cops, would you?"

"Are you kidding?"

Leo, the bartender, came up. "Her boyfriend stiffed us, boss. Thirty bucks."

She was a curvy little brunette and Tommy loved her legs. He wanted her to turn around so he could get a look at her ass.

"I didn't get a dime. If you want to search me, go ahead. I've had worse nights."

Mike turned to Tommy. "You want to search her?"

"Sure."

"Will it cover the thirty?"

"He'll be the judge of that," Mike said.

"Give me another five," she said to Tommy. "To cover the cab fare."

"If you walk, honey, we'll both get home for nothing."

She had a crooked front tooth. She smiled. "But you'll be riding.

"I don't pay for my mounts. It's a family tradition."

She turned to Mike again. "Do I get another drink?"

He laughed. "You have to get something, don't you?"

"That's the picture."

He waved to Leo. She carried the drink through the dining room and past the piano player and the blonde who sang, and when Tommy had the door of Mike's office closed behind them, he said to the girl, "If you touch that drink, you'll owe us for every cent on that bill."

She brought it up to her lips, but she saw him staring at her.

"What are you going to do to me?"

"Nothing. I'm not going to touch you."

"Not ever? Not at all?"

"You don't fool me. What's your name?"

"Dolores. And you don't fool me either."

"Doesn't matter. I won't pay for it. Now give me that drink."

She sat up on the desk. "Will you share it with me?"

"You sound like a kid. How old are you?"

"Twenty-two. How old are you?"

He was close to her. Her underpants were wet on his fingertips. "I'm eighteen," he whispered in her ear.

"What a liar," she breathed, and wiggled closer. "You got a hand like a safecracker."

"It's true." He was kissing her on the neck and pulling at their clothing. "Why don't you figure I got the combination?"

She looked into his eyes. "I was told that this would happen, that some kid would come along and really give me a thrill."

"Sure," he said in her ear. "Why the hell not?"

She lived on East Fifty-sixth Street and he got over to see her in the afternoons and when he was off on Sundays. She wasn't too smart, and she had convinced herself that he was a kind of milestone in her life. She wanted to give him money, but he told her he had plenty, even when he didn't. There was a daffy blonde in the building who saw in his dark eyes the sensitive expression of an artist, and she wanted to paint him. The way she looked at him, he figured she meant in the nude, and when he saw her on subsequent occasions he was circumspect and, given the situation, modest. He wasn't in love with Dolores, but he knew he was sweet on her, as dumb as she was. He didn't want to hear what she did or how much she got for it. She would have settled the thirty-dollar tab at the store with Mike if it had been necessary, and Tommy understood that he would be a sucker if he forgot it.

Still, he thought she was playing straight with him, and when Mike announced that he was going to keep the place open after hours to do a little special cooking, or Kate and Charlie decided to have people up to their place for a few drinks, if Tommy could find Dolores, he would bring her. There was always a good crowd, and if people knew what she was, they knew what they were too. There was Kate herself, who grabbed his sleeve one night and pulled him down to whisper something.

"Do you like doing business with an old established firm?"

"The last thing it's going to be is business."

"Doesn't she have little gifts for you?"

He looked at her. "I can't take that stuff."

"By turning her down, you're only making her feel like a whore. I'll bet you want her to get her tooth fixed, too."

"What's wrong with that?"

Kate smiled. "She'll never do it."

"Are you going to tell me why?"

"She doesn't think you love her enough."

"You mean that, one way or another, I got to settle up with her?"

"With all of them," Kate said. "Didn't your father teach you there's no such thing as a free lunch?"

"You knew my father pretty well, didn't you?"

"Not as well as I knew your grandfather," she said, and winked.

He kissed her cheek. "Dolores will have the prettiest smile at Vassar before I believe that one."

"I could tell you stories." She held his sleeve again. "Don't underestimate yourself, Tommy. Don't sell yourself short." ˙

"Thanks, I'll remember that."

"You must! I mean it!"

It was a time when he was getting a lot of praise and he thought about what she said but only in passing, and he went on about his business. The realization that she had been intimate with his father grew more slowly. He would look at his mother and remember how she had cut Kate dead after his father's funeral, and everything he had ever been taught about the old man would stir up in a muddy confusion. When it was done, however, he thought more of the old man and felt more comfortable with himself, even superior. He could look at his mother and understand that she really had grown worse over the years—she was the woman his father had taken on the lawn down at the lake, according to Mike's story. That had been twenty years ago, and she had spent the last ten alone. If his father had rejected a woman like Kate—a redhead then, according to Mike and Charlie, and beautiful—because she had been a pro, it had been his mistake. Tommy was unwilling to pursue Dolores not because of what she did but because he didn't love her.

Dolores didn't get her tooth fixed and then she drifted out of his life, and the following July he ran into her again in N.T.G's Hollywood Club, where she was with a bald guy throwing his money around as if he wanted to be the next Daddy Browning. She gave him the snub as she went by, but at the table as she got a dollar from the jerk for the ladies', she gave Tommy the eye, and he moved away from the bar and met her near the phone booths.

"Hello, Tommy."

"Hello, Fatass. Where've you been keeping yourself?"

"Are you going to be a bastard, Tommy? Tell me now. I don't want to waste my time."

He rocked on his heels. "You knew where I was."

"I thought you didn't want to see me. Do you want to see me, Tommy? I saw that look when I came in."

"Sure. Let's go." He took her elbow, but she resisted.

"I got a job. Come on."

"Come on, hell. Don't shit me, kid."

She stepped back. It was strange—she was as wildly, irrationally angry as he was. He didn't know why they were suddenly exploding with a rage neither of them could have expected. She showed him her crooked tooth. "Tommy Westfield, you can kiss my ass!"

He chucked her under the chin. "I'd rather run my tongue around the end of the Holland Tunnel."

Of course he never saw her again, not that he imagined he would, for that night he took a page from his brother's book and got as skunked as he could stand, throwing up in the gutter on Columbus Avenue as a Packard rolled by and some pretty brunette, the image of Lillian, whooped, "Jesus, there's a kid who's done for the night!" He wasn't thinking of Lillian, but of Dolores, and he knew that at odd moments she would pass through his thoughts for the rest of his life. He had gone around to her place in the mornings, when the bed still smelled of her sweat and powder. She had a flaw in the fat of one of her buttocks, not quite a dimple, a flat spot that embarrassed her. Kiss her ass? He had done it a dozen times, and now they were enemies because neither of them had been honest about what they had been taking from each other. More than pleasure—harder to give than pleasure. Joy—it had run up on them. He was not going to forget it.

VI

Charlie pulled him out of Mike's place and put him to work as a driver. Tommy was a damned good wheel man; he had quick reflexes and that soft touch that was now a running joke between Kate and Lillian. Occasionally he was·needed to get a truck in from the country, but mostly Charlie wanted Tommy on call for himself. Charlie said he was tired of driving, but there were times when Tommy could see that he and Kate were really keeping an eye on him or possibly grooming him for a real spot in the organization.

Charlie liked to go fast. He had a new Chrysler sedan with a high compression engine, and on Tommy's suggestion he had taken the car around to a machinist to grind the rough edges off the gears of the transmission and rear axle. As a result, Tommy could bang through the gears without bothering with the clutch; Charlie didn't even notice until Tommy pointed it out to him, that they clicked forward without the neck-snapping lurches of normal shifting. Charlie didn't understand the intricacies of choosing the shift points; all he wanted was speed, and Tommy let him have it, eighty miles an hour on Astoria Boulevard, eighty-five on the Pompton Turnpike over in Jersey, three figures on Sunrise Highway running out to Montauk.

It was a good summer. Mike and Lillian took the kid up to Saratoga; they asked the baby's grandmother, but she declined. Amy and Georgie Howe became engaged—George seemed to be mellowing. In mid-August Kate suddenly confessed that she had never been to Saratoga in her life, and the next day the three of them and Sissy were driving up Route 9, the luggage rack of the Chrysler so burdened down with trunks that Tommy had trouble holding the car on the road, the rear end fishtailed so much. The maid was sitting up front with Tommy and she had some reefer; Charlie had champagne and cavier in the back and he prepared a tray for the front seat. If Kate had any of her snow, she wasn't saying, but Tommy didn't think so: she was the only one in the car who didn't seem to be afraid of being arrested. Sissy and Tommy were smoking, but with the window open. Kate hated the smell of "that goddamned shit," as she always called it, but she was having a good time. She had not been so far from the flat on Riverside Drive in more years than anyone could remember. After a while Tommy started to hear them giggling back there, and then Charlie leaned forward and said in Tommy's ear, quietly, "You and Sis just enjoy

yourselves up here for a little bit, all right?" And they went at it, moaning
and breathing hard, Charlie and the old lady, while Tommy and Sis blew
another stick of tea, north of Hyde Park somewhere, rolling past monas-
teries and mansions. Tommy put his hand on Sissy's thigh and she said
something and he put her hand on his pants and then he got his buttons
open and took his eyes off the road long enough to see her shiny, dark
fingers wrap around him—time enough for the car to cross the center line.
There was a yell from the back seat and then a silence as Tommy jerked the
wheel to the right again.

"I'm gonna get hell for this," Sissy whispered, her head on his shoulder.
"That old woman carry on like a schoolgirl whenever she in the mood, but
all the time I have to set back and pretend nothin' is happening." She was
working him like a milkmaid. "I love that woman, but there are times when
I don't understand her. Or like her much neither."

"Be quiet up there," Kate said.

"You be quiet later," Tommy said.

"That goes for you, too, kid. You're worse than your father."

There was no more conversation, but there was noise from the back
seat—and then noise from the front seat. After a while Tommy realized
that the two in the back were sleeping, and he kept the speed down to give
them a smoother ride.

"How old is she?" he asked Sissy.

"She say sixty-six. Whenever she can get a day in the sunshine, she look
fifty. Workin' for her is a burden sometimes, but I love her."

"I love you, too—*now* will you be quiet?"

Kate had been awake all along. A second later they heard her say, and
obviously it was her intention to have them hear her, "But Charlie, oh,
Charlie, I have always loved you the best."

They stopped for lunch south of Albany. Sissy had to eat in the car and
Tommy felt he was betraying her, staying in the restaurant, but he wanted
to ask Kate about what she had meant by saying that he was worse than his
father. A day in the sunshine wasn't the only thing that made Kate look
younger than her age; so much tension was gone from her face that she
looked as if she had been on vacation for a year.

"You're smarter than your father, that's what makes you worse. You
don't even know how smart you are. Charlie doesn't see it, but I'm not sure
he understands what I mean. I told you not to sell yourself short and I said I
meant it. Your brother will sell himself short for the rest of his life. But
you—someday it's going to dawn on you how much you know. You're
smarter than your father ever was."

"I want to go out and keep Sissy company."

"I know you think I'm harsh with her, but I'm the way I am because I remember everything that ever happened to me, and I'm not just talking about dreaming about those people with knives and waking up in a cold sweat—"

"She has dreams about her sister," Charlie offered.

"I dream about niggers with knives, for Christ's sake! And when I wake up I can't help thinking about dying. I don't know why it is, it's just the way I am." She kissed Charlie. "Ah, you're a saint, Charlie, to put up with me."

Charlie actually blushed. She leaned over again, as graceful as a girl half Sissy's age and kissed his cheek. "I keep telling you, when I go, you get somebody in her twenties, somebody like Lillian." She turned to Tommy. "I love him. He's my best friend. He's the best friend I ever had in my life."

Tommy grinned. "If you two want a rematch, I'll try to talk Sissy into playing a doubleheader." He got up. "I'll wait for you in the car."

Sissy had found the .45 automatic that Charlie kept in the glove compartment. "I know how big this is! I come from South Carolina!"

"Where this car goes, that's better than the Automobile Club."

"Do you know how to work it?"

"Sure. Charlie don't like to take chances. Now put it away. I'm sorry about you having to be out here, but I got out as soon as I could."

"Don't trouble yourself. I'm thirty-eight years old, maybe thirty-nine, nobody remembers, and I'm used to this. I just don't want to catch hell from her. She can be a bitch on wheels when she want to be. I enjoyed myself. I'm old enough to do what I feel like doing, and I felt like doin' that. Besides—well, the besides is my business."

"I was just thinking—if the dope who owns this joint looks out the window and sees us, what is he going to think?"

"Hm? Chauffeur and maid, I suppose."

He was smiling. "But if we were kissing, really kissing, if we were holding on to each other—"

"I'm listening."

"Well, if were doing it right, we'd never even notice him."

"I knew at the last moment that you were going to say that, and now I'm really going to be in trouble with that woman."

In Saratoga he stayed with Mike and Lillian for a couple of days, but he began to get itchy feet, quickly made his good-byes, and caught the boat for New York.

Mike called a week later to tell him to come back, bringing their mother with him, but she did not want to leave the city, she said; they knew what was really on her mind. Tommy decided to stay with her. One Sunday they took the open-air double-decker down Broadway and Fifth Avenue to

Washington Square. It was a sunny day and there was a fine breeze blowing out of the shade in the streets. The bus filled up and emptied out twice on its way downtown, and there was plenty of time to talk. He knew about the apartment his mother and father had shared off Irving Place, and that they had walked up Broadway in the evenings for dinner in any of dozens of excellent restaurants; but it seemed to him that she had not been in such an expansive mood in years, and so he let her go on with the anecdotes he had heard more times than he could remember. The result was that new details—or perhaps embellishments—emerged: that she had worked in a settlement house on the Lower East Side and even knew a few words of Yiddish and Italian. He had not known that she had been to Europe as a girl, and that she had never spoken of it either before or after his father's death struck him as so curious that he wanted to ask her about it; but she was on to something else, something about his father's boyhood, and the moment passed. He heard the details of his grandfather's suicide again, that he had been quite a man with the ladies (his mother blushed when she said that), and while Tommy wondered what Kate could tell him about it, his mother went on to say that his father had been quite a man with the ladies, too, before he met her. "We fell in love at first sight," she said, and he wondered again if his father had ever deceived or betrayed her. She seemed so stupid—the old man had been a gambler and a hustler, yet she went on talking of him as if there had been no more to him than the gallant suitor who brought her candy and flowers and took her off to Delmonico's in a carriage. His father had been able to break the seal on a new deck of cards, toss away the jokers, shuffle and cut the deck, then deal the other six players at the table full houses—all second-best to the straight flush he dealt to himself. An easy trick, he said. (In fact, it was; but it still took skill. Sensitive hands? The hands of a safecracker.)

"You never talk about the girls you see," she said. "I know you're seeing them because your shirts smell of powder and perfume."

He was grinning. A kid had just run through the flock of pigeons down by the fountain, and the birds had whirled upward in one expanding arc. Did they always fly in the same direction? Did anybody know? He felt so sorry for her; when he had come back from Saratoga she had asked only about grandson David. She didn't know that Kate and Charlie were anywhere near their lives. She still thought Tommy worked in Mike's restaurant; she had not even made her peace with the idea that they sold liquor there. "Ma, if you knew the girls I'm seeing, you wouldn't talk about them either."

"You're always so smart—too smart for your own good. You're going to wind up like your brother."

"Hey, if I buy you dinner, will you tell me more?"

"You know there's something wrong there."

"There's a terrific spaghetti joint over on Sixth Avenue. They do a chicken cacciatore Mike still can't touch. There's nothing wrong there, Ma, believe me."

"She was the one who hurt him. I'll never believe anything else."

"They're married and parents and trying to make a go of it. Let them have a chance. They say it was an accident. If she hit him, she hurt him only because she had her legs set. You could do it yourself, if I showed you how."

She was crying, but now she giggled through her tears. "She does have big legs."

"Sensational, Ma. Only the best."

"You like them?"

"I'm telling you straight, Ma. I like everything about Lillian. Let's try the chicken and then go uptown and see what's playing on Broadway. I've got a couple of extra bucks."

Suddenly she was worse—inconsolable. "I didn't want you living this way, any of you. I know what Amy's doing!"

"She's engaged, Ma!"

"To what? I see through him as well as anybody. She's right across town. I'm not allowed to stop by. Why can't I call her? What is she ashamed of?"

"She's on her own. She wants her privacy."

"I'm not fooled by her either. I didn't want any of you living this way. I didn't live like this as a girl."

"We're not anything to be ashamed of, Ma."

She put her hand up to her mouth. "I'm ashamed of *myself!*"

He put his arm around her and walked with her back under the Arch and hailed a cab. Halfway uptown she said she would be all right and tried to tell him to get out and let her make her own way home. In front of their building she remembered the chicken cacciatore and told him to walk over to Broadway for something to eat, but he could see that she had only figured out another way to torture herself. When they got upstairs he wanted to fry some eggs, but she chased him out of the kitchen so she could do the job herself.

He decided he wasn't going to tell Mike any of this, and naturally there was no point in telling Amy. At this point in her life their mother wanted to blame herself for everything that happened. She saw a dark cloud behind every silver lining. Lillian was no good. George Howe wanted Tommy to go to a ball game with him—he was starting to act as if he wanted to be part of the family: and their mother chose this time to announce that she was not fooled by old Georgie.

Did she hate other women or did they all hate each other as part of their common madness? Big legs. Not a Tooth in Her Head—*that* woman had been mad. Dolores went around defying men to love her in spite of her disfigured smile. Lillian broke Mike's nose and now she was yelling at him, but when she was alone with Tommy she wanted to talk about how much she believed in her husband. And when Amy was on the telephone with her mother, she made faces and curled her lip. Tommy couldn't make sense of any of it. Of them all, he liked Kate best, or he had the most faith in her; but the way she treated Sissy bothered him, and the cocaine— although Charlie said that she was one of the very few people he knew in the world who might have the intelligence to be trusted with the stuff. Still, it frightened Tommy, who sometimes looked at Kate and wondered what she thought about. Tommy knew he was afraid of women, but he knew it was because he had never been able to make sense of any of them and come away with a feeling of real admiration or, for that matter, confidence. Tommy figured that unless something special happened, he would be alone for a long time to come.

One night in October Charlie had Mike call him at home. It was after eleven o'clock and their mother was in bed; Tommy himself would not have been awake but for the late-night chance to fiddle with the radio. He had a ground tied to the radiator and an antenna strung around the dining room: he could get Pittsburgh and Wheeling, West Virginia, with ease, but on certain nights, when atmospheric conditions were right, he could dial through the static and eavesdrop on the mysterious world of Chicago.

"Charlie has to go out to Long Island. He could take somebody else, but he says he likes your eyes. Meet him down here at the store in an hour."

An hour gave Tommy time for a cup of coffee before he caught the Broadway local downtown. He was at the store when his mother appeared in the doorway.

"Who called?"

"Mike. He has a friend who needs a car delivered to Long Island."

"At this hour?"

"Rich guy, I'm going to get a hundred bucks. Mike's got the money in his pocket."

"I don't like you doing things like this. You're nineteen years old. Your brother should know better."

"Ma, please. Maybe this guy is important."

"You're lying to me! You're laughing at me!"

"Call Mike—ask him! That's the best I can do for you!"

"I'm going to do just that!"

And she was gone. It was always bad to skirmish with her, if only because she had to have the last word. There were times when it seemed to raise the skin right off his back—it made him want to smash her. "I'm doing the best I can," he muttered over his coffee.

The Chrysler was parked outside the store when Tommy came along, but the sidewalk was still so crowded with drunks and their girls that Tommy didn't see that Charlie was sitting in the passenger's seat until he was almost beside the car. Charlie motioned for him to walk around to the driver's side.

"I have to go to Howard Beach. We're not due there until two-thirty, but I want to get there early, so take the shortcut through Fresh Pond Road and Metropolitan Avenue."

"Why didn't you have me meet you uptown?"

"I didn't come directly."

The water temperature gauge was all the way over to hot. Tommy started the car and rolled it out into the line of eastbound traffic. At Sixth Avenue an elevated train passed overhead and Tommy's first question had to wait until they were heading toward Fifth. If the traffic kept moving, Tommy could fall into the pattern of one block over, two blocks up, all the way to the Fifty-ninth Street Bridge. When Tommy turned into Fifty-fourth he watched the rear-view mirror to see if they were being followed. The light changed and the crosstown traffic surged into the intersection.

"What's this about my eyes?"

"Kate's right about you. You don't tell her about tonight, though, get that straight. We're going to get reorganized after this, and we'll be doing nothing but retail. If we can't make a living, we'll all have to get jobs. Being a small fry is big enough for me."

"You get all this from my eyes?"

"Georgie Howe was shot at last July. Did he tell you?"

"Never mentioned it. Jesus, he's full of surprises."

"The hell. He's been scared to death." Charlie started to tell the story, but for a moment Tommy couldn't help remembering Georgie's inviting him to the ball game, or telling him that he had hired a decorator to produce drawings of a joint he was thinking of opening. No, Georgie *was* full of surprises—when he ʰhought he had to, Georgie could really keep a secret.

He had been bringing a fishing boat loaded with Scotch through the Shinnecock Inlet one night, when three men in a speedboat, one of them with a machine gun, fired shots at him. He cut the throttle so they could pull alongside and board; he had a pistol, but he let them take it away from him. Charlie said, "He told me that as soon as he heard the shots he knew he was giving up. One guy could have taken him, and he wasn't ashamed to say so. It wasn't worth dying for. They got the boat and ten thousand dollars' worth of booze, but that was the end of it. Now he's looking for something else to do."

"I know."

"Well, Mike saw his drawings," Charlie said. They were on the bridge, and the car was difficult to control on the steel grid of the roadway. "The drawings were awful, and Mike didn't tell you about them because he feels sorry for the guy and doesn't want to make fun of him."

"Mike doesn't like to see him picked on, but people are always going to pick on Georgie Howe because he's a jerk."

"I don't know what Amy sees in him," Charlie said.

"That's because he always keeps his pants up around you. I know my sis—"

Suddenly Charlie opened the glove box and pulled out the .45. "Do you remember what I taught you about this?"

"Sure."

Charlie checked the clip, and then put the gun away. "There's no moon tonight, but on the way out I'd like to try running with the lights out."

"Now I get it. If you'd said something, I'd have had carrots for dinner."

"I didn't know I'd be going out here until an hour before I called you. This isn't the way I like to do business, and after what happened to Georgie, plus some other things I've heard, I don't want to take any chances. With you along, you can be sure that I'm not going to let anything happen to either of us."

"That's nice, but if I don't know what's going on, I won't be any good for anything else—and on those terms, I don't want to go."

"I wouldn't do that to you."

"I don't want to hear the old song about my father either."

"The reason Kate says all that stuff is because she knew him when he was your age. Maybe she's ready to tell you what kind of a young man he was, but maybe you're still too young yourself to hear it. As for me, your father more than anybody besides Kate taught me how to live my life, and I didn't think you'd be upset to hear that I would do for you what he did for me, if I ever get the chance. And finally, even though Kate and I have been together for more than twenty years now, we have no children of our own. I have two children, but they always belonged to my wife, and there was no sense fighting her for them because she was the kind of woman who thought every fight was part of the one long fight to the death—"

"Kate doesn't fight?"

"Sure she does, but she likes to lose as much as I do. Let me finish. Kate and I talk about you and Mike more than we would if you were our own kids. You have to understand that—*try* to understand it."

"Where are we going?"

"I put out twelve thousand two weeks ago for a load of Scotch that was due last week, but they started calling ten days ago saying they were delayed getting out of Nova Scotia, and then tonight they said that they were able to get the stuff to the garage in Howard Beach, but because of all the crap they went through, they want another three thousand, which doesn't bother me, but the order isn't right either, they tell me now, with Canadian and gin. There's more of a count, of course, but they want me to come out and satisfy myself that I'm getting a good deal.

"At this stage, kid, I don't give a shit. If they want to rob me, fine, or if they want to hijack the booze, that's okay, too, but I'm scared of getting hurt, and even more scared of getting killed. These guys sounded scared themselves, calling about their delays and mixups, and they may be just setting me up, but the whole thing is no way to do business."

"Do you know these guys?"

"Yeah. Tough customers, coming up in the world. I don't want to do business this way, kid. Down in Brooklyn they took a baseball bat and broke a guy's hips and knees and put him on the couch so he faced the wall."

Once they were beyond the cobblestoned streets of Long Island City, Tommy tried running without lights. They were on Borden Avenue down behind the cemeteries, headed toward Maurice Avenue, where there were still small truck farms, and chickens sometimes got out on the road. Tommy liked it out here. It was open country, hilly, with plenty of trees, a grocery store here and there. The houses were nothing special, under ten grand. It was going to fill up with families and kids, and already there were enormous public schools towering like medieval cathedrals over the surrounding two-story semiattacheds.

On Woodhaven Boulevard Tommy opened the throttle, getting the speedometer to wind past sixty before he put the headlights out. The road looked like velvet in the darkness, but Tommy really couldn't see a goddamned thing.

"Put them back on again," Charlie said. "To hell with it."

"You said you didn't come directly."

"I wanted to make sure we weren't being followed—"

"I checked on that when we left Mike's."

"You're some tough kid. I'd tell you to stick your head in your shorts, but you'd probably chew your dick off."

"Where did you hear that?"

"Your brother. Up at the Spa. Somebody wanted to go up against some cowboy and that's what he said to the guy and the fight was over."

"I should have stayed. I don't live right."

"You'll learn."

Most of the streets in Howard Beach were still unpaved, a graded yellow dirt that was almost sand. Tommy saw that it would be easier to drive blacked-out here, but the closer he got to the actual possibility, no matter how he wanted to make a joke of it, the more it made his palms sweat.

He knew the way to the garage. He wanted to hear Charlie say something, but they kept rolling down the long sandy street in silence.

"Come up easy."

Tommy let the shift slip into neutral. There were lights on in the garage.

"Keep the motor running. And your eyes open. Call me if you see something."

"I don't like this, Charlie."

"I can't let them walk off with the twelve G's without at least barking at them, can I?"

He got out of the car. They had been waiting for him across the street, and now a door swung open. Tommy saw two guys as Charlie made his way over. Tommy thought of something, and as he kept his head as still as he could, he pulled the automatic out of the glove compartment.

There was no telling where the guy was going to come from. Tommy looked around. There was no light coming into the car and the lights outside were far away, so that from most angles he offered no silhouette. He was sure he was losing his mind, but the wetness of his hands, his rapid heartbeat and the chill in his bowels made him crazy with fear. He slipped over the back of the front seat onto the rear floor. As an afterthought he rolled down the rear door window and then unlocked the door itself.

The guy came right up to the driver's door. Tommy brought the automatic up through the open window. "Stick 'em up. I ain't kidding. I'll kill you."

"Okay, okay."

"Don't back up." Tommy got out of the car. The guy had a revolver.

"Hey, you're just a kid."

Tommy brought the barrel of the .45 down on the crown of the guy's fedora. His eyes rolled back and his knees sagged, but he needed more and Tommy hit him again and the guy went down around Tommy's ankles. The door across the street opened.

"Everything all right, Walter?"

"Just a kid," Tommy said in Walter's voice.

"Well, get him in here," the guy in the garage said, and shut the door.

Tommy hesitated. He had seen two and that had made him figure one more, but now he questioned his judgment. He stepped over Walter and kept low as he approached the garage. When he cleared some dust away

from one of the windows with his fingertips he could see two of them
inside, one of them with a machine gun. Charlie was standing in front of
them, his hands at his sides. Tommy stepped lightly in the dirt outside to
the door and eased it open. The guy who had come to the door half-
turned to him. "Get him in here, Walter. I want to get this over with."

"Walter's taking a nap."

Charlie had seen it coming, Tommy taking aim on the machine gunner,
but he didn't move until the others' heads started coming around.
Tommy would see it again and again for years to come, the man's eye just
perceiving Tommy as Tommy squeezed the trigger. The top of the man's
head vanished in a sheet of pink spray even before the gun kicked up.
The other guy stood there motionless, his gun down, and Tommy shot
him, too, aiming for the spot where his tie tucked down into his double-
breasted suit. The guy flew back screaming, and went on screaming, flat
on his back, kicking like an infant. Tommy stood there gaping, his ears
ringing, and Charlie grabbed his arms. "How do you like that? He froze!
You did it, kid! Come on, let's get the hell out of here!"

He pushed Tommy into the passenger seat and swung the car in a
U-turn. The headlights picked up a guy standing in the middle of the
road. It was Walter, his face bloody, pointing his revolver at Charlie.
Charlie saw him, but he stepped on the brakes as Walter shot, and the
bullet came through the windshield on that side, and Charlie yelled.
Walter turned and ran, and Tommy pushed the knob that controlled the
headlights. Charlie sat back with a hole in his overcoat, above and to the
right of the point of his lapel.

"Oh, my God."

"You'll be all right. Can you get over here?"

"Don't get out of the car! Don't leave me!"

"Got to get you home, Charlie." He had seen Walter running away,
but he went around the back of the car anyway. Charlie had no use of his
right arm at all. Tommy pushed him the rest of the way and got the car in
gear.

"It hurts! Oh, God, Tommy, it hurts!"

Tommy kept it in low gear, lights out, for half as far as he thought
Walter could have run, and then he stepped on the gas and put the lights
on at the same time. Maybe his own ears were ringing from firing his gun
or the blows to the head had him confused, but it was as if Walter had not
heard the car coming and he turned around with surprise on his bloody
face.

"Kill him, Tommy! Kill him!"

"I'm trying!"

Walter saw what he was doing and got the gun up again, but Tommy put the accelerator to the floor, clicked the gear lever up to second and got his head down. Another bullet came through the windshield and Tommy flicked the steering wheel and caught Walter in the center of the radiator. The collision was worse than he thought and he saw Walter hit the top of the windshield and heard him roll back over the roof.

"Keep going," Charlie said. "Right to Kate's."

"You bet your ass."

VII

"They were the three who went after Georgie."

The air was coming through the holes in the windshield and Charlie tried to get out of the blast. "You figured it out before I did. The voice on the phone was the guy I met two weeks ago. To hell with it—just get me home."

One headlight was out and the hood was twisted up like a snarling lip, but the needle on the temperature gauge was holding steady, indicating that the radiator wasn't leaking. The wind had Tommy chilled, but when he started trembling, he knew that the wind had only reached something forming inside him. He could still see it, everything that had happened, every moment. Charlie groaned and Tommy asked him if he was all right, but there was no answer immediately; then he said that it was getting numb.

"Did the bullet pass through?"

"There's something grinding in there. I don't know. I don't want to talk about it."

He was asleep—or unconscious—before they reached the bridge. There was nothing Tommy could do for him or the condition of the car but keep on going and hope. They weren't stopped. Tommy supposed that the law might decide that they had acted in their own defense, but the rendezvous itself had been held for the purpose of committing a felony, which made it different. The electric chair. He couldn't think clearly. He kept seeing the guy with the machine gun turning toward him, the other guy thrashing on the floor, and Walter going over the roof of the car. The images were making him tremble how, and he could hear the explosions of the .45. He could feel the car bucking as Walter hit the radiator and the top of the windshield. Tommy had to clutch his teeth and tighten his stomach muscles. If they passed the police on their way uptown, he didn't see them. The front of Charlie's coat was soaked with blood. When he reached Riverside Drive, Tommy realized that he could not remember driving up Broadway at all.

"Charlie, wake up and help me get you up the stairs."

Without opening his eyes Charlie reached over his left hand and opened the door on his side. There was blood all over the door and the seat. "Shit. Ther's blood sticking inside my shirt and down my sleeve. And you gotta get rid of the car, too."

"One thing at a time."

He had to hold him up in the elevator, and on the way out he looked behind them to see if Charlie had bled on the floor. There was nothing to see, but it made Tommy realize that he had more to do than simply dispose of the car. He saw just how close they were to getting away with it, and when Kate opened the door, he was almost smiling.

"Ah, for Christ's sake!"

"He's alive. It's in his shoulder."

"Are you all right?"

"Sure. The car's a mess. You better get Mike. I've had enough for the night."

Sissy came out from her bedroom on the kitchen end of the apartment. "Oh, will you look at that? Who would do a thing like that to such a nice man?"

"Does Mike know a doctor?" Kate asked.

"I don't think so."

"We bring him in the kitchen," Sissy said. "On the table we cut all those bad clothes off him."

"Do you know about these things?" Kate asked her.

"My uncle the barber do this work once in a while."

"Get him," Charlie breathed. "If Mike knows a doctor, we'll pay your uncle anyway."

They helped him into the kitchen while Sissy called her uncle and then Tommy got Mike out of bed and told him that Charlie had been shot. Mike didn't know a doctor who could be trusted, but he thought he would be able to hide the car. When Tommy returned to the kitchen, the women had Charlie stripped to the waist and were trying to sponge the dried blood off his skin. The skin around the wound was swollen and blue, which meant that he was still bleeding inside, and the bullet hole itself had puckered out so that you could see the white bubbly layer of fat beneath Charlie's skin, Charlie's own personal fat. Tommy suddenly felt that he was violating more than the older man's privacy, and it made him want to withdraw.

"Charlie told us what you did," Kate said. "You were with us. Sissy and I will go all the way down the line for you on this."

Tommy was looking at Charlie again, wondering if the whiteness of his belly was normal; the fear he felt for Charlie made him see the man with the machine gun turning toward him. If Tommy had not shot, how much longer would Charlie have lived? How close had he been to death himself? Was death going to take Charlie? Tommy saw then that Kate was looking into his eyes, and then his teeth began to chatter.

"Go into the living room and lie down. We'll get you a blanket."

When Mike arrived, Tommy was on the couch with a blanket up around his neck, but he was still awake and he was still shivering. Kate took Mike aside to tell him what happened, but she made no attempt to speak softly, and Tommy heard her say, "Charlie was able to tell me that he killed them all."

"How's Charlie?"

"He's breathing. He's on the kitchen table; Sissy said that's where her uncle will want him."

Mike got down on one knee beside the couch and brushed the hair away from Tommy's forehead. "How are you doing?"

"I started to get the shakes."

"They're normal. In the war, if you didn't get them at least once, there was something wrong with you. I want you to understand that we're with you, kid. You weren't anywhere near Jamaica Bay tonight. Don't worry about the car. I'm going to take a look at Charlie. Do you want me to get you anything?"

"No, I'm all right."

When he came out again, Mike called Georgie Howe at Amy's and told him to come up and help with the car. George might have something else to contribute, too. The doorbell rang while Mike was saying good-bye, and Kate admitted Sissy's Uncle Rupert, the barber, a big man with conked hair and a waxed moustache. He had big teeth and eyes and a doctor's instrument bag, but perhaps because he was in the home of white people he was so extremely circumspect that he was not even something so dignified as a barber anymore, but something else, a figure out of a Punch-and-Judy show or pantomime, an old spectacle. He indicated that he usually received two hundred dollars for something like this, and Kate, her eyes narrowed, said that they were good for it. Uncle Rupert wanted to see the patient. He looked at Tommy shivering on the couch and smiled, then went into the kitchen.

Uncle Rupert asked Sissy for a pot, and once he had his instruments on the stove to boil, he methodically rolled up his sleeves and washed his hands with soap he had brought himself.

"This soap strong enough to take the skin off. If I get any in the hole in that man's shoulder, he gonna sit right up."

"You haven't even looked at it," Kate said.

"I seen it good enough, but I'm gonna take a good look now. He lost a lot of blood, but he a fat man and that usually a help. He probably gonna live, if he don't get infected."

"Jesus Christ," Kate muttered. Uncle Rupert didn't know it, but he was driving her crazy. He stood over Charlie's shoulder, touching the bullet hole with the nail of his little finger. Now he touched the area that was swollen and lifted Charlie's arm. Charlie let out a moan and came wide awake.

"Meet Uncle Rupert," Kate said.

"Nice clean shot," Uncle Rupert advised. "Good thing you didn't try to duck, or you mighta got it in the eye. The glass it came through slowed the bullet down enough so it didn't break your shoulder, so all in all you a pretty lucky man."

"What are you going to do?"

"Well, the bullet has to come out, but I can't just poke around in there hoping to find it because I might cut something important, and then I got to clean all that dried blood out of there and get the flesh back together the way it's supposed to be, or close enough, and then I sew you up. You understand that I got to cut you a little to do this right."

"You got anything for the pain?" Kate asked.

"I got a little morphine and a little heroin, and he can have his choice."

"Heroin," Charlie said.

"I like morphine myself 'cause it's closer to natural, but suit yourself."

"How do you know all this?" Kate demanded. "How do you know what to do next?"

"I just follows what an old nigger taught me years ago, and it pretty much always works. I took one out of a lung one time and the lady lived."

" 'Pretty much always,' " Kate repeated. "For Christ's sake, Charlie, let me call a real doctor."

"So he can fix me up for the chair? What about the kid? Come on, Rufus, do your stuff."

"Rupert. The ones that die, they don't die because I killed them. They die for the damnedest reasons, including just wanting to."

Kate let out a snarl of disgust and stepped backward into Tommy. She turned to him, close, finding his eyes almost at once. "You—"

He opened the blanket. "Get in here and keep warm."

"I don't have to tell you who you remind me of."

"Yeah, yeah. And you don't have to say what you're really afraid of. Relax. Rupert says that he'll probably live. He's giving you an honest count, you have to say that for him."

"If he can count as straight as you, okay. Now I owe you something, Michael, and I won't forget it."

Everybody heard the name, maybe even Charlie, slipping into his heroin funk; Mike looked around, and Sissy's head came up. Kate saw none of it, at last accepting Tommy's offer of the blanket or, actually, a hug, a momentary holding. He had never had her in his arms before, and

in the shock of having heard her call him by his father's name, he could
almost believe that he was holding the woman his father knew, young as
she had been thirty years ago, certainly longer—Charlie said his father
had known Kate at the age Tommy was now. She felt delicate and terribly
light; it was so strange, becoming aware of her in two ways at once, and
he could feel his fear of getting too close to her, of stirring his father's
vengeful dust. Had Kate been his father's mistress? Had she been his
father's lover before—*before*, like Lilith, in the old legend? But now he
knew that his father had been in her debt somehow, and the first thing he
thought of was money. What would the old man think of his kid, now,
the classy old gambler, always traveling first class? Now Tommy saw that
Kate was the only one who would tell him what he wanted to hear. The
old man's vengeful dust was stirred already, if it was ever going to rise at
all. Tommy could remember the old man smelling bad from the cancer
holding him the way he was holding Kate. Charlie had said that his father
had taught him how to live, yet the old man had been in this woman's
debt.

"What is he doing?" Kate asked.

"He's terrific. He's better than Bojangles."

Rupert looked up from his work and smiled. "You have a nice way
about you."

"You should have seen my way a couple of hours ago," Tommy said to
him.

"Not my business," said Rupert. He was probing for the bullet with a
pair of thin tongs, and Tommy could see it when he met the resistance of
bone. "Here she comes," Rupert said. The bullet dripped with red goo,
and he put it on a dish towel on the counter. "Lots of folks like to save
these, have them made into rings and things."

"Ah, you son of a bitch," Kate growled, and pushed out of Tommy's
arms toward the dining room. For a moment her old woman's body had
tightened into an angry knot, and she had surprised Tommy with her
strength.

"You got your hands full, working for that lady," Rupert said to Sissy.

"You have to know her," Sissy said.

"Nobody does that," Rupert said. He was sewing Charlie. "Not even
this feller knows that woman. He'll be sore for a while and won't want to
move, but when the soreness wears off he might try something a little too
soon and open himself up inside. After a week of so if there's been no
trouble, snip out these stitches with cuticle scissors and pull the threads
out nice and easy with your fingertips. A little bleeding then is all
right—just be careful. The other thing is all that blood he lost. You go
down to the slaughterhouse and bring back a pint of fresh warm blood

every day. If you can get it back here with the original heat still in it, so much the better, but don't go heating it. You do that for a month, he have his strength back in no time. It's the best thing for him. Best thing for everybody."

Tommy was laughing at the prospect of Charlie trying to get cow's blood down his throat. "You drink that shit, Rupert?"

"Every day," he said proudly. "I'm sixty-eight years old."

"You're older than our friend in there," he said, motioning behind him.

"I thought I was. That's why I say you people don't know that woman. I got a few secrets myself. Take my advice and keep a few yourself."

Mike had brought some cash from the roll he kept at home, and while he settled with Rupert, Tommy went to find Kate. She was in her chair in the living room, facing the window.

"The way Rupert is acting, he thinks Charlie is going to get better. How are you doing?"

She nodded. Her eyes were red. "You have blood on your jacket. Charlie would be dead if you hadn't saved him."

Mike was showing Rupert to the door. "Good-bye, Missus."

Kate raised her hand. When Mike opened the door, another figure was standing in the hall: Georgie Howe.

"You did what anybody would have done," Kate said to Tommy. "You did what you were supposed to do."

"What's going on?" Georgie Howe wanted to know when the door was closed.

"In the kitchen," Mike said. "I couldn't tell you on the phone because you got wise to it out at Shinnecock. They made the game."

It was true, Tommy thought. They had not gone to Howard Beach to kill anybody. But it didn't stop what seemed to be burned into his eyes or rising in his chest with a force that frightened him. Kate was staring at him. And he remembered again that his father had owed Kate something, but he could not imagine what it was, that this would have her nearly reliving it. The terror he felt was becoming twisted up in it; it throbbed through his entire body.

They had Charlie conscious enough to let Mike walk him into the bedroom, his left arm around Mike's shoulders. Georgie hovered behind, his hands almost on Charlie's waist. Kate stood up, but Charlie, if he was aware of her, didn't have the strength to look over. She cried out and tried to move toward him, but Tommy blocked her way and then took her in his arms.

"Give yourself a break. Isn't that what you want me to do?"

"I don't want to lose him. I'm not lonely with him."

"I'm going to remember that, old woman."

"He's always loved me for what I am, never what he wanted me to be. I had to wait until I knew who I was before he came along, and that took a long time. I don't want to live like that again."

"I don't think my father loved my mother the way Charlie loves you."

"You don't know enough to be able to say that. She isn't what she was—she went through a lot. They went through a lot together. Charlie went through hell for me. He was a lawyer and he walked away from it. He didn't lie to himself about how unhappy his other life made him, even though the people in it said they loved him. Insisted. In public. But Charlie was honest, and everyone he knew turned against him, but as much as I yell, and as tough to live with as I can be, he's never let me think that he's ever regretted it. He was still a young man when I met him, but he was the one, of all the men I ever knew, including your grandfather, and I'm saying more than I ever will again on the subject—Charlie was the one; he gave up something for me. The rest were just talk."

"You're all the same," Tommy said. "Dolores wanted me to kiss my way around her fucking tooth."

"Oh no, it's all of us, men and women. Years ago, before your brother was born, before your father met your mother, I had a housekeeper who was an old whore, like me, and her name was Gert, and she said the whole world was whores and customers, but she could hardly ever tell which was which."

He shook his head. "I had a tough night."

"When you want something, you'll be willing to pay for it," she said. "But then, when you've paid, you might find that you've got more than you've bargained for. You see, Gert was right; with Charlie and me, neither of us can figure out who's paying."

Georgie was standing behind her. "He wanted us to get him into bed before we let you in. He's really cooking, considering what he's been through."

"You missed Uncle Rupert—that was him on the way out. But that Charlie is such a sticker on being seen properly that he wears pajamas to bed." She was looking at Tommy now, this white-haired old woman, nearly in tears, and she kissed him on the lips, the fuzz on her upper lip touching the corner of his cheek. "Thank you," she whispered. "You angel. I love you. Thank you."

Georgie waited until she was out of the room. "Mike told me about it. He told me you were upset and that he'd throw me out a window if I rubbed you the wrong way. But he said that you were sure they were the three guys who hijacked me out on Shinnecock Bay. How did you figure that out?"

"Something made Charlie tell me about that on out way out. He was wound pretty tight."

"Well, maybe now we can relax."

"Don't be stupid, Georgie. What more do you know about it now than you did before?"

Georgie stared at him, his eyes narrowing—sometimes it was a mistake to call him stupid. "I don't understand," he said slowly.

"Lay low," Tommy said. "We don't know who they were or who they were working for, if anybody at all. Charlie doesn't want trouble. He was talking about getting out of wholesale. Lay low until he's feeling well enough to think about what he wants to do next."

Mike wanted to get the car to the East Side without further delay. There was light in the sky, but it was still too early for many people to be on the streets. Georgie led the way in Mike's Buick, stopping to let Tommy out at the door to his mother's apartment.

"I want to say thank you for what you did tonight."

"I don't think I want to talk about it. You better get going. There's been enough trouble for one night without Mike getting stopped."

Mike rolled up behind him in the battered Chrysler. One headlight nacelle was missing completely, and the bumper looked like a harelip. "Get your rest," Mike said. "Don't worry about anything. Call me when you feel like it."

"You think Charlie will be okay?"

"Absolutely. Listen, this was a hell of a thing to happen to a kid. You know that. Forget about it. Put it out of your mind. You better get that jacket out of sight when you get upstairs."

"The shirt, too. It's on the cuff. I wish the old man were alive." He wanted to talk with Mike about what their father may have owed Kate. Maybe Mike hadn't thought about the meaning of her words, but he had heard them, too.

"If the old man were alive, none of this would have happened. Our lives would have been completely different."

For some reason Tommy suddenly could not imagine it. He said good-night to Mike and went into the building. As the elevator carried him to the fourth floor, he realized that if he wanted to know how his father would have reacted to this, all he had to do was ask Charlie—or Kate. And as much as he wanted to know the answer, he could see, too, that he dreaded the old rogue's condemnation, or, worse, incomprehension, too much to think anymore about pursuing the issue. The old man, stone dead, was the final authority; and, for the moment Tommy couldn't even bring back the image of Walter going over the roof of the car.

There was a light on in the living room when he opened the door, and his mother was sitting on the couch with her hand over her eyes. He closed the door quietly and then got out of his jacket. He was unbuttoning his shirt, tiptoeing across the room, when she brought her head up abruptly. "What is this? What are you doing?"

"I'm going to bed, Ma."

"What's wrong with your shirt? Why is your jacket folded up?"

He tried to go past her to his bedroom, but suddenly she lunged at him, catching enough of his sleeve to expose the stain on the cuff.

"That's blood! I've seen blood in my life!" She reached for his face, but he pulled his head back. "You're not hurt! Whose blood is this? What have you done?"

"Leave me alone, Ma. It's nothing. Let me go to bed."

"No—no! I won't have this—it's six in the morning and you're nineteen years old!" She grabbed at the jacket with both hands, but he held it tightly.

"Stop it, Ma! I don't want to fight with you!"

She struck him on the chest. "I won't have it! What have you done? Tell me!" He put his hands up and she pulled at the jacket again. The sleeve was covered with blood and she could see that now, too. "Are you a thief? What have I done to deserve this?" She was crying, screaming. He dropped the jacket and tried to hold her, but she pulled away, cringing as if he had been beating *her*.

"Ma!"

Now she wanted sanctuary in the back of the apartment, but he held her arms tightly. She kept turning her head away from him.

"Ma! *Please!*"

"Take your hands off me!"

He looked at her. Her face was twisted as if she expected him to strike her to the floor.

"To hell with you, Ma," he said quietly. "It's Charlie's."

"Charlie who?"

"Charlie Duran. I work for him. Somebody shot him tonight and that's how the blood got on my sleeve."

"I don't believe you."

"Charlie Duran, Ma, whether you want to believe it or not." He stepped back. "I don't care what you believe. You're a crazy old woman and I'm sick of lying and sneaking around—" He was six feet away from her. He knew he was out of control; he wanted to tell her to call Mike. He even wanted to tell her that she would have to wait until Mike got rid of the car. "To hell with it. I'm sorry, Ma." He was still backing away. "I told you the truth." Now he could see those men dying, while he was looking into her eyes. He turned and ran.

By the time he called Mike, two hours later, the streets were filled with people going to work. It was Indian summer, and already the sun was strong enough to have men removing their jackets and opening their collars. Tommy was in a cafeteria on Fifty-seventh Street, and the place was crowded with office workers grabbing breakfast. There was the smell of freshly baked pastry, and over the hubbub of voices you could almost hear the bacon and ham frying. From the telephone booth Tommy could see the short-order men dancing slowly in front of their griddles and cutting boards. As they reached for this and flipped that over, they shuffled their feet and shifted their weight, and it looked like a dance. It was still too early for anything to be in the papers, even the latest editions. Possibly by noon, the first afternoon papers. The telephone booth was in the front of the cafeteria, and if he looked the other way, Tommy could see the traffic bumper-to-bumper in the sunshine pouring down Fifty-seventh Street, the exhaust rising through the rays of the sun.

"Did you tell Lil?"

"Yeah. She cried. Tommy, look, I'll square it with Ma, no matter what you said to her. I heard what you told me. Lil and I don't want you out by yourself, not now. There's room for you here."

"Nah. I've had a chance to think. If I'd stayed in bed last night and just woke up early because the weather was nice, I probably would have come to the same conclusion. I want to be on my own for a while."

"We don't want you disappearing on us."

"Not a chance. Let me check into a hotel and get a day's sleep, and then I'll call you. When will you hear from Kate?"

"Noon. Don't worry about Charlie, kid."

"What do you mean, Lil cried?"

"Well, I'll tell you. She was awake when I came in, and I sat her down in the kitchen, and she stared, and then she got sick in the sink, then in the bathroom. She's like me; she figures it was something that happened to you, and she wishes to hell it hadn't. We don't want anything to happen to you, Tommy. We love you, both of us."

"Okay, okay. I'll call you later."

Once he was on the sidewalk again, he hesitated. His clothes felt as though someone else had been wearing them. He was so tired that it took him almost five minutes to realize that there were any number of hotels on the side streets in the forties and fifties that could give him a room in the back away from the noise of the avenues. It had occurred to him that a big hotel could find him a girl—something in him made him think he wanted to get his ashes hauled, no matter how incapacitated or tired he felt. He couldn't even think of old Walter going over the hood. Tommy wanted to be alone now, but what were he and Mike going to do about their mother? Possibly that was a small problem; for all he knew, the electric chair he was going to die in had already been built, waiting for him to surrender himself to it. He wanted a woman? *Sit back, kid, I'll take care of you.*

He checked into a hotel on Fifty-fourth. They gave him the eye, and the elevator operator told him there was a girl available, but Tommy stuck to the plan he had made in what he regarded as his last coherent moment, three blocks to the north. In the room he closed the drapes, freed the blankets from their hospital covers, stripped to his shorts, and got into the middle of the bed. The mattress was lumpy, but the sheets felt clean. With his eyes closed, he could still feel his hands on the wheel and the wind blowing through the holes in the windshield. At least Charlie was alive, and on the bridge, and hacking up to Kate's place, Tommy had not been too sure.

It took him hours to fall asleep, and then the kid dreamed of his father.

VIII

Charlie recovered; they had a good Christmas, at Emily's as well as Kate's. Mike was able to convince Tommy that he had eased their mother into an understanding of what had happened to them all since the war; and so Tommy came up to the apartment on Christmas afternoon, but he kept his distance—ashamed, humiliated, whatever: everyone could see it. Lillian thought it was a blessing. The boy was having a very bad time, and his feelings kept him from seeing how much his mother had suffered, too. It was not just a matter of how much he could stand. It was not his fault—if there was responsibility to be parceled out, all of them could take a share. At the beginning, during the worst of her hysteria, Mike had wanted to blame himself, and it had taken Lillian to remind him of what was part of the family history now, something she had never seen: that Emily had turned her back on Kate as soon as his father was in the ground. Lillian thought he could see it clearly, but at times she wondered. Mike was too good to his sister, for one thing, considering she was willing to do nothing to help her mother all these months. Amy knew what Emily knew, according to Georgie—nothing about the killings; but that wasn't the issue, for her behavior was just more of what she had been giving her mother for years. Mike had Georgie managing one of Kate and Charlie's joints, and that had something to do with it; but for Lillian it was simply one more example of the concessions that were being made all around for the sake of peace, or the illusions each thought the other needed.

So they tried to make it an old-fashioned Christmas, seven of them at the table, including David in his high chair and Georgie, for whom Christmas appeared to be a new experience. Mike had offered to have the cooking done down at the store, but Emily would not hear of it. She was so tense that he had to go out to the kitchen to help her, something he hated to do because it was rude and insulting; but he had spent too much time with her since October not to know how to turn his intrusion into the reassurance she seemed to respond to. The food got on the table in good order, and if she was not a good cook, the food was still good enough for the males to help themselves to more. David was big enough to pick up turkey pieces to chew on, and he smeared himself and his chair with fat and mashed potatoes. Emily had him spoiled: he knew where he was and that he could get away with anything, and when Tommy gave him a wing, David decided to see the reaction he would get if he jammed the thing into his milk. The milk went flying and he needed cleaning, and in the excitement he started crying. He would be restless for hours and hard to get to sleep, but, worse, it would be days before he forgot the episode and the idea that mealtime was playtime, messtime.

It was a dark night outside, and cold; Mike had brought a bottle of Grand Marnier, and the evening ended with the adults sitting in the living room sipping liqueur and listening to Christmas music chiming tinnily over the radio, while David ran from one to the other, passing out walnuts from the bowl on the table.

Kate's party three days later was only slightly less subdued. Charlie was feeling better but was still very stiff, and the cold weather was bothering Kate's back; but they still had the tree up and presents underneath it, the apartment seemed to be filled with food, and David was in another party mood, banging on the table and yelling at the top of his lungs, prompting Kate to remark that he brought to mind certain customers, including a gentleman who went on to become a bishop of his church. After she made a joke like that, Kate would sit very still, her lips pursed to conceal her own merriment, while her eyes darted around the room to make sure that everybody was laughing like hell.

Tommy had a room in a brownstone walk-up on the other side of Eighth Avenue. The place was full of old people, but there was a girl on the top floor who worked the avenue, and Tommy could hear her taking the customers up the stairs. Her room was in the front and Tommy's was in the back, and once she closed the door, that was the end of it. His windows looked out on the trash-littered back yards, and he knew that it was only the cold weather that kept down the noise and the shouting from the neighbors. Once in a while there would be a yell and the sound of a bottle breaking, and it would only be worse in the summer, when the windows were open and tempers sizzled.

He was working for the Hudson Fur Company, but he was on the lookout for another job. The fur company was a con; they had him upstairs with forty other guys in a boiler room, all of them wearing telephone headsets and dialing numbers out of pages of a reverse directory, working their way up one street and down the next.

He was Mr. King: that was the name he used when he was talking to potential customers. It was his job to convince them that a fur expert would be calling on people in the neighborhood to appraise fur garments. Perhaps Madame would care to make an appointment? No cost or obligation. All Tommy had to do was get the woman to agree to see the "fur expert" and the company paid him a quarter. It was up to the expert to sell the dame the remodeling or dye job and get her coat the hell out of there. She could have it back when she paid her bill. The job was lousy and it was an awful thing to do to people, but Tommy was good at it. The Mr. King was unnecessary; no one ever complained that he was rude or too aggressive, and the boss never came down the row wanting somebody to confess to being Mr. King.

The guy who had told Tommy to use a name he wouldn't have to repeat but one the boss couldn't trace—not Mr. Field or Mr. West, obviously—gave Tommy some comfort while they fleeced the suckers. The guy was a family man in his forties and he was in over his head with payments on furniture, a Kelvinator, and one of the new Fords that he had on order—even he couldn't keep track of it all. He had another job nights that he walked to through the dinner hour, saving carfare. He had a meal ticket for a big lunch that had to last him until he got home again after eleven o'clock. Food would be on the table waiting for him; his wife had to rise early to get the children off to school. Tommy figured out that he saw his wife Saturday afternoons and Sundays. The guy's collars and cuffs were frayed and his socks darned; there was nothing of value he could call his own, including time, but he did not seem to have lost his spirit. He read the stock tables as if he had thousands on margin, discussed horses as if they knew him all over the clubhouse.

Tommy played dumb. If Mike couldn't understand why he wanted to be on his own for a while, working harder for less dough, then Tommy was beginning to see that he himself didn't understand people who were really living hand-to-mouth. He had Mike to fall back on, and Charlie now, too: when this guy fell, he went right off the edge of the earth. What Tommy didn't understand, and what somehow gave him comfort, was how the guy wasn't out of his mind with rage and terror.

At times Tommy realized that he had it backwards, that the guy probably wouldn't understand him or how he kept from going nuts, wondering if the cops had figured out something, or if someone else had begun looking for him. It had all faded now, receded, grown smaller, but the light it radiated had, if anything, grown more intense: in his room, hours from the fur company, Tommy would sit up all night, listening to the whore's footsteps on the stairs, occasionally the suspicious mutterings of her soured, overstuffed clientele. Tommy had slept through that first day and then had let Mike follow the case for him in the papers, and so he never found out, for instance, if Walter had been a family man or was just middle-aged and alone, like the heavy-legged victims who trudged up the stairs after the Queen of the Third Floor. No matter: Tommy could still see Walter's expression of surprise as he came flying back toward the top of the windshield. In that split second before the roof struck his skull, the awareness that he was about to die must have been rushing up in him. It made Tommy think of that afternoon after Christmas his father waved to him from upstairs, hours before his death. Had the old man known? Tommy had a clear memory of sitting on the sled and squinting into the dark, reflecting glass of his parents' bedroom window, finding something moving inside, realizing that it was his father waving. A message of love. Tommy could see that he was torturing himself. He had wanted to be alone? He was not fit for human company.

In the spring Charlie folded the last of the other joints, put Georgie in the Steak Cellar as full-time manager, and eased into a restless semi-retirement, lunging for the telephone when Mike had some news about the new big joint on Broadway. Georgie had found a third-floor loft on West Forty-eighth Street, a big room with a high ceiling that had been everything from a sweatshop to a dance hall. There was never any question about who would manage the new place; Mike thought that Georgie understood that better than Charlie knew. From Mike's point of view Charlie was a little apprehensive about Georgie, as if he figured Georgie was a guy who would always spill the fat on the cat, but Mike thought he had a pretty good eye on Georgie at the Cellar. Georgie had a grip on the operation—better, he had the right attitude. The place was going over to the new ownership in a couple of months, but Georgie was still trying new things to keep up the interest.

As for the new place, Mike had thrown out Georgie's plans and come up with some sketches of his own. Because people were always rubbernecking and paying attention to one another's business, Georgie had the idea that they liked coming out at night to see and be seen, but that wasn't entirely true. In varying degrees, some wanted to see, and others wanted to be seen. The main room was going to be an amphitheater, with three levels, in the latest modern style, facing a semicircular dance floor. The bandstand would protrude from a proscenium arch. The dance floor would be the most brightly lighted area of the room, naturally, but as you moved up the sides or to the back, the place would darken dramatically. The partitions between the banquettes on the upper tier would be slightly higher than the partitions in the middle. When Georgie first saw the sketches, he wanted to go to bold colors, black walls and ceiling, but Mike explained things to him. The walls and ceiling were going to be rose, and the beige and dark red of the linens of the upper tier would give way to cream and pink around the dance floor. People liked luxury and comfort, which weren't the same thing, and they appreciated a bargain or, at least, the belief they were getting one. That was why the bar was going to be very dark mirrored glass, small, and up behind the third tier next to the kitchen. You'd be able to see the show from there, but not well, and when you turned the other way, your reflection in the mirror over the back bar would be so dark that it would have you almost convinced that you weren't there at all. Two-dollar minimum at the tables? No cover? A steal if it meant that you were going to feel that you had finally joined the party.

Kate wanted to call the place the Colorado Club—not even Charlie knew exactly why. She had been to Colorado years ago, she said, and it had been good for her. One name was as good as another, as far as Mike was concerned—the success of a place really depended upon the management, and they had enough of a following to get them off to a fast start.

In all, Mike thought that it was going well. At Kate's insistence, he and Charlie had gone over the shootings at Howard Beach a dozen times, trying to reconstruct everything that had happened in the weeks before, rereading the clippings from all the newspapers Mike had bought in the weeks that followed. The guy with whom Charlie had made the original deal had disappeared without a trace. Given the fact that nothing else had happened since, Mike and Charlie could not help coming to the conclusion that Tommy had killed the whole bunch, the same three who had scored so easily against Georgie. Georgie was still nervous and Kate kept saying she knew better, that things like this had to be settled, but Charlie quieted her by asking if they were supposed to stop living. The newspaper clippings identified the three as small-timers from the Bronx—the one with the machine gun didn't even have a record. The bodies hadn't been found until six the next morning, but the police had the machine gun. If anyone else had been in the garage after Charlie and Tommy, he hadn't known the value of the weapon and therefore was no one they had to worry about. Kate said she could see that everything argued that the thing was over, but they still did not know how the three dopes had found out about them, or about Georgie bringing in his boat the previous summer. Charlie and Mike had been over it, of course, not just in general conjecture but in unpleasant specifics—whether Georgie had shot his mouth off or whether a bartender or someone in one of the kitchens sold them out—and it had led nowhere. For all of his faults, Georgie knew how to do business, and none of the employees had beat it or behaved strangely after the word had got around that the boss had had trouble. It took months, but finally Kate acquiesced, and if Mike and Charlie harbored thoughts that perhaps she was getting old, they decided between them to withhold from her the information that Georgie Howe had carried a gun for protection for two months during the winter until Mike had seen it in his belt and had taken it away from him.

On Tuesday evenings Mike had dinner with his mother, and at least once during the week he made it his business to talk to Tommy. The kid was out of the fur business, fit news to be passed along on a Tuesday evening, but he was still pitching on the telephone, which was not. He was working for the Grand Street Hospital, which did not exist, soliciting for the building fund, which did. Tommy was getting ten percent of his gross, and he usually quit every day at noon, fifty to a hundred dollars ahead, enough for the rest of the day at Belmont or Jamaica. The kid was not having the best time of it. He was living downtown now; he'd gotten involved in a brawl between his landlady and a whore and wound up telling the landlady what she could do with her building. He was going through the hardest part of all, Kate said. What kind of a world was it if you could get away with murder? She didn't think it was murder, nor did Charlie or Mike, but she knew what Tommy thought it was. Tommy called her once in a while to see how she was doing, he said. It was one good sign—at least he was lonely. But aside from the job and his trips to the track, no one knew what else he was doing. One night over dinner in a hash house Mike asked him if he was seeing anybody, but the kid curled his lip and shook his head, as if to say that this was not a time in his life that he could do himself any good, and he knew it. For Mike the clearest message was that his brother wanted to be on his own, and if Mike felt hurt and could not understand the kid, at least Kate said that she was not worried about him; and the reluctance with which Tommy discussed himself made Mike's dealings with their mother that much easier for him.

What had started as a sandwich one evening when she had been all but out of control had grown into a custom that the woman anticipated from one Tuesday to the next; when the conversation slowed one week, she would ask him what he wanted to have for dinner the next. The cooking was worse, lamb chops simultaneously burned and greasy, mashed potatoes lumpy, the vegetables cold, but she insisted on doing it. She did not want to hear about business or, for that matter, not much more about

Tommy than that he was all right. She wanted to hear about David, his comings and goings. She hardly ever asked about Lillian. Mike knew that his mother had sustained another serious injury, and he knew, too, that Amy had a grasp of the truth when she said that he was wrong to coddle their mother, but the woman's pain was real. How old was she now? Nearly fifty-five? She looked sixty, and if that were not enough, Mike believed that if someone tried to engage her serious attention on the subject of remarriage, she would run out of the room with her hands over her ears. Mike could understand Tommy's situation, but he could not forgive Amy. The girl knew their mother was a sick woman, but it did not matter to her; she refused to admit that her mother's heart was open to her. So it was Mike: it was up to Mike to carry the burden. He was at the apartment off Central Park West every Tuesday a little before six, often with some trinket in hand—more likely than not, something Lillian or even Kate had picked out, a lace handkerchief, a cameo. For all he knew, he was the only person she ever touched or spoke to all week. Tommy's radio was still in the living room, and there was always a program schedule somewhere in view. From experience he knew that she was partial to WEAF, for the dial was almost always set to that station, and that when the weather was pleasant, she spent the hours in Central Park. The stories she told—tidbits, really, not even anecdotes—led him to the understanding that she loved to walk, lost in her thoughts. She talked about the Shakespeare Gardens and the boat lake, the duck pond and the zoo. He knew he could not bring himself to think about what went through her mind during those afternoons in the sunshine. He carried it with him, though, and if he entered the park on the other side to give David a stroll around the playground, he would be aware of the possibility that she was near. He dreaded that he would see her coming down the path, her mind elsewhere. Her eyes were so poor that he doubted that she would recognize him more than ten feet away. He dreaded seeing her when she thought she was alone. He dreaded discovering her as she really was.

Early in May, Charlie came down to the new place, watched the kitchen simulate a dinner hour, and gave his approval. Mike was ready. He had one hundred thousand membership cards printed, including ten thousand embossed "special member" versions for distribution in detective squad rooms, newspaper city rooms, backstage at the theaters, through the Brill Building, and in the locker rooms at Yankee Stadium, the Polo Grounds, and Ebbets Field. Tammany and Walker already knew about the place; if the boys wanted to have a look, they would be along. Ed Sullivan came in. Legs Diamond. Ruth Etting. It was a wonderful start, and in June they almost broke even. Charlie was satisfied. So was Mike. When they shut down at the start of the summer, waiters, chefs, and musicians clustered around the bar until eight the next morning, pronouncing the club a success.

IX

The fall season went beautifully. People wanted to come out. There had been three good years in a row, and it made no difference that Al Smith was beaten so badly—the smart money had expected as much anyway. If the city could not have one of its own in the White House, then it had its other heroes, starting with Hizzoner Himself; Ruth, Gehrig, and the rest of the Yankees; Dempsey and Tunney; Jolson, Cantor, and Georgie Jessel; Berlin, the Gershwins, and Cole Porter. People wanted to dance. Mike had wanted to showcase young comics and singers, but there was too much stirring at the tables that made the kids look bad; when their initial contract ran out, he didn't renew and brought in a piano player who could croon show tunes while the band was out on the fire escape passing the boo around.

The work was settling into a routine. Mike was tired, and he was still caught in the Tuesday night revolving door, but he saw that he was giving his mother something to do. Sometimes he would start feeling sorry for her again, and wind up getting drunk. Georgie was able to run the club now. Mike would sit up half the night, slowly getting drunk, letting something boil out of him—he said that to Lil once, and she seemed to understand. The drinking frightened her, but she kept it to herself. At least they did not have to worry about business. Or Tommy: when he felt like it, he took home three hundred a week—and home was a two-room suite in an apartment hotel on East Twenty-third Street. He was dressing better, and once in a while he mentioned a girl.

They made real money in December, but it grew cold after the holidays and the rivers froze over. On the third of January, Charlie Duran disappeared. The ice broke with the thaw and answered the question of what had happened to him. He had been missing for ten days. His body bobbed up between the floes, swollen to twice its normal size and so stiff they couldn't bend the arms when they wanted to get him into the wagon.

No one doubted that he had been shot; and when he thawed out, they found the bullet holes, two of them, hidden in the icy hair on the back of his head, holes so small that the gun that made them could have been hidden in the palm of his killer's hand.

Old Woman

I

"There's no doubt in my mind now that she knew everything," the voice said. "She knew what her husband did, or at least understood that it was something he couldn't bring himself to tell her. She understood, too, that it was the thing that had destroyed her parents' family. And she kept quiet not because she was frightened or because she trusted him, but because it was her part of the bargain. They never spoke of it and nobody drew up anything to sign, but it was a bargain all the same, conscious and as real as the light from that fire there."

If that had been the intention, the spell was broken; and as she had said, the wind had come up so suddenly that it felt alive as it buffeted them. Her voice was now so small in the contracting firelight that their ravaged imaginations perceived themselves (later they compared) shrinking, too, slowing down, as if they were on the edge of disappearing. "She read the papers. Her son came home with blood all over him and the story that her old crush, Charlie Duran, had been shot; and the next day the papers had it that three men had been killed in an apparent gangland slaying—newspapers used to write things like that in those days—so let's not kid each other: she knew, the old woman knew about Charlie Duran. And there was the last thing," the voice said softly. "No one ever knew what she really understood about it, not to the end of her life."

II

The police never solved the crime. They questioned everybody a dozen times, getting nastier and then trickier with each succeeding

481

interview. They never learned anything more than they could see when they pulled Charlie out of the river that blustery, mild afternoon. The cops found Charlie's wallet right where he always wore it, and if they dipped into the wad of cash he usually kept in his pocket, it was only for a windfall hundred here and there. Charlie never carried less than a grand and sometimes as much as twenty-five hundred, and when he disappeared, one of the first thoughts everybody had was that some mug had made his roll and tailed him. But the cops turned in seventeen fifty, and so robbery was not the motive. And since they could never learn anything else, and because they believed that the victim had had a more adventurous life than any of his friends seemed willing to say, the cops kept coming back. Mike wanted to hire a lawyer, but Kate advised against it. If the cops felt they were getting real resistance, they would go back over everything and maybe turn up some old employee who had a grudge and wanted to tell the cops that Charlie had been shot fifteen months before. As it was, the condition of the body had apparently led the coroner to conclude that the scar on Charlie's shoulder had been an old wound. If they learned the truth and went back over their own files, they would have been looking in an hour for the kid who had driven Charlie's car—they would have known; somebody would have talked. The weeks went on, and the cops never knew that Tommy Westfield existed.

Kate wouldn't even let him call her. He met Mike for dinner one night at Gallagher's, his first night north of Twenty-third Street in months. He had not seen Mike since Charlie disappeared, one of the old woman's first precautions, and the big guy looked lousy, drawn and pale. The corners of his mouth were turned down in a way that made him look old.

"She doesn't think you're in any danger," Mike said, "but she wants you to lay low for a while longer anyway. She knows you're worried about her, and she wants me to tell you that she's going to be all right."

"Is that the truth?"

"She sits in her chair. She talks about the old days. She told one on the old man that I'd never heard before. He wanted to get something on a guy, and suckered him up to a hotel room where a couple of Kate's girls were waiting. The photographer was along a moment later, and that did the job."

"Maybe she shouldn't be talking about that kind of stuff. It's only going to upset her. Did you ever stop to think that the old man lived in a more innocent time? You heard Charlie say that he as much as Kate taught Charlie how to live. The old man didn't teach him how to defend himself. Charlie got shot the first time because he froze when he saw Walter in the headlights. So forget the old man. The guys in the garage froze, too, and that's why I'm alive. I learned something in that garage. I can't tell you what it is—I can't even describe it. But Kate knows what it is; she learned it a long time ago."

"Where do you get this stuff?"

"We're not worried about each other's safety. We're worried about what's going on up here." Tommy tapped his head. "It's like going to different schools together, if you know what I mean."

In deference to the old woman Mike had agreed to take certain precautions when he met Tommy—making sure he wasn't being followed, and so forth—and he had been shocked to find that the kid had been a step ahead of both of them: as he had come up to the restaurant, Tommy had suddenly appeared beside him. "Why did you stop for that shine? That kid taking your bets?"

"Hey, I got my shoes shined an hour ago."

"Wanna hear what you had for lunch?" He pushed his brother through the door.

Now Tommy leaned across the table. "Think, Mike. After Charlie called you that night, did you tell anybody that I was going with him?"

"No. I didn't even take the phone away from my ear from the time he called me to the time I called you. I was alone in the office. Look, you're forgetting that Charlie himself could have spoken to anybody."

"Not that night. He was very tight that night."

"Kate says you've got nothing to worry about. If somebody wanted you, they could have had you any time. Things quieted down and we forgot about it. That was our mistake, and Charlie paid for it. It was business, strictly business."

"So where does that leave you?"

"Kate says that if it had to do with the club, we would have felt it there long ago. She thinks it's some old score Charlie never told her about. She learned a lot about him after he died. She had to start looking through his papers right away. He was a lawyer once, you know. Everything was in order. He left her a letter. He took care of all her business, but when she had to go to his desk, she said it was like being given a tour. He made sure that she would be able to understand her situation the first time she set eyes on them."

"That's one thing he learned from the old man," Tommy said ruefully.

"I suppose so. He left his papers in order. She said she turned the business over to Charlie before the old man died, so that's how long he managed them—all her properties, mortgages, leases, stocks, bonds. She's worth more than five million, by the way, according to tonight's closing prices. But she said she could see that there were many, many deals he didn't tell her about, that the figures account for but don't explain. She doesn't know who was involved. Charlie never wrote down a man's name in his life, or at least not after he met Kate."

"Writing down names don't bother me," Tommy said suddenly. "I got a list of everybody who knows I was in the car that night with Charlie."

"Including me?" Mike said.

"Including Ma! I gotta believe my eyes! I'm alive and he's dead because I was alert that night. He froze at the wheel and got shot for it—don't you think the same thing happened to him again? Mike, he got *outsmarted!* Somebody walked up behind him and went pop, pop." He made a gun of his fingers. "Be careful it doesn't happen to you."

Mike looked unhappy. "You know, all those people who knew you were in the car are accessories after the fact. Including me—including Ma. I just hope you don't have it labeled so that somebody can figure it out."

Tommy saw that he had to let it go. He was scaring Mike, but not in the way he had hoped. It was as if Mike wanted to run away and hide from it, yet Tommy thought he could see that Mike had never been different. Of course Mike was drinking again—now Tommy understood the look in his eyes. Mike still thought the old man was going to solve all his problems for him. Tommy knew from Kate that Lillian thought that their mother had Mike wrapped around her little finger, and Tommy was surprised because he had thought that Lillian had a brain. The two of them, mother and son, were bound together by the mortal wounds of their grief. If the old woman thought God was punishing her, then the man believed that he had already made the mistake—sometime, somewhere—that marked him as a failure forever. Amy had walked away from their ritual self-savagings, those almost silent sessions in which the one would scuttle from room to room on useless errands while the other would sit in the easy chair in the living room in an agony of politeness—their mother drove them crazy, Mike said, but it never even occurred to him that he could tell her, much less do something about it. If Tommy called her the next day, she would complain that she had not been able to sleep the night before and that she worried about Mike and David. Never Lillian. And if Tommy called Mike—he had done it several times, and for more than just to prove the point to himself—it was always Lillian who answered the telephone. Sometimes she'd lie and say Mike was asleep, or down in the park with the kid; but once in a while it would be too much for her, and she would tell the truth. "He made a mess of himself again last night, and this afternoon he went overboard when he tried a couple of shots for his headache."

Tommy hoped to God there was nobody after Mike.

III

They had him, all of them, the whole damned family, even Amy, and that made him the worst of the bunch, the craziest. Their hold on him was his deepest secret; Tommy did not even discuss it with Kate. He wanted to run away from the city and start his life over again, but he could not, because of them, because he was afraid that they would need him. Kate knew that part, that he wanted "to see more of the world." He knew where she had been. She had been urging him to go last fall before he got word to stay away from her; because he had not been completely honest with her about the depth of his need, he had always allowed the subject to drop.

The rest of it she knew: that he was living in a hotel because he didn't want to own anything, that he stayed in the room at night listening to the drunks and whores in the halls rather than trust himself outside. Tommy wasn't afraid that someone was coming after him or, for that matter, what he was liable to do in a bad situation, like an argument in a speakeasy. He told Kate that his nerves were shot. It was everything he could do to get to work. If he went to the track, it was only another way to be alone. Kate heard it all. For a long time he thought it was never going to stop, even after she assured him that it would have to, for the simple reason that a living human being could not continue in such a condition indefinitely. When he started talking about going out West, she showed him that the process of changing had begun. It was true. But when Charlie died, everything had changed again.

Tommy went uptown again in July. He didn't call Kate. It was a hot day, up in the nineties, and he took his time walking from Broadway over to the Drive. In the corner of his mind was the notion that he was not going to go upstairs, that he was going to hang around across the street for a while. He loved the old woman, and more now because he hadn't seen her. Some of it was pity because Charlie was gone, but only some; Tommy could recognize his own need. He didn't know why he wanted to be in her company, and so the thought of standing across the street made him feel safe.

The elevator boy did not speak until he had the doors closed. "I thought something happened to you."

"Nah. I took a little trip, that's all."

"Those detectives were here again and again, asking me if I ever noticed anything. I noticed that the old woman and Mister Duran always treated me with respect and gave me fifty dollars for Christmas. I noticed that, but since those detectives didn't seem interested in that kind of thing, I kept my mouth shut. I'm going to keep it shut, too. What do you think of that?"

They had reached Kate's floor. Tommy stepped outside, turned to him and grinned. "I think you're banging the maid."

"I remember you good now. It's no easy time with that maid, I'll tell you that much," the operator said, and let the door roll shut again.

The lady in question admitted Tommy to the apartment. "The old woman's taking a nap," Sissy whispered. "Does she know you're coming? Are you supposed to be here at all?"

"Who is it out there?" Kate yelled. "Who's at the door?"

"Harold Lloyd!" Tommy yelled back. "And if you don't get out here PDQ, I'm going to fall off this damned window ledge."

"Give me Buster Keaton any day. He's the one with sex appeal."

"Let me see if she needs anything," Sissy said. "She'll be right out. Fix yourself a drink. Everything's right where it always is."

He made one for Kate first. A year ago she had asked him if he was drinking, and he had told her the truth: no. "I like myself better when I just lie there and sweat," he had said. It was still the thing that frightened him most about being alone. Now he poured a light Scotch for himself. He really had nothing he wanted to tell her, but he wanted to loosen his tongue anyway. He would see a Dayliner out on the river, dazzling white in the sun, and it struck him that he might not be sober by the end of the day.

It took her only a few more minutes, and when she came out, he kissed her. A few minutes later he got out of the chair and kissed her again, and she told him to freshen the drinks. He said that he had not had so much as a beer in more than fourteen months, and she told him that she was not his mother. Sissy brought them lunch and told her that there were no steaks, if Mister Tommy was going to stay for dinner. Kate had six things to say about Sissy calling him "Mister Tommy," given the fact that she had been in the back seat of a car on a certain day almost two years ago.

"And what were you doin', old woman?"

"This is what I have to put up with," Kate said to Tommy.

"You deserve it."

"Do we always get what we deserve?"

"No." He seemed to deflate: they were through the preliminaries.

"Why don't we get what we deserve?"

Without taking her eyes from him, she handed her glass to Sissy for another refill. Trying to keep up with her was not just senseless: if he tried, there would be no need of steaks for dinner; the "evening" would be over within the hour.

"I've been thinking about it," he said. "I don't know what the answer is."

"Well, for a long, long time I've believed that the life I've lived started when my sister got killed—when that black man used a knife on her—and off and on through the years I've had it in my head that it would end the same way. You know that; you've heard me rant and rave about it." Sissy was in the room, at the serving cart, and now Kate waved his attention away from her. "After her Uncle Rupert was here, something in me started getting ready. I didn't know how it would come, but I understood that I was going to wind up alone, just as I began. That night completed the circle in more ways than you realize. I didn't start crying that night, but it wasn't long after. She'll tell you."

"It's true," Sissy said. "She told me why she was crying, and I told her that it was just an old woman talking and that she should shut up."

"Really?" Tommy asked.

"Oh, I never took as much of her shit as she wanted all you people to believe."

"She has her ways," Kate said.

"That's right, I do. Now, should I call about those steaks?"

"Yes, but make sure they cut a small one for me. I don't want a longshoreman's dose."

"You'll eat what I put in front of you." While Kate smiled gaily, Sissy said to Tommy, "See? She don't eat like anything but a bird anyhow, so I got to kick her old behind."

"You're a hard woman, Sissy, everybody knows that."

"He's got your number!" Kate cried. "He's got your number!"

"Well, it's my time to lie down," Sissy said. "If you folks want anything else, you either get it yourselves or just wait."

"I cried a long time," Kate said when they had heard Sissy close her door. "He'd be asleep and I'd come out here. I knew he was dead when he didn't come home the night of January third. I had thought that I was done crying, but I hadn't really begun. I found that out. Your father told me about it a long time ago, when your grandfather did himself in; but I had to find out for myself."

"I'm losing my taste for my father. Charlie left you in good shape. Look at my mother."

"Don't misunderstand your father. I knew him longer than anybody."

"When were you two lovers?"

"After his father died. We needed each other. We were never really suited. He was a bit younger than I was, and I felt that. I wasn't as smart as he was, and he felt that. There wasn't much to it, and because we were honest, we stayed friends."

"Sissy's sleeping with the elevator operator, in case you didn't know."

She laughed aloud. "In case I didn't know? Where do you think they do it? I have to listen to them!"

"When I was a boy in Mountain Lakes, my mother found some French postcards that I had hidden in a drawer. When she tried to talk to me about it, she ran out of the room and wouldn't talk to me for a week."

"Couldn't talk to you, you mean. She was ashamed. I know her longer than the rest of you, too, don't forget that. She feels ashamed whenever she comes face to face with something she doesn't understand. It's not just sex, it's everything. She was that way when your father was dying. It's a long, complicated story, but she fell out with me basically because she was ashamed.

"Listen, Tommy listen to me. I got my education in a whorehouse. I thought I was learning what was pleasing to the customers, but what I was really learning was what human beings have in their hearts. Your father learned it in other ways, just as you're learning it now, and maybe Mike will never learn it. That's why I say don't misunderstand him. You're more like him than anyone else I've ever known. I didn't see him from the time he was twelve until he was twenty one or twenty-two, and you're not that old yet; sometimes I think that in you I'm seeing him as he was when I didn't know him."

"Why is my mother crazy?"

"She was raised to be crazy. Now if you'll get me another drink, I'll tell you *why* she fell out with me—why she felt ashamed. I might as well get drunk and tell some of the dirty secrets. That's what you came here for, isn't it?"

"You're the only person I can talk to."

"Ah, you know you haven't told me a thing, don't you? Just like your father, just like him."

He fixed her another drink and made another, lighter one for himself. Still, his head was buzzing, and he knew that he wasn't fully appreciating the significance of what she went on to tell him, that when they had first met, his mother had been smitten with the handsome, dashing Charlie. They were nearly the same age, and on a train to New Orleans—when? in the winter of '07? '08?—his father and Kate had held their breaths while Tommy's mother showed the symptoms of a genuine infatuation. "She could have turned Charlie's head. She doesn't know to this day how she tested Charlie's character."

Mike had told him that their mother cried when she heard the news about Charlie. Mike had said nothing after the disappearance, and then he had had to get around to her place in a hurry before she read the story in a newspaper.

"How're you doing with the girls?" Kate asked.

"Nothing. I want to meet somebody, but there was that long stretch last year and now I've lost my confidence. Maybe I'm just rusty."

"Find yourself a pro and tell her the truth."

"Nah."

"You and your father—"

"They don't make them like you anymore, Kate."

"That's right, they don't." The old lady beamed. "You cannot imagine how good I was. I had red hair."

He had heard the story of how his father had forsworn whores and alcohol because of his own father's abuses, but not from her point of view, and so he listened intently as she covered the familiar ground. For the first time he realized that he was older now than she had been then; he had only a rough idea of how many years his grandfather had lived, but if he went on the assumption that Grandpa's birth preceded that of his oldest child by less than twenty-five years, then the old madman had been nearly forty when he had met Kate. It made Tommy believe he could smell the old goat's whiskey breath. "Did my father help my grandfather through all those drinking bouts because of the pain it caused him?"

"Your father? No, he did what he did because he alone in the family loved and understood the old gentleman."

"But my father was hurt in his boyhood."

"Yes, he was."

"This is the first time I can sense what he was like as a boy. There was none of that left when I knew him. He was just—up there. He knew everything. He had the strongest hands in the world. But I still don't understand why he married my mother. If he had been younger when he met her, I could."

"Tommy, your father and mother were a boy and a girl for many years after they were also man and wife, and father and mother."

"How did you know him when he was twelve? I mean, you were his father's mistress, and unless he tried to take you home—"

"No, he didn't," she said with a smile. "You know, sometimes I wonder why I was put on this earth. I've seen more than my fair share, wasn't smart enough to have a kid when I had the chance, and now I'm alone again. That bitch in there kicks me out of the house once in a while and I tell her I walked up to Broadway, but all I really do is go a block down the Drive and back. I have a lot of money, Tommy, and I'm going to leave it to you and Mike and Amy. It gets you even. While I'm alive you're the only family I have. No, I'll tell you the truth: everybody else I know is dead. But please, do I have to answer all your questions?"

"I'm sorry."

"I gave a speech because I love you." Then she added, "You're asking too much when you expect us to confess all our sins to you when we kept so many from each other."

They went on like that, less coherently, less importantly, and then

Georgie showed up with the steaks. Sissy had told him that Tommy was visiting, and Georgie wanted to say hello. He stayed for a drink. He said that he and Amy were going to Lake George for the month of August, when the club would be closed. He wanted to take it easy this year, he said; he wanted to get some rest, so they had rented a cabin.

"Why don't you come up for a weekend, kid?"

"And do what? Listen to the bears fart?"

"We're two of a kind, Georgie," Kate said. "You couldn't get me up there either."

"Kate, if I thought it was your cup of tea, I'd buy the joint so you could use it all year round."

"Georgie, you have no gift for bullshit."

He smiled. "Amy says the same thing."

"Was Mike at the club when you left?"

"Oh, sure."

"Was he all right?"

" 'Fit as a fiddle and ready for love.' "

"Well, have him give me a call when you get back."

After Georgie had gone, Tommy asked Kate what she thought was going to happen to Mike.

"I didn't know what you knew about it," she said. "I've already told him that he's going to lose his wife. Lillian is not the kind of woman who will go on cleaning up after him forever. If he doesn't straighten himself out, you'll have your troubles with him for years. I don't envy you. Your mother only makes him worse, and of course your sister will do what she always does. I haven't seen her in months. Where the hell does she think my money is going to go?"

"My sister is a very unhappy girl," Tommy said.

"When did you see her?"

"Six weeks ago. Georgie called and said they wanted to have me over for dinner. As long as they weren't trying to fix me up with her old roommate or something like that, I thought it would be all right. It wasn't. The two of them were at each other's throats all night."

"She wants to get married, doesn't she?"

"She wants to get it nailed down anybody can see that, but after a while it dawns on you that she doesn't even like the guy. She's constantly telling him how stupid and clumsy he is."

"You feel sorry for him?"

"Yeah, a little. I can't warm up to him. I don't care if I see him and then I don't want him crowding me when I do."

"Well, I think the man is nothing. I used to get paid for going to bed with creeps like him, and you can believe me when I tell you he's empty inside. He's playing a dangerous game with your sister. When he marries her I'll know I'm about to die, because he knows that once I'm gone she'll be able to shop around for something better. She'll do it, too. She doesn't know that about herself, but she can turn around faster than you can snap your fingers. She may be a unhappy girl,and you can feel as sorry for her as you want, but nothing bad is ever going to happen to her." She leaned around in the chair. "Hey! What the hell happened to those steaks?"

"You want your potato baked an hour and ten minutes, or don't you?" the voice came back from the kitchen. "You can't even smell them damn things yet," she grumbled. "Now, do you want a tomato on your salad?"

"Not if it's been in the icebox! You know they make my teeth ache when they're too cold!"

"What a rotten old woman," the voice grumbled.

"I love her," Kate said to Tommy, beaming.

Mike called at nine and Tommy got on the telephone for a while. You could hear the band going in the background. Mike sounded fine. Tommy asked him if he wanted to think about taking Kate to Saratoga.

She was in the kitchen and Tommy was free to talk. "Might as well. I talked to Ma, and she said she might want to do it further down the line, whatever that means. Maybe Kate will feel up to it. I didn't think so."

The old woman had wanted to prepare the dessert herself. "When I sold the house in Brooklyn and set myself up again here in town, I had a customer who got himself in the mood with this—strawberries and orange sections in orange juice and Grand Marnier. He had a beard, and it wasn't until he got it nice and juicy that he was ready to get down to business."

"You liked your work."

"I made him do it right. Oh, I see what you mean. Yes, I did. I loved my work, once I understood that the men who came to me needed me to share their secrets—that they had no place else to turn. When I was young, I tried to outsmart them and all that stuff, but then I learned that I could make more dough giving them exactly what they wanted. It took me a long time after that to realize that I wasn't just important in the scheme of things, I was necessary. Many of my customers helped build the city. When I saw that they needed me to keep going through the craziness of the rest of their lives, I stopped being ashamed and began to love my work. Do you know why I used to sniff cocaine? Charlie. He was afraid of the stuff, and it made me seem mysterious."

"He got a thrill out of buying your underwear. Mike told me that."

"And that's why he deserved a little mystery, whether he thought he needed it or not. I'm not going to tell you all a woman's tricks, because then you won't have any fun of your own, but I will tell you this: every woman knows that the first job is to make the man pay attention."

"*Every* woman?"

She laughed. "Sure. It's the most natural thing in the world to be a whore." She picked a strawberry out of the dish, and while she sucked on it, she winked. And then she blushed.

I V

Kate went to Saratoga with Mike, Lillian, and the baby, who delighted her with his running around and yelling. The nights were damp and she could feel it in her shoulders and back, but when the sun got high, around eleven o'clock, she would sit outside for an hour, and then she would be ready for the track.

Tommy came up on weekends, even though there was no racing on Sunday. He took the train on Friday nights and the last boat on Sunday afternoon. The kid's spirits were picking up, and Kate asked him if he still thought about going out West, and he said that maybe he was getting like his mother because he kept seeing it "further down the line."

"Why don't you just go out and look around? A month isn't forever."

"Nah. What would you guys do without me?"

"You worry too much, kid. You've got the weight of the world on your shoulders."

"There are no secrets from you, are there?"

"I know *all!*" She giggled.

"So why can't you pick a horse?"

"I don't have the right bloodlines, and bringing up the subject makes you a smart aleck, you little bastard."

As if to prove his point, he came up on Thursday before the Travers, and on the next afternoon had five winners in a row and thirty-two hundred dollars in his picket. Dinner that night took four hours and cost two hundred dollars, with tip, and on Saturday the kid won another five; but when Kate got back to town he called her to report that he had moved out of the hotel and into a cold-water walkup on Thompson Street, on the edges of Little Italy and Greenwich Village. If it seemed like a step downward, it wasn't: he had met a girl, he said, a little Italian with no tits and a terrific ass.

Kate laughed. "Wonderful."

"Well, it's a start."

Twenty minutes after she put the telephone down, when she was long past thinking about the kid's agony these past two years, Kate began to cry. She wasn't sure she understood the reason for it, but then she realized that she was thinking of the kid's father.

In October the market collapsed, and Kate's broker—a young man with no experience except that of the long bull market of the previous seven or eight years—advised her to cover her positions during the long slide that cold winter, believing as so many did, or so many told him, that it was only a technical correction and that there would be a rally in the spring. In that way many millions were lost, not just Kate's. She recognized what was afoot before the broker did, but for a couple of weeks she let him talk her out of selling everything, and then it was too late. She could not hold him responsible; it was worse than anything she had ever seen. Unimaginable. And as people started to lose their jobs, she could see that the thing had begun to multiply, that it would consume the world—it was just a matter of time before her real estate was swallowed up, as more and more businesses defaulted, and so on up the line, until the river of money dried up completely. She had Sissy sit down and listen to an accounting of her new situation, that in a few months or years there would be nothing at all but those few things she owned outright, her personal property, jewels, the furs in cold storage—the furniture, if it came to that. She might even have to take a smaller apartment to cut down on the rent. "I may need every cent to stay alive. I don't know how long I'm going to live; nobody in my family ever lived this long that I know of. I always thought that I'd be able to take care of you—I was going to give you a cut off the top, if you want to hear the truth. That's the way I saw it. But I'm an old woman, and I have no way of making a living. I have to think of myself first. So if you can get yourself a better deal, take it."

"Let's just see how it goes. You and I both know that it won't be easy for you without me. I got to satisfy my conscience, too."

"Help me, Sissy! I want to stay alive!"

"You should. Hold still while I kiss you now, and if you tell me I'm the first nigger ever to lay hands on you, I'll laugh right in your face, you old whore."

"That's what I am," Kate said, weeping. Sissy thought that the old woman cried a lot these days.

Mike understood the situation. For the time being, fortunately, the club seemed safe. In some ways a financial panic was not the worst thing that could happen to a nightclub, for while the real patrons were drying up, there seemed to be more people who wanted to spend a hundred dollars for a bottle of carbonated hard cider and apple juice—for those who didn't know what champagne tasted like, vintage Moët and Chandon. It was a lot more potent than the original, which gave it the virtue of putting the suckers out of their misery quickly. It wasn't something Mike enjoyed, but, these days, it was a necessary part of the business.

He had leveled with Kate: the best they could hope for, unless there was some kind of turnaround, was to keep the place running until they headed down through the break-even point, and then take what they could get for the fixtures. He could see people who were out of work hanging around on the streets and he didn't want to fire anybody until he absolutely had to; the first place he intended to economize was in the amount he and Georgie were drawing out of the place—more than they needed, money to burn, in fact. Kate knew that he had been paying his mother's rent for the past six months, but what he was hoping to be able to do was pull enough money out of the club for all of them to live on, especially Kate. After her capital was gone, she would be helpless. He would have to take care of his mother first, and if there was anything left over after that, then he could think of her. But that would be a third household on his back. His mother was all but broke; she had a few pieces of jewelry and a paid-up insurance policy. Kate understood everything. Tommy had lost his job long ago, but at least he had caught on at a garage where Georgie knew someone. The kid was fixing cars. He was making ends meet and he said he liked the work, but it was fixing cars all the same.

Beyond that, Georgie was not much help. For a long while after things started going sour he was almost out of his mind, like one of those men on the *Titanic* who put on women's clothes to save themselves. One night he and Mike got drunk; the place was closed and the band was gone, but the porters were working in the main room and there was the usual late-night, early-morning noise coming out of the kitchen. When Georgie got drunk, his hair fell over his brow, his eyelids went to half-mast, his mouth fell open, and for some reason you took more notice of his Adam's apple. He was afraid the world was going to roll right from under them. "Like in the circus; you know, those big balls the tigers get on? Have another shot. Those big balls they get on and backpedal, but the ball goes forward?"

"You better get married, Georgie, if you're getting balls on the brain."

"Ha, ha." He grabbed the bottle and filled Mike's glass. "I'm talking about the world, I'm talking about human civilization! Everything's sliding away! People who have worked and planned all their lives are finding that what they've been heading for has just vanished. What the hell are they supposed to do?" Suddenly he let out a shout and slapped the bar. "Mike! You tell me! What are they supposed to do?"

Mike turned toward him. Georgie was staring at himself in the smoked mirror over the back bar. He was in a mad rage—but at the same time he was more in love with himself than ever; Mike could see it so clearly that he would remember the whole incident when he was sober.

"Maybe you need a shower before you go home tonight, Georgie. Let a cab take you to a bathhouse."

He slapped the bar. "No, damn you, take me seriously! You, Michael Westfield, you tell me what these people are supposed to do!"

Mike hadn't been called Michael since the Mountain Lakes School for Individual Instruction, and it made him realize how drunk he was. Perhaps it was better to give Georgie what he wanted. "Well, start over, I suppose. Try to get a new slant on things. Take what you can get. Isn't that what we've always done?"

"The game's a lot more serious, Mike." He was still looking in the mirror. "Did you ever stop to think that maybe things are going to keep getting worse? That they were getting worse even before the crash and we didn't know it? There's going to be another war, you know. This time they're going to bomb cities. They can't wait to try it. The whole world could go up in flames."

"I thought you were the guy who was going to live forever."

Georgie glowered at Mike. The story about that had gotten around a long time ago, but apparently he still didn't like being reminded. He reached for the bottle again and tried to pour Mike another shot, but Mike got his hand over the top of the glass. "Come on," Georgie said. "You might as well. You're too drunk now to do anything but keep drinking."

"A light one." Georgie poured a good two fingers. "You're drunker than I am, you stiff."

"Oh, no," Georgie said slowly. I'm never as drunk as you. That's one thing you can depend on. You'll never catch me as drunk as you."

Mike rocked back. "You're an insulting son of a bitch. That was an insult, wasn't it?"

"Naw. I was only kidding. Where would I be without you? You and Charlie taught me this business."

"We thought we were getting Tommy, but we got you instead." He lifted his glass. "Hell, we don't even have Charlie."

In the mirror he could see Georgie watching him, his eyes hooded over like a bird's. Georgie was obviously having thoughts of his own, and Mike had a moment of real unease.

He remembered it the next day, looking at his tongue in the mirror, and when he was on Riverside Drive and Kate asked how Georgie was doing, Mike thought of it again when he answered that he thought Georgie was doing fine.

Now Georgie had swung over to the other side, to a kind of wild optimism. He wanted to believe that they could save the club—he wanted to build up the place. But at the same time he wanted to work the suckers, push the champagne, kite the tabs, cut back on the food, buy cheaper cuts. He needed constant dissuading. Mike would roll home at four in the morning, bouncing off the walls as much from exhaustion as drunkenness, and he wouldn't be able to get out of bed the next afternoon before five o'clock. At that time of day, there was only one thing he wanted for breakfast. And if Lillian was in the kitchen, she would stare, or have something to say. Most of the time he was better off keeping his own mouth shut.

"Don't you think you're overdoing that stuff?"

"Leave me alone, for Christ's sake. Don't you think I have enough problems?"

"You're living on that shit! I notice you don't go over to your mother's smelling of liquor!"

"The hell I don't! Shut up, will you? I'm trying to keep us all alive!"

"Don't shit me! You're trying to kill yourself. You know you're not your father—can't you get it into your head that you're not your grandfather, either?"

He might stop for a couple of shots on his way to his mother's, but if she ever smelled anything on his breath, he had not detected so much as a glance from her. Not that that made his life much easier; now his mother expected to see David at the weekly dinners. Because he heard so much yelling at home, David was afraid of his father, and that made Mike feel guilty and tense. He would try to talk to the kid, but David would pull away, and then Mike would pull away, and Mike would start thinking of the other David—once he caught himself thinking that it was the same thing all over again, but he didn't know what he meant by it.

And then getting the kid home again was a problem, because Lillian would be there—again, with something to say. She would not make her peace with the weekly dinners. She would say nothing about them now, but there was always something else. She did not like staying at home; she did not like missing all the "excitement," as she called it. He knew she was young and he knew, too, even if he would not admit it to her (she accused him of it), that he was avoiding her. And it was not just so he could stop at a speak on the way downtown, although that was true. She did not seem to see what was happening to him, or she would not believe it, which was worse. He wasn't succeeding. He wasn't holding things together. The club was eventually going to close; he didn't know what they were going to do then. All she could do was complain, and the complaining made the kid worse. She wouldn't listen to reason. Mike didn't know why he was alive. If he walked into the club and found everything running smoothly, he'd want to stay all night.

Georgie said he was having the same trouble. He wanted to talk less about it because Amy was Mike's sister, but the truth was that she would call up to check on Georgie or drop in because she "just happened to be in the neighborhood."

"You know what your sister does all day?" Georgie asked him one night. "She sits around reading magazines all day. The pile of magazines tipped your brother off. Boy, he's a bright kid. When he was over for dinner that time, he just called her on it. 'You spend all day reading this shit, don't you?' he said. She hasn't worked in eighteen months; she's never just in the neighborhood. She figures that if she can catch me saying I'm here when I'm not, she'll have evidence that I'm two-timing her. You know how I'm sure? I noticed something about her. You won't believe this. She won't come out of the flat at all unless there's a meal in it. And then she asks me, 'Is my ass getting fat, Georgie?' I don't know what would happen if I told her the truth."

Mike laughed. "If she thinks you're stepping out on her, all she has to do is ask me. Doesn't she think I'd tell her if you were?"

"I don't know if she'd believe you. She probably thinks we're in something together."

"That's a sickening idea. Tell her I'll punch you in the nose. She'll believe that."

"Maybe, but it'll keep. I'm going to sit here awhile. Keep me company." He poured another couple of drinks.

It went on like that through the winter.

"You're saying now that she knew this, too? That she knew what was going on and still she did nothing?"

"No, what I'm saying is that she saw that something was happening, which is different," the old woman said, her voice small in the darkness. "At that point, the rest of us were only aware of so much. The important thing is that she kept silent."

"Why?"

"Well, there was the thing between us. Now I can understand how she saw me. Maybe she believed somewhere inside that it could be begun over. And finally, you have to remember that her humiliation was complete. Mike paid her expenses, gave her cash, listened to her complaints. I'm certain that she knew she was a complainer, but now I can see that she was in genuine emotional pain all of her life. She was broke and alone, helpless, exactly as her father had predicted. Given what her son was doing for her, I'm sure she felt she had no right to speak. I don't know, I'm beginning to suspect that she didn't know how."

"What did she do with herself? How did she occupy her time?"

"She shopped. She walked for miles. It was the depression, remember. This part of it, before Mike moved back in with her, took two full years. It was very subtle. The other one was always two or three moves ahead."

The young man saw that she did not want to say the man's name. It was not hatred or guilt, although it seemed clear that she felt those things: no, she had decided that he was never going to touch her again, even from beyond the grave. She was glad he was dead.

"Maybe he used that, too, the way she was, what she did, the orderliness and regularity of her habits. She always read the Herald-Tribune *in the mornings, and after the* World *folded, she bought the* World-Telegram. *It wasn't the same paper, but that was the way she did things. She loved the radio. Radio was still new then and there was an excitement about it. She was the one who told us to listen to Amos 'n Andy. In her own way she kept up with things, the things that made life better anyway—more than any of the rest of us she could see how life was changing, not just the hard times but the permanent changes. These gave her comfort.*

"I remember that she would go through the newspapers for the best prices, even taking the Journal-American *or the* Mirror *out of the trash baskets for the advertisements, and that night she would plan her rounds for the next day. She had a cloth shopping bag, but sometimes she had her arms full when she came home, two or three miles. It was her way of helping. She had holes in her shoes. I understand that during the war she would wait in line for hours for cigarettes, sugar, and coffee."*

"I came along after," the young man said, *"but I heard the same stories."*

"What was she like to live with at the end of her life?"

"I remember hearing the radio late at night. There were five of us in that little house in Hempstead and she had the smaller of the two bedrooms. We kids had the big bedroom, and my parents slept on a folding couch downstairs in the living room. She'd be awake day and night. She had something the matter with a nerve in her face and it caused her a lot of pain. Are you afraid that she was bitter?"

"I know she was bitter, but she had no right to be. She was told the truth."

"She knew?"

"Tommy told her—excuse me, that's how I knew him. He was always Tommy to me, and I'll remember his smile for the rest of my life. But he told her right away, and she stared at him as if he were crazy. He didn't see her for years after that, and then later she never acknowledged that conversation. She wanted the romantic legend to go on. If she acknowledged the sins of her children, then she would have to acknowledge the sins of her husband, too, as well as her complicity in them, and she wasn't in a position to acknowledge the sins of anyone."

"Why not?"

"After a certain point in her life she was unable to accept responsibility for anything she did, and so she did not understand why any of these things happened to her. You see, everything conspired to make her feel helpless, and finally she lost the thing that her husband had cherished in her above all."

"And what was that?"

"It took me a long time to understand it. It was the thing that gave her value in the scheme of things. What she lost was her faith. Life was more cruel to that whole generation than any of them ever dreamed."

V

The gas station laid him off, and Mike offered a slot in the club, but Tommy said no and the big guy didn't press him for an explanation. Mike knew that Tommy was keeping away from him, and he knew why, too; but he was too ashamed of himself to allow the kid to put his feelings into words. Tommy was keeping away from his mother for the same reason. And Lillian, too: her panic had turned her into a shrew. Tommy had tried to talk to her once, but she cut him off. "Oh, no! I'm not putting up with that stuff! I've seen this all my life and I know all about the way a drunk can lie, whine like a baby, and then steal the pennies off your dead grandmother's eyes! I've already seen my share!"

"You're going to ruin your life," Tommy said disgustedly.

"That's my business, kiddo! That's my business!"

So, except for visits to Kate, he stayed downtown. Kate saw that Mike was worse, but there was nothing she could do. As angry as Lillian was, she was not wrong about her husband. Kate herself did not feel much sympathy for him, for there were too many others who were suffering and not responsible for it. There was a Hooverville right beneath her window, down by the river. She had not see children fed and dressed so badly since her own childhood, and there were men sleeping under newspapers on the park benches—Hoover beds and Hoover blankets, they called them.

When he lost his job, Tommy did not tell her, hoping that he would catch on somewhere; he didn't, and one afternoon when he returned to his apartment, he found that the landlord had put a padlock on the door. Tommy wanted to call Mike, but this was his night at their mother's, and Tommy did not want to deal with them together. He had only a dime in his pocket anyway, half of it for a telephone call, the other half for a subway ride. Kate told him to come up right away.

For the next six months she covered his rent and he felt terrible about it, not just because he was taking her money, but because he felt that he had maneuvered her into indulging him. If he had avoided the subject of moving into her spare room, becuase he did not want to see Mike on his visits here, then he had made it clear that he wanted to stay downtown to conclude his business with Angela. Beneath the surface of every love affair is a battle-to-the-death, and this one cost Kate Regan nine dollars and twenty-five cents a month. At those rates, she said, she was glad she didn't have to see his place.

"Is she feeding you, at least?"

"Angela? Sure. I'm over there twice a week; she comes by at least once. I come up here. Occasionally I see my mother. Sometimes I go over to the Bowery and get on a breadline. I ain't ashamed of that. What makes me sick are the people who think they're too good to get on a breadline."

"Cut it out. You do things to yourself that you wouldn't do to a dog."

Angela worked for New York Life and lived in Little Italy. She'd been a virgin when they met and had cried bitterly when he'd pulled her pants down and forced himself into her; but now she was the girl who performed fellatio on him in her kitchen while her parents slept on the other side of the wall and who shrieked so much in bed that the poet across the airshaft told him that he had not heard such carryings-on in a Berlin whorehouse. She didn't want to let go of him, but at the same time she was not willing to solve their problems. Birth control was a sin but as long as he had the rubber on, the sin was on him. It was that kind of love on both sides. She did not love him enough to do anything about it, and the only real pain he felt was in the knowledge that she really was getting the best of it by telling him he was important to her when all she was doing was placating him. For a while at the beginning he had thought they had something going, something sweet, and now it made him feel as if he were in prison.

In the fall he went around to the local Democratic headquarters and told them that he was an alderman's grandson with experience on the telephones, and they booted him uptown where he made five dollars a day hammering contributions out of the party faithful. He also met a girl from the Lower East Side named Marsha Feldman, who said she was a Communist. Kate knew what he was up to, but as she said, at least she was starting to get something for her money. He told her that he had lousy thoughts about himself, but she misunderstood and said that it was only normal for his age. Marsha kept telling him that a great world crisis was coming, and Angela was sure that Christ was coming. Between the grunts of one and the shrieking of the other, Tommy had his own opinions. When the Roosevelt money ran out, he let Marsha take him around to a publisher on Eleventh Street. He had more of the stuff

Tommy was getting from her, what the ruling classes were doing to the downtrodden masses. One night he figured out that Marsha was even less than she had ever hinted. They were riding the trolley across town after some kind of discussion group when he realized why so many guys who were not fairies had been staring at him, and he got up and reached for the cord that rang the bell that signaled the operator.

"Where are you going?"

She had stiff, unwashed hair and Tommy suspected that she outweighed him by twenty pounds. He was suddenly heartsick over Angela, whose dumbness at least was the dumbness of good intentions. He leaned over the wicker seat and looked into Marsha's eyes. "Did you know, if you were a guy, you'd be a creep?"

That was the night he went down to Angela's and knocked on the door—after midnight, all of them asleep. He did not know what was wrong with him. Mr. Sabella did not speaka da English so good, but he got Angela out of bed. She came to the door in her nightgown, no robe, not awake, and asked Tommy what he wanted. *You're not supposed to be here now; why are you out of your place?* written all over her. That her dumbness had his visit in uncannily exact perspective only made him angrier until he saw that this was the measure of him, running back and forth between these two klutzes. He was as big a loser as his brother. Before the night at Howard Beach he had been living with his mother, a kid, like a kid; he would be there yet—or he would have manufactured an incident that would have allowed him to break with her the way he had, which was childishly.

Angela woke up enough to realize that he was upset about something, but if she became alert enough to see that she wasn't getting a straight story from him, she kept that to herself. When she said good-night to him an hour later, she was telling him she loved him and that she'd be worried about him until she saw him the next afternoon.

Three weeks later he received a postcard from Marsha's publisher friend. Apparently he didn't see much of her or had been given a different picture of the relationship than the one Tommy had. He wanted to see Tommy, and Tommy went up there the following week, and the guy offered Tommy a job. The guy was about fifty-five, with curly gray hair, and he smoked English Ovals. Tommy had forgotten that about him.

"I want to get one thing straightened out. I haven't seen Marsha in three weeks, and that suits me fine."

"It's none of my business."

"I need work," Tommy said. "I don't want any trouble."

The man lowered his eyelids in a way that reminded Tommy of Georgie Howe—it was the look of being harpooned. With Georgie,

Tommy had learned that you could not let up if you wanted to make sure the message got across.

"I want the job. I'm honest and I work hard. I like to keep moving. I'm a good salesman and I'll make money for you, but I got to have this understanding. I don't want you thinking Im beautiful or something."

"You're a lout."

"But I'm no fag." Tommy laughed. "Hell, I ain't even a Communist, but I can sell this crap. I can sell anything."

"Really?"

"Really. Want to pay me a commission?"

"Want to take less salary?"

"You'll change your mind after a month."

"Take my offer and we'll discuss it in *three* months."

"I'll see you Monday."

In a month Tommy was given a raise on the understanding that there would be no more talk of a commission, but perhaps it meant that he had reached the low-water mark. Four years ago he had been making fifty dollars a day; now, with his twenty percent raise, he was making six dollars a week, and glad of it.

In June, Angela told him she was pregnant, and he did not waste any time with her. Nothing had changed between them; they had not even had an intelligent conversation in weeks. He told her that he was not going to marry her, and that what she wanted to do about the baby was up to her, but that he would cover her expenses.

"Where are you going to get the money?"

"I'll get it, don't worry."

"Where? From your boyfriend?"

"Maybe the parts you think I'm missing are the parts that make babies, kid. Be graceful, cut your losses."

"I hate you!"

"Go sleep with your rosary beads."

Mike gave him the number of a doctor in Brooklyn, a real doctor who was probably tired of getting paid in promises, and because she was only two weeks late, he gave Angela a shot and told her to go home and soak in a hot tub. Tommy walked her to her door—under the circumstances, she said she didn't want him to come inside; he knew he was being had, but he felt just awful anyway—and then he didn't see her again for four days.

He knew they were finished, but she wanted to pretend a little longer. She had had a heavy and painful menstrual flow, and insisted to him that she had "seen something" in the toilet. Lillian had told him that a fetus was microscopic at that stage, but Angela would have none of it. He saw that she only wanted to punish him, He told her not to come around anymore, to see other guys, and she went away looking as if he had just sentenced her to death.

His pity overwhelmed him ten days later and he left work an hour early and went uptown to wait for her at the Fourth Avenue entrance of the New York Life building. She didn't see him, and he had to chase after her for thirty feet before she turned around. He had been through it with her so many times in the past that at once he could see that he had stepped back into a life that he had wanted to end because so many tiny elements of it drove him frantic.

She seemed glad to see him, although a bit hesitant, almost frightened of him. He took her to a diner, and at first he thought that he had made a mistake, because the place started filling up with its dinner regulars and the noise of the conversation and hailed greeting and clattering dishes made it impossible to hear her; but then he saw that she was purposely sitting back from the table and keeping her voice low—she had something to tell him, she said. As he sat there listening, he had to ask himself how long it would have taken her to get in touch with him to tell this story, which was about "being talked into' going out on a date the previous weekend, and the man she met. Angela had difficulty saying the words, and there were things that she couldn't remember because she had gotten drunk; but she felt different now, she said, and she supposed she was going to see the fellow again. Tommy stayed silent, waiting to see how long she dared extend the moment. She wanted Tommy to expose the pain she thought she was inflicting and surrender to her forever. She lived her life as if she were still a little girl in school, doing everything expected of her; she had her stories and she stuck to them. The pain he felt was nothing like what she might be thinking. He was trying to accept the fact that she had no character, and maybe not even decency.

He walked with her to the subway station and stopped at the top of the stairs to tell her there. She seemed to think that he was going home with her, or taking her to his place.

"I don't want to see you anymore. This was a mistake. We're only going to hurt each other."

For a moment she was in a panic, but then her mouth tightened so much her lips turned white. "Go to hell, Tommy Westfield! I hope you never have another day of luck in your life!"

So he was not surprised the next week when he learned from Kate that Lillian had thrown Mike out of the house and that the big guy, drinking all the time now, had moved across town to Tommy's old room and was giving their mother a hell of a time.

VI

He didn't go around to Lillian's until after he had talked to Mike first; Mike saw that he was attending to the question of family loyalty, but what Tommy really had on his mind was getting both sides of the story. She said that she was finished with Mike, and because Tommy had already seen the condition his brother was in, he was not prepared to argue.

He was not prepared for her rage either. She did not want to hear how Mike was; she said she had warned him for years that she had had enough drunken binges in her childhood. Tommy remembered. He could remember, too, telling her that her yelling was making things worse for Mike. But Tommy had just come from the apartment across town, where Mike was liquoring up for another evening of the weeps. He loved her. Didn't she know what she was doing to him? This was halfway through the bottle. Toward the end of the night he might throw himself into a fury—there was already a broken lamp; their mother said it had been an accident, but Tommy knew that his brother had taken some kind of half gainer over his own feet. Their mother thought that Mike was going through something and that he would get over it, but Tommy had to believe his eyes. His mother was consoling herself with a lie the same way his brother was doing it to himself with booze.

"He smells!" Lillian yelled. "Stinks! Dirty, filthy—! That's when he thinks he can put his hands on me. Did you smell his breath? What do you think he can do when he can't even stand on his own two feet? Well, she can have him. They can sleep together, for all I care. They deserve each other."

He couldn't recall anything of the feeling he had had for her when she had been Mike's girl. She had smiled more—now Tommy wasn't even sure he liked her.

It took Mike a week to get back to work, and he was shaky on his pins all that first night, but he kept it under control, going one step at a time, until the band blew its last riff. Georgie had done a pretty good job; at least he had not served the customers any horsemeat. They had made the decision to try to hang on until Repeal, and now they did not know if they had done the right thing, for there were some weeks when Mike, Georgie, and Kate had less than forty dollars to split among them.

The next night was better, and even the glass he kept at the end of the bar looked better. Georgie had some friends in, and when the doors closed, they kept going, sitting around a table, Georgie running up to the bar for drinks. They heard about Mike's troubles; they had stories of their own. One guy had been through a particularly messy divorce, and the prospect of going through a similar ordeal with Lillian revealed a new dimension of despair to Mike. Georgie took him home, stopping for a shot at an after-hours along the way. Georgie brought him upstairs. Mike decided not to go to bed right away, but to find something on the radio and sit for a while. He kept the Scotch on the top shelf of a cupboard in the kitchen, more for the sake of keeping it out of his mother's sight than out of her reach—she wouldn't do what Lillian had done, pour the stuff down the toilet.

He was up for another couple of hours and did not get into bed until nearly five o'clock. He was sick the next day and did not get into the club until after eight o'clock. Georgie told him to go home—he looked as bad as he felt.

Instead, he called Lillian. He had not seen David since she had told him to get out.

He had sent her a check; she had received it, she said.

"I can't stand this, Lil. This is hell for me."

"I won't even discuss it with you until you quit drinking. You're no good to yourself or anybody else the way you are. Hell, you've been drinking today. I can hear it. I can hear it when you've had only one—but how many have you had today? Do you even know what day it is?"

"You know, I don't have to take this from you. I haven't done anything that lets you wreck my life simply because you feel like it. I can move back in any time I want. And you can't stop me. It's the law."

"We'll see about that, I'll have the cops here, and we'll see."

"You're my wife! I can do what I want!"

"The hell you can! You haven't been *able* to do anything for months. You're not going to treat me this way. I'm a human being and you're going to treat me with respect!"

"You haven't got an ounce of sympathy in your whole body."

"Not for a drunk, I don't. Listen to you, for Christ's sake. You haven't got any respect for yourself, drooling and sitting in your own stink. Even your own brother is disgusted with you. You want to see David? What is he going to see? A filthy, unshaved drunken bum, which is who you are. And you know it. You haven't got the honesty to admit it."

"I'm hurt inside!"

"I've been hearing that for years. When are you going to grow up? Your father's dead and Charlie's dead. I miss Charlie as much as you do, but I've gotten over it. What the hell is the matter with you? You'd rather spend your time sitting in that club drunk and sorry for yourself. These are bad times for everybody, not just you."

"You're full of shit. I sold my car, I go to work with a dollar in my pocket, I haven't had a new pair of shoes in three years. I've been supporting three households—"

"Don't take credit for Kate. It was her money that got you started—

that got you out of the gutter. Do you know what she thinks? If you haven't had the courage to face it, I wouldn't be surprised. She's seventy-two years old, Mike. She tells me that you break her heart every time she sees you. The best she can say about you is that 'it's the way of the world.' Do you hear that, Mike? She was willing to close the club—remember? You and Georgie wanted to keep it open. You wanted to hang on, you said; it's the phrase you always used. What are you holding on to? What is so precious that you're allowed it to crush you?"

"Is this the best you can do for me?"

"Don't give me that martyr crap. You're a drunk."

"What the hell are you? Not even a whore treats a man this way."

"The only reason Kate didn't treat Charlie this way was because he had some self-respect and he loved her."

"He had something to love."

"Don't come around here, Mike. You're just ugly," she said, and hung up.

He was out of work another week before he could get himself straightened out again.

Tommy had a vacation coming, and Mike talked him into taking the middle two weeks in August so that the two of them could go up to Saratoga at least one more time. He thought he would have trouble with his mother, leaving her alone, but she told him that he needed a vacation after what he had been through. He sent Lillian the cash he had, a little over a hundred dollars, and pawned a gold watch she had given him in the old days. It raised a surprising hundred and fifty dollars, enough to get the two of them started.

He was pretty well dried out now, he thought. He would sip a little beer during the day if he felt like drinking, and at night he would pace himself, one highball an hour—no straight shots, nothing on the rocks. Some mornings he was even clearheaded. He had lost weight and he felt weak, but he knew he would get it all back, eating right and taking some exercise. The worst was on his face, and he knew it: he looked drawn, and the bags under eyes had sunk into permanent, though faint, webs of wrinkles. There was a vein on his nose that concerned him, too.

The kid hadn't seen him in a month, and there was no concealing his shock and despair. Mike threw his arm around Tommy's shoulders.

"We're going to have a rest. I'm going to build myself up."

"Suits me. But tell me when you're going to start roadwork. As soon as you're out of the room, I'm going to roll over in bed and start squeezing my banana."

"Well, maybe we'll get lucky in that department, too."

It was the first thing Mike had said about other women since the breakup, and it made Tommy think that maybe he was beginning to really come around.

They had not tried to pick horses together in years and their limited bankroll made them cautious, and on the first day they did little more than make their expenses, but on Tuesday Mike built a three-horse parlay and put their roll up to more than six hundred. It gave Mike some confidence, and at the end of the week they had enough to get Tommy a seat in a card game at their hotel. The game was strictly seven card hi-lo, and after he got a feel of the game, Tommy ran a string of perfects and near-perfects that had people folding their cards and sitting out in the hope he would cool off. The old man had taught Mike that a hot streak could last only as long as the player's energy and concentration did not flag, and Tommy lasted about an hour before it started to run the other way and the two of them realized he had to tighten his play. When Tommy ran second-best a half hour later with two thousand dollars in the pot, he picked up what remained of his pile and passed it over his shoulder to his brother. One of the old bookmakers at the table wanted to know how much the kid had won, but Mike said they weren't going to count it until they were in their room. There wasn't going to be any trouble, but it was a good idea anyway—you never wanted it getting around that you made a big score. The man took a look at Mike and decided to back off. Mike had been having such a good time this week that he had forgotten about drinking for days at a time, with the result that he was as sober as he had been in months. Even Tommy said he looked more like himself.

In the room they spread the money on the bed for easier sorting, and then it took them ten minutes to count it all. Eight thousand. Now Mike thought of a drink. But the money had him thinking of other things as well, and he started talking as they put the notes into neat piles again.

"We put it all in the safe downstairs. Leave ourselves enough for a good steak somewhere. I don't want to make a mess of myself. Why don't we think about not talking about this? If we do what we've usually done, giving this one a grand and that one five hundred, we're going to spread it too thin for it to do anybody any real good. In these times, eight grand is an important chunk of money."

Tommy smiled. "I'm listening."

"I don't have any ideas yet," Mike said, "but if we start thinking, we might come up with something. We can think about clearing out tomorrow, too, while we're ahead. Who knows, maybe our luck is finally starting to change for the better. I'm sick and tired of being behind the eight ball."

Tommy was still smiling. Mike could see that he liked everything he had heard.

The next day they decided that there were too many good horses at the Spa this year for them to quit before Tommy had to go back to work. But they decided, too, to go easy on their stake, and not carry on like a couple of sailors—or cowboys, as their father used to say. They had a fair week, going down five hundred Monday and Tuesday, getting it back on Wednesday, winning exactly one dollar on Thursday, five thousand on Friday, and throwing back another thousand on the Saturday of the Travers. They had twelve grand. Without making any announcements, Mike allowed the last of the booze to boil out of his system. In the mornings he walked all through the village, stretching his legs, making his muscles work. He was thirty-four and he had turned his body into a prison. But he could feel himself getting stronger, and he could see that his attitudes were changing.

He felt lousy about Lillian, and now that he was a couple of bucks ahead, he felt guilty, too. He had seen David once in the eight weeks of the separation—the kid had a toy sailboat, and they took it into the park on the Fourth of July—and now that he had his head clear, Mike understood how much the boy added to his life.

He had not seen Lillian since the holiday, either. Or talked with her. The tension had been too much for him, and after he got David back to the apartment he headed to the nearest speak. And when he had his snoot full he got her on the telephone and started calling her names. She told him that she was tired of his bullshit and wanted him to keep away from her for good. She hung up, and when he called back, she told him she meant it; she was not going to put up with a drunk. She didn't want David seeing what his father had become. He was silent and she asked if he was listening. He said yes. She said good-bye.

The next day he was worse, having convinced himself that as long as he didn't call her again to confirm what he had already heard, it wasn't really true.

But now he was sober. The first thing he was going to do was redeem that watch—he had begun to feel badly about that, too. Then he wanted to send Lillian five hundred to make her life a little easier. Tommy could make even better use of five hundred. Mike wanted to keep the account straight, and the kid needed clothes. That left eleven thousand, which was plenty.

VII

"You'd better call your sister," their mother said.

"What's wrong?" He had Tommy with him. They had stopped at a bakery for one of her favorites, a mocha cream layer cake. Their mother was sitting on the couch—she looked as if she had not moved in a week. The place looked just as bad. It was Sunday evening and the drapes were drawn; there was the smell of dust in the air and the newspapers were piled on the end table. She had not taken out the garbage and there was that smell, too, coming out of the kitchen.

"Call your sister! I just don't want any more trouble!"

"Is somebody dead?" Tommy asked. "What's wrong?"

"Are Lillian and David all right?"

"Yes, yes, I suppose. Call your sister—please! I don't want any more trouble. I am sick at heart over this."

"Ma, if it's that serious, why the hell didn't you come up to Saratoga and find us? We were having lunch every day in the clubhouse—you would have walked right to our table."

"Let me call Amy." Mike said.

Amy picked it up on the third ring and he identified himself. "Ma told me to call you."

"Not me, brother! I'm as dumb as you are! Are you drunk or sober? Tell me now."

He cringed with humiliation. "I'm sober."

"Well, call Lillian! Let her explain it to you. She won't talk to me. Yeah, that's right, call her. And don't be surprised by the voice you hear!"

"Come on, Amy, what the hell is this?"

"Don't pull that on me, you drunken bum! If it wasn't for your goddamned drinking, none of this would have happened. You don't know how much trouble you're in!"

"Well, thanks for the help. I come home and find Ma sitting in a mess—"

"To *hell* with her! Let this be the end of it. I hate your guts. I hate all of you—you, her, Tommy, and most of all, that old man you love so much. Talk to Georgie. Oh, go to hell!"

"Georgie?" The line was dead.

"What's this about Georgie?" Tommy asked.

"I'm going to find out, kid." He wasn't fooling anybody; suddenly he was scared to death. He knew what was happening a moment before it actually occurred: he dialed his own number, and Georgie Howe said hello.

"This is Mike. Let me talk to Lillian."

"She doesn't want to talk to you, Mike."

"Don't give me that shit! Put my wife on the phone!"

"Those days are over, big fella. Now why don't you meet me down at the club? We'll talk about it there."

"We'll talk about it *there,* where I can see her face!"

"She doesn't want to see you, Mike. She told you that. You and I have other business to talk about, so why don't you meet me at the club? If you come here, you're only going to make trouble for yourself."

"Is David there?"

"You're in no position to ask questions. Meet me at the club in, oh, two hours, and maybe you'll be able to salvage something of this for yourself."

"An hour," Mike said.

"I have something to do," George purred. "I'll see you in two hours. Don't come here—somebody's liable to get hurt."

He was gone and Mike put down the receiver. He could feel Tommy staring at him. "When do you see him?"

"Two hours."

Now Tommy moved. "I got the picture," he said. "Let me at that phone. You lost your wife some time ago. This guy is really stealing something else—and not just from you. This is serious."

Mike watched Tommy dial Kate's number. "Hey, yeah, it's me. I'm calling from my mother's, but never mind that. Are you all right?" He listened. "Yeah, we won twelve grand, but what does that mean now? Tell me how you got the news." He was silent again. "We just walked into it now. Mike's going to meet with him in two hours." Another pause. "You're damned right I will. And I'll call you just as soon as we're out of there." He said good-bye. "Georgie didn't break the news to her until he was sure we were going to take the second week up at the Spa. You'll like this. He showed up at an old woman's apartment with a pair of goons. I'm going with you."

"No, you're not. He's mine. I own him."

"No!" their mother cried. "I don't want anybody going to jail!"

"What the hell is the matter with you?" Tommy yelled. "The guy waited until Mike was out of town to move in on his wife and child and business. What he didn't figure is that Mike would come back sober. Look at him. What do you expect him to do about this, sit down and have a drink?"

"Don't talk to me that way!"

"Georgie poured a lot of booze into me," Mike said.

"We underestimated him. He's not only smart, he's tough."

"The toughest of the bunch," Mike said. "He's going to set me up."

"He's going to try," Tommy said.

"He knows I'm sober. He heard my voice. He knows I won't stay away."

"There's only one other way to do it," Tommy said.

Mike looked at him sharply. "They say that at an electrocution the smell is like roast loin of pork. I'll be the first guy they'll be looking for."

Tommy laughed. "At the right time you'll be having dinner with the cardinal, the mayor, and the police commissioner."

"I don't want that kind of talk!" their mother shouted. "I don't want that kind of talk in my house!"

Tommy turned on her. "What the hell do you think we are, a couple of Eagle Scouts?" He snapped his fingers in front of her eyes. "Wake up, Ma, you've been hypnotized. The old man might have been able to laugh it off and take you to Delmonico's for dinner, but we can't—we don't know where our next meal is coming from!"

She got up from the couch and tried to make for the bedroom, but tommy grabbed her arm. She was in tears, and he let go of her at once. "I keep thinking about that baby," she said. "I'm sorry, but I do."

He grabbed her again and turned her around to his brother. "Look at this baby, Ma! He weights two hundred pounds and we're all trying to keep him from taking his next drink, but he's your baby—you think of him! You think of him now!"

"Leave her alone," Mike said. "This is my problem. I want to handle it myself."

"You'll have to fight me first, Mike, I mean it."

"Fight!" their mother cried. "Fight! That's all you know."

"There isn't going to be any trouble, Ma," Mike said. "There isn't," he said to Tommy. "Georgie doesn't know anything about the twelve grand. He doesn't know our position. He wants to see me—he had it all figured out. But if I were him, I'd see the situation in exactly the same way. If anything happens to me, the first one they'll come looking for is Georgie Howe." He stopped. "Go inside, Ma."

"What are you going to do?"

"I'm going to stay alive, and so is everybody else. When you add it all up, including David, it's not worth dying for, not this way; and it's not worth going to war for, not the part I could get back—and that includes David, too. I want to see what this guy says, and then I'll figure it out from there." He waited until she was gone, and then he turned to Tommy. "I'm not going down there early. That's too easy. He expects it, and anyway I've lost too much time to be sure of beating him—or the goons he took to Kate's."

"You better figure that there are three."

"How do you get that?"

"Downtown, you can leave a car unattended. Uptown, you leave a guy downstairs to keep an eye on things. You remember the guys Georgie used to run with, silk shirts and custom shoes. If he's the guy he now wants us to believe he is, he's the guy he was years ago. He's been with us for the ride."

"That doesn't change much," Mike said. "I'm going to wait until I'm sure Georgie is set up at the club, and then I'm going to call Lillian. I'm going to tell her where I'm going, and that I want to live through it. I know Lillian. She'll hear my voice and she'll know I'm sober. If this is the way she wants it, fine, but even she knows there's no point in making it worse than it is."

Tommy was staring at him.

"What's wrong?"

"I'm going with you. When I'm along, the right guys come out alive."

"Not Lillian," Mike said. "I know her."

"Did you ever hear of an accident? What is she going to do about it if Georgie does it right? And who's going to support her and the kid? She'll be thinking of that. Maybe she won't like it, but she'll have to. You have a lot of money. Who do you want to bet it on, yourself or somebody else?"

"Do you have a gun?"

"No. But I don't think we need one. What are we going there for? You don't know what kind of a hold he has on the place. Or on Lillian. But you'll find that out when you talk to her. You're in for a bad night. I don't think you've begun to feel it yet."

Mike stared at him.

"You have only his word for it. Leave it to her to give you the details. That will make it real for you. Georgie isn't going to make it pleasant. You'd better think twice and make sure you know what you're going to see him for."

"Lillian will give me a better idea of what I can expect. Kate and I have an equity in the place. We can't defend it in law or by force, but unless he's willing to kill me—and Kate—he knows that I can make a lot of trouble for him without going to the law. I just have to talk to people."

Tommy was staring at him again. "You'd better give me the twelve thousand," he said. "We'll leave it here. Georgie has no reason to bother Ma. No matter what happens, she'll have something to tide her along."

"You really think I'm a dope, don't you?"

He hesitated. "You'd better figure that if there are three of them, Georgie is carrying some heat."

"Georgie's too yellow to carry a gun. What did you say that to Ma for, that stuff about being hypnotized?"

"I started out just saying, 'Wake up,' but as usual when I talk to her, I lost control of myself."

"Well, lay off her, will you?" There was a sharpness in his voice that he had not intended, and he apologized at once. "Let's wait a little longer. I want to be sure Georgie's out of the house before I talk to Lillian."

"And when you're done, after we're out of here, I'm going to call Kate."

"Why don't you do it from here?" He gestured toward the bedroom door." She won't hear you. What difference does it make now anyway?"

Tommy winked. "I wanted to talk to her privately."

In a half hour Mike called Lillian. "Is what Georgie told me true? I want to hear you say it."

"You sound sober, but you're not."

"I'm sober. Tommy's here with me. He'll tell you—but first you tell me: is it true or isn't it?"

There was no answer at all. He felt a rage he would not have believed could exist inside him. "He wants me to meet him at the club. He had it all arranged. Now tell me what you know about it."

"I told you not to call me."

"I'm not going down there to get killed!"

"Stop it! He's going to tell you that he's going to continue to pay you your share. He's going to send it to you. He told Kate that she would go on getting her money, too. I called her and checked. She repeated to me just what he said he was going to tell her."

"Did she tell you about his two hoods?"

"What hoods?"

He was so sick with his hatred for her that he had trouble breathing. "Just one more question, whore. How long has he been slipping it to you?"

She hung up.

"That lacked polish," Tommy said.

"I can say what I want to her. What do you think?"

"If you waste time worrying about it, you'll be doing exactly what Georgie wants."

"He's got her believing him. She thinks he's going to take care of Kate. Who's going to count the money?"

Tommy stood up. "We're going out the back way. You don't mind climbing a fence, do you?"

"That's pretty cautious, kid."

"I'm alive, Mike. I'm only doing what I think I should."

There was a Cadillac V-16 parked at the curb a few feet up from the entrance of the club. Tommy stepped over and touched the long hood with his hand. "It's been here for a while. They're making it too easy."

While Tommy had been talking to Kate from a pay telephone, Mike had bought some envelopes and stamps. Now he took three of the envelopes, already stamped and addressed, and gave them to his brother. "Don't look up. They can put a guy at the window and we wouldn't be able to see him, but he'll see this. You're not the only one who's thinking."

The envelopes were addressed to Winchell, Sullivan, and the district attorney.

"What do you have in there?" Tommy asked. He had hefted their weight convincingly, and now Mike was pleased with himself.

"Pages of the Manhattan directory. Drop them off in the box on the corner. I'll wait."

"Sure, why not? It's worth a try."

Someone in the window would be able to see that the envelopes were real, and that there was something in them. He would be able to see Mike clearly enough to shoot him, too, if that was the intention. If it was, Mike wanted it done now, while Tommy was at a distance. Mike never looked around. The Lillian/Georgie thing had cooked him, and there was no reason to tell the kid. Tommy still wanted to play cops and robbers. Mike could see that the battle was already over, and that Georgie had won. If you couldn't hold on to what had been handed to you on a plate, you didn't deserve to keep it. He just wanted to find out what Georgie wanted. He wanted to hear what Georgie had to say. There were people who could walk out and scheme some revenge even if it took ten years, but Mike knew himself too well for that. He was done with the whole thing.

Tommy came back. "Now what?"

"We get on the elevator. You can still walk away if you want."

"Who, Bring 'em Back Alive Westfield? I'm still the best insurance you have."

Upstairs, the doors to the club were wide open and there was noise coming from inside. Suddenly they heard Georgie's voice.

"Here they are! That was them. Come on in, boys, We're up in the bar."

"You're right," Mike whispered. "He's got a gun."

"It's that kind of confidence," Tommy said. "Oh, I'm right about him, all right."

"Come on upstairs," Georgie called. "I was just mixing drinks for the boys. What's your pleasure?"

Mike went up the stairs first. As Tommy had predicted, there were three of them, one of whom Mike recognized as one of Georgie's Brooklyn friends, and another guy who was at least two inches taller than Mike. Enormous. He looked as if he weighed two hundred and fifty pounds. The three of them were sitting at the far end of the bar, close together, as if they were out on the town and didn't have a care in the world. Georgie had a gun. He was giving the orders, and he thought he was safe.

He was in his shirt-sleeves. He liked to have his shirts heavily starched and pressed crisply. He introduced his friends; the big guy's name was Karl. Mike let his eyes pass over him, because Karl was taking his measure. Mike had been in the restaurant business too long to give himself away so easily. "Come on, Mike," Georgie said, "what will you have? Hello, kid," he said to Tommy, "I didn't expect to see you here."

"It stood to reason. You saw me down on the sidewalk."

"Oh, that was Jack here. He didn't know who you were."

Jack, the smallest of the three, gave a little salute. "What did you put in the mailbox, kid?"

"Insurance policies. How are ya? Nice to see ya."

"Bright kid," Jack said.

"You in the insurance business now, Tommy?" Georgie asked.

"It's still only a sideline. The commie book business is showing too much profit."

"See?" Georgie told Jack, "He *is* a bright kid."

"Let's get down to cases," Mike said.

"No drink?"

"Not today."

"Kid?"

"Not me, I'm holding the nickels for the subway."

"Can't you talk straight?" Karl asked.

"If I'm going too fast for you, stomp your foot three times."

"Don't overstep yourself, Tommy," Georgie said.

"Well, if you're going to back him up, okay."

"That's enough, Tommy," Mike said.

"I want to get this over with," Georgie said, suddenly tense. "It's nice to see you sober, Mike, but let's be realistic: it isn't going to last. It's only a matter of time before you fall off the wagon again. You've been a disgrace around here for a year and a half, and there are too many people who depend on this place for their livings for them to let you pull it down around you on another one of your binges. So you're out. I'll send you a check. Get yourself set up somewhere. Try to get a new start. That's it. Do you need cash? I want you out of here."

"Did you decide all this before or after you started fucking my wife?"

Georgie smiled. "What do you think?"

"I thought I was going to be able to walk away from this. Now I want to squeeze your head like an egg."

"Let's go, Mike," Tommy said. "Out, *now!*"

"Not so fast, kiddo," Karl said, getting up.

"Get out, Tommy," Mike said. "They won't do anything to me if you get out."

"Nothing doing."

"I'll take you on," Mike said to Karl. "You want to go Duke City with me? You leave the kid out of it."

"He can leave," Georgie said. "For that matter, so can I—it's even less my business. Isn't that so, boys?"

"*He* challenged me," Karl said, pointing a finger.

"Do you get it, Tommy?" Georgie asked with a smile.

"Sure, but all the same, I want to keep my eyes on you."

"Oh, I wouldn't want to get Lillian mad at me. When it starts with you waving your dick at a woman, you want to keep it just as it is."

"Look out, Mike!"

Karl came around the bar faster than Mike would have thought possible, but Tommy's warning gave him time, and he was able to back up enough so that Karl was forced to take one step too far. Mike caught him off-balance with a jab, high, and he hit Mike on the side of the head with a heavy right hand. He was bent so far forward that he gave up his height advantage entirely, and as they grappled, Mike saw that Karl kept backing his feet away, leaning his weight forward. It was like trying to stop a truck from rolling downhill, but then Mike saw that the guy was trying to protect his belly, or his balls. Mike took more of his weight, straightened up and kneed him once, then again, then a third time. Karl had been hurt there before; Mike could feel the fight going out of him even as he struggled and punched. Mike moved as if to kick him again, and as Karl shuffled back Mike pushed him hard. He was able to stop himself at once, and Mike stepped into him with two lefts and a right. He had a cut lip, and he was still standing, like a tree. The side of Mike's head was aching—he wasn't going to be able to take many of those sledgehammer right hands. Mike moved toward the guy's left, and again Karl begin to crouch, losing his height advantage, bringing his hands up like a wrestler. Mike feinted a hook twice with his left, and Karl went deeper into his crouch. Mike planted his feet and threw his right with his back into it just as Karl turned to make his charge and Mike's knuckles caught him flush on the hairline. The sound in the room was like a gunshot as Karl's head seemed to compress into his shoulders and the bones in Mike's wrist splintered like a handful of walnuts. The guy never looked up but pitched forward like a side of beef that somebody else had dropped there.

"You got the wrong guy, Mike," Georgie said.

"Look out, Mike, he's got a gun!"

"I can see it." He tried to raise his hands, but his right fell over like an empty balloon. In a rush the other two guys were off their stools at the other end of the bar.

"What the hell is that? Is he dead? That's my cousin!" The other rolled Karl over. "What's that pink shit coming out of his nose?" the cousin yelled. "What the hell do you call this?"

"He's alive," the one bending over Karl said.

Georgie gestured to Mike. "You can have him if you want him, but you don't kill him, not here."

"Don't forget what I put in the mailbox," Tommy said.

Georgie pointed the gun at him. "Kid, you live a charmed life. Why don't you just step back and let this run its course? Broken wrist and all, your brother is going to get out of here alive—why don't you figure that some of your luck has already spilled onto him and let it go at that?"

Tommy was watching the muzzle of the gun. Mike had never seen him so frightened. "Leave him the hell out of it," he said to Georgie.

"Hell of a punch," Georgie said. "Didn't travel eighteen inches. Your wrist hurt much?"

"Plenty."

"He's still breathing," the guy tending Karl said.

"Don't move him," Georgie said. "I think his skull is fractured."

"I'm going to break this guy's other fucking wrist."

Georgie smiled. "I don't think so. How will he be able to get a glass up to his lips? Work his body if you want to; just don't make a mess of the rug. We'll give him a drink before he goes—just to get you started, Mike. We'll all feel a lot more comfortable with things back to normal again. And you stand and watch, kid. You don't know what kind of a bank account you have with me. For all you know, I may want to put one of these little poppers right in your heart."

The cousin hit Mike in the solar plexus, then in the kidney, then low on the ribs. Mike held onto his right hand and curled up and kept his legs closed. The cousin hit him in the nose and broke it again. The numbness brought Mike to his knees and the cousin put the toe of his shoe smartly in Mike's lower abdomen. The other guy punched him on the temple and as Mike landed on his side the two of them kicked him until they were tired. A couple of ribs were broken—it was an odd thing, but he drew in from the pain like a kid huddling under the covers on a cold night. He kept waiting to pass out, but he never did. They stood back from him for a moment. Mike felt he could move, but that it would be just asking for more.

"Let's have a look at him," Georgie said. "The only way this is going to work is if it's a fair fight. We have to get Karl to a hospital. Mike, we're going to do you a favor. We'll tell them that Karl got in a fight. Of course, if Karl dies, we'll have to give them your name. The only defense you'll have is looking like you really mixed it up with the victim. We're going to have to hit you in the face a couple of times, so you might as well have your drink now."

Mike shook his head.

"Okay, it'll be waiting for you when they're finished."

They hit him and then Georgie told Mike to pick up the shot, and Mike refused; the cousin hit him again and Mike took the drink.

"Have another," Georgie said.

"Come on, Georgie," Tommy cried.

"Shut your fucking trap, kid. I already gave you all the warnings you're going to get. Can't you see that the guy wants the booze now? Don't you, Mike?" He pushed the bottle toward the cousin. "Now he's looking right. See if you can get him smelling right, too." The cousin pulled Mike's head back and poured the whiskey into his open mouth. Georgie said, "Every once in a while in school we'd get a guy like this. Did you do this at your school?"

"Oh, sure," the cousin said.

"This guy wants to hear about his wife now."

"I suppose he does."

"Well, I always liked Lil anyway, so I don't want to say anything bad about her. You forgot what a woman is, Mike. A little of this and a little of that and you have them where you want them. You know that. All I had to do was wave my dick at her—it's the truth. Oh, maybe I was a little rough with her, but that's not the important thing. You know your sister, and Lillian's no different. Now you go about your own business, you fucking drunken bum. Ah, give him another drink! You get yourself together and maybe you'll be fit to see your kid. Now get the hell out of here. Get this fucking garbage out of here, kid, before I change my mind!"

He couldn't really walk; Tommy took his arm and got his weight on his shoulders and eased him down the stairs. The elevator was where they had left it.

"I hurt too much to talk. I'll be sick."

"You took a hell of a beating."

"Think he'll die?"

"No one will know. Georgie wanted to kill you, Mike."

"Not a mark on him. He got away clean. Those guys always do."

Tommy seemed to shake his head. "You're coming down to my place. They don't know where I live. We'll tell Ma you went to Europe or South America."

"It scared him to see me sober."

"Don't think about him until you're over this. Let somebody else do the worrying for a while."

"Yeah, that's right."

Tommy leaned him against the side of the building while he hailed a cab. The pain was getting worse; for the time being it was a kind of insulation from everything else. But that would not last the week, and Mike knew himself. The kid was grateful and he wanted to help, but he was still young enough to believe that human beings were worth something. What would he think of his brother if he knew how much Mike was already thinking of climbing back into the bottle? Couldn't he see it? That his brother was past the point of being able to deal with anything at all?

VIII

Their mother didn't believe Tommy when he told her that Mike had taken a trip, and they fought over it; but he could make her back down easily now, and after he had the better of her he got the twelve thousand from behind the couch cushion and stuffed it down into his pants. It wasn't going to help her to know about any money, not at this stage of the game. He did not remind her of his address, either. Georgie would still hear of them through Kate or Lillian, and they would be better off if Georgie could enjoy the security of not knowing how close to him they were.

The money, most of it, went into the branch of the Bank of Manhattan Company on East Forty-second Street. Tommy had begun to think things over again on the way downtown. He wanted to believe that things would change if he told Lillian what had been done to Mike, but now it was clear to him that he was still clinging to something out of his childhood. She knew where he lived. If Georgie started getting nervous again, it would be nothing for him to wheedle the location out of her—and that was putting the best face on it. So he was going to move. He would tell his mother later. And the bankroll would be there when they were ready to do something with it.

He found a furnished floor-through in a brownstone on a sunny street in Chelsea. It was on the second floor, airy and spacious, with high ceilings and a real fireplace in the front parlor. Tommy wanted to keep Mike's spirits up. The doctors at Saint Vincent's had set his nose, taped his ribs, and prescribed codeine for the pain, warning them that it was addictive. Tommy thought that it didn't make a hell of a lot of difference in Mike's case, and kept him doped up until he could get to the bathroom under his own power, and then he cut him off cold. Mike was so sore that he never noticed. He had four broken ribs and there was blood in his urine, though less each day. Tommy had watched the doctors mold the nose like clay. Mike had been silent all through the beating, which Tommy had taken as a sign of defiance and pride; but the silence had continued and now Tommy could not read it at all.

Once in a while in the new apartment he caught Mike staring off into some melancholy place inside himself or standing at the kitchen sink, waiting for the water to run cold from the tap, his hand shaking with nerves—or terror. Tommy could see that he wanted a drink, but he could see, too, how much the guy was fighting it.

Mike didn't venture out of the apartment until mid-October, when there was a nip in the air. He still had some pain and the cast on his hand was as big around as a small ham, but the marks on his face had faded and he said he wanted to walk; so one clear Sunday afternoon Tommy accompanied him down Eighth Avenue and Hudson Street to Canal and on through the Washington Market, closed and deserted for the day; then he wanted to see City Hall, and they trooped up Warren Street to Broadway. Tommy thought he was going to hear something new about the old man's lunches with the alderman down at the old Astor House, but instead Mike started talking about himself. He said he still could not understand what had happened to him. Charlie had given him the chance of a lifetime, and in the end he had not been able to prevent a weasel like Georgie from taking it away from him.

They walked across City Hall Park and Park Row and down Spruce Street toward Peck Slip. Mike said he wanted to see if there were any of the old sailing ships tied up at the piers. The fresh air took the sting out of Tommy's fears. For the first time in years he wanted to hear Mike try to make the old man reappear before their eyes—playing cards, buying a horse, taking the family from the house in Flatbush down to Coney Island for seafood. Tommy could see it for what it was now, that his brother had been able to find some consolation in who he thought he was or might have been. There was still that romantic notion inside Mike, not that life had dealt him a cruel blow but that he was something special, some kind of drunken lost prince. But now there was none of it—and because Mike had mentioned what had happened to his business first, Tommy could see that his brother was more defenseless than ever.

There was a four-masted square-rigger in, its bow out over the street. It was an old, old thing, the rusted stack of a steam engine rising amidships, the hull encrusted with heavy black paint, and Mike wanted to have a good look at it.

"The worse is that I still love the Lillian I met years ago," he said. "She was just a kid, and what I liked best, and what I believed in first, was the way she looked at me. When she looked into my eyes and really smiled, I felt all right—*all right,* you know? I don't know if I'll ever accept the idea

that the person is really gone. I can't think about what's going on. I can't
think about David. Maybe it isn't a lucky name. I don't know what's
going to happen to him. I used to have good feelings. I used to have
happy thoughts about what the future was going to bring. Not even that
run of luck up at Saratoga could bring them back again. I've always been a
drunk, even when I was a kid. During the war. Kate and Charlie pulled
me out of the gutter. I met Lillian when I thought I had my life pretty
well straightened out. Now I know better. And Georgie stalked me for
years. He latched onto me pretty early.

"Did you know that the old man knew a lot about the sea? He told me
that when he was a little boy, no more than five or six or seven, his father
would take him down here on Sunday afternoons and tell him about the
ships and where they went. There were dozens of them in here at a time,
the old man said; it was a completely different world. The old man told
me that he was a happy little boy, and that his memories of being taken
down here by his father were still vivid. That was when he was sick. He
told me then that his mother taught him to read."

"I hated that woman."

"Yeah, I know, but even the years you knew her are a long time ago."

"Kate told me that the alderman was a great dreamer. She said that she
could always see those distant places in his eyes."

"Not toward the end. Something broke his spirit. He clapped Tommy
on the back. "Let's walk up to Chinatown. We'll get some crisp duck.""

"Sure. I think I wanna buy a duck."

It was a reference to Joe Penner. "You said it, brother. We're the guys
who want to buy a duck. He just hasn't been able to find us yet.

The end came fast. Not long after that Sunday Mike started drinking
again, and not long after that he found the bankbook from the Bank of
the Manhattan Company. That was a Tuesday; on Thursday the mailman
delivered a thick, soiled, and crumpled envelope containing the
bankbook, with the notation of a withdrawal of two thousand dollars.
Apparently Mike had forged his brother's signature on a withdrawal slip.
There was no note in the envelope, no explanation. Mike showed up at
the flat in Chelsea a month later, on a bitter night, so dirty he stank; and
Tommy got him into bed and kept him there until the guy felt strong
enough to bathe. He hadn't seen their mother in five months. Tommy
had a telephone now and she would call him, or he would ride up
there—twice a month, no more; she didn't know that she was drawing on
their Saratoga stake, which was down to seven thousand—and she would
ask if he had heard from Mike, and he would say he'd gotten a card from
Miami Beach, where Mike was cooking in a hotel and getting his strength

back running on the sand. Tommy didn't know if she believed him, but he didn't listen very carefully to the nuances of her mumbled responses. He gave her money that he said Mike had sent him, and she complained about her sinuses. She never had any questions. She liked to tell him that Lillian had called to say that David was fine and progressing nicely in the second grade. Tommy could not imagine what sort of elaborate mutual hoax the two women were working on each other, but then he could not understand what his mother really believed about her older surviving son. For a time he thought of telling her that Mike was in Havana, then Venezuela, and on to Buenos Aires, propelling him on a zany world tour; but then one evening she said that Mike had come by one afternoon—she would not say if he had been drinking. What was the use? She had her radio programs, Will Rogers and Bing Crosby movies, patent medicines and her afternoon walks to the zoo and the boat lake, and, at the center of her existence, all those sleepless nights and daybreak sessions on the toilet. Tommy had moments when he wept for her, but none when he understood her. It had been years since he had kissed her. He never thought of the split second of failure when he arrived at her apartment or said good-bye, his belly filled with scorched chicken and the voices of Mother and Father Barbour scratching out of the radio. Couldn't she see that her son was killing himself? When the elevator door closed, Tommy would punch at the air, swinging his arms and throwing his fists, snarling and snorting, and once he ran all the way down to the subway on Broadway, like a kid, and his heart hammered in his chest for twenty minutes.

In the spring she had something else to turn her attention to when Amy announced her engagement to a divorced insurance man from New Jersey. It was six months before Tommy learned that the loving couple, long past their honeymoon by then, had known each other before. Since the bridegroom was a puffy individual with sweaty hands and an unpleasant smell, Tommy concluded that the long interment of that information offered a clue to what had actually happened between them. And sure enough, Mike was able to remember Arthur Donaldson from ten years before, after Amy came to New York and before she ran into Georgie, one of the many who had been through the revolving door that probably reflected those giddier times more than anything else. Donaldson considered Tommy a juvenile, but he felt pleased with himself for having married such a handsome woman, and took it upon himself to tell Tommy that Amy had written him a long letter to renew their acquaintanceship. Tommy did not see his sister as handsome; in fact, he thought that her selfishness had made her ugly. So the story was really no surprise—Kate had predicted something like it. But as part of her campaign Amy allowed Donaldson to believe that she was the dutiful daughter, and the result was that their mother was drawn into all kinds of senseless journeys across the Hudson—to meet his family, to participate in a weekend at Atlantic City. She wanted to take this largesse of attention as the dawning of a new era, and if Mike had been secretly invited to stay away from the wedding, she was willing to accept as consolation for his absence the fact that the ceremony itself, though modest, had gone off smoothly. Kate wanted to hear none of it. At seventy-four she was too old for such shenanigans, and she announced that she wanted to hear no more of Tommy's mother or sister. Mike had already been in and out of Bellevue and Kings County; whether his mother knew it or not, he had given up the last pretenses of respectability. The five dollars she gave him when he came by at odd times during the week was as much a part of his regular income as the visits themselves were part of the larger tour that took him to his brother's and Kate's—he had no real address of his own. He wouldn't bother with a story anymore: "Let me have five, will you? A couple of bucks anyway, to tide me over." There was no way to refuse him, because it was clear that if he was refused he would only do something desperate. He liked to say he was getting work here and there, but he wasn't even fit for diving for pearls in a mission on the Bowery. In January 1935 he fell down the stairs of the entrance to the Seventy-second Street station of the east side IRT, and he spent six weeks in Metropolitan Hospital, then two months more at a farm upstate. He couldn't remember why he had been uptown in the first place, or so he said. When he returned to the city, he had regained some of his lost weight and there was a little color in his face, but it was obvious to all who saw him that he had been a sick man. People hoped that he would be able to hold himself together for a while, but in June he disappeared again.

There was no word until one evening in late September when the police found his wallet in the pocket of his jacket; death by misadventure, even when death itself is expected, is always an especially vicious shock. The body had fallen twelve stories, from the window of an empty office, landed on the hood of a DeSoto Airflow, and then rolled onto the pavement of Nassau Street. Given the time of night, after eight o'clock, and the location, so far downtown, there were no witnesses. The police could not reach the victim's wife, and so they were forced to telephone the other number in his wallet, belonging to his mother. The old woman came down and identified the body. They did not have to be told that he had had a drinking problem, for even in death he reeked of the stuff.

Given the circumstances, Tommy tried to make as little of the arrangements as possible, but three of the newspapers ran small stories of the death of the onetime speakeasy operator. One was able to discover that he was the grandson of an alderman who, curiously, had died in a similarly tragic incident. The size of the stories probably indicated to people that they need not attend the funeral, and there were only a half a dozen signatures in the guest book. The estranged wife did not make an appearance; she and her lover were out of town on an extended holiday. Only Tommy went down to Brooklyn to the cemetery, and when the graveside rite was over, he waited until the gravediggers had covered the casket before he walked back to the limousine.

"Your father buried Kate, too," the small voice said, "that old woman he spoke of to you so many times but never identified. He used to tell us what he told you, that he had once known an old woman who knew so much and said such outrageous things. I can only imagine what you know of death with the experience you've had, but at my age I can tell you honestly that it is possible to die happy, and Kate told Tommy—your father—that that was the way she was going to go to her grave."

"She tried to get rid of Sissy," the old woman said. "This was in the fall of 1936, when Kate was seventy-six years old. She was as frail as a bird. We don't think of seventy-six as a very great age anymore, but the majority of people still don't live that long. Kate was always the realist—she always knew what she was and what her possibilities were. But Sissy wouldn't go, even when Kate told her she was going to die. Sissy told your father all this at the funeral. During the war he went up to Harlem to see if he could find her, but her Uncle Rupert was dead and the barber shop closed and no one was willing or able to give any information. So by the time of the war everything we knew, all of that old world, was gone, and for your father, it was simply the fulfillment of Kate's last prophecy. I call it that even though what she told him was more the result of her realism and sense of herself than any mystical divination. She said the world was moving on beyond her and the feeling she had about trying to preserve her small corner of it was only evidence of the fact that, whether she wanted to or not, she was giving up her claim to her indivisible share of the whole. She told your father that your grandfather reported having feelings like hers at the end of his life, even before he became ill."

She stopped talking so suddenly that the young man in his own exhaustion thought that she had lost track of what she had been trying to tell him. The fire was all but out, cracks of light in the blackened coals: occasionally one would pop and send a geyser of sparks upward, like a prayer, like the breath of a man sleeping on his back. The young man could not believe how cold the air had become after the mild temperatures of the afternoon. He had hated the cold since his childhood, and even now it still represented the viciousness of the universe, but the old woman, more frail herself than perhaps she wanted to admit, looked comfortable in her sweater and hillbilly zippered jacket. She started to smile. "I just remembered something. Before he died—you'll like this—your grandfather told Kate that the country was going to be ruined by the income tax and the automobile. He really said that. With the income tax the government would always know where you were and what you had; but as long as you had your automobile, you would at least have the illusion of freedom, with your ability to rush all over the landscape. He said that the trouble would start just as soon as the government tried to take away the automobiles."

The young man and his girl laughed.

"Kate died in January 1937. She'd had a stroke in the November of the previous year. It was a warm day and Sissy took her downstairs to the park. She moved very slowly then. What she liked was to sit in the sun. At the end she didn't get out enough to remember the people she saw in the neighborhood, and so she just asked Sissy to get her in a spot where there was sunshine and she could see children or young people. She didn't like old people; she said they had no life in them." Now there was another smile. "Well, on that particular afternoon she complained to Sissy that she felt lightheaded and wanted to go home, and by the time they got upstairs she had a real headache, but as Sissy was trying to make her comfortable, while they waited for the doctor, the old lady seemed to relax. She said to Sissy, 'Don't worry about me anymore,' and that was the last thing she said, because by sundown she had lost the power to speak, and from then on she was in the hospital. The hospital had your father on record as her son, and he visited her three times a week. He thought she recognized him. He was still a young man then, not yet thirty, and he was her friend to the end of her life. Your father was a very special man. He was there the Sunday before she died. He told her what was new and he read her from the newspaper. She had a radio, but she couldn't sit up. The side of her face was drawn down from the stroke and she drooled, too, which embarrassed her terribly. From her symptoms as your father described them I would have to say that she was degenerating faster and faster at the end. He said that she seemed to understand him, nodding and trying to raise her hand. He kissed her good-bye, kissed her on the forehead, and stroked her hair—I suppose she was almost bald—and she tried to say something, couldn't, and cried, which is typical of stroke victims. The next evening they called him to say that she had died while he had been eating his dinner and reading the sports page of the New York Post."

Book Five

THE NEW WORLD

Serenade

I

In April of '46 Tommy moved out to Queens. He was working for the telephone company, in the Boerum Street office in Brooklyn, and the trip from the furnished room on the West Side just took too much of his time. A guy in the office found the place for him, a converted basement in a two-family semi-detached in Sunnyside. Tommy had to walk down an inclined driveway, really an alley, to get to the "private entrance," and his living room was occupied mostly by a whitewashed furnace which he tended when he was home—when he was out, the landlady, Mrs. Galucci, let herself in through the interior stairs—but Tommy knew what he was doing and the place fitted his needs perfectly.

He took the bus on Laurel Hill Boulevard to Court Square to catch the GG crosstown into Brooklyn, and when he came back from visiting his mother on the Upper West Side he was able to get off at Ely Avenue and catch the same bus home. The street he lived on was lined on both sides with houses like the one he lived in, set back behind tiny gardens and brick porches. Trees arched the street and they made it dark at night, but as summer came people spent more time out of doors, and the streetlights shining through the leaves were actually lovely.

The area was almost completely built up now with a few empty lots here and there. In the mornings Tommy could hear a rooster, and on one of his walks around the neighborhood he found him, an old bird presiding over a dozen hens in a large cage next to a corner house two blocks away. Kids roller-skated in the streets and the little ones played with

wooden swords. There was a big, flat lot up on the next street where
older boys played hardball on the sand, and on the near corner, like a
sign announcing the entrance to a village, was the street's World War II
Honor Roll, with certain names preceded by gold stars. Tommy never
bothered to count how many. Most of the blocks in this corner of the
neighborhood were like the one he lived on, but a little way up to the
north was a shopping district, with supermarkets, five-and-tens, small
clothing shops, and no fewer than four movie theaters. There was a
playground in the middle of it all, and on Sundays the veterans pushed
the kids off the handball courts and played quarter-a-man elimination
tournaments, doubles and singles. It was a place to get the fresh air; when
the other spectators had seen Tommy for a couple of weeks they started
calling him Sailor because of his clothes, and they invited him to get into
the betting. He had been watching the players, so he won a couple of
bucks, which made them curious about him. They took note of the gray
in his hair and his glasses and wondered aloud what the Navy had wanted
with such an old, blind man, and he gave them a smile and said no,
Merchant Marine; and when they wanted to know how long, he said
seven years, still smiling: and after that they waved to him when they saw
him, and when he missed a Sunday they asked where he had been.

   The job was all right. The work was easy and routine, but he had to
stay alert and use his head. He knew cars and radio, but the telephone
system was a different technology, electromechanical, and genuinely
primitive. One of the old hands in the office, a man who had installed the
first underground cables, told him that it was just a matter of time before
the whole apparatus disintegrated under the weight of increasing traffic.
They were at the end of the telephone company's second generation—
for the first fifty years, most of the lines were overhead and operators had
to connect every call. Now, only twenty-five years after that, it was all
going to have to be built new for the third time. The guy was fifty years
old and had been on the job since the age of seventeen, and there were a
lot more in the company like him. And there were still thousands upon
thousands of operators, women who had gone to Catholic schools and
knew their geography. Once you were in, you were in for life and the
company took care of you; but the pay was twenty-five percent too low
for the work, and the company demanded loyalty—the union was in-
house and the management fought outside organizers.

   So it was not perfect, but Tommy knew he could live with it; and if his
seventy-five a week did not go far after taxes, expenses, and fifteen
dollars a week to his mother, he still had enough money to live com-
fortably. He could have roast beef, mashed potatoes, carrots and peas,
coffee and cheesecake at the Thompson Hill on Queens Boulevard for

less than a dollar, and if he still had any energy after seeing his mother, he would take the IRT Flushing line home, pick up the *News* and the *Mirror* and walk across Forty-sixth Street to Bickford's for coffee and apple pie. The sign on the lamppost said Forty-sixth Street, but the elevated station had the old name, which Tommy had thought hilarious years ago: Bliss Street. He got off at Bliss Street.

One of the movie theaters was called the Bliss, and for a while Tuesday night was dish night. It was a way to fill the cupboard. He hated to cook for himself and for days at a time he would have nothing in the old Kelvinator but a quart of milk and half a loaf of white bread. He had no books, either—he had learned at sea not to accumulate the bulk and weight of books. There was a storefront public library a long walk away, heavy on Louis Bromfield and extra copies of *A Tree Grows in Brooklyn*. There was a copy of *And Quiet Flows the Don*, but there was no point in running the risk of making Mrs. Galucci nervous. All through that spring Tommy worked days, and so he could get to the library only in the evenings. The school across the street was open for the kids who wanted to play basketball, and one corner of the schoolyard had a crowd of wisenheimers in pegged pants sneaking cigarettes. There was a line of stores the next avenue down, two funeral parlors, a dance studio, candy stores, and a bar bearing an Irish name on every block. By midsummer their doors were wide open, and the smell of beer poured out ino the sidewalk like the smell of rotting vegetables from the grocer, or the smell of blood from the kosher butcher's halfway through the whole long gauntlet—the butcher was the cantor at the local synagogue Tommy learned. The last bar was Burke's which had an adjoining room of empty booths with a sign outside saying Ladies Welcome, and the last German delicatessen was Burfiend's, where the Mister had no hair, the Missus was full-bosomed, and the sandwiches were thick. Tommy would get a roast beef on a roll and a quart of Ballantine to wash it down. The beer would keep him awake, but he would have something he wanted to read anyway. Because the alley would carry the sound upward he would have to play the radio softly. After midnight he would listen to "The Milkman's Matinee," with its endless commercials for I. J. Fox and Barney's "the only store of its kind in New York."

When the warm weather came Tommy heard from the guy upstairs about the radio, and then when a heat wave set in he couldn't get enough air moving through the apartment even with an oscillating fan. The next week when the temperature started climbing again he stopped in Bickford's for a salad before going on to the library, and he turned in at Burke's before taking on the last three blocks home. There were a couple of vets from the playground handball court sitting at the middle of the bar, and they waved him over. They still did not know one another's names, and they introduced themselves. One was named Halley, the other Flannery. Halley was down at Delehanty's studying for the cops, and Flannery thought he wanted to become a high school teacher. When Tommy had come in during past weeks he had stayed for two or three ten-cent Rheingolds, one more if the bartender picked up a round; but it was an hour and a half before he rolled out of the place this time, dizzy and bilious. He worked the following Sunday and forgot about the two young Irishmen until he passed Burke's the following week and Halley, who had freckles and yellow hair, called out to him.

"Hey, Tom! Are you going to pass us by? Where were you Sunday?"

Tommy told him. Halley was out on the sidewalk now, a glass of beer in his hand. He was sober; he wasn't more than twenty-five and it was another warm night in the middle of a long summer.

"Come on inside," Halley said. "Meet some people."

There were nine or ten men and women, most of them young. Flannery introduced him around. Halley wanted to join the cops, but Flannery was the bigger of the two, a brawny athlete and the natural leader. He was in that much better spirits than Halley and introduced Tommy as an old man who had fought more war than both of them put together. The girls seemed no more than twenty-two or twenty-three years old, and Tommy could see, even if Flannery couldn't, that he was a figure more frightening to them than impressive.

"Seven years in the Merchant Marine," Flannery said to everyone.

"Were you torpedoed?" the tallest of the girls asked. Tommy said no and the girl blinked, as if she didn't believe him. She was taller than him, he realized, perhaps by more than an inch. She had honey-colored hair, freckles and green eyes, a flat nose and broad cheekbones, the kind of face people called the map of Ireland. Flannery passed Tommy a beer and acknowledged Tommy's salute.

"How old are you?"

"Thirty-seven." He was smiling. She glanced at his books and he handed them to her, *Two Years Before the Mast* and *The Red Pony*. She said she had read *The Grapes of Wrath* after she had seen the movie with John Carradine and Henry Fonda. Tommy said he didn't think Steinbeck knew anything about politics.

"My uncle wouldn't see the movie for the same reason," the girl said. Flannery had said that her name was Mary Dougherty. "My uncle was in the Easter Rising and he said that only poets appreciate the horror of politics, and William Butler Yeats best of all."

Tommy was smiling. "Is your uncle still a two-fisted revolutionary?"

"He says he'll do his duty." She smiled back. "And you? Where will you be when the great shout goes up?"

"Tell your uncle that you asked me that question, and tell him I said that I would distrust the man who thought he had a choice."

"You sound like one of his friends. They get together in the kitchen with their quarts of beer and fan the old flames together."

Tommy emptied his glass. "Tell your uncle, too, that I told him to read *Nostromo* by Joseph Conrad and *The Possessed* by Dostoevsky. I can't stay. I haven't had my dinner yet."

"I'll tell my uncle what you said."

Flannery stopped him from putting a couple of bucks on the bar and there was a ragged chorus of disappointed-sounding good-byes. The sun was down now and the air felt cooler. Across the street, a bus squealed to a stop and let out a backfire. Tommy was on the corner when he heard his name being called. It was Mary Dougherty. She certainly was a big girl. She half ran, half walked the distance to him. He had to look up into her eyes, but she tilted her head and assumed an attitude that made him think of a little girl about to beg a favor of a respected male relative—oh, an uncle, for instance.

"What was that word?"

"*Nostromo*." He spelled it.

"Why are you so frightened? Are your secrets that dark?"

He laughed. "I'm just too old for that stuff. I have to go to work in the morning."

She smiled. "Even Flannery knew you were lying about being torpedoed. No one in there would bother you about that. We all know too much."

He took his time answering her. "By the time I got around to being torpedoed the first time I had seen so much death and dying that all it did was remind me of how much I wanted to get the hell away from it all. I went into the Merchant Marine because the services wouldn't take me with a punctured eardrum. I'm dead in the left ear."

"I'm sorry."

"Nah." He winked. "Your uncle has nothing on me. I'd lost my desire to die." He was smiling again. "I could have quit, but I thought, I was too valuable where I was. By then, I was the World's Greatest Radioman. Why did you ask me how old I was?"

"I don't want to tell you."

"It's time you stopped playing with kids anyway." He stroked her arm. "Come on, let me tell you how many times I was torpedoed. I'll buy you dinner. Tell your friends that you're going to be with me."

"I knew you were smooth. Sure, I'll be right back."

"You know, I'm used to running around with midgets. You're the biggest thing I ever saw in my life."

"That's the first thing I thought when I saw you, that you didn't like women who were taller than you."

"What was the next thing?"

"Go to hell."

He grinned, "I'll bet you and I could take care of it in a phone booth."

She blushed, then she ran back to tell her friends what had happened to her. She ran with long strides, her hair swinging behind her.

II

The first person who didn't like it was Mrs. Galucci, who banged on the pipes when they started making too much noise. They? She—Mary Dougherty. She was twenty-three. All the women he had ever known in his life had been small and he had been able to control them physically, and she made him feel uneasy at first. So she was right, he didn't like taller women, but she had a sweet way about her, and a lovely smile. It occurred to him that she still thought he was afraid or suspicious, but her liveliness forced him to accept her on her own terms. She didn't want to fool him, she said: her friends had laughed out loud when she had come back to say she would be with him. "He wants us to know you're safe?" Flannery had asked. "And he thinks he's seen action on the North Atlantic?" It was more than a joke. After Tommy had begged off, Flannery had caught her trying to get a look at him leaving. "Ah, she's checking his buns." She had hesitated only a second more before going after him.

She had lived in Sunnyside almost all her life; she had been out of the city only twice. She was still with her parents, in a two-bedroom apartment in one of the rows of walk-ups owned by the Metropolitan Life Insurance Company, six blocks from where he lived. The rooms were so tiny you could not take three steps in any one direction, but there were five people in the place, including her brother and uncle, who slept on a daybed in the living room. She had gone to Saint Theresa's Parochial School and Bryant High and she worked as a secretary for the Otis Elevator Company on the West Side. A kid—she was a big kid. He could see that she hated every bit of it, living with her parents, being a secretary. She wanted to flirt and play with words. They prattled on, and he actually told her that he had been born in New Jersey and never been married.

He took her to the Queen of the Sea on Queens Boulevard and flirting became more intense and she allowed him to understand that, while her group of girl friends included a war widow and a divorcee, they looked to her for the kind of leadership that took them to Rockaway Beach in the summertime and the good bars and cocktail lounges in the city in the winter. He asked her why she wanted him to know all this, and she said, "What the hell"—a lacerated battle cry, he thought; but suddenly she wanted to know the truth about the number of times he had been torpedoed, and he told her, four, and she sat back.

"I don't know anything, do I?"

"You know you're not happy with what you think you know, or you wouldn't have come after me. I'll tell you something: the only thing you don't know is that everything you need to know is already inside you."

He took her back to his place and made love to her, trying to please her. She was a big kid, beautiful, and when old lady Galucci banged the pipes, Mary looked alarmed. "What the hell," he whispered, and she hugged him hard enough to make him wonder about her strength.

Mrs. Galucci didn't like it, and Mary's father didn't like it, and then her uncle, and eventually her friends' parents. All of them thought Tommy was too old for her. Mrs. Galucci took to standing back from him when he paid the rent.

Mary liked to talk about her adventures, the men she had been with, the money they had offered, the places they had wanted to take her. More than anything, he thought, she wanted to grow up. When he asked how she felt about the way her family and friends' families were reacting to him, she told him she didn't care what people thought.

"Why not?

"I know when I'm happy. I don't need other people to tell me."

"You're pretty tough."

"Yeah." She stretched herself out like a cat. "I raped you, didn't I?"

That was in another bar on Queens Boulevard, the Merry-Go-Round, which billed itself as "the largest revolving bar in New York." There was an Italian restaurant with watery spaghetti, a kosher deli, and a no-English Chinese storefront offering takeout only. She would meet him at the el station at Forty-sixth Street and they would grab a quick meal and a movie, a double feature, newsreel, and a Pete Smith short; or he would travel from Brooklyn into Manhattan and meet her on the West Side. They would go uptown for a first-run movie and a stage show. They saw Dick Haymes, June Haver, and Dan Dailey. Mary understood that Tommy had not done these things in years—it had taken him weeks of encouragement to get her to call him Tommy. He wanted to go out—he told her about himself. He told her about his father and brother, his mother and sister. He had not seen his sister in years. Amy had wanted the opportunity to sever connections with him, and after Kate's death he had given it to her. He told Mary about Kate, who was buried next to Charlie, up in Woodlawn. Charlie had been the one who had introduced him to Sunnyside. Tommy knew that he would have to tell Mary eventually about the battle in the garage in Howard Beach. He thought she already understood that he had killed, but he could not tell if she would make the dubious distinction between killing during war and killing in a time of peace. She knew what his politics had become, and possibly her uncle and his Easter Rising cronies had taught her that all killing was the same, brother against brother; but it was one thing to learn it in the abstract and another to attempt to overwhelm one's own sense of powerlessness. In the end Tommy's brother had been reduced to fighting over scraps like a dog: for years the two of them had been fighting simply to stay alive. Tommy began to see it for what it was that evening he carried his brother away from the club. He kept his thoughts from Kate all those months through 1936—the more important thing was that she was not alone at the end of her life. He had understood from his silence that he had not really taken it all into his heart, the reading and lectures, discussions and arguments, and for a long time after that he told himself that he was still holding something in reserve.

A lie, he told Mary. What he believed had more to do with his own condition rather than the validity of a series of assertions about history. He told her everything—everything that had laid waste to him inside. Now he knew that the assertions were true, that people were made to suffer unnecessarily, but he had fought his fight, his share of it, at least. What he had believed did not matter; it was what he believed now that was important, and he thought he would have difficulty living with himself if he had not fought. He told Mary all of it, on one of those nights that drove Mrs. Galucci frantic. They could only wonder what went on in her mind when she heard the water thundering into the old cast-iron bathtub—Mary wanted them to bathe together, or, more the truth, she wanted to bathe him. He was burned on his back and on the back of one thigh, and on the first night he had been apprehensive—she was almost fifteen years his junior. Now she said the scars of his back were like the color of his eyes and the gray in his hair. He wanted her to understand that he was still really living as much by his wits as when he'd had to run for his life across the Pyrenees into France, or when he'd turned Charlie's Chrysler into Walter while Charlie told him that bullets hurt. Tommy had to be sure she understood that he had never walked away from anything in his life, that he saw life as one whole, continuous thread. He had been a boy trying to prove something when he had gone to Spain, and now that he was a man he knew that the truth of what he had been trying to prove was something else entirely.

"Look at the way you've changed since we met. You carry yourself better. You're more beautiful."

She heard all this while she scrubbed his back—"scrubbing the elephant," she called it—and he could feel and hear her beginning to cry. He looked over his shoulder and winked.

She sniffed, "I'll be all right."

"Good. I love you because you can keep up with me. When you get like that, your face looks like a catcher's mitt."

She sniffed, "I didn't know they had baseball when you were a boy. I thought you kicked a skull or something."

The first time she saw him nude, she said, "You're what I've wanted all my life. When I was young, I thought it was a pony."

"And when you were older, you thought it was a high school teacher, and after that an Italian sailor."

"It was the Italian who taught me not to pass up shorties like you." And she pulled the covers over her head.

Another time she complained that she had to go to the bathroom. He jumped out of bed. "I'll do it. You're so big it'll take you three trips."

But he thought she was gorgeous, and told her—told her after he knew she was in love with him, although he thought she was a bit ahead of him on that score. And when he realized that he was thinking that he had to be careful with her feelings, he saw that he was only kidding himself about his own feelings, and he took her uptown to meet his seventy-one-year-old mother.

By then it was October, and he had a car, a '37 Dodge four-door with a welded block and brakes Tommy had rebuilt in the back yard of one of Mary's uncle's cronies. Mrs. Galucci had told him that she didn't want the noise in her yard, and his competence with the Dodge and its scored brake drums had put him in solid with the old Irishman who stood behind him that weekend, opening one quart of Knickerbocker after another. You had to prove you were all right, but by Sunday night he was so sick from beer that he couldn't be really sure that the brakes were actually fixed. He had instructed Mary that her people were never to hear about Spain, whatever they could guess. History had to repeat itself, he had told her; the two great world powers had to confront each other, and individuals on both sides were going to be used like pawns. He had no intention of confessing or recanting or implicating anyone, but at the same time he saw no reason to offer himself as a sacrifice to historical process when silence and a little cunning would allow him to avoid the whole matter. He wanted other things now, and if they were important enough to involve her, then they were important enough to engage everything he knew about staying alive—he believed he had learned that much from life.

She had less confidence in his judgment, where it concerned his family. He could not talk about his mother without feeling a tightness in his throat, and he had nothing at all to say about his sister. At first his mother resisted meeting Mary, and then when he asked her to come out with them for dinner, she said no, she didn't want him spending money on her that way. His mother struggled against all changes now; she was afraid of anything new; he said he felt sorry for her, but Mary could see it went deeper than that. Except for the radio, there wasn't a stick of furniture in her apartment less than twenty-five years old. On Sunday afternoons she listened to the Hartz Mountain Canaries—birds chirping on the radio. Tommy was thirty-eight years old and Mary could see that his mother still made him shrivel up inside and want to crawl away from her. He felt honor-bound to tell Mary that she could deal with her family with more maturity than he could muster for his own—his age did not matter, he said, or what he knew, or all the things that had happened to him. She thought it was pathetic, but she could see that it was true. He would sit in the dust and waste and utter defeat of his mother's life, and rage inside at her mewling and complaining. Mary knew in advance what she was going to meet. After nearly a month the old woman relented, or had the light dawn on her, and she asked Tommy why he didn't bring his "lady friend" up for dinner some week.

It was arranged. His mother had regarded him as the villain or the curse of her life for so long and for so many reasons that he expected her to commit some unimaginable, unforgivable horror, drawing Mary's razor-tongued wrath. Instead, it was an evening of small talk, souvenirs, and photo albums, and finally, the hoary old legends of Mountain Lakes, Flatbush, and the elegant two-year courtship. And the next time he saw her, his mother wanted to know Mary's age—she could guess her religion and background—and then said that Mary seemed terribly young. But then she was silent, and Tommy took it to mean that she was washing her hands of the matter. He called Mary from the Fifty-ninth Street subway station, and fifteen minutes later he transferred at Court Square for the IRT and twenty minutes after that he found her waiting over apple pie and coffee in the Bickford's at Bliss Street.

He wanted to tell her how crazy he still was, as old as he was; after everything, how uncontrollably unhappy he could become. He had to be sure she understood that he had not been able to have a family life in more than ten years, that he had not had a real home in almost twenty. She listened and told him to sit where he was, and then she got up and went to the counter for more coffee; and when she brought that back to the table she said she would be another minute, and she went outside. When she came back she had the *News* and the *Mirror;* she gave him the *News*, and the next time she spoke it was to read something about Hedy Lamarr from Winchell's column on page ten of the *Mirror*.

They found an apartment on Thirty-ninth Place near Forty-seventh Avenue, a grim and dirty block with a splendid view of the Empire State Building. Tommy had to give the landlord, an old German cabinetmaker, an extra two hundred under the table, but they were lucky to get anything at all. Mary's father reported that they were putting up Quonset huts in the empty lots near La Guardia Airport, and he had to be reminded that Tommy wasn't eligible for them. It didn't matter that they already had an apartment; Old Man Dougherty was that kind of guy, wanting to help but always a day late and a dollar short. They had the place furnished and he was still seeing chairs for five bucks, and a kitchen set, slightly used, for seven-fifty.

Tommy signed the paper agreeing that the children would be raised as Catholics, and the wedding was performed in the church in the basement of Saint Theresa's School. Flannery was the best man. Tommy said he didn't care who was the best man, provided he hadn't slept with the bride, which let out Halley for sure; so Tommy asked Flannery, and then Mary remembered a night when Flannery had been home on leave which, if it didn't exactly qualify, came close enough. What the hell, Tommy told her, he would just give the guy a smaller gift.

They observed the traditions and it was a wonderful wedding. The banns were read and the rehearsals held while the bride watched; there was a bachelor party of sorts, veal parmigiana and spaghetti on the Boulevard, and getting drunk in Paprin's up on Roosevelt Avenue, and the betrothed couple declined to copulate the night before the wedding. The bride wore white, a dress long enough to conceal her flat shoes, and when Tommy lifted her veil he had trouble getting it over her head until she ducked a bit. Her eyes were wet and she had used makeup in a way he had not seen before, so that her freckles were hard to see; when they kissed her lips were warm and the powder prickled spicy and sweet in his nose. This woman was his wife. He had awakened in midmorning nearly mad with uncertainty and disbelief, but now he could see how happy he was. He started to cry and when he looked around everybody else was crying, too, Flannery and the maid of honor, all the bridesmaids, even his mother, down front by herself, wearing a gray straw hat adorned with a tiny, pretty sprig of dried wildflowers.

III

They were clearing almost a hundred a week after taxes and the money he gave his mother, and the rent for their two-bedroom second-floor rear was forty-seven fifty a month. The landlord like to cheat on the heat, but they bought an electric coil and turned on the oven in the mornings before they went to work. When the weather broke he pulled the block from the Dodge and dropped in a rebuilt and spent the spring seeing that the rings took a nice set. In the summer he started working nights again—he would come home at nine in the morning to find a sandwich in waxed paper on the kitchen table. Sometimes there would be a note, and on Mondays the bankbook with their weekly deposit. Mary was fierce about saving; she wanted an end to living hand-to-mouth even more than he did. He was the one who wanted to drive out to Jones Beach instead of just down to Rockaway, or wanted to spend his night off at Steeplechase instead of on Queens Boulevard at the Center, which called itself "The Home of Proven Hits," where the two of them could see Marie Dressler in *Tugboat Annie* and Spencer Tracy in *Captains Courageous* for less than a buck. He told her he couldn't help himself, he had champagne tastes, but that wasn't it: at every turn he found her still so trusting and vulnerable that he could not help wanting to treat her better. The changes in him made him wary of himself, too—he could see that he had held back feelings he had kept buried for years. He would sleep during the day and cook her dinner in the afternoons, and if they made love before he went to work, it would be in the middle of the evening, when there were things he wanted to do but couldn't because he didn't have time. In spite of what she thought was her experience, there was a lot that she didn't know, and he wanted to hold her and take care of her. Their fighting never lasted long and usually led to new understandings. They were different from each other in age, religion, and background, but not in temperament, and finally they understood that their sensitivity to each other saved them more times than they knew.

She had a diaphragm, but she went to Mass, saying that it made her feel better, and often enough on Saturday afternoons she walked down through the shady streets to Saint Theresa's for confession, which meant that she felt the need to receive Communion. Tommy left her alone. During their courtship, she had said that she didn't like the feel of rubbers any more than he did, and after they had been married a week she told him she had been to a Jewish doctor, Samuelson, over on Forty-eighth Avenue, for a fitting. Mary knew her husband now, knew him better than he had ever allowed anyone to know him, and she knew he worried about intimidating her, but then something would happen to show him that she was ahead of him in many sly, subtle ways. She loved him so much that it taught him how to love her, in ways he couldn't even describe.

When the summer ended they started house-hunting seriously and in December they put down a binder on a two-story wood frame house in Hempstead not far from the Long Island Railroad station. With what he had put away during the war, they had over seven thousand saved; he figured they could make a down payment of four, set aside a thousand for repairs, and be out ahead in less than two and a half years—mortgage payments, interest, commutation, and taxes amounted to only half of their rent in Sunnyside and what they had been putting in the bank week after week; but when they got lazy one night and tried withdrawal instead of a trip to the bathroom, and the next month she complained of a cold. The symptoms were different from her usual cold, and he told her what he thought, and when she missed her second period they knew.

She was the best friend he had ever had, and he told her so. She worked for as long as she could, but they soon realized that she was not going to carry easily. There was more money for him in night work and overtime now, too; but there was a strike brewing at last, a real strike, and as he told her, it was going to be a long one. She had quit work but they stalled another couple of months, mostly sitting in the kitchen over coffee cups, satisfied with the fact that, by pluck and luck, they had bound themselves to each other forever, until death.

One night she told him that when she was a kid, her father and uncle, and even her brother, would sit in the kitchen having farting contests. "They'd want their corned beef and cabbage and their quarts of Piel's and then they'd sit there, swollen up like balloons, farting away and giggling like idiots. My mother would stand over the sink, pretending to enjoy it. It was lousy, dirty—I wanted to kill them all."

"Well, forget it," Tommy said "If Mike and I had tried anything like that at the dinner table, my old man would have stood up, glared, and ordered us to our rooms. I was young, but I remember how he dealt with my brother when he stepped out of line. That man insisted on a decent life, and the older I get, the more I understand how he did it, and the more I appreciate it, too."

The first child was a boy. They named him Michael, and if Mary's uncle chose to take pleasure in it, that was all right. The child's name was Michael M. Westfield III. The strike came and the executives locked themselves in the central offices, to keep the telephones in service, they said, but really to break the union while making themselves look like martyrs—they had their pictures in all the papers. Tommy took his place on the lines, following his captain's orders, and spent the rest of the time working on the house, sanding the floors, painting and papering, and replacing the moldings. Mary's father found him some car repair work, and her mother came our for a week. She was not a well woman and told Tommy that Mary was the first person in her family as far back as she could remember to own her own home. Then her mother confessed that she had not been sure of Mary's decision to marry a man so many years her senior, but now she saw it all differently. His own mother, by contrast, came out only one Sunday and was uncomfortable through the entire afternoon. When he had called her about the baby's baptism back at Saint Theresa's she said that she was not feeling well, and it seemed to Tommy that she was unnaturally reserved in Hempstead when the child was presented to her. Tommy knew that it was just more of her fear of anything unknown, but his anger boiled up nevertheless. There was nothing he could do, and because he really understood that, he did not let himself dwell on it. The baby was four months old and they were afraid that Mary was pregnant again, but when Tommy walked with his mother up to the station, he decided that drawing her into his confidence would only cause more pain on both sides, and he said nothing. It was a breezy night, and he walked with her on up to the platform. She said she didn't need money while he was not working, and he told her not to worry about it. The train came into view, and probably because Mary had opened him to his feelings, for the first time in years he moved to kiss his mother. She was unprepared and then embarrassed; she used some kind of fine powder on her cheeks that felt almost slippery against his lips. As he walked home again he pictured her sitting alone on the train as it rocked back toward the city—what did other people think of her sitting there by herself? Who did they think she was? He could not guess, and he could feel a terrible pain spreading inside him. Did people look at her, with her bitter little crescent slash of a mouth, her stooped shoulders? He looked at other broken old woman, and he did not want to imagine what went on in their hearts.

Mary was pregnant again and she became desperately unhappy. The strike ended, but they were down to less than five hundred in the bank. Later they remembered it as the summer they sat on the porch. The baby took after her side of the family and his skin was sensitive to the sun, so they could not just get into the car and drive out to Jones Beach. They did it one night when Mary's mother was out to visit and wanted to sit with Michael. It was a humid night and they came back with all the windows and vents open—the Dodge looked like a yacht going wing-and-wing as it sailed down the road. It had a radio now, a big push-button job Tommy had pulled out of a Buick, and they had it tuned to "The Milkman's Matinee" on WNEW. Mary was showing again she had put on weight and her back hurt. They had planned to have dinner, but the heat and the motion of the car had made her sick, and they had had to settle for a walk under the lights near the water tower. As they rolled up the Wantagh Parkway at forty-five miles an hour with Helen Forrest singing

"All the Things You Are" on the radio, Tommy felt the former Mary Dougherty beginning to cry. He reached over to pat her knee, and she broke down, sobbing. In another moment he realized that he had not heard a woman weep so bitterly since the death of his father, and he pulled over and cut the engine and held Mary quietly in his arms.

They named the new baby Annie after Mary's mother and as soon as she was old enough to sit up she was in the kitchen sink for her bath with her older brother. It was harder for Tommy to work nights with the two of them squealing in the house, but it meant more money, and working every other weekend meant more money still. That summmer they left the kids with Grandma in Sunnyside and took the Dodge up Route 7 through Connecticut and Massachusetts to Burlington, Vermont, staying at motor courts and inns along the way. Mary had looked forward to the trip for months, planning and writing for brochures. The doctor had put her on a diet to take the pressure off her back, but she needed a cushion behind her when she drove, and there were nights when she did not sleep well. The friends of her girlhood had drifted away and she had made new friends on the block; but most of the husbands were younger than him, go-getters, and Mary did not force them upon him. He supposed they wondered about him anyway, an older man married to a lively girl with a bawdy sense of humor. The young executives saw the Dodge up on blocks and heard through their wives that Tommy was replacing the transmission, or that the radio that sounded like a concert hall had been pulled from a wreck, and they came around. But while he was talking over the fence, Mary would come out to rub his back, or ask if he wanted coffee or a beer. It was clear that she loved him, a woman who could hold their attention even when they didn't want to give it to her, and he could see them appraising him. There was no real mystery. One night when he told her that no woman had ever made him feel so cared for, she burst into tears. They were best friends. She had told him long ago that he knew things about her that the priests didn't know, the sorts of things other men, including priests, held against a woman's character.

She had told him too, that she thought that he was a great teacher. He liked that; it made him smile. He was the kind of man who needed time alone to remain the man he wanted to be. He knew more about himself than she thought people could know. There were things that upset him. He had trouble with one of his bosses, an oppressive little man who hated any kind of independence. Tommy hated to shop for himself and left it to her to keep him in clothing. None of it weighed in any kind of balance—how could it? She had almost forgotten that he had taught her how to use a knife and fork properly. On one anniversary she sat in fascinated terror while he told the wine steward that the bottle had begun to turn, only to find that the steward agreed with him. "The old Westfield class," he said, and winked. He thought it was a joke, but it wasn't to her. On Christmas and his birthdays she shopped for books for him; now that he expected books, he told her what to buy, and she would take the list into the city not knowing which of them he meant for her—*Strange Fruit* by Lillian Smith, *Freedom Road* by Howard Fast.

Mary was pregnant again when they came back from Burlington, and after Mary Louise was born, Mary had her tubes tied. That was the summer everyone realized Emily could no longer care for herself, and she was moved out to New Jersey with Amy. There was a reconciliation between Amy and her brother, at least for the purpose of family business; and instead of visiting his mother week nights for dinner, once every two or three weeks he drove out Route 46 to Dover where Amy and old Arthur were living. Tommy never stayed for dinner. Amy and Arthur liked their martinis in the parlor, and guests two or three times a week. Tommy could see how unhappy his mother was, but there was nothing he could do. He could not help coming home wrung out. Mary would push a beer in his hand and make him sit down. They had a television set now and he would try to get home for "Garroway at Large," which was the only thing he could watch.

Emily's death took a long time. She became incontinent and Amy gave up on her, saying that two and a half years was plenty. It was decided that Michael could crowd in with his sisters, and it was done, and the old lady with the last of her belongings, was brought from Dover out to Hempstead.

She hated New Jersey and now she hated Long Island, and she lasted two more years, puttering in the kitchen for hours in the morning with her breakfast, sitting in front of the television set all afternoon, not quitting until Howdy Doody came on for the children. Mary had to change her sheets while she was downstairs and there were whole weeks when the two women did not speak. The old woman was grim and resentful of everything and everyone except Michael, who accepted quarters from her and heard her call him David, which he took to be more of her craziness. He knew that she favored him over his sisters, and he felt uneasy about it, but his mother told him to forget it, and after a while he saw it as a kind of compensation for being crowded in with his sisters. His sisters hated their grandmother enough to whisper in their beds that they were going to poison the old witch, but even a child knows that a family is only a group of people bound together by the secrets they keep from one another, and so Michael forgot about it; and then the quarters stopped and the place really smelled of medicine and urine, and finally, as he told his friends when they asked about the ambulance, "They carted her off to the hospital." It didn't take her as long as he thought to die, and the next weekend they were all in the funeral parlor again as they had been for his mother's Uncle Mike, only this time there were very few people there and his father stood over the coffin and wept out loud.

IV

They sold the Dodge for a hundred dollars and picked up a '49 Chevy two-door torpedo back, a handsome car, and in the summers of '56 and '57 after Mary Louise was old enough to travel, the family drove through New England up into Canada. Tommy had been in and out of Halifax a dozen times during the war, and on the second motor trip he saw it again. His hair was beginning to thin in the back and he had a ten-pound paunch. His years at sea had reduced what he had known of Spain to a few memories of light and dark, day and night; and a decade of marriage and family had left him with only a few glimpses of the face of the sea itself, shining in the quiet of afternoon, looming out of the darkness in the hours before the dawn. He had already told Mary that at this stage of his life he remembered his childhood better than any of the rest of it, just as in his youth he had hardly been able to recall his childhood at all—he could see that she was still so young that she could not imagine how her own childhood could ever be important to her again.

She was going to go back to work. The children were very nearly old enough. It was part of their plan. They were comfortable on what he was bringing home, but money was not the issue. When she had stopped crying in the car that night on the way back from Jones Beach he had reminded her that they had come as far as they had because they had had a plan.

"But now it's ruined," she said "We're broke, we're always going to be broke."

"I was never broke in my life, and I'm not now. Didn't I tell you my old man gave me the key to the vault?" He had his arm around her. "Remember? Do you want to hear it again?"

"I love you."

"He always had a plan."

So they had agreed to have the third child right away, and now, even with the house less crowded and Michael back in his own room, the place was bedlam. Theirs was the house in which their children's friends congregated. The grass in the back yard was trampled flat. A model plane was pinned to the workbench and there were electric trains on the cellar floor, a dollhouse on the side table in the dining room and pencil marks recording the children's heights on the jamb of their parents' bedroom door. Sometimes there were blanket-tents in the hall. The girls brought home a pair of kittens, and for a while Abner and Daisy Mae rode back and forth on the wash line in a pair of Daddy's socks. Socks were useful at Christmas, too. At Easter Mary wanted the hats he had stopped wearing long before—after a while, Easter was the only reason he kept them. He loved it—he was the one who read to the children. When Michael started the first grade, the teacher discovered that he knew how to read. "My father taught me from comic books," he said. Public school. Tommy wanted that, but Mary did, too. She said that her happiest childhood memories were surpassed every day in the Hempstead household. She liked the neighbors; her husband could see that she was good with people. Sometimes he was able to get home early and he would find her in the kitchen hearing some woman's marital confession while upstairs Michael had turned his bedroom into the Planet Mongo and was preparing for interstellar war by blocking the door with his dresser. Michael cried when the Giants moved to San Francisco, and swore to his father that he would never play baseball again.

"Don't say that," Tommy told him. "Don't ever try to hurt yourself."

"I don't care," Michael said. He was sitting on his father's lap. He was getting big—he was a husky kid.

"Do you know how much I love you?" Tommy asked.

Michael rubbed his nose. "How much?"

"Does it make any difference where Willie Mays is? What did you say to me? That when he gets done playing center field, there won't be any left?"

"I heard that on television."

"Well, he's still out there, isn't he?"

The sudden change in his father's voice made Michael look up. His father was crying. For the second time in his life, Michael saw his father in tears.

In the fall they started looking farther out on the Island for a larger house. Mary came home late one weekday night, saying that she had found a place, out beyond Farmingdale, on the other side of the Suffolk County line, a split that was finished and landscaped outside, but only roughed out within. The owner had tax problems and wanted to sell everthing. He wanted seventeen thousand. Tommy offered thirteen and they split the difference. It took a second mortgage on the Hempstead house and a first mortgage on the new place, but by spring, when they sold the Hempstead house for twenty-three-five, Tommy and Mary's brother had been able to finish the master bedroom. All that spring the children could see one another through the two-by-fours of their walls, and the dust did not settle completely until Thanksgiving, when Mary's parents came out with her brother and his fiancée, a gum-chewing little redhead from Astoria. At the end of the day there was a great fire going in the fireplace in the family room, but only the children were enjoying it while they watched television. So much of the day had been spent showing the in-laws the work that had been done that the adults finished in the kitchen, with bottles of White Label and C. C. in the center of the table, a line of buckled beer cans stretching out in front of Mary's brother. The old man was getting frail now, although he was still going to work every day for Con Ed, and he didn't need many C. C.'s to begin to feel sentimental. He wanted to thank Tommy for taking such good care of his little girl.

"When the hell did any of you ever think I was little?" Mary wanted to know.

"You got the wrong guy anyway," Tommy said to him. "I'm not the one who made this happen."

"I still don't know one end of a hammer from the other" Mary said.

"Not you," Tommy said. He reached for his mother-in-law's hand. "Right, Annie? You're the one who wanted to see this. You worked all your life for this."

The old woman's eyes filled up and her lips pursed, and then she nodded.

"It isn't everything," he said.

"No, it isn't."

"But it was still worth doing."

She held his hand tightly. "Sometimes I have my doubts."

The whole family was watching them. "Your grandchildren have never been hungry, Annie, not like you and your mother and her mother before her."

"Back in Ireland," she amended, to absolve her husband of the blame for her hunger. "You hope to God they never go through it, but sometimes you worry if you're right."

"You have to have faith, Mama."

The old woman looked up. "It'll be your bad luck, Mary, if you ever come to see that that's the hardest part."

"Count your blessings, Mama."

"Oh, I do, I do," she said, and suddenly, impulsively, she pulled Tommy toward her and kissed him wetly on the cheek.

There was a wedding, and then a couple of funerals. Arthur Donaldson had a heart attack, and then there was talk of him and Amy following their older daughter down to Florida. There were two Donaldson girls, married and young mothers; every winter Christmas cards would come up from the South, but there was no real communication, and no one knew what anyone else looked like. At fourteen, young Michael was almost five feet four, slimming down and he was losing the pug nose of his childhood. He had red hair and freckles, but Mary insisted she could see something of the tall dark-haired man in the photograph they had found among Emily's things, but it only made Tommy uncomfortable. He loved all the kids, but Michael made him glow, and more than anything Tommy wanted Michael to discover himself on his own terms. Michael hated school now, but at least he had his baseball. Tommy went down on Saturdays to watch him play. The kid was a showboater. He liked to dig in when he came up to the plate, and then lean back like a gentleman when the pitcher tried to tuck one under his chin.

Tommy saw more of his family in the girls, who had dark hair and faces that were oval even in their childhoods. Mary Louise had the same fierce blue eyes as her mother's brother, but Annie, who was slim and straight, had the dark, dark eyes of her father's family. They were both Daddy's girls, and those first few years in Suffolk when he wasn't spending his Saturday afternoons at the baseball field, Tommy was touring the shopping center with the girls. Mary was working Saturdays then, clerking in the local library. She worked three days a week, and although payday came only twice a month, her check was still so small that it was not unusual for her to spend all of it in a single trip to the supermarket. But she was learning public administration, municipal budgets and the ways of small-time politicians. One of them came into the library one night and tried to talk funny to her, but she could fix a man with a stare, and she never bothered to mention it to Tommy. She was a different kind of woman now, too busy to hear the complaints of neighbors in her kitchen. The job was making her known in the community, and people from the church and the PTA were calling her for community work.

Tommy was almost as old as his father had been when his father had died, and she owed it to herself to go as far as she could. Tommy had a pension as well as his social security, life insurance, mortgage insurance, telephone company stock and savings; but all of that plus the equity in the house and the scant value of her mother's jewelry would not carry her and the kids more than five to seven years. She was over thirty-five with only subsistence skills and practically no experience. He had told her years ago never to believe that they were on solid ground or that there was such a thing as progress. One night when the children were asleep he told her what he had been thinking and why. There was nothing wrong with him and he felt fine, but he wanted her to be realistic. She went out to the kitchen for her Canadian Club, telling him that either he smelled her breath or watched her cry.

He felt better after that winter was over. She saw to it that he got to Belmont and Roosevelt more frequently and he said he wanted to take the kids to Saratoga that summer. And as sum.ner approached, his mood grew more and more expansive, and she heard him telling the kids stories of his old man that even she had not heard before. One Sunday in June he took them out to Mountain Lakes, and they drove past the old enormous house—as far as he could tell, he said, nothing had been done since the Westfields had left. It took them hours to get home again in the Sunday traffic, and he was quiet that night; but the next morning he made love to her and said that he had hoped that there would have been time the night before to take the family down to the beach. She told him to take the day off, if he wanted, and go to the track, and he did, taking Michael with him. The two of them had a wonderful lunch, lost seventy dollars, and came home happy. In July, two weeks before they went to Saratoga, he took the family to Palisades Park and they spent the night going on all the rides they wanted.

That was the summer before Michael fell in love, the year before Mary was appointed administrative assistant at the board of education. They bought a second car, an Olds, and occasionally when he worked nights Tommy drove in on the Southern State, picking up the Expressway in Queens and crossing into Brooklyn over the Kosciusko Bridge. He and Charlie had come back and forth this way in the old days, when it was all country, and he had met Mary in Sunnyside just to the north, and even that was beginning to change. In the mornings as he went the other way he watched the lights of the cars streaming into the city, hundreds of thousands of them, and more than once he remembered that he had grown up on the dirt roads of Mountain Lakes as his children were growing up on—what?—ribbons of light? Kate had told him that his father had finally felt estranged from it all; and at the end she said that she could feel the same thing happening to her. Perhaps it started when you saw that your children knew nothing of the world you had left behind.

The winter of his senior year, Michael hitchhiked down to Florida to try out for the Detroit Tigers, but they weren't interested, and in the spring Tommy helped him get a car in shape to take him to Hofstra, the only college in the area that would accept him. He was an awful student, but he was going to give it a try. The girl he had been going with had treated him badly and Tommy could see that he was floundering, but the kid wanted to keep it to himself. That summer Tommy would follow the extension cords out to the back yard where Michael would have the portable turned to the Mets on Channel 9. The kid would open a beer for him, but the conversation would have to do with the game, or the car. That was the summer before the kid flunked out and was called up for the army. The following winter, while Michael was still safe on Okinawa, Tommy took Mary down to Florida, and spent an uncomfortable evening with Amy and Donaldson—an evening because they did not want to waste an afternoon they could put to better use at Hialeah. At the end of the night Tommy realized that he had done it out of some long-dormant respect for their common dead. Amy was an old woman who was the image of her mother, and Donaldson had angina, and carried his nitroglycerine tablets around in the pocket of his shirt.

V

They brought Michael into Da Nang by helicopter after they gave him the news, and allowed him the opportunity to call his mother and clean up before they put him on the Pan Am 707 for home. He got high before he boarded the plane, and kept it going until he reached the West Coast, when it seemed like a good idea to clean up. Sure enough, a son in mourning or not, they searched him; but there was a four-hour layover before the transport bearing coffins left for New Jersey, and some red-neck rotating out laid another number on him, and Michael slept until he was past Omaha. The plane was above the clouds the rest of the way, flying toward the sunrise. He had called one of his friends from California and together they rolled up the Turnpike in the gray, rainswept morning. The friend had still more details of the accident, that one of the kids in the other car had lost an eye, that the driver had been booked on a variety of charges—Michael knew he had to hear it, but it did not alter the emptiness he felt. Fifty-nine. What was one fifty-nine-year-old phone company man, more or less? And even given the circumstances, what was there to complain about? "He didn't suffer," Michael's mother had said. So why this deepening emptiness? Long Island seemed as small and remote a part of the world as the one Michael had just left, and he could see that difference between the one and the other, and the people, including his dead father, was only what he made of it. People on the next block hadn't known Tommy Westfield, as if they were all Vietnamese rice farmers. Michael and his friend rolled through the intersection in Amityville where the kid had turned his Riviera in front of the Olds. The intersection possessed no new magical properties—there was not so much as a scratch in the pavement to mark the spot of his father's death.

He was on time for his father's funeral. He figured out the miles and the hours in the air, almost halfway around the world, and he was still on time. The numbness was only beginning to wear off, his mother said. She had Annie under sedation and Mary Louise screamed and punched the wall, but his mother insisted that they would be all right. There was nothing to do but let the lawyers and the insurance companies settle it. Michael was not to worry—she was not going to be a fool. Still, Michael wanted to do something. He went to the police station in Amityville and read the accident report and learned exactly how his father died. He watched his mother's eyes the night before he had to fly back. "We're going to be all right," she said. "I don't want you to worry. Your father and I talked about this many times. 'Make a plan,' he said. Remember? I'm not going to let him down, and neither are you."

And then he was going back to Vietnam. He had another nine months to serve.

He was home for good the following year. Annie was at the State University at Stony Brook, and she kept him in smoke until he got his bearings. They would sit in her room talking, not terribly high, wasting the summer. Annie smoked like a bird. She was worried about Mary Louise, but Michael thought she was not that well herself. Their mother knew they were smoking; she didn't like it, but there was nothing she wanted to do. Mary Louise had gone haywire since their father died—the neighborhood was changing for the worse, and Mary Louise had started running with a tough crowd. Their mother thought that as long as she was working in the schools, she could keep some kind of watch on her younger daughter—Annie didn't have to tell Michael how foolish that was. Annie looked so thin to him that he felt obliged to ask her if she was doing speed. She said no and he felt ashamed for intruding. She was only the same as her sister, and he thought she probably knew it better than he could imagine.

He borrowed her car and went up to Cape Cod, but he was alone and found others traveling in groups, and it made him feel more alone than before. One night he called home, hoping to get Annie, but their mother answered. Annie had a date, his mother said. Michael was in a phone booth outside a gas station on Route 6, and he could watch the insects swarming up into the lights. He was almost twenty-one, and he had been drinking, trying unsuccessfully to pace himself, since five that afternoon. He asked what she was doing and she said she was watching a movie— God, she didn't know what it was; something about a family vacationing in a van on a beach, and being attacked by hippies.

He was silent a moment. "I don't know what I'm going to do with my life, Ma."

"I know. It will come to you. You have to be patient."

"What did Daddy have to say?"

"About you? When you were away? He couldn't see into the future. He knew that school never made itself interesting enough for you. He thought you didn't know how smart you are, that you hadn't begun to find out about yourself. Well, you miss him the way the rest of us do. I don't think you really know how much he loved us."

"I hardly knew him."

"No one was more aware of it than him. He said it was because he started his family late in his own life, and because life isn't organized the way it used to be."

"I think he would have been disappointed in me."

"No, he would have been proud of you all, especially the way you're trying to stay together. He said it would have been easier for you if you had had a brother. There was a lot you didn't know about him."

"I knew about his brother."

"No, I mean there was a lot he might have wanted to tell you."

But he was no better; only because he understood what they were trying to do for him, he let his mother and Annie steer him back to college. He had the GI Bill, and he saw that if he lived at home and held down his expenses, he would be able to make it from month to month. He told himself that he would help keep an eye on Mary Louise, but all he really did was throw her a good word when she was passing through on the way to her room. He knew it was worse than nothing at all, and he allowed that to work on him, too. Once college had been too hard and confusing; now it was too easy, or he saw how much of it was garbage. He took *Maggie, A Girl of the Streets,* from his father's library, and *The Adventures of Martin Eden,* but didn't finish either one. As often as not, he cut his classes. Many of the veterans would spend the afternoons in a bar or in somebody's apartment getting high. On weekends somebody would be brave or foolish enough to throw a party, or Michael would spend the night in one of the gin mills on Sunrise Highway. He ran into plenty of people he knew, other guys back from the war, girls from high school who already had stories of marriage, children, adultery, separation, and divorce. At home he would find his mother up waiting for Mary Louise, or Annie sitting cross-legged on the couch in front of Alice Faye singing "You'll Never Know" or Jimmy Cagney raving on top of a gas tank or her dreamboat, John Garfield, in *Under My Skin,* or *Body and Soul.* Michael knew about his father's years in the Merchant Marine and he was fairly sure that he had fought in Spain. The rest of it was what Annie called legend—the older brother, their grandmother's Apollo of a husband, and on, and on. Now the Westfields were a houseful of women who never used the living room. And him. Annie played the guitar and sang in a voice that buzzed the eardrums when she forgot that people were listening, but that was rare, and the stuff she wrote told nothing of what she knew of life. She was a woman, but everybody else, including their mother, seemed to know it better than Annie. "She'll only admit she understands the little things" was the way their mother put it, and Michael told Annie that the letters he had read in 'Nam reached deeper feelings, which was supposed to remind her that she had written *"Oh I love him! We fuck and fuck and fuck!"* Michael imagined that she was still the family's best hope—the countryside was overrun with spooks like him. Annie had a song called "Big Brother" that had to do with a fellow who played baseball and went to war and when was his suffering going to end, oh Lord, and so forth—that was him. That was his contribution. The first time he heard it, he told her to stop smoking that stuff, but he felt really very honored, and did not hide it.

They had one of those nonfamily, restaurant Christmases, the four of them over their shrimp cocktail, prime ribs, foil-wrapped baked potato—and a six-dollar bottle of two-year-old Beaujolais. The old Westfield class. On their living room floor was an array of phonograph records, best-selling books, sweaters for everybody, shirts for him, nightgowns, and the other things that women fearlessly bought for one another. The three women seemed to be enjoying themselves, and they did not see that they could not help pushing him away.

At the end of the next month he moved out of the house and in with three other vets near the campus. They had a colonial four-bedroom that was tied up in a property settlement, and installed in the living room was an old slate pool table so heavy that the floor flexed when they walked around it. Through the veterans office Michael got a job in the college library, and although it had to be rated first as the best place in the world to meet girls, it was a pretty good job, too, easy work if not especially free of dust. One night one of his housemates came in with a girl, a slim, brown-eyed brunette with smooth skin and a thin nose, and Michael could see that she was watching him. When the fellow went off on an errand, she came up to the desk and told Michael she knew Annie, who had said that the redheaded clerk was her brother. Michael's disappointment showed and the girl's laughter stung him, but then she said that his housemate was not important to her. Michael was smarting from her laughter, and so he told her that he would rather have it out front; and she said of course, ask him, and walked away. He did. She had told the truth, and she was back the next night, smiling; he saw that there was still some unresolved business, and he was wary. She was Jewish, her father was a history teacher, and her name was Natalie. When he was alone with her she grew shy, tense, and her behavior became artificial, but she didn't stop him when he wheeled the car into a Holiday Inn on Jericho Turnpike. He expected to hear some long story, but there wasn't any; and when Michael saw his sister on the weekend, he thought she would have something to say, but it turned out that Natalie was only someone she knew from a modern dance class. Yes, she had told Natalie that she would find her brother in the library, but they had been talking about their brothers—Natalie's brother had spent four years in the navy fixing jet engines, and now he wanted to do nothing but play basketball and smoke dope. Michael told Annie what had happened and he wondered aloud—he knew in the same moment that he was being an asshole: he sounded like a literature professor—if Natalie was using him, and Annie laughed in his face. He had the message at once, he didn't have to hear it, but she said it anyway. She was sitting in the middle of her bed, her legs folded under her, the vein in her neck showing while her cheeks seemed to glow red. "Don't you know how *cute* you are? Oh, Michael, she just wanted to take your pants down!"

"Well—" He was blushing.

"How much did it cost you?"

"Shove it up your guitar."

"I think I will!" And she grabbed her toes and rolled onto her back, laughing.

Michael did not have the chance to confront Natalie; she was in the library on Monday night with a note she slipped into his hand, something about missing him on Sunday night, and then he made the mistake of whispering something to her in the reading room. She was waiting for him at his car at ten o'clock, and he took her for a drink—she sipped her beer, which made him boil. She told him that she had done what she had felt, and she thought it was really lousy of him to demand that she explain her feelings. She wasn't asking if he loved her. Was she? What could she expect to hear? What did he want of her?

When he told her that he thought she had misled him about how well she knew his sister, she told him to go to hell and walked out of the cocktail lounge—one of those jet-black, candlelit places in the middle of a row of stores closed for the night—and he did not catch her with the car until she was across the parking lot. There were four lanes of traffic whizzing by on the highway.

"I won't put up with your Irish Catholic bullshit!" she cried.

"That's only the part you can see. Come on, get in the car."

"For what?"

"There must have been something you liked."

Her mother didn't approve. In spite of his status as a veteran, she thought Michael Westfield was a bum. Her opinion only made him more determined. Natalie's brother approached him cautiously, got high with him one night on his own really good Colombian, and then finally gave him a lecture on the history of the Jews. That was another night, a night they were drunk, and Michael said he thought Jesus Christ was the best Jew who had ever lived. Natalie's father liked him. He had been in the South Pacific during World War II and had been impressed with Michael's father's record. He was a short, square, muscular man like Michael's father, although many years younger, and Michael volunteered that his father had fought in Spain. Natalie's father put his arm around Michael's shoulder.

Annie played and sang at what they called their reception. There was no wedding—they were just moving into a converted summer cottage on the North Shore together. Mary Louise and her boyfriend were there, and Natalie's brother and his old high school flame, the veterans Michael had been living with, more girls, twenty other people, food, tequila, wine, a water pipe, a bong, a small quantity of hashish, and in the middle of it all, a discreet distance from the illegal substances, drinking her own Canadian Club, Michael's mother. She did not cry until Annie drove her home. Annie was supposed to call Michael when they were safely in the house, but she was too busy with their mother for too long, and he called them.

"She's all right," Annie said. "She was telling me what you were like when you were a baby, stuff for Natalie to hear. Hell, we were babies together. Tell Natalie that we had a lovely time."

"What's wrong?"

"Mommy and I just managed to get a lot on our minds in a short period of time. I love you, Michael."

All she was saying was that they had their hopes for him, but he could not lie to himself about what he was doing. He was not sure what he felt. He knew he was frightened and he could see that he had become a bully. Natalie wanted to go to California; her friends were there and in her mind it had become the means by which she was going to escape her mother. Natalie made it clear that she loved him, but she would not let him forget that he used her to rid himself of his own anger. He was not ready for marriage, she said—and perhaps she was right, because he knew that he would have allowed himself to be drawn into marriage if that had been what she wanted in spite of what he understood of his feelings. They were already so far along that he could see how marriage would have turned out, but—as she said—he didn't want to acknowledge the truth of it to himself. She had a sharp tongue—she was not perfect. They were still fighting over the first things that had happened to them. He did not think she was being honest with him yet, and she accused him of the same thing. One night she said that he wanted her to love him first, without equivocation, before he would commit himself. It stung him, although he did not let her know it—it remained a fact that she would not let him see how much she loved him. Oh, Natalie was not perfect. She was willing to live with him, but she would not admit to what he could see in her eyes.

She was twenty and had never been in love before. She was slim and girlish, and liked to put her arms around him, pat his stomach, and squeeze his butt. When he fixed her car, she was thrilled; and when he took one hundred seventy dollars from his friends at poker, she was amazed. Late that night he showed her the tricks his father had taught him, and on Saturday he took her to the racetrack for the first time in her life. They lost, but she loved that, too.

"My mother doesn't know how to enjoy herself," she said, "and she overwhelmed my father."

"I know."

"That's why she thinks you're a bum She knows I can't control you. Not even she can control you."

"How do you feel about it?"

"Today was a lovely day."

He thought he would give her a break and not ask her what that meant. He knew. If he began working on her, he would only be evading what she was telling him, that as far as she was concerned, he was free to do as he pleased with his life. It was no reassurance when he did not know what he would do with the whole world if it were given to him. He did not know who he was.

They had to be out of the cottage by May. In March her brother was arrested at a party, and charged with thirty-seven others with possession of marijuana. It was not going to amount to more than a fine, but he used the escalating tension as an excuse to move out of his parents' home, and that put pressure on Natalie. Annie had the second lead in the spring musical at the college, and Mary Louise changed boyfriends again, Michael heard. He went home less and less. He and Natalie had not decided on what they were going to do in June, although Natalie kept saying that after her girl friend's wedding in the middle of the month she wanted to go to California. She had known the girl since grammar school and it was going to be a big wedding. Natalie wanted to suggest that there was some measure of obligation in her response to the event, but he knew better. She was like his sisters about weddings, which meant that she could not wait to get there. For him it meant a haircut and getting together reasonably appropriate clothes, and then conducting himself as inconspicuously as possible under the circumstances. He had thought she was going to tell him it would be easier if he didn't go at all, but she said she was not going to act ashamed in front of anybody. He thought she was letting out a little of the anger she felt with her mother, but Annie said it was more serious than that—if he didn't believe her, why didn't he ask their mother? He didn't. Closer at hand was the decision he had to make about California, and closer still was the problem of where they were going to live for the two weeks before the wedding. It was a busy, confusing, upsetting three months for Michael; he might have missed Annie's performance if he had been left to himself, but Natalie had it down in her book.

He went up to the campus afraid for his sister, that she would be timid and let others push her aside; but she gave a performance, creating a real character, and her voice was the best of the cast, just beautiful, and it filled the theater. There was nothing small about her. She looked lovely, so lovely he felt uncomfortable with the idea of so many men staring at her; but in the second act she wore a dress that was cut low in front and the audience paid that much more attention to her—and it was obvious that she loved it. He had never seen her so happy, and when she took her bow he was cheering her joy as much as he had been cheering her singing and acting. Natalie was in tears. His mother had told them that there was going to be a party at the house afterward, and now he saw that he didn't want to be anywhere else.

The place was filled an hour after the theater emptied. The people were mostly Annie's friends, but neighbors came in, too, and people who had been in the audience—his mother's co-workers, it turned out. Michael wound up behind the bar downstairs, and after a while Natalie came down with a sandwich, salami and swiss on rye, heavy on the mustard, and couple of chicken legs heavily doused with vinegar-and-spice sauce.

"Your mother loves you," she said. "Can I have a whiskey sour, or are you too busy?"

"Watch me."

She stepped back to let him work. "She asked me if we were going to stay here until we leave for California. She said it exactly like that. I haven't said a word to her, Michael. I told her that I'd have to ask you."

"And you say my mother loves me?"

"No, she says. She said, 'Tell him his mother loves him.'"

"The message is clear. Annie must have spoken to her. What do you think?"

"I know you haven't made up your mind."

He could see that his mother had put her in a bad position, and that she had been trying from the start to make the best of it. "Do you want to stay here?"

"Do you want me to?"

"Yes." He still couldn't say it well, and both of them could hear it. She hesitated before she got up on her toes to kiss his cheek. He held her by the waist. "You'll have a good time," he said. "I promise you."

She smiled. "I felt something for you tonight that I never felt before."

"You're not going to tell me."

"No, you have to figure it out for yourself." She was on the other side of the bar now. "Oh, your mother told me that when we got to this stage of the conversation, I was to tell you that she's glad that you're going to California, because she has something she wants you to do for her along the way."

"When we get to this stage? What's going on?"

There was a gust of laughter from upstairs.

"Actually, she said when and *if.* Your mother's no fool. She said that if I couldn't talk you into going with me, I'd be better off going alone, and you know as well as I do how right that is."

"You'll do fine here." He took the cherry out of her drink and bit it in half.

"You wish. Oh, I love it here already," she said, and danced off.

15

Cross-country

I

His own car wasn't up to the trip. It needed upper and lower bushings and new drums all around, and at least two new tires, probably three before the trip was over. Her car was out of the question, too. It was a Volkswagen, and he simply couldn't fold himself into it for that long a period of time. He sold it for nine twenty-five, and then he was able to get five hundred for his own car, and an additional twenty-five for his snow tires and extra rims. He put in the cash to make up the difference, and then they put up another two hundred apiece when he found a '67 Firebird with a good-sized V-8, the big Turbohydramatic, air conditioning, and all the power accessories. She didn't like the car, but it was hers—they registered it in her name to save on the insurance. It was not a pleasant time. The Firebird was the best car he had been able to find, but all she could say about it was that he had forced it on her.

"I'm trusting you with the ownership, aren't I? Why can't you trust my judgment about the car?"

"It's not a matter of your judgment. The whole trip is becoming your trip anyway."

He wanted to tell her that she was on a trip already. They were like that right up to the Saturday of the wedding. It was a hot day, and they drove to the synagogue in the Firebird with the air conditioning on, and he won the small victory of hearing her admit that the thing had its uses after all.

As the day went on and got better for him, he saw his pettiness for what it was, but he could not help feeling that he had been driven to it. He wanted to talk to her about it, but it was not that kind of day for her, either. A Jewish wedding was a new experience for him, but he thought the way the Rabbi could say what he pleased was lovely, and Michael made sure she heard him say so. She gave him that little smile that was supposed to let him know that he was making her happy, and later, at the reception, after the cocktail hour, she said she could tell that her girl friends thought he was handsome.

"I want to have a good time," he said.

"I'm having one."

He had meant the trip. They were leaving Monday. There was only a little packing to be done tomorrow. The doors to the main room opened, the full band struck up, and she started to move to the music.

"Do you want to dance?"

"Yes," she said. "I do."

"Good." He put his arm around her. "We're going to make this our own party."

Before they left, he called his mother, told her they would be late, and took Natalie to their Holiday Inn on Jericho Turnpike. He made love to her and then they slept, and then they made love again. They slept through the night.

His mother said good-bye to them before she went to work, and they finished the last of the packing by ten o'clock. Annie had rolled a couple of real boomers to get them started, and she and Mary Louise shared a third with them before they kissed them good-bye, and waved and yelled from the driveway. The car was loaded down, the tiny trunk filled, the back seat piled up to the windows with suitcases, a pair of knapsacks, and a bag of food. Michael told Natalie to light another number as they eased onto the Southern State, and then she hid the second, their last, in the bottom of a box of Tampax. He thought it was a lousy place to hide anything, and that told him he was feeling both joints, and he kept quiet. He saw that she was pretty high, too, and they rolled toward the city silently. They had a book of maps with the route marked, and she had the package his mother wanted them to deliver for her—his mother had given Natalie all the instructions the night before, and he didn't have to think about it for another two thousand miles. They rolled over the George Washington Bridge at eleven-thirty, and an hour and a half later they were crossing into the rising hills of Pennsylvania. It was a good day, with a blue sky and high, small, white clouds. They had already been into the food, celery and carrots, then cookies. Neither of them had ever driven so far west before. She had been up and down the East Coast from Lake George to Fort Lauderdale, and she knew that he had overflown the country four times. He wanted to keep going. The road wasn't as good as he had hoped, but he thought he had the energy to go all night, even if she wanted to sleep. She said she was awake. At three o'clock she took the wheel, and he closed his eyes but hardly dozed. At five they were a little more than halfway across Pennsylvania. They had been on Route 80 since they had left New York; in Ohio they were going to cut south to 70, and then take 70 west to Saint Louis before heading southwest to Oklahoma. The land grew progressively more steep as the light faded, and when they stopped for dinner they looked at the map again. It barely showed the mountains, only a few thin plus signs and numbers here and there, and a telltale twisting of the highways. Did he remember the French and Indian War, she asked him, and Fess Parker crossing the mountains? Dan'l Boone killed him a b'ar when he was only three. She looked a little tired, but she was in a good mood. She wanted to save the last joint, but he had seen too many boy scout hats and smoothly shaven, steely faces underneath them to want to be bothered with living dangerously any longer. She understood—and after they attended to the car and got rolling again, she started fishing in the Tampax box. The engine stumbled, or backfired, the box went flying, and it was five minutes before all the paper-wrapped cylinders were picked up, and another five before the joint was found.

The marijuana slowed them down and made them tired, and by then it was nine-thirty and very dark, and the lights they passed offered only gas and lodging, or towns somewhere out in the dark. There was nothing to see. It was now really too cool for the air conditioning, but they had to leave it on because of the humidity. The insects were like snow flurries. The car had a windshield washer, but Michael had only checked the fluid level, and the jets were clogged. They were near the Ohio line, too deep in the mountains to get anything on the radio but static. To stay awake, Michael told her about the war. He had been in 'Nam three months when his father died, three months of being frightened and getting high. This stuff was garbage compared to what they had smoked over there. His father's death made a mess of him, he said; going back, he tried to promise himself that he was not going to talk to anybody, except on orders, for the rest of the tour. Natalie knew where he had gotten that from; she had spent an afternoon with his sisters, who had told her why he was Michael Westfield III. She knew all about his drunken late uncle, the wife who ran away, and his elegant, suave grandfather, and the two-year courtship—she had come back to the cottage eager to discuss the gentleman in the yellowed photograph, and instead she heard about his old man, who had never even raised his voice to him, who had taught him so much. How did a man like him come out of a background like that? He had thought the war was a gag—Michael supposed that Natalie had heard all this; he could not discuss the war without discussing his father. They were in Ohio now, and all they could see were interstate highway signs under purple lights, and oil company emblems afloat in the darkness.

" 'Hey, listen to me,' he said," Michael repeated—he knew she had heard this. " 'You don't have to go. I'll back anything you want to do.' He said that to me. And then he said, the last thing he wanted me to understand, 'The most important thing is to stay alive. If you want to know why it's politically important, the best thing I can tell you is that the war has nothing to do with your destiny as a human being. Stay alive,' he said. 'If I could make you obey me the way I was being raised to obey my father, I would do it. My great-grandfather kept my grandfather out of the Civil War that way.' I told you this, Nat, but I want to tell you again. There was nobody as tough as he was—he could laugh at anything. He could! Because he laughed then, and said, 'That's the story about your great-grandfather anyway.' He looked at me and said, 'Come back and live your life.' Do you know what happened then?"

"No, what?"

He had his pants unbuttoned. He liked to have her scratch his belly with her long fingernails, and now he kept still while he stretched in the seat and she dug in and scratched hard. "Well, Swoboda went fishing for a curve ball again with the bases loaded and the Mets took the field in the top of the ninth and went on to lose the game."

"Bastard."

"My old man had terrific biceps. It was the way he worked. He said he fell into working with his hands and then he found, after a long period of time, that it suited him."

"You didn't tell me what happened to you when you got back to Vietnam."

"I did exactly what he said, which was everything I could to stay alive. I was out of my mind. I can't think of it without thinking of him. I just stayed alive. I don't think I ever killed anybody."

"Are you sure?"

"Natalie Burger, Miracle Mile psychiatrist. Yes, I'm sure, I don't think I ever killed anybody. I don't know. People shot at us and I shot in the same direction as everybody else. I never actually saw anybody I was supposed to shoot at. All the time I was there I hoped to God I never would see anybody. And I never did."

"I'm sorry."

"If you had any honesty, you'd be in Israel now taking your basic training."

"Don't remind me," she said.

He felt threatened enough to want to make a wise remark, because he knew that her feelings were real. She had made it clear at the beginning that she was glad she was a Jew. Her children, whether he liked it or not, were going to be Jews.

"And if they're baptized and confirmed?"

"You don't understand! They're still Jews because they come from *me!*"

He did understand—he understood that this had started because he had started talking about 'Nam. At the wedding on Saturday he had wanted to talk to her about the fact that he never felt that she was giving him any *help*—by the time he realized that he really wasn't angry with her, she kissed his cheek while she reached into his pants briefly, and told him she was going to get some sleep.

She was still asleep when he stopped for gas in Columbus, and she didn't feel the engine stumble again as they moved out onto the interstate again. There was something wrong with the car, he knew, and he began to listen to the way the thing was running. He got lost in Indianapolis and went around in circles for a while until he found the right signs and arrows, and then Natalie woke up, ate an apple, and said she was ready to drive. It was four in the morning, and the moisture in the air was like ice. He had gone through miles of darkness, and now they were passing through another bank of purple lights and bureaucratic intersections. He pulled over to the side and ran around the back of the car as she got herself over the transmission hump; it was so cold now that they had the temperature control moved over to the position marked HEAT. He pushed the passenger seat back and covered himself with Natalie's coat. The car started rolling again. His eyes were closed and in spite of the pain his position was inflicting on his back, he could feel himself falling asleep.

When he woke up, it was daylight. They were pulled over to the side again, and Natalie was asleep behind the wheel with a sweater over her and her head against the window. He didn't know where they were. The land was flat and the road, all four lanes, went straight out to the misty horizon. A truck went by, rocking the car. Michael's watch said seven-thirty. A car went by, its license plate reading, *Land of Lincoln.* Then a camper: *Live Free or Die,* which Michael knew was from New England. Two more cars, both reading, *Land of Lincoln.* All right, Illinois. He got out of the car, waited for the road to clear, and took a leak.

She was awake in a few minutes, a little stiff, and went around to the passenger side. He started the car and put the defroster on, then moved the selector lever into DRIVE. The car got going nicely, stumbled, and then bogged down so badly that Michael instinctively feathered the throttle. Then the car started to roll again.

"It did that last night when I stopped for gas."

"Like this? Was it as bad as this?"

"I don't know."

"Well, you just felt it."

"Don't raise your voice, Michael. I had to pull over because I was seeing spots. Christ, you don't even ask about that!"

At sixty miles an hour, the engine coughed. He backed off again. "I'm hoping I can get you to a gas station. You have to go, don't you?"

They drove the next twenty miles in silence, at fifty-five miles an hour.

There was only a kid on duty at the gas station, and the mechanic—the owner, in fact—wasn't due until nine o'clock. Michael was sure the problem was fuel delivery. He had put in new plugs, points, and condenser, checked all the cables and vacuum hoses. Now he got out his tools and pulled a couple of plugs and took a look at the points. Natalie brought him a cup of coffee from the machine in the office. He started the car and it ran. Fuel delivery—he wanted to be methodical. He took off the air cleaner and worked the throttle by hand. Plenty of gas. He removed the fuel line and blew out the brass fuel filter. It looked clean. The kid was watching him and volunteered that often fuel filters were put in backwards, which sometimes restricted fuel flow. Michael wanted to check the fuel pump. The kid got a bucket, and while Natlie cranked the starter. Michael watched the fuel gush into the bucket.

"Nothing the matter with that," the kid said.

"Maybe we picked up some dirt." Michael put everything back together again and ran the engine hard. Natalie was watching him. "Anything wrong with this car?" he asked the kid.

"Shit, no. I'm about to make a bid on it myself."

Natalie got in the car. Five hundred yards down the road, the engine faded and then caught again. It stumbled—if anything, he had made the problem worse.

"Did you put the filter back in the right way?"

"Jesus Christ, yes! It was in right to start with!"

"Don't yell at me, Michael!"

"Did you see anything wrong? Did you see anything wrong with this fucking car? It's the fuel pump. It's got to be the fuel pump. It can't fill the bowl under load. Don't put the air conditioning on."

"Pull in at the next place."

"I intend to."

The "mechanic" was on duty, and Michael told him what he had done. The man said it had to be the ignition. Michael asked him if he had an analyzer, and the man said no, but if Michael wanted him to advance the ignition so he could make it to the big truck stop fifteen miles up the road, he'd do it. Michael said thanks, but no, thanks, and got behind the wheel again. He wanted to feather the throttle while getting them up to speed—it had to be the fuel pump. Natalie had heard everything in the gas station, and she chose to speak a moment before the engine coughed—he was watching the speedometer: forty-five miles an hour.

"Why didn't you let him advance the ignition?"

"Because the points will burn out in ten fucking minutes, that's why! That damned hillbilly doesn't know shit about cars!"

"Where's the hill? Now *calm* down!"

In another moment he slammed his fist down on the steering wheel.

"Don't do that! It's my car, too! My name is on it!"

"And if it ran right, I'd throw you the hell out of it!"

The car was getting worse. When he looked over, she was trembling. "I'm sorry," he said.

She covered her eyes with her hand. "I don't know why I got into this with you. You can have the damned car. I'll catch a bus or something. Anything will be better than this."

"Come on, I'm sorry."

"You know, when I saw you cheering your sister, I thought you were the nicest guy in the world—really, number one. I'm trying to understand why you can't treat me the same way—"

"Why do you have to give me that stuff about your children being Jews?"

"Michael, you're going to have the face the fact that you're not going to have your children alone."

"I'm sorry. Don't get out of the car, please. I mean it."

But she said nothing, and as they rolled off the highway at the next intersection, the engine died completely, and wouldn't start again. The sign said the town was one mile down what looked like an endless straight road. The traffic on the Interstate was heavier now, and the sun was out. It was going to be a nice day. Michael opened the hood and removed the air cleaner. The carburetor bowl was full. He went back to the driver's door.

"I don't know what's wrong," he said to her.

"I know."

"If I can get it started, we'll go to the first gas station."

"All right," she said.

"I'm sorry."

"Stop it now," she said.

The car started, and at twenty miles an hour, and then bucking, the car rolled toward a rising cluster of gas stations. The first was on the right, and it was big, with three bays. Michael was relieved. If it had been the town junkyard, he would have had to go past it, and he didn't know what she would have thought.

Another kid. Michael told him what they had been through, and asked if he had an analyzer. The kid told him to drive it in. They had to push it.

Inside, in neutral, it ran. The oscilloscope showed the ignition timing on the nose. The kid didn't want to go further on his own, and the mechanic was in town—no, this wasn't the town. There was a diner across the road. Michael said they would be over there having breakfast while they waited.

When they came out of the diner half an hour later, there was a beat-up old Lincoln parked beside the gas station building, and inside, an old man was curled delicately over the engine compartment of the Firebird.

"Merle, this is the feller who owns the car."

Merle was sixty. He had no hair, few teeth, and a whistle in his nose when he exhaled.

"It's her car, too," Michael said.

Merle gave Natalie a little smile, then he scratched the white fuzz behind his ear. "Well, she seems to run all right in here, but she don't seem to want to run under load. We tried it. Sonny says you checked the fuel pump."

Michael nodded. He glanced at Sonny.

"Old Merle don't look like much," Sonny said, "but he sure knows his shit."

Merle had another little kindly smile. "I want to have a look at that carburetor."

Michael was suspicious, but he couldn't see that he had a choice. He didn't want to be caught exchanging glances with Natalie, either. "All right. Say, is that your Lincoln out there?"

"Quarter of a million miles on that old tanker," Sonny volunteered. "Merle gets his money's worth. Look at those tires. Fifty pounds of pressure."

Merle was already at work. He fiddled with the throttle linkage. "When did you get the rebuild?" He put the accent on the first syllable of the last word.

"We just bought the car. It's got forty thousand on it."

"Well, you've got a rebuilt carburetor just the same. Come here." With his rag he wiped the base of the casting. Michael could see that the gasket wasn't a factory installation. "I'll have to have a look. I never liked these four-barrel carburetors anyway. We had a lot of trouble with them right after the war. That's a two-barrel out there." He motioned toward his dented old car hunkered down on its monster tires. Michael told him to go ahead and then he turned to Natalie to tell her what was happening. He led her outside.

"I have no idea if he knows what he's doing, but I don't see that we have a choice. In any event, he's already seen something that I didn't see."

"Do you think we have a bad car?"

"I don't know. Natalie, I don't know what I do know. I'm sorry—I'm not going to make this worse for you."

"I told you to stop it."

"I better watch old Merle."

Merle had the carburetor off and they waited while Sonny bathed it in kerosene and blew it dry with the air hose outside. "You never know what you're going to get with a rebuilt," Merle said. "You get one done in a factory in a city, and the feller just opens the box and screws in the parts. An old country boy like me will look in the book to see what the right parts are before he goes into town to get them. Now we'll have a look-see."

"I'll tell you," Sonny said, "this old boy really does know his shit."

"Why do you let him talk about you that way?" Michael asked.

"Well, he's only a boy. I know he likes me."

Now Merle took the carburetor apart, rolling it over in his hands, removing one screw after another, one piece after another. "Here we go," he said. "I've seen this before. I'll bet she ran fine around town. Get her out on the road and let everything get nice and hot under there, and you're not going to have nominal values anymore." He had the book open now, Pontiac—1967, and he paged through exploded views of carburetors. "It's not even the right carburetor. It'll do the job, but not even the jets inside it are right. I'll tell you, son, they can do you twice and you won't even know it once. I can do a rebuild and have you on the road in an hour."

"That little car will run like the village idiot," Sonny said.

"How far are you going?" Merle asked.

"California."

"I think you'll be all right."

He wanted to buy the parts himself, and Michael and Natalie went into the office to wait. After a few minutes the owner of the station came up in a Cadillac, a young man, maybe thirty, with thinning, sandy hair. He said hello and asked them where Merle was, and they explained everything;

and the owner, listening as he went through the work orders, said, "Well, that old man don't piss around." He wanted to know where they were going, and he told them that he wanted to sell and clear out himself—he had inherited this place from his father, and now he wanted to go to the Virgin Islands and live on a sailboat. He supposed he would have to do a little chartering to stay alive. Michael asked him about Merle.

"He's some kind of a fucking genius, I guess. But if you want to see him turn all shitfaced, tell him a joke that's a little off-color. He's the kind of jughead who likes it here. Sonny's another, the two of them just as dumb as trees and happy all the time. Me, I can't wait to get the hell out."

Natalie was laughing out loud. "Nominal values—I heard him say nominal values."

"Oh, he gets that shit from *Mechanix Illustrated.* Can't wait for the next moonshot. You saw that Lincoln. He'll chew your ear off all day about tolerances. I'd go crazy if it wasn't for Saint Louis."

Which was where they wanted to stop, they decided when they were on the road again, an hour and a half later. Sonny had had to road-test the car, and that had taken the extra time. The car was running perfectly. Michael ran it up to ninety miles an hour, and there was still plenty left. The truth of the matter had been that Merle would have been willing to talk their ears off on tolerances or anything else mechanical, and it had occurred to Michael that he could have got Merle going on moonshots, but he didn't even consider it. It would have been ungrateful, disrespectful, and unloving. The whole bill was thirty dollars, and Michael gave Merle a five-dollar tip—the idea of a tip had seemed disrespectful, too, but Merle had seemed glad to get it. At the same time, Michael told Natalie, he thought they owed it to themselves to spend the night in Saint Louis.

"He was an unhappy soul," she said about the owner.

"I liked him. He wasn't so unhappy that he had to cheat us. His engine analyzer cost two thousand dollars used, and he didn't try to make us pay for all of it. We'll stop in Saint Louis because I want to take his advice."

"You feel better already."

"Yes, I do."

They checked into a downtown motel at three o'clock, and they showered together, soaping one another down, letting the water draw the tensions out of their bodies. They made love and slept until seven o'clock, made love again, and went downstairs to the nightclub for dinner. He thought they were spending a lot of money, but she said no—she wanted him to have a steak anyway, she said; and when they were up in the room again, she made love to him, getting on top. It was the way that gave her the most pleasure, and after she was asleep, he turned on the television set and took another look at *Invasion of the Body Snatchers,* or the first half of it, as if he hadn't had a fretful moment in a year.

He woke her up at five-thirty, putting her on her back. She was getting sore now, but it didn't take much this time, and as they lay there laughing about it, they realized they were wide awake, and she asked him if he wanted to get going.

He did. They were rolling out of the city by seven-fifteen, and one hundred miles to the southwest by a quarter to nine. This was rolling land, cultivated and benign. On the radio a funeral parlor sponsored a reading of the local obituaries. Signs announced souvenirs of the Ozarks, and they passed a perfectly preserved 1954 Mercury hardtop with the see-through plastic roof. Michael turned around to look at it—Natalie was driving—and thought of his father, because it was the kind of thing that he would have enjoyed seeing again.

The sky was overcast today. They were forty-eight hours out of New York, and the days were running together in his mind. She said she felt the same thing. They were not tired. In the early afternoon they passed south of Saint Joseph, Missouri, which Michael remembered from the westerns as the portal to the Southwest, and on into Oklahoma, cowboy country, Indian country. DO NOT DRIVE INTO SMOKE the signs said, but now it was raining lightly, and the wipers thumped across the windshield.

She took the wheel again in Oklahoma City, close to dinnertime. They had driven out from under the rain, and there would be daylight until nine o'clock. They had fallen into a comfortable rhythm, changing places when they stopped for gas, every two hundred and fifty miles or so. They had decided to go straight through. The car was humming. The land was flat again, flatter than Illinois, and treeless and dry. They could see for miles—it was like the ocean on a calm afternoon, frozen forever. The book of maps indicated that it was going to go on like this most of the way to Flagstaff, Arizona, their first destination, eight hundred miles away. They would run out of interstate in the Texas Panhandle, and from there they would be running on long sections of the old Route 66. Natalie was a good driver. She said she was having no problem with her energy. Her period was due on Thursday afternoon and it usually had her uncomfortable and tired the day before. Under the circumstances, she said, she expected a heavy flow. But she said she was all right. He figured that they could take it easy through the night and be in Flagstaff by two o'clock in the afternoon. She said they would be there sooner, and he took that as a measure of what she thought she could do.

They had dinner in Shamrock, Texas, and passed through Amarillo an hour and a half later, and stopped for coffee in Tucumcari before midnight. New Mexico. It was mostly a two-lane highway now, and the motels, restaurants, and gas stations were smaller, older, and farther apart; and although they could see nothing out beyond the lights along the highway, they began to feel the emptiness they were making their way across. People had come out here in wagons, and now that they could see what it was, they were filled with wonder. Even now civilization seemed like hardly more than the track of a snail across a rock. Michael told her that the West reminded him more of the rest of the world than of the eastern half of the United States—they could feel the East behind them, secure and content in the darkest part of the night. This was close to the ground, like the rest of the world, and it felt poor in the same way.

At three-thirty he took the wheel again. He had slept a bit, but he was more weary than he had expected. His arms felt heavy. The road began to climb again, and after she curled up to sleep they passed a sign advising of dangerous crosswinds. After a while he could see glittering necklaces of light spread out on the horizons—towns, but he couldn't imagine how far away. The sky was clear, and sometimes when the road was empty he dared to look up. If the primitives thought we hung motionless beneath the stars, he could understand why. He turned the radio on low and listened to a cousin three states away play country music for his "friends and neighbors."

Then around the mountain, twisting left and right, the transmission in second, down into Albuquerque, three miles of downtown, porn theaters, and Indian jewelry wholesalers. Natalie woke up, heard where she was, and turned over again. Then they were in the desert, climbing.

The fellow on the radio talking to his friends and neighbors gave way to another who wanted to speak to his "brothers and sisters." Yes, sir, The word of the Lord. The Kingdom of God is at hand, brothers and sisters; if you seek, you shall not fail to find it. Michael listened for a while, and then he began to see the silhouettes of the mountains in his rear-view mirror.

They had breakfast in Gallup, and Natalie took them on into Arizona. Did they have any produce or live plants? They remembered the agricultural inspection in *The Grapes of Wrath.* The sun was up, and the land looked as if it had been asleep for a million years. The bottom of an ancient sea, home of Geronimo. They could see a freight train that looked at least two miles long.

In midmorning they stopped at the Painted Desert and the Petrified Forest, and took pictures of each other standing beside the car. A while later they felt tired again, and drove past the sign that pointed to the Meteor Crater two miles to the south. They could get Flagstaff on the radio, and the map showed that it was at seven thousand feet, just south of the highest mountain in Arizona. Grand Canyon was a few miles to the north. There would be plenty of motels in Flagstaff, and Michael was ready to stop. He wanted to sleep before he did anything else.

Natalie was sitting on the foot of the bed, fully dressed, when he opened his eyes. She anticipated his question and told him that it was three-thirty. He had not been asleep that long.

"Did you sleep at all?"

"I closed my eyes," she said. "Are you awake? I called those people for your mother, and they're expecting us. It's only about fifteen or twenty minutes to the south, they said. I have all the directions."

"Do I get anything to eat first?"

She had a white paper bag. "I bought you a burger and a shake across the street."

"What are you up to?"

"Los Angeles is just another five hundred miles. I don't want to waste time. We can be there tomorrow."

"I don't want to be rude to these people. What did my mother tell you about them?"

"That she's never met them. Come on. I thought you knew. Guess what arrived right on schedule? And no problems. Saint Louis was good to us. Eat your burger before it gets cold."

"You're my Burger."

"Shut up. Unclean."

He drove—she said that she had not written down everything she had been told. It seemed to take longer than the time she said, and she made him drive slowly while she read aloud from her notes. She had the package in her handbag. They were supposed to stop at a gas station before they turned off the road and went up the hill.

"What the hell for?"

"Something we have to pick up. They only have one car and the lady of the house has it back in Flagstaff."

She had them doing ten miles an hour before they went around the curve that brought the gas station into view. She had Michael tap the horn twice. A young man with dark hair came out of the office. He had a paper bag full of groceries.

"Are you Tom?"

"Sure enough. You Natalie?"

"Yes, hello."

"Hello. I got the call. He's all excited." He looked over at Michael. "Hello in there. How're ya doin'?"

"Okay," Michael said, laughing. Natalie took the groceries. Michael put the car in gear. "You've been a busy little devil, haven't you?"

"One call, Michael. Now stop it."

"Don't get excited." Tom was laughing at them—or him. Michael looked at him sharply.

"Take it easy," Tom said. "I'll see ya."

"Turn right at the second telephone pole," she said to Michael. "It's about a mile and a half. It's a kind of mobile home, but it's down on a foundation. Double-sized, whatever that means."

"Double width. What are you so tense about?"

She sat back. "I'm beginning to realize what's going to happen to me. Just keep driving."

They came to a little crest and there, just over the top was the mobile home, with a little landscaped plot around it. In front was a little dirt turnaround for cars. The house faced southeast, and on the other side of the turnaround the hill dropped abruptly fifty or seventy-five feet to the road they had just taken, and beyond that, in a series of lengthening steps, the hill gave way to a valley that extended for a dozen miles to a wall of red cliffs. There were more red cliffs beyond that, and the effect made you believe you could see twenty-five, thirty—maybe even forty miles.

She was going into her pocketbook. "Your mother told me to give you this here. You're supposed to take it to the old man in the house. Don't worry about the groceries. I'll bring them in."

"What old man?"

"Him." She was about to burst into tears. "This was all for you, my darling. Michael, I love you!"

"What the hell is going on?" He turned in the seat, expecting to see a little old man tottering down the steps, but this man filled the doorway and stood there, waiting. He was six feet two or three, and even as old as he was, his back was straight and he had to weigh two hundred and ten pounds. Michael got out of the car. He looked back at Natalie, but she waved him on. The package fit in his hand, and was hardly heavier than the empty wrapping would have been.

"Michael!" the old man called. "Michael Westfield!" He came down the steps. He had a full head of straight gray hair and large, sad pouches under his eyes. "Don't you know who I am?"

Michael shook his head.

"Do you still cry about Willie Mays?"

Michael stopped. The old man moved forward, squinting in the afternoon light. "Well, my father gave me the same name as your father gave you. I'm your father's older brother. He saved my life years and years ago, so come here now, and let me say hello to his son. I thought I'd never see you."

II

With one arm around Michael's shoulder, the old man opened the door for Natalie. She had the groceries. "You had no trouble with his cousin," he said to her.

"Oh, *he* had fun," Natalie said. "He wanted to know how Michael was doing."

"My cousin? I thought he was looking for trouble."

The old man said, "You have four altogether, and they can't wait to meet you. Westfield's not our name out here. You call us Regan. Their mother and I took that name when we came West."

Michael gave him the package. "We brought this for you."

"We'll open it later," the old man said. "You're staying for dinner, you know."

Michael turned to Natalie. "How long did you know about this?"

"I started to find out the night of Annie's party."

"Annie's my sister," Michael said.

"I knew that the day she was born." The old man smiled. "She stole the show this spring. Your family out here knows about you. Would you like to see your photographs? We have them going all the way back."

"You really are his brother—"

"That's what I said." His voice broke. He grabbed Michael and held him by the shoulders briefly. "You're my brother's son."

"We both cried over Willie Mays," Michael said. "Now I know why."

"He told me. He used to call us at night from the job in Brooklyn. We lived in Los Angeles until four years ago. The telephone would ring in the middle of the evening, and I'd hear the hiss in the wires, and then I'd hear him say, 'Hey, it's me. How the hell are ya?' "

"He saved your life? Why was it a secret?"

"Did he ever tell you about a man named Charlie Duran?"

"The two of you worked for him."

"Your father figured out who killed Charlie."

"He never said anything about this."

"Not to you. Your mother knows. He told her before they were married. He didn't want you to know, you or your sisters. You see, at the same time, he learned that my father—your grandfather—had kept a secret from us. Later, your father decided secrecy was the right thing for him as well. The night after your father was killed, the night you were flying back from Vietnam, I brought my children together and told them the whole story. They knew I had a brother, but that's all. We had a rule in the house about who picked up the telephone when I was home. They didn't know we were in touch, just as you didn't know, and your father and I talked on the telephone almost every week for twenty years. He called us from Boerum Street. When the improvements started to come in, all he had to do was plug in his test equipment and dial, he said. We were talking to each other all the time you were growing up, right up to the night he died. Well, I told my kids everything that next night. Natalie, I'm going to say this in front of you because I want Michael to know that what his father did was nothing to be ashamed of. He and I disagreed about it for twenty years. My father wanted to keep his secret from his children forever, and so did my brother, for the same reason. But I told Tommy when he was alive: he saved me. The man who killed Charlie Duran was a man named Georgie Howe, and your father figured that out, and saw that Georgie was just waiting for the chance to kill me, too. Your father gave him that chance, and Georgie fell for it, and your father and I threw Georgie Howe out a window."

The old man's eyes held him. "My kid brother was the best man who ever lived."

"If he were here, he'd say your face looks like a catcher's mitt."

He smiled. "Do you want to know where that came from?"

"Sure."

"You sound like him. How about a drink? Your father said you're a pretty good bartender."

"He used to talk about the places you ran."

"Well, you won't eat for at least an hour, so it won't matter what you drink. Your aunt is up in Flag, probably putting a torch to the place. She's become some piece of work in her old age."

Michael held Natalie's arm. "What's her name?"

The old man was opening a package of frozen strawberries over the blender. His big hands worked with care, as if the package were a miniature. "Lillian and I were married forty-four years this spring." He looked at them and grinned. "And we've earned it. You have to tell me how these taste. I haven't had a drink in twenty-six years, which may be the achievement of my life. Everybody in Boyle Heights in LA knew Mike the drunk, but everybody in the San Fernando Valley still remembers Mike Regan from AA. I put more drunks in the hospital in the Valley than anybody else, from 1946 to 1962." A can of frozen lemonade concentrate went on top of the strawberries. "Use the lemonade can to measure the rum," he said to Michael. "A can and a half. Then fill the blender with ice. You'll like the strawberries in California. They're almost as big as baseballs and just as sweet as you want."

"You still cook."

"You're getting marinated steak with fruit and vegetables. Does your mother keep kosher, Natalie?"

"Sort of."

Michael could see that she loved him already.

"I was going to make an avocado or carrot-and-leek soup, but they both take milk, and if your stomach isn't used to it, you can have trouble." He turned on the blender, and in a moment the glass pitcher frosted over. He took champagne glasses from the cupboard. "So I made a mild, thick, finely diced gazpacho."

"You're his brother, all right," Michael said.

Mike poured slowly and handed the glasses over the counter. The glasses were heavy, and felt like ice in their hands. "I was going to tell him where his father learned a certain remark," he said to Natalie.

"I remember. This is delicious, not too sweet."

"Enjoy it. No one your size has ever been able to finish two. Well, it was the last time I saw my brother, during the war. I was still drinking, and he had the chance at a travel priority. In those days it was hard to make a cross-country call, and it took him an hour to get through. I was sober when he called, but I was drunk by the time he got here. We lived in Boyle Heights then, and you'll pass it as you head out to West LA. The train smelled of sweat all across the country, he said. I opened the door and there he was. I was drunk, as I said, and Lillian was standing behind me, and he made a remark to her about me, and she said, 'Yeah, his face looks like a catcher's mitt again.' And that's where it came from."

"What was he like during the war?"

"He read. He loved the sea. He wanted to be by himself. It changed him. Georgie Howe had tried to kill Charlie Duran back in the twenties, and your father, who was nineteen at the time, figured that out, too. When the war ended, I wanted him to come out here, but he said there were things he wanted to do back East. He didn't want to leave your grandmother to my sister. We never could take your Aunt Amy into our confidence. Your father tried to tell your grandmother once, after a woman named Kate Regan died, before your father went to Spain, but your grandmother always thought your father was one of the ways God was punishing her. For years after I left New York, she wouldn't speak to him. It was a terrible thing, the worst thing she ever did in her life."

"I never liked her," Michael said. "I'm sorry, but she made life miserable for all of us."

"In Brooklyn, when I was a little boy, she was so beautiful she glowed. She was a passionate woman."

Hey, how the hell are ya? His father had used the same phrase when he had called home. Willie Mays? The man his father had saved was alive, growing into his old age, while his father was dead. Yet his mother had sent Michael here. Natalie put her drink on the counter. The old man understood and led her to the hall that gave access to the bathroom. The house was pleasant, pressed wood, plastic, and formica wrapped in an aluminum skin, and it looked mass-produced, but clearly it was what the occupants wanted. The kitchen extended the width of the structure, and the dining area was crowded with plants. The living room gave access to a heavily planted patio in the rear. Mike came up beside him.

"Your Aunt Lillian told me to go easy on you, but your mother said that it would only get us off on the wrong foot with each other. I wanted to go East when your father died, but your mother thought that it would only make things harder for everybody. Your father never wanted you to know any of this."

"Why?"

"He wanted to put it behind us all. I'm going to tell you about your grandfather, too. Your grandmother may have glowed in her youth, but there was no two-year courtship, and very few carriages. I know you heard all that. My father went through his own hell. I didn't learn any of it until the middle of World War Two, when your father came to Boyle Heights. Your father argued that we weren't the first generation to try to bury the violence of history, but that was all the more reason to try. But you've already been to war. My father wanted to keep his secret, but he was overruled by his best friend, Kate, whose name your aunt and I took. Your mother has decided to overrule your father for the same reason. You need to survive. A half hour before I took the beating of my life, your father called Kate Regan and told her that Georgie Howe had seen years before that we were all pushovers if he planned it carefully enough, and she asked him if he were sure, and he said yes. He engineered the beating, by the way, by acting like a smart kid—that's what saved my life. After his call, Kate said, she sat there looking out at the river for almost an hour. She told your father later that she was remembering everything she knew about Georgie. 'Now I know what was in your father's heart,' she said. 'He would tell you not to do it.' And she told him what your grandfather had been through. And then it was your father's turn to be quiet. He told me that he was trying to put it all in the balance as well as he could, including the future of my son David and the beating I had just taken. Charlie had been Kate's lover. He looked at her and winked. She thought he was going to say he understood, or he would at least think about it. But no; your father played a dangerous game for months. Come outside. You've got five hundred miles of desert to cross before you get

to Los Angeles, and you might as well have a look at it before the light
fades." He opened the sliding glass door. Out beyond the patio wall the
land fell away in a long, gradual slope—it seemed absolutely bare; mile
after mile of crumbling yellow and purple, sun-blasted rock. "We started
coming here after the war. For years we camped in a tent." There was a
stone fireplace in the corner of the patio. "I want to get the charcoal
started. Your father said to Kate, 'I'm not going to make the mistake my
father made with Sullivan. I'm going to take my time killing this son of a
bitch.' "

Hey, it's me. How the hell are ya? Natalie found them. The air coming up
from the desert was hot and dry, and the strawberry drink made wonderful sense. Natalie wanted to know how he was feeling. Michael did not
know. His Uncle Mike was beginning to tell the story of Michael's
grandfather now, and of how Kate Regan had know him. Michael could
imagine his father whispering through the long-distance wires, whispering across the country. It was all true, and this man was his father's
brother, talking of the elegant gentleman in the photograph as a boy on a
street that no longer existed, born on a ship in the North Atlantic during
the Civil War. Not Westfield. Monk, what their common middle initial
stood for. Running through the streets in the snow, blood on his hands.
   The fire was going. Mike stepped inside, and then the young man
became aware of Natalie watching him intently.
   "I didn't know any of this," she said.
   "Why am I afraid, Natalie?"
   "We can leave."
   "You brought me here."
   "Michael, nothing is permanent. That's what he's telling us. That's
what he's telling me."
   "You don't know how naked I feel."
   "I know you don't think I do. But don't bother yourself with that.
Instead, ask yourself if you think I'm your friend."
   "Now?"
   She blinked. "I'm sorry, but you have to. Not even this will make you
think of it on your own."
   "I can't believe it. You pull this shit on me now?"
   "Every time you feel pain you take it out on me! I'm not throwing shit
at you! I am holding up a mirror!"
   The glass door rolled open. "I thought you were a scrapper," Mike said
to her genially.
   "I'm sorry," she said.
   "Are you satisfied?" Michael asked her.

Mike handed him his glass. "I did what you're doing long before you were born."

Michael backed up. "I'm sorry, man, but I don't need your shit, either."

The old man smiled. "Not all those drunks *wanted* to go to the hospital, youngster."

Michael eyed him. "Did you hit your kids? I want to know."

"Michael!"

"No, no. I know what he's driving at," Mike said. "His father never hit him. He knows I know that. He thinks—well, look how he fights. The answer's no, and now that we cleared that up, let's go back to the idea that I'm your uncle, and not your father."

"Not all those drunks wanted to go to the hospital, Michael."

He looked at her: *don't you understand?* her expression asked.

Mike said, "I spoke up when I came through the door, because of the real reason Lil is out. I had her on my mind and Natalie reminded me of her. There's a part of this that my wife doesn't want to be reminded of, and I don't have any choice but to get to it directly."

Michael was hot with anger, but he knew he could fight no longer without risking the last of their respect for him. He surrendered to the stupor of the defeated. Lillian with Georgie Howe—who was Lillian? Michael didn't know why he should care. His father, only a few years older than he was now, keeping track of his brother, making sure through his mother and Kate (and Lillian, deceived) that Georgie was not concerned with Mike. This man. This old man telling the story of a young man named Tommy—he had dropped the *your father;* Lillian, the mystery woman, apparently was on her way—Tommy watching, waiting until his older brother was about to sink into alcoholism completely, and then one night spiriting him up to Kate's, getting him into the elevator, and then tying him to the bed in the guest room. The alcohol took a week to boil out of him, with Kate and her maid spooning soup into him and changing sheets underneath him, and then Tommy appearing at the foot of the bed on Friday evening to tell him quietly that Georgie had done more than secretly engineer Mike's collapse. The little pistol he had pointed at them had killed Charlie Duran. Because Georgie had been endlessly patient, it had been impossible to see the pattern until he had emerged on top of them all.

"The first thing I thought of was that it would be pointless to tell Lil, the kind of thing I thought in connection with her years before she threw me out. Oh, I wrote the book. Tommy had already told her. She was outside in the living room, afraid to face me. She was breaking down. And there I was telling myself that she was no longer human. She knew what was going to happen, what Tommy planned to do regardless of what she said or did. He wouldn't let me see her until he told me what he had said to her. If she didn't go to the police, she would be an accessory to murder, but if she did, Georgie would have gotten away with Charlie's murder. We had no proof. I want you to understand, this almost destroyed my wife, and as Tommy said that night, none of it would have happened if it had not been for me. She was already at the point of collapse; I couldn't say that I wasn't going to face myself. This is only a hint of how bad a man can get. Tommy had to tell me that he was going to stop right there unless I showed some understanding of what I had done to that woman."

Tommy sent Sissy across town for David, and when she called from the back of the barbershop in Harlem to say that the two of them were safe, Tommy gave the telephone to Mike, who called Georgie at the club. Lillian had come back to him, Mike said, and now that that was settled, he wanted to discuss the disposition of the club.
"I'm listening," Georgie said.
"I'll call you tomorrow where you are," Mike said, and hung up. In the apartment on the East Side, Sissy had taken the phone off the hook. There was no answer when Georgie called Kate's apartment, either. They could hear the telephone ringing as the elevator started down to the street.

A kid. A boy. *Hey, it's me. How the hell are ya?* Michael could see his father leading the others through the streets of a city that had all but vanished—what was left of any of it? What was the use of it? And Lillian. Michael's father had talked about his older brother's wife, a tall, leggy, lovely brunette: she had to be close to sixty-five years old today. His father and his father's brother had thrown her lover from a window, but what had they imposed on her? Who was she now?

Tommy had a passkey to a building downtown. He knew Georgie's routine and habits. The next evening, Mike called the club at seven o'clock, and Georgie appeared on the sidewalk three minutes later and got into his car alone. When the car was rolling, Tommy sat up in the back seat. He put the gun to the back of Georgie's neck. "Make a U-turn. Here. Now. You figured we'd be watching the place, but you made the same mistake as your late friend Walter. Now keep your hands high on the wheel. The boys around the corner are just going to have to figure that you never left. Take Eighth Avenue downtown. You always underestimated me, Georgie. Charlie and Mike weren't stupid; they were just trusting. Me, I trust you to kill me, the way you killed Charlie."
"Don't wise off, kid."

"Turn that mirror so I can see out the back. How'd you do it, Georgie? What did you tell him that made him let you put holes in the back of his head?"

"I forget."

Tommy pushed the gun barrel into Georgie's flesh. "It doesn't matter. My brother and I are going to kill you regardless. Lillian knows. In another hour, you're going to be dead. Your body doesn't know that, though. There's a mark where the gun is. Your body thinks it's going to live. In an hour, it's going to be garbage."

"Maybe I did the world a favor," Georgie said. "You want everything. I know what you're up to. Go fuck yourself. You're not going to see me beg."

At that hour on a Saturday the streets were empty, and they were downtown in ten minutes. Tommy got Georgie out of the car and walked him into the building, where Mike pulled open the heavy, brass-trimmed door.

"Hello, Mike."

"Get his gun first. And don't stop with that."

Georgie had a thirty-eight in his jacket pocket.

"Look for the peashooter," Tommy said.

Mike found the little one up between Georgie's legs—like a load in his pants, in his shorts, behind his crotum.

"What do you say, Georgie?" Mike asked. "Are you going to come across?"

"Why don't you get on your knees, like your wife?"

Mike kneed him in the groin.

"He says he's not going to beg." Tommy told him. "I lied to you, Georgie. This is where you die—now, not an hour from now. Tell your body how soon it's going to be smashed out here on the sidewalk!" He hit Georgie on the side of the head, hard enough to take more fight out of him, and together the brothers muscled him into the elevator. Mike opened his pants and got the gun, and then in disgust hit him with it. There was blood. "We're not going to be able to put him in your clothes," Tommy said.

"Jesus Christ!" Georgie yelled. "My God!"

"Now you're begging, you bastard! You did the world a favor, killing Charlie? Now the world is going to pay you back!" The elevator stopped. The door to the empty office was open, and beyond that, the window was up.

"Please! Don't do this!"

"Get the stuff in his pockets," Tommy said. He wheeled Georgie around. "You die sooner rather than later—what difference, eh?" He hit him again with the gun, backing him up, Mike grabbed him, and pulled his jacket off. His own clothes were in a suitcase on the floor, and Mike got Georgie into them quickly. Georgie was drooling, moaning, when Mike poured the whiskey on his jacket. We'll do to him what the Alderman did to himself, Tommy had said—it had required no more explanation than that. In another moment Mike had Georgie ready. "My brother thinks he's going to push you, but he's

not. I've been waiting for this since you pointed that gun at me, you mother-
fucker! You killed Charlie and made a killer out of me! Go to hell, Georgie.
You're going into the ground forever!"

Georgie grabbed for the window frame. "Please! I want to live!"

Tommy put his foot against Georgie's chest and pushed him through the
window.

"But we did it, the two of us," Mike said. "Tommy didn't see it, but I
was there, realizing that we couldn't allow Georgie to be seen struggling
in the window. I had my hands on him. Tommy could have disappeared
off the face of the earth at that moment, but Georgie was still dead."

Michael was staring at him, breathing through his mouth.

"Then your father turned to me," Mike said slowly. "He turned to me.
'Did you see his eyes? They were on me all the way down. He never
made a sound. Ah, Mike! Mike!' " The old man sat back, his hands in his
lap. "I told this to Lillian, and then to my kids when he died. The first
time, with Lil, was terrible for me. The second time, I wanted to tell it.
Eager. I wanted my children to know about this man. Your father was
crying, but he grabbed Georgie's clothes and me out of the office and into
the elevator. He had a plan. The building was the one your grandfather
had had his office in, and it had a side entrance. Your father had a car
there, bought with the last of the money we had won at Saratoga two
summers before. He was to take Georgie's car back in to the East Side
and park it in front of my old apartment. Kate, Lil, and David were on
Riverside Drive, Kate waiting for the police to call and ask if she had a
son named Michael Westfield, and Lil and David for me. But in the
elevator, your father began trembling and turning gray. I knew what was
happening to him—I saw it during the war. The car was registered in my
name, and I decided to leave it there, even though the police would
never be able to understand what happened to the ignition keys, if they
thought of them. I had to push your father into Georgie's car, and all the
way uptown he was doubled over beside me. He thought he was having a
heart attack, it was so bad. And it kept coming, in waves. In those days
there weren't any tranquilizers, only opium, but we both knew we could
get that from Sissy's uncle. That's what I had in mind, but I wasn't really
thinking, and your father knew it. He put his head back against the
window and talked. He told me to call Kate before she heard from the
police and tell her what had happened to him, and to have Sissy get Lil
and David out of the apartment to meet me somewhere. I wanted to
change the plan, but he wouldn't have it. But he couldn't get out of the
car. He couldn't move. I called Kate and told her that we were all right,
and the others came out to meet us. They were standing on the northeast

corner of Eightieth Street and Broadway. David, of course, was very confused. He was eight years old. Later he remembered that he saw his uncle the day we left New York, but he didn't know what anything meant. Your father wanted him in the car, where he couldn't hear what was said on the sidewalk. Your father couldn't stand up straight. He wanted to curl up against the wall. Lillian thought he was hurt. Sissy knew what it was. She looked at me and gave the sign that she would deal with it. But we could see that he was coming down with something right there."

"He's dead. You have to run or Mike and I will both get the death sentence. And Mike's innocent. Hear me? He didn't do it. I did. I pushed Georgie out. I thought I was trying to make everything right, but I was kidding myself. I found that out just as soon as I had the chance. Oh, boy. It's starting again. What's happening to me?"

"You'll be all right," Sissy said.

He smiled. "I'm going to trade on our friendship."

"We'll see."

"You got a heart like a turnip. See? She's right. I know what's wrong with me. I had it before, and that's what I wanted to get him for. And now it's back, worse than ever."

"My uncle knows all about it," Sissy said.

"He can cure this?"

"No, it's more like he invented it. Why do you think he's so smart?"

"Sure." He turned to Lillian. "Last tag. If you don't take him and run, we both die. I don't know about my brother even now. I don't know what kind of life you can have. But you get another chance, whatever it's worth. If you take advantage of it, I'll get mine. I'm responsible. I did all this. Spit in my eye if you want, but your husband's innocent, at least of murder. What he's done he's already dying for." Tommy took a breath and stood up straighter, holding his stomach. "I love you, Mike. When I was little, you always took care of me. But I can't take care of you now. We both know that. And don't ever think that I was trying to take care of you when I kicked Georgie out the window. I know what was in my heart. You can't take care of me now, either, and I know that better than you. Well, the hell with it. Get going. Don't call, don't start looking at the newspapers to see how you're doing. Just go. I don't even know how far this car is going to take you. The one I set up will run forever." He smiled. "I guess it's mine now. Okay? I'm still thinking."

"Come with us," Lillian said.

"Kate's getting old. She's done a lot for the Westfields—I'll tell you about it some time. Go on. When it gets bad I'll go up to Mom's for dinner and get some of her good cooking."

Lillian kissed him. "I won't quit."
"We'll see each other. I promise."

"Your father had a breakdown after that. Kate appeared downtown as your grandmother and said that Georgie was me, and then she went home to help your father. I found out later that he spent weeks on Kate's sofa, doubled over like that, in the grip of terror. He told me later that he didn't want his children to know that he had been through anything like that—never mind the reason why. He went to the funeral. He wanted to make sure Georgie was really dead, he said, and I believe that. The following year, Kate had her stroke. Your father tried to tell your grandmother the truth, but the deception was too much for her. What did she know about police procedure? She lived the rest of her life as if I were dead. Your father reminded her of too much, going all the way back. She treated him terribly. And he never stopped giving her money and the money that I sent. Your father had a post office box, number 351, New York 1, New York, and I'd send him cash wrapped in paper. For her. I didn't know what they were going through. He didn't tell me. Not then. That came later.

"The club closed, of course. Your father wanted to stay away from there, and he never found out what, if anything, anybody thought of the disappearance of Georgie Howe—and his girl friend. All we ever knew about him was that he came from Brooklyn and had changed his name. My wife understood him the moment she saw him, and if you need an explanation for the other things that happened between them, all I can tell you is that I was never better than her worst fears. When we drove away from that corner, she told me that she was doing it for your father—she had a lot to answer for, she said, but she was not going to her grave with his death on her conscience. She wanted to say something else, and I thought I knew what it was, but I couldn't find words for it. She said, 'I would rather kill you than see him suffer any more. Don't give me cause to kill you, Mike. I mean what I say!' And that's the way we started out here—how we came clear across the country, with only the clothes on our backs and the money in our pockets. And that's one of the reasons why I told you about your grandfather first—I would have wanted to tell you the way your father told me, but Lil's heard it all, and just as much, that was how your father heard it, in the middle of his own trouble. Maybe it will help you understand him better. Kate made no mistake in telling him. But now at least we don't have to mention the other man's name again. The only chance I had with her years ago was to let her forget the past. I made up my mind to that. She didn't hear his name again until 1943, when your father came out to tell me about your grandfather. I read the old New York papers when we made it to LA, and it seemed safe to call Kate to find out how your father was doing and to tell them where we were. Long distance was expensive and difficult in the late thirties, and the next time I called, Kate's telephone was disconnected. Your father and I had already made the arrangement concerning your grandmother, and week after week, I sent cash wrapped in a piece of paper, and later, when it all got to be too much for me in LA and I started drinking again, Lil did it."

A car was coming up the hill.

III

They were in the living room waiting for her. Michael watched her get out of the car. He was a poor judge of the height of women, but Lillian was not that tall, or as he saw as she gathered her packages, that straight, either. She was thin, and her color was pale, almost jaundiced. Her hair was straight gray, and bound in a bun behind her. She raised her head and saw them watching her, and she smiled. Michael went to the door.

"Hello! Give me one of those packages."

"Oh, they aren't heavy. Give me a kiss instead. Say hello to your old aunt. Have you heard all the dirt?"

He laughed. "I doubt it."

"He does run his mouth, doesn't he?" She let Michael take everything, and then she saw Natalie. "Oh, I know who you are. I do want to say hello to you."

"They're already booked into a motel in Flag," Mike told her.

"It was the best I could do," Natalie said. "We came straight through from Saint Louis, and it was no time for surprises."

"I'm sorry," Michael said.

"Maybe you'll decide to stay another day. There's lots to see." She took a glass of the strawberry mix from her husband and accepted his kiss. "They adjourned without a decision," she told him. To the young people, she said, "Everything you hear about Arizona politics is true. It's the frontier. You'll feel it in California, too, even if you only stay for the summer."

"I want to start the vegetables," Mike said.

"He's chasing us," Lillian said. "Tom said he would stop by later. Your cousin. He's afraid he scared you."

They were going outside again. "I didn't exactly understand the situation," said Michael.

She turned to Mike. "Did you tell him about his cousins, old man?"

"Nope. I saved all that for you."

She closed the door on him as he went to his work.

"I love him," Natalie said. "He's the nicest man in the world."

"Is he like your father?"

"Yes," Michael said. "In his way."

"How many children do you have?" asked Natalie.

"Four. David, who's old enough to be your father—he has two teen-agers. They all live in Marin County, California, north of San Francisco. Charlie lives in Woodland Hills, California, which is Los Angeles, and he has three children and a wife who's a trial. Kathy lives in Santa Monica, and she has two boys. She's divorced. And Tom, our cowboy, who decided that this was for him, too. Rat poor. Two children and another on the way." She smiled. "Pretty good for an old wreck like me. I had two heart attacks and now I have plastic valves. Did Mike tell you?"

"No. I'm sorry."

"They're in there five years," she said. "They work beautifully, I think. He does the housework, the wash, and the ironing. And he tends his garden. I could do it all, but he wants to. He said he came back here to be by himself, and he meant it. I have to have activity. I found that out when we got to California. I wanted to work. Did he tell you what we were like in those days?"

"No, but you don't have to."

"Well, we had David, who was old enough to know that something serious was wrong—again. We had to tell him we were changing our name because we were going to start over. Mike gave me the money, saying he wanted me to trust him; and I asked him if he thought he merited it. We were like that. Neither of us even liked the other's smell. It went on in that fashion for a long time. We stopped in Chicago, but it was too much like New York, and at that time in our lives, such a thing was much too nerve-racking. We took the Lincoln Highway west. We traveled with the people from the dust bowl. We were as poor as any of them, but we had a good car and one set of decent clothes apiece. We thought we could avoid trouble if we looked as respectable as possible. Those were hard times. Mike worked as a dishwasher and a short-order cook. I worked nights as a waitress. We were trying to stay alive. He was laid off, and I knew what was going to happen, but he held on for a long time before he started drinking again. This time it was different. He would sit in the kitchen by himself. For a while I thought he was doing it that way because he was afraid that if he went out, I'd disappear on him. No. I decided that I would live with anything except physical abuse. It was on one of those nights that he told me he still loved me, and a while after that I realized that he was trying to tell me something else—that he'd been faithful to me, as his father had been faithful to his mother, and as, later, your father was faithful to your mother."

She became pregnant with Charlie, and then conditions improved a little, and Mike found work again, cooking in an all-night cafeteria. He lasted about a year before he went haywire again—she made mistakes dealing with him, Lillian told them. Michael liked her eyes. She was talking to Natalie as much as to him, and he could see that Natalie was listening with care. Their marriage came alive again, Lillian said. Tommy had been in Spain and come back; he had broken with Amy over it—she had threatened to go to the FBI. Kathy was born in 1940. Mike went to work for Lockheed in Burbank, traveling in a car pool through the Cahuenga Pass—now there was a freeway. For a while he was sober, working two jobs, cooking at night, building Hudson bombers by day. Mike Regan. Then he was drinking again. And Tommy, because he had the money and the opportunity, came out to see them.

"There was nothing boyish left in him by 1943. Even though Mike was drinking, we weren't actually doing that badly. He had given up the short-order work at night because I could make more on the swing shift at Lockheed. Mike and I would pass each other going over the hill. That would be in the late afternoon, when David was home taking care of the two younger ones. And overtime, the two of us working sixty hours apiece some weeks. We knew we were working too hard, but it was a time to make money, I thought. Mike was only drinking to knock himself out, but then he was reeling when his brother arrived."

Mike was ready to broil the steak, which had been slit through the middle and stuffed with vegetables. Natalie wanted to know all about it, but he told them to go inside and start eating—questions later. When she had the door closed behind them, Lillian said that Mike was really very demanding when he was cooking, but that he was not different from others who thought cooking was art. "He knows exactly what he's doing and why. There are never any choices or substitutions, either. He'll talk to you forever about it. He never stuffs you, always keeps your palate clean—" She smiled. "He begs for compliments, so don't be shy."

"The soup is delicious," Natalie said. "Everything is so precisely chopped—it looks beautiful."

"Always. He will spend hours preparing something for the stove, only to cook it so briefly that you wonder, why did he bother? Until you taste. People have it backwards, he says. They think cooking is standing in front of a stove looking at steam. Oh, he has maxims, too."

"He ought to write a book."

"David has his recipes. When Mike thinks he has a good one, he has me send a Xerox to David. Mike doesn't want to be bothered with that side of it. He says he doesn't want to worry about some other old geezer recognizing him. Bing Crosby took a long look at him at Santa Anita back in the late forties. Mike knew a lot of people back in New York."

The steak flared up, and in another minute or two Mike was inside. "Everything all right? I think this is going to be a good one. Natalie, for your information, the meat is away from the fire. The heat is just being allowed to get to the vegetables." He was getting things out of the refrigerator. The women started laughing. "What's wrong?"

"You shameless old man. Everything is just wonderful and you know it."

"Aw."

Salad. Limestone lettuce and translucent slices of cucumber in oil and vinegar. Dishes of diced fruit, which he identified as pickled watermelon rind and lightly cooked apples. Lillian said he really was in his glory, and it was true, he was having a grand time, telling them that the fruit belonged on the steak, and that it had to be kept cold until the last minute. He wanted Michael to try the wine. Then he went for the steak.

"How often does this happen?"

"Holidays. Sometimes when Tom and Debbie come up, he'll put on the dog. And every great once in a while I'll be able to talk him into having company. He doesn't want to waste his time with most people now—says he knows what they're up to. Some of it is getting old, of course. And he doesn't want to be without me. He knows I have to see people, but he gets lonely and afraid that he's going to have to be without me."

"Don't talk like that," Natalie said.

"It's just something we both know. It's really why Tom is here."

The door opened and the steak was carried in, seared black all over, steaming. Mike carried it to the counter, then hurried around to the other side so they could see what he was going to do. "I don't want it to split open," he said.

"It won't split open," Lillian said. "What are we having for dessert?"

"Pears Hélène."

"That isn't much."

"Do you want an explanation?"

"Here it comes. Yes, I do."

"Be quiet." The steak was sewn together on one side. With small scissors he severed the cord at one end, and then with his fingers pulled the cord gently, wriggling, out of the meat. The meat parted over a fraction of an inch, and there was another little billow of steam. Michael could smell the food now, a deep, clear, cooked, bloody odor, and it made his mouth begin to fill with saliva. Mike brought the platter back to the table. "Natalie, the potatoes and rolls are in the oven. Potholders are on the stove."

"I'll get them," Lillian said.

"Sit. You did enough today. Take your time, Nat. I won't slice this without you."

"I was going to ask you to wait, don't worry."

The knife was made of that dark, carbon steel that Michael's father had favored, and Michael was not surprised to see what made Natalie's eyes bulge, the knife going through the meat in one swift stroke. The steak was uniformly pink all the way through, dripping blood, and the quarter-inch layer of vegetables glistened with heat. Suddenly Michael was afraid he wasn't going to get enough. Mike was telling Natalie about the vegetables, onions, zucchini, and carrots sautéed in butter and sesame seed, thin strips of pimento, pepper, spices, small amounts of horseradish and ground anchovies. The potatoes were pan-browns left over from Sunday's roast; he always made extra and put them away. The rolls were tiny. He said he liked very small, very hot rolls with steak, no matter how he prepared it.

He wanted them to use only a little of the fruit with the steak. Michael had to swallow before he could open his mouth, and then he wasn't prepared for what happened, hot and cold, sweet and sour, the meat tender, the vegetables crisp. The icy fruit tasted of mustard and clove. He could just feel the horseradish up through his nose.

"It's delicious," Natalie said with her mouth full. "I can't believe it."

"Don't ever cook anything too much," Mike said.

"Is it always like this?" Michael asked.

"Always," Lillian said.

"You used different oil and vinegar in the marinade," Natalie said to Mike.

"Everything goes together," Mike said, beaming.

Lillian winked at Michael. "If you let him, he'll serve a loin of pork in a bed of apricots and dandelion leaves. I'd go crazy if everything didn't taste so good."

Michael smiled.

Kathy was pretty; she wanted to be in movies. After the war Lillian took her on the Red Car down to Culver City for extra work. Later she was in Disney's *Song of the South* and Losey's *The Boy With Green Hair*. By then the Regans were living in the Valley. Tommy was married; the Regans had celebrated with another child. Mike was sober two years. The whole saga, the last twenty-five years, David in Korea, David at

Berkeley under the GI Bill. They had a house and two cars. Charlie at UCLA, then Kathy. Mike had his gall bladder removed in 1962. They had spent most of the previous ten years' vacations coming to Flagstaff and Cedar Canyon.

The Pear Hélène was finished; Mike had tried something with the chocolate ice cream—he still wasn't satisfied. He told them to go outside while he cleared the table. Lillian put on a jacket and gave Natalie a sweater. The sun was down and now the sky was turning from pale green to dark purple. The air was cold. Lillian poked at the coals in the fireplace. They watched the old man at work in the kitchen.

"Years ago he told me that when Kate and Charlie gave him his start, they put him in the kitchen, and the chefs made him work—oh, they made him work! He was living at Kate's place, and he'd get home in the early mornings thinking about something he had seen the pastry man do, and when Kate and Charlie got up, there'd be some whipped cream thing waiting for them. Do you know what he does now when he gets upset? He cooks. He'll call Debbie at three in the afternoon and tell her that she's serving chicken breasts stuffed with crab meat, drawn butter, and walnuts when the kids wanted Spaghetti-O's."

Mike came out with another tray, with Irish coffee for the kids, he said, and Sanka for Lillian. The package Michael and Natalie had brought was on the tray, too, but Mike wanted to wait until Tom arrived before he opened it.

"You know, for a long time after your father came out here during the war, I didn't believe what he had to say about your grandfather. I went on drinking—I wanted to; what the hell, what good are you if you're not stinko by midnight?"

"All right, old man, it's not an AA meeting."

"I'm just trying to tell them the kind of things a drunk thinks. I was a drunk. I'm still a drunk. I remember the taste of all of it. You know that."

"You *talked* a lot of drunks into the hospital," Michael said.

"This crazy old man is a spellbinder when he wants to be," Lillian said.

"She's been calling me old man since I was fifty," Mike said happily. "But when your father was here, the two of them got me sober for a while, and he talked to me about my drinking and what I was doing to myself, and what he understood of it. 'Christ,' he said, 'I've been hurt as badly as you. I've hurt myself. The old man did the same thing. How long are we going to be chumps for every hustler who comes along?' It started like that. We started talking to each other that way. He would send us a postcard with a clue to where he'd been, or what had happened to him. Once we got one that said, 'Mary Jenkins runs again,' and it wasn't until after the war that it had meant that he'd been torpedoed still another time. For many years, he told me, he had wanted to die. He felt he had to give himself back to the long historical process—what the hell, I could never read that shit. We had fought about it, but my brains were stewed half the time until 1943 anyway. But then he told me what Kate had told him. I could see he was feeling different about himself, even if I didn't want to face it. He told me he wanted to live his own life, and he didn't want to see me die of booze just as he was getting himself together. He wanted to stay close to your grandmother, and he would work out some way for us to stay in touch. I think he already had everything worked out. Except for those years when he was knocked for a loop, your father always had a plan. He called it the key to the vault."

"He said that your father taught him that."

"My father made a lot of mistakes. He told Kate as much. He shouldn't have done a lot of the things that he did, and he should not have left undone so many other things. In a lot of ways he was a wonderful man, but Julie's second husband skinned him alive. And he had those two years alone to think about Sullivan, a boy named Andy Fletcher, and his own lost love. No, your father had more than a plan, he had an idea about himself, and when you were in Korea, he told me that he was going to see that you understood something of the way he saw life."

"Vietnam, lover," Lillian said.

"What did I say?"

"You said Korea."

"My mother does that," Michael said.

"What do you expect of me?" his uncle asked. "I'm an old man. I can remember everything from forty years ago, but don't ask me what happened yesterday." He leaned forward. "Do you know what your father taught me? That I'm real. That I have a physical, biological, and historical identity that goes deeper than politics and beliefs. It didn't make any difference if my name was Monk, Westfield, Regan, or whatever. He told me that he wanted to make his own life, that it was the one lesson he could draw from your grandfather's life, and the only thing we could possibly understand of the people who came to this country during the Civil War, your real great-grandparents, the people from Birkenhead and Liverpool. You are real, Michael. Make your own life, and do it as well as you can. There won't be any future for you unless you create it. Your father told us that if we succeeded in our second chance, he would succeed in his, but he was hustling us. We didn't have to succeed for him; all we had to do was disappear. He said that he thought we were coming around to the point where he'd have to give you a push, but he wanted to do it his way, leaving out all the things that happened to us, and your grandfather. Well, your mother overruled him, and not least because you must know what happened before you were born in order to know who you are. Your father made his chance, and so did your grandfather. Your grandfather thought he was trying to build the thing his parents had wanted, but the fact is that they had no real idea what they were coming to. They were just washed ashore, but they believed in themselves enough to want to make their own lives. Your father said that we only stopped using wood for fuel a few generations ago—that for six thousand years, the human race had been living on interest, and that when we started to dig coal, we started to spend capital. But it was necessary. After this continent was discovered, it began to dawn on people that life could begin all over again, that there was a second chance for us all. More than anything else, that was what this continent and this nation gave to all mankind. And in many ways we made the most of it—not perfectly, to be sure. And not accidentally, the world changed in my father's lifetime, and it changed twice more since I was a child. You have your own life to invent out of what you find around you. Since the beginning of history, people have been told that they were better off leaving those decisions to others, but this new land allowed us to see the truth about ourselves. We were *meant* to be free, and anything else is a way of stealing your right to make your own future. I used to wonder what my old man would have thought of my sons David and Charlie, but I gave up. David is in public administration, and Charlie teaches the fifth grade. Neither plays cards or goes to the track. David has a sailboat, which might have pleased my father. They're living their own lives. And he lived his. That's the real revolution, your father said, and it started here. It's your heritage and your duty to pass it on to your children."

"You have to mention the other two," Lillian said.

"Kathy decided that she didn't want to be a movie star, and now she's a nurse at UCLA Medical Center. The last one fell in love with the first girl he ever met, and he's still in love with her."

"That's Tom," Natalie said.

"It was your father who told us to get out of his way," Lillian said. "Tom and Debbie were married when they were seventeen. You don't need a learner's permit to live."

"And Tom's late, as usual," Lillian said. "Why don't you open the package?"

The old man reached for it. "He won't give a damn anyway."

"Yes, he will. You like to bitch."

"He's the one who never saw me drink," Mike said, peeling the tape from the paper. "You want to know what this thing is. Before my father died, he told Kate the details of the night his parents were killed—he told her everything, I suppose. Well, hell, she had a lot of it figured out."

He was turning back the corners of the paper. "In any event, he told Kate about this, and your father told me while your grandmother was alive, and I told him that we were bound to find it among her things. He did. We never wanted to send it back and forth in the mail, and at the end he talked of bringing it out to me. Your mother wanted me to see it. The night my grandparents were killed, my father took something with him. He hid it until Westfield came for him, and for the rest of his life he kept it in the top drawer of his dresser. When he died, my mother put it with her things. My father told Kate that he took it from his mother after she was dead. For years, he told Kate, he would pick it up and hold it in his hand to remind himself of who and what he was."

Mike held it up: a small, tortoiseshell comb.

"There," Lillian said.

"The comb he described to Kate."

There had been an evening in the back yard on Long Island, the portable television set or the folding chair, the extension cords running across the grass and up through the kitchen window. The beer cans were lined up on the ground next to Michael's chair. His father came out and turned another chair around beside his son's.

"Is this worth looking at?"

"Kranepool just hit into a double play."

"You're just trying to fill the time."

"I know."

"I hate to see you like this. You're not even enjoying your life."

"I'm all right, Pop. I'm going to be okay."

The voice whispering across the continent. *Hey, it's me.* He had held himself back to spare his son. His father had told Michael that he would support him in anything he wanted to do about the draft, and Michael had been able to see that defying the government would only invite disaster later. "Whether you kill in war or in peacetime," his father had said, "you're just killing your brother, and usually because you've allowed yourself to be hustled into it." Georgie Howe. Michael Monk— his father must have seen what they had shared, the little there was. His father had wanted to spare him, and now Michael began to realize why: the burden of it was descending on him with the weight of a mountain.

Headlights shined over the roof of the house and onto the tops of the trees around the patio. Their son Tom. "We don't get up for him," Lillian said. Natalie had the comb now. A comb. The boy running through the snow. As Michael reached for the thing itself, it was as if his hand had become his grandfather's, and it shook and turned wet with perspiration.

What had his great-grandfather been through in England that had made him want to come to America?

Tom let himself into the house, waved to them through the glass doors, and went to the refrigerator. When he came out to the patio, he had a sixteen-ounce can of beer in his left hand. Debbie had had to babysit while a neighbor took a child to the doctor. Tom kissed his mother on the mouth and his father on the forehead, and then he came around to shake hands with Michael and say hello to Natalie.

"Well, did he feed you all right?"

"Yes," Natalie said. "I don't feel full, but I don't think I'll have to eat until Saturday."

"He knows how to do it to you. Well," he said to his father, "did you get a look at that comb? Does it seem like the real thing?"

Smiling, his father pointed to the comb on the table. Tom took it into the light.

"I was thinking of taking it up here to the university," he said. "Maybe somebody up there will be able to tell us something. Chances are they won't even know what it's made of."

"I was hoping your cousin would take it out to Kathy. Nobody has a picture of the woman she was named after, and she wants to see anything from Kate's world." Mike turned to Natalie. "The original was a slender woman whose red hair turned white as she grew old. Kathy is a big, blonde California girl."

"Aged thirty," her mother said. "With two children."

"I came up to see if these two are going to be around tomorrow, and if they'd like to meet Debbie. It's just one long day's drive to LA, and if they do it Sunday, they can spend the last three hours caught in the traffic."

"We'll spend at least one more day," Michael said.

That was all. Tom had wanted to see how his parents were doing. He told them that Debbie would be by in the morning on her way up to Flag. His father got up to walk with him back to his car.

"Don't let him frighten you about Los Angeles," Lillian said. "He doesn't like it, and your father didn't like it, but Mike and I told your mother that you might be pleasantly surprised. All the time we lived there, it made Mike think of what your grandfather told him about New York in the last century—New York came up out of the ground in his lifetime. Your father didn't like Los Angeles during the war because it wasn't a city yet, and Tom doesn't like it now because it became a city in the time since. We watched that happen, maybe we even helped, and it gave us a great deal of pleasure and satisfaction."

"Of course you helped make it happen," Natalie said.

"Los Angeles is full of former New Yorkers. All the time we were there, we were seeing people who looked familiar to us."

"We see them now, here," Mike said. He came over to Lillian's chair to give her a kiss. "I'm getting a little tired."

She held his hand. "He goes to bed early and gets up early," she explained.

"What time do you get up?"

"When it starts getting light." He picked up the comb again. "Thanks to both of you for bringing this out."

Michael stood up and extended his hand. "I didn't know what I was doing, but I'm glad it turned out well."

"Natalie, you're more rare and precious than you know," Mike said.

"I'll remember that," she said, "that there's more to me than I realize."

"That's the idea." Lillian looked up at him. "Do you want me to come inside?"

"I'm all right." He kissed her again. "You two call in the morning and tell us what you're going to do."

"We will," Natalie said.

It was growing colder. "There's more," Lillian said. "There's more that Mike wanted to tell you. He's always felt that your father gave him this life. Your grandmother treated your father badly from the time he was an infant, but it didn't stop him from loving her."

"I know," Michael said.

"Your father loved you, me, and his brother. He loved his wife and his daughters. He told Mike that he was a happy man. Mike wanted to take more of the burden of your grandmother, but your father insisted that it would only lead to trouble. He didn't trust your Aunt Amy.

"Your grandmother knew. She knew everything. What she didn't know about your grandfather, she suspected from the start. Their marriage was her attempt to live her own life, but she was crippled before the two of them met. Kate saw that but she also saw that your grandfather wanted her that way. For better or worse, he allowed a dream to develop inside him, and then he tried to make it come true. You're going to do the same—you have to, or your life won't be your own. And then your children and grandchildren will be left to make sense of it for themselves. Your grandfather did the best he could, but he married your grandmother in silence. And your grandmother knew what he expected of her. So it was a bargain, but a bad bargain for her. Not even the death of his son could force him to abandon what they had started, and when she faltered, he forced her to continue. But she didn't believe it anymore;

she thought she was being punished for yielding to what she was taught to believe were selfish passions. It may have even crossed her mind that she was being punished for her complicity in the things he had done. There was the silence, and she must have seen that she bore her share of the responsibility for that. When she told him that there was no reason for him to speak of his real origins again, she was giving him exactly what he needed to have in order to smuggle the rest of himself into a supposedly legitimate life. They fell in love at first sight, and they were both very eager to seduce each other."

Natalie got up and kissed her.

"But there was that silence, and it continued into their marriage, and even after the death of their child. He thought he was doing the right thing, but he never really calculated the price his wife was paying. Because of what he had done, he did more than push the moral education of their children onto her. He allowed her to decide what they would be. She taught her oldest son one set of values, but by the time her youngest came along, she was, as your father put it, under siege. He told Mike that he could see in his childhood that she wasn't paying attention when she was teaching him to say his prayers. She no longer believed. Your father said that it took him until World War Two to realize that she had stopped believing in life itself.

"They were as much her sons as his—but at the end, she didn't even believe that. It was true. Your father's understanding of his mother was one of the things he needed to have to get to Sunnyside and your mother. He told us. He told his brother. Your father saw himself as a man who had sustained a wound. Some of the arrangements he made for himself after the war were expensive for him, like looking after his mother the way he wanted to do, or that job—repetitive work, alone, in the middle of the night. When we wanted him to make a change, he would laugh and say he liked things just the way they were, or that he didn't want to take on any more, or that he had all he could handle. But we saw, and your mother saw, that as time went on he was reaching for more and more, the trip to Halifax where your great-grandparents first set foot in the New World, and the trip to Florida when you were in the service."

"He was waiting for me to come home."

Lillian started to cry. "The old man in there is saying his prayers. All his life he has said his prayers just the way his mother taught them to him. He had an awful time confessing that to me when we were first married, but I knew what he was doing. I could hear him whispering in the dark. When your father came out to the coast during the war, the two of them talked about her loss of faith. What your father understood helped Mike; what Mike understood helped your father. They were truly brothers. Even then I wanted to think that everything could be somehow brought under control through the force of my own will. But Mike started to change, and then he began to try to sober up. He said that this time was different, but for a long time I reserved my judgment. One night I found him in the living room by himself. 'I'm praying for my father,' he said. 'And my mother and brother and you—' He named all the people he could think of until he broke down and sobbed in my arms. 'What good am I? Look how much all of you have given me.' And he hasn't had a drink since. He changed, and so did I. You can't imagine how many lives that man has saved. He would come home with his clothes covered with some drunk's vomit. He sat up with scores of men, telling them a lot of what he told you. And more. 'I don't have all the answers,' he'd say, 'but look at me. I'm sober.' " She began to weep again.

Natalie said, "You don't have to go on. He'll be upset if he finds you like this."

"Michael, your grandfather told Kate that he was afraid that what he had done had cost him his soul, and in the attempt to prevent your father from going through the same hell, Kate told him everything your grand-father told her. When he and Mike talked of it later, your father said he could remember your grandfather with the Bible. This was in the autumn before his death, after Kate saw him for the last time. We don't know if your grandfather was able to forgive himself—he told Kate that God loved us, but Kate thought it was the talk of a man trying to face his death with dignity. 'God loves us all,' your grandfather insisted, and he said he was without fear. Mike says it's true, and now I know that I'm not afraid to die. I believe. Your father would never admit to any belief—he saw himself as someone who was scarred. We do know that he was at peace with himself. He'd argue with Mike that there was a lot we couldn't know, and that he was happy just to let it go. But he never closed the door, he never asked Mike to stop talking about the subject. He'd call and say 'How the hell are ya? You still have me on your list?' which meant, 'Are you praying for me?' and Mike would always answer 'Sure,' the way your father used to grind out that word and the way you do now. He said he couldn't do what Mike had done, open himself that way, but he didn't feel the need, and he said that maybe he was being looked out for, after all. He didn't say that to make Mike feel good. They never lied to each other. They loved each other."

"Maybe we should stop," Natalie said.

Michael rose—he felt a little dizzy, and then it passed. They carried the dishes inside. Lillian said she would take care of them, and she walked with them to the door. "Call us in the morning. Breakfast is just breakfast here, so you don't have to spend your money someplace else."

They kissed her, and a moment later, when he was wiping the windshield, he looked up and saw her working in the kitchen. He did not want to leave. He knew it, but he got into the car anyway.

He lay awake in the motel room, the lights out, Natalie asleep. The others were asleep, too—his aunt and uncle. And his mother, whom they had forgotten to call, was asleep at the other end of the country, where it was later in the night, or earlier in the morning. He thought of the immense distance he and Natalie had just crossed, all of it rolling under the darkness of the early summer night. He thought of his sisters. *You have me on your list?* Michael's heart began to pound, and he got out of bed. He felt dizzy again, and he put his hand on his chest. In his childhood he had had moments of dread—that paying attention to his heart would make it stop. He knew what was happening to him. He threw back the drape. The room was on the second floor, in the back of the building, and there was nothing below but the parking lot, and beyond it, the woods that seemed to run up the side of the mountain itself. Michael thought of the couple whose wedding they had attended the previous weekend, and then remembered how he and Natalie had finished that night. It was a season presumably succulent with promise. *Still have me on your list?* The whispers across a continent still mostly empty, dreamless and uninvented. Natalie rolled over and, in her sleep, pulled his pillow against her stomach. Michael would have to retrieve it later; he had told her that getting his pillow back from her was like trying to get an octopus out of a washing machine. *How the hell are ya?* Michael could see his father as if he were standing in the room, not unhappy. Smiling. Michael wept. *List? Sure.* Forever. *My old man gave me the key to the vault.* "So did mine!" Michael cried, and Natalie sat up, and rushed to his arms.

November 12, 1973–May 16, 1977